Ariana

Ariana

EDWARD STEWART

CROWN PUBLISHERS, INC.
NEW YORK

Published by Crown Publishers, Inc.,
One Park Avenue, New York, New York 10016 and
simultaneously in Canada by
General Publishing Company Limited
CROWN is a trademark of Crown Publishers, Inc.

Manufactured in the United States of America

Library of Congress Cataloging in Publication Data
Stewart, Edward, 1938-
Ariana.
I. Title
PS3569.T46A89   1984   813'.54   84-27443
ISBN 0-517-55728-2
10   9   8   7   6   5   4   3   2   1
First Edition

With unflagging generosity and skill,
Alexandra Hunt made available to this project
her splendid musicality and operatic experience.
She has been of invaluable assistance
in not only the technical
but countless other aspects of
the preparation of the book.
My thanks to her.

When an inner situation is not made
conscious, it happens outside, as fate. When the
individual does not become conscious of his
inner contradictions, the world must perforce
act out the conflict and be torn into
opposite halves.

Carl Jung

Prelude

FEBRUARY 7, 1979

BY 9:00 A.M. THE LINE OUTSIDE ST. PATRICK'S CATHEDRAL stretched ten blocks north along Fifth Avenue. These were the ordinary people, without passes to the funeral.

Some had brought books to read; some, cameras; some, tape recorders; a few, food. Some held shopping bags; some wore jeans and wool jackets; some carried little bouquets on the off chance of passing within tossing distance of the coffin of Ariana Kavalaris—the woman who had given them some of the finest evenings of their lives.

Policemen told them to stay behind the striped sawhorses, to keep the cross streets clear. They obeyed grudgingly, then at the first chance pushed forward again.

Beginning a little after nine there was a constant stream of faces into the cathedral: the supporting singers, the chorus members, the nonstars who had worked with Kavalaris.

At 9:30 a group of almost a hundred women carrying pickets surged east along Forty-ninth Street, taking dead aim on the cathedral. THE POPE NEVER HAD TO RAISE AN UNWANTED KID one sign proclaimed; another, NEW YORK MOTHERS FOR FREEDOM OF CHOICE; another, WHAT JESUS HAD TO SAY ABOUT ABORTION—NOTHING!

A phalanx of police, pushing sawhorses in front of them, managed to drive the mothers back across Fifth Avenue. They took up position around the statue of Atlas in front of Rockefeller Center and began chanting, "Sepa-*rate* church and *state!*"

At ten sharp celebrities began to arrive for the funeral.

There was Giorgio Montecavallo, who had sung with Kavalaris— dapper in morning clothes; and Rodney Maxwell, who owned newspapers and TV stations on three continents; and Tad Brinks, who hosted the CBS evening news; and Adolf Erdlich, director of the Metropolitan Opera, where Kavalaris had had so many triumphs.

A little after 10:30 a group of two dozen priests and nuns began moving west on Forty-ninth Street. Their voices could be heard intermittently above the tumult, singing "Salve Regina." Their neatly lettered placards all said the same thing: THOU SHALT NOT KILL.

It took only ten policemen to push the public back from Forty-ninth Street, making a narrow path for the small, dignified procession.

A dozen other policemen kept the steps of the cathedral clear, making way for tycoons, actors, actresses, diplomats, bank presidents, society hostesses who had risen far earlier than their accustomed hour and whose hairdressers had too; the widow of an ex-President ("She doesn't look a day over forty-nine!"); last year's Wimbledon male and female

3

champions, rumored to be having a romance; rock stars; two United States senators and their wives. . . .

Across Fifth Avenue, the nuns and priests quietly took up position north of the mothers.

By 10:30 every fifteen seconds brought a fresh Lincoln or Cadillac limousine to the steps, a Bentley or a Rolls, and—after a moment's hesitation adjusting fur or overcoat—out stepped a new celebrity to fatten the crush.

"Sepa-*rate* church and *state!*"

Necks craned, recognition flared into screams of names, flashbulbs went off, TV minicams scanned.

An ambulance sped down Fifth Avenue, siren wailing.

A custom silver Mercedes pulled up at the cathedral steps. Everyone recognized the Hollywood actress who had won an Oscar the preceding year—her borzoi tried to follow her out of the car. Instructing the animal to be good and wait in the back seat, her escort (Who *was* he? He looked like that new soap-opera heartthrob on CBS) gripped it by its jeweled collar and handed it over to the chauffeur.

Some of the well informed recognized Count and Countess Nicholas von Hohenschmidt-Ingolf, tanned from the Costa Brava and blond and among the minority who had worn mourning. They had flown in from Denmark to represent the royal family.

Ambassadors arrived in limousines flying the little fender flags of their nations—Paco and Pilar de Guzman of Mexico; Sir Robert and Lady Fitzmorency of New Zealand; Ali Ben-Golah of Algeria; dozens of others.

"Sepa-*rate* church and *state!*"

The mayor arrived and waved somberly to reporters.

The governor and his wife arrived and did not wave.

Representatives of the great opera houses were there: the directors of the Paris Opéra, of Buenos Aires's Teatro Colón, of Covent Garden, of Milan's La Scala.

The world of international fame and luxury had turned out for this, Ariana Kavalaris's last public appearance. They all passed up the steps and through the cast-iron doors like images on a TV screen, flashing faces, names, smiles, greetings, cheek-to-cheek kisses.

As the hour of the mass neared, the crush thickened. Between 10:45 and 11:00, in less than fifteen minutes, over $15 million in jewelry and fur and high fashion streamed into St. Patrick's.

Through the open cathedral doors, rising faintly above the turmoil, came the unhurried, unhurrying notes of an organ. The church air, sweet with the smell of wealth and fame, bloomed and buzzed like a dark garden.

Within, everything was movement, stir, color.

The pews gradually filled up and the cathedral became a sea of designer hats. Heads turned. Kisses were exchanged, greetings murmured.

Earrings and necklaces threw out pinpoints of light. Beneath sable and mink, Galanos and Saint Laurent and de la Renta originals rustled silkenly on famous bodies.

A whisper swept the pews as Nikos Stratiotis came striding up the aisle alone. The owner of six world corporations listed among *Fortune* magazine's top hundred, he had been the dead woman's lover and, later, her betrayer.

He stopped and for an instant faced the altar. Kneeling quickly on one knee, he crossed himself in Orthodox fashion, forefinger touching right shoulder before left. He stepped into a pew and as he knelt again the light outlined his solid frame and graying, leonine head. Eyes shut, he began moving his lips in silent prayer.

Everywhere, fabled gems flashed against velvet and silk and satin and pampered flesh.

The coffin, covered with a burgundy-colored pall, lay in the center aisle before the steps leading to the altar. There was a great cross of white lilacs on it, with clusters of red roses at the four extremities.

Heads turned as an usher led Kavalaris's arch-rival, Clara Rodrigo, to her pew. With Kavalaris's death, Rodrigo was arguably the most famous living soprano in the world. She walked in white mink, head held high, her eyes heavily mascara'd and watchful. She turned toward the altar and—giving the flap of her mink an outward fling—dropped to one knee. With great deliberation she touched a jeweled finger to her forehead—*"En el nombre del Padre"*—to her bosom—*"del Hijo"*—to her left shoulder and her right—*"y del Espíritu Santo."*

The Greek ambassador to the U.N., seeing she would be some time in that position, stepped respectfully around her.

Clara Rodrigo finally moved into the pew. She opened her purse—the catch gave a click like a tiny firecracker—and took out a large rosary of onyx and ivory beads the size of walnuts. She knelt again. Grasping the shining gold medallion of Our Lord, her voice low-pitched but prevailing over the murmurs around her, she began reciting the "Padre Nuestro."

Boyd Kinsolving, Kavalaris's husband for seventeen years and her conductor for twenty-one, now music director of the New York Metropolitan Opera, bowed his head and whispered the words of the Twenty-third Psalm: "Yea, though I walk through the valley of the shadow of death . . . "

Beside him, Richard Schiller, who had been Kavalaris's agent for almost a quarter-century, sat silently, head angled downward, eyes resolutely averted from the movement and activity around him.

The last mourners to arrive finally found their places. The thousands were now still, waiting.

An expectant silence fell, like the hush before the curtain rises in an opera house.

A procession of altar boys filed in from the sacristy doorway, led by an acolyte in white, swinging a gold-chained censer. Then, like a sort of royal procession, came the Roman Catholic cardinal and archbishop and—slightly behind them, in a plain black suit—the Episcopal bishop who was to speak the eulogy over Ariana Kavalaris.

He was a handsome man, dignified and gray-haired, and emotion choked his voice.

"The woman we mourn today opened for us the doors of a different world. She not only cheered us and stirred us with her gift of song, colored our lives with her mastery, she lifted us, gave to our mortal ears the only image of eternity they will ever be able to perceive. She gave us music. In some ways hers was the sort of music that sounds strongest in memory. We never really hear it till it is gone. Like light that we see only by the shadow it casts, we hear her—know her—mourn her—only by her silence."

The bishop turned and stepped away from the lectern.

For a moment no one moved or breathed.

From somewhere high in the rear of the cathedral, a thread of sound wove itself into the stillness. Softly at first and then with increasing volume, a soprano was singing the "Et Lux Perpetua" of Verdi's *Requiem*. The sound filled the arches of the cathedral like light from a glorious summer sky.

There was a stir, a surge. A wind of shocked recognition blew through the crowd.

There was no mistaking that voice. It was the voice of the woman who had died . . . Ariana Kavalaris.

Even before the last notes died the air trembled in glassy ripples. A forest of heads whipped around. Eyes fixed on the choir loft. Dozens of mourners rose and on their faces were expressions that ranged from bafflement to terror.

In the twelfth pew Richard Schiller turned to peer through the crowd.

"Is it a recording?" he muttered wonderingly.

Beside him, Boyd Kinsolving froze. For an instant he sat staring straight ahead, his face a pallid oval of disbelief, and then he turned and saw the woman standing in the loft.

"That's no recording," he whispered. "Who is she?"

Two pews ahead, Nikos Stratiotis shut his eyes. The voice caught at his throat and sent a trembling along his spine. Suddenly he wanted to cry.

Slowly, he turned to look.

The voice came like a hard hit to the pit of Clara Rodrigo's stomach.

Disbelief shot through her. The blood drained sickeningly from her head.

There were indefinable stirrings in the crowd around her, a silence that was like a whisper of alarm.

Her head spun around.

The Episcopal bishop looked up.

And suddenly something came unmoored inside him. He began to shake. His sight became blurred.

It was like a dream seen through shivering layers of memory.

She was standing in the choir loft. The light had somehow changed; the area surrounding her had dimmed out and a white spot seemed to be focused on her.

Her face engulfed him.

A dazzling brightness spread from her and it was as though she were alone, silhouetted against a dark sky.

She seemed to be someone else, someone he had known long ago. He rose, reaching out to her.

And then the light changed again, and he saw her blond hair, parted down the center, hanging in two long tresses that framed the oval of her face.

He staggered as though he had been struck.

An acolyte helped him back to his seat.

"Mark?"

It was night now. A woman's voice cut into the bishop's thoughts. He turned in his chair and saw his wife standing in the doorway, a small, neat-looking woman of fifty-six, her face lit by the glow from the fireplace.

"Yes, dear?" he said pleasantly. He had had a tiring day. It was good to be home, enclosed again in familiar Episcopalian walls.

"Coming to bed?"

"Not just yet. I think I'll sit by the fire a little longer."

His wife gazed at him. "She meant a great deal to you, didn't she?"

"Who?"

His wife smiled a gentle little ghost of a smile. "You don't need to pretend, Mark. We all have our memories to keep a little springtime in our hearts."

The bishop rose from his armchair and went slowly over to the desk. Embarrassed, he busied his hands lighting a pipe.

"I didn't mean to intrude," his wife said.

"You never intrude, my dear."

"I love you, Mark." She blew him a kiss and closed the door.

"I love you too," he said softly, speaking to someone who was no longer there.

The fire, beginning to die, filled the old room with flickering shadows.

The bishop stood alone for a moment in silence. He went over to the shelf where recordings were kept. He searched a moment, chose one, and placed it carefully on the phonograph. He went back to his armchair by the fire.

Slowly, he sank down.

The needle dropped to the disk. A faint crackling hiss filled the warm, drowsy air.

The bishop's head began nodding in rhythm to Puccini's melody.

From far across the years the rich, never-forgotten soprano voice soared through the darkness.

"Tu, tu, amore? Tu?" It was the great Act Two duet from *Manon Lescaut.*

The tenor entered and the music swelled.

The bishop shut his eyes, letting the present melt away.

In his memory, chandeliers bloomed into light and the past lived again; he was a boy of eight and once more, for the first time, he saw her.

Part One

PROMISE: 1928–1950

1

IN 1928 HERBERT HOOVER WAS ELECTED PRESIDENT OF THE United States, Amelia Earhart became the first woman to fly across the Atlantic, and—at the old Metropolitan Opera House on Broadway and Thirty-ninth Street—Mark Rutherford saw his first opera, Puccini's *Manon Lescaut.*

He quickly grasped that opera was profoundly different from life. On the stage, grown men and women threw away everything for a kiss. In the audience, grown men and women—including his own parents—sat believing, approving, applauding.

The first three acts gently lured him into the dizzying melody-filled space of a universe whose existence he had never suspected.

During the final intermission he wandered onto the grand tier promenade. He felt curiosity, dissatisfaction, a seeking for the things he had glimpsed on the stage.

Suddenly, far away on the edge of the brilliantly milling crowd, in a thicket of pillars with heavy gilt coils twisting up them, he saw a tiny figure. He saw her for just an instant, silhouetted against the red velvet wall. She was standing near the water fountain.

For that flicker of an instant her eye caught his. She was like a dream, like something on the opera stage. He had never seen such a beautiful, strange girl before.

The light from the chandeliers scattered little sparkles through her thick black hair. Parted in the middle, it hung in two long braids. Her face was slender and dark and glowing. She wore a white skirt, white gloves, knee-length cotton socks. Her tiny red purse on its gold-colored chain was small enough to be a doll's. She couldn't have been more than six years old.

All that he saw in a glance, till the crowd closed like seawater around her. He moved through the throng till he could get another glimpse of her.

The pink ribbons on her hat fluttered nervously behind her as she turned her head. It came to him with astonishing certainty that she was frightened, perhaps lost, in need of help. His help.

He was eight years old. Old enough to help.

The opera was whispering to him: *Go ahead.*

He made sure the brass buttons of his navy blue school blazer were buttoned. He moved a little to the right, then to the left, as though he were strolling nowhere in particular. Just as he was about to pass her, she raised her head.

For an instant her eyes, strangely sad and gentle, looked directly into his. A pain like none he had ever felt before squeezed his heart. She smiled at him. He was standing in front of her.

"Hello," he said. He felt he should be singing, not speaking.

She answered softly, "Hello."

It was as though they already knew one another. Something surged out of him. He stepped toward her, kissed her swiftly on the forehead. It was a kiss out of a fairy tale; a kiss out of opera.

She pulled back, giving him a tiny grin.

"Ariana—there you are!" This from a woman in black, seizing the girl's hand, dragging her away toward the stairway that led up to the balconies.

"Mark, why in the world did you run off like that?" This from his own mother, glittering in pale blues and greens, pulling him toward the stairway that led down to the orchestra.

Just before the girl vanished she turned to look back at him and smile.

He didn't see her again for eighteen years.

By then a depression and a world war had ended. He had graduated from Harvard, done his basic training at army camp in North Carolina, and—thanks to a gift for languages—had served three years on the staff of General Dwight D. Eisenhower.

In 1946 the world had changed but didn't yet know it. Everyone was trying to get tickets to see Ethel Merman in *Annie Get Your Gun;* Joe Louis was still heavyweight champion; in Fulton, Missouri, Winston Churchill gave a speech saying that an Iron Curtain had dropped across half of Europe.

And Mark Rutherford—deciding he not only had a calling to the ministry but a damned good singing voice—went to an open audition of the Domani Opera Company, a semipro, which was to say a totally amateur, totally unpaid opera company of young hopefuls. Affectionately known as the Mañana Met, the Domani was headquartered in a former bar next to a filling station in a run-down neighborhood on lower Third Avenue that looked as bad as anything the Allies had done to Berlin.

Over a hundred young hopefuls had crowded into the small, makeshift auditorium with its folding wooden chairs and uneven wooden benches and unswept corners. The auditioners sang on a stage that was little more than planks, with a dirty little frill of a drop cloth attempting to disguise the sawhorses beneath.

As each hopeful auditioned the others waited in silence, sipping coffee in soggy containers from the deli across the street. Between numbers—"Mi chiamano Mimi" and "Pres des remparts de Seville" for sopranos and mezzos, "Celeste Aïda" and "Piangi, Piangi" for tenors and baritones—there was a low buzzing of whispered conversation. Mark realized immediately he was an outsider: there was no one for him to buzz with. Moreover, he was ridiculously overdressed in his Brooks Brothers suit—the other young men were wearing jeans or corduroys.

Most of the young women were dressed in black skirts and black turtlenecks and wore their hair pulled back in ponytails.

But there was one young woman sitting up close to the stage who was different. A glow from the light on the rinky-dink piano threw little sparkles into her hair, which hung dark and soft and loose. Dressed in a blouse of sparkling white, she was reading a score. Not a ripple disturbed the surface of her concentration.

He saw her and right away something about her gave him that once-upon-a-time feeling. It was just a tiny nagging hint of a feeling, except it wasn't tiny at all. He knew he knew her.

She saw him watching her and he dropped his eyes in confusion, pretending to be looking at his own score.

And then it came to him where he had seen her. He rose from his seat and walked up the side aisle.

"Excuse me." He leaned toward her with quick eagerness. "This sounds trite, but we've met before. A long time ago."

She had a fine smile, knowing and warm. At the same time it was girlish and it made him feel protective. "You used to have blond curly hair," she said. "Now it's auburn and straight."

"It was at the Metropolitan Opera, right? You had long hair?"

"Down to here." She touched her shoulder.

"I kissed you. What a pushy little brat I was."

She dropped her eyes.

There was a silence before he spoke. "Mind if I sit down?"

She slid over on the bench, making room. She looked over at him.

"Do you come to auditions often?" he said.

"As often as I can," she said. "And you?"

"I audition now and then when the urge hits. I'm really just a bathtub baritone."

He liked her laugh. Something about her fitted something in him. Tumblers moved and it was like a key sliding into a lock.

He held out his hand. "I'm Mark Rutherford."

"Ariana Kavalaris."

They shook hands and that hurdle was passed.

"How about a cup of coffee afterward?" he suggested. "We can catch up on the last two decades."

"I'd love it," she said.

And then someone was calling her name.

"Excuse me, Mark."

She got up on the stage. Her eyes signaled the accompanist. The piano hit a thunk of a chord. She lifted her head and her throat was a milk-white patch barely hollowed by a shadow.

She began a tone, and it was like a very tiny hole emitting a point of light that gradually swelled and then went sailing through the silence. What she did wasn't just an aria: it was a performance; eyes big and wondering and vulnerable, hands clutched around her, she became the tubercular little Mimi.

The voice soared. The tone was fresh and sweet and pathetic and absolutely appropriate to the role. When she finished applause slammed down in a solid wall.

It would have been an impossible act to follow. Luckily, there were seven sopranos and three tenors before Mark's turn came.

He felt like a fool standing on that wobbly stage in his three-piece suit, felt like a worse fool when he missed his entrance and the accompanist had to start again.

He got twelve bars into "Piangi, Piangi."

The woman running the audition had been standing in the wings listening. Now she stepped out of the darkness into the stage light. "Mr. Rutherford," she said, cutting into the aria, "thank you."

He left the stage guiltily. There was no way he could face Ariana Kavalaris. He sneaked out the fire exit, sneaked across the street, sneaked into a booth in the coffee shop with a view of the Domani entrance.

Five coffees and a terrible headache later he saw her come out with a group of six other young men and women. They were laughing.

Ariana stopped a moment, looked around. There was fleeting disappointment on her face and then she was laughing again, linking arms with the others, bounding up the street.

Ariana Kavalaris, he thought. *I'm crazy about you. And I made an idiot of myself.*

She stayed with him, like a lingering image on film: Ariana Kavalaris. The sunny months of June and July and August dissolved into a sea of swimming and sailing and parties and aimless melancholy. There wasn't a minute in the entire summer when he didn't feel lonely for her and just plain dying for her.

He began his studies for the ministry that fall.

There was nothing else in New York quite like the Episcopal seminary, a peaceful cloister with stepping-stone paths and light-dappled oaks, open to the blue sky. The dark, ivy-twined brick buildings and high Gothic tower of the chapel gave the impression of something ancient and consoling that had survived a century of upheaval.

For two months he pulled himself through St. John Chrysostom's sermons and Hebrew waw-consecutives.

And then one cool day in November his old friend Nita Farnsworth phoned. "How'd you like to go to an opera Friday?"

"Okay," he said.

They agreed to meet in the seminary garden. She arrived wearing blue jeans. She had the understated blond American good looks that come with money moving coolly and uninterruptedly from generation to generation, and she carried herself like an heiress.

Mark had put on his tux.

"Didn't I tell you?" she said. "We're not going to the Met."

"You didn't tell me."

"Sorry. You look great."

They'd grown up together. He had escorted her to her first prom, her second prom, her coming-out at the New York Infirmary Ball. She'd gone to Chapin and Farmington and learned her horses and tennis and French alongside Vanderbilts and Rockefellers and heiresses from Brazil. One night three years ago she had proved astonishingly good at kissing, but he'd decided to leave her a virgin and keep her as a sister and pal. And there matters had rested.

They took a taxi. He recognized the old brick building that had once been a bar. He recognized the precarious wooden chairs, the tattered blue curtain, the upright piano jammed against the concrete wall. Nita had brought him back to the Domani Opera.

"Why are you interested in an amateur outfit like this?" he asked as they found their seats.

"The girl singing Annina is Mom's goddaughter."

The lights went down. The audience was shushing and rustling expectantly. The piano struck up the Prelude. *Traviata*, misplayed.

And then in Act One the young woman playing Flora stepped forward wearing feathers and jewels in her hair.

It was Ariana.

Mark sat sweating, breathing too rapidly, hands trembling, heart pounding.

The performance was a long, agonizing route through a maze of poor singing, tottering sets, bad direction.

After the curtain calls Nita turned to him apologetically. "I know it's an awful nuisance, but I promised I'd go backstage. Do you mind?"

He managed to stammer that no, it wasn't a nuisance, no, he didn't mind at all.

There were a dozen people already in the women's dressing room. The visitors were standing, the performers sitting, crowding for mirror space to pull off fake eyelashes and to cream off their stage blushes.

"Shoog, you were fabulous!" Nita hugged the chubby girl who had sung the maid. "Mark—Shoog. Shoog, Mark."

Mark met Shoog's gaze, but he was searching for Ariana. He heard a voice behind him say, "Mark—Mark Rutherford."

He turned. Ariana's glance touched his so gently that the look was a caress in itself.

Why does it hurt when I look at her? Why is there a tightness in my chest when I see that the skin of her arm is the color of honey?

"That was a wonderful performance," he said. He remembered to turn back to include Nita. "Nita, this is Ariana," and then, with a foolishness that surprised even himself, "Ariana sang tonight."

He could feel Nita wondering who, what, how, why, all sorts of things, and he could feel Ariana wondering the same things.

Nita was making appropriate well-bred sounds, and he stood there wishing he could muster the bad manners to ask Ariana for her phone, her address, do something to let her know that though he was with Nita he wasn't *with* her.

But he was a gentleman. Politeness held him back.

Then there were goodbyes all around and Ariana gave him that look again, that dark questioning caress of the eyes.

"Who's Ariana?" Nita asked in the cab.

"I can't say I really know her. We met last spring at an audition."

"I didn't know you still sang."

"Sometimes I do."

They rode eight blocks in silence. Nita said, "She's pretty."

"Do you think so?"

"Yes, I think she's very pretty."

2

HARRY FORBES STARED AT MARK WITH EYES OF UNDISGUISED shock. "You've lost weight."

Mark and Harry had roomed together sophomore year at Harvard, and tonight they were sitting in Harry's brownstone floor-through on West Tenth. Harry was working for a brokerage house on Wall Street. He'd had two raises in six months and grown a mustache and gained fifteen pounds.

He asked about Mark's studies.

Mark told him about Ariana. "I can't get her out of my mind."

Harry mixed a second pitcher of stingers and settled back into the armchair and listened to Mark for thirty minutes. Then he reached for the telephone.

"Who are you calling?"

"I'm about to arrange the rest of your life." Harry dialed and in his finely chiseled voice inquired, "Operator, do you have a listing for an institution known as the Domani Opera? . . . Thank you." He dialed again. "Hello, may I speak with Ariana Kavalaris, please?"

Mark's eyes came up in a glaze of disbelief.

"Do you know where I might reach her? . . . Thank you." Harry broke the connection. "Operator, there's an institution known as Fennimore's luncheonette on Ninety-third Street and Broadway? . . . Thank you." He dialed. "Ariana Kavalaris, please? Hi. This is Mark . . . Mark Rutherford, remember me?"

Mark jumped out of his chair. Harry waved him back.

"How've you been? Look, I don't want to keep you from all those starving customers. But I have tickets to the opera next week. Would you be interested?"

He covered the phone and whispered. "What night?"

Mark mouthed, "Tuesday."

"How would Tuesday be? . . . Where shall I pick you up? . . . At work? Fine. Seven-thirty. See you then. Looking forward to it."

For a moment Mark was speechless. "You can't just—"

Harry twirled the stem of his stinger glass. "Somebody had to before you die of malnutrition. Now hurry up and get yourself a pair of opera tickets for Tuesday night."

Mark arrived at Broadway and Ninety-third Street at 7:15. Fennimore's was all neon lights and Formica and signs announcing specials du jour.

He watched Ariana through the window. She was wearing a crisp white uniform. She smiled at the customers, she smiled at the cook, and a stab went through him because she wasn't smiling at him.

At 7:25 he went in. He sat down at the counter and smiled till the smile ached. She served two red Jell-Os and one malted and refilled three coffees without even a glance at him. Finally with a flip of her pad and a pencil tucked over her ear she came to take his order.

"We have a special on stuffed pepper." She stopped. "Mark. Omigod, Mark!" She had the most beautiful smile he'd ever seen. "I just have to take care of two customers. Have a coffee on Fennimore's. It's an experience."

He sipped. She was right; it was an experience.

"One of these days," she said, "I'll make you some Greek coffee."

At her suggestion—"Taxis take hours this time of night"—they took a subway. The Metropolitan was a solid nineteenth-century building completely out of place among the skyscrapers of the garment center. She led him to the stage entrance, where painted flats were propped on the sidewalk four-deep against the ornate stone wall.

"There's not enough storage space for them inside. I love trying to guess which opera they came from. That one's *Forza del Destino*." She searched for the grease-pencil scrawl on an arched castle window. "I was right. Act One."

He glanced at his watch. "Ariana, we'd better hurry."

"Just a minute. Act confident—as though you belong."

Smiling a hello at the guard, she pulled Mark through the stage entrance and over to the switchboard. A tiny woman in a huge mink was coming down the curving wooden staircase. "That's Lily Pons," she whispered. "The best coloratura *ever*."

He stared, and it really *was* Lily Pons.

"Good evening, Miss Pons," Ariana said cheerfully.

The little woman smiled back at her. "Good evening, my dear."

Back on the sidewalk, Mark shook his head. "You have guts."

"Why? I have as much right to walk in there as anyone else—after all, I'm going to sing at the Met one day."

They rounded the corner on to Broadway. The huge clock above the large, square canopy said there was one minute to get to their seats. They hurried through the lobby as the last bell was sounding. There was a moment's blaze of tasseled dark red plush and gold trim, of diamonds and evening gowns and dinner jackets, and then in the dimming lights they dashed down the aisle to their seats.

"I'm not dressed!" Ariana whispered.

"They were the only seats I could get," Mark lied. He'd gotten the orchestra seats to impress her.

"What am I complaining about. They're the best seats in the house."

She took off her woolen coat. He led the way past subscribers' knees into their seats. Jeweled dowagers peered at the young man in the three-piece Brooks Brothers suit and the girl in the Penney frock.

With an explosion of woodwinds and strings, the opera began. The Metropolitan's great golden curtain rose on the courtyard of the inn at Amiens. It was the same production Mark had seen years ago. The sets, the melodies, the actions had not changed. He had grown into a man, but *Manon Lescaut* was not a day older.

As Mark watched the singers, time seemed to fold back on itself. He sensed that these characters had gone through these motions a thousand times before: Manon had stepped out of the coach bearing her to the convent, glimpsed Chevalier des Grieux, and fallen instantly in love. He knew people never had such emotions, let alone belted them out at the top of their lungs, and yet four thousand people were sitting here in the dark with him believing every note of it.

He looked at Ariana, saw her face caught in the light from the stage, framed in long dark hair. Her attention had the intensity of prayer and it altered his own perceptions, as though he were seeing with her eyes, hearing with her ears. He had sat through dozens of operas, but for the first time in his life the characters and the situations on the stage seemed wonderfully, terrifyingly real.

He understood that what he was seeing was not life, not even an attempt to mirror life. It was a dream, the dream of the girl beside him and of the other people sitting in that theater. *I've been listening too long with my head,* he realized. *This stuff was written for the heart.*

He was especially impressed by Ricarda DiScelta, the soprano singing the lead. Though in her late forties or early fifties, she managed to project all the youth and sensuality and raw innocence of Manon. Any actress her age playing the part would have been ridiculous, but singing it, she was absolutely convincing.

During the first intermission he took Ariana to Sherry's on the grand tier. With its old-fashioned paintings and sculpture and red-flocked wallpaper, the restaurant had a fading nineteenth-century elegance. At a little table next to one of the mirrored columns, they lingered over high-priced pastries and thick black coffee.

"You seem to work awfully hard," he said. "That job at the luncheonette and then all the roles at Domani . . . "

She speared the last of her Napoleon on her fork. "Everyone says I'm working too hard, stretching myself too thin."

"Is it true?"

"If I expect to get anywhere in this world I have to have a plan and I have to stick to it."

He felt that he and this dark-haired girl lived in two different universes. "Your world sounds like a lot tougher place than mine."

"Of course it's tougher. I'm an opera singer."

"Don't you ever get any relaxation?"

"Relaxation never built a career."

"But tonight you're enjoying yourself, aren't you?"

"Tonight I'm learning by listening and watching. Next week I'll come back and follow the performance with a score." She described the desks for score reading at the top of the house, placed in such a way that the study lights could not disturb the rest of the audience. "If you lean forward and sideways you can see a little bit of the stage." She said she saw most productions at the house twice, watching one performance, following the score the next.

The intermission bell sounded. As they dashed down the grand staircase she gave him her hand and it was marvelously soft.

He felt the touch of her arm on his shoulder as the tenor was singing "Pazzo son'." "He's forcing his high notes," she whispered. "He won't last another season."

Mark tried to muster a frown of intelligent agreement.

After the opera they took a cab. There was a giddy feeling of fullness just below his chest. He was thinking, *I could kiss her right now. She wants it as much as I do.*

"Right here," she leaned forward to tell the cabbie. "The house on the corner."

They got out and she began looking through her purse for her key.

He darted a kiss onto her cheek. She gave him a little smile that was almost shy, and then she handed him a piece of paper. "This is my landlady's phone. If you can't reach me at work or at Domani you can always leave a message."

He folded the paper into his wallet. When he told her his phone number she wrote it in her address book.

Good, he thought. *She's making me permanent.*

She hesitated. "Goodnight. And thanks. It was wonderful."

He watched her unlock the front door. She turned and gave him that same shy little smile again. He smiled back.

The next day Mark had lunch at Harry's club. "Why didn't she ask me in?"

"Maybe she didn't want to seem forward," Harry said.

"Would it have been forward to offer coffee to a guy who'd taken her to the opera? Or a drink? Or at least a glass of water?"

"Maybe coffee keeps her awake. Maybe she doesn't have liquor."

"Maybe she doesn't have water?"

Harry put a hand on his friend's shoulder. "Stop it, Mark. You've got to be sane about this."

"How the hell can I be sane when I'm losing my mind?"

"By *acting* sane. Life, in case no one ever told you, is ninety-nine percent acting."

❅   ❅   ❅

Mark phoned Ariana at the landlady's. At Fennimore's. At the Domani. At the luncheonette. At the Domani. So much for acting sane.

And then he settled down to a state of sheer unrequited misery, realizing he was going to spend the rest of his life waiting for a girl with dark eyes who was never going to phone.

It was 7:30 and he was in his room at the seminary when the phone rang.

"Mark?" It was Ariana. "You phoned."

"Eight times."

"Nine."

"I guess I lost count. How've you been?"

"Busy. Dead. The usual. And you?"

"Oh, the usual. Busy. Dead. I enjoyed yesterday."

"Me too."

"Maybe we can do it again."

Two beats of silence. Ominous.

"I have a friend who ushers at the Met, he could get us in to a performance. It would be family circle."

"Sounds great," he said. "When?"

"Week after next?"

Why not the century after next. Stay cool. No gibbering now.

"Damn," she said, "there's my cue."

He heard a piano in the background, strident and out of tune.

"I'll phone when my friend can get passes," she said, "okay?"

He spent the next two weeks not studying, not hearing from her, somehow managing not to go crazy.

3

AUGUSTA RUTHERFORD PHONED BREATHLESSLY. "MARK, HOW quickly can you change into something decent? We're going to the opera."

"Mother, I have a pastoral theology exam tomorrow."

"But you already know theology. Be at the Metropolitan in half an hour. Harry Havemeyer has given us his box. DiScelta's singing."

The opera was Mozart's *Don Giovanni*. Mark's mother had invited Nita Farnsworth and he understood that this was part of the Plot to Get Mark Married to the Right Girl.

"Hello, Mark." Awkwardness rose from Nita like mist.

"Hello, Nita."

Mercifully, the houselights dimmed and the curtain rose on a set depicting seventeenth-century Seville. Tonight, without Ariana beside him, Mark found Mozart's graceful score hopelessly at odds with the depressing tale of the sex-obsessed Don Giovanni and his string of female victims.

In intermission he took Nita strolling on the grand tier promenade. They found embarrassingly little to talk about before the bell called the audience back for Act Two.

It was close to midnight by the time the stage-flames of Hell swallowed up the unrepentant Don and the curtain fell to tumultuous applause. Augusta Rutherford, gathering up her fur, seemed to be struck by sudden inspiration.

"Wasn't that delightful? Mark, why don't you take Nita home?"

Mark's immediate thought was of a two-hour round trip to Lloyd Harbor, Long Island. Nita smiled and took his arm.

"Don't worry. I'm at the Barbizon. I can get home by myself."

"You'll do no such thing!" Augusta cried. "Mark would love to take you. Mark?"

In the back seat of the Checker cab Nita kept rearranging the folds of her skirt. Mark fumbled for conversation. "I didn't realize you were living in town."

"I've been here for a month. I'm working for Digby Welles. They're a small advertising agency. I'm really just a trainee. But it's a good excuse to live in New York. I like being on my own."

He wondered how much on her own she really was. The Barbizon had a sign in the lobby: NO GENTLEMEN BEYOND THIS POINT. The woman at the reception desk wore her hair knotted in a tight gray bun, and as she handed Nita the room key she raised a doubtful glance at Mark.

"Friendly place," Mark said. "I'm allowed to see you to the elevator, aren't I?"

"But not one step beyond." She kissed him quickly on the cheek. "It was good seeing you, Mark. I go home weekends, but maybe we can get together some week night?"

"That would be great."

Ariana phoned Thursday, ten minutes before their date. "Mark, it's a real disaster. Laurie was standing by for Sue, but Sue got stranded in Pittsburgh, so Laurie's going on, and I have to stand by, so I can't make our date tonight. I'm sorry. They phoned me two minutes ago. Raincheck?"

"Sure," Mark said. "Raincheck."

He sat on the unmade bed, absolutely still, trying to empty his mind of the hundred thoughts racing in it. His arm stiffened and swiped a book from the bedside table. Seven hundred pages of Dom Gregory Dix's *The Shape of the Liturgy* flew across the room.

Harry listened, half smiling, half nodding, and then he went calmly back to buffing his patent leather shoes.

"Mark, did it ever occur to you maybe she's telling the truth?"

"Standing by for a standby? Come on. She changed her mind. She got another date."

Harry looked at his friend like a doctor gazing at a patient. "Or it could be she's testing."

"Testing what?"

"Testing you, nitwit. Seeing what you'll put up with."

"Girls do that?"

"Everybody does it."

Mark sighed. "I don't think I can handle it."

Harry refilled the wineglasses. It seemed to Mark the wine tasted a little smoother than it had an hour ago.

"Harry, just tell me what the hell I'm going to do."

"You're going to go after her. It's obvious she's not going to join the seminary. So you'll have to join the opera."

"I tried that."

"But this time you're going to succeed."

Mark phoned the Domani Opera. The call was answered by a woman with a Park Avenue accent. She said her name was Mabel Dowd and she could see him that afternoon at two. "Be prompt."

He was prompt. Nervous and prompt.

Mabel Dowd's gray-streaked hair was pulled back in a no-nonsense ponytail. She wore pearls, a baggy sweater, and blue jeans. "What do you do—or hope to do? Operatically speaking?"

"Just about anything."

They were sitting in her cramped office. She chain-smoked Camels and told Mark what she didn't need.

23

"Baritones, tenors, dancers, pianists who can't transpose."

"I could paint flats," Mark said.

Domani performed two operas per month, Thursdays, Fridays, and Saturdays. In November they did *Il Trovatore* on a budget of $82 (Mark painted flats of castle turrets and gypsy tents) and *Adriana Lecouvreur* on a budget of $120 (he painted flats of boudoirs and drawing rooms).

He learned how to make doors of canvas and windows of cellophane and trees of cloth. He went for coffee. He swept floors. He turned pages for the pianist. He worked the lights.

He saw Ariana.

She was always chatting and laughing and kissing people, and his heart turned into a burning stone in his chest.

Once he managed to speak to her. The stage was ten feet deep and there was no crossover. The singers had to cross through an alley behind the theater. It was raining and he held the umbrella for her.

She said, "Hi," and smiled.

He said, "Hi," and smiled back.

End of conversation.

But not end of incident. As he returned to his place on the other side of the stage, one of the other sopranos asked him to fasten a hook in the back of her gypsy costume. Her name was Clara Rodrigo and she jiggled against him and her voice was low-pitched and mocking. "I think you have a crush on Ariana, yes?"

Mark had observed Clara Rodrigo. She was the sort of performer who held notes longer than her tenor and stole extra bows and spent intermissions misplacing rival sopranos' props. If you had a strong enough voice—and Clara Rodrigo could outshriek a fire siren—that sort of thing was called temperament.

"I think it's none of your business." Mark fastened the hook and gave her a friendly little push away.

"You're a nice boy," Clara said with poisonous sweetness. "Don't get involved. She'll hurt you."

Mark knew better than to put any faith in the word of a troublemaker like Clara. And besides, Ariana smiled at him during a choral rehearsal of *Nabucco* and waved during the soloists' rehearsal of *Die Fledermaus*.

But she also smiled and waved at a tenor called Sanche.

"I hate Sanche," Mark said.

It was a chilly day in February 1947 and he and Harry were having port by the fireplace in the Knickerbocker Club.

"Who the hell is Sanche?"

"He's the man Ariana's flirting with."

"Who the hell could flirt with a man called Sanche? Mark, it occurs to me that in certain matters you're an idiot."

Then came *Bohème,* and Ariana spent rehearsal time next to a balding baritone called Herb.

"Don't look surprised," Clara Rodrigo whispered, brushing past Mark backstage. "I warned you."

"She's interested in a balding baritone called Herb," Mark told Harry. "She's always next to him at rehearsals."

Harry gazed into his glass of ruby port. The steward had lit a fire and their shadows danced on the wall of bookcases.

"It could be Domani's short of scores and they're just sharing," Harry said.

Mark checked with a friendly contralto called Mildred. She said there weren't enough piano-vocal scores to go around, so the soloists had to double up. Mark was relieved until he saw Ariana standing at the water cooler with Max, the prompter.

Max was fifty years old and had arms like Popeye, and Ariana was smiling at him.

Slowly sipping his port, Harry listened to the tale of Ariana and the weight-lifting prompter. Then he cut Mark short. "Friend, I told you to pursue, not sit on your duff sobbing."

"How the hell can I pursue when she's interested in every male in the company but me?"

"Ask her for coffee."

Mark gazed at him uncomprehendingly.

"Coffee—the stuff you put milk and sugar in."

"Milk, no sugar," Ariana said.

"Same for me," Mark told the waitress.

They let their coffee cool and spent ten minutes discussing Domani politics: who was angling for what role, and whose aunt was putting up the money for the *Cavalleria Rusticana* costumes.

"I wanted to ask you for coffee before," Mark said, "but you always seemed busy."

She smiled. "Well, I've got voice lessons every Tuesday and Thursday at the Manhattan School of Music; French and German Monday and Wednesday evenings at New School; Wednesday mornings I clean for a little old countess who gives me Russian lessons in exchange."

"Russian?"

"Sure—a lot of opera houses do *Boris Godunov* and *Eugene Onegin* in the original. I have to be prepared."

"So that leaves—Monday, Wednesday, and Friday afternoons."

"Which are the days I tend counter."

He persevered. "And Tuesday and Thursday evenings?"

"Tuesday I study stage movement at Stella Adler. Thursdays I get piano lessons from a teacher at Mannes. We barter. I clean her apartment Monday mornings."

"And how do you fill the long hours between?"

"I study scores, learn roles. There's always something that needs doing, believe me."

Part of him believed her, but part of him thought, *She's giving me excuses. She knows I'm angling for another date and she's saying no, a nice reasonable no because she's a nice reasonable girl.*

With unreasonably beautiful dark eyes that kept glancing away from his.

He lifted his cup. "Even soldiers in the front line get rotated once a month. Sounds as though you're always on call."

"I have to be. Ninety percent of the people who start out in opera never make it. They don't know a role when the soprano gets strep throat, or their German's no good. That's not going to happen to me. There are no excuses in opera."

They sat a moment in silence and Mark wondered about her. "Where do you get your determination from?"

Her eyes met his, dark and speculative, and he realized the thing they were speculating about was Mark Rutherford and his naïve-sounding questions.

"I suppose I get it from growing up on 103rd Street. Ever been there?"

He shook his head. Guiltily. He knew nothing about the slums of north Manhattan, nothing about this girl with the dark hair and eyes and the strange-sounding name. All he knew was that he was falling and powerless and he hated it.

And loved it.

A beautiful white smile came shining out of her face. "But if I want to sound ritzy, I can claim Fifth Avenue. My mother went into labor on the sidewalk in front of Flower Fifth Avenue Hospital. I was born in the emergency room. It's a great address to be born, don't you think? Fifth Avenue at 106th Street."

For a moment she stared into her coffee, not speaking.

"One summer we had a sublease on Ninety-sixth. That was elegant, because the railroad tracks were underground. But we moved back to 103rd. My mother still lives there."

"Tell me about your parents."

"Mom is French. Dad was pure Greek peasant. Most of his family still live in the Peloponnesus. He came to this country when he was sixteen. He was going to strike it rich. He was good with his hands—woodwork, gardening, there wasn't any kind of machine he couldn't fix. When I was a child he used to carve me little dolls out of soap. He was a night watchman for the Ruppert brewery for twelve years, and he saved enough to open a little restaurant. The mob told him he had to pay protection. He was Greek. He refused. They blew it up. End of my dad's career in cordon bleu moussaka."

"What happened to him?"

"He died later." Her expression turned serious, and he sensed she was holding something back.

After a moment he broke the silence. "How'd you get into singing?"

She brightened. "I always wanted to be a singer. When I was a kid I was lucky enough to have a couple of good teachers. They loved music. They even loved me."

She stared out the coffee shop window at Second Avenue with its trucks and taxis speeding past. She seemed to be remembering.

"They encouraged me. I studied hard. I worked hard. Last year I won a Guggenheim grant to the competition in Toulouse. It wasn't enough to pay for scores or clothes, so I became a very quick study on how to waitress in fast food joints. I went to Toulouse, I sang my heart out, I didn't win a damned thing, but I got a chance to hear my competition. And no matter what the judges said, I know I'm as good as anyone else my age singing today. Better."

She said it simply and without conceit, as though it were no different from saying the earth was round or two times two was four.

"I respect you," Mark said. "I respect you tremendously. And I think it's damned unfair that it has to be so hard for you."

She gazed at him. "Unfair? That's not the way I see it. I have the advantage over all the others with the rich relatives and patrons and the scholarships and the state grants. I know what I can do, I know what I have to do, and I know how to work for what I want. And I'm going to get it. It's going to happen because the only person it depends on is me."

Mark could feel pride and hope and certainty radiating from her like heat, and in himself he felt a tiny shaming bite of envy. He couldn't help thinking, *I wish I were as certain of my calling as she is of hers.*

"And now that we've covered me," she said, "what about you? How do you fit into opera?"

"I don't. I just like it."

"What do you like about it?"

You, he thought. "The tunes. The stories."

She gazed at him. "What do you do when you're not painting flats for Domani?"

"I study."

There was a momentary blank in her eyes. "Study what?"

Instinct warned him not to tell her everything too quickly. To her, the word *minister* might have implications of *priest* and *abstinence* and—who could say?—*guilt.* Save it for later, he told himself.

"I study languages." After all, Biblical Hebrew and Koine Greek were languages, weren't they?

"Why—to teach?"

He smiled. "That's right. Assuming anyone wants a teacher like me."

A smile tiptoed across her face and it was as though a light had come on. "They'll want you," she said.

She likes me, he thought.

She stood and suddenly she was getting into her coat.

She doesn't like me. She can't wait to go.

"This was fun. Let's do it again." She gave him that smile again, and it slid through him like a soft knife.

"Let's," he said.

The bill at Domani was Mascagni's *Cavalleria Rusticana*—Rustic Chivalry—and Leoncavallo's *I Pagliacci*—the Clowns. Opera houses the world over invariably paired these two short masterpieces of blood, thunder, and melody, and singers and fans affectionately referred to them as "Cav and Pag."

"Cav" always came first.

Tonight Clara Rodrigo was singing the heroine, Santuzza. She had a brief moment offstage during the "Intermezzo" when Max, the prompter, knocked on her dressing room door.

"Did you notice the bald man in the gray suit in the back row? He was taping the performance."

"Who is he," Clara said calmly, "this bald man?"

"No one knows. He left in a purple limousine."

"He left?" There was but one possible interpretation to this information. The stranger with the tape recorder had obviously attended the performance not to hear *Pagliacci*, but to hear *Cavalleria*, which was to say to hear Clara Rodrigo.

"Max, if the limousine is here tomorrow, will you let me know?"

The next evening, during the "Intermezzo," Max stopped Clara in the wings. "He's back."

Clara put on a dramatic red shawl to give the man with the tape recorder a new reason to look at her. She sang full-out, holding high notes, interpolating high C's. After seven curtain calls she changed quickly into street clothes. By the time she reached Second Avenue a faint drizzling haze lay across the city and a purple limousine was pulling away from the curb.

Luck was with Clara—a Checker cab sailed past, free. "Could you follow that limousine, please?"

The cabbie gave her a glance in the mirror.

"I'll give you five dollars above the meter."

The limo stopped on Central Park West at a corner building with chateau turrets. Clara paid the fare and, reluctantly, the tip.

A bald man stepped out of the limo and hurried into the building. Clara watched him exchange greetings with the elevator operator.

She darted into the lobby. It was clean, Art Deco, and for the moment deserted. The indicator on the elevator stopped at eighteen. Her eye ran down the line of buzzers. There were two names on the eighteenth floor: *H. Ross* and *R. DiScelta.*

Clara had to rest against the marble wall to catch her breath. Ricarda DiScelta, the leading soprano of the Metropolitan Opera, had sent a man to tape her voice!

She turned and walked slowly from the building. Her feet seemed scarcely to touch the pavement.

She wondered what role the Metropolitan would offer her.

In the music room of her Central Park West penthouse, Ricarda DiScelta sat steely black in the armchair. The voice of Clara Rodrigo singing "Voi lo sapete" poured from the little tape recorder: a surprisingly large sound from such a little machine.

"Such wonders nowadays," DiScelta murmured. "Too many wonders."

She listened. A wave of fatigue swept her. The voice on the tape was like a blank, unfeeling gaze. It revealed nothing of the soul of the music.

She rose from her chair and sat at the piano and stared at her hands: young hands once, but now the only young thing about them was an emerald ring that the King of Yugoslavia had given her in 1927.

She stared at James Draper, bald and gray-suited, serene behind his cloud of freshly exhaled cigar smoke.

Finally the burden of her thoughts came out in a sigh. "For a quarter-century I have trusted you."

"Stop staring as though I betrayed you."

"As though after thirty years I even have time to notice your betrayals."

"Ricarda, it is the voice you asked me to tape."

"It is not. The voice I heard on the tape of the Toulouse competition had fire and a top and a middle and a bottom. This top has no color. The middle has no force below a mezzo forte. The bottom sounds as though it belongs to an entirely different singer."

"It's a young voice."

"The problem is not youth. This woman simply is not the singer I heard on that tape."

James Draper shrugged and poured himself another port. "I sat through two dreadful performances and I did what you asked."

"And you failed. Which means I myself shall have to sit through a third dreadful performance. Will there be a third dreadful performance?"

"Next Thursday."

"Thursday of all nights. I'll have to cancel dinner at the governor's."

✿　✿　✿

Ricarda DiScelta arrived two minutes before the announced curtain time. There could not have been more than thirty people in the audience. She took her seat in the back row.

An out-of-tune piano struck Mascagni's opening chords.

She watched the performance with a mixture of nostalgia and pity. It reminded her of her own student days. She paid hawklike attention to the Rodrigo girl. She watched the face move across the stage, through the darkness and the light. She was more than ever convinced: *This is not the voice I heard on the Toulouse tape.*

She sat through the opening scene and wondered why these youngsters offered themselves so willingly to opera. What power did it possess? It did not go out of its way seeking them, it was not a lover, not a father. In any given year fewer than 150 opera singers would earn a full-time living in the United States, and she doubted that even one of them was singing at the Domani tonight.

Her mood began lifting when she noticed the second soprano, a dark-haired girl who played the role of Lola. Something in the voice caught DiScelta's attention. It was not a formed voice. But it was a presence; it had spirit. She angled her program toward the light.

The girl's name was Ariana Kavalaris.

James Draper noted DiScelta's fretfulness when she returned from the performance. She stared at him balefully, then slipped a tape onto the tape player and pushed a button. The soprano solo from the Verdi *Requiem,* "Et Lux Perpetua," poured from the speaker. Finally the voice on the machine ended and became part of the silence in the room.

DiScelta sighed. *"That* is the voice. The Toulouse program says it belongs to Clara Rodrigo, yet I have heard her, and it is absolutely not her voice."

James Draper rose. "One of the singers scheduled before Rodrigo must have dropped out after the programs were printed. The voice that caught your ear belongs to whoever sang immediately after her."

DiScelta crossed to the rolltop desk in the corner of the music room. She rolled back the desk lid and found the Toulouse program.

She fitted her collapsible spectacles to the bridge of her nose. The print that had looked like tea leaves at the bottom of a cup came into focus. She scanned down the column of names. "The singer after Rodrigo . . . her name . . . her name is . . . "

She sank into a chair.

"What a fool I am, James. When I saw her at the Domani I was too stupid to make the connection, but I knew there was *something.*"

"What's the name, Ricarda?"

"Kavalaris." Ricarda DiScelta said the name slowly, as though reciting the syllables of a poem. "Ariana Kavalaris."

* * *

Clara waited six days.

There was no phone call, no word, no contract, no agent, no dinner invitation, no introduction to the management of the Metropolitan Opera. Nothing.

But on the seventh day *he* was there.

She saw him as she stepped onto the Domani stage as Rosalinda in *Fledermaus:* the bald man with the suntanned hands and head and the dark stockbroker's suit. Sitting where he had sat before, in the last dark row of the almost empty theater.

She sang her greatest Rosalinda. Triumph beat in her. The small audience—it was raining that night—called her back for four bows.

Afterward she sat in the women's dressing room, taking a very long time removing her right eyelash, waiting for him.

A man's voice said, "Excuse me."

She looked up. Her most charming smile flooded her face.

"Is one of you Ariana Kavalaris?" he asked.

Clara felt the disbelief that dwells on the edge of murder.

"I am," a voice said.

"Could I speak with you after you've changed?"

Clara's left eyelash came off much too quickly. The mirror told her that her features had hardened into a stony remoteness.

Something had changed forever. It wasn't exactly that the universe had caved in upon her, but she was suddenly aware of a large empty space above her head where two minutes ago the sky had been.

4

RICARDA DISCELTA WAVED HER VISITOR TO A HIGH-BACKED chair, keeping the brocade armchair for herself.

Ariana Kavalaris sat down lightly, smoothed her long dark hair, and arranged her hands neatly in her lap. DiScelta knew the girl at a glance. She was young—what girl wanting to sing wasn't—but her dreams were old, as old as song itself.

"Tell me," DiScelta said, "do you happen to know the 'Et Lux Perpetua' from Verdi's *Requiem?*"

Ariana was silent. Her gaze took inventory of the room: the Chinese vase of cut flowers, the marquetry tables, the elaborately framed oil of a cathedral at sunset. *So this is what comes with success,* she thought. *I wonder if I'll ever have anything like this room.*

After a moment she nodded. "Yes. I know the 'Et Lux Perpetua.' "

"Do you need the B-flat chord?" DiScelta gestured toward the Steinway. The keyboard lid was closed like a coffin's.

"No, thank you. I know what a B-flat chord is."

"You enter, of course, on a G," DiScelta said.

"I know what a G sounds like, too."

"Do you know by the sound?" DiScelta asked.

"My throat tells me, by the tension. Each note has its own tension, don't you find?"

DiScelta smiled. "Please. 'Et Lux.' "

The girl got up from her chair. The strong column of her neck swelled. Her voice rose and began to inscribe in time the spiritual shape of one of Verdi's most simple, most inspired melodies.

DiScelta listened, her eyes shut.

There were a thousand voice students in New York who were the cream of the best voices in America, in the world. And of the thousand there were at most thirty who would break out into international careers, who would shape for themselves recognizable international identities, who would record, perform, whom people would not only want to hear but would be willing to pay and pay exorbitantly to hear; and then, in every generation, there was *the* voice.

And Ricarda DiScelta was certain. This was that voice.

The girl had a slight breathing problem at the "Et Domine," the descending B-flat minor arpeggio.

"It doesn't matter," DiScelta said. "I can teach you all about that later. Go on, go on. Just keep singing. Don't break the line."

Ariana Kavalaris finished and there was silence.

DiScelta rose. She wore a knitted lace shawl fastened at the collar and beneath it, on a thin gold chain, an antique gold locket set with amethysts and rubies. Her fingers sought the locket and touched it now.

She turned to face the girl. "Singing makes uncompromising demands. There are many hardships, few rewards. It requires a leap of blind faith. Are you capable of leaping into the dark?"

A little drum of nervousness was tapping at the base of Ariana's throat. "Yes."

"Then I shall teach you," DiScelta said. "Much that I ask may strike you as unreasonable. But I shall ask nothing of you that you cannot do. As for the fee, well—"

"I'd give anything to study with you."

"Anything will not be enough. You must give *everything.*"

Their first lesson began with DiScelta asking, "What is opera? In one word?"

Ariana hesitated. "Music."

"No. Opera is theater. Its roots are musical, but its flower is human conflict. And that is why so many great operas are bad music. And why so much good music is dull opera."

They were discussing Mozart's *Don Giovanni.* Ariana worshiped Mozart. DiScelta obviously had her reservations.

"In Mozart," DiScelta said, "we see too many symphonic elements. Well, he came early in the history of opera. He has to be forgiven." She called his musical, as opposed to dramatic, forms oppressive, his key relationships "useless"—"As though it mattered to an audience whether an act begins and ends in D!"

With Mozart, she said, the singer was always in danger of putting the audience to sleep. "Arias follow patterned forms, acts are broken into separate numbers, recitatives interrupt the flow and are simply dead. True, there is invention, there is genius, but it is all delicate, tiny, a Dresden figurine. No blood. You have only one ally in Mozart: melody. But it is a treacherous ally."

DiScelta explained that Mozart's vocal melodies were based on instrumental models. "The challenge is to make his melody human. You must get into the characters—otherwise the music is boring."

They analyzed the opening scene. DiScelta pronounced it an unbroken music span. "Symphonic, not operatic." She praised Donna Elvira's first aria with its crazed leaps and pauses. "Here the music finally gives us character. There is wit. The serious and the comic come together. Audiences like it."

She pointed out the amazing ball scene that ended Act One, where three orchestras on stage simultaneously played a peasant dance, a contredanse, and a minuet. "A dramatic idea. Unfortunately, too harmonious. He is writing music, not theater."

She praised the supper scene in Act Two where a stage band played numbers by three different composers. "But again, too harmonious."

She criticized the finales of both acts. "Long movements held together by tonal relationships. The idea of ending a tragic opera with a cheerful sextet is straight out of the symphony, with its bright rondo finales."

She made a face. "Nonetheless, the opera can work—and does—provided the voice supplies the emotions which Mozart, in his perfection, did not. So, let us start with your character, Donna Anna. She is a woman in love with the murderer of her father. A neurotic. A woman torn. Put *that* into these pretty melodies and you will be giving us opera, not concert music. Which, after all, is the only reason audiences are paying today's criminally high ticket prices."

Ricarda DiScelta made a point of visiting her old teacher, Hilde Ganz-Tucci, once a week. Today her teacher greeted her at the door, frail as old parchment, but neat and clean and tidily dressed.

"Ricarda, what a pleasant surprise."

"It's not a surprise at all. You know I always come Tuesdays."

The table had not yet been cleared.

"I see you've had lunch," DiScelta said.

"Alone," Ganz-Tucci sighed.

And no wonder, Ricarda thought. Hilde Ganz-Tucci was a boring old woman. She was always complaining. She was doing it now. Her joints, servants, the Metropolitan Opera, back pains, inflation.

DiScelta interrupted. "Hilde, I believe I have found the one."

Hilde Ganz-Tucci suddenly looked very alert. "You're sure?"

"I do have a modicum of judgment. I can recognize talent."

"But can she be *the voice?*"

"I believe she can be. But time alone will tell."

"Sometimes," Ganz-Tucci grumbled, "you are a paragon of inertia."

"And of caution."

"Ricarda, we do not have forever. You risk a few hours a week. But I risk eternity."

"It's a risk," DiScelta remarked coolly—she had, after all, survived decades of her teacher's manipulations—"that we'll both have to take."

After two months Mark hadn't phoned Nita.

After four months she told herself to accept the fact that he was a childhood friend, *period;* she had plenty of work to keep her busy and she had beaux who *were* interested in her and it was silly to keep daydreaming of a guy who obviously wasn't daydreaming about her.

After six months she picked up the phone in her room in the Barbizon and gave the operator his number.

"Mark? Nita."

"Oh. Hi." He sounded like a very distant echo of a voice she had once known.

"Haven't seen you in a few light-years," she said.

"I'm sorry, Nita. I've been swamped with exams."

Exams all year, she thought. *Why am I phoning him? It's not as though I were eighteen going on fifty-six. It's not as though I didn't have other friends.* "Are you busy tonight?" she said.

"Tonight? I can't. Not tonight." And then, "Not for a while."

She couldn't help smiling at herself. *I couldn't take a hint. I had to phone. I wish to hell I didn't love him.* "Well, maybe some other time."

"Absolutely," he said. "Absolutely some other time."

"Goodbye, Mark. And good luck with all those exams."

She replaced the phone firmly and sat for a moment thinking.

Say goodbye to him, Nita. It was fun wrestling him when you were six and fun necking with him on sofas when you were sixteen but that was long ago. Now he's got a friend with dark eyes and dark hair and a beautiful voice and a strange last name and that kind of lets you out.

For a month Mark had kept his evenings free on the off chance that Ariana would be free. It didn't happen very often. Usually she called at the last moment, breathlessly apologizing that a waitress hadn't showed or a soprano had strep, and would he forgive her if . . .

He always forgave her.

But two days after Nita's call he was able to nail Ariana down to dinner.

"Nothing fancy," she said, and they went to a Chinese restaurant. They sat on a glassed-in terrace on Bleecker Street and stared at each other in silence.

"I'm sorry," she said. "I haven't spoken much."

He smiled to show it was all right, and the smile was a complete lie. It wasn't all right at all.

Dessert came and they showed one another the messages in their fortune cookies. His said *Now is the time to work* and hers said *You would be wise not to overextend your commitments.*

Afterward they strolled along MacDougal Street.

"Would you mind awfully, Mark," she said, "if we cut it short?"

Dear sweet Jesus, he thought, *cut what short? Here it comes, she's met a tenor.*

"Ricarda DiScelta has taken me as a pupil. She's hearing my 'Una voce poco fa' tomorrow." Excitement was radiating from her. She said it was the first time that the music world had given her a clear and unambiguous sign that she was part of it. "I want to be my best."

"What's 'Una voce poco fa?' " he asked.

"Rosina's aria from *Barber.*" She saw his blank look. *"Of Seville."*

"Oh."

"You don't mind, Mark, do you?"

"I mind like hell but I hope you have a great lesson."

"Will you help me celebrate—afterward?"

"You'd better believe it."

Ariana sang "Una voce poco fa."

DiScelta listened. After an endless silence she folded her hands in her lap.

"With Rossini, Bellini, and Donizetti," she said patiently, "we come to the flowering of melody. What is artificial in these works is what is artificial in song itself. No one makes love or commits suicide in verse, refrain. Except in this school of opera. But it doesn't matter. These melodies touch the heart. Or, rather, they *must* touch the heart if anything is to be believable. Harmonically and orchestrally they are laughable—Wagner called them guitar music—but, properly sung, their emotional pull endures."

She had moderately kind words for Ariana's performance. "But you must let more spirit and wit shine through. The aria is rhythmically alive and melodically inventive and the cabaletta never fails to delight. And there are even dramatic orchestral touches."

She pointed out the famous "Rossini crescendo" that occurred throughout the score—the orchestral phrase that appeared unobtrusively in the strings, then throughout the orchestra, moving upward in register, gaining in volume and power, till the voices joined in and all musical hell broke loose.

"Say what you like, naïve it may be, obvious it may be, but it is a device that always works in the theater. Rossini knew how to get applause. And therefore he is every singer's friend."

Moving on to Bellini, DiScelta became less enthusiastic. "A throwback, but he wrote extremely long melodic lines such as no one else before him or since." That the melodies were all cut to the same pattern of two-bar units, that his rhythms rarely varied, that he dwelt endlessly on the third degree of the scale—none of this mattered.

"His melody has power. It seems simple, but it is not. Enormous breath control and *mental* control are required. The phrase must *never* be broken. Even when you are silent in this music, you must be singing. *The silences are part of the melody.*"

DiScelta pointed out that later composers had made Bellini's handling of emotions seem pallid. "But his emotions are never pallid in their own context. Look at the aria 'Casta Diva' from *Norma*. The climax—very unusual for this period—is postponed till the end of the aria, and when it finally arrives it is pure ecstasy. Chopin based his *piano* writing on this climax. It is anything *but* pallid. But because the melody is exposed, because there are no harmonic or orchestral supports, the delivery must be perfect. Straightforward music is always more treacherous than complex music. The voice has nowhere to hide."

Which led to three hours of drilling in staccato runs, roulades, and trills. Which led to Donizetti.

"Again," DiScelta said, "melody is all. Donizetti is nothing in the way of harmony or orchestra. He uses the same devices over and over, and no other composer dared to wring so much sadness from plain major chords."

She pointed out other deficiencies: arias that climaxed too early, overuse of repetition, expanded cadential formulas that invariably ended in the major. "But he is brilliant, he is expressive, he achieves drama by shaping the vocal line—and he always lets the audience know exactly when to applaud. In opera this matters. Donizetti can still build careers."

As Ariana rode down in the elevator her thoughts were spinning. She had prepared one tiny aria and her teacher had rewarded her with a three-hour seminar of which she could remember not one word.

Am I studying with a madwoman? she wondered. *Or am I a simpleton?*

And yet that night, in her dream, she heard a voice singing "Una voce poco fa"—singing it with wit and spirit and proper style.

When she awoke, she recognized the voice.

Her own.

5

FOR THE CELEBRATION DATE MARK TOOK HER TO LA JACQUERIE, a "neighborhood" restaurant of the sort that only a neighborhood like Fifth Avenue and East Ninth Street could afford.

Ariana's fingers touched Mark's arm as they entered the restaurant. He felt her hesitate at the sight of the softly glowing place settings and the well-dressed men and women quietly conversing in three different languages.

"Panagia mou," she murmured, *"ti kano edho?"*

"How's that again?"

She smiled. "Just a Greek way of saying 'Wow!' Literally it means 'Virgin Mary, what am I doing here?' "

She glanced at herself in the mirrored wall. With a barely detectable movement she brushed her hair forward to cover her earringless ears. Jacques, the owner, welcomed them personally. He bowed to Ariana, called her "Mademoiselle," and then, joking with Mark, led them to a pleasant table in the corner.

Ariana asked Mark to order for both of them, and he ordered champignons à la grecque followed by a blanquette de veau à l'ancienne. Jacques solemnly advised a bottle of Pouilly Fuissé, and when that was gone he gave them a second, courtesy of the house.

Ariana spoke of her plans, her hopes, her disbelief that out of hundreds of students, Ricarda DiScelta had chosen *her.*

Mark listened and smiled and thought how beautiful her eyes were.

With their dessert soufflés he ordered champagne.

She lifted the glass and stared at the bubbles rising from the long stem. "I've never had champagne before. A little vin mousseux in Toulouse, but never real champagne. And this is my first real restaurant. Last November was my first orchestra seat at the Met. I'm doing a lot of firsts with you, Mark. It probably shows. Do I embarrass you?"

The question amazed him. "How in the world do you think you could possibly embarrass me?"

"We come from very different backgrounds. It must be pretty obvious by now if it wasn't before."

"What difference does that make?"

"Maybe a big difference, maybe just a lot of little differences. But still a difference. Maybe I'm using the wrong fork. Wearing the wrong dress. Talking with the wrong accent. Maybe I'm asking the wrong questions, like whether or not I embarrass you."

"You could never embarrass anyone. You're one of the most tactful, sensitive people I've ever met."

She looked at him, her eyes moving carefully across his face, and then her gaze turned to the glass and with absolute dignity she lifted it to her lips and took a tiny swallow. It struck him at that instant that she was not Ariana Kavalaris from East 103rd Street, but Verdi's Traviata or Puccini's Manon, and that this was a moment not from life, but from opera.

"All my life I'll remember this evening," she said with a seriousness that surprised him. "Nothing will ever change it."

A little ache went out from him toward her. Their glasses touched.

"I'll remember this evening too," he said. "All my life."

And he did.

Afterward they strolled down Fifth Avenue and through the soft evening. They stopped at a sidewalk café on Bleecker and had cappuccinos.

She gazed up at the glowing night sky. "In almost three years it will be 1950—the second half of the twentieth century. Do you realize the fifties will be our decade, Mark? I'm going to be somebody, and you're going to be somebody."

They toasted one another in cappuccino.

"To us," he said. "To the somebodies we're going to be."

He walked her back to her room on Sullivan Street. They held hands crossing Houston, and at the door of 107 she handed him the key.

He followed her into the narrow front hall. There was a smell of sandalwood and old books.

"Three flights up," she said. "Sorry about that. My landlady's a light sleeper, so tiptoe."

He went up behind her. She opened a door on the fourth floor.

"The bulb's out. Do you mind candles?"

She vanished. By the streetlight from the window he could make out a decoupage screen of opera singers, opera programs, jackets of opera albums. A cabinet squeaked open and shut, and then she reappeared holding what looked like two votive candles. She placed them on the wicker table.

"Make yourself at home."

In the dimness of the room he could make out a daybed with a flowered print spread, a bentwood rocker, a spinet piano, bookcases overflowing with vocal scores. He opted for the rocker.

She reappeared holding a small cylindrical brass pot with a long handle.

"What's that?" he asked.

"A *briki*—it's for making Greek coffee." She lit a can of Sterno, held the *briki* over the flame till the water came to a boil, then poured in some rich-smelling ground coffee and sugar. In a moment the mixture foamed up. She blew out the Sterno and tipped the coffee into two Venetian-blue cups. "Specialty of the house."

As he took a cup their hands touched. A gentle explosion went off inside him.

She sat on the bed.

He sipped the incredibly thick coffee and heard her talking about the freak high F above the staff in *Lakmé* and the freak G-flat below the staff in *Salomé*, and what did he think of Wagner sung in English?

Something came out of him that must have sounded like an answer, but all he could think was: *I love you. I want you.*

And on a deeper, more disturbing level, he was thinking of the promise he had made when he entered seminary—not to marry till after ordination.

"When you've finished," she said, "you put your saucer over the cup, like so—and turn it upside down. And then you can tell your future." She lifted the inverted cup and stared at the pattern of coffee sediment in her saucer.

"What do you see?"

"Success. Good luck. Let's see yours."

He inverted his cup and saucer and lifted the cup.

As she bent to read his fortune the candle flame drew her face out of the shadows. "Success for you too."

She was leaning close to him now. With the movement of hand he could have brought their mouths together.

"I'd better go," he said suddenly.

She seemed surprised.

"Heavy day tomorrow," he said.

She saw him down the stairs. At the door she offered her cheek and he kissed her quickly, lightly. Her hand clung to his a tiny extra moment and then she stepped back and closed the door.

He crossed the street. When the faint glow in her window finally winked out, he turned away.

After three steps his fingers felt something in his pocket. He pulled it out and stood staring at a hard little point of light burning in the palm of his hand.

The key to her front door.

He hesitated only an instant, then crossed the deserted street and pushed the buzzer. One endless moment leaked into another.

The door opened. The moonlight fell on her face like a glow on a pale flower.

"Your key," he said.

Their hands touched. The key fell to the pavement with the ringing sound of a coin.

He put his arms around her and drew her toward him. They kissed. How long they stood pressed against the wall of the narrow hallway he had no idea. It could have been minutes. Years.

"The key," she whispered.

He knelt and picked up the key from the sidewalk.

This time one of the steps on the second flight squeaked. He half expected the landlady to come flying out of her room on a broomstick. But silence closed in, sealing off the moment.

Ariana shut the door of her room behind them, closing them into a space separate from the world.

She brought a candle to the bed and as she set it on the table a little circle of light slid down her face. They sat there gazing into each other's eyes, smiling. He drew her toward him.

It began awkwardly, tenderly.

At first he was satisfied to touch her breasts through her clothing, but then she took off her blouse and skirt and unhooked her bra. Following her lead, he undressed too. His eyes never left her and he almost tripped over his trouser leg.

His hand returned to her breasts. They were small and firm. The brown nipples seemed to become larger when he began stroking them again.

His eyes dropped to her flat stomach, her full thighs. He kissed her on the mouth.

Gently, instinctively, she pressed his head down. His lips touched her nipple. She had never felt the sensation before. The idea came to her, *I'll never in my life need more happiness than this.* She wished time would stop them, that this instant could become their eternity.

And something changed.

She wasn't instructing him any longer. His hands caressed her everywhere and his mouth was everywhere at once. He bent her backward onto the bed and positioned himself above her and she could see his eyes gazing down into hers in the candlelight.

And then he hesitated. "Am I going to hurt you?"

"No," she whispered, "you won't hurt me."

"But what if I get you pregnant? You'd better just take me in your hand."

Without thinking, letting her instinct rule her hand, she guided him into her body. Pain came in a rush. She held to him and it passed, leaving only an unfamiliar warmth.

Then he was whispering, "Ariana, oh, Ariana," and she felt him slide into her, strong and thick. He began moving easily and she arched in answer and her eyes shut.

"You're in my body—in my body," she murmured.

He held back, not wanting to rush the moment, and then she was begging him and the moment was there.

"Mark," she cried, "oh, yes, oh, Mark!"

There were tears on her closed eyelids, glistening in the candlelight. He kissed them away.

"Oh, Mark," she sighed, "that was beautiful."

"It was for me too."

She pressed meltingly against him. Later they made love again: tender and solemn and gentle and over and over.

In the morning daylight streamed through the dormer window. An alarm clock went off and she swatted a hand out and silenced it.

"You make the coffee," she said, "I'll run the bath."

They bathed together, like children. She soaped him and squeezed the sponge over him and warm water rained down on him.

He said quietly, "I didn't tell you everything. There's something you have to know about me."

She looked at him curiously and stepped out of the tub. "You're married," she said.

He smiled. "No. I'm going to be an Episcopal minister."

Her gaze fell on him strangely and there was an instant's silence and then she broke into laughter. "My dear beautiful Mark."

"It doesn't bother you that I—believe in God? That I want a church and a parish and I want to spend my life—serving Him?"

"But don't you see—I believe in the same thing, only I call it music?"

He looked at her and suddenly it was all possible: his dreams, her dreams, the world. He crossed the room and hugged her. "I'm going to hold you in my arms every night and keep you safe all your life."

"It's funny, but I have the feeling I'm the one who's going to have to keep you safe."

It was close to midnight, and a young flashily dressed man of twenty-five or so was leaning idly against a car parked outside the luncheonette. Ariana knew it wasn't his car. How she knew she couldn't have said, but she knew. He was wearing a stiff-brimmed fedora cocked at a theatrical angle. It left his face half in shadow, but she sensed even without seeing his eyes that he was watching her.

He waited till the shop was empty and then he pushed open the door and came in. Ariana began memorizing, deciding how she was going to describe him to the police after the holdup. He had deep brown eyes and curly hair and a broad, olive-dark handsome face. No scars.

He slid one haunch onto a stool and settled down at the counter. "I'll have a cup of coffee—hot, regular, and made this week."

"You're going to hate ours." She poured a cup and slid it across the counter to him.

He seemed to chew the coffee. "What else you got?"

"What do you like?"

His tongue flicked over his lips. "Anything you like, baby."

She couldn't tell. Maybe it wasn't a stickup. "I like opera."

"Funny thing. All my life I've wanted to go to the opera." His hands went up to fool with the knot of his cream-and-tan striped tie. He smiled. "Just to see what it's like. You sing in the opera?"

"I sing in *an* opera. It's not the same as singing in *the* opera."

He stirred his coffee. "Where are you from?"

"My part of the world."

"I was born in Armenia," he said, "but my father was Greek." He told her that he had emigrated to Uruguay at seventeen. She wondered why he thought she'd be interested. "The coffee's a hell of a lot better down there."

"So why are you up here?" she said.

"New York's got possibilities. What time do you get off work?"

"Forget it. I have a friend."

He got up from the stool. He slid a $20 bill across the counter. "Take your friend to the movies. On me. Say it's a present from Nikos."

Ariana and Mark went to the movie at the Waverly the next night, *Gentlemen's Agreement.* "Put your money back." She slid a $20 bill through the cashier's window. "Tonight the show's on Nikos."

"Who's Nikos?"

Later, in her room, making coffee with the *briki* over a Sterno, she told him who Nikos was. "Just about the handsomest Greek-Armenian thug you ever saw."

Mark was standing by the window looking up into the cold milky wash of stars. "And you took money from him?"

"It was a tip."

He couldn't explain what was happening to him. He was two people at once, one of them loving her and the other wanting to twist her head off. "A twenty buck tip for a cup of coffee? *That* coffee?"

He turned to stare at her, to try to understand why she was putting him through this terror.

"Mark, what's wrong?"

Rage almost strangled his voice. "Don't you know I love you?"

"Panagia mou," she murmured.

"Why do you have to bring the Virgin Mary into this?"

"Panagia mou doesn't always mean 'Virgin Mary.' Sometimes it means—*prove it.*"

He proved it; perhaps a little too energetically. Ariana phoned the next day and said the landlady had heard them. "She laid down a new law. No visitors. It's a renters' market. Rooms are hard to find."

"Don't lose your room. Pacify the old bag. I'll think of something."

"Why not use my place?" Harry Forbes said. "I go to Vermont weekends. That gives you two nights a week."

They were sitting in the Knickerbocker, sipping port by the fire.

"Harry, I couldn't ask—"

Harry scrunched a hand into his pocket and pulled out a key ring.

43

"Relax, I'm taking advantage of you. The deal is, you feed the cat and change the litter, okay?"

And so Mark and Ariana took up weekend residence in the Tenth Street apartment of Harrison Forbes. The flat had a huge living room with walnut paneling and a beautifully proportioned marble fireplace that actually worked. There were yards of bookshelves loaded with novels and poetry and there was even a little spinet piano tucked into a shadowy corner of the hallway.

Ariana struck a resounding chord. "Guess what, Mark. You get to hear me rehearse."

Those weekends were full of light and lightness. Mark discovered a whole dimension of existence he'd never known before. There was time to thumb through books he never intended to finish, time just to sit in a chair and savor a sensual rush of warmth and well-being and above all time to be with the person he loved.

For those first seven weekends, Mark Rutherford Junior had never known a deeper feeling of peace and joy. And neither, he had every reason to believe, had Ariana Kavalaris.

On the eighth weekend, as Mark slipped his borrowed key into the tricky upper lock, he heard voices, and when he opened the door Harry Forbes and Ariana were sitting in the living room, chatting away like old friends.

There were cocktail glasses, one in Ariana's hand and another in Harry's, and ice and a lemon twist were waiting in a third glass on the tray, right next to a half-empty martini pitcher beaded with condensation.

Ariana rose, uncurling one limb at a time from the sofa. "Hi, hon." She came unhurriedly across the room and kissed Mark.

She had a cigarette in her hand. Mark had never seen her smoke before. He supposed Harry had arrived unexpectedly and offered Ariana a cigarette and she'd accepted out of politeness.

"Hi, Harry," he said. "Nice to see you."

"Allegheny Airlines canceled my flight to Woodstock," Harry said. "Ergo, I'm staying at the Knickerbocker Club and had to come by for a change of undies. Didn't mean to barge in."

"It's your home," Mark said, and he had a sense the words sounded churlish.

"I invited Harry for dinner," Ariana said.

"Correction," Harry said, "I invited myself."

"Great," Mark said. "That's great." He tried to see Harry as Ariana saw him, and he saw a beautifully dressed, beautifully built young fellow who was lazy, good-looking, aristocratic, completely at ease and completely irresistible. "I want to hear all about Vermont."

"And I want to hear all about you two." Harry's eyes had the glint of empire.

Despite himself, Mark's guard went up. He did his best to hold up his part of the chitchat for a few moments and then he went to the bathroom for an aspirin—Harry's bathroom with all the right male colognes arranged in just the right way on all the right shelves.

Ariana followed him. "Are you okay?"

"Just a little headache from squinting at small print." He gulped two Bufferins and a handful of water from the tap. "Harry likes you."

"He has to. I'm your you-know and he adores you." She kissed him and left him dousing his face in ice-cold water.

When Mark returned to civilization Ariana was in the kitchen tossing unmeasured herbs and spices into baking pans and salad bowls and Harry was smoking a pipe, propped in the doorway, looking on.

Dinner was a great success. Ariana somehow threw together a cool green salad of arugula and avocados with lemon and salt and a beautiful leg of lamb au poivre and baked potatoes scooped out and mashed with butter and parsley and bits of bacon and then stuffed back into their crispy skins. There was a bottle of more than decent Burgundy and for dessert fresh pears, unbelievably perfectly ripe, and a block of Stilton cheese that Harry had brought from a specialty shop on Cornelia Street.

It was a gourmet feast, the sort of evening that years from now they would remember as the good old days.

But tonight Mark could find nothing good or old about it. His mind was a beehive of uncertainties, stinging and buzzing. He ate little and he never took his eyes from Harry, and Harry never took his eyes from Ariana, who was busy serving and filling glasses and bursting with conversational brilliance.

Mark got the message. She was the perfect hostess. No need to hide her from anyone.

Afterward, as Ariana was in the kitchen making espresso, Harry said in a lowered voice to Mark, "You're happy, aren't you?"

"Happier than ever in my life."

"So's she," Harry said. He was silent a moment, his eyes appraising Mark. "Have you asked her to marry you?"

"Not exactly."

"What do you mean, not exactly?"

"I have a feeling if I asked now she'd say no. Or not yet. Or something evasive."

"What gives you that feeling?"

"She has some notion about our backgrounds."

"What about your backgrounds?"

"That they're different."

"That's not a notion, that's a fact."

"She has some notion that it matters."

"Are you sure you're not the one with that notion?"

Mark was silent.

"Mark, that background nonsense was fine in the nineteenth century, but today it's just plain beside the point. Ariana is head and shoulders above any deb you or I ever waltzed at the Infirmary Ball. If you don't grab her right now, you're a fool."

After Harry had gone and they were washing up the dishes Mark said, "I adore you, you know that?"

"Of course I know, what kind of idiot do you take me for?"

"No kind. I'm the idiot, not you."

Ariana broke into a smile, and her face lit up the kitchen and all of his world. "Come here, idiot."

They kissed and a china gravy boat almost broke slipping back into the sudsy sink water.

"Could you ever fall in love with a bimbo like Harry?" he asked.

"How do I know? I've already fallen in love with a bimbo like you."

"Could you ever marry a bimbo like me?"

"Maybe. If a bimbo like you ever asked me."

"Will you marry me?"

"Ask me the day after tomorrow."

"Know something? You're a tease."

She tossed him a dish towel. "Let's get these dishes done and then we'll see who's a tease."

6

HARRY'S BROKERAGE HOUSE DECIDED TO SEND HIM ON A FACT-finding tour that summer. "I'll be hitting the fact centers of the world—Kenya, Singapore, Paris, Helsinki," he explained wryly when he came to the apartment to tell Mark and Ariana they could have it for the summer. "All I ask is you mind the cat's litter."

Which solved the problem of summer and how Mark and Ariana were going to manage to spend it together.

Mark enrolled in a course in clinical pastoral care at St. Clare's Hospital and Ariana found that DiScelta was willing to come in from the country to coach her twice a week. "You're making progress," her teacher said, "and now would be just the wrong time to take a break."

For ten weeks Mark and Ariana were utterly hardworking, utterly together, and utterly happy.

The August heat that summer was the worst on record in over a century. Unlike Mark, Ariana had trouble sleeping. As a result she was underprepared for her second lesson of the month and was still reviewing a tricky cadenza in the score of *Lucia di Lammermoor,* and she didn't notice the floor when the elevator stopped.

Two men got in, talking.

She glanced at the taller of them: a black-mustached giant in a gray suit and red-and-black-striped tie.

She felt a needling speculation in his eyes. An instinct she couldn't quite define told her not to look again at him. She concentrated instead on the dynamic markings of her score.

The door whooshed shut and the elevator began moving down, not up. With a grimace of irritation she realized she'd missed her floor.

The tall man noticed her confusion and his dark liquid eyes were looking nowhere but at her. "Enjoy the movie?" he said suddenly.

"I beg your pardon?"

"You took your friend to the movies on me, remember? Nikos. Nikos Stratiotis. We met at that diner last spring."

He'd changed astonishingly for such a short time: put on better clothes and a lot of money. He seemed to enjoy her surprise, and what had started out as a smile on his face broadened into an uncontrolled grin. He was holding out a hand. It carried too much jewelry too expensive and too obvious for a man.

"And may I have the pleasure of presenting my good friend Mr. Richard Schiller? Richard's an agent representing concert artists." He added, "My young lady friend here sings, Richard. In the opera."

The agent's balding head had a thick, almost unruly fringe of jet-black hair. Ariana sensed interest in his eyes.

"Very pleased to meet you, miss."

"Now if only I could remember this young lady's name," Stratiotis said, "we'd be all set—and who knows, you might even have a client, right, Richard?"

"Ariana. Ariana Kavalaris."

"You study with DiScelta?" the agent asked.

She wondered how he knew. "Yes, for over two months now."

"Small world," Stratiotis said. "Richard and I were just up in DiScelta's place having a talk with her. Nice apartment."

Ariana tried not to show amazement. "You don't seem the type who'd be interested in classical music."

"I like classical everything, right, Richard? I used to read classics when I was a kid—Plato and Shakespeare and Molière in falling-apart paper editions. Now I read them in bound editions. Just between you and me, they lose something in leather." He laughed.

"You're late," DiScelta said.

Twilight had come to the apartment, blessedly air-conditioned and cool, but the fading day still sifted dimly through the high windows with their view of the park.

"I got stuck in the elevator," Ariana said. "With those two friends of yours."

"Ah, did Stratiotis discuss his scholarship?"

"He didn't discuss anything. He stared at me."

"I'm not surprised. You don't dress like a lady."

For an instant Ariana could not believe her teacher had said such a thing in front of the accompanist. But Austin Waters sat motionless and silent at the keyboard, as though he were no more than part of the furniture.

"I dress the way I can afford," Ariana said. "Nikos Stratiotis is rude and I'm surprised you receive him."

"My dear," DiScelta said, "you don't think Nikos Stratiotis is a friend. He has no value to me except money. And money, as it has been since the time of the Caesars, is a necessity. With what Stratiotis is offering you could dress properly. You wouldn't have to serve coffee on Broadway. You wouldn't have to buy used scores. You could take taxis to your lessons and be on time for a change."

"Are you suggesting marriage?" Ariana shot back. "Because the only thing he's proposed to me is prostitution. And frankly with Nikos Stratiotis I wouldn't consider either."

Austin Waters flicked her a glance, and it was as though he had shouted, *Attagirl, show her you're not going to be pushed around.*

A movement of DiScelta's hand held her mute. "Stratiotis has made an overnight fortune in real estate. At least he *says* it's real estate. Now he wants respectability. Someone has put it into his head to establish a scholarship for deserving artists. He contacted an agent, the agent contacted me, and we spoke for half an hour. I said I might possibly be able to think of a deserving student. The offer is, I assure you, quite legitimate."

Ariana's voice felt raw and ugly as she answered, "No."

DiScelta sighed. "Very well. Show me what you've done with *Lucia.*"

It was their last week in the apartment before Harry returned. Ariana had settled on the sofa with a cup of chamomile tea ("Fresh from the cliffs of Greece and very soothing—sure you don't want any?") and a piano-vocal score of *La Gioconda.* Mark crouched by her legs and laid his head on the cushion beside her.

"Marry me," he said.

She closed the score and pulled away. *"Panagia mou.* This isn't the time. There's too much that still has to be done."

"Like what? I get the bishop's permission, we marry."

She sat staring into her tea. "You once said you wanted to give me everything in the world."

"I still do."

"Then give me time."

"Time for what?"

"I don't even know where the break in my voice is. I haven't learned a complete major role. I don't know what my real top is. What if I'm a mezzo with a freak high?"

"What does all that mean?"

"It means not yet!"

"Not yet is not an answer."

She took his hand. "Till I have my own answers, I'm not giving anyone else any. I'm a singer, Mark. I'm a singer who wants to be your wife and one day will be. What I am not, what I will not be, is a wife who wants to sing. There are ten million of those. I want you to be proud of me."

"I'm proud of you now."

"Then let *me* be proud of me. Otherwise you'll have a bitch in bed and you'll hate me."

The situation, he decided, left no choice but to introduce Ariana to his family and show everyone concerned—especially Ariana—that he was Very, Very Serious. He phoned home that afternoon. "Mother, I'd like to bring a friend down for you to meet."

"Is this friend important?"

"She's important to me."

"Oh, dear. Then it's your father's and my duty to meet her. Does she eat chicken?"

"Of course she eats chicken."

"Then bring her Sunday at one o'clock and she'll get some."

"Why did she invite me?" Ariana moaned.

"You're blowing a simple lunch all out of proportion," Mark said.

"It doesn't sound so simple. Your mother thinks I'm trying to marry you."

"You don't have to go if it makes you uncomfortable."

"Doesn't she know I have a career?"

"I'll tell her you have a career and can't come."

"No, I'll tell her I have a career. You tell her I'll be delighted to eat chicken."

Sunday he found her in front of the bathroom mirror. "Does this neckline hang like a noose?"

"It hangs like a neckline."

"If I open my mouth I look like a pushy rabbit. How did I never notice? No wonder I failed the audition at City Center."

"You're not going to an audition, the neckline is great, and you don't look like a rabbit. And we're going to be late."

"Mark, will you please get out? I have ten minutes to perform a goddamned miracle."

Four minutes later she came out of the bathroom. Her face seemed to radiate light.

"You look great," he said. "How did you get that glow?"

"I slapped myself—hard."

Harry's car, for once, didn't stall. There was no traffic and the weather was perfect and the Hudson north of the George Washington Bridge was a painting of sailboats and mist and bright October light.

She took his hand and clung to it.

It wasn't just a drive forty miles upstate; it was a ride twenty years into the past, into a world where nature was clean and well behaved and the air smelled of apples and burning leaves and freshly tarred back roads. On this particular sunny fall day, the moneyed counties north of New York seemed to Mark to be as close to the Peaceable Kingdom as mankind was ever likely to get.

Three miles north of Oswick, Mark turned the car off Route 3 onto a curving rhododendron-lined drive.

"I've never seen gravel so white," Ariana said. "What do they do— wash it every week?"

"It's not gravel. It's oyster shells."

She had eyes of shock. "Who eats the oysters?"

"There's always someone willing to eat oysters." He nosed to the edge of the drive and flicked off the ignition. "Let's walk a little."

They got out of the car. She squeezed his hand and they crossed a long lawn. It was smooth and close-trimmed as the dark velvet of a billiard table. Mark felt they were rolling backward in time. The grass stretched down a hill to a wading pool with a little bronze faun cavorting in the center.

"This little fellow was my best friend," Mark said. "He knows all the times I was hurt, all the times I was happy. This was my good luck place. I used to come here to dream."

He was stalling, hoping she wouldn't turn, wouldn't look and see what was behind her.

But she turned, and a gasp came out of her.

Till now orchards and oaks and twelve-foot boxwood hedges had blotted the house from sight. But from the little sunken pool there was no way of not seeing it on top of the hill, at the apex of all converging sightlines, a mountain of slate tile and sandstone blocks and leaded windows, crawling in four decades' growth of ivy that had been nurtured to look like a century's worth.

"Jesus, Mark."

He knew what she was feeling. The twin turrets gave it all away: the eighteen-foot entrance hall and a dining room for thirty and two living rooms and six bedrooms and five and a half baths and a semidetached wing for servants. He felt like the son of capitalist pigs.

"My parents named it Avalon. You know the old song? That was their song. When they were in love."

She wasn't letting go of his hand. "Can I call it Avalon too? Do I approach curtsying?"

"Let's approach briskly and get it over with."

At the flagstone terrace she hesitated. "I'm dressed wrong."

"Don't worry. They're just rich, not fancy."

"That's the problem." She took off her earrings and bracelet and brooch and tucked them into her purse.

He swung the door open. Without alerting a single servant, they made it past three carved marble fireplaces, a Hepplewhite secretary, two Carpaccio portraits and a Ruysdael still life.

Ariana sucked in her breath and pointed to a tiny landscape hung in the shadow of a grandfather clock. "Is that a Corot?"

"Yes, it's an early Corot."

It was not Mark who answered, but a tall, powerfully built man who seemed to have popped out of the paneling. "My mother bought it in Paris in 1893." His full gray head flicked out a bow and his blue eyes appraised Ariana with all the finesse of ice picks.

"The man with the silent tread is my father," Mark said. "Father, this is Ariana Kavalaris, a good friend of mine."

51

Ariana and Mark Senior shook hands.

"Delightful to meet you," Mark Senior said in a tone very much like a bank manager refusing a loan.

Mark put a protective arm around Ariana and switched to loud, bright gear. "And in yon large sunny den, doubtless watering her prize azaleas, is my mother."

But Augusta Rutherford was not watering plants. She was seated by the window with a leather-bound book. Mark peered at the faded gold lettering on the spine. *"Paradise Lost?* Now, Mother, you don't expect us to believe you've reached the middle of that."

"Why not? It's perfectly *lovely."* Augusta's vowels came not from the throat but the jaw. She rose to her feet, a confident, well-groomed woman in her fifties with graying hair and a hint of outdoor suntan. She smiled firmly and held out a hand to Ariana. "Hello. I'm Mark's mother."

Mark wondered what you could tell by looking at Augusta: that she slept with a copy of the *Social Register* by her bedside? bred champion poodles and champion roses? had a dealer's eye for diamonds but never wore them before sundown? "Mother, this is Ariana Kavalaris."

Mark estimated that the handshake his mother gave Ariana was only a split second longer than a nod she would have given a shopgirl.

"You have a lovely house," Ariana said.

Error, Mark thought. *In Dutchess County, polite souls never comment on houses, diamonds, or age, except behind the back of the person concerned.*

"Thank you." Augusta smiled, showing tolerance. "Was your drive all right? We heard the roads were slick from last night's rain."

Mark Senior suggested drinks, and Ariana asked for sherry. Mark Senior made the drinks and passed them, and Mark wondered why Peters the butler hadn't appeared in full monkey suit to do the honors and intimidate the newcomer.

Augusta sipped and smiled comfortably.

Mark Senior asked what Ariana thought of Princess Elizabeth of England marrying Lieutenant Philip Mountbatten.

Mark took note of the subjects avoided in the next ten minutes. His parents did not ask where Ariana was from, who her parents were, or where she had made her social debut. He tried to imagine their reaction if he were to say, *Mother and Father, seated in your drawing room is Ariana Kavalaris of the East 103rd Street Kavalarises. Her father Pete ran a greasy spoon before his untimely murder. After pursuing studies at P.S. 45 and Henry Newbolt High, Ariana made her debut as a singing maid in an amateur performance of the Domani Opera Company. Her primary residence, when she can afford one, is a rented room in Greenwich Village. She does not pal with Rockefellers or Havemeyers. Her*

greatest dream is one day to sing an adulterous Druid priestess on the
stage of La Scala.

And I love her.

A uniformed maid floated in with a tray of clams individually wrapped in bacon strips. She moved like the tip of a glacier, and Mark wondered if Ariana could sense lurking beneath the Arctic waters the backup team of cook, laundress, gardener, and Norwegian couple—not to mention Peters, and by the way, where was the old corpse? Wasn't it usually his job to pass the clam goodies?

It was Augusta who finally, sweetly, worked around to the interrogation. "Mark has told us very little about you." (Translation: *He's told us nothing.*) "Are you a graduate student too?"

"I'm a student," Ariana said, "but not a graduate."

"Ariana studies voice," Mark said.

He sensed a missed beat, a ripple of hesitation before his father picked up the ball.

"That's admirable," Mark Senior said.

"I always think of Winston Churchill," Augusta said, "when I think of voice."

"Are you doing original research?" Mark Senior asked.

"Ariana *sings,*" Mark said.

Augusta touched her lips to the surface of her Scotch. "Ah. *That* sort of voice."

"Music is a high and legitimate calling," Mark Senior said, and Mark winced. His father was being democratic. "Where do you study?"

"Ariana studies with Ricarda DiScelta," Mark said.

"We heard DiScelta at the Met," Augusta said coolly.

"Wonderful voice, just wonderful," Mark Senior chimed in.

"Have you been studying long?" Augusta asked.

"One way or another, all my life."

"You sound admirably dedicated," Mark Senior said. "Augusta here studied piano when she was a girl."

"I never got any further than the 'Moonlight Sonata.' I didn't push myself. I'm sorry, now. It would be so nice to have a creative outlet."

"Music is a language," Ariana said. "Not everyone is a native speaker."

Smoothly omitting any reaction to what was just possibly a jibe, Augusta asked, "Will we be hearing you at the Met, Ariana?"

"Not for a few years, I'm afraid."

"You'll be hearing her in two years," Mark said. "Ariana's going to be the leading dramatic soprano of our age."

"What's a dramatic soprano?" Mark Senior said. "I thought they were all dramatic."

"Not all the voices are," Ariana said. "Only the personalities."

"Is your teacher dramatic?" Augusta asked.

Ariana smiled. "I'm afraid she is—in every respect."

"Sounds as though she beats you," Mark Senior said.

"She's capable of it."

Mark Senior grunted. "I don't care much for temperament. On the stage it's fine, but flying loose around the room—no, thank you."

"Luncheon is served, Mrs. Rutherford." The maid, not Peters, made the announcement.

"Bottoms up, everyone. Ariana?" Mark Senior offered his arm.

It was a short stroll to the dining room. Augusta seated Ariana on her right and Mark on her left. Mark tried to gauge the impression Ariana was making. But he had too much of himself tied up in her. All he could see was a glow where she was sitting.

"Would you care to say grace, son?" Mark Senior asked.

It was as though he had said, *Would you care to bring suit, counselor,* or *Will you perform the appendectomy, doctor?*

Mark's eyes glided down to the mahogany dining table and its four perfect place settings. The maid had laid the plain white Wedgwood: always simple, always suitable. Two dozen Revere spoons and knives and forks sparkled like implements ready for surgery. There were fish knives, and he knew there would be finger bowls. He realized he and Ariana had never discussed finger bowls.

He shut his eyes and tried to concentrate on gratitude.

"Bless this food to our use, O Lord, and us to Thy service, in Jesus' name, Amen."

His parents' amens came neatly synchronized and Ariana's came a half-beat later, musical and oddly sincere.

The maid passed butterballs and hot sourdough rolls and then she served the clear soup that had been Sunday lunch first course since Mark's childhood. He blew on a spoonful and asked where his parents were hiding Peters. "I want Ariana to get a look at the man I used to think was Dracula."

"Peters died," Mark Senior said quietly.

Mark set down his spoon.

"He had a long illness," Augusta said. "Didn't I write you?"

"No one wrote me."

"Peters was with us twenty-five years," Augusta explained to Ariana.

Shock hit Mark. Without warning, a part of his childhood had been amputated. He fought the water that pooled, salty and sudden, in his eyes.

Augusta Rutherford moved on quickly to brighter topics. "Dodie Bingham married and now she owns five racing stables."

For an instant Mark found himself hating his mother, this cold, handsome matron who would never soil herself by expressing any family or personal sorrow in front of a guest, and who implicitly forbade his showing any. He stared down at his plate.

Conversation went on, an hour of bringing Mark up-to-date on schoolmates and old flames he'd spent ten years trying to lose track of. Just the sort of stuff to fascinate an outsider. It occurred to him that possibly that was his mother's point: to remind the outsider—politely, of course—just how hopelessly far outside she was.

At the appropriate moment Augusta smiled and suggested, "Let's have coffee in the other room."

She never called it the library. It was always the other room, as though library would have been vulgar or boasting.

They sat sipping demitasse amid two tons of leather bindings and gilt lettering. Tiny spoons tinkled on bone china. Skirts and trousers were smoothed, legs were crossed. Augusta guided the small talk from the weather to roses to, "Do you sail, Ariana?"

"I've never been sailing in my life."

"What a shame. You must."

It would have been the perfect moment to invite her for a sail on *Chant de Mer*, the family sloop. The moment passed.

"I wish I had more time to get outdoors," Ariana said. "But there's so much to be done—voice lessons, theory, piano, language. I hardly have time for reading. And of course there's my job."

"You work?" Mark Senior asked.

Mark braced himself. *Uh-oh, here it comes.*

"I tend counter. Part-time."

There was an instant's glazed neutrality, and then Augusta managed an almost hopeful tone: "In one of the department stores?"

No, Mother, Mark wanted to say, *she's not working in Bergdorf's for a lark.*

"In a luncheonette. I don't know why they call it that. It's open for breakfast and supper too."

Mark's parents did not look at each other. It wasn't that they avoided one another's glance, but in that instant something passed between them that was far more fundamental than any look or word.

"You sound very busy," Mark Senior said.

"I may have to stop German lessons. For this year, at least."

"Tell me, Ariana," Augusta said, "what are your favorite roles?"

"I wish I had the voice for them all. I'd love to sing Violetta, Aïda, Isolde, Mimi, Turandot."

Augusta was smiling steadily, but Mark could see her thinking it sounded like a cotillion of very questionable young ladies.

"And when my voice develops, I'd like to try Elektra."

"But Elektra's so *unpleasant!*"

"No law says opera has to be pleasant."

Augusta gazed at this girl who tended counter and who had contradicted her, this serene child whose hands lay in her lap as calm and soft as fresh snow. "The operas *I* like are all pleasant."

Ariana drew herself tall in her chair. "But opera can be so much more than that. It can stir you, it can seize you and terrify you and seduce you—it can do all the things to you that people do."

People did not do that sort of thing in Augusta Rutherford's world, and Mark could feel his mother wondering about the people in Ariana Kavalaris's set. "Well, I certainly wish you luck."

"I wish everybody in the world luck," Ariana said. "I wish their dreams could all come true the way mine are going to."

Something uncanny reverberated in the silence. Mark felt it and he could feel his parents feeling it too. It was as though this girl with the dark eyes and wild dreams and crazy last name knew her own future, knew it the way psychics and saints are said to—innocently, completely, without doubt and without fear.

It was Augusta who spoke. "More coffee, anyone? There's just a little bit left in the pot."

That little bit left in the pot was a signal that, charming as the afternoon had been, Mr. and Mrs. Mark Rutherford Senior had given just about as much time as they intended to this particular interview.

Mark glanced at his watch as though for the first time that day. "How did it get to be four-thirty? We'd better get a move on if we expect to beat the traffic."

Chatting about traffic conditions on Route 3, Augusta steered Ariana out of the library. Mark Senior stayed behind to tamp tobacco into his pipe. Mark realized the afternoon was not quite over.

"Your Miss Kavalaris is very pleasant."

"Thank you, Father."

"You obviously haven't known her very long."

There was a question mark at the end of his father's statement but Mark let it dangle.

"You know, Mark, your mother and I feel you're treating Nita a little bit casually."

"Why do you and Mother insist on pretending I'm engaged to Nita Farnsworth or even want to be?"

"She's very fond of you."

"I'm very fond of Betty Grable."

"We think it's a little casual of you and we're surprised. That's all I have to say."

"Wait a minute." Ariana put her hand on Mark's knee. "Don't start the car yet." She rolled down the window and looked back at the house. The wind made a sighing sound in the oak leaves. The cidery smell of

October drifted across the lawn from the orchard. "This is what I want my old age to be—this light and this air and these trees."

"Marry me," he said in a joking tone that wasn't really joking at all, "and you'll have it all."

She shook her head. "I'm not taking the risk."

"What's the risk?"

"Little things like children."

"I said marriage, not children."

"What do you think marriage is? Marriage is children."

"You are maddening and simplistic. There don't have to be children."

"Then there doesn't have to be a marriage."

"Then let's get a place of our own and live together."

She didn't answer.

Congratulations, Mark. The parents weren't bad enough. You had to top it by insulting her.

He started the car and they drove in silence.

It began raining outside of Oswick and one of the windshield wipers wasn't working. He had to squint at the Taconic Parkway through a rippling Niagara.

"You weren't serious about living together," she said. "You couldn't be. You're a minister."

"I'm not a minister yet and possibly I never will be. I know what I want now, and that's to have a life with you. Today. While we're here and young and alive. Before I turn into Mark Senior and before you turn into whoever you're going to turn into."

"What would your parents say?"

"Who cares what they say? What do you say?"

"Maybe you'd better see who I'm going to turn into. Come meet my mother."

"She may not approve of me."

"She doesn't have to. Just say hello to her. It's an ancient Greek formality."

57

7

AS THE CAB SLOWED TO A STOP ON EAST 103RD STREET, IT SEEMED to Mark that they had landed on another planet. Ariana's mother lived in a neighborhood of crumbling six-story tenements and storefronts and a few, very few, scrawny trees.

Ariana stood a moment, just looking around, her eyes solemn and dark with remembering. "I used to walk up and down this street with my mother when I was a child. My brother and I played stickball over there in that vacant lot. It all seemed so big then, and now it seems . . . shrunken."

"You grew up," Mark said. "That's all."

"No. I went away. That's a very different thing from growing up."

She took his hand and led him across the sidewalk to 108 East 103rd Street. The building smelled of mysterious, spicy cooking. She led him down a half-flight of stairs to the rear cellar apartment.

"Mark, there's one thing Mama may mention—she usually does. I had TB when I was a kid."

He didn't know how she expected him to react. "What difference does that make?"

"The doctors got me over it, so I guess it doesn't make any difference. But she likes to bring it up. Be prepared."

Ariana knocked.

The door opened and a woman stepped out onto the threshold. She was in her mid-fifties, neatly dressed in a pale cotton print with a lace collar. She reminded Mark of the kind of waitress who would kiss the regular customers.

Mother and daughter embraced. Quickly. Very quickly. Ariana said, "Mama, this is Mark. Mark, my mother, Yvonne."

Yvonne Kavalaris angled her fine-boned, pert-nosed face upward, studying Mark. Finally she held out a hand. She had a very gentle grip, surprisingly soft skin.

"How do you do, ma'am?" he said.

"Very pleasant to meet you." Speaking with a slight French accent, she turned to her daughter. "It's a long time since we've seen each other. Why is that?"

Ariana shifted weight a little guiltily. "You know how it is, Mama. My studies, my work . . ."

"Strangers see one another more often." Yvonne led them into the dark little apartment. She served cakes and cookies and candies and coffee.

Mark complimented the cookies.

"Mama baked those herself," Ariana said.

"Il est très gentil," Yvonne said to her daughter. She turned to Mark and said, "I was telling my daughter that you're a very nice boy."

"Thank you."

"Of course, I knew you were nice the first time we met."

Mark registered bafflement as politely as possible.

"You don't remember? It was at the opera. You were standing at the fountain with Ariana. You were wearing one of those private school blazers, with shiny brass buttons. That's how I knew you were nice. Though I have to admit, when I saw you kiss my daughter, I wondered. But you were only eight years old or so. So I let it pass."

"That's right." Mark remembered now. "And you were wearing—"

"Black. It was two months after Ariana's papa died. I shouldn't have been at the opera, but Ariana begged me and begged me. We sat way up in that balcony. Are you an opera fan?"

"I love opera."

"I've never understood it. But it's a living." She glanced at her daughter. "At least they say it's a living."

"You'll see, Mama. It's a living."

At that moment there was the sound of a key in the lock. The door opened, and a young man with a narrow face and dark eyes sauntered in. He was wearing a wide-shouldered black pinstriped suit that could have come from a thirties' gangster movie, and he sailed a fedora onto a chair halfway across the room.

"Hey, Sis!" he shouted.

"Hey, Stathis!" Ariana ran to hug him.

He lifted her and gave her rump a pat. "Eating a little zabaglione, Sis?" His gaze took in Mark. "Hey, we got company?"

"As if Mama didn't tell you I was bringing a friend."

And out came a flood of Greek, two pairs of dark eyes focusing on Mark and leaving no doubt who was being discussed. Finally Ariana said, "Mark, this is my brother Stathis. Stathis, Mark."

Mark accepted a tough handshake from her brother. What hurt was not the bone-grinding grip, but the sandpaper calluses.

"Mark, you got yourself quite a girl."

"I told him already," Ariana said.

Following dinner a chocolate layer cake was produced, oddly tasteless after Yvonne Kavalaris's home cooking, and Stathis—his mouth full—proudly explained that it came from the bakery he ran public relations for.

Yvonne tried to have a serious talk with Mark about the Episcopal ministry. "You can earn a living at that?"

Ariana, who had taken over the serving, called from the kitchen, "Mama, we'll be secure, okay?"

"Sure *you'll* be secure, but what about your kids?"

"We're not going to have kids."

"No kids? Because of your lungs?"

"Mama, I happen to have terrific lungs."

Yvonne glanced at Mark. "You know what I mean."

A sigh came from the kitchen. *"Panagia mou, voithia!"*

"I won't have that Greek cursing in my house."

"Just because it's Greek doesn't mean it's a curse."

"I may not speak Greek but I know a curse when I hear one."

Ariana came back into the room and bent to kiss her mother. "Relax, Mama, we're just not going to have kids right away."

"Of course not right away, no one has kids right away, but—"

"What Mama means," Stathis cut in, "is when you do have kids will they be Catholic or Protestant?"

"We're leaving the church out of this," Ariana said.

Yvonne's face drained of color.

"Mama, we're not going to get married. Not right away. We're going to live together, just to see how it works. Like you and Papa did."

A silence flowed by. "That's fine," Yvonne finally said.

Stathis rose gloweringly from the table. "Hold it a minute, that doesn't sound so fine to me."

"Stathis, it's what they want, it's what they'll do. So shut up. Who wants coffee?"

"I'll get it, Mama," Ariana said.

"You sit. You've done enough."

While Yvonne was in the kitchen clattering saucers Ariana exchanged what-can-you-do raised eyebrows with Mark.

After a very long time Yvonne returned with the coffee. Her eyes were red. She bent down to hug her daughter. "I'm happy for you, Ariana. You too, Mark. I hope all your fairy tales come true."

In the taxi going back downtown, Mark asked Ariana how she felt the evening had gone.

"They'll get over it," she said.

"About your young friend, Ariana . . . she's a charming girl."

They were sitting in a softly lit corner at the library of the Union Club. Mark Senior had left the brokerage house early, Mark Junior had cut hermeneutics in answer to his father's summons.

"You're in love with her?" Mark Senior asked.

Mark nodded.

"Might I ask what, if any, are your intentions?"

"I have no intentions, Dad. Hopes, yes. Intentions, none."

"Is she pressuring you?"

"To marry her? No."

"Then I have a suggestion. Miss Kavalaris is an attractive young woman. You're a healthy young man. She's willing, she doesn't expect marriage." Mark Senior raised his cup of bouillon and carefully sipped and set it back noiselessly in its saucer. "Have your romance with Miss Kavalaris. Get her out of your system. Finish your studies. And in time you'll meet the right young woman."

"You're overlooking one thing, Dad. I *have* met the right young woman. And I love her."

"I'm sure you believe that."

"Have you ever been in love, Father?"

"Of course I've been in love. Everyone's been in love."

"Were you ever in love with Mother?"

Mark Senior stared out the tall club window at Fifth Avenue. A double-decker bus went by. "Your mother's a fine woman. She's made me very happy. And someday, if you don't make a grave mistake with your Miss Kavalaris, some fine woman will make you very happy."

"I'm not certain that's the sort of happiness I want."

"I'm not certain you're completely sensible at this stage."

"Father, I could bear your honest disapproval far more easily than this queasy tolerance of yours."

"Your mother and I only want what's right and happy for you."

"Thank you, Father. And please thank Mother too. Because that's exactly what I want too."

Mark told Ariana about his talk with his father.

"That does it," she said. "We're going to find an apartment."

They searched Hell's Kitchen, the Upper West Side, the meat-packing and warehousing district just south of Chelsea, and finally they found a two-room apartment on Perry Street in Greenwich Village.

As such things went, it was cheap. The building, pink stucco with a garden courtyard that had a fountain with a prancing Pan, had originally been a two-family townhouse, and was now converted into flats. The super, a limping old woman with dyed red hair, led them up a flight of stairs and pushed open a door on the first landing.

"Perfect fourth," Ariana said. "The hinges sing do-fa. The first two notes of 'Amazing Grace.'"

She explored. There was a bathroom with a tub that—if you hugged your knees tight—you could just manage to crouch in. Tucked away in what had obviously once been a closet was a two-burner stove and a two-shelf refrigerator and a sink. There wasn't a right angle or a window that slid easily or a straight-hanging door in the place. But there were two rooms, and a door between.

"I love it," she said. "Let's live here."

They paid the red-haired old lady $37 deposit—all the money they had in their combined pockets—and asked her to hold the apartment for a week.

At her next lesson, Ariana asked DiScelta what sort of strings came attached to the Stratiotis scholarship.

"None. He simply wants to support the arts."

"How much support?"

"He mentioned $300 a month."

"I've changed my mind. I'll take it."

Two days later Ariana presented the landlord's agent with a certified check for a month's rent plus a month's security. The next day she and Mark moved into 89 Perry Street.

They scrounged for paint and beat-up old tables from the warehouses on Tenth Street. They argued dealers into giving them mark-downs on worn rugs and battered lamps and scratched pots and an old oaken armoire with a cracked mirror.

In three weeks, they had the beginnings of a home. It was cramped and cluttered with musical scores and New Testaments and falling-apart Hebrew-English lexicons and a third-hand sofa and an upright piano from a Brooklyn warehouse and a brass bedstead Harry Forbes let them have from his barn in Vermont. Though they couldn't afford anything to eat but pasta, they were happy.

"Magda hates me," Ariana remarked over a bowlful of their Thursday evening special, tortellini marinara. Magda was the super with the limp and the bad dye-job. "I caught her looking at our mailbox. There are two names."

"That's logical. There are two people."

"Two people who aren't married. She looked at me like I was leading you astray."

"If you ask me, Magda shows great accuracy of judgment."

Ariana made a slingshot of her fork and flicked a spatter of marinara onto the exact center of Mark's forehead. "Watch it, smarty, I'm pretty accurate myself."

Richard Schiller entered Ariana's life with little steps.

First there was a polite note on Americana Artists Agency letterhead, asking if she remembered him, a friend of Nikos Stratiotis, asking if she might be interested in singing Annina, the maid, in a St. Louis production of *Traviata*.

She talked it over with DiScelta, who said, "This agent is hungry. He'll work for you. Do it."

Then there was the phone call asking her to stop by his office. A receptionist walked her to a windowless cubicle where a heavyset man with a fringe of black hair was speaking on two phones at once.

He saw her and hung both phones up, and right away she liked him for making her feel important.

"What would you think of Micaela in Atlanta?" he said.

"I'd think yes."

"I'm going to like working with you."

He got her jobs: Mimis in the Midwest, Musettas in L.A., a Rosalinda in Kansas City. Every month there was a check in the mail from his agency, and every month it was a bigger check.

The checks changed a lot of things. The Perry Street apartment bloomed in little ways: a shower attachment in the bath, lace curtains on the windows, a small eighth-hand Persian rug in front of the rocker. When Mark passed hermeneutics with a straight A, they were able to celebrate by going out for dinner.

After a Rosina in Louisville, Richard invited Ariana to lunch at the Russian Tea Room.

"Why are you knocking yourself out for me?" she asked.

"It's my job."

"Other clients are more important. Why me?"

"With you, Ariana, I hear the distant winds of fame blowing. I have a stable of warblers and hoofers and keyboard tinklers and fiddlers, and of the whole bunch you're the one sure thing. Which is why I want to ask you a question. Will you sign with the agency? Three years, exclusive. And I'll work for you. Really work."

"You mean you haven't been really working?"

"I mean you'll see some results. And I mean *real.*"

"Sure. I'll sign."

They went back to his office. It was still on the seventeenth floor but now it had a window looking at the seventeenth floor across the street. He gave her a three-page document and she signed without even looking at it.

"It's nice to be trusted," he said.

She gave him a glance of her brown eyes. There was a glint of another color in them, a changing color like the shimmer in a peacock's feather. "You're easy to trust," she said.

He went out of his way to book dates for her, pushing and lying and hustling just a little harder than he would have for anyone whose eyes didn't have that extra glint. She never let him or the agency down and, more important, she made him feel good about his own judgment. He knew she had a voice and he liked to think he was nurturing her.

He didn't like to think he might be in love with her; and the thought only crossed his mind once or twice a week.

Besides which, he'd been married for eight years to an angel by the name of Sylvia who gave terrific back rubs.

Stepping into the apartment on West Fifty-ninth Street, DiScelta kissed her old teacher. "How are you, my dear?"

Hilde Ganz-Tucci managed to suggest a great deal of suffering with a simple shrug. "With back pains life is not always comfortable."

DiScelta sat on an overstuffed chair. She bent forward to search through slices of cake arranged fan-style on a Dresden platter and selected the one with the most almonds.

"I dozed this afternoon," her teacher said. "I had terrifying dreams. Sleep frightens me. It's too close to death, and I can't afford to die yet."

DiScelta chewed a moment in smoldering silence. "You spend your life worrying."

"What have I to do except worry?" Ganz-Tucci closed her eyes. Her hair was sparse and totally white. "I've accomplished my task. Now why don't you accomplish yours!"

"If I go too fast with Ariana it will be a botch."

"Your standards are artificially high."

"No more so than yours. I used to leave this very room in tears."

"And now you're having your revenge."

DiScelta sighed a sigh of conciliation, of compromise. "All right. I'll start her on *Tosca*. Will that satisfy you?"

Ariana saw the announcement in the *New York Times*. Due to health problems, DiScelta was canceling three *Tosca*s at the Met and two at Covent Garden.

Yet at their next lesson DiScelta seemed perfectly robust, feisty as ever, with no diminishment of bad temper. They began with cadenzas from Sabaggi's *Solfège des Solfèges*. After the seventh cadenza, a killer, DiScelta looked at her.

"See?" she said. "You're not even winded."

It was true. There was still breath in Ariana, a reserve that had never been there before.

"You found your breathing that time, just as you came to the A-flat trill. Isn't that so, Austin?"

It was the first genuinely encouraging remark DiScelta had ever made about Ariana's singing, and she seemed to be calling on the accompanist as much to witness her own generosity as her pupil's newfound skill.

Austin nodded. "Yes, madame. She did very nicely." His dark eyes met Ariana's. *And I mean it,* they said.

"It happened because you stopped trying," DiScelta said. "You let the music take you."

There were other oddities during the lesson. A "Nice, very nice," when Ariana came off a pianissimo high D-flat. A hand touching her shoulder, warning her to save strength for the next roulade. She was aware of dozens of infinitesimal gestures and inflections, veiling the shape of some hidden, mysterious change.

At the end of the lesson her teacher leaned quietly against the great

Steinway, wrapped in her cobalt blue woolen shawl. "I won't be singing Tosca anymore."

"I saw in the *Times*," Ariana said. "I'm sorry you're not feeling well."

"That was just an excuse. I'm tired of the role."

Ariana's eyebrows went up.

"Tired of singing it," DiScelta said quickly. "Instead, I would like to teach it." She took both Ariana's hands between her own. She smiled gently and said, "I should like to teach it to you, my child."

Ariana wondered at the thickening layer of doubt that seemed suddenly to fall on her. Doubt where there should have been excitement. Hesitation where there should have been eagerness. It was one of the greatest roles in the entire repertory. "I'm honored," Ariana said softly.

"It will be work, you realize."

"I can work."

"I know. That's why I chose you." DiScelta's eyes held Ariana's strangely. "I will never sing the role again. You will be my Tosca." And then she added, "You will be the world's Tosca."

DiScelta's *Tosca* lessons began with a somber warning. "Puccini has ruined more young voices than any other composer. Though his characters are youthful, his melodies take strength and maturity to sustain. The accompaniment is rich, the lines are long. A deadly combination for untrained voices. He is the killer of youth."

She pointed out the dangers of the often-sumptuous orchestration. "See how he doubles the vocal line in the orchestra. Sometimes he triples it, even quadruples it, sometimes he even plays it in the bass. The listener thinks, what luxurious sound! But that sound is your rival. You must be heard above it. And the secret is not volume, but enunciation. Keep your consonants crisp. One thing the orchestra can never take away from you is your consonants!"

They attacked the score through the personality of the heroine, Floria Tosca.

"She is a creature," DiScelta said, "like all Puccini's heroines, who lives and dies for love. And she is the center about which the entire action revolves."

DiScelta pointed out how every one of Tosca's arias sprang directly from the drama, expressing the character's fluctuating psychology at any given point in the action. "The prime example, of course, is 'Vissi d'arte.'" DiScelta emphasized the treacherous simplicity of this aria: the descending scalelike melody in even rhythm, the theme taken up by the orchestra while the voice glided in on a repeated note. "What you are singing is the situation—not the scale, not the repeated note. Without the situation, the aria is nothing. Project the situation, and the aria has all the warmth and radiance of Verdi."

DiScelta went on to say that she could understand critics who found Puccini's music questionable. "After all, he is a man of the theater. He is drama using music, not music using drama. Nadia Boulanger once asked me, 'How can anyone like such awful music?' I said, 'It has emotion and energy and it always tells the truth.' But that is its musical weakness. When there is a choice between musical and emotional priorities, Puccini will always choose the emotional path."

That was the reason, DiScelta said, that so many of his harmonic progressions sounded like the pop music of a half-century later.

"Which proves not that he was cheap, but that he articulated the real feelings of real people long before they themselves did. Well, enough talk. Let's get on with your 'Vissi d'arte.' Make me cry."

Mark eased open the door. His first glance told him that, housekeeping-wise, it had not been one of the great days. Breakfast dishes were still piled on the table; pots and plates still poked through the soapy water in the sink and a jetsam of coffee grounds floated on the surface.

He tiptoed through the apartment. Ariana was sitting in the bedroom at the spinet.

It was almost four, and the last rays of winter daylight were slanting down on her. She was wearing her bathrobe. Head back, lips wide apart, she was mouthing the most horrendous scale he'd ever heard, each note like Sisyphus pushing his rock up the slope.

She saw him and started. A book of vocal solfèges slammed onto the keyboard with a terrific dissonance. "Damn—what time is it?"

He made a show of pulling back his cuff and squinting at his watch. "At the tone it will be practically tomorrow. Beep."

"I meant to clean and shop and . . . " She tightened her robe. "There's not a thing in the house for dinner."

"Sounds great. For appetizers we'll have fresh not-a-things on the half-shell. They're in season, you know. For the main course, not-a-thing soufflé. For dessert, not-a-thing compote."

He was joking, but she sensed mystery behind his half-closed eyelids. "You've got a secret," she said.

"Says who?"

"Says your face. What's happening?"

"I'm divorcing you. You're a lousy housekeeper."

"I'm a lousy housekeeper with a fantastic top extension. DiScelta told me today I have E above the staff easily, maybe even F."

"Well, how would you like to pack up your top extension and your E and your F and take them to Paris?"

"Paris—France?"

"I'm not talking about Paris, Missouri."

"When?"

"Spring recess."

It took a moment for that to sink in, and then she said, "Why?"

"Because I have been duly elected American Seminarian representative to attend the ecumenical congress at the Pro-Cathedral under the sponsorship of His Grace, the Archbishop of Canterbury. For your information, that is a very big honor and a chance to meet some of the movers and shakers of the church."

She looked out the window. The worst of winter was over. The little Pan in the fountain had shed his icicles. "Paris," she said dreamily.

Her mother had always spoken of Paris as a sort of lost Paradise of lights and champagne, the Seine halo'd in a Toulouse Lautrec glow, echos of bal-musettes and funny auto horns. And food. Pounds and pounds of butter-fat suicide.

"You're sure it's—all right for me to go along?"

"Honey, soon I'm going to be mired in some parish in eastern Appalachia. You're going to be raising our triplets and flying off to give concerts to garden clubs in Houston. This is our chance. Maybe our only chance till we're retired. We're free, we love each other, and my airfare is paid and yours will be off-season low-price-special. I say let's do it."

She got out the *briki*, made Greek coffee, and peered at the sediment in her saucer. "Okay. We're going to Paris."

Richard was waiting for her at his office door. She angled her cheek and they exchanged a warm client-agent kiss.

"Richard, there's been a change of plans. I'm going to Paris in three weeks."

Richard frowned. A sharp line jagged down between his eyebrows. "Things are just beginning to move for you. It took me months to set up those dates."

"I'm going to Paris."

"And I'm supposed to phone New Orleans and L.A. and say my client just had a hankering to see the Eiffel Tower? What do you think I was put in this world for, to eat, sleep, and spend twenty hours a day shifting dates for dizzy clients?"

There was surprise on her face, and he realized he was shouting. The walls were paper-thin and it wouldn't do to have every secretary in the agency know he couldn't handle his clients.

"What's wrong with you, Ariana?"

"I love . . . someone."

"And this someone wants you to screw up your career."

"No, it's my choice. And I don't see that two dates with small companies are going to matter one way or the other."

Richard Schiller closed his eyes and thought of the canceled dates; the long-distance screams; the lost deposits and returned advances and commissions down the drain. He should have been furious; screaming; ripping up her contract. But the truth was, when he allowed himself to face it, he was fond of this dark-haired girl with the too-big eyes and the big, big voice. He wanted to be part of her.

Thirty years from now, he wanted to be able to say, *I shaped her. And face it*, he told himself, *she's young, she's at that age when love matters, when Paris matters. Better she should get it out of her system now.*

"I suppose I can put something together," he conceded.

"Thanks, Richard. I know I'm a nuisance. I won't forget this."

DiScelta held Ariana in the darkest of dark gazes. "So, you are not only living with this man, you are rearranging your life to suit his."

Today was one of their occasional lessons without Austin Waters. DiScelta had accompanied. She had done it poorly and with a metallic touch, and now she slammed the lid of the keyboard and sent a ghostly dissonant chord jangling through the music room. She fixed her pupil with the unblinking, unpitying eye of a potato.

Ariana realized suddenly that the next moments were going to be remarkably silent.

"Don't look so serious, my child," her teacher said. "Don't you see, you must laugh. You must laugh because it is laughable, grotesque, that a person of your gifts would squander one instant of her career for this—this lovers' tryst on the banks of the Seine. It is accordion music. Mandolin concerto. It is comic."

Ariana kept her eyelids down, hoping DiScelta would not suspect she was holding back tears. But the tears came, unwanted, unbidden; and her teacher's hand stole about hers.

DiScelta spoke softly, mother to child. She described the heaviness of her own heart. She painted the future in the darkest possible shades. She prayed that Ariana's own good instincts would come to the rescue.

She harangued till Ariana felt very small and very lonely standing there, lips set tight, chin held firm.

But DiScelta's efforts were to no avail.

"I'm going to Paris," Ariana said.

"Then I am sorry for you. Sorrier than you will ever know." DiScelta waved, as though brushing aside a sheet of filthy newspaper that the wind had fluttered at her. "Go."

She waited for the sound of the door closing, then went to the telephone in the study. She composed the number with a rigid forefinger that hurried the dial along.

"Richard Schiller, please . . . Ricarda DiScelta, urgent."

It took a moment for him to come on the line. She sat forward in her chair.

"Richard? Ariana can't be dissuaded . . . Yes, a dreadful mistake. On the other hand, it may give us an opportunity."

❖ ❖ ❖

Ariana answered the phone. "Hello?"

"Hi, it's Richard." He sounded too cheerful, too forgiving. A wall of wariness went up in her. "They're doing three *Bohèmes* at Covent Garden the week of April 12. That's just a hop across the Channel from Paris. They need a replacement for Musetta. Interested?"

She sank slowly into the chair. She had to close her eyes a moment. She heard Richard talking and her mind was racing now, her thoughts trying to catch up with the sudden pounding of her heart.

"That's wonderful, Richard. Thank you."

When Mark came into the room he saw a shocked little girl crouched in the chair, gazing at him with enormous, wide-open eyes.

"They want me to sing in Covent Garden."

"Great." He kissed her and she clung to him. "When?"

"That's the unbelievable part—it fits in with our trip."

"Hey, no crying now."

"I just feel so damned lucky."

"If you ask me, Covent Garden's lucky."

"No, Mark, I'm lucky. I have you."

8

FOR THREE WEEKS DISCELTA SUBJECTED ARIANA TO A CRAM course in *La Bohème*, which amounted to a continuing seminar in Puccini.

"The opera is pure emotion. The melodies no longer follow a musical logic. They follow the emotional line of the words themselves."

She pointed out that Puccini's use of the orchestra, for all its "lapses into lavishness," was masterful, and economical as well. "Note in *Bohème* how the harp is used. Often it cannot be heard, but it can always be *felt*. It plays the role of italics in a page of prose. It emphasizes without adding fresh material."

And she pointed out how the typical Puccini aria was made up of different melodic kernels, each succinctly expressing an emotional state—and that these were linked together to form a melody which was not so much a "tune" in the Verdian sense as the working out of the character's state of mind. "His melody sweeps us with its feeling rather than with its exact notes. What counts here is the passion."

Ariana nodded, trying very hard to absorb.

"Now Musetta," DiScelta said, "is not a typical Puccini role, but it is one of his most effective. You have one show-stopping number: the waltz. Don't be afraid of it. It is a popular tune—sing it like one. Opera audiences are always grateful for a popular tune. This is your chance to be loved more than the heroine. Take advantage of it."

Ariana stood in the gallery of the Racquet and Health Club and watched the squash match.

Nikos Stratiotis played savagely, with a street-ball overkill, sending the ball on unpredictable trajectories that caught his opponent time after time in just the wrong place. The match ended with Nikos slamming a hard shot high onto the rear wall. It ricocheted past his opponent's lunging racket and took three bounces and died. Nikos's opponent came up and shook his hand.

The door to the court opened and an attendant went over to Nikos and pointed to the glass window. Nikos looked up at Ariana.

Two minutes later he was standing beside her, swinging the head of his racket against his bare leg with a hard slapping sound.

She handed him the check.

"What's this?" he said.

"My Covent Garden guarantee."

He smiled. "That's terrific. I knew you'd be a great investment."

He tried to hand the check back. She didn't take it.

"You loaned me money," she said, "remember?"

"Did you certify it?" he asked.

"No."

He ripped the check into neat quarters and let them sprinkle down among the cigar butts in a standing brass ashtray. "That was no loan. That was a scholarship." He was smiling, bending down to massage the muscle in his thigh. "Which means you don't pay it back. What's more, the scholarship wasn't from me, it was from the Stratiotis Foundation for the Fine Arts."

She heard herself murmur, "All right. You're very kind."

"The hell I'm kind. And let's get something else straight. You've got no responsibility to me. You've got no responsibility to some cocka-mamy foundation my lawyers drew up. Your responsibility is to excellence alone."

She stared at this muscular man in sweaty squash clothes, dark curls plastered to his skull as though he'd just been diving in the Aegean, and she had the confused sensation of not quite seeing him. "That doesn't sound like you," she said.

"It's not meant to. I'm taking lessons. An actor's teaching me how to sound like him. Minus the British. British would be too much on me, don't you think?"

"I don't know. But I'll tell you something. I don't care what you say or how you sound. You *are* kind."

She kissed him quickly, a light brush of lips against cheek. As she hurried away she caught her reflection in the squash court windows. It gave her an idea what he was seeing, a tall girl with a determined stride and long jet-black hair that whiplashed her shoulders. When she glanced back from the elevator he was staring at her. *A funny man*, she thought, *a kind thug.*

It was a good time to travel abroad. The dollar was strong, and Europe had almost recovered from the devastation of the war. Though there were still ruins in the heart of London and Rome, they were clean ruins, not the smoking rubble Mark had left three years ago.

He and Ariana made the reassuring discovery that they could not only sleep together eight hours a night, they could be happily conscious together the other sixteen, traipsing through Vatican City, standing in awe before the doors of the Cathedral of Chartres, losing their way in the Scottish Highlands, settling any and all disputes as to where-next or what-next by consulting appropriate passages in *Baedeker* and *Michelin.*

They saw four countries, attended three international conventions of Anglican and Protestant-Episcopal youth, and stuffed themselves on fettuccine al pesto in Venice and on bangers and mash at a pub in London's Portobello Road, and one night—just to be able to tell their grandchildren they'd done it—glutted themselves on tournedos Rossini at the Savoy.

Mark picked up his glass and before bringing it to his lips raised it toward Ariana. She mirrored the gesture. It was their nine-hundredth wordless toast to love, to each other, to happiness, to now; and they were beginning to get a little bit tipsy. He washed down the remnants of his poire belle Hélène with the last of the wine and settled back in his chair.

"What?" she said.

One thing he'd noticed in the last week was that she was quick to pick up on his moods and even on his fleeting thoughts. "What, what?"

"You're wondering something."

"No, I'm not." He grinned.

But she was right. Beneath the grin he was wondering if life would ever be this good again.

They paid the tab with a wad of travelers checks, which hurt, and then they went and sat on a terrace with a view of the Thames and the floodlit houses of Parliament and Westminster Abbey. An orchestra was playing and between Grand Marniers they danced.

Ariana was wearing an evening dress that her agent had bought her two weeks ago, when he'd finally reconciled himself to her going. It was silvery gray silk, very simply cut, and only a very beautiful or striking woman could have worn it. The silk picked up all the colors around her and blended them into a soft shimmering iridescence.

"Tomorrow I have to rehearse Musetta," she sighed.

"Tomorrow's a long way away."

As they danced he pulled her tight against him and they kissed.

He whispered in her ear, "Let's go to bed. I want to make love."

She smiled. "Now?"

He nodded. "Now."

They could afford to eat at the Savoy—barely—but not to sleep there. They rode to their hotel in S.W. 3. in a London cab whose back seat seemed larger than their entire living room.

The next day was her first piano rehearsal at Covent Garden; the day after was her first stage rehearsal; and the day after that her first and only rehearsal with full company and orchestra.

Wearing her red gown and ermine stole from Act Two, she watched the first act of the dress from the third row of the house.

Puccini's opening measures, catching all the eager high spirits of youth, rang out from the orchestra. The curtain rose on a delicately shabby set that had the flavor of a hand-tinted nineteenth-century engraving.

It was a Christmas Eve in the 1830s.

The poet Rodolfo and the painter Marcello were freezing in their bleak Paris garret. Rodolfo—sung by Lucco Patemio, a three-hundred-pound former wrestler with a rough and friendly face—lit the stove with a draft of his play. Two friends arrived: Schaunard, a musician, bringing wine and food, and Colline, a philosopher. The four began to feast. (Patemio, saving his voice for the performance, sang mezza voce—half-strength—the others sang full-out.)

The landlord entered, demanding his back rent. In a broadly comic scene the young men plied him with wine until, drunk, he began telling them of his extramarital loves. Pretending to be outraged, they threw him out.

While the others left to celebrate Christmas Eve, Rodolfo stayed behind to work on a newspaper article. Mimi—a beautiful young neighbor sung by a two-hundred-pound Bolivian—knocked at the door. Her candle had gone out—could Rodolfo light it? Suddenly she had a fit of coughing and, almost fainting, dropped her key. Rodolfo helped her to a chair. A draft blew out both their candles.

In the dark, they searched for the key. Rodolfo found it and hid it. Their hands touched. Mimi's was icy. He took it, warming it. "Che gelida manina," he sang—"What a frozen little hand." They told each other about themselves and—as inevitably happens between tenors and sopranos in opera—began to fall in love.

From outside, Rodolfo's cronies called him to come join them. Embracing, voices pouring out joyous octaves, Mimi and Rodolfo left the garret arm in arm.

Act Two took place moments later in the Latin Quarter. Ariana watched from the wings as Rodolfo, Mimi, Colline, and Schaunard mingled with a huge crowd of extras in front of the Café Momus.

I am Musetta, she told herself. *I am Musetta.*

The strings and winds sounded her mockingly coquettish cue.

With a toss of the head, waving hands, gay laughter, she became her character and entered on the arm of Alcindoro, a baritone and a rich and very elderly admirer. She stopped short at the sight of Marcello. He used to be her lover, and with a lingering glance, she made it very clear that she still cared for him. Angry when he pretended not to notice her, she broke into a luscious waltz reminding him—and the gathered public—of her charms: "Quando m'en vo"—"When I go through the streets."

Shrieking suddenly that her foot hurt, she dispatched Alcindoro to buy new shoes. She and Marcello embraced. While a military parade distracted the crowd and the waiters, Musetta and Marcello and his young friends slipped giddily away, leaving Alcindoro to pay their café bill.

While the stagehands shifted sets for Act Three, Lucco Patemio took Ariana aside. "You do splendid work for a novice."

She couldn't quite believe that the world's most popular tenor was complimenting her. "Thank you," she said shyly.

"You have a delicious voice, my child," he said. "But in this house the high B in Musetta's waltz is a waste. Take it an octave down."

The suggestion shocked her. "But the high B *is* the aria."

He leaned across the table to touch her wrist. "Save it for La Scala, where such things are appreciated. And, my child, if you do as I say, you will be singing at La Scala. I'll see to it."

Darkness was falling and Ariana could feel London closing around her as she hurried through the artists' entrance the night of the performance.

From the moment in Act Two when she flounced, laughing and flirting, onto the stage, she had a strange, almost disorienting sense that she was no longer singing Musetta's music or creating her character: Musetta's music was singing *her*, the character was creating *her*.

Disregarding Lucco Patemio's advice, she took the high B in Musetta's waltz . . . because that was what Puccini had written and that was what Musetta would have done. The house rewarded her with two minutes of bravas.

There were even more bravas in Act Three.

The scene was the Barrière d'Enfer, one of the Paris tollgates. It was a snowy February night as Mimi met Marcello and told him Rodolfo had left her for good. When Rodolfo came out of the inn, she hid and overheard him tell Marcello he still loved her but was afraid her poor health would kill her if she continued living in his cold, damp garret. At that moment a fit of coughing seized her, and Rodolfo, recognizing her, rushed to embrace her.

Musetta's laugh rang out infectiously from the inn. Marcello dashed jealously inside. An instant later he and Musetta emerged, arguing furiously. Musetta exited in a scenery-chewing fury.

(The audience applauded, holding up the action.)

In a final lyrical duet, Mimi and Rodolfo decided to attempt a reconciliation—at least till spring.

The last act took place back in the garret. Rodolfo and Marcello—single again—sang regretfully of their old sweethearts. Colline and Schaunard arrived with a loaf of bread and a salted herring—the day's food.

Musetta, agitated and trembling, burst in with the news that Mimi, dying, had left her viscount and wanted to spend her last hours with Rodolfo.

Rodolfo helped Mimi into the room and settled her on the bed. She was touchingly happy to be back, but wished she had a muff to warm her hands.

Realizing this was probably her friend's last wish, Musetta volunteered to sell her earrings to buy a muff and medicine.

Alone, the lovers remembered how they first met—the dropped key, their hands touching in the dark. The others returned. For a moment Rodolfo thought Mimi had fallen asleep, but then—from his friends' expressions—realized she was dead. Sobbing, he threw himself across her body.

The curtain slowly fell.

Afterward, when the cast had taken its bow, Lucco Patemio approached Ariana with a thin smile. "Do you mind, my dear," he said, "only the principals will take solo calls."

"Musetta *is* a principal."

"Not tonight."

And suddenly she understood. Greed was speaking through him. "It's because they like me, isn't it?" she said. "You sang poorly and I sang well and the audience knows. And you're scared that if I took a solo bow I'd get more applause than you."

It would be two years before she learned that no one, not even a prima donna, talks to a tenor that way, but that night she was young in the ways of her profession and she spoke as she had sung, with all the truth in her being.

"You will not bow," he said, "because the audience has seen enough of your silly cowlike simpering."

She did not bow, but she stood behind the curtain, out of sight of the audience, applauding the other principals, and except for Lucco Patemio they smiled at her and applauded back as they returned to their dressing rooms.

She spent exactly one night hating, refusing to talk to Mark, refusing to make love or even to kiss, and then the hatred was lifted. Her reviews the next day were good.

Lucco Patemio's were not.

Her second Musetta was Friday. Saturday morning she and Mark took the boat train from London to Paris. They spent the afternoon walking hand-in-hand in glorious sunshine along the Seine, exploring bookstalls and flower stalls and junk stalls.

Sunday morning at eleven they joined the well-dressed American and British expatriate throng at the Pro-Cathedral and heard the Archbishop of Canterbury preach a sermon on nuclear disarmament.

There was a reception afterward in the cathedral garden: tea and tiny gâteaux and a sea of very expensive Easter bonnets.

The Archbishop grasped Ariana's hand warmly. "I heard you sing."

Astonishment took her. "You heard my Musetta?"

He smiled broadly. "No, I heard your 'Christ the Lord Is Risen Today.' Your voice inspired the whole congregation." And he took Mark's hand. "My compliments. You have a lovely wife."

Ariana sensed something very much the matter when she and Mark got back to their borrowed apartment on the Rue de Fleurus. She put a cup of chamomile tea down on the table in front of him. She listened in silence while he explained as coherently as possible—and it seemed hard for him to be coherent—that he must go home today. Right away. No delay.

"Panagia mou, why?"

He didn't seem to be able to come up with a why.

"What's the matter, Mark? Is it you? Is it me? Is it us?"

She went to him, sat on the arm of his chair, slid an arm around his shoulder. He gazed at her a long moment, and then he took her hand with a tightness that surprised her and pressed it to his astonishingly hot, damp mouth. When he finally spoke his voice seemed to come from a thousand miles away.

"I love you. I really do love you. And . . . I want to live my life with you and I want to marry you and . . . "

"Mark, we've been through *those* wants. Why are you upset? Is it because the Archbishop thought we were married?"

"I have to go home. That's all."

"You have to go home today?"

"That's right."

"And I still have a Musetta to sing at Covent Garden, not to mention three Rosinas in Düsseldorf where I've never been before in my life and where I kind of hoped we'd be together."

That afternoon, silently, they shared a taxi to the airport and took separate planes, she across the English Channel, he across the Atlantic.

Rosina was the last assignment in the world Ariana felt capable of at that moment: the youthful, lighthearted heroine of Rossini's *Barber of Seville.*

Fortunately, audiences invariably loved the amiable idiocies of the libretto and the deft humor of the melodious score. *Barber* was all surface, charm, and comic precision.

In the first scene Count Almaviva sang a serenade beneath Rosina's window. Figaro, the town barber, entered boasting of his various remarkable skills. Almaviva asked his help in winning Rosina. Figaro warned that her guardian, Dr. Bartolo, guarded her jealously and intended to marry her himself. Rosina dropped a note to the serenader, asking his name and intentions. Almaviva sang another serenade, claiming to be "Lindoro," poor but full of love. Figaro suggested that the count disguise himself as a soldier and ask to be billeted in Bartolo's house.

The second scene took place within the house. Rosina wrote a letter to "Lindoro." Her soliloquy—"Una voce poco fa"—"One voice does but little"—and its spectacularly leaping, filigreed cabaletta constituted one of the best-loved coloratura arias in the soprano repertory. Ariana sang exactly as DiScelta had taught her, and the audience applauded warmly.

She tucked the letter into her bosom as Bartolo, her aged guardian, entered. Basilio, the music teacher, warned that Almaviva had arrived in Seville to court Rosina; he recommended a slander campaign to drive the count away. But Bartolo had no time for slander and wanted to marry Rosina immediately. He asked Basilio to help him draw up a marriage contract.

Figaro, who shaved Bartolo daily and thus could come and go in the house as he pleased, entered. Rosina gave him her letter to pass on to "Lindoro." Bartolo returned, glanced at the desk, and accused Rosina of writing to someone.

At this point there was a knock at the door. Berta, the comic maid, admitted Almaviva, who was impersonating a drunken officer.

Almaviva whispered to Rosina that he was "Lindoro." Bartolo demanded to see the letter Rosina had written. She handed over a laundry list. Bartolo exploded in anger.

The resulting fracas attracted a police officer, who arrested the count. Almaviva gave the officer his card. The officer, snapping to attention, arrested the doctor instead. A rousing final chorus brought the curtain down to appreciative applause.

In the next act Count Almaviva returned, disguised as a music master replacing Basilio, who he said was sick. Bartolo was suspicious until the count handed him Rosina's note, saying he had intercepted it before it could reach Almaviva. Bartolo summoned Rosina and stayed in the room, snoring, while the lovers, going through the motions of a music lesson, plotted their elopement. Figaro arrived to shave Bartolo and stole the balcony key from his pocket so that the lovers could escape that night.

Basilio arrived unexpectedly and was on the verge of upsetting everyone's plans when the count bribed him to pretend to be sick. Bartolo, finally realizing he was being duped, pursued Figaro and the count from the house.

He then returned and showed Rosina her letter, saying that Lindoro was merely a go-between courting her for the count. Believing herself betrayed, Rosina agreed to marry Bartolo, who went to summon the police.

The count and Figaro entered via the balcony. Rosina accused "Lindoro" of deceiving her, but he revealed himself as Almaviva and they fell into each other's arms. Basilio arrived with the notary, but the quick-thinking Figaro presented the count as the prospective groom. By the time Bartolo returned with the police, Almaviva and Rosina were married. Told that he could keep his ward's dowry, Bartolo resigned himself to the turn of events, and the opera ended in general jubilation.

The Düsseldorf press gave Ariana three nice little mentions, and after two more Rosinas she returned to New York. The hinges sang out two notes of "Amazing Grace" and she plunked her bags down.

Mark kissed her. It wasn't the kiss she'd expected. He looked sober and drawn. There were dishes in the sink. And unchanged sheets tangled up on the bed. And shirts tossed into the bathroom hamper, overflowing onto the tile floor. Collar shirts. Shirts with stays and neat little buttons.

She picked one up and studied the label. Brooks Brothers.

"You never used to shop at Brooks," she said.

"They were having a sale."

It had been twelve days since they'd said their silent goodbye in Paris, and—subtracting the weekend—that left ten working days. There were ten blue broadcloth shirts.

"You wear these to class?"

"I haven't been going to class."

She looked around the apartment, carefully now, sensing that the coziness had gone out of the chaos. Everything was wrong. Stacks of *Barron's* weekly teetered on tabletops instead of homily outlines. *Wall Street Journal*s lay crumpled in the corner where three unread weeks of *The Church Times* should have been nesting. A Dun and Bradstreet sat on the shelf beneath the coffee table where the Hebrew-English lexicon used to be wedged.

"So what have you been doing?" she asked. "Playing hooky in button-down shirts?"

"I've been working."

"You took a nighttime job?"

"Daytime. Harry Forbes got me a position with his brokerage house. I've quit seminary."

She stared at him, not wanting to believe what she'd just heard. "You're doing this because of me, aren't you," she said quietly. "Correction—you think you're doing it because of me."

"Maybe we should talk," he said.

"Maybe that's the first intelligent idea you've had in twelve days."

She sat at the table. He brought two cups of tea; two threads of steam wisped up into the air and he bowed his head.

Then, it spilled out. He'd been having doubts. Not just about the divinity of Christ or the tripartite God, not just about the formularized prayers that turned a conversation with the divinity into something only slightly less rigid than an exchange with Mrs. Vanderbilt . . .

"Mark." She laid her hand on his. "Get to the point."

For one instant their eyes met. His were large and hurt and there was shame in them, and she had never before seen shame in the eyes of Mark Rutherford Junior. He told her about a student who had invited a girl into his room—perfectly innocent, a second cousin—and whom the seminary had thrown out as though he'd been committing all the sins of Sodom and Gomorrah.

"Mark, I may be an opera singer, but what do you take me for, a lovesick moron? Sure you're having doubts, but they're not about Apostolic legitimacy and they're not about somebody's ninth cousin, they're about us."

For an instant he sat absolutely still.

"Or maybe," she said in a softer voice, "maybe they're about me."

He began pushing out denial that had all the weight of a tombstone. "Honey, I swear, of all the things in my life I never doubted—"

"Will you quit lying to yourself and will you please quit lying to me? Are you so scared of wounding me, so scared of making me feel you can't trust me? Or maybe you don't trust me? Is that it, Mark? Do you take me for some kind of coward or idiot? A piece of singing fluff, pretty to listen to, nice to sleep with, but count on her when the bills come due, not on your life? This didn't happen over a weekend, and it didn't happen because some administrator in that seminary went on an antisex crusade. This has been coming ever since we met. And let me tell you something, Mark Rutherford Junior, I will *not* be the reason you make yourself unhappy! Be a minister, be a garbage man, but don't blame me!"

"Hey, hold on, who's blaming who?"

"You!" she screamed. "You're blaming me! A minister can't be married to a singer because a singer performs on the stage and everyone including the Archbishop of Canterbury knows that's one step up from streetwalking; and so to spare my feelings and my career you're sacrificing everything and selling yourself to those Wall Street goons peddling stocks and bonds and futures and debentures and all that manure so you and I can continue in unwedded bliss while I warble my way to the top and you *shlep* the number six train to Wall Street every day for the rest of your life!"

"You're hysterical. Maybe we should both shut up."

"The Rutherford way? Don't talk about it and maybe it will curl up and die?"

"This has nothing to do with the Rutherfords."

"This has everything to do with the Rutherfords and even though you've made it very clear that it's none of my business, I'm going to ask anyway. Did your father cut you off?"

Amazement washed across Mark's face.

"Did he tell you it was me or seminary tuition?" She took his silence for admission and she began shooting words at him in a voice so low it was almost a stinging whisper. *"Panagia mou, voïthia!* Goddamn it, Mark! If we can't trust one another, what the hell are we doing in each other's life!"

He didn't seem to have an answer for that one.

"Don't you think you can count on me for *anything?*"

Or for that one either.

She lifted her teacup and sent it eight feet through the air, smashing into the wall behind him.

He ducked, half expecting a kettle or a lamp to follow. But nothing followed except silence, and when he looked her way she wasn't there anymore.

"Ariana?"

She was not in the bathroom, not in the bedroom crying, not on the landing outside, not in the courtyard downstairs, not out on Perry Street hailing a cab.

She was gone.

And except for the stain dripping down the wall and the two suitcases standing inside the door, it was as though she had never come back to Perry Street at all.

9

ARIANA WENT TO RICHARD SCHILLER AND TOLD HIM SHE NEEDED $2,000 quickly.

"I can book you into *Andrea Chénier* next July in Cincinnati."

"Richard, I need the money *now*. Can't you get me something fast? Maybe some television commercials?"

"No way I'm going to let you do commercials. Absolutely not."

When Ariana stepped into her brother's office he was tilted back in a swivel chair, wingtip shoes crossed on the desk top. "Hi, Sis. I only have a minute." He made a proprietor's gesture toward a chair.

She sat. "Quite an office." It was cheap, tacky stuff: mass-produced Danish modern.

He smiled. "I picked the color scheme myself." He stopped smiling. "What can I do for you?"

"You're handling publicity for these people?"

"I'm president in charge of public relations."

"I want to do television commercials for you."

He shook his head. "We have an Italo-American product, an Italo-American market. You're Franco-Greek."

"I look Italian and I sing Italian. What's more, I sing legit, and one thing Italians love is opera. We could take the big arias, like 'Un Bel Di,' 'Celeste Aïda,' change the lyrics to cookies and breadsticks. I can really belt. I've got what they call a high extension, that's an E-flat you wouldn't believe."

Sitting there in the chair, moving nothing but her jaw, she let him have the E-flat, sixty-three seconds that swelled from a whisper to a lampshade-jangling fortissimo.

He was staring at her with amazement. "How much do you want?"

"I'll do it for two thousand dollars."

Ariana didn't come back for three days, didn't phone, and Mark went out of his mind. On the fourth morning he called in to work sick and went to the precinct and asked what to do about a missing person. A chubby sergeant with red hair said, "You check the hospitals, and if she hasn't showed up in five days you file a report in the precinct where she vanished."

"How do I know the precinct where she vanished?"

"Wait five days, okay?"

"She could be dead and you guys are telling me to sit on my ass?"

"She could also be sorry about the argument and decide she's scared you enough."

"What argument?"

The sergeant gave him a look. And a shrug. "Go home."

Mark was in his bathrobe when he heard the gate squeak in the courtyard, that special squeak it always made for her and no one else. He made a dash for his regular chair, grabbed a section of the *New York Times*, opened it, and arranged his face.

The apartment door swung open, the hinges singing out the two notes of "Amazing Grace." Steps came halfway into the room.

"Water's running," she said.

Now he looked up at her. Slowly.

She just stood there motionless, beautiful, and then she took off her coat and hung it neatly on the coat rack and peeked into the bedroom. "Tub's overflowing," she said.

There was a long strangling pause while they looked at each other.

"I went crazy," he said.

Her smile opened up like a fan. "Are you going to take that bath? I'll soap your back." She took his hand and led him into the bathroom.

"Where were you?"

"Home."

She soaped his back in long circular strokes.

"This is your home," he said.

"Sometimes."

"Where were you?"

"I met a millionaire in the Oak Room at the Plaza."

"Where were you?"

"My mother's."

"Doing what?"

Her look was almost a smile. "How's the brokerage house?"

"I hate it."

"Good. I don't want you working there."

"Sometimes we don't get what we want."

She squeezed the sponge over his head and warm suds rained down over his face. "Mark, it's going to be all right."

"You could have phoned."

"You could have stayed in school and not gone to work for those dumbheads."

"Are we going to argue?"

"I have a better idea. It's been four days. I'd like to make love. Okay?"

He tried but he couldn't be angry. The three lousiest days of pain and craziness he'd ever dragged himself through in his life didn't matter. All that mattered was that she'd come back.

"Okay." He got out of the tub and came toward her. Still dripping bathwater, he lifted her and carried her into the bedroom and set her down gently on the small brass bed.

She let him undress her and then he slid his moist hand between her thighs and parted them. He arched her back against the blue-and-white comforter. She closed her eyes. He began to devour the soft flesh between her legs. She could feel his teeth, light and teasing, and then not light, not teasing.

She moaned.

He crouched over her, squeezing her nipples, and he took her with an intensity that she had never known in him before.

She reached orgasm quickly, so quickly it almost frightened her, and then she felt his lean hips working, building her up to an even higher level of excitement. She had to bite into his shoulder to keep from screaming.

When the second wave broke, the room seemed to be whirling, the whole world spinning. He cried out and collapsed against her.

Seconds later she felt a more muted, sustained orgasm. She lifted his head and kissed him. "If you're going to make love to me like that, maybe I should run away more often."

"Don't you dare."

The day that the check from Stathis's bakery cleared the bank, Ariana phoned the seminary. The dean's secretary said she could have an appointment in nine days.

The dean was waiting for her, the door of his office ajar. "Miss Kavalaris?" He rose from his studded leather chair, a burly man six feet tall with a thick head of white hair. He wore a dark vested suit and his hand was extended in a welcome so automatic as to be chilling. "Please." A pause, and then, with a gesture leaving no doubt which of the three chairs was to be hers, "Sit."

They took up positions on opposite sides of the carved teakwood desk. She brought the money out of her purse calmly, clean $500 bundles.

The dean's nostrils seemed horrified. "What's this?"

"Mark Rutherford's tuition. For next term"

"Mark Rutherford has not applied for readmission."

"He has now," Ariana said.

Two days later, at three in the afternoon, Ariana was practicing her sight-singing when she heard a knock at the door.

Mark's father was standing on the landing. "May I come in?"

She felt winter in her blood. "Of course." She stood aside.

He took spectacles from his pocket and slipped them onto his nose and then he strode around the apartment. "Charming," he said.

The bedroom door was half open. He glanced through it. "You've been imaginative with very little space."

"Thank you." She offered tea.

"No, thank you."

"Sherry?"

"Perhaps a little sherry, yes."

She poured two tiny glasses. He glanced at the label on the bottle. He sipped with almost dainty displeasure, staring at her.

"Don't think I don't understand you." Sitting back in his chair, one knee crossed over the other, he nodded tolerantly. "I don't question your aim. I certainly don't reject it. Many young unknown girls have become great singers. But let's examine your plan."

"Why? Why should you and I examine my plan?"

"Because I'm concerned."

"That's kind of you, but there's really no need. I can't expect you to care if I fail or succeed."

"I care if you succeed in one thing only—harming my son."

She tried to mask a flash of anger. "I'll never harm Mark."

"You've already begun to. Until the dean of the seminary phoned me I'd no idea Mark had dropped out; no idea he'd rented this apartment; no idea he was—with you. Oh, I knew he was sleeping with you, but living with you, no. You're Catholic or Greek Orthodox?"

"Catholic."

"You may be unfamiliar with Mark's church. The clergy are permitted to marry."

"I know that."

"On the other hand, the Episcopal Church is not the lyric theater. Episcopal ministers may marry, yes, but live with a woman, publicly, unmarried—out of the question. Why do you think Mark dropped out of seminary?"

"I don't think it had anything to do with me."

"It had everything to do with you. He had to choose between ordination and you. He chose you."

"He told you that?"

"Of course not."

"Then you can't know it."

Mr. Rutherford's upper lip curled. "This is going to sound old-fashioned to you. But ministers must set examples. And though ours is a liberal age, a man and woman living together out of wedlock is not yet considered exemplary behavior. Particularly when the man has promised his bishop not to marry till after ordination."

Ariana rose. She went to the window and stared down into the garden. A robin had perched in the fountain on Pan's shoulder.

"Leave him," Mr. Rutherford said.

"Leave him?" She saw that to Mark Rutherford Senior life was a completely solved equation, with no room left for unknowns or variables.

"It'll be an expense. I'll help with the costs, of course."

"That's very kind. But I'll have to talk it over with Mark." She moved slowly about the apartment, touching things, drawing reassurance from the lampshade, the rocking chair, the polished tabletop. "I think Mark would prefer to marry. I know I would."

Mr. Rutherford carefully took his spectacles off, blew on them, resettled them on his nose. "Young lady, I'm not judging you. But I'm talking life, not opera. Even if the bishop were to agree, which I find highly unlikely, there's a financial consideration. To support a wife and family, to feed and clothe them and send the children to decent schools, Mark will have to become bishop of a large diocese: New York or Chicago."

"Then he will."

"Not if he's married to a singer. No diocese will tolerate a bishop's wife performing on the stage. He'll never advance above village minister and his family will starve."

The eyes of Ariana Kavalaris met those of Mark Rutherford Senior. "Isn't there another option?"

She saw that she had aroused more than his disdain. For that instant at least, she had caught his interest.

"After ordination Mark could marry a rich woman," she said. "Surely Episcopal ministers have done that."

"No doubt. But how does that fit into your plan?"

"I have no plan, Mr. Rutherford, except to be the best singer I possibly can be."

"And let him be the best minister he can be?"

"Of course."

"Then we agree?"

"On that much, Mr. Rutherford. I'll do whatever I can to help him."

"By leaving him."

"By staying with him."

Mr. Rutherford lowered his head. His shoulders hunched and for an instant he was a silent, glowering bulldog. "Then you're determined to destroy my son."

"No. I'm determined only to be a successful singer."

"I can almost admire your candor. You admit you care for nothing but yourself."

She drew herself up full height and wished she were two feet taller, that she could look down on this immaculate gray-haired man with the narrow ice-blue eyes and chiseled nostrils. "What do you know of successful operatic singers, Mr. Rutherford?"

"Enough."

"Then you know that if your son is my husband, he and his family will eat and be clothed. His children will go to the same fine schools you

85

did. He'll want for nothing, he'll have nothing to be ashamed of, nothing to regret. And neither will you. You have my word."

Mr. Rutherford picked up his hat from the chair by the door. "You sadden me."

"You ought to be glad to know I'll never threaten Mark's happiness."

"You've probably destroyed it."

"Visitor?" Mark said that evening when he saw the two sherry glasses.

"Visitor."

"Should I be jealous?"

"Concerned."

"I hate you."

"Could you marry a woman you hate?"

"Sure."

"Then let's marry."

"Fine. I'll have to ask the bishop's—"

"Mark, I want to marry secretly. Right now."

10

BUT RIGHT NOW TURNED OUT TO BE NOT QUITE THE SAME THING as right away.

They wanted a church wedding—a ceremony performed by an ordained minister in a building with a steeple and a cross over the altar—and the only sect liberal enough to give them all that plus secrecy was the Unitarians. Ariana phoned the Church of All Saints and asked how soon the minister could perform a marriage. "A mixed marriage, we're both Christians and neither of us has time to convert." She'd meant it as a joke. She was told, unjokingly, that the minister was on another line and would have to call her back.

But when the phone rang it was Richard Schiller, eager. "How's your *Barber of Seville?*"

"Pretty damned good."

"You've got three days to get to St. Louis."

By the time she got back to New York the Unitarians didn't have an opening for three weeks. But in two weeks Richard pulled a Santuzza in *Cavalleria* out of the hat—"Buenos Aires, a very important opera town," and that meant a six-week wait till the Unitarians had chapel time available.

Two weeks before the wedding date Richard phoned and said Maria Callas had canceled four dates in Mexico City. "How's your Aïda?"

"*Panagia mou*—not ready."

"You've got nine weeks."

"Richard, a friend of mine is marrying in nine weeks and I've promised to be there."

"Tell them to postpone. Lucco Patemio this early in your career is a catch."

"I've had Patemio, thanks, and he hates me."

"He's still Lucco Patemio and he hates everyone. And this could make you. I mean, make you. I'm going to move heaven and earth, okay?"

For three days Richard burned up long-distance wires. Patemio's agent said Lucco was not a launching pad for amateurs. If Lucco couldn't have Callas he wanted Alima Harvey.

DiScelta told Richard, "Give him Alima but book Ariana as the cover. Alima will pull out. She's my student and she obeys me."

So it was set.

Which is to say it was set until 6:20 Friday evening, August 23, when Richard Schiller was sitting in a bar on Fifty-fifth Street. Two hundred voices were shouting in a space where the sign on the wall said: MAXI-MUM OCCUPANCY 108 PERSONS.

And then on top of it all one voice was singing.

Richard stopped jiggling the ice in his drink. He knew that voice. He looked up, and on the television screen above the bar Ariana Kavalaris's eyes were dark with sparkling points. She was belting "O Mio Babbino Caro," except the words were "Oh, try my delicious breadsticks" and the accompanying saxophone band sounded like a tub of schmaltz.

"Christ," Richard Schiller groaned. He took his drink and elbowed to the phone booth in the corner. He dropped a nickel in the slot, dialed. "Turn your television on. Your pupil's on Channel Seven."

"Everything you do—every breath, every word, every act—either sows the seeds of a career or it is useless."

Ricarda DiScelta stood in the center of her living room and with an exactly poised forefinger accused her pupil.

"Patti, Tettrazini, Melba, Ponselle, Callas, don't you think they had their years of struggle, of sacrifice? But did they ever stoop to advertising cakes and breadsticks?"

Ariana tried to think of something to answer, something to deflect the justness of the charges, but there was nothing she could say. "I'm sorry."

"Why did you do it?"

"Money."

"But if you need money, why didn't you ask me?"

"I had no right to. The money wasn't for me."

"Then who was it for?"

Ariana explained.

DiScelta listened, rose from her chair, moved with decisive steps to the window. "This young man you want to marry, this Mark Rutherford, does he love music?"

"He loves me," Ariana answered.

"That isn't what I asked."

"May I ask you a question, Mr. Stratiotis?"

"A question? Why not?"

DiScelta had summoned him to her living room. The curtains were drawn, as in a house where a death had just occurred.

"Do you genuinely want to help Ariana Kavalaris?"

"Certainly I want to."

What a voice, DiScelta thought. *What a baritone he would have made.* "Ariana has made a foolish mistake."

Nikos listened in silence as Ricarda DiScelta described the television commercials. He nodded. "Don't worry. I'll get the films back."

He called on Stathis Kavalaris at the bakery. "Your sister wants those commercials off the air."

Stathis studied his visitor carefully. There was a long moment of eye-to-eye contact.

"It'll cost you to get them off the air," Stathis said.

"It'll cost you more not to."

A bakery in Queens was firebombed that night.

The commercials were withdrawn the next day.

In the taxi going to Wall Street, DiScelta saw a photograph in the *Times*, a frozen instant of rubble and destruction. Her mind hovered uneasily over the possibility of a connection.

Mark Rutherford was waiting for her in the reading room just off the main entrance of the Downtown Association.

He was exactly what she had expected: a handsome, well-dressed young man, appropriately deferential. He suggested cocktails.

"Why not wine with our meal?" she said.

They took a small circular table in the dining room. She said she was not at all satisfied with her present broker; she had some stock options that needed looking into; and since Mark was Ariana's friend . . . "I feel I can trust you," she said.

He had expected a ladylike dragon. Instead he was seated across a lunch table from a motherly figure in a gray print dress.

"It's impressive," DiScelta said, "that Ariana can sing both Lucia and Aïda, music so different in character. Do you have any idea how scarce dramatic singers are? They're scarcer than good stockbrokers. You are good, aren't you?"

"I do my best."

She lifted from her head a little black pillbox hat that was at least three decades out of date and placed it on the empty chair between them. It crossed his mind that this woman was not Ricarda DiScelta, but simply one of her character changes, pulled out of the closet and put on for the occasion.

"Ariana said you're a minister. I hope that means you're honest."

"I studied for the ministry. I try to be honest."

The waiter took their orders. Through soup and shad roe they talked of stocks and the coming split in IBM. Mark sensed that DiScelta had too firm a grasp of the market to need his advice and that she must have had another purpose in asking to see him. With coffee, conversation shifted back to music.

"Two months ago I would have said Ariana will be one of the great voices of our century. Now all I can say is, she may be."

"Why are you suddenly uncertain?" Mark asked.

"Because you stand in her way."

He felt atoms of color beginning to drain from his face.

"An operatic career," DiScelta said, "is not just one or two performances, any more than an opera is one or two arias. An operatic career is a life. It cannot be divided."

"But there are married singers."

"Yes, the stable ones. But Ariana is not stable. Look at the evidence. She canceled engagements in order to travel with you. She made those television commercials to put you back in the seminary."

"She never told me that was the reason."

"Twice she compromised her career and came close to ending it." DiScelta leaned forward, and shadows seemed to gather around her. "I believe in her talent. I believe in her voice. But her nature is volatile, divided. She lacks the ability to dedicate herself one hundred percent. And she's competing with people who dedicate themselves one hundred-ten percent. An operatic career requires, above all, emotional concentration."

Mark did not answer. Very carefully, he buttered a roll that he had no intention of eating.

"I'm not denying," DiScelta said, "that she loves you and you her. That is not the issue."

"Then what is the issue?"

"I see in Ariana a woman who could be one of the most dedicated servants of music this century has known. That is what I want for her. I make no secret of it." Her eyes were blazing into his. They were the color of night. "And you, Mark—may I call you Mark?—what do you want for her?"

"I want her happiness."

"Or is it her love you want? What if they're not the same?"

Mark had a feeling that a great wave of will was pouring out from DiScelta, almost engulfing him. "What does Ariana want?" he said. "Doesn't that count?"

"Each of us gets one chance." DiScelta held up a single finger, and a diamond sparkled. "Only one. This is Ariana's chance. She may succeed, she may fail. But if you make her give up her one chance, she'll always wonder what might have been. She'll be unhappy for the rest of her life. We all know what happiness is—songs and poetry tell us—but what about unhappiness, lifelong unhappiness—do you have any idea what that is?"

"How do you know she'll be unhappy?"

"I've had students. I've seen careers. I've seen marriages. I've had marriages. I know. For a real artist, and I believe she is a real artist, there is only one satisfaction, and that is to share her God-given gift with the world. As you, were you a practicing minister, would share yours with the world."

He felt inexplicably depleted. It was as if every impulse of joy and youth in him had suddenly died.

"You realize, don't you, Mark, that she would give up her career for you? Is that what you want? Is that what you're asking of her?"

A cold, irrational foreboding took him. It was as though when he looked at this woman in black another person were speaking through him. "No. I have no right."

"Then I propose a bargain."

He sat, powerless to move, and Ricarda DiScelta calmly stirred half a sugar lump into her coffee.

"In a little more than eight weeks," she said, "Ariana will sing *Aïda* in Mexico City. This will be her international debut—the test of whether or not she can carry the major role of a major opera in front of a major audience. Can you be at that performance?"

He knew everything depended on his having the strength to muster a *no*. But he heard that other person speaking through him. "Of course."

DiScelta smiled and took a little catlike sip of coffee. "If, after that performance, you believe she has the makings of an international star, you will step out of her life; give her up. If you honestly believe she hasn't the makings, I will respect your judgment. I will urge her to give up all hope of an international career, to devote herself to lieder, to recitals, to teaching; to bury herself in the small satisfactions of music. To marry you. The nightingale will clip her wings and become the parson's wife. With my blessing. The choice—the decision—will be yours."

He could feel a grave closing over him. "That's quite a responsibility you're thrusting at me."

"All responsibilities are dreadful."

"Give me time to think this over."

"You have one week. And then, one way or the other, the arrangements must be final."

That evening Mark sat in the rocker, hands writhing in his lap.

"Supper in five minutes!" Ariana called brightly.

"Ready and waiting," he called back, faking cheerfulness.

A smell of spaghetti marinara filled the little apartment, and a moment later in the next room Ariana was accompanying herself at the little spinet in a passage from *Norma*.

Mark stared desolately at the floor. It seemed to him that one pure soprano voice lifted in song went further toward God than any prayer he could muster.

Mark phoned his father and asked if they could talk. They met the next day in a quiet corner of the Union Club, and for twenty minutes

Mark Rutherford Senior stirred his coffee and listened to his son. And then, with eyes that were hard but kind, in a voice that was aloof but gentle, he answered as best he could.

"I look at you and I see a young man who loves tennis and rowed in the Harvard crew, a young man who feels a calling to the Episcopal Church and, in my honest opinion, doesn't give a damn about Puccini. Gilbert and Sullivan is enough for him."

"And I love Ariana."

"As what healthy young man wouldn't? She has admirable qualities. She has intelligence, she has spirit, she has determination. I look at her and I see an undeniably attractive young woman who loves music, who loves the stage, and who—with the love that's left over—loves you. But is that going to be enough for either of you?"

"I don't see how I can live without her."

"You have to realize, Mark, as people change—and life changes us all—love changes. In some cases, love dies. And lovers have to go on living. Are you quite sure you'll always love her just the way you do now? Or she you?"

"I'm sure of it."

"And you're sure nothing hidden in the future—or in the past—can ever shake your faith and beat you down and break your heart?"

"I don't know what you mean."

Mark's father smiled. It was a smile of remembering, of kindness, of youth recalled. "You're both highly gifted young people. But the artist and the minister have very different gifts. There are bound to be moments of serious conflict."

"Don't all lives have moments of conflict? You and Mother—"

"Deeper than that. Conflicts of vocation. I'm using the word in your sense, Mark. Does that surprise you? All human endeavor—law, medicine, the ministry, the arts—has to be seen in the light of vocation."

Mark felt growing suffocation, as though DiScelta had closed the grave and now, with every reasoned, tolerant word, his father was shoveling topsoil over it.

"You and Miss Kavalaris worship different gods."

"If you mean she's Catholic—"

"Let's not be parochial. I'm talking about opera and the church. The score of *Traviata* and the Book of Common Prayer."

There was a moment of silence while the stooped old waiter, unbidden, poured them fresh steaming coffee from a tall pewter pitcher. Mark stirred a lump of sugar into his cup.

"She's called to music," his father said. "And you're called to the ministry. I doubt that both callings can exist in the same marriage."

Mark sat there quietly, like a schoolboy taking punishment from the headmaster.

"You have an obligation to consider not only the people you may one day serve with your gifts, but the people she may one day serve with hers. If you let her." With that, Mark Rutherford Senior drained his coffee cup, signaled the waiter to bring the chit, and signed. "I'd better be getting downtown. Can I give you a lift?"

That evening after work Mark crept into the chapel in his old seminary. Evensong was in progress, and he slipped unseen into a seat in the rearmost pew.

His soul was in pieces as the last rays of day bled through the stations of the cross onto his folded hands. He felt more remote from God than ever before in his life.

His lips formed a voiceless supplication.
Dear God, please guide me. Thy will be done.

Mark phoned DiScelta from his office the next morning. He said two words.

"I agree."

"Alima!" Ricarda DiScelta clutched the receiver close and shouted across the Atlantic from her living room to the Villa Graziella in Palermo. "Don't sing the Mexico City *Aïda!*"

"I can't hear you," came the faint and incredulous voice.

"Don't sing *Aïda!* Save yourself for *Norma* at Scala! Besides, the Mexican *Aïda* is a terrible production and Tumolti has organized the critics against you!"

"I didn't want to sing it in the first place, but my agent—"

"Good! You've always had sense! I'll take care of your agent! Enjoy your vacation and be sure to bring me back a box of those delicious Milanese macaroons!"

For eight days Richard Schiller negotiated over crackling long-distance wires.

The Mexican Opera, committed to an elaborate and costly spectacle, swayed by international reviews which Richard shouted to them over the phone, accepted Alima Harvey's understudy as Aïda. But Patemio's agents refused what they called "the breadstick singer." Richard pointed out that she had sung Musetta to Patemio's Rodolfo. The agents phoned back a day later, saying their client would absolutely, but absolutely, not sing with the "television salesgirl."

Which left Giorgio Montecavallo, a tenor who if not over the hill had certainly passed the crest. A resident of New York, Paris, and Gstaad, he happened to be in New York at the moment; more important, he happened to be a client of Richard's agency. He viewed himself as the equal of Patemio and had made a profession of stepping into his rival's cancellations.

"But of course I will sing with Kavalaris," he told the press and photographers in his East Side apartment. He was wearing only his blue-striped gym shorts, and his body of muscle-going-to-pudge glistened with a light glaze of sweat. "I have heard she is splendid. No true artist would be frightened of appearing with such a talent."

11

"WITH VERDI," DISCELTA SAID, "OPERA BECOMES MODERN. WE have freer form. Arias do not always return to the opening verse—and why should they? Do our thoughts and emotions repeat?"

She pointed out that the early Verdi operas were beautiful melodies over an oom-pah-pah accompaniment. "Sometimes he sent a work into rehearsal with nothing more than the vocal parts, the bass line, and a few instrumental cues. His early scoring was formula. The aria opened with string accompaniment. Winds were added as the melody climaxed. And that was the Verdi style."

DiScelta went to the bookcase.

"And then he changed." She pulled down two leather-bound volumes and handed them to Ariana. "These are yours."

Ariana opened them and was astonished to see that they were DiScelta's own heavily marked editions of *Aïda* and *Traviata*. They were not the piano-vocal reductions that she and her teacher usually worked from, but full orchestral scores.

"With *Traviata* and *Aïda*," DiScelta said, "Verdi added a character to the opera: the orchestra."

And so Ariana had to learn to read orchestral clefs and transposing instruments, how to hear in her mind the difference between clarinet and bassoon on the same low E, between viola *tremolando* and violin *sul ponticello*.

And she had to learn a new vocal style.

When she first sang Aïda's aria "Ritorna Vincitor," DiScelta slammed the keyboard lid shut and waved her silent.

"What do you think you are giving the audience—beautiful technique?"

"I was trying to," Ariana stammered.

DiScelta sighed, made two cups of herbal tea (this week it was lemon verbena) and sat Ariana down in the armchair by the window.

"Beauty," she stated, "is for tunes, not for *Aïda*." She explained that Verdi conceived his mature operas not as strings of songs, but as dramas told through music. "The drama never stops for the music, and the music never stops for the soprano. Always keep this in mind. In *Aïda* you are an actress who sings, not a voice that happens to act."

She explained that beyond a certain point in Verdi projection of the words and a commanding stage presence were far more important than vocal polish or flash. "You must base your performance on the dramatic situation and the text. *Nothing else matters.*"

Ariana felt like an idiot. "I was only trying to please you."

"Never try to please anyone but the composer. Finish your tea and let's take 'Ritorna Vincitor' again, not as a soprano would sing it, but as Aïda would."

Mark sleepwalked through the next weeks, stunned, bewildered, stupefied. And then it was The Day. Eleven A.M. Time to go.

He picked up two suitcases and she picked up the other two and the hinges went fa-do as they swung the door shut and locked it, and they struggled down the stairs with their luggage.

He prayed for there not to be a cab, but when he raised his arm a Checker cab swerved around the corner of Perry Street and slowed toward the curb.

It was an unpleasant ride to the airport. Not just the traffic, the jolts, the red lights, which he welcomed (*Maybe we'll miss the plane . . . maybe we'll miss the performance*), but the feeling of complete powerlessness, of total inability to control what was happening.

"Mark," she said. "What's the matter? I'm the one who should be worried, not you."

He tried to smile. "Nervous for you, I guess."

"Don't be." She patted his thigh. "I'm going to be the greatest. I'm going to knock Mexico City on its ear."

Eight hours later she was tapping him in the ribs. He had dozed off on the flight. His dreams had been awful.

"We're here—Mexico." She said it with an "h," the Spanish way, jokingly.

A limousine was waiting to whisk them to their hotel. Mark stared through the window at broad avenues that seemed to be Paris with palm trees.

The sun burned more powerfully in this latitude; plants and sky and even buildings radiated color, like excess energy. He felt a tiny chill—inexplicable, for the car was hot and underneath the sweater that he had foolishly worn he was perspiring.

Black palm fronds stirred against the evening sky as Mark and Ariana arrived at the opera house. He stayed with her while she vocalized, turning pages at the little spinet in her dressing room.

"I thought you hated hearing me warm up," she said.

"I love it."

"*Panagia mou*, now you tell me!"

The dresser arrived. He left Ariana and the little old woman fussing with a black wig, wondering why in the world a black-haired soprano needed a black wig to sing Aïda. He went into the corridor to smoke a cigarette.

The shape of a jeweled woman appeared in the shadows. DiScelta. "The green room is empty," she said. "We can talk there."

He followed her into the deserted room. He felt he was walking through a nightmare.

She chose an armchair, deposited herself on it with an odd little shimmy of possessiveness. Her gaze fixed him. "Each step in life—our actions, our failures, our successes—is an act of faith."

"You sound like one of my teachers," he said.

"No, I sound like her teacher." Her eyes were dark with something more than night. "Whatever happens tonight," she said, "you must never, ever tell Ariana of our agreement. May I have your word?"

He finished his cigarette, stubbed it out. "In for a penny, in for a pound. You have my word."

DiScelta rose. "There's just time for you to wish her luck."

He went to the dressing room and found Ariana gulping down chamomile tea. He hugged her from behind. "It's going to be fine," he promised.

"It's going to be awful. I don't even remember my first notes!"

He set down her cup, took her hand and held it, lifting it into the space between them. "See this hand?"

"Yes, all too clearly—it has palsy, like the rest of me, including my so-called voice."

"God has placed in this little hand a little light to lead you."

"Mark Rutherford, of all times for you to turn minister on me . . ."

"No kidding. And this little light is the hopeful and believing soul of Ariana Kavalaris. All you have to do is follow it."

He kissed the hand and gave it back to her. She stared at the hand, then at him, and there was wonderment in her eyes. "You couldn't have said anything more perfect." She managed a sort of half-smile. "But I still have this terrible feeling. As though if I kiss you it's goodbye."

"Then don't kiss me."

"But I want to."

And she did. Lightly, on the lips.

And he returned the kiss, lightly, on the crown of her wig.

He watched the opera from the wings. The first act went well for Verdi, well for the Mexicans who had paid a hundred pesos a seat, well for Ariana Kavalaris.

But terribly for Mark Rutherford.

The setting was the palace at Memphis in ancient Egypt. The high priest told the warrior Radames that the goddess Isis had decreed him leader of the Egyptian army against the Ethiopians. Radames loved the beautiful slave girl Aïda and sang of her in one of the world's best-loved tenor arias, "Celeste Aïda"—"Heavenly Aïda."

Amneris, the pharaoh's daughter, entered. She loved Radames, but sensed he did not return her affection. Aïda appeared. Ariana looked magnificent. Jealously watching Radames and the beautiful slave, Amneris began to suspect that Aïda was her rival for Radames' love.

The pharaoh entered with his court and appointed Radames commander against the Ethiopians. The crowd rejoiced, wishing him a victorious return.

Aïda remained behind, torn by the knowledge that her beloved must meet her father, the Ethiopian king, on the battlefield, and that one of them must die. Ariana wrung every drop of pathos from the scene. The audience loved her "Ritorna Vincitor," they loved her "Numi, Pietà," in which she implored the mercy of the Ethiopian god. They loved every note she sang.

And so, in a terrible way, did Mark. He had never heard tones purer, more sustained, more effortlessly floated. The rapturous Mexicans called her back for four bows after her first curtain.

In Act Two, word reached the court that Radames had won the battle. Amneris lied to Aïda, saying that Radames had been killed. Aïda's grief-stricken reaction told Amneris all she needed to know. In cold fury, she revealed the truth and warned that she would be a pitiless rival.

The scene shifted to the gate at Thebes, where Radames led his army into the city to the strains of the Triumphal March. Amneris placed the crown of victory on his head. The pharaoh bade him name his reward. He asked that the lives of the prisoners be spared. Among them Aïda recognized her father, the Ethiopian king, disguised as an officer, but he begged her not to betray his identity.

Over the priests' objections, the pharaoh granted Radames his wish—and gave him Amneris's hand in marriage, proclaiming him heir to the throne.

Watching the spectacle swirling on the stage was like looking down from a bridge into swift water. Mark felt as though his hands were bound with a cord behind his back, as though Ariana's voice were a noose encircling his neck.

She sang even more beautifully in the next act, where Aïda met Radames at the temple of Isis and begged him to flee with her to Ethiopia. He said they could escape through the Napata Pass, which was unguarded. Aïda's father stepped out of the shadows, revealing his identity, and announced he would lead his army across the pass. He offered Aïda's hand if Radames would side with Ethiopia.

Amneris entered with the high priest. Confessing that he had betrayed Egypt's plans to the Ethiopian king, Radames gave himself up to the priest.

As Mark applauded tears blurred his vision. He had the sensation of both his life and Ariana's bounded in time, his moving toward a strange sort of death, hers toward something he would never know, let alone be part of.

There was one more act.

Amneris begged Radames to renounce Aïda, promising he would be pardoned. But he insisted on being punished for his treason. The priests condemned him to burial alive.

In the final scene Radames was sealed into the crypt in the Temple of Vulcan. As the stone closed over him forever, he discovered Aïda waiting for him in the dark. While Amneris stood weeping in the temple above him, the lovers embraced and sang farewell to the earth.

There were fourteen curtain calls, followed by a celebration party. The noise in the restaurant was a constant, deafening scream, and perfect strangers came up to Mark to tell him that his wife would be one of the true greats of her age. Every time he looked at her she was radiating joy and he knew it was true.

How many times during the night can you get out of bed without waking the woman sleeping next to you?

"Hey." And she was standing beside him, lit by a wave of light rippling in from the balcony. "Since when did you start smoking?"

"It's something I do now and then."

She took the cigarette from him and held on to his hand. They stood there silently, side by side, gazing out over Mexico City.

"When your hand is in mine," she said, "I feel nothing can ever hurt me."

That week of three performances brought rave reviews in all the local papers, even a glowing mention in Milan's *Corriere della Sera* that arrived by airplane, and a deepening certainty in Mark.

There was an empty sensation high up in the middle of his chest. For the first time in his life he craved unconsciousness. He began hanging out in the hotel bar, and it was there that he became drinking buddies with Ariana's tenor.

It was hard not to love Giorgio Montecavallo. Short, muscular, with a sheet of corpulence over the muscularity, his thick black hair beginning to gray handsomely, and he flowed into the bar as regular and as imperial as the Nile, at eleven o'clock every morning.

"*Buenos días*, my friend." He clapped a hand on Mark's shoulder, then gave a fingersnap and a smile to the bartender. "Two double tequilas, *por favor*."

Giorgio Montecavallo might not have been the world's greatest tenor (even Mark recognized that some of those high B-flats in "Celeste Aïda" were hefted, like a Soviet athlete on steroids jerking six hundred kilos at an Olympic competition) but he was certainly a nonstop talker, just the man when you didn't want to hear yourself think; and he also turned out to be one of the world's most charming, most willing tour guides.

"You haven't seen the pyramids at Cuernavaca?" His eyebrows rippled in disbelief when Mark and Ariana informed him of this astonishing fact. A glance at his $2,000 Omega wristwatch—"We're in luck, there's time before rehearsal"; a snap of his fingers summoning the waiter to summon the concierge; and within minutes a car and private guide had been hired, and two hours later the three of them were clawing their way up steeply stepped Aztec burial mounds, sweating and gasping beneath a burning Mexican sky, pausing at the top to take snapshots of one another.

"You have to admit it's extraordinary," Monte said. (That was what he'd asked them to call him: "No one calls me Giorgio.") "Here we are on top of a crypt in Central America that was built two thousand years before Mozart, and in a week I'll be four thousand miles away in Scala singing Verdi, and Ariana will be—where will you be, Ariana?"

"Back in New York singing scales."

"Nonsense, you'll be in Vienna singing Queen of the Night. One more, keep smiling, there we are. Now, Mark, could I ask you to do me the honor of taking one of me and my delicious Aïda?"

Mark managed to hold together till two minutes before the final performance. He was in Ariana's dressing room when his whole body began to shudder. He bent his head and kissed her on her wig.

"Knock 'em dead," he said.

There were eighteen curtain calls after the final performance, three thousand men and women leaping to their feet to scream and clap and cheer. Ariana felt she was living a scene from someone else's life. Nothing seemed real, not the dressing room, not the voices rippling outside the door, not the dresser's hands helping her out of her costume. And not the envelope that her dresser held out to her.

"Señor Rutherford left this for you."

She had a sudden, overwhelming fear that something dreadful had happened to Mark. Opening the envelope, she sank into a chair.

> My dearest Ariana,
>   These are the hardest words I've ever had to write in my life. I feel more strongly for you than I've ever felt for anyone or anything, including the church. And that is the problem.
>   I realize now that the church is not just my career—it is my life, the best part of me. It is everything that is good and strong and honest in me.
>   I made a promise, Ariana. In my heart I betrayed that promise. My very act of loving you betrayed it—and betrayed you as well. That betrayal would sooner or later kill everything we love in one another. I could not bear that.
>   I am returning to the church. I can never see you again.

You have made me happier than I ever deserved. Please forgive me, Ariana. I shall never forget you.

Mark

She couldn't believe he had written it.

The handwriting was his, but the words were someone else's.

Suddenly she understood. It was a joke. It had to be a joke. Some sort of Mexican tradition of scaring the prima donna to death.

"Where is Señor Rutherford?" she asked.

"He went to the airport."

"The airport . . ." *Could the letter be real?* she wondered. *Could this really be happening?*

She read it again, and once again, and each word struck her like an earthquake burying a little bit more of the past, a little bit more of the future. She saw herself in the makeup mirror, a thing still living that had just been dealt a killing blow. She could see belief seeping, like death, into her face.

She tried to stand. She had to think each movement, execute it one minuscule exertion at a time.

In the distance a bell was ringing.

She screamed. The world had just ended.

"Señora! Señora!" The dresser was holding her down in a chair.

A grave-faced man with a black bag was hastily assembling a hypodermic. Ariana felt the cold kiss of alcohol on her arm, the quick sting of a needle, the slow inflooding of false relief.

After that time passed with a strange, unnatural flow. She felt hands undressing her, washing her, dressing her, transforming Aïda back into Ariana.

And then a voice came through a fog: "The best investment I ever made."

It took Ariana a moment to recognize the dark eyes and drooping mustache and suntanned skin of the man standing in the doorway. "Nikos," she said.

He embraced her lightly. "Music makes me hungry," he said, "doesn't it you? Let's go someplace wonderful and eat."

Her mouth began to shake and then her face and then she could feel herself going entirely to pieces.

He sat down beside her. He took her hand, so lightly she didn't even notice that he was holding a part of her.

He let her talk. "I'm taking you home," he said gently.

He took charge. With two phone calls he had a limousine waiting at the opera house and a private plane waiting at the airport. It was peaceful and quiet in the ten-seater plane. They were the only passengers. He sat beside her all the way to New York, holding her hand, listening when she spoke, listening when she didn't.

Another limousine was waiting when they landed at Idlewild. A chauffeur drove them to Perry Street.

Nikos hugged her. "Your bags will be here tomorrow. Try to get some sleep. You'll feel better. Here. Don't forget your passport."

She kissed him, a kiss of thank-you, nothing more.

She unlocked the front door.

Mark will be here, she told herself. *It was all a misunderstanding. In two minutes we'll be laughing about it.*

Her feet took her through the squeaky gate into the little courtyard with the lonely little Pan in the fountain.

He's home. I know he's home waiting for me.

She hurried up the flight of steps to apartment 2-A.

He's just on the other side of this door. He's embarrassed and he's sorry and he's afraid I'm going to be angry and maybe I will be, just for a moment.

The door hinges sang out the two notes of "Amazing Grace" and she looked around the darkness. She turned on the light.

He wasn't in his chair in the corner, lifting his eyes from a page of New Testament Greek, rising to kiss her.

She crossed the room and turned on the bedroom light.

He wasn't in the bed, holding out his arms to her.

She went into the bathroom to find an aspirin. The odor of his aftershave lotion came floating out of the bathroom cabinet, and for a brief, stabbing instant she stood recalling that eternity ago when there had been love and tomorrow had really existed.

She phoned his parents. Augusta Rutherford answered sleepily. "Yes, Ariana."

"May I speak with Mark?"

"Mark's not here. He said he was going to Mexico with you. Ariana, what's wrong?"

"Nothing. I'm sorry to wake you up. Goodbye."

She dialed Harry's number. He didn't know where Mark was. She felt her life slipping away. "If you hear from him, would you ask him to phone me?"

"Of course," Harry said gently.

Her mind clenched and unclenched like an empty fist and a spiraling emptiness pushed through her. She knew her life had changed forever, and the only question was how long forever would be.

She stared at the phone. It didn't ring. It didn't ring. Didn't ring.

And then she was hurling pans at the piano, kicking over lamps, screaming, and five minutes later Magda, the concierge with dyed red hair, was pounding on the door and angry neighbors were peering onto the landing, and a policeman was saying, "Isn't there anyone who can take care of her?"

❊   ❊   ❊

DiScelta arrived forty minutes later.

She looked at the mess. She looked at the girl.

"I'll handle this."

Ariana showed her Mark's letter.

"Sad," DiScelta said. "Very sad. He's through with you."

"But *why?*"

"Who knows why? Sometimes I think even God doesn't know why."

Ariana cried convulsively for almost two hours.

DiScelta spoke gently, patiently, like a mother. "Face it. Accept it. Mark is gone. The person you loved is no longer part of your life. Don't think about him. Don't think about the past and don't worry about the future. Though you don't believe it now, there *will* be a future." Her touch was soft on Ariana's face. "And don't try to contact him. It will only prolong the pain."

But Ariana did try. She phoned Harry the next day, whispering so DiScelta couldn't hear in the next room.

"Have you heard from Mark?"

"I'm sorry, Ariana. I'll be in touch the minute I do."

"Harry, can I see you? You're his friend and I need to talk. Please."

"I'm leaving for London this very minute, but maybe when I get back . . ."

"When will you be back?"

"I don't know exactly. A few weeks . . ."

Ariana phoned Harry's number the next day.

When Harry answered she hung up without speaking.

DiScelta canceled pupils, canceled parties, even canceled performances to stay with Ariana—cooking, cleaning, and always, always listening and soothing.

When Ariana began crying because the apartment reminded her of Mark, DiScelta answered, "You'll stay here till you can stand it, because if you don't, the street outside will remind you of him, and the city will remind you of him, and the world will remind you of him. Once you start hiding no place in the universe is safe."

So they stayed in the apartment, teacher and pupil, and for almost a week Ariana was a hopeless mess: crying, sleeping, crying, not sleeping, crying, remembering, crying, not eating, crying. For those first seven days there was nothing in her life except DiScelta, nursing, listening, helping her through her angers and fears and loneliness.

Gradually the first sorrow, the first unlivable-with grinding ache faded, and a mechanical sort of life began to flow back into her again.

"It's time to work," DiScelta said. She struck a chord on the piano, turned her commanding gaze on Ariana. "Don't just stand there. Vocalize."

Ariana flew into a disbelieving rage. "What am I supposed to do? Go perch on a bough and sing for an emperor?"

DiScelta looked at her from a great center of calmness. "It will come, my child, it will come."

At first it was difficult. There was a tightening in her throat. DiScelta was patient with her.

"The voice wants to rise under stress, but you must resist, my child. Hold the note."

Ariana obeyed. There was no choice. The only barrier between her and insanity was do-re-mi and la-la-la.

Gradually, music took her back. It challenged her, dared her, absorbed her, stimulated something in her will to live.

After two weeks DiScelta moved out, and Ariana felt a bone-soaking loneliness. She kept at her music. Three times a week she went to her teacher's apartment for her lesson. Twice a day, at DiScelta's insistence, she chatted with her teacher on the phone. "Never isolate, my child, never isolate. Only contact with the world can heal."

It was a month since she'd last seen Mark when she swallowed her pride and phoned Harry Forbes again.

"Harry, it's Ariana. How was London?"

"Wonderful, as always."

An awkward silence.

"Have you heard from Mark?"

A pause. "I'm sorry, Ariana. Truly sorry."

Harry hung up the phone and turned to gaze at the figure slumped in the easy chair.

"It can't go on like this, Mark."

For weeks Mark had holed up in Harry Forbes's apartment, drinking, smoking, smoking, drinking, never changing the sheets on the sofa, never washing a plate, never taking a shirt to the laundry, never leaving the apartment except to go to work and never returning except to drink and smoke and stare at bookshelves.

"I'm not complaining," Harry said. "I don't mind helping a friend. I don't mind listening and cleaning and cooking. But I do mind lying to that poor girl."

"Sorry," Mark said in a dead voice.

"You've been sorry a hell of a long time. Why don't you stop being a fool and pick up that phone and call her?"

Mark sighed.

Harry crossed the room and handed him the phone.

In very slow motion Mark began dialing: three digits, a fourth, two more . . . and stopped, like a mechanical toy needing winding up.

"Do it," Harry prodded. "Tell her you want to see her and you want to see her tonight."

This time Mark dialed seven digits. There was a pause and Harry watched his friend's face.

With absolutely no change of expression, mummylike, Mark said, "Hi, it's me."

There was a long silence while Mark sat listening, but his face still didn't change.

"I have to see you," he said.

"Tonight," Harry whispered.

"Tonight. How about O. Henry's steak house on Sixth Avenue and Fourth?"

Mark slowly hung up and sat absolutely motionless, staring at bookshelves.

"What did Ariana say?" Harry asked.

"I wasn't talking to Ariana."

"Then who were you talking to?"

"Nita. You've met her."

"Mark, what the hell are you doing?"

"Relax, Harry. I've worked it all out. Everything's going to be just fine."

"Will you marry me?" Mark asked.

Nita's eyes fixed Mark's, trying to see if he was being honest. For she knew questions, like statements, could be lies.

"Say that again, Mark?"

They were sitting with two steins of beer. The butcher-block tables at O. Henry's were crowded, and the waiters in their long white coats and straw hats looked harried and tired.

For a long moment there was only the murmur of other customers, the faint nattering fingers of rain against the plate-glass window with its ye olde gold lettering in reverse.

He said it again. She wasn't imagining.

"Will you marry me?"

Surprise caught her and she could feel tears swelling the corners of her eyes. For a moment she writhed with her memories, with all the bright, brave decisions she'd made about putting away childish things, first and foremost among them her crush on Mark Ames Rutherford.

She couldn't believe there had been many who had touched the face of the earth quite so gracefully as the man now waiting for her answer. She'd dated a dozen others in the last year and she'd almost been to bed with three and she'd seriously considered marrying one of them.

But she'd always compared them to Mark. She didn't know why. Maybe because he'd been the first to kiss her. Maybe because he'd played Schubert duets with her when they were twelve-year-olds. Maybe because even a goodnight brush of his lips made her weak in a way no other man's kiss did.

A dark voice warned her that he was only asking because he wanted to heal a wound before it festered, a wound that had nothing to do with her. The voice told her to get up from that table, to get out of Mark's life and stay out.

But what did dark voices know?

"Yes," she said. "Oh, yes, my darling Mark. I'll marry you."

12

RICARDA DISCELTA KNEW THERE WAS A SOLUTION FOR ARIANA. That the solution was, broadly speaking, work and music and time, she had no doubt. She saw, over the weeks, how the little mercies of routine gradually began to reclaim her student. Yet an element was missing, and the element, she decided, was Boyd Kinsolving.

DiScelta found Boyd boring but his father was Amory Kinsolving of Kinsolving Steel, and his mother, the former Marjorie Biddle of the Philadelphia Biddles, served on the boards of the New York Metropolitan and the Chicago operas. Connections counted in Ricarda's world. When you were young they helped you get roles, and later, when you had the roles you wanted, they still helped you get your way.

She invited Boyd to lunch at the Café Chambord.

"I've a student you ought to meet."

Boyd Kinsolving asked who and why.

"Her name is Ariana Kavalaris. I don't know whether you read her reviews last month, but she's considered a very promising voice."

"What sort of voice?"

"Dramatic soprano with a very high, brilliant top."

"Does she know the final scene from *Salomé?*"

Boyd had contracted to guest-conduct a fund-raising mishmash for the New York Philharmonic in March, and his scheduled soprano—a notoriously unreliable Hungarian prima donna—had canceled. He had had trouble signing a first-rate substitute.

"If you're willing to use her, Ariana will learn the scene."

"When can I hear her?"

"Tomorrow at four. You can eavesdrop on her lesson."

"I'll have to reschedule my haircut."

"Ariana is worth a haircut."

"I'll be there."

"And Boyd, if you like her, you're doing a *Rigoletto* in Mexico in April? She got a very good press in Mexico."

"We'll see. If I like her, it's possible."

He listened from the study. He liked her.

"The concert and *Rigoletto?*" DiScelta whispered.

He nodded, and his blond bangs fell at an elfish angle across his face. DiScelta swept him into the music room.

"Ariana, I took the liberty of inviting a friend—Boyd Kinsolving—he loves you."

Ariana turned and her mouth fell open just a little. *Why not, Di-*

Scelta thought, *he has blue eyes and pink skin and big shoulders and long straight legs and he's dressed like a model.*

DiScelta made introductions and told Ariana that Boyd wanted her for his concert.

Ariana's face fell. "But I don't know *Salomé*," she said.

"We'll learn it," DiScelta promised.

Afterward, when they were alone, Ariana wheeled on her teacher. "I can't learn that music in a month. I've never sung Strauss. The tessitura's wrong for me. That low G-flat is out of the question. I'll never project with a hundred musicians on the stage behind me."

DiScelta smiled, hearing the reasons but not accepting them. "You've had too many months of nothingness. You need this."

Richard Strauss's *Salomé* had been, at the turn of the century, a shocker. The Kaiser had advised Strauss not to let it be performed. The financier J. P. Morgan had once paid the Metropolitan Opera a fortune *not* to stage it. But the public had always adored this opulent portrait of a murderous Levantine Lolita, and Ariana resolved to give it her best vocal shot.

"With Strauss," DiScelta said, "the clarity of the words comes first. You must project over the loudest orchestration in the world—and the vocal line never stops."

Though DiScelta obviously had reservations about his music, she regarded Strauss as the operatic giant of the twentieth century.

"He is the supreme melodist. He is able to stuff his vocal lines to the limit—and they still hold. He is also the greatest writer for the female voice any century has produced. I do not mean the music is always first-rate—far from it—but the effect is always sublime." She cited the final trio of his *Rosenkavalier*, where three sopranos (though one was often sung by a mezzo) melted together in a soaring, ten-minute-long melody that crowned not only the opera but nineteenth-century music itself.

She sighed. "But today we are dealing with less sublime matters."

She opened the score of *Salomé*.

"Of course, *Salomé* is really a tone poem with voices, rather than pure opera. Which is why it holds up in the concert hall as well as on the stage. Strauss commands the Wagnerian apparatus of sound and the full range of post-Wagnerian techniques. As a result he is a master at communicating psychological states."

She grimaced. "Particularly morbid states. In this work, you and the orchestra are partners in psychoanalysis. The voice expresses the conscious psyche, the orchestra lays bare the unconscious: every impulse, every complex, every mental twitch and fleeting thought is articulated—often simultaneously."

She said there had probably never been a richer tapestry of operatic sound than Strauss's *Elektra* or *Salomé*.

And again she grimaced. "Whether they are pleasant tapestries is another matter. They have power. That is enough."

Ariana plunged into a study of the libretto. It was essentially a gory anecdote. Salomé's stepfather, King Herod, had imprisoned Jokanaan, John the Baptist, in a cistern of his palace on the Sea of Galilee. Fascinated by the prophet's voice, Salomé had the guards bring him before her. Smitten with desire at the sight of him, she begged to kiss his lips and fondle his hair. He scorned her and returned to the cistern, leaving her stung by rejection.

King Herod emerged from the palace. Lusting for his stepdaughter, he entreated her to dance for him. At first she refused, but when he promised any reward she wanted, she consented to perform the Dance of the Seven Veils.

Boyd Kinsolving planned to begin his concert excerpt with the dance, which was masterfully lurid hootchy-kootch and had inspired the scores of hundreds of Hollywood Biblical extravaganzas.

After shedding her seven veils, Salomé demanded payment: the head of Jokanaan. The horrified king offered her anything else, but she was adamant. Finally Herod gave the signal. The executioner descended into the cistern and a moment later handed up Jokanaan's head on a silver charger.

This section would be omitted in the concert performance, and Boyd would cut directly to the final scene, where Salomé—in an erotic ecstasy—gloatingly fondled the head. As she smeared the dead prophet's lips with kisses, Herod, revolted, called to his guards, "Kill this woman!" They crushed her beneath their shields.

Herod's line would be omitted, but the audience would get the point from their programs.

For four weeks DiScelta drove Ariana twelve hours a day, drumming the tortured vocal line into her memory and into her throat muscles.

At the first orchestra rehearsal Carnegie Hall echoed with the brilliant chaotic dissonance of instruments tuning. It was a closed rehearsal, but the forward seats of the first and second tiers were filled with women with dazzlingly perfect hair and jewels and rich furs dumped over the backs of their seats. Friends of Boyd's, Ariana supposed.

Boyd smiled at her, then raised his baton.

Ariana stood beside the podium, awaiting her cue.

The clarinets rippled a shrill, birdlike arpeggio. Horns brayed. Her entrance. She stepped forward, her mouth projecting the opening vowel above the orchestral din.

"Ah! du wolltest mich nicht deinen Mund küssen lassen, Jokan-

aan!"—"Ah! you would not let me kiss your mouth, Jokanaan!"

She could feel the orchestral fabric pulling together behind her: the wind prickles really prickled, the brass explosions truly exploded, even the evil little percussion rattles punctuated the texture with just the right snakelike sinuosity.

After the final catclysmic fanfare of brass and timpani, the tiers of socialites broke into applause. Boyd laid down his baton and mopped his face with a monogrammed handkerchief.

A woman came running up with an ermine slung over her shoulders and kissed him on both cheeks. "I just adored it," she cooed. Her vowels were rich, confident, depraved. "I'm *tingling*."

"Can you believe it's Ariana's first try at the part?" Boyd said. "Ariana, you know Keekee deClairville, one of my great great chums?"

The woman turned to Ariana. Diamonds shivered at her ears. "My dear, you're a natural. You bring out the bitchiness in that Jewish princess *perfectly*."

"Thank you," Ariana said.

The rehearsal broke up. Boyd reached for Ariana's hand. "Have you got dinner plans?"

She had none.

"Come on. My treat."

The morning after the concert Boyd's houseboy brought him the reviews with his coffee. He glanced over them.

The *Times* critic felt that Boyd Kinsolving *showed complete mastery of his orchestra, evoking in a thousand sure and telling details the beauty and damnation that inhabit these pages.* . . .

Boyd blew out a soft, disbelieving whistle.

The critic was equally kind to the soloist: *Ariana Kavalaris—a young woman endowed with great personal as well as vocal beauty—would appear to be well on her way to becoming one of our major dramatic vocalists. She attacked the role with assurance and accuracy, brilliance and fury.* . . .

Boyd knotted the cord of his maroon satin robe and walked to the window. He stared a long, long moment across the peaceful square at Gramercy Park. The winter-stripped trees and iron picket fence stood out with extraordinary distinctness against the snow, like lines in an etching.

Together, he thought, *this little girl and I could conquer the world.*

The limousine cut neatly across the evening-cooled plaza. In the purple mist that had begun enveloping the palm trees and statues, the opera house loomed like the shadow of a gray giant.

Ariana huddled deeper into the seat. *"Panagia mou—ti kano edho?"*

Boyd understood the tone, if not the words. He patted her hand. "Courage, sweetums. You'll do just fine."

The stage entrance smelled of a recent mopping with ammonia. Ariana had come this far with a sort of numb resignation, but as she stepped into the elevator panic gripped her. *This is where Mark left me. I'll never be able to walk onto that stage.*

"Sweetums, you're perspiring just a tad." Boyd gave her his handkerchief. "Drink a little tea, vocalize, and lie down. You'll be fine."

They had given her the same dressing room as before.

Here, she thought. *Here is where my life ended.*

The little spinet was tuned flat, and she felt uneasy having to vocalize to it. She drank chamomile tea for her nerves. By the time her dresser arrived cold sweat prickled her forehead and her eyes felt as though they were burning with fever. As the old woman bustled around her, fitting her into the layers of her Renaissance dress, the overture crackled through the loudspeaker on the wall—the ominous motif of the curse, followed by the giddy merrymaking music that set the scene at the Duke of Mantua's palace.

Ariana listened with half an ear as the duke, a libertine and tenor, revealed to the hunchback Rigoletto, his jester and confidant—sung by a splendid baritone—that he hoped to seduce a beautiful girl he had seen at church. Rigoletto laughed approvingly. While the courtiers danced a graceful minuet, Count Monterone burst in, enraged and grief-stricken that the duke had seduced his daughter. Rigoletto mocked the count, who hurled a curse at him.

In the operatic equivalent of whispering—swift, lightly accompanied recitative—Marullo, one of the courtiers, revealed to the others that Rigoletto kept a young woman locked up in his home. Supposing her to be his mistress, they decided to play a joke on the detested hunchback by abducting her.

The applause that came through the speaker was loud and generous. The audience seemed to be in a good mood.

There was a knock at the door and a voice called, *"Diez minutos."*

Ariana waited in the wings and watched the beginning of the next scene. In the secluded street in front of his house, Rigoletto crossed paths with Sparafucile, a professional assassin, who offered his services whenever they might be needed.

Ariana moved quickly from the shadows of the wings onto the glaring light of the stage. Now she was the jester's daughter Gilda, the joy of his life, and she was running to meet him.

Beyond the orchestra pit the audience was still and cold as dark water: not a ripple disturbed them.

Ariana sang her first lines. They had to be projected over a blanket of horns. Rigoletto questioned her about her activities. Her tone felt pinched, her breath short.

As Rigoletto told the nurse to watch his daughter carefully, the duke slipped unseen into the house, tossing the nurse a purse, and hid.

After her father left, Gilda told the nurse of the handsome young man who had been following her at church. The duke stepped into the open, motioning the nurse to go. Gilda recognized him. They sang a love duet, and—lying—he told her that he was a student, that his name was Gualtier.

As Ariana lifted her face to the audience, acknowledging their polite applause, a light seemed to catch her eye. In the third row of the orchestra she saw a man with an empty seat beside him. His eyes were fixed on her in a kindly, encouraging way. He had dark hair, a clean-shaven face, a tiny cleft in his chin. He was wearing a minister's collar.

It was Mark. For an instant her heart stopped. He signaled her with his eyes. *I am here. You are safe. I'll protect you. Sing.*

She drew air into her and it was like the first breath she had breathed in months.

The duke left, and Gilda—rapturously in love—sang "Caro Nome"—"Dear Name." The music seemed to soar out of her of its own volition: there was no sense of strain or panic.

The applause was warm, sustained, sincere. There were bravas.

Ariana felt her heart pumping, tears threatening to run down her face. *Mark.* Still there, still smiling.

Now the courtiers gathered outside the house. Rigoletto returned, and Marullo told him they were stealing another man's wife and needed his help. Pretending to mask him, Marullo blindfolded the jester. Rigoletto held the ladder while the courtiers entered his house and carried Gilda away. Tearing off the blindfold, Rigoletto realized he had been duped. "The curse!" he cried, and the curtain fell.

Ariana passed the intermission in a state of mixed terror and excitement, almost afraid to step back onto the stage.

Act Two took place in the palace. The courtiers told the duke they had stolen Rigoletto's mistress for him. He went to join her. Rigoletto entered, but the laughing courtiers encircled him and blocked his way. Revealing that Gilda was his daughter, he pleaded for their compassion. They mocked him.

Now. Now was her entrance. Now she was Gilda again. She rushed onstage, sobbing and dishonored, and flung herself into Rigoletto's arms. Still loving the duke, she begged her father not to swear vengeance.

From the audience Mark's gaze came up at her, a warm glow.

She had no memory of reaching the end of the act. All she knew was that the curtain was falling, and rising, and hands were pushing her to the apron of the stage.

She heard Mark's voice above the others, shouting "Brava!" Her eyes met his and thanked him.

In the next intermission she spoke to an usher. She told him where Mark was sitting. "Would you ask the gentleman to come to my dressing room after the performance?"

Act Three began with a storm building. Gilda and Rigoletto watched through a crack in the wall as the duke entered the house of Sparafucile, the assassin, and asked for wine and a room. The duke sang "La Donn' è Mobile"—"Woman is Fickle"—and flirted with Sparafucile's sister, the prostitute Maddalena. Gilda was heartbroken.

Rigoletto ordered his daughter home to change into men's clothes and precede him to Verona. Sparafucile came outside. Rigoletto gave the assassin money—half his fee for murdering the duke. The rest would be paid at midnight, when Rigoletto returned for the body.

Maddalena, attracted to the duke, now pleaded with her brother not to kill him. Gilda returned, dressed in male clothing and determined to save her faithless lover. She overheard Sparafucile agree that if another man arrived before midnight, he would kill that man and substitute his body for the duke's.

The storm was raging in full fury as Gilda knocked on the door, entered, and was struck down by Sparafucile's dagger.

Rigoletto arrived. Sparafucile handed over a body in a sack. At that moment the duke's voice could be heard offstage singing "La Donn' è Mobile." The jester tore open the sack and discovered his daughter. With her last breath, Gilda begged his forgiveness. He collapsed over her lifeless body, crying *La maledizione!*"—"The curse!"

The curtain fell. The cast took their bow, and then the soloists.

Mark got to his feet and led a standing ovation. It seemed to Ariana that all the wealth and glitter of Mexico City were cheering her. The din refused to die away and even after a dozen curtain calls the audience still would not let her go.

Mark's eyes stayed fastened on hers and there was a promise in his glance.

Her eyes questioned. *Did you get my message?*

His eyes answered. *I'll meet you. Soon, my darling, soon.*

The audience called her back eleven times. Bouquets and torn programs rained down on the stage and Mark was there beside the empty seat, his eyes promising.

The dressing room overflowed with well-wishers, packed thick as trees in a forest, but Ariana didn't see Mark.

"Didn't you deliver my message?" she asked the usher.

The usher nodded toward a large man in a dark suit. His gray hair was full and curling and the lines in his face seemed intelligent and kind. But he wasn't wearing a clerical collar and he didn't resemble Mark in the least.

He was waiting for Ariana's glance. He approached, his hand outstretched, a smile blazing out of his dark, tanned face.

"Miss Kavalaris, what a sublime performance." He bent over her hand and she felt the shadow of his lips. He said his name was Raul Rodriguez. "May I present my wife, Madalena?"

The woman beside him murmured, "*Encantada.*"

Ariana stared at the woman. The seat beside Mark had been empty—she would certainly have noticed if Señora Rodriguez with her ash-blond hair and diamonds had been sitting there. "You were in the third row? Third seat to the right of the aisle?"

Señor Rodriguez reached into his vest pocket and from behind his gold watch pulled two ticket stubs. "Usually my brother-in-law uses the seats, but he is in Geneva. His bad fortune was our good luck."

Ariana could only nod in dumb embarrassment. "I'm sorry, I made a mistake. I thought you were someone else."

"I hope you are not disappointed that it was only my wife and I. Could we trouble you to autograph my wife's program?"

"Of course." Ariana took the pen that Señor Rodriguez held out and splashed a signature across the cover of the program.

It took twenty minutes to get rid of all the visitors, and a desperate loneliness welled up in Ariana.

Boyd smacked a kiss on the side of her face, his white teeth flashing. "It came together, sweetums, it came together!"

"Did it?"

He looked at her. "Don't tell me you're glum. You should be dancing on ceilings."

"I'm a little disappointed, I guess."

"Then you're the only disappointed person in Mexico City."

"I thought someone was here. And he's not."

"So? Big fat end of the world? What does it matter, sweetums, so long as you sang like a goddess?"

Ganz-Tucci squinted at the bootleg tape that one of her informants had smuggled in from Mexico.

Her vision was blurring with age and her entire body ached but she managed torturously to slip the reel onto the player. She found the button that made the tape go forward.

She shut her eyes, listened to the entire recording, and went to the telephone and dialed a number.

"Ricarda? Get over here immediately."

"Are you a criminal or just an imbecile?" Ganzi-Tucci was poking the air with her arms like a furious old monkey.

DiScelta watched, unimpressed. "Whatever I am, you taught me to be."

Ganz-Tucci fumbled with the tape player, and motioned the younger woman to be quiet and listen.

A voice glided upward, filling the room. At moments it had tones like shadows slanting away from the sun; at others it had the brilliance of a diamond. Ganz-Tucci stood by the window and with the edge of her folded spectacles tapped time on the sill.

The tape finished.

Ganz-Tucci gave DiScelta a dark look. "Your pupil?"

"My pupil," DiScelta acknowledged. "How did you get it?"

"There are people willing to help me. You are not my only friend. Happily."

DiScelta did not answer. Something congealed in the silence.

"That is the sound we've been searching for. I feel it here, inside me." Ganz-Tucci rapped her spectacles against her heart. "Ricarda, *that is the voice.*"

DiScelta was silent.

"Are you going to answer me, or are you just going to stand there and flaunt your ignorance and incompetence as though they were gifts from God?"

DiScelta looked at her teacher. *She's aged*, she thought. Even by the glow of sunset creeping through the curtained window she could see that Ganz-Tucci was a very old woman with stiff white hair and painfully brittle movements.

At that instant Ricarda DiScelta loved her old teacher with a melancholy, almost overpowering tenderness. She wanted to rush across the space that separated them and embrace her. She wanted to spend the evening talking about their careers and their youth and all the music they had ever made and all the singers and composers they had ever known and loved.

But that was not the way they behaved with one another. They were teacher and student, still, even after all the decades they had shared.

"I hope you're right," DiScelta said with forced coolness. "I hope she is the voice. Soon I'll know."

"We haven't time for your inertia!" Ganz-Tucci screamed. "I could die tomorrow!"

"That would be very sad, but I am the judge of her readiness," DiScelta reminded her teacher, "not you."

13

"IT'S DIFFICULT TO PUT INTO WORDS. I'VE WORKED TWICE WITH Ariana. And both times I've sensed an improvement in my work. The second time I knew it was no accident. It was her."

Only the skin of DiScelta's throat reacted to what Boyd Kinsolving had said. It pulsed rapidly just above her pearls.

"With Ariana," he said, "my ear is sharper, my control of the musicians is firmer."

"I know, I know," DiScelta said. "You think a shading or an accent, and it's there. You are the music and the music is you."

They were sitting in her apartment. He had requested the audience. She had granted him ten minutes between pupils.

"You have power over her," he said.

DiScelta did not deny it.

"I thought you might encourage a collaboration between her and me."

A silence fell. DiScelta sat in absolute motionlessness.

"She sang only eighteen performances at major houses last year," Boyd went on. "She has only sixteen this year. If she works with me, she'd double her performances. In two or three years she could be singing eighty to a hundred."

"And you would be conducting those eighty to a hundred?"

Boyd nodded.

"Ariana will be the greatest voice of our age. You are developing into a good conductor, but you will never be considered one of the greatest."

"I can't deny that. On the other hand, I could save her ten years' struggle for recognition. In return, she would be an enormous help to me later, when I've peaked."

"No. I'm against it. She's giving you too much, you're giving her too little. Unless . . ." DiScelta paused. "Why not marry her?"

"Marry her?" Boyd frowned thoughtfully. "Look, you're perfectly aware I'm not attracted to women. Sexually, I mean."

She shrugged. "There have been marriages of the spirit, especially between artists. As husband and wife, you would be attractive to audiences. The exclusivity would make sense: agents and impresarios would cooperate, whereas if you were unmarried they would resent you. And Ariana would have a home. She wouldn't waste time looking for emotional security."

Boyd hesitated. "What makes you think she'd accept me?"

"Perhaps she wouldn't, but what do you risk by trying? Propose to her, but don't force a reply. Give her whatever time she needs—a week, a month, a year. Plant the seed."

There were too many intriguers at the party, too many small people ready to condescend: "Would I have heard you sing at the Met?" and then that startled look when she said she'd sung three Butterflys that season. "Oh, we gave our *Butterfly* tickets to the maid."

A hunger for fresh air drove Ariana into the garden.

"You look lovely and lonely," a voice said.

She turned. Boyd Kinsolving, not quite steady on his feet, was holding out two glasses of champagne. She took one of them. They sat on a bench and sipped for a silent moment.

"What do you think of me?" he asked.

"Oh, I think you're probably drunk."

"At the moment I think you're probably right."

"But I also think you're a promising conductor."

"Thank you. And personally?"

"The truth?"

"Please."

"I think you should spend more time with your scores and less with rich and famous fools."

"You don't like our fellow guests?"

"Half of them have names, half have fortunes, none have minds. They bore me and I'm going."

"They bore me too and I'll help you find a cab."

He walked out to Beekman Place with her and hailed her a cab, and then he asked if he might ride with her because New York always looked so beautiful through the windows of a taxi. After three blocks he took her hand and said, "Would you consider marrying me?"

She turned in the seat, surprised.

"It's only something to think about," he said. "Nothing needs to be decided today."

"I don't love you," she said.

"You may come to. I'm quite lovable, you know."

"Boyd Kinsolving proposed marriage to me."

Ricarda DiScelta leveled a long, smoke-colored gaze at her pupil. But she did not answer. She opened the score of *Barber of Seville* and laid it carefully on the music rack.

"It's a ridiculous idea. Boyd and I are completely wrong elements for marriage."

"Elements are strange. From horse tails and cat intestines you can get a string orchestra."

"You think I should marry him," Ariana said. In her eyes was a mingled expression of disbelief and indignation.

"An artist's life is solitary and difficult. It can be a great help having a

117

companion who shares one's values. Boyd Kinsolving knows his deficiencies. And he knows your qualities."

"You actually want me to marry him."

"My child, you must do what makes you happy. But never forget that love, what you call love, once made you very unhappy. With this man you would never have to endure that again."

"Ricarda, he doesn't even like women."

"But he likes *you*. And he's offering you companionship, a shared interest, and professional support." DiScelta glanced at her watch. She smoothed her skirt, lowered herself to the piano bench. "Fascinating as your emotional life is, we have more important problems to discuss. You're breathing wrong in the cadenza to 'Una voce poco fa.'"

By the first Sunday in November autumn had come with sharp windy gusts to the little park on Bleecker Street. But the sun was sparkling and the children in the playground made a cheerful noise, and Ariana decided to take a bench and read her Sunday *Times* outdoors.

She went through the entertainment section first, studying the music reviews and the announcements of upcoming concerts and operas. Then she searched through the news section for late reviews.

The name *Rutherford* leaped out at her from the society page.

Miss Farnsworth Weds Mr. Rutherford.

She stared a moment at the bride's photograph. She read the article slowly.

Nita Farnsworth had married Mark Rutherford at her family's estate in Lloyd Harbor, Long Island. The ceremony had been performed by the rector of Phillips Exeter Academy, one of the groom's alma maters. The bridesmaids—among them the daughter of the Vice President of the United States—had worn cream taffeta.

Ariana ached as though there were nothing in her life except his absence. It was an hour before she could gather herself together and stand and tell herself that Mark Rutherford was gone, that a chapter of her life had ended forever.

She phoned Boyd Kinsolving and asked him to meet her at the Palm Court in the Plaza Hotel. She chose the Palm Court because it seemed the sort of place where people who went to weddings in Lloyd Harbor might take afternoon tea. She asked Boyd if he knew a family called Farnsworth.

"I used to date a girl called Nita Farnsworth. She got married last week. Poor Nita."

"Why poor Nita?"

"She married a minister. Nice fellow, but—" A waiter passed and Boyd beckoned. "Ariana, what are you having?"

"Aren't we having tea?"

"God, no, it's much too early in the day for tea. Have you ever had French seventy-fives?"

French seventy-fives turned out to be an enormous cut-glass bowl of brandy and champagne. Boyd ladled two glasses full. He sipped and sat back and looked over at the pianist and violinist playing Fritz Kreisler waltzes.

"Do you know Nita Farnsworth's groom?" she asked.

"He went to Buckley, I went to Allen-Stevenson. He went to Exeter, I went to Groton. He went to Harvard, I went to Yale. Our ships kept passing in the night. I see him sometimes at the Knickerbocker Club. We say hi."

The bowl of French seventy-fives went on forever, like a magic pitcher in a fairy tale, yet instead of feeling drunk or giddy Ariana felt distant and isolated. Suddenly she slid over on the bench next to Boyd and laid her head beside his.

"Do you still want me to marry you, Boyd?"

He stared at her. She had the impression shock had suddenly sobered him.

"I want to marry you, Boyd. We'd be good for each other. I'm making my debut at La Scala next month, singing *Lucia*. We could get married afterward; in the spring."

"Not till you sing Isolde." He gulped the rest of his drink, and then he smiled and put both hands on her shoulders. He held her at arm's length and kissed her very deliberately on the tip of the nose. "I could never marry a woman who hadn't sung Isolde."

"No one sings Lucia *and* Isolde."

"You could."

She sensed he was drunk. "Boyd, I need a friend."

"You got one, sweetums." He snapped his fingers in the air. "Waiter—more French seventy-fives here, please."

"Boyd, do you think we ought to?"

"Of course we ought to. We're celebrating our engagement."

"He wants me to sing Isolde," Ariana said.

DiScelta shrugged. "First things first. We start with Lucia."

For the next month DiScelta lashed Ariana and herself like workhorses. She demonstrated whole sections, hammering out the beat with her fist on the piano top.

"You have to find a terrible crazed quality for the voice. After all, you are mad. The voice is the role. You must find the voice, and then you will have Lucia."

Her demands were often almost beyond reason. "Who told you to breathe there, Donizetti? Show me in the score." Her fury at Ariana's mistakes was murderous—"*Cocente, cocente,* not *concente*"—her praise for Ariana's successes only moderate—"Very well, Austin, we will move on to the arioso."

And, during the final week of preparation: "Forget the notes. You know the notes, the audience knows the notes—pay attention to the character!"

On March 15, five days before the first performance, Ariana and her teacher boarded Alitalia Flight 612 for Milan and hurtled toward La Scala, toward *Lucia di Lamermoor.*

"I have not been kind to you, have I?"

It was moments before the performance and DiScelta was sitting beside Ariana on the little pink sofa in her dressing room. DiScelta spoke slowly and gently. The dark wooden walls, so good for vocalizing, cupped her voice in soft resonance.

She took from around her neck the ruby and amethyst locket that Ariana had so often seen her wearing, the locket of large heavy stones glowing softly in their gold setting. It seemed to pulse with indecipherable mystery.

She pushed a spring, and the locket snapped open with surprising force. There was a miniature portrait of a woman inside.

"What an extraordinary face," Ariana said. It was difficult to resist the steady gaze of those painted eyes.

"Her name was Alberta Gesualda. She was said to have the greatest voice of her century. Her voice was so beautiful that she moved even the Pope. It was said that she was the first woman to have his permission to sing upon the Italian stage. He gave this locket to her. She gave it to her pupil, who gave it in turn to her own pupil. It has been passed down from teacher to pupil ever since. It belonged to Grisi, to Patti, to Melba, to Ganz-Tucci, who was my teacher, and for twenty-five years it has been mine. I have never given a poor performance while wearing this locket. They say no one has. I don't know the reason. Perhaps there aren't reasons for such things. But I like to think that some of the greatness of its past owners is still living in it." DiScelta's eyes met her pupil's. "Perhaps it would give you courage to wear it tonight?"

Ariana sensed that this was not just the handing over of a lucky charm, some rabbit's foot or laminated four-leaf clover: something was at stake.

Her glance traveled across the little piano where she had warmed up. In the full-length mirror she saw a scene that had the stillness of an old engraving. Two figures, one in sixteenth-century Scottish costume, one in twentieth-century evening clothes, sat on a sofa. A locket on a chain hung between them.

Ariana heard herself answer, "I want to wear it."

"Then it is yours." DiScelta paused. "But there is a promise you must make."

A curtain had been drawn over the open door to the hallway. The two costume ladies who sat outside with needle and thread, ready for any summoning, could be heard discreetly chatting as they sewed.

"The promise is the most important part of all," DiScelta said, "for it ensures the continuity of the line. You must take a student—the most gifted student you can find. Note by note, role by role, you must train her in your repertory. Once you have taught her a role, that role is hers—and you must never perform so much as a note of it again. Within twenty-five years of tonight, you must promise to have turned your entire repertory over to your successor."

The locket hung unmoving in the space between them.

"At some point—you may choose the moment—before you renounce your last role," DiScelta went on, "you will give this locket to your pupil—as I give it to you—and you will bind her to the promise I now bind you. Once she has sung that last role, you will never sing on any stage again—just as I shall never sing on any stage again."

The air in the room seemed suddenly hot and humming.

"Do you accept?"

The locket drew Ariana's eyes, held them. She thought of the ordeal ahead of her, the most demanding audience in the world, a role with one of the highest tessituras in opera, the cruelest critics in Europe. Every childhood terror, every superstition she had ever known rose up in her. She whispered, "I do."

"You swear by Almighty God and on your soul?"

Ariana nodded mutely.

DiScelta slipped the chain around her pupil's neck.

"Then—for twenty-five years—the locket and the voice are yours."

Ariana did not appear in the first scene of Act One. She watched from the wings as Lord Enrico Ashton, in a grove outside his castle, received a disturbing report: his guardsmen had seen his sister Lucia meeting in the woods with Sir Edgardo di Ravenswood, Enrico's sworn enemy. Enrico, hoping to restore his family's fortune by marrying his sister to the wealthy Lord Arturo Bucklaw, vowed to let nothing obstruct his plan.

Scene Two took place that night at a moonlit fountain in the castle gardens. The cue came for Lucia to enter with her companion, Alisa.

Ariana crossed the narrow walkway that led onto a set misty with sixteenth-century Scottish gloom. At the instant she stepped onto the stage where Grisi and Patti, Callas and Melba and Ponselle had sung the greatest Lucias in operatic history, a nameless fear clutched at her heart. She took one blinding glance into the spotlight and opened her mouth. Something came out. She had no idea what.

There was silence, darkness just beyond the light. She felt the darkness judging her.

Paralysis swept over her. Her hand went to the locket beneath her blouse.

As her fingertips secretly touched the metal, a warm current seemed suddenly to pour from it into her whole being. Strength came flooding through her. Suddenly the stagelights were a blinding boundless sun beaming its power upon her.

After her first aria, "Regnava nel Silenzio," she heard clapping. Someone was applauding.

She realized it was *they*. The Milanese public was applauding her, applauding the little girl from East 103rd Street in Manhattan.

And then it came to her that they were applauding Lucia, not Ariana: Lucia who stood resolutely by the fountain as Alisa pleaded with her to break off her friendship with Edgardo.

Lucia refused.

Edgardo entered, handsome and in an overweight way dashing in his doublet and boots and sword, saying he must seek safety in France but would return for Lucia. Their duet, "Verrano a te," brought a storm of bravos. The lovers exchanged rings as token of their marriage before God.

Act Two opened in Lucia's apartments. Enrico showed her a forged love letter purportedly from Edgardo to another woman. Believing herself betrayed, Lucia agreed to sign the wedding contract binding her to Arturo Bucklaw.

The action moved to the castle hall. Just as Lucia put her signature to the fatal contract, Edgardo pushed wildly through the celebrating guests to hurl an accusation of faithlessness at her.

The main characters poured out their conflicting emotions in a sextet, *the* Lucia sextet, the most famous vocal ensemble in all opera. Lucia's despairing voice rose to a high E-flat that soared effortlessly over the others.

When the applause finally died down, Enrico seized the signed contract and brandished it in Edgardo's face. Cursing the Ashtons, Edgardo drew his sword and threw himself at Enrico and Arturo. The chaplain separated them, and Edgardo fled.

The next act opened in a raging storm at the tower of Wolf's Crag, the Ravenswood castle. Entering on the back of a not very well-behaved horse, borrowed, a stagehand told Ariana, from the police, Enrico challenged Edgardo to a duel. The two men agreed to meet at dawn in the cemetery.

The next scene returned to the wedding celebration in the great hall of the Ashton castle. The chaplain interrupted with horrifying news: Lucia had gone mad and stabbed her bridegroom.

The audience gasped as Lucia appeared at the head of the stairs in a blood-splattered wedding gown. This was the Mad Scene, the great solo moment of the opera. The crazed heroine passed among the stunned guests and—in an aria that alternated heartbreaking pathos with explosions of coloratura fireworks—she imagined herself being married to her true love, Edgardo.

The applause lasted four and a half minutes.

Ariana watched the final scene from the wings. Edgardo waited in the graveyard, resolved to let himself be killed in the duel. A death knell sounded. A procession passed, and one of the hooded figures told him of Lucia's madness and death. Edgardo flung himself onto his sword.

Ariana had twelve curtain calls after the opera—a record, someone said, for a debut, or for an American, or for a Lucia. She was too confused to follow all the Italian babbling, but the next day, the Milanese critics praised her ineffable sense of character, her innate musicality, the splendor of her technique.

That rarity of rarities, they called her, *a young voice that is also a perfected voice.*

"It's strange to think they're praising me." Ariana closed the newspapers and laid them down on the breakfast table.

DiScelta looked up from the roll she had been smearing with apricot preserves. "Why is it strange?"

"I didn't feel it was me singing last night."

"It seemed to be someone else singing through you, didn't it?"

Ariana stared at her teacher. "How did you know that?"

DiScelta smiled. "When a singer is healthy, rested, prepared, and calm; when everything is going absolutely right and all conditions are optimum; when the voice is working technically correctly, then there is sometimes the sensation of another voice singing through you without your having anything at all to do with it. All singers know the sensation. Or think they do."

"You experience it too?"

DiScelta buttered another roll. "I used to."

"How often does it happen?"

"For most singers—twice in a career, if they're lucky."

"And for me?"

DiScelta's gaze met hers. "So long as you keep your promise, that voice will be yours till you give the locket to the next."

Ariana Kavalaris's second Scala *Lucia* was carried to North and South America by shortwave. Huddled under three shawls in her bed in her apartment on West Fifty-ninth Street, Hilde Ganz-Tucci followed the performance with her score.

Twice she muttered "Excellent," and after an act and a half she closed the score.

"*Ecco*," she whispered, "*ecco l'artista.*"

And she was satisfied.

She closed her eyes. The score slid softly to the floor.

When the cleaning woman let herself into the apartment the next morning, the radio was blasting static and Hilde Ganz-Tucci was sitting up in bed, smiling like a bride on her wedding day.

Her hands were ice-cold. Her heart had stopped.

The funeral in the Lady Chapel of St. Patrick's Cathedral was sparsely attended. The young priest who, Ricarda DiScelta thought, could not possibly have heard Ganz-Tucci perform, said that the dead woman had been opera itself, with all its ancient traditions and glories, all its beauty and wisdom.

The burial was in the graveyard of Our Lady of the Sorrows in Queens. Fresh snow blanketed the cemetery in thin cleanliness.

Ricarda DiScelta stood shivering with the half-dozen other mourners at the grave. *Now I know more dead people than living,* she thought.

Trudging back to her limousine, she was haunted by her last glimpse of Ganz-Tucci's face in the open casket at the viewing. It had been more the face of a peaceful young woman than of a hypochondriacal old nag, a face peaceful and unlined as though all care and fear had, at the end, been lifted from her.

And now it is up to me, DiScelta thought. A sigh went out of her, hanging in the air before her like a ghost. *God help me.*

It was time, DiScelta told Ariana, to face up to Wagner. "You will need endurance, and—when you sing Isolde—comfortable shoes."

She called Wagner the longest symphony in all opera. "And the voice is but one melody among many."

She showed Ariana how the musical texture was built on motifs: tiny memorable kernels of sound, each intended to arouse a specific idea in the listener's mind. "The Wagnerian 'aria,' which scarcely exists as a type, is like human thought itself, with a thousand associations flowing together."

She explained that Wagner had undermined the most basic assumptions of opera and of music: the division into set pieces, tonality, the traditional sequence of harmonies and keys. "He exploited sound for its own sake. He used harmonies that had no relation to one another except their psychological effect. He invented new instruments to achieve the sonorities he wanted. He called for unprecedented virtuosity from his players and his singers. And what is the result?"

DiScelta sighed. "Flux. Endless flux. The music never comes to rest. For many it is hell to listen to. For all of us, it is hell to memorize. You ask what key it's in, and the answer is—all keys. There are no boundaries. His music is infinity—too much infinity. Yet he was serious, and though he was a horrid little man, the operas have dignity. Sooner or later a singer with your gifts must face up to the challenge."

Ariana faced the challenge. Though she was not comfortable with the role, she sang four Isoldes in Vienna and three at La Scala.

Boyd Kinsolving sent two dozen roses to each performance: *To my luscious Lucia, my sole Isolde—from your own loving boy, Boyd.*

The critics called her remarkable, *a lyrical Titan. One would like to hear this artist's Brünnhilde.*

Which, DiScelta explained, was acclamation.

"And now you must marry."

The sun was shining with unseasonable brilliance, and long lines of Lincolns and Rolls-Royces were double-parked in front of St. Bartholomew's Church on Park Avenue and along Fiftieth Street. The sidewalks were thronged with men and women of the press, autograph hunters, celebrity watchers, and innocent strollers-by caught in the riptide of celebrity.

Inside, the pews swelled with hundreds of beautifully dressed members of the musical world and the international set, as well as the aristocracy of Philadelphia, the more important hosts and hostesses of New York, and an impressive sprinkling of British and French titles.

At 12:15, in a Protestant-Episcopal ceremony performed by the Reverend Mr. Charles Grissom, Ariana Kavalaris and Boyd Kinsolving exchanged vows to love, to cherish, to honor, to keep one another, and so were joined in holy matrimony.

The reception was held a half-hour later at the Colony Club. Ricarda DiScelta had to fight her way through the crowd to congratulate the bride. "This is yours now," she said, handing Ariana a thick package wrapped in silver paper.

Ariana experienced a queasy feeling in her breast. "What is it?"

"My score of *Gioconda*. With Ponchielli's own corrections. Ganz-Tucci gave it to me, and Nordica gave it to her."

"But I can't accept—"

"My dear, I'll never sing *Gioconda* again. I'll never sing anything again. It's your turn now." Turning to the groom, DiScelta added, "I wish you all the happiness in the world. It was a lovely ceremony."

Part Two

GLORY: 1966–1969

14

THEY HAD A GOOD RELATIONSHIP. THEY SHARED INTERESTS; THEY knew how not to get on each other's nerves. It wasn't the glorious insane sort of love Ariana had once known; but she had companionship. She had warmth. She had predictability. Things that counted.

She supposed she was happy. After all, she and Boyd were rich; they were famous. Their performances sold out. Their agents were able to book them two years in advance.

They had three homes: a co-op in Manhattan, a chalet in Gstaad for Christmases, and what the French called a chateau on the Mediterranean shore three miles from Cap d'Antibes, a twelve-room house with red tile roofing where they spent their summer vacations.

She liked her husband. She did most things in her life thinking, *This will be fun to tell Boyd.* And when her mother died in 1957, he was supportive and understanding, a great comfort to her.

Years came and went like waves. Dukes invited them; they received barons; the Queen of England had them to a Buckingham Palace garden party. Everything was the best: hotels, clothes, Steinways, stereos, Bracques, food, friends. Reviews were always good, ovations the rule. And there were honors. Many, many of those.

In the tenth year of their marriage, after five performances of *Pélleas and Mélisande* at the Paris Opéra, they were awarded the Légion d'Honneur for service to the glory of France.

In the bedroom of their suite at the Georges Cinq, Ariana's eye went to the mirror, to the locket hanging on its gold chain around her neck.

The promise she had made so long ago stirred like a faint dissonance in her mind. "*Panagia mou,*" she sighed.

"Something wrong, sweetums?" Boyd came in from the sitting room with two highballs.

"I should take a pupil," she said.

"Why? You're in your prime. You'll have plenty of time to teach when you're an old wreck."

"I only have fifteen years," she said. "I promised DiScelta . . ."

"That old nuisance. Whatever you promised her, it's nothing you have to do this year, is it?"

She decided Boyd was right. She didn't have to take a pupil that year. She didn't take a pupil the next year either.

Or the year after.

In April 1966, at a ceremony in the White House Rose Garden, President Lyndon Baines Johnson awarded Ariana and Boyd Congressional Medals of Freedom for their services to music.

It had been sixteen years since they had married; sixteen years since she had put on the locket and made her promise to DiScelta. She still had not taken a pupil.

"In this hour of uncertainty," the President intoned in his Texas drawl, "music is needed to lift this nation to courage, to strength, to faith. For over two decades, Ariana Kavalaris and Boyd Kinsolving have given us that music."

That fall, after two *Normas* at the Teatro La Fenice, they were awarded the Order of St. Mark's of the City of Venice.

"A voice is needed," the Mayor of Venice declaimed in sonorous Italian, holding out the little gold lion as hundreds of reporters and citizens of Venice looked on, "a voice to lift mankind to courage, to strength, to faith. And that voice is—Ariana Kavalaris."

She let him pin the lion to her pale blue Chanel. It was not good for the cloth. She thanked the mayor, thanked Venice, thanked Italy.

By the time the ceremony ended it was dusk and Ariana and Boyd were tired of being the world's most famous musical couple, tired of dodging photographers and interviewers and musical hopefuls.

"Let's be tourists," she said.

"Let's," he agreed.

She put on a black kerchief and dark glasses. For a half-hour they avoided the main malls and waterways and walked down narrow streets and along back canals. No one bothered them.

Suddenly Ariana exclaimed and caught Boyd's hand and pulled him back to look in a shop window.

"Look!" she cried. She was pointing at a framed photograph. "Hilde Ganz-Tucci."

All Boyd could see in the garish frame was a fat woman dressed like a grande dame out of a Marx Brothers movie.

And then something in the window moved. It took him a moment to realize that a reflection in the glass had shifted.

He turned around and looked behind him.

A man stood by the awning of a café, half in shadow, tall and grave but disturbingly coarse in his striped red shirt and dark trousers. A cigarette smoking in the corner of his mouth drew his lips down to one side.

The man was staring at Boyd with extraordinary concentration. Not at Ariana Kavalaris, not at the most famous soprano in the world, but unmistakably at her husband. At first it occurred to Boyd, *He knows me* . . . and then he realized, *No, we've never met. He simply knows who I am, what I am. Italians are quick to pick up on these things.*

"Damn," Ariana said. "The store's not open for another half-hour. They take such strange siestas in this city. We'll have to kill a little time and come back."

Boyd took her hand. "You don't mean you actually want to buy that awful thing?"

"Naturally. Hilde Ganz-Tucci was my teacher's teacher."

"And if they recognize you and ask a fortune for it?"

"Well, I'll just have to sing another *Norma*."

Boyd glanced again over his shoulder. The man in the striped red shirt was still staring. He pulled Ariana along quickly to an arcade leading to St. Mark's Square. A bandstand had been set up by the campanile and a crowd had gathered. A cloud of pigeons swooped overhead.

"That must be the civic band." Ariana listened a moment, and her nose wrinkled. "It sounds like Donizetti, but which one?"

"*Maria Stuarda*. Come on, let's get a table at Florian's."

"But, Boyd, those awful *trumpets*."

"I'm thirsty. I'll buy you an aperitif."

They threaded their way through tourists to Florian's café. Ariana lifted her dark glasses just long enough for the waiter to recognize her and give them a table on the piazza.

The man in the red shirt strolled past their table and glanced lingeringly at Boyd. Twirling his glass stem in embarrassment, Boyd looked at Ariana to see if she had noticed. She was sipping her vermouth, listening to brass-band Donizetti.

"You know," she said thoughtfully, "even in those awful oom-pah arrangements, that music holds up."

Across the square from Florian's café, near the shadow of the campanile, stood a man who had never earned a cent from Donizetti and who detested every note of it.

It was business that had brought Nikos Stratiotis to Venice. He had come the day before. The place had immediately disoriented him. The blindingly blue air overhead and the canals below made him feel he was hanging between two skies.

His deal had fallen into place far more quickly than he'd planned, and now he had two empty days ahead of him. He was a man who lived life for its storms, and he didn't know what to do between hurricanes. And so he had wandered into St. Mark's Square.

Tall and well-dressed, he made a handsome figure. His shoulders were sturdy and there was no thickening of the stomach. His hair was just beginning to show flecks of iron-gray. But there was restlessness in the way he shifted weight from foot to foot.

He had not counted on the pigeons, or the crowds, or—worst of all—the municipal band, a hundred strong, thundering out operatic potpourris. He grew bored, wondered how people could crowd together and endure such stuff.

And so he began to stroll aimlessly. He turned down an unmarked passageway. The oom-pahs of the municipal band vanished as abruptly as if a needle had been lifted from a phonograph record. The evening air was damp and still.

For an instant he was alone and then in the deserted arcade ten feet ahead of him a dress flashed like blue fire. A head turned fleetingly in profile.

Though he had not spoken to her in how long—seventeen, eighteen years?—he immediately recognized Ariana Kavalaris. How could he fail to? She'd been in headlines and magazines for almost two decades, and there were posters advertising her four appearances at La Fenice plastered all over the city.

He deduced from the way they were talking, heads close with careless intimacy, that the man beside her must be her husband. Nikos Stratiotis believed in few things, but he did believe that destiny sent signs. At that instant his boredom lifted. He drew back into the shadow of the arcade.

Kavalaris and her husband stopped at a window farther up the arcade. They discussed something with excited hand movements, and then they went into the shop.

Nikos crossed the passageway with measured slowness. From the opposite arcade he saw Kavalaris standing in a small, dusty shop. She was holding a frame of elaborate gilt. Her husband hovered at her shoulder, nodding more like an echo than an independent opinion. Finally she came straight to the window and angled the frame to the light.

Nikos stepped back quickly from her sightline. A moment later Kavalaris and her husband emerged from the shop, empty-handed.

Nikos waited till they had turned the corner. Then he went in. The shop smelled of crumbling paper and old leather bindings.

The salesman approached. "Signore desires?"

"What was she looking at? The woman who just left?"

An instant's surprise flitted across the man's face and then his features readjusted themselves into business. "A beautiful piece."

"May I see it?"

The salesman hesitated, then produced the framed photograph from a drawer beneath the counter. He held it for Nikos to admire. "A signed photograph of Hilde Ganz-Tucci. Most unusual."

Nikos studied it. "How much are you asking?"

The salesman shrugged apologetically. "The lady made a deposit."

"How much?"

The salesman named a price. It fascinated Nikos that anyone could believe this faded photograph of a fat woman with its decidedly grotesque frame was worth the equivalent of $2,000.

"Who is Hilde Ganz-Tucci?" he asked.

There was a flicker of condescension before the salesman answered.

"Ganz-Tucci was the greatest dramatic soprano of the post-World War I era."

Nikos found himself wondering: *What does Ariana Kavalaris feel toward this photograph? Why does she want it so much?* "I want to buy this," he said.

The salesman's face tightened. "As I explained to signore, Madame Kavalaris and her husband made a small deposit—"

Nikos handed back the photograph. "My name is Nikos Stratiotis. I'll pay whatever you ask. I must have this photograph."

The salesman made a quick, respectful bow of the head. "If signore will wait, I shall speak with the owner."

Ariana and Boyd returned to the shop at noon the next day. The salesman greeted them as though they were old friends. He opened a drawer beneath the counter and searched a moment. He shook his head in perplexity. He called the owner. The owner consulted a ledger.

"I am sorry." The owner turned the ledger around to show Signore and Signora Kinsolving the entry. "Sold by mistake."

With sincerest apology, the owner returned the Kinsolvings' deposit.

As they walked back to the Hotel Danieli, Boyd realized he must steer his wife's thoughts away from disappointment. He took her hand. "We could stop in the bar for a Bellini," he suggested.

"*Panagia mou,*" she murmured. "It's an omen."

"Sweetums, it was only a photograph. It doesn't mean anything."

"If it doesn't mean anything, why did it disappear?"

"Accidents happen."

"There are no such things as accidents. Aristotle says chance is simply a cause hidden from human understanding."

"Aristotle did not understand bel canto." Boyd snapped his fingers. "Bartender. Two Bellinis, please."

They took a table on a terrace overlooking the Grand Canal. Ariana sipped at a bubble of peach crushed in champagne that had risen to the edge of her glass.

"Tonight," she said, "will be my worst *Norma* ever."

That evening Nikos Stratiotis paid a scalper for a stall seat to the Teatro La Fenice. He had seen opera before and it had always struck him as a stretching emptiness. Tonight, he began to fear, would be more of the same.

He gathered from the program that the scene was ancient Gaul during the Roman occupation. In the sacred forest of the Druids, by the foot of the stone altar, Pollione—Roman proconsul—told his friend Flavio that he had betrayed Norma, the Druid high priestess, and loved Adalgisa, another priestess of the temple.

Nikos covered a yawn as the Gauls trooped onstage to celebrate their sacred rite.

And then he sat forward. For suddenly she was there: Ariana Kavalaris, wearing the slim white toga of a pagan priestess.

The Gauls urged Norma, who alone could declare war, to give the signal to drive out the Romans. But she had secretly wed Pollione and, unwilling to endanger his life, she called upon the chaste goddess of the moon—"Casta Diva"—to bring peace.

Kavalaris as Norma bewitched Nikos. Her voice moved through the orchestra and chorus like a spot of pure sunlight cutting through clouds. He watched her face in the small circle of light. Even after eighteen years, time seemed barely to have touched it. Of course that could have been due to makeup or distance or light or the very fact of the music itself playing upon the emotions.

As she sang the long, arching melody of "Casta Diva," the notes spun out of her, melting together like a cool flame. He sensed something almost religious in the quality of the audience's attention. At the end of the aria, slowly lifting her arms, she sent a note through the theater that was wild and sweet at the same time.

Slowly, the arms descended. For an instant the hush was deep and still and then the house screamed with bravas and applause.

She bowed, and he suddenly saw her not as a woman but as an achievement. Finally there was silence and the stage cleared.

Adalgisa and Pollione met in the deserted clearing. He begged her to run away with him. In the next scene Adalgisa confessed to Norma that she had broken her sacred vow of chastity. Norma was ready to forgive her until she learned the name of Adalgisa's lover. In a furious torrent of melody she cursed both Adalgisa and the faithless Pollione.

Kavalaris took six curtain calls.

In the next act Norma resolved to kill her two baby sons by Pollione. But watching them in their sleep, she was unable to raise the knife. Adalgisa entered and, moved by Norma's plight, offered to persuade Pollione to return to his wife. Norma entrusted the two infants to her.

The scene shifted to the temple. As Adalgisa performed the sacred ceremony, Pollione tried to seize her. Norma entered and, outraged, struck the sacred shield to summon the Gauls. She declared that Irminsul, the Druid god, commanded war against the Romans.

At that instant, as Kavalaris's voice called down the powers of heaven, a shiver went through Nikos. He felt himself in the physical presence of a mystery. He saw that Kavalaris wielded power, perhaps the purest, the most naked form of all because it was not power commanded, like his, but power given.

The woman fascinated him. Her hold on the audience fascinated him. He wondered if it was a gift, to be loved like that.

The Gauls seized Pollione as a victim for the sacrifice, but Norma, ripping the sacred wreath from her brow, confessed her own guilt. The Druids prepared the sacrificial fire. Pollione, moved by Norma's nobility, begged to die with her. Together, their throats pouring forth music, they ascended into the flames and perished.

The curtain fell. Nikos did not wait in his seat to applaud. He bribed an usher to take him backstage.

"Ariana Kavalaris?"

She had given orders that visitors were not allowed, and as soon as she heard the voice she whirled around, ready to be furious.

A man stood in the doorway. The steadiness of his gaze suggested that he owned the theater. His hair had begun to turn gray, but little else about him had changed.

"Nikos," she said, surprised at the genuine pleasure she felt.

He gave a barely perceptible signal to the dresser, and the old woman gathered up an armload of linen and scurried from the room.

Ariana saw that Nikos Stratiotis was used to being obeyed.

He took her hand, bent over it, and brought it to his lips. The movement might have been a bit of stage business from an opera, but their eyes met and lingered just a second longer than would have happened in any performance. His were luminous under thick dark brows.

"So," he said. "You've kept up with your singing."

"Some people arc kind enough to say so. And I hear you're very busy making fortunes."

"And losing them. But it averages out."

"You look as though you're doing far better than averaging out."

"So do you."

"I read somewhere that you're married?" she said.

"Separated. And you're still happily married to your conductor?"

She smiled, aware of the irony of the remark and flattered that he should want to goad her. "Very happily. Boyd conducts all my performances. You heard him tonight."

"A talented man."

A slender man in evening clothes rapped on the door and Ariana turned.

"Boyd darling, we were just saying wonderful things about you. This is Nikos Stratiotis—an old friend from—why should I lie?—from my days at the lunch counter. And my first sponsor. And an opera lover."

Nikos took Boyd's hand. "Your wife pays me a compliment I don't deserve. It's not opera I love. Only aspects of the art."

"Ah well," Boyd said, "taste takes time to acquire."

Nikos glanced toward Ariana. "Anything worthwhile takes time to acquire."

* * *

Nikos and the bearded informant were alone in the conference room of the Venice office of Minerva Società Anonima, a wholly-owned Stratiotis subsidiary. Nikos got straight to the point. "What does this famous couple do when they're not performing?"

Embarrassment rose from the informant like the unclean mist from one of the city's canals. "Parties. Ceremonies."

"That much I know from the newspapers."

The informant consulted a small notepad. "Yesterday Kavalaris stayed most of the day in her hotel room."

Nikos's fingertips drummed on the desk blotter. "And Kinsolving?"

"He spent most of the day . . . strolling."

The information did not fit. Nikos Stratiotis distinguished only two kinds of people: those who possessed power and those who did not. Ariana Kavalaris belonged to the first group because she had fame. Her husband belonged to the second because he possessed only his wife. And yet it was the husband who strode through Venice like a conqueror and the wife who sat in a dark hotel room like a captive. "Where did Kinsolving stroll?"

"Along the Rialto. By the bridges near the Fondamente Nuove."

"Was he alone?"

"He arrived alone, but he met someone . . ."

Nikos leaned forward. "He went to the Rialto for sex?"

The informant nodded.

"Who was the woman?"

The informant's silence trailed clouds of implication.

Nikos rose from the desk. "He met a *man?*"

The informant nodded again.

And at that moment Nikos Stratiotis understood the wife, the husband, the marriage, the existence. He understood that Ariana Kavalaris lived in the dark. And that he, Nikos Stratiotis, had the power to turn life on for her like a motion picture film and project it onto the largest, most silver screen in the world.

He smiled and handed his informant the 500,000 lire that they had agreed upon. He added another 500,000 as a tip. "I'll be requiring another service of you."

Boyd was irritated with the heat and the shops and the crowds on Fondamente Nuove. He turned left into a street whose name seemed to translate as Passage of the Dwarf.

He stopped at a stand and bought a bottle of pear juice from an old woman. It was a small bottle and he emptied it in two parched swallows. As he handed it back he was aware for the first time of a shadow sliding like smoke behind him. It occurred to him that he was being followed.

He wanted to look back. Instinct told him not to. He paid the woman, smiled, kept walking. As he approached a dark passageway steps echoed against his own. And then there was dead silence and a man stood beside him.

"*Scusi, signore.*"

Boyd looked at the man. He was broad-faced, tanned, with a mustache that seemed to smile. There was an odd stab in Boyd's heart and an absurd thought crossed his mind.

I've seen this man before. He's been following me. He was wearing a red striped shirt and dark trousers. But today he's wearing a business suit.

The man spoke again. "*Lei parla inglese?*"

"Of course," Boyd said.

"Have you light?"

A hundred indecisions preyed on Boyd's mind, but his body did not hesitate. He reached into his pocket for the gold Van Cleef and Arpels lighter Ariana had given him for their second anniversary. He flicked flame from it.

The man was standing beside him, too close, in the way Latins have. But instead of bending to accept the light, the stranger pushed his hand very firmly against Boyd's groin.

He had a rough, friendly voice. "My name is Egidio."

When Boyd came into the room she was lying on the bed, one hand clasped over her eyes.

"Ariana, sweetums?"

She did not move.

He tiptoed to the bar. He poured himself a generous double Chivas, opened the ice bucket and tonged three cubes into it.

The space where Ariana lay sleeping seemed sad to him. He bent down to kiss her. Her eyes opened and she looked at him.

"I love you," he said. "I don't think I've ever loved another human being so much."

She stared at him with groggy wondering. "Your cheeks are so red. Have you been in the sun?"

The glass with the Danieli decal slipped slowly from his hand and tapped down onto the table. He lit a cigarette. "I have to go out tonight. I'm sorry. It will only be for a while."

She raised herself to a sitting position. "But we were going to have dinner at . . ."

He sighed. "Yes, but you're tired." He was careful not to exhale cigarette smoke in her direction. "And the orchestra has called another rehearsal."

"Another?"

He nodded, eyes not quite meeting hers. "Will you be lonely?"

"Of course not. I love Italian television. They have the strangest

137

game shows. And besides I could use the rest. The dampness in this city tires me."

They were silent.

"We should never have agreed to four *Normas*," he said.

"You're right," she said. "You're always right, my darling."

He bent over her and gazed at her silently. They kissed and said goodbye and a moment later a door closed.

As she sat up she caught sight of herself in the armoire mirror. She stared curiously at the woman in the glass, the woman they said was the greatest soprano in the world, this woman abandoned for the night like a lonely child.

She tried to understand the face that stared back at her, and the soft creases in her skin deepened.

Aside from touching up an infrequent gray hair, she'd never tried to make a secret of her age. Yet there was something young in her movements, in the transparent play of emotion on her features. Like a little girl. As though something in her had stopped growing eighteen years ago.

What makes me think of eighteen years? Seeing Nikos the other night?

She approached the glass. The closer she got the less familiar the reflection seemed to her.

I don't know myself, she thought. *I haven't known myself for eighteen years.*

She reached out a finger and traced the shape mirrored in the cold glass.

Who are you? Are you alive? Are you happy? Angry? Lonely? Are you a voice? Are you a career? Are you a woman? Do you wish you'd had a real husband? Do you wish you'd had children?

There were no answers in her. Only questions.

And hunger.

At least she knew how to deal with the hunger. *Prosciutto*, she thought. *I'll have prosciutto.*

15

ARIANA FINISHED HER PROSCIUTTO SANDWICH. SHE GAZED FROM the balcony out at the city. Slender church spires flecked the starry sky. The bedroom seemed immensely empty, immensely quiet. The hands of the grandfather clock by the marble fireplace pointed to five after nine.

A sigh came out of her. *Only five after nine,* she thought.

She heard the ringing of a bell. She hurried to the door.

The same bellboy who had brought her dinner was holding out a huge basket of flowers. Carnations, roses, lilies, gladioli. *How sweet of Boyd,* she thought. The bellboy set the flowers on the table. She tipped him 10,000 lire.

She searched through the stems and found a heavy cream envelope. The handwriting of the note was large and bold.

> I am downstairs in the bar. Will you do me the honor of meeting me for a drink?

It was signed *Nikos S.*

For a moment she was amazed. And then she knew exactly what to do: pick up the phone and tell the switchboard that Madame Kavalaris sent her regrets.

But instead she went to the armoire mirror and undid the sash of her bathrobe. Her eyes played over her bare midriff. There was no slack. *Not bad for an opera singer,* she thought. She opened the armoire and from her thirty-six dresses chose a blue silk cocktail gown.

Ariana glanced about the lobby and saw a scattering of Japanese tourists. Her eyes scanned the bar. Nikos Stratiotis was not there.

A hand suddenly waved from the terrace. Nikos was sitting at a corner table beneath a striped umbrella. His smile glowed against his tanned face. He rose and came striding toward her. She wasn't aware of moving toward him, but they met on the threshold.

His lips touched her fingers. "Thank you for joining me."

"Thank you for the flowers."

"I didn't know what you liked, so I told them to send a little of everything."

She laughed. "They sent a great deal of everything."

He motioned toward the table with the umbrella. "Shall we?"

They sat facing each other across the table. He ordered drinks.

He kept looking at her. "You're not at all what I'd imagined you'd be."

"I'm flattered you've found time to imagine things about me."

"I'd heard you were high-strung, short-tempered, utterly ruthless and completely unpredictable."

Her thoughts went back two decades to that eager, hardworking girl in the Broadway luncheonette whose idea of happiness had been a fifty-cent tip and a standing room ticket to the opera.

"Are any of those things true?" he said.

How does he see me now, she wondered, *as the little waitress or the world-famous diva?*

"Everyone says the same things about anyone who's famous," she said. "To tell the truth, I've heard rumors about you. You drive yourself and everyone around you, you're utterly ruthless, and you're the despair of women and accountants."

He was watching her, half smiling, half challenging.

I must look older, she thought ruefully, and then it occurred to her, *maybe not so much older. Maybe I haven't aged any more than he has. He still has the same eyes, the same smile.* The accent was different from that first night, but the music of his voice—its suggestion of confidence and irony and intelligence—was the same as it had been twenty years ago. The only real change was his clothes: gone were the padded shoulders and rakishly tilted fedora. Instead there was a carefully understated opulence to his tailoring. *But he still dresses as though he were onstage*, she thought.

"Tell me," she said. "Are any of the rumors about you true?"

"The rumors about the accountants are true."

I haven't changed, she thought with sudden happiness. *He's staring at me the way he did then.*

Drinks came. The glasses were tall and frosted.

"Then we're the same," she said. "The only difference is that I sing and you make money."

"Or more accurately, you make your money by opening your mouth and I make mine by keeping mine shut."

She raised her glass to her lips and a pleasantly sweet liquid passed coolly down her throat. Suddenly there was singing and laughter and the splashing of oars, and a party with lanterns glided past on the canal.

"I love Venice," she said. "I always have."

He raised his eyebrows. Two dark eyes flashed. "Why?"

"It calms me to think that beautiful things can last."

"Would you like to live here?"

"No. It makes me too sad to know that Venice will last and I won't."

"Then where do you live?"

"Mostly New York. Boyd has a contract with the Metropolitan, and with the Philharmonic, and it's . . . easier for us there. And where do you live?"

"Everywhere. But I think of Paris as my home. Have you dined?"

It occurred to her to lie. But he had known her hotel room number;

he had known she was alone that evening; and it was a good guess he knew precisely what had been on the dinner trolley that room service had rolled into her suite.

"Thank you, but I had a small snack."

"So did I. Well then, would you care to see a little of the city you love so much?" He angled a nod toward a gleaming motorboat with mahogany coaming moored in the canal. "My driver's waiting."

She hesitated. "But my husband . . ."

"Has a rehearsal. I'll have you back in plenty of time."

"You've been spying on me."

"Naturally."

She looked at him, wanting to be outraged, and all that she could muster was laughter. They got into his boat.

He gave orders in Greek, and the driver took them gliding past the ancient stones and leaded casements of the sinking palazzi.

"There's a place I want to show you," Nikos said.

A bend in the canal carried them into the bay. A wind was creeping up. The waves leaped and the night warmth was suddenly shot through with ripples of coolness. She felt Nikos place a shawl over her shoulders. His touch made her uncertain who she was.

The driver cut the motor and made the boat fast to a jetty. Something like thunder rumbled overhead and she realized they were shooting off fireworks on the Lido. Nikos helped her onto the pier.

A cloud passed, and iron bars and carved stones were suddenly patterned and silvery with the light of the full moon. She saw he had brought her to a graveyard.

"All the best people are here," he said. "Come on."

He guided her along deserted paths. They stood at a grave and he lit a cigarette lighter for her to read the inscription.

"Alberta Gesualda." *Gesualda's portrait at my throat*, she thought, *and her body at my feet.* "Why did you bring me here?"

"In a way, she's your ancestor—the first woman to have the Pope's permission to sing on the Italian stage."

She looked at him sharply. "How did you know that?"

"Your *Norma* inspired me. I did some research this morning. Gesualda loved opera and she loved Venice. She was like you."

"No. She wasn't like me. Gesualda has lasted."

"I'd say on the contrary she's been forgotten."

"There are those . . . who remember."

"Only a few books in the library remember. For Alberta Gesualda it's all over. Just as one day it will all be over for you and me: happiness, misery, Swiss banks, flowers, love, lawsuits, wine."

She could not move her eyes from his face. "You're a cynic."

"And you're not?"

"I'm a realist. And as a realist I have faith."

He smiled as though she were a child. "In what? God?"

"In music. But it's the same thing."

"I was educated by nuns, and they never taught me that."

"Certain things can't be taught. They're given."

She had a sense he was going to take her hand and it surprised her when he didn't.

"We'd better go," he said. "Mr. Kinsolving's rehearsal must be just about over."

At the hotel pier he bent to kiss her on the cheek. "I'm glad we're friends," he said.

"Thank you, Nikos. I'm glad too."

When she let herself into the suite, Boyd had not yet returned.

At ten o'clock the next morning a bellboy came to Ariana's door with a small, flat package. With the point of the pencil she used for marking scores she tore the envelope open. The note bore the crest of the Bauer Grünwald hotel. This time it was written in Greek.

Efcharisto—Nikos. A thank-you from Nikos. She couldn't help smiling at the thought of Nikos Stratiotis, his gifts, his millions, his pirate's mustache, his life like the blurb on a paperback novel.

She neatly began to tear an opening in the wrapping. Understanding came in pieces. At first she realized only that she was holding a carved wood frame. In the frame was a photograph of an overweight woman in a flowered dress with a feathered hat.

The woman's eyes held hers. There was a gentleness in them stronger than any force in the world. A dream rippled out from those eyes like light.

As Ariana stared at the photograph a serenity seemed to cloak her. She became aware of something unvarying, something permanent in the flow of things, like a rock submerged in a turbulent stream.

Hilde Ganz-Tucci is dead now: she is history. Her voice is silent. But she was alive, and my teacher was alive with her, and she lives in my teacher, and through my teacher she lives in me.

"Whatcha got there?" Boyd stood in the doorway rubbing his eyes. He saw the picture. "Well—so the old dame turned up after all. Where'd you find her?"

She had never lied to her husband before. "The shop made a mistake," she said, "that's all."

He squinted. "What a terrible frame. I know two fellows in Greenwich Village who can change it."

"I'm not changing the frame. I want it exactly the way it is."

"And what in God's name do you intend to do with it?"

"I'll hang it, of course."

"Not in our living room, sweetums, or I'm going to move out." He kissed her quickly. "Only joking."

She took the picture from him, protecting it. "Boyd, I don't know what you were drinking after your rehearsal, but it's foul. Go brush your teeth."

In a moment water was running in the bathroom pipes. She moved instantly to the phone and asked to be connected to the Bauer Grünwald. "Nikos Stratiotis, please . . . Ariana Kavalaris calling."

"I'm sorry, signora, he checked out this morning."

Ariana and Boyd left Venice the next day, after the last *Norma*. They plunged into a long winter of touring: *Otello* in Stockholm, *Ariadne auf Naxos* in Hamburg, *Medea* in Genoa, *Tosca* in Prague, three *Aïdas* at the New York Met.

The critics praised them, as always; society lionized them, as always; but Ariana was beginning to feel like a migrating bird. In odd little ways her life seemed lonelier than ever before—three embassy receptions, thirty indifferent meals in a dozen first-class hotels, a hundred meaningless conversations with strangers, and at the end of every long day a goodnight kiss exchanged with Boyd.

The thought kept coming to her, *It's not enough*.

More and more often she found herself gazing out windows and envying the clouds.

Five miles above Lyons, on Air France Flight 607, Boyd folded his London *Times* shut. It was all too depressing: demonstrations around the world against U.S. involvement in Vietnam; students in Madrid battling Franco's police; Red Guards in China protesting God only knew what. Israel and Jordan at it again. Pope Paul VI planning to meet with the Soviet foreign minister . . . talk about mad tea parties . . . No wonder people needed opera.

Boyd glanced up and noticed that Ariana had spent the last half-hour staring out at the evening sky. "Sweetums, what in the world is so interesting out there?"

"The sunset."

She'd seemed preoccupied lately, and he was beginning to worry. She had a lot of high C's still to get through. And it was her top and not his conducting that brought in the $50,000 fees.

"You're looking at that sunset as though you're memorizing it."

"I am. That's the last color we'll see for a week. It will be raining in Brussels."

She was right: it was pouring in Brussels. They had to run to their limousine under a porter's umbrella.

"Three *Dinorah*s," Ariana sighed. "In this place."

"This place," Boyd said, "happens to love you." He put his hands on the sides of her neck and massaged her shoulder blades. He could feel the tension in her like piano wires. "And so do I."

She reached up and held tight to his hand. "Thank you, darling. Please never stop."

A rough wind was bending the almost leafless trees in Place de la République when they arrived at their hotel.

Georges Guiraud, their Belgian agent, was waiting for them in their suite. He looked sad. He kissed them both. "You didn't get my cable in Hamburg? The *Dinorah*s have been canceled."

Boyd's eyes heaped disbelief upon the dark-mustached little agent. "*Canceled?*"

"Decision of the Ministry of Culture. *La Fanfarade* has . . . preempted."

"And what the hell is *La Fanfarade?*"

"It's an opera by a young Belgian composer."

"And what do you suggest we do for one week in this town? Go to the goddamned zoo?"

"You are at liberty. Your fees have been paid to your Swiss corporation."

"You could at least have tried to let us know a little earlier than Hamburg."

"It was all . . . very fast."

"I don't believe you, Georgie. Nothing in opera is fast. Least of all you."

Ariana was only half listening. She'd finished glancing through the mail that the hotel had stacked on the writing desk. "Boyd, we have a cable. Nikos Stratiotis would like us to join him in Nice."

"Perfect!" the agent cried.

It struck Boyd that it was all a little too perfect: the cancellation, the cable, Georges's *cri de joie*. He stared at the cable Ariana had handed him. "What the hell language is this?"

"Greek. He'll keep a plane waiting for us at the airport."

"He can keep his damned plane waiting a month for all I care."

A flush of defiance was beating at the base of Ariana's throat. "I'm not going to spend a week in this rain while you hire lawyers to battle the Ministry of Culture. I want rest, I want sun, and frankly I think $150,000 for not singing three *Dinorah*s is pretty generous pay. I'm going to sleep now and tomorrow I'm going to Nice."

She crossed the room and kissed Georges's bald pate. "Goodnight, Georges, and do thank the ministry for me."

It was not the ministry that Georges Guiraud thanked the next day but Nikos Stratiotis, by collect phone call from the Brussels airport. "It took all my persuading, but they'll be arriving in two hours."

Stratiotis's voice was cool. Either he had no conception what, besides money, was involved in rescheduling a week at the state opera or he was used to buying miracles. "Your Liechtenstein account will be credited with the sum we agreed on."

"It was my pleasure, Mr. Stratiotis."

Nikos met them at the airport. He was bare-chested and very muscular and tanned. He flung one arm around Ariana and the other around Boyd and then he gave Ariana a flickering glance.

"I'm delighted you could make it. Good flight?"

"Mercifully short," Boyd said. "The champagne was excellent."

Nikos smiled and Ariana couldn't help smiling back.

"Where are your baggage stubs?" he asked.

Boyd found the stubs and Nikos handed them to a servant.

"If we hurry," Nikos said, "we can catch the sunset."

Nikos drove them in a Karmann Ghia convertible with the top down. The Mediterranean blurred by in a glow of swimming-pool blue. The highway was only two-lane, and he passed trucks on blind curves.

"I invited a few friends," he shouted. "I hope you don't mind."

His yacht was moored in Nice harbor. It was the size of a small ocean liner. They had to take a speedboat to get to it. A steward helped them on board. Several guests were clustered around the swimming pool and Nikos made introductions.

"Why don't we make this easy," he said. His hand was lightly touching the hollow between Ariana's shoulder blades, lightly staying there. "This charming couple is Ariana and Boyd, and these charming people are Karim and Inger and Anatoly and Marlene—did I get that right?"

"You always get it right." A Swedish-looking blond woman in a bikini smiled.

"Then please excuse me while I show our new arrivals to their room."

Ariana sucked in her breath at the sight of the damask-and-walnut-paneled suite with its silk-covered chairs.

"If there's anything you need, you just give the bell there a yank." Nikos gestured toward a gold brocade bell cord. "We'll be having cocktails in the salon before dinner. You can meet the others then."

"When's *then?*" Boyd asked.

"Any time. And meanwhile, please make yourselves at home."

"*Mi* ship, *tu* ship?"

"Precisely." With a smile, Nikos was gone.

"Our zillionaire host has got a good body," Boyd said. "And he seems quite touchingly impressed that some classical musicians have fallen into his web of rock stars and rickety nobility."

Ariana put her head out the window and sniffed the view of Nice harbor.

"He must work out," Boyd said. "He probably has a gym on the ship."

It was a soft, sweet May evening, with pleasure craft moored neatly like flowers in a formal garden. "The sky seems higher here," Ariana said.

Boyd had found the liquor on the sideboard. With a comfortable sigh and a full highball glass he sank back onto an enormous velvet sofa. "Sweetums, *everything* is higher here."

Ariana went into the bathroom. The bath was an immense black marble tub with seashell fluting. The spigot was a craning swan.

A moment later Boyd heard her scream. "What is it, didja fall in?"

She came back to the door. "The toilet seat—it's gold. And the faucets too."

Boyd shook his head. "Gilded bronze, love. Gold would be vulgar. And these people are *jamais* vulgar."

"I can't believe any of this."

"You're not supposed to believe it. Just love it. Like opera."

She bathed and their luggage arrived and she asked Boyd to help her select a dress.

"The beige organdy. It'll be perfect. Now straighten your hair."

She sat at the dressing table. She brushed a moment, then let her finger run across the carved walnut surface inlaid with marble and tulipwood.

"It's French," Boyd said. "Sixteenth century."

"How do you know?"

"Oh, one develops an eye for these things."

"I never have." She was silent a moment, pensive. "I don't think I could ever get used to it."

"You'll be used to it in three hours and in four you'll have forgotten there's any other way to live."

She checked her cocktail dress one last time in the mirror. What an ordinary dress, and what a spotless reflection.

A uniformed steward opened the huge cypress doors of the salon to them. The room was mobbed, but there was not even a moment to feel orphaned or lost. Nikos was there, making introductions.

British titles, a television talk-show host, an ambassador, and politicians sped past Ariana like the view from a train. No musicians, thank God.

And then a change came into Nikos's voice. "And may I present a dear friend and collaborator—Egidio DiBuono."

The man who stood before them was tall and well-built, with chiseled features and dark hair. He was wearing designer camouflage overalls. Boyd had been in the act of lighting a cigarette. His lighter stopped in mid-air. Ariana sensed shock and then a sudden, hushed politeness whooshing like air into a vacuum.

"How do you do," she said.

"I am honored to meet such an artist." Egidio DiBuono's eyes glued themselves to hers.

During the instant of silent appraisal, she sensed not the elegance of a yacht's drawing room but the savvy of the Naples waterfront. DiBuono took the hand she offered and bent slightly. The tip of a tattooed palm tree peeked out from under one of his overall straps.

"Egidio advises me on books," Nikos said. "In fact he helped me put together the little library on B deck."

"Books?" Ariana had never seen a librarian with such a tan. It suggested months spent sleeping on beaches and decks.

DiBuono smiled and his teeth looked almost unnaturally clean. "Yes, I am what you call a real worm of the books."

Boyd threw back his head and laughed.

"Forgive my English," DiBuono said. "It is grotesque, yes?"

Boyd clapped DiBuono on the back. Ariana had never seen her husband clap another man on the back, friend or stranger.

"Not at all. It's like the Rossini translations they sell at English opera houses. Isn't it, sweetums?" Boyd turned to Ariana. If ever a smile was too loud, it was the smile he gave her at that moment.

Why is he forcing? she wondered. She sensed something not quite genuine going on but before she could home in on it there were more introductions: a Lord Tony, a Dame Giselle Something-or-other, a Royal Ballet prima ballerina with her arm in a sling, a British film director who'd won his second Oscar that year.

And then chitchat: We-love-your-Turandot.

And then, at long long last, dinner.

The tables were set for eight, with pale green cloths and hibiscus centerpieces. The place cards put Ariana next to a viscount, and she noticed that Boyd was two tables away next to the Swedish woman, who appeared to be laughing at something that the DiBuono man was whispering to her.

There were bisque and trout and quail and a dozen other courses, and the viscount told Ariana the majolica dinner service had been made by Patanazzi for the marriage of the Duke of Ferrara in 1597.

"This salt cellar," he said, "is also sixteenth century. The plaques are Limoges. You can tell by the blue. It never fades."

"How nice that there's something that never fades. Tell me, Lord Sandly, who is Mr. DiBuono?"

The viscount's mustache suddenly seemed perplexed. "Who is who?"

"Do you see the Swedish woman over there?"

"Ah yes. She has controlling interest in SAAB."

"The man on her left who keeps whispering."

"Very rude, all that whispering."

"Who is he?" *And why is my husband staring at him?*

"Someone told me he's a book salesman. Doesn't look the type though, does he?"

After dinner the party moved to the great lounge.

"Ariana—cara!"

She turned. It was Giorgio Montecavallo—Monte. She hadn't seen him since her three last *Adriana Lecouvreurs* in Vienna. He snatched her into a quick hug. He'd gained fifty pounds.

"What in the world are you doing here?" he whispered.

Surprisingly, he offered her a cigarette. She shook her head.

"The same as you," she said, suddenly feeling she'd had too much flying and food and partying. "Enjoying myself."

"It's uphill work having a good time, isn't it?"

She smiled, glad he had said it, glad he understood. "Especially after three months jetting around the world performing."

"Don't worry, you'll get better at it. Like me."

It took her a moment to realize she had said the wrong thing. In the last three years she hadn't heard of Monte jetting anywhere performing anything. She vaguely remembered hearing of a *Pagliacci* in Dubrovnik, scathing reviews for his scene-chewing Canio, and since then . . . silence.

"Sing with me," he said suddenly. "Please, Ariana. Just this once."

"Monte, you're not making sense. Sing *what?*"

He looked at her. "Don't you understand? My God, you don't. You think I'm a guest on this cruise."

"Of course you're a guest, the same as all of us, aren't you?"

"Am I?" Monte pointed an unsteady finger. "That man owns all the jute mills in India. That woman owns the largest sapphire in I forget where. That one designs jeans. But I'm Monte. I used to sing opera, and now I sing . . . after dinner. I'm the entertainment."

Ariana was too surprised to answer.

"Well, cara, 'Vesti la Giubba.' " Monte bent to kiss her. He smelled of Scotch. His legs took him the wrong way and he banged into the Uruguayan ambassador's chair.

There was laughter and an apology and he finally managed to get to the piano. The accompanist awaited eye contact before rolling a three-chord introduction.

Monte fortified himself with a visible deep breath. Too visible. He began to sing "Granada." Badly.

Ariana sank deep into her chair, wishing she were in Brussels in the pouring rain.

The Baroness de Chesney leaned sideways and asked a rock star to light her cigarette. After-dinner mints and coffee and cordials were passed. An Austrian film star loudly said *"Scheiss"* when there was no apricot liqueur. Joints were passed. There were whispers and jokes and gossip and little explosions of laughter in four languages and a German automobile magnate noisily invited eight companions to his stateroom to snort some truly excellent coke.

Monte brushed the dampness off his forehead and kept singing.

Ariana tried to hide behind her brandy snifter of sparkling water. As he approached the F-sharp, the high note in the second chorus, he lunged instead for an A: she had been afraid he might.

It would have been a good way of recapturing his audience, but his voice cracked and what came out was not a note, not a sob, not even one of those pitchless emotional gasps tenors trade in. It was a clear, unmistakable burp.

There was a millisecond of shocked silence. An Egyptian minister cried, "Gesundheit, Monte!" and the room broke up in guffaws.

Suddenly an eardrum-perforating sound drowned the laughter.

A clear A above the staff rang out, climbing to a ringing high D. Projecting the final line of the song as though she were singing to the galleries in La Scala, Ariana moved through the chairs toward the piano: *"De lindas mujeres, de sangre y sol!"*

She took Monte's hand and together they bowed to screaming applause. "What pigs," she whispered. "Let's give these bastards what they deserve. 'Be My Love' and 'Smoke Gets in Your Eyes.'"

They did.

And "People Will Say We're in Love." And "Wunderbar." And "Why Do I Love You?" And a dozen others. Monte took melody and Ariana spun fioratura in the stratosphere above him. When his voice cracked or his air ran short she dipped to melody, covering till he caught up.

"Funny," she said when the howling jet-setters finally permitted them a break. "I never thought I'd be singing 'Melancholy Baby.'"

He kissed her and his eyes were glistening. "You could have a second career, cara."

"Thanks. But one career is murder enough."

It was three in the morning by the time Ariana found Boyd and got him back to their stateroom. The air was sweet from a bouquet of blue and white arum lilies that a chambermaid had placed on the table.

There was a little note attached in Greek script. *Efcharisto.* Ariana recognized the handwriting.

"You're sad," Boyd said.

"Yes. I suppose I am." She stood listening to the gentle roar of the Mediterranean. "I wonder if the world is always gaudy. I wonder if it's always dying."

"Come *off* it, sweetums. What's the matter?"

"Monte and me, tonight. Those people. Laughing, and Monte thinking they were applauding."

Boyd plopped down on the edge of the bed. His face reddened with the effort of prying his foot out of a patent leather pump. "Oh, stop being operatic. It wasn't so bad as all that."

"But it was. Monte used to be an artist. And now . . ."

"Say, lookie here." A bottle of Mumm's rested in a silver cooler beside the bed. Boyd popped the bottle open and overpoured two glasses. He offered one. Ariana declined with a headshake and watched her husband drink them both.

"Boyd. Who's DiBuono?"

"Who's who?"

"That librarian at your dinner table."

Boyd scratched his ear. "Oh, him. He strikes me as a nobody."

"What's a nobody doing on this ship?"

"Maybe he's a somebody to somebody."

"Did you know him before?"

"Sweetums, I'm not the bookish type."

"Neither is he."

"Then you know more about him than I do."

"I don't trust him."

"I don't think I can stay awake for this conversation. G'night, sweetums."

16

OVER THE NEXT THREE DAYS ARIANA NOTICED THAT BOYD SPENT a great deal of time in the bar drinking with the DiBuono man. She spent most of her time with her little electric piano, reviewing scores; not because she needed to, but because all the chatter and people were beginning to get on her nerves.

The fourth day, after sunset, she came out of the stateroom in an evening dress. Through the window of the main salon she could see diamonds and tanned shoulders. The roar of a party drifted faintly onto the deck.

Three smokestacks loomed into the evening. Rolled canvas was lashed to the railings. Nikos Stratiotis stood in evening clothes in the dying light, his image faintly reflected in the droplets of spray that covered the deck. He approached. "Enjoying yourself?"

"Marvelously, thank you."

He looked at her. "Your husband seems to . . . It's none of my business, but you're alone a great deal."

She laughed. "We see plenty of each other during working hours. This is our vacation. He goes his way, I go mine." She gazed down at the Mediterranean, at the wind blowing the water white and moss green.

"In my opinion your husband goes his own way a little too much."

"Boyd has a great deal on his mind."

"And you? Is your life all opera and travel and practicing? Isn't there ever ice cream or dolls or roller coasters?"

She shrugged. "I don't have time."

"Silly things matter."

She looked at him. "Do you have silly things?"

"I have a collection of over eight thousand World War II comic books. Mint condition. You've never wanted anything silly?"

Waves made a lapping sound at the hull. "Well, sometimes I've thought I'd like to wear the best underwear in the world."

"Why don't you? You can afford it."

"Silk and lace aren't important."

"They're important to you. And aren't you important?"

"Oh, I don't know how important I am. Music is important, and opera is important, but I . . ."

"Aren't you important to yourself? If you're not, you'll never matter to anyone else." Suddenly he gripped her arm. "Let's go to Monte Carlo right now. Let's buy you some underwear."

She loved the idea and hated herself for loving it. *He takes me for a child.*

"But, Nikos, you have guests waiting for dinner."

"Let's insult them."

She hesitated only a moment. "All right. Let's."

They took the launch to shore, and Nikos drove them in the Karmann Ghia with the top down. They curved through the bright mile of shops and nightclubs, hotels and casinos, past the villas and mansions of the legendary rich. They slammed to a stop in the parking lot of the Grand Hotel Monte Carlo. He strode into the lobby, pulling her with him.

"Nikos," she pleaded, "the shops are all closed."

"Don't worry, I own sixty-six percent of the place."

He made the manager open the Hermès lingerie shop. They bought armloads of pink silken underwear, soft and delicious and glistening.

"We'll take the nightgown with us," Nikos told the manager. "Send the rest to my ship."

A well-dressed crowd had gathered as they came out of the shop. Jeweled fingers pointed. There were excited whispers: *Stratiotis! . . . La Kavalaris! . . .* A young reporter standing barely three feet away exploded a flashbulb in their faces.

Nikos's hands swung up. The camera crashed to the marble floor in a glittering nest of torn wire and chrome. Nikos handed the reporter a 50,000-franc note. "No pictures, please. Madame Kavalaris is on vacation."

He took her arm and led her to a table on the terrace. The sound of laughing voices and violins drifted into the cool night. Ariana felt surprisingly safe with him, safe in a way she'd never felt with her father or brother, or even with Boyd.

He ordered the same delicious fruity drink they'd had in Venice. When she set the glass down she realized she was giddy.

"I feel as though I were a little girl again."

"Don't," he said with surprising firmness. "You had a bad childhood. Like me. We're very much alike. Life has marked us."

"How do you know?" she said. "Have you researched me?"

"Of course."

"Then you have an advantage. I know nothing about you except what I read in the cover stories in *Time* and *Der Spiegel*."

"They tell what happened. They don't tell what it was like."

"What was it like?"

"Prison."

She listened, and for the first time she heard the bitterness and the loneliness in his story. He had been born in Armenia, and at age six had moved to an Athens slum, the youngest of five sons and three sisters. "My father wore grease-stained overalls all his life and ended up right where he started, on the bottom. I emigrated to Uruguay at seventeen, to the United States illegally two years later. I was twenty-five before I ever saw the clean side of a dollar, before I even knew there *was* one."

A cloud passed over the moon and there was a silence.

"What do you make of me?" he said. "Twenty-five words or less."

"I admire your grasp of how life really works." She gazed down at the esplanade planted with palm trees that followed the curve of the bay, wondering how moonlight managed to turn reds and greens to such shimmering pale blue. "But you judge people."

"To stay ahead I have to judge and judge quickly."

She didn't answer. There was a warm breeze from the sea.

"Let's walk," he said.

They took the stairs down to the sea and took off their shoes and walked along the damp sand in their evening clothes.

"What do you hate most in life?" she asked.

"I suppose—feeling I'm not needed, feeling there's no reason."

"You feel that too?"

"Sometimes. It's a horrible feeling."

"What are your hopes?" she asked.

"Hard to say. Hope is like a horizon. The closer you get to it the farther away it moves. I've always hoped to find someone who . . ." They had reached the parking lot. "You have a smudge on your cheek. Stand still a moment." He drew out a handkerchief and slid the tip across her cheek. "There. It's gone now."

"You were saying, someone who . . ."

"I was being a teenager."

He gave the attendant the ticket for the car, and they drove back to the ship. Their hands almost touched on the front seat. Almost.

"I enjoyed our talk," he said outside her stateroom.

"So did I."

It was 2:00 A.M., and she felt pleasantly exhausted. He seemed to understand that.

"Goodnight," he said. There was not even an attempt to kiss her.

"Goodnight."

She bathed, slipped into her new nightgown, and fell asleep without a glance at the empty space beside her in the bed.

Nikos and Ariana were together after that.

He took her shopping in Nice; shopping in Juan-les-Pins; showed her how to scuba dive off Portofino; sat with her in the corner of the ship's bar and sipped fruity drinks and asked her questions about opera and answered her questions about finance.

The crew and staff treated her with new deference. They rushed to open doors for her, fought with one another to carry her little packages, were constantly asking if there was anything she needed and looking so crestfallen if there was nothing that she began making up needs just to avoid hurting their feelings.

The guests treated her differently too. She was sunning alone on A deck when a woman pulled up a deck chair beside her. "Darling, are you going to tell me?"

Ariana took off her sun-goggles and looked at the woman, who was wearing a pale blue Galanos and had beautifully maintained ash-blond hair and smooth skin without a hint of sunburn. She sounded like New York, the exactly right sort of New York.

"You and Nikos look as though you have a secret."

"Maybe we do," Ariana said.

"I detest maybe's."

"I don't. I think maybe's are beautiful."

"Darling, I really haven't time. I'm dummy this hand and the baroness has bid five no trump. Are you sleeping with him?"

"You're a gossip."

"And a damned effective one. If I were to say the right word about you and Nikos, these people would respect you."

"Are you offering that as a favor?"

"I collect people and you'd be my first decent operatic soprano. You'd be envied. Invited. Imitated."

"You make your friends sound like monkeys."

"That's not an answer."

"I can't give you an answer."

"Can't or won't? Everyone's seen the way he watches you. Everyone's talking and everyone's wondering."

"You're the only one who's wondered about it to me."

"I'm the only one with the sense to be direct. By the way, we haven't been seated together at dinner yet. My name's Carlotta Busch." She looked Ariana straight in the eye as she shook her hand. "I hope you'll come to dinner when we get back to New York. I'll invite Nikos too. Must run. I hear the baroness growling."

That evening at dinner the other guests were extraordinarily courteous to Ariana. She was keenly aware of secret, envying glances from women at neighboring tables. The glances warmed her.

Two days later the maid was making the bed as Ariana came into the stateroom.

"You needn't bother," Ariana said. "My husband and I will be leaving the ship in an hour." She opened her suitcase on the bed. She began bringing dresses from the closet. The maid helped her.

"Mr. Stratiotis will be very sad," the girl said.

Ariana's hand paused on the zipper. "Will he?"

The maid lowered her voice. "Madama is his favorite."

Ariana tried to maintain her composure. Suddenly this little servant was the most important critic in her career. *He told her to tell me*, she realized. She crushed 10,000 lire into the maid's hand. "Please finish the packing and ring for the porters."

She hurried out onto the deck. Nikos and Boyd were waiting. Nikos came forward to place his hands on her shoulders. He kissed her cheek, lightly but warmly.

They stretched their goodbye to ten minutes, eyes meeting, probing, lingering. She was aware that halfway down the deck the Baroness de Chesney had straightened in her chair and was craning her neck.

"Keep in touch, both of you." Nikos's arm went around Boyd's shoulder, and his hand closed around Ariana's, tight and secret and for a moment almost causing pain, and then she and Boyd and five uniformed porters and eight pieces of Vuitton luggage were moving down the gangway and into the waiting launch.

Ariana and Boyd picked up their tour with four *Aïda*s in Copenhagen and two *Semiramide*s in Athens. They gave themselves two days to shop and unwind in Paris. She did no shopping and no unwinding at all but sat in the Ritz wanting to phone Nikos's number.

And then they flew back to New York, back to the co-op on East Seventy-eighth Street with its marble entrance hall and phones ringing and doorbells buzzing and secretaries and agents and managers and housemaids all demanding, all needing, all talking at once.

Ariana tried to study scores but kept staring into space, kept seeing Nikos's large brown eyes. She kept thinking, *Maybe he'll phone, maybe he'll write.* She found the transition back to routine unbelievably painful. She worked on her cadenzas in *Lucia*.

He didn't phone, didn't write.

That winter Boyd began going on weekend retreats in the country with his Mahler scores and the weekends would run as long as Tuesday.

One morning at two, when he still wasn't home from a Philharmonic concert that should have ended at 9:30, she went into the living room to find a magazine. She heard something and realized it was Boyd, slipping through the front door like a thief. He tiptoed into his study, and then he was on the phone, whispers muted. When she heard the receiver go down she knocked.

"Boyd, is something the matter?"

He was sitting staring into space. There was distance in his eyes. She searched his face.

He took a sip from his pony of brandy. "I've got a hell of a load with the Philharmonic and the Chicago guest series and I still haven't heard from Amsterdam about the Concertgebouw."

"You've had heavy work loads before. You've never reacted this way."

"I'm being piggy, aren't I. And I'm taking it all out on you." He rose from the chair. He was wearing the patent leather slippers that had been her gift on Father's Day and they made a soft squeaking sound on the carpet. Suddenly he drew himself up short. "I'll rent a studio. A little place where I can take my sulks out on the four walls and not on my adorable wife."

"Boyd, I didn't mean—"

He cut her short with a wave of his cigarette. "It's settled. Tomorrow I start searching the real estate ads for a little padded cell large enough for me and a Steinway and a few thousand scores."

Thursday afternoon six weeks later the doorman handed Ariana an envelope. It was a cable for Boyd and she could see through the cellophane window that it came from Amsterdam. She opened it. The Concertgebouw orchestra wanted Boyd for three Mahler concerts.

She quickly let herself into the apartment, ran to the phone and began dialing. Her finger stopped at the seventh digit.

He'd been waiting and hoping months for the Amsterdam contract. The news was too good for the phone. She'd surprise him and take the cable to his studio.

The blue sky was darkening and the air held a hint of snow as she stepped out of the cab in front of the converted brownstone on Greenwich Street. There was no answer when she buzzed. She let herself in.

Boyd's little apartment had only two rooms but they were jewels, and there was a little garden in back with big old elms that you could see from the window. She had helped him choose a pale green for the walls, and the effect was delicious, like the inside of a grape.

"Boyd?" she called.

There was no answer, which surprised her, since he had said he would be working late. Her eye scanned the empty room. It was medium-sized, with just enough space for the Steinway, the shelves of musical scores and the stereo equipment, the two comfortable chairs.

The door to the next room was open. She walked to it. The windows were shuttered. As her eyes adjusted to the dark she saw two bodies intertwined on the couch that had been opened into a bed.

She turned back to the living room. Two pairs of galoshes sat side by side on the stone hearth. A man's jacket lay carelessly tossed on one of the chairs. She could see at a glance that it was not the work of Boyd's Savile Row tailor.

Through a half-open closet door she could see two overcoats hanging. She recognized only the camel's-hair that she had given Boyd. The other, a broad-belted Aquascutum, she had never seen before. Half the clothing in the closet was new to her. There were three suits in broad checks, not Boyd's style at all; cashmere scarves and sweaters she had never seen him wear.

As she swung the closet door shut she heard a voice behind her.

"Oh, it's you, sweetums. Sorry the place is such a mess." Boyd stood in the bedroom door knotting his bathrobe.

"I should have phoned, but I wanted to surprise you." She handed him the cablegram.

Boyd kissed her quickly on the cheek. He opened his cable. A catlike look of hunger satisfied came into his eyes.

"You have someone living with you," Ariana said.

Boyd glanced back at her and nodded.

"Why did you keep it secret from me?"

"Now, sweetums, please don't be hurt. I wanted to tell you, but . . ."

"You deceived me, Boyd. And you didn't need to. You said your work was upsetting you. You said you needed room to be alone when you really needed room to be with your lover. I felt I was letting you down and now that I know the truth I feel humiliated."

"I was rotten to you, sweetums. But I didn't know how to tell you."

"Tell me *what?* I know you meet men. I know you need things I can't give you. We've lived together eighteen years—credit me with a little understanding!"

"But I love Egidio. And it's not just an affair."

"Egidio?" She frowned. In her memory, the name stirred distrust.

Another man stood in the bedroom doorway, groggily slipping into a maroon silk bathrobe. "Ariana. It's so good to see you."

"You remember Egidio DiBuono," Boyd said. "From the cruise."

The man came forward into the room, hand extended.

For Boyd's sake she took the DiBuono man's hand but the handshake was a lie. She wanted it to end.

"We were talking about you all afternoon," the DiBuono man said. "Wondering how to tell you. And now"—he gestured—"there is nothing to tell. You have made it all so easy."

He bent forward to kiss her on the cheek.

Ariana studied the face, the carefully styled hair, the mannerisms of movement and speech. The man struck her as utterly false.

Through the window she could see night beginning to seep through the garden. "Boyd, can you and I go outside for a moment?"

"Will you excuse us, Egidio?"

They stood in the little garden, husband and wife, and stared up at the smoky purple evening sky.

"Well, Boyd, what do you want to do?"

"I want to live with Egidio."

There it was. The truth. "Then you want to leave me."

He nodded. There was sadness in the nod, but firmness too. He told her his reasons. He censored nothing.

As she listened she felt his need in all its sad and awful nakedness, a need she would never be able to satisfy. But she felt something else as well, a mysterious illogic in Boyd's decision, a sort of fatalism coming off him like a mist. And in herself she sensed a fear that she wouldn't know what to do without him.

She pleaded with him. She reminded him that they had agreed to face the world together, as a couple, each lending the other what little strength or hope or experience he or she possessed.

He agreed with every word she said. But . . . there was always a *but*. Always a glance thrown back toward the half-open window. "Everything you're saying is right and wise. But I love him. I can't help it. I don't want to help it."

"You don't even know this man. And he doesn't know you."

A laugh came out of Boyd that was oddly jaunty. "He'll just have to take his chances. And I'm not such a bad bet, am I?"

She saw discussion was pointless. After a moment she sighed. "How do you want to arrange the divorce?"

His head snapped around. "Who's talking divorce?"

"You and I are—aren't we?"

Something wounded came into his eyes and he took her hands. "Good God, sweetums, no. We're a great husband-wife team and I want to keep it that way. Of course, if you want a divorce, I'll understand. But it seems a shame to break up our . . ."

"Our façade?"

"Call it what you will, it's worked for eighteen years."

"Till you met Egidio six months ago."

"It can still work. We can make it work."

"What's the point, Boyd?"

"Career."

"And with all our careers, do we ever get a life?"

"We have more than most people."

"At this point I somehow can't give much of a damn about most people. I hurt, Boyd. This hurts. You're throwing away eighteen years. Maybe you're right to. I don't know. But you have him, and I have . . . nothing but hurt."

It was drizzling and dark by the time Ariana came home. Tonight was the maid's night off, but she called anyway, making sure.

"Sonya?"

No answer.

She sat in a living room chair and tried to cry, telling herself tears were therapy, telling herself if she let go of her feelings she'd be free of them.

She let go and she wasn't free.

She wandered through the apartment, the showplace that it had taken her and Boyd twelve years and three and a half-million dollars to put together. She remembered the parties, the arguments with decorators, the prices. The place seemed cluttered and pointless. All the expensive furniture struck her as stage trappings, shapes without use or meaning. Nothing interested her, not the piano, not the paintings, not television, not books, not records.

She took two Seconals with a glass of water.

DiScelta refilled teacups and brought endless slices of hazelnut cheesecake to the table. For three-quarters of an hour she listened and did not interrupt once, not even with her eyes.

Finally there was nothing left for Ariana to pour out. Silence flowed through the kitchen.

DiScelta steepled her fingers together and gazed at her pupil. "You *will* die if you sit still with all your remembering and regretting and looking back. It would be better to water plants and scrub the kitchen floor. Do anything. But keep moving. Movement is the basis of all life."

"Tuesday I'll be in Hamburg, Sunday in Zurich, Thursday in Paris— you call that sitting still?"

"I call that sitting still on an airplane. You must have movement."

"*Aïda* isn't movement?"

"For you, *Aïda* is repetition. You must learn new movements."

Ariana raised a wary eyebrow. "There's some strange new Czech opera you want me to learn."

DiScelta waved the idea aside as though it were a fly trying to get at her cheesecake. "I'm thinking of a new role *off* the stage. Now is the time for you to reach out to another person."

Ariana sighed. "I've spent all my life trying to reach out to other people."

"You reached from your weakness, not your strength. Which is why you failed. This time you will reach from your strength."

Ariana slammed her teacup into its saucer. "Haven't you understood a thing I've been telling you? I'm scooped out. Hollow."

DiScelta shrugged as though nothing on earth had the power to impress her, not pupils, not hysterics, not even a cracked Wedgwood saucer. "Music is your strength. You will reach out from your music."

She lifted a hand to touch the gold and amethyst locket that hung around Ariana's neck.

"Over eighteen years ago you promised to take a pupil. You must delay no longer. For your own sake, find her. Teach her. You'll see. It will make all the difference."

17

ARIANA PUT OUT WORD, DISCREETLY, TO THE MUSIC SCHOOLS: Juilliard, Mannes, Manhattan. For over two months, two days a week, she auditioned a flood of applicants. She listened, she said "thank you," "very nice," "good luck." And after each one had gone she exchanged sad shrugs with Austin Waters, planted on the piano bench.

But in the second month a slim young girl called Vanessa Billings entered Ariana's music room.

"What are you going to sing for me?" Ariana asked pleasantly.

"I'd like to sing 'Et Lux Perpetua' from the Verdi *Requiem*."

Ariana knew it wasn't an accident. She knew it had to mean something that the girl had chosen that piece.

She looked at the girl as she would have a photograph. The face was unlined. From beneath the blond, neatly arranged hair arced a broad, intelligent brow with penetrating gray-green eyes.

The girl handed her music to Austin Waters. As he played the unaccompanied choral parts on the piano, her unfaltering voice shaped the line of the glorious, soaring soprano solo: *"Requiem aeternam dona eis, Domine, et lux perpetua luceat eis"*—"Give them eternal rest, Lord: and may perpetual light shine upon them."

She has the gift, Ariana thought. It was all there: the timbre, the projection, the thousand instinctive touches of musicianship that could never be taught, but only given by the Creator.

"I want to teach you," Ariana said. "When can you start?"

The girl smiled. "Right now."

Though she had taken hundreds, Ariana had never given a lesson before. From time to time, in that first lesson, when she felt a moment's uncertainty, her finger touched the locket, and somehow the right question, the right instruction, came to her lips. Within forty minutes, she began to understand what DiScelta had meant. When she taught, she forgot herself.

For three hours a week after that, the pain and the emptiness were gone. But except for those three weekly hours, spring was a season of *Norma* and *Traviata* and feeling like dry leaves waiting for rain.

And then one morning in late May Ariana caught her new secretary, Roddy, a thin gangling blond boy, throwing an envelope into the discard tray.

"A Greek-American fund-raiser," he said. "You're in London that night. It's your second Covent Garden *Manon Lescaut*."

"I still like to know what I'm refusing." She opened the invitation and read down the list of patrons. "Wire them and cancel the second performance. I'm flying back."

Roddy squinted as though he were seeing a crazy lady. "But—"

"No but's. I'm singing at the Waldorf for the benefit."

Because it was her duty as a Greek-American. Because the air was heady with the fragrance of gardenias from the bowl on the desk.

Because the chairman of the fund-raiser was Nikos Stratiotis.

Covent Garden screamed, her agent screamed, and DiScelta was on the phone to her the very next day, demanding, "Why?"

"For God's sake, Moffo cancels. Callas cancels. Why can't I?"

"The real reason is Stratiotis. Admit it."

"What of it? I'm tired of being lonely."

"You're lonely because you know too many people. And you'll be even lonelier if you start moving your life around to suit this pirate. I forbid you to fall in love. He's in too many headlines."

"I shall not fall in love. But I shall sing the benefit."

Ariana kept only half her promise.

At 10:30 she made her entrance at the Waldorf down a red-carpeted staircase and was greeted by a standing ovation. She began with the Greek national anthem and then sang two folksongs: "The Olive Tree," and "When the Dolphin Returns." The Waldorf dance band accompanied. For an encore she did Puccini's "O Mio Babbino Caro," transposing it up a third to show off her high C.

The applause went on for twelve minutes.

Afterward she glimpsed Nikos moving gracefully through the crowd. He nodded at her twice. He didn't smile. Didn't approach. Didn't congratulate her or thank her. What she felt was worse than disappointment: it was physical shock, as if he had driven a knife through her chest.

She tried to listen to a movie tycoon and a senator arguing whether Israel could beat the Arabs in under a week. She made polite murmurs, sipped retsina and nibbled lamb and watched Nikos across the room whispering to a woman in blue and vowed *I'll never do a thing for him again.*

After the program he came over to her table. He greeted the others and then he greeted her. "Hello, Ariana." He bent down and his lips brushed her cheek.

She was too startled to organize her resistance. He took her hand. "Can I give you a lift home?" he asked.

"Thanks, but I have a car waiting."

"I took the liberty of sending your car away."

She sat looking up at him, wanting more than anything else in the world to be furious at him, but suddenly there was no anger in her.

Suddenly the only thing that mattered was that Nikos Stratiotis was offering her a ride home.

She gathered up her purse. "There's no sense calling another car. We might as well take yours."

It was a magnificent custom-built gray Mercedes limousine. It had a bar, a tape player, color television, two phones. He pushed buttons, pulled down panels. "This turns into a writing desk."

She asked what he was writing.

"My memoirs."

"Am I in them?"

"I hope you will be."

He gave the driver her address. It pleased her that he knew it without asking. She felt herself sinking into a warm sea of safety. She wanted to lay her head in Nikos's lap.

"Thank you for performing," Nikos said. "You canceled Covent Garden."

"Yes."

"You're living alone now."

"Yes."

He pressed a button and raised the partition between them and the driver. His fingers went grazingly over her forehead. He slid an arm around her waist. His lips touched her mouth, her face, her throat.

The car coasted to a stop. "I'd like to come up," he said.

She wrapped her hand around his.

They went upstairs. He closed the apartment door behind them.

"A drink?" she offered.

"I didn't invite myself here for a drink." He stood smiling down at her, his burning brown eyes at once devouring and tender.

Suddenly aware how long she had been imagining this moment, she led him into the bedroom. She pressed her mouth against his, her tongue hungry and impatient. She was astonished to sense a holding back in his kiss. Even his embrace was light.

She met his eyes and could not read them. He seemed preoccupied.

"Wait," he whispered. "Just a minute." He went into the bathroom. To her surprise she heard water running in the tub. He came back to her, a slight smile on his face.

"Let's undress," he said. He began to open her gown.

Her hands reached and grappled blindly with his collar button, his diamond shirt studs and cuff links. Each newly bared inch of his skin received a touch of her lips—not a kiss but an acknowledgment.

She came to his cummerbund and her fingers trembled. Her hand explored the inside of his leg, brushed against his thigh. She felt a swelling in response.

Can he tell that I've never unzipped a man's trousers before?

She tugged his Jockey shorts down. Every muscle of his corded belly was clearly defined. Her hand enclosed his testicles. She gazed at his penis, watching it contract and expand as blood pumped through its blue veins.

All her reserve, all her timidity, burned away. She knelt before him on the carpet. She gripped his thighs. She had never known herself to be so open, so heedless of all but the need to give and receive love. She kissed the tip of his penis and probed the sensitive slit with her tongue. She pressed her nose into the thick, clean-smelling mass of his pubic hair.

Nikos gave a tiny gasp and pulled back. "No—not yet."

He held her a little away from him. She could hardly bear the momentary separation of their bodies. He dealt smoothly with her bra and then surprisingly gently with her hose, as if he knew how easily they could be snagged.

When they were both finally naked he took her into the bathroom. He bent to test the water. When its warmth suited him, he pulled her toward the tub, still smiling his slight smile. "Come."

She stepped into the tub and slid down to her knees, letting him treat her like a little girl. He sponged warm water over her shoulders and breasts, slowly, ritualistically, as if he were subjecting her to a delicious sort of punishment.

He got into the tub beside her and straightened her legs so that she was stretched almost full length. The water came to her shoulders. He caressed her with the soap from hip to ankle—first the outside of her legs, then the inside. Each stroke brought his hand closer to the waiting, pulsing place between her thighs.

She lay back and closed her eyes. His fingers slipped into her and something like light went through her legs.

Now she felt his mouth on her lips—more insistent, a little less gentle than before. He raised her to her feet and helped her from the tub. He took a huge, soft towel and knelt, drying her legs and feet with long strokes. He pulled her toward him. He buried his face between her legs. Gradually, millimeter by millimeter, his tongue entered her.

Electricity shot through her. She had to grip his warm, hard shoulders to steady herself. With one movement, he rose and swept her up, carrying her to the bed.

As his lips and tongue moved down her rib cage another spasm thrilled through her. She felt his knee separating her thighs and a gentle pressure as he lowered himself on top of her. She yielded like melting wax to his stocky, graceful strength, his weight, his smiling confidence. Her body glowed with total happiness as it savored the wonder of this moment, this man.

Nikos's plunging pace gradually quickened. "Are you comfortable?" His words came through the darkness.

"Yes, oh, yes. Yes, my darling."

She looked up into his face. The long-lashed dark eyes were watching her. The same odd little smile played on his lips.

"Nikos," she murmured.

His hand reached for her breast and in that instant she came, gloriously, knowing a fulfillment she had never imagined possible.

And then amazement. *God*, she realized, *he's not stopping*.

She could feel him still inside her, firm as ever, going on. Continuing. Entering and withdrawing with a zest and eagerness that made her whole body quake. He was better than she had ever imagined any man could be.

"You like it?"

She heard herself give a long, low moan. "Oh, yes, Nikos, yes."

He slammed violently into her. She gave a strangled, exalted shriek. He brought her to a climax again, and then again, with his hand, and again, with his mouth, and then he entered her again. . . .

His last words before he left in the morning were, "I'll phone."

She found excuses to stay home, canceled her lunch date, canceled Austin Waters. (She had taken to working more with him and less with DiScelta, who found fault not only with her singing but with every other aspect of her life as well.)

She sat at the piano and stared down at her hands. She didn't vocalize, didn't play. She wanted to hear the phone when it rang.

It rang, but it was never Nikos.

She sat on the terrace in a spill of evening light. Without turning her head, she could see the phone in the study. In less than twenty-four hours her entire world had shrunk to the hope of hearing his voice.

He didn't phone. Not that day, not the next.

Tuesday she flew back to London for her final *Manon Lescaut*. Somehow she had expected he would call or send a cable or note or bouquet. But there was no message, no cable, no bouquet.

The London audience was polite. The reviews were not.

The next week she sang a dreadful Isolde in Berlin; the week after she pulled herself together and managed three decent *Hoffmanns* in Zurich. But she kept remembering his eyes.

She was in Hamburg to sing three *Lulus* when the phone in her hotel suite rang. "Ariana?"

There was a strange suicidal thrill in her stomach, as though she had stepped into an elevator shaft with no elevator.

"I've missed you terribly. Tell me you've missed me too."

Instinct warned her that this was the wrong time to let Nikos know the power he had over her. "I enjoyed our evening," she said.

"Can you meet me in Paris next Tuesday? I've booked a suite at the Georges Cinq."

It astonished her that he never even considered the possibility of her having her own life and her own commitments. She let him bubble on about theaters and nightclubs and a country week at Baron Rothschild's, and then she said in what she hoped was exactly the right tone of not giving a damn, "Nikos, I can't. I have to be in New York. We're blocking the new *Pelléas* at the Metropolitan."

An instant's disbelieving silence came across the line. "It's that important?"

"Yes, Nikos. It's my career and it's that important. When I make promises I keep them."

"You're angry with me. Won't you please let me explain?"

"I have a performance in three hours and I've got to get ready. Goodbye, Nikos."

She broke the connection quickly, before her resolve could falter. There was a click and then the lonely hum of a dial tone and suddenly she was very much alone in a strange hotel room in a strange city on a strange continent. She seized up the receiver again.

"Operator, we were cut off, can you reconnect me?"

"It's difficult, madame, the call was coming from Moscow."

Control returned. "In that case never mind."

The *Pelléas and Mélisande* dress rehearsal went disastrously.

Ariana was trying for a special vocal quality, soft and supple enough for Debussy's elusive heroine, yet full and powerful enough to fill the four-thousand-seat Metropolitan. But the director, Gian-Sebastiano Ferelli, an elegant composer and fashion designer (and current darling of the Texas millionairess bankrolling the production) was taking his virgin plunge into opera staging. He nagged about senseless details and kept pulling Ariana off her characterization.

"Ariana, you have to be on the yellow mark at '*Votre chair me dégoûte!*' And when Golaud seizes you by the hair, let yourself go—don't fight it."

"It's my scalp he's pulling, not the wig."

"There should be a wig strap."

"There's not."

Gray hair fluttering, Gian-Sebastiano whirled on his heel and screamed, "Props!"

Three voices relayed the scream backstage and eventually two prop men, a seamstress, and two electricians arrived. What with union regulations and imbecilic stagehands, it took half an hour to straighten out the wig strap and the tiny piece of yellow cloth taped to the stage.

Finally Boyd rapped his baton and gave the upbeat.

A characteristic Debussian effect—two clarinets playing a dissonant major second—rose from the orchestra pit. The sound hovered in the air like a single note that had split into two warring halves and could not pull itself back together. Ariana found the sound agitating, stirring, troubling, like a premonition that could not quite be articulated. It seemed to her that with those two clarinets Debussy had caught all that was wordless and subliminal and troubled in the twentieth-century psyche.

The clarinets died and a menacing silence filled the hall.

"Gentlemen, please." Boyd rapped the music stand again.

There was a sudden sound of joking and laughing, a scraping of chairs, a shuffling of feet and squeaking of stands. The musicians rose, instruments under their arms, and crowded in a disorderly mass toward the two exits.

"Gentlemen," Boyd cried, "what the hell is going on?"

It was the bass-clarinetist, union spokesman, who answered. "We're taking a coffee break."

"I haven't given you a coffee break. If you leave now, you're walking out."

They walked out.

"Panagia mou! Ti kano edho?" Ariana strode to the footlights and stared at the empty desks shining in light-framed quadrangles. "For God's sake, Boyd, I flew three thousand miles to be here today. Can't you control your musicians any better than that?"

"They're not my musicians, sweetums."

Blind rage flooded her. She ran to her dressing room, slammed the door, stood shaking, wanting to scream. With an unthinking sweep of her hand she took vengeance on the dressing table, sending brushes and hairpins flying to the floor.

A movement in the mirror caught her eye. The reflection of a man in a dark suit was rising from the reflection of a chair. She spun.

"I brought you a present." It was Nikos, holding out a package.

They were alone: no dresser, no seamstress. Electricity began to rise up the back of her neck.

His eyes were on her, hungry and steady and pleading. All thought, all anger flew from her head. Silently, she took the package. She removed the expensive Madison Avenue wrapping.

It was a small oak clock veneered with ebony and Boulle marquetry of brass on tortoiseshell. A museum piece.

"It works," Nikos said. "I had the parts replaced."

"It's lovely. Thank you."

Suddenly his hands were on her shoulders. His mouth clamped onto hers. A roaring of waves filled her ears. All strength drained from her legs. They began buckling under her.

She tried to push him away. But he shoved her down onto the daybed, began pulling her costume off. She dug her teeth into his shirt. A muffled groan came out of him. She raked her nails down his face, but they were too short, powerless to draw blood. He wrestled her to the corner of the bed, held her pinned.

"I love you," he whispered.

He held her till she stopped resisting, then sank gently into her. The sensation that filled her was so strong and so sweet, it carried her so far outside of herself, so far from musicians and walkouts and telephones and pain, that ten seconds of it would have been worth ten years of her life.

Afterward they lay side by side, quiet, floating.

Gradually, the walls of the dressing room returned and beyond them the sounds of workmen shouting and scenery moving.

"You paid the musicians to walk out," she said.

He didn't deny it.

She sprang up from the bed. "You're intolerable! You think money can get you anything you want!"

"And you're an idiot if you think it can't."

"It doesn't matter to you that hundreds of people worked thousands of hours to prepare a performance. All that matters is your whim, your desire."

"And yours. You enjoyed making love as much as I did. Perhaps even more."

"How dare you!"

"What do you expect me to say? I'm perfect for you and we both know it."

She stared at the brutish cunning in his face. A heart-thumping fury came over her. She seized the little oak clock from the table and hurled it at him.

It struck the side of his head.

He stood a moment feeling his face. When his hand came away she saw that his cheek was torn open under the eye.

She seized a makeup towel and pressed it to the wound.

"You've destroyed a very rare clock," he said.

"I'm sorry—about the clock."

"It doesn't matter."

"Nothing matters to you, does it?"

"You matter. I love you."

"Get out. And tell the musicians to get back to work. I have an opera to rehearse."

At the performance the next night Ariana's voice moved through Debussy's shifting harmonies like sunlight pouring through the rose window of a cathedral. She communicated something extraordinary to the audience, something that went far beyond the notes in the score and the words in the text. It was a blend of effortless musicianship and uncanny acting. One critic said you could hear her shadow moving across the stage.

After the final curtain the wide waiting silence of the audience exploded into a seventeen-minute ovation.

She took eight curtain calls, the greatest number of any Mélisande in the history of the Metropolitan.

And yet something was wrong. She knew it, and DiScelta knew it at their next lesson.

"I admire the tree; I dislike the fruit." DiScelta drew in a deep breath. She turned to Austin Waters, erect and silent as ever at the keyboard. "Austin, thank you very much. That will be all for today."

"Yes, madame." He gathered up his scores and shot Ariana a glance that said, *I've seen her in this mood before—you're in for it.*

There was a moment of silence after he left. The surfaces of DiScelta's face seemed to shift and move as she gazed at her pupil.

"You're taking shortcuts. Something is diverting you. Or perhaps someone." DiScelta rose from the piano bench. "Stratiotis, yes?"

There was no point in telling a lie that was not going to be believed. Ariana met her teacher's gaze. "I'm tired of living in parts and particles."

"Ah, the truth is beginning to glint through."

"What in the world does my personal life have to do with my singing?"

"When I pour twenty years into you, and this merchant changes your voice, yes, that has to do with your singing. And believe me, I can hear the difference. You who are a great voice are turning yourself into an interesting and pleasing one."

"That's nonsense."

"My ears don't lie! You are becoming ordinary!"

"Maybe I *am* ordinary. What do you expect me to be, a nun?"

"If your voice requires it, yes!"

"I have a right to love."

"This man isn't giving you love, he's giving you lovemaking."

"And I love it! It takes the jaggedness off life. It softens things. For a moment I can relax."

DiScelta stood shaking her head. "A moment. What is a moment compared to a career?"

"Sometimes a moment can be everything."

"And sometimes you are a fool! This man has millions, he invites you on a yacht, he introduces you to people you read about in gossip columns, and to you this is the real world at last. And what does he feel for you?"

Ariana looked down at her hands. "He's fond of me."

"My poor child, you must face the truth. He could have any woman in the world, and he has chosen you. Why?"

"I suppose because he prefers me."

"And why does he prefer you? There are hundreds of millionaires' wives who make conversation better than you, thousands of jet-set courtesans who make love better, but you have one quality none of them can match."

Ariana swallowed. "And what is that?"

"Fame. And when he has stripped you of that, he will throw you aside like a gnawed steak bone."

Ariana was silent. Her heart thudded against her chest. "Are you trying to frighten me?"

"I'm trying to terrify you."

"You've managed very nicely."

Summer came, swollen with festival dates—Edinburgh, Florence, Athens, Mar del Plata. It took every ounce of resolve Ariana could muster, but for three months she didn't see Nikos.

He tried.

There were cables and phone calls at every hotel. He sent flowers: two dozen vivid violet hyacinths every Monday, two dozen scarlet roses every Tuesday, two dozen of one beautiful sort of bloom or another every day of every week wherever she went.

But DiScelta's warning followed her like a shadow, and her teacher took to mailing her, without comment, gossip columns ripped jaggedly from the gutter press of the world.

Nikos was escorting actresses, heiresses, other men's wives, a twenty-five-year-old beauty who would one day inherit controlling interest in General Motors.

He can't be trusted, Ariana thought.

But one September evening in Barcelona she returned from an exhausting *Traviata* at the Teatro Lirico and found an emerald necklace lying on her pillow.

The note with it said *Efcharisto, Nikos.*

She was tired, so tired that sleep refused to come. She stared at the empty pillow beside her and thoughts kept crowding into her mind. Was she a fool to keep putting him off? He said he loved her. She loved him, she was sure.

Almost sure.

They met that fall at a dinner in New York. Most of the guests were worried about the Soviet invasion of Czechoslovakia that had taken place the night before.

"You realize, this could be World War III," a CBS news anchorman told Ariana.

"I hadn't realized."

She hadn't noticed Nikos among the guests until she saw him standing on the terrace alone in the shadow.

"You shouldn't have sent me flowers," she said. "Or jewels."

"*Shouldn't* is a strong word. Why did you run from me?"

"Because you bribed the musicians. Because you attacked me in my dressing room."

"And because of what you call an attack, you gave one of the greatest performances of your career."

"It wasn't me performing. It was something you unleashed in me."

"It's called woman."

"You can be banal in the most insulting way."

"And your eyes show contempt in such a pretty way."

"I'm sorry. I didn't mean for it to be pretty."

"I wish you'd stop acting as though I'm a bigger bastard than God."

"Maybe I will when you stop acting as though you're richer than God."

"You're wearing the necklace."

"That was an oversight." She unclasped the necklace and held it out to him. Instead of taking it, he gripped her hand and pulled her tight against him. For one instant she could feel their two hearts beating wildly out of synchronization. She yanked loose but he caught her arm.

The necklace made a slapping sound as it struck the terrace.

Nikos retrieved one of the stones. "You've lost an emerald."

"It's yours now." She kicked the rest of the necklace toward him.

As he stooped and picked it up light struck his face.

She recoiled. "Your cheek is scarred."

The whiteness of his teeth went through her like a knife. "What do you expect when you throw an oak clock at a defenseless man?"

A wave of hesitation washed over her. "But can't the doctors—"

"I'm too busy to waste three weeks on such a little scar. And besides, it has sentimental value. It's the only thing you've ever given me."

He's perfect, she thought. *Dear God, why does he have to be perfect?*

"You've got to have it taken off," she said.

"On one condition."

And even before he named the condition, she knew she was going to say yes.

A month is a strange thing. It can change all the years that have gone into a life.

Nikos rented a beautiful estate for them in New Jersey. He showed her how to ride horses, how to play tennis and bridge, how to meet people. She'd never had such nurturing from a man. Overnight she was mixing with media celebrities, European nobility, international millionaires, NFL commissioners, baseball pitchers, artists, singers, dukes, men and women she'd never have met in the narrow world of opera.

And something astonishing happened.

They accepted her.

She couldn't believe it: Ariana Kavalaris, the little girl from East 103rd Street, was being treated as an equal by people who she'd thought existed only in headlines and on the evening news.

It was a time of discoveries, of finding out how much more there was in her than just a voice. She found she had the wit to make small talk with a cardinal from Venice, the charm to flirt with a glittering Mafioso, the quick grasp of information to make intelligent conversation with a Swiss financier and a Latin-American *presidente.*

And the courage to stand up to society lionesses like Marge Macintosh.

It happened one night at a dinner for sixty at the home of a TV newsanchorwoman. Ariana was standing alone on the terrace looking down at Park Avenue when Marge materialized next to her and in a rather mysterious voice said, "Congratulations."

Marge was the wife of the second-largest TV network in the country and the daughter of the third-largest oil company, and she was not given to congratulating people.

"Thank you," Ariana said, "but what for?"

"I do believe you've tamed the world's least tamable playboy. Nikos used to have a compulsion for dazzling women, but since he met you he's given all that up."

Ariana recognized the odor of malice. "You're very kind."

"Not kind at all. Just a poor loser."

"You were in love with Nikos?"

"Three times in the sack, is that love?"

Ariana looked at this woman in the $3,000 Adolfo and the $250,000 diamond necklace. *She's dangerous. Not because she has power, but because she has jettisoned pride.*

"For some people it might be," Ariana said.

The woman's eyes fixed her and the loathing was undisguised. "Not for Nikos, obviously. Tell me, dear, I know so little about opera, what should my husband and I see you in? Have you got any good roles?"

"I'm superb in everything. Including . . . how did you put it? . . . the sack."

There was an instant's recoil and reappraisal before Marge spoke again. "Enjoy it while you've got it."

"Thanks. I intend to."

When Ariana and Nikos returned from a vacation at Carlotta Busch's estate in Barbados, she hit an A-major chord on the Steinway and tried

171

to sing the arpeggio. Her voice made a stretched, creaky sound like old piano wire. She had no control over timbre or pitch.

"Darling, I love you," Nikos said, "but do you have to make that noise?"

"That happens to be the noise singers make when they're trying to get back in shape after much too long a vacation."

"But you don't sing till next week."

"Nikos, I'm singing *Turandot* next week."

"Is *Turandot* hard?"

She stared at him with his wonderful dark curls and his wonderful ignorance of everything operatic. "Come over here and hug some sense into me and make me forget about music."

And he came to her and took her in his arms.

"Why are you so good to me?" she said.

His mouth was grazing along the back of her neck. "I want you to need me. More than you've ever needed anyone."

"I do. You know I do."

"Then I've found my reason to live."

She had to laugh. "Nikos, how can you say things like that? You're worse than opera."

At that moment he had the look of a hurt little boy. "I'm *better* than opera."

She tried to find words, but there were too many feelings all at once. It was as though she were home at last—as though she'd found her father, her lover, her friend. "Oh, Nikos, what will I do when you're not here?"

"But I am here." His arms tightened around her and then his tongue touched the inside of her ear, where nothing but music had ever touched her before. "I've found you, you've found me. Nothing else matters."

For the next six months, the elements of her life were in perfect harmony: the parties, the travel, the performances, the reviews. The *Hamburger Zeitung* called her Marschallin "God-sent"; the Milan *Corriere della Sera* said of her Tosca, "Not since Callas." Her days and nights turned into a feast, and she realized how much of her had never lived. She felt as if she had finally awakened from the long sleep of childhood.

Life and business were going well for Nikos too. He was able to acquire controlling interest in the North American uranium cartel. He began real estate projects in Majorca and Sardinia as well as a major push to take over the property surrounding Manhattan's Union Square. In June 1969, after one of his foundations gave their law school a new dormitory, he received an honorary doctorate of philosophy from Harvard University.

Ariana attended the ceremony. It was a cloudless blue day and she sat with the 25,000 parents and graduating students who had crowded into Harvard Yard. She gazed proudly at Nikos holding himself like a king among the honored dignitaries on the platform in front of Memorial Church. With the eyes of the Eastern establishment upon him, he seemed absolutely at ease in the scarlet robe that covered his Savile Row suit and his Turnbull & Asser shirt and tie.

Ariana let the endless speeches flow over her, a contented reflection of the light projecting from her lover.

And then a young man in a black robe took the microphone at the center of the platform and began addressing the gathering in Latin.

Ariana's heart struck a sudden blow under her throat.

The Latin bouncing off the façade of Widener Library had the rhythm and melody of another voice. She had not heard that other voice in almost a quarter-century, but still she recognized it as though it had greeted her only that morning.

She opened her program.

Address in Latin, she read. *Mark Ames Rutherford III.*

She sat forward in her chair. *Mark's son!*

She had followed Mark's career from a distance. She knew of his service as chaplain in Vietnam and rise to bishop. She had read his letters and his Op-Ed pieces in the *New York Times* and seen him on television panels. She had never known that there was a son.

The young man was handsome and well-built, with Mark's pale blue eyes and light brown hair.

She was able to follow the parts of the Latin that resembled operatic Italian. He was making a good-natured speech about sons of Harvard and their mission to civilize the world.

There was a great deal of laughter, loud applause when he finished. After the ceremony she hurried through the crowd and caught him. "Excuse me, Mark Rutherford?"

He stopped. She could feel celebrity recognition going out like a wave. Heads turned and young men whispered, and she knew they were saying, *Isn't that Kavalaris?*

"Yes, I'm Mark Rutherford, usually called Ames."

"Bishop Rutherford's son?"

"That's right."

She held out a hand and managed to keep it from trembling. "I'm Ariana Kavalaris. I knew your family once. Long ago."

Suddenly her whole past seemed to be present in the young man staring at her speechlessly. A tide of recollection rushed in on her. She smelled the trees through the open window of the apartment on Perry Street, she heard the old spinet, she saw Mark frowning with concentration as he turned the print-black pages of a student Bible. A feeling of loss went through her, sharp and immediate as a stab: *This boy might have been my son.*

She smiled her kindest smile, inviting his, and slowly he smiled back.

"My family's here today," he said. "Would you like to say hello?"

She felt her smile about to stream down her face. "It's been so many years. They've forgotten me."

"Dad hasn't. He collects all your records. Come on and say hello. He'd love it. He worships you."

For a moment she couldn't force words through the tightness in her throat. "Maybe another time."

Ames Rutherford grinned good-naturedly, accepting the rebuff. He reached beneath his robe and pulled out a tiny notepad and a chewed pencil. "In that case, could I have your autograph?"

He held the pad steady and she signed. Then quickly, she kissed him on the side of his face.

He gazed at her a moment. "Thank you."

There was nothing more to say; there was everything more to say. She saw Nikos approaching through the crowd. "If you ever get to one of my performances come backstage, please."

"I'd love to," Mark's son said.

But the crowd was pulling them apart, and she knew she would never see him again.

Nikos's hand touched her lightly. "Who was that you were talking to?"

She smiled. "No one. Just the son of an old friend."

Part Three

BETRAYAL: 1969–1979

18

AT SEVEN O'CLOCK IN THE EVENING AMES RUTHERFORD SAT IN A chair in his club, staring at his friend and classmate Dill Switt. Mustachioed, impressively overweight, Dill was drunk. Not drunk drunk, but wisely drunk: a Harvard senior and former *Crimson* editor who had just been handed the world rolled up in a diploma.

"It's all bullshit," Dill said. "Law school and business school and being part of the ruling caste—what good's all that?"

"As long as there are laws, there'll be lawyers," Ames said.

"But why you? Why the hell do you have to join the power brokers? Can't you see what they're doing to this country?"

Ames and Dill were alone by the fireplace. The clubhouse was a litter of glasses and bottles and cigarette ashes.

"Maybe once some of us get a little power we can do something a little different for our country," Ames said. He was thinking of Ariana Kavalaris, who had given her voice to the world and who had made the power brokers bow down to beauty.

Ariana Kavalaris, who had stepped out of a crowd and kissed him.

That kiss still felt warm on his cheek. And it filled him with a glowing hope like none he had ever felt before. For the first time in his life, he could almost believe that the world belonged to him too, that his dreams had a place in it.

"Of all the people I never expected to sell out . . . you, my best friend." Dill was shaking his head, slurring his words now.

"I'll always be your best friend," Ames said. "And I'm not selling out. Some lawyers are decent people, you know."

Dill's eyes fixed Ames's with sudden shrewdness. "Name one."

"Me."

That summer, for graduation, Ames's parents sent him abroad.

"You'll never be this free again," his father said, shaking Ames's hand at the airport. "Enjoy yourself, son."

There was a remembering in Mark Rutherford's eyes that was so sad and loving that Ames grabbed him and hugged him.

"I'll enjoy myself, Dad. Don't you worry."

"Be careful." Ames's mother, immaculate in her bishop's wife blue cotton suit and trying very hard not to look too maternal or too concerned, embraced him tightly.

"I'll be careful." Ames smiled, kissing her.

But he wasn't careful. He had the time of his life. He loved the Old World with its countryside that exuded the smell of time, its ancient buildings that looked like paintings, the unfamiliar music of foreign languages, the taste of the food and the unbelievably clean sunlight.

He loved the people. He had affairs with girls he hardly knew—French girls, Belgian girls, English girls. He drank too much wine. He ate at some of the best restaurants and some of the worst, slept in good hotels and rotten hotels and five of the most beautiful parks in Europe. He didn't budget. He loaned a hundred dollars to an Australian painter he met in front of Chartres Cathedral who had the best hard-luck story he'd ever heard. He wasn't exactly surprised when he ran out of money two weeks ahead of schedule.

It was at the end of an overactive night at the end of that wonderfully overactive summer that he found himself, broke and contented, stretched on the lawn in the palace gardens of Fontainebleau, an hour's train ride southeast of Paris. A silvery sound kept butting into his hangover.

He rolled over and opened his eyes, and saw a girl crouched between the marble paws of a chinoiserie lion, playing a flute. She had long dark hair and she was wearing a long skirt and a Victorian lace blouse. He propped himself up on his elbows and watched and for five minutes she did a good job of not noticing him.

"*Qu'est-ce que c'est la musique?*" he called, realizing it was not quite the right way of asking, "What's that music?"

Her eyes were on him a moment, and in that early morning light they were pure undersea green. She seemed not particularly surprised to see a young man in jeans and Brooks Brothers shirt lolling on the palace grounds at sunrise, and not particularly interested either.

She lowered the instrument and answered in perfect patrician American English—why did he think it was Delaware?—"Badinerie from Bach's third *French Suite.*"

The flute went back to her lips, and out came another silvery piping note.

"It's pretty," he said.

She sighed. "You obviously aren't a musician. The music is beautiful and the performance stinks. My lesson with Mademoiselle Boulanger is in two hours, so would you mind if I practice?"

"Go right ahead. Would you mind if I listen?"

He stretched out on the grass. Silvery Bach drifted over him. When he opened his eyes again, the sun had moved up to the jonquil beds and the girl was gone and an old peasant type was steering an electric mower across the lawn.

He took his queasy headache and fierce stomach to a sidewalk café. He was nursing a thick little coffee when two students sat at the next table and ordered *omelettes fines herbes.* They were chattering in American English.

Eavesdropping, he gathered there was an American school at the chateau where college graduates studied architecture and music. The café appeared to be their meeting place, and it occurred to him he might see the flute player again if he could just stretch his coffee long enough.

For four hours he endured the waitress's stares. It was noon rush hour when he saw the girl standing on the sidewalk waiting for a traffic light. He slapped his last coins down on the table and rushed into the square. She was still carrying that flute case.

"Say, are you an ambassador's daughter?"

She looked at him with undisguised skepticism and he remembered he hadn't shaved since Torremolinos, where he and three thousand other tipsy young Americans had gone to see if the locals were still running the bulls as they had in Hemingway's *Farewell to Arms*. They were.

"You're not from the school," she said.

"No, I'm not from any school."

"What are you doing here then?"

"Here Fontainebleau or here France?"

"Here anywhere."

"Chasing you."

She gave him that look again, longer and more probing this time. "Would you like to have some coffee?"

More coffee was the last thing on earth his stomach wanted, but it was a way to be with her. "I'd love to, but I'm broke."

"So am I till Friday."

That seemed to settle that. They walked past hedges and gardens. "We could have coffee in my room," she said.

It was a lovable little room, for all the music manuscripts scattered about and the drying undies that she quickly snatched off the backs of chairs. Coffee was American instant, made on a hotplate, served in unmatching tin cups that looked as though they were meant to measure laundry detergent. She assumed a lotus position, told him about the American summer school of music and fine arts, about Nadia Boulanger, who she said was the world's greatest teacher of music, about her own talent, which Mademoiselle Boulanger had said was decidedly not virtuoso calibre.

"Mademoiselle says with a lot of hard work I may be good enough to teach children."

"Is that what you want to do?"

"I have a keyboard harmony lesson in ten minutes, and what I want to do is meet you here afterward."

He grinned, not believing his luck, and there was a little anticipatory surge of sexuality in his groin. "What do you know. That's exactly what I want too."

That evening he explored her, awakening nerves under her arm, beneath her nipples, finding hidden vibrations that linked breasts to labia. She moaned with happiness, taking his swollen cock as it lay pressed between them and massaging it.

Then he twisted around to kiss her between the legs and, pressing her more firmly against him, began to penetrate her.

"That's nice," she said. "So nice."

Love with her was rich, abandoned, inventive. Almost musical. Themes and variations.

They got into astonishing positions. She threw her legs up around his neck and he took her on the rug and then he took her on the bed with her head hanging back over the edge, her dark hair brushing the floor.

And then he took her in the shower.

That evening he found out everything about her. Her name was Fran, she read Henry James and identified with Fleda Vetch in *The Spoils of Poynton*, and she could cook astonishingly tasty veal cutlets on her little hotplate.

He spent the weekend with her. He began to notice a look in her eyes. He realized she was falling in love with him. And he realized he hadn't fallen in love that summer. Not once. Right now, here, in this sweetly messy little room with her, was the closest he'd come.

He wanted to fall in love. Not falling in love under these circumstances was like driving a car with the handbrake on.

He asked about spending the week and a light seemed to come on in her face.

"That would be wonderful," she said. "Just act like one of the students if Mademoiselle sees you."

For two weeks he knew the greatest satisfaction he'd ever known with another human being, and yet there was always that damned handbrake holding him back.

Why don't I love her? he wondered. *Why can't I love her?*

And then he looked at his fourteen-day beard in the mirror and realized he had a return ticket to America and seven days to get his ass to Harvard Law School. "I have to go home," he told her.

She turned, flute in hand. "When?"

"This week." He saw whole cities crashing in her eyes. He crossed the room and threw his arms around her and pulled her bone-crunchingly hard against him.

I'll love her, he thought. *I will. It's going to happen.*

"Come with me, Fran."

After much juggling of reservations, trading-in of tickets, and excuses to Mademoiselle Boulanger, Fran and Ames tipped the porter 1,200 francs and took occupancy of a cabin in what amounted to steerage on the *France*. Fran's eyes took in the walls—white and smooth and shining like the insides of a hospital—and then she peered out of the tiny porthole.

"Ames, what in the world are we doing here?"

He put his head next to hers and stared at the bright blue sky and industrial-green waters of Le Havre. "Fran Winthrop, flautist extraordinaire of Chestnut Hill, Delaware, is having an affair with Ames Rutherford of New York, a promising young student whom she met in Fontainebleau, France. They are moving their headquarters to Cambridge, Massachusetts, where Mr. Rutherford will pursue his legal studies and Miss Winthrop will be very, very happy and that's a promise."

"Oh, Ames, I *am* happy, but . . ."

He kissed her on the nose. "But what?"

"This isn't me. I'm a good Episcopalian girl. I had a scholarship to study with Nadia Boulanger."

"And I'm a good Episcopalian boy and my father's a good Episcopalian bishop and that makes it okay."

"I'm having a guilt attack."

He kissed her on the forehead. "Then let's go find the dining room and drown our guilt in pâté campagne. The rooms may stink on a French ship, but the cuisine *jamais*."

19

THE TROUBLE BEGAN AT DINNER AT CARLOTTA BUSCH'S TOWN-
house the Thursday after Labor Day. In a voice strained
through Newport and three packs of cigarettes a day, Carlotta brought
Ariana up-to-date on her new acquisition: fun couple Principessa Maggie di Montenegro and husband.

Ariana observed a young woman across the garden, laughing in a circle of men. She had wide, hard eyes, and her long caramel-colored hair
swept smooth shoulders left bare by a strapless blue Adolfo evening
gown.

"She was engaged to Prince Olaf of Norway, but she ran away ten
days ago with another man and was married by the captain of the
France. You're at her table by the way—I mean, she's at yours."

"Who did she marry?"

"Him." Carlotta pointed with her eyes toward a young man with
dark brown curly hair. He wore a beautifully tailored navy blue blazer
and he was bent over the diamond-bloated hand of one of the Rockefeller wives. "Philippe du Chat, du Chose, du-something. He's a divine
cocktail pianist."

"If you've seated me with amateur musicians, I swear next time
you're at our place I'll seat you with a reporter."

"I've seated you very well, and you'd better be grateful."

Dinner was indoors, and Ariana's companion turned out to be Adolf
Erdlich, the gray-haired director of the Metropolitan Opera, who lost
no time in describing his upcoming production of *Traviata.* It was to be
a gala, with new sets, new conductor, new *tenor.*

Ariana listened, feeling a slight ache. "Adolf, I can't do it."

"Why not?"

What was she going to say? That she had made a promise to a dotty
old *strega,* that she had already turned the role over to her pupil? "I've
sung it too often."

"Who can sing Violetta too often?"

Across the table, a shriek of laughter broke from Principessa Maggie.
Ariana's eyes went to the dark-eyed girl with the not-quite convincing
hair and the not-quite convincing little upturned nose.

"Am I the only one out of eighty guests who notices that there's
something very strange about that girl?"

"More than a few notice. You with your admirable directness are the
only one who mentions it."

"Is she on drugs?"

"Cocaine, I'd think," Adolf said.

"What have you heard about her?"

"She's spoiled. She's bored. There isn't anything she wouldn't do to experience a new sensation. Ergo her engagement to the Scandinavian prince. Ergo her elopement and marriage to a café society pianist. Some people want to shock the bourgeoisie; little Principessa Maggie aims higher. She wants to shock the aristocracy—what there is left of it."

After dinner there was a five-piece band and dancing in the garden. At the first break in the music Principessa Maggie left her husband and came over to the table where Ariana and Nikos were sitting. Her dress made a rich swishing sound.

"Hello, Nikos." Her eyes were half open and very bright.

"Hello, Maggie. Do you know my friend Ariana?"

"I'm so pleased to meet you," the principessa told Ariana with a smile that included a drop of her eyelids. "Ever since I was a tiny little girl I've loved your performances."

"You're very kind."

Nikos turned to Ariana. "Would you mind if Maggie and I dance?"

Ariana felt a burn crawling up her face. "Of course not."

Riding home in the limousine, Ariana was silent. Nikos tried to hold her hand but she pulled free.

"You're angry," he said.

"You like her," Ariana said. "You like that principessa."

"Her father's a friend of mine. I have to be nice to her."

"How long have you known her?"

"I've known Maggie since she was eleven or so."

"I hear she uses drugs."

"Naturally. Don't all the smart young things these days?"

"I hope you're not going to be a fool."

"I can promise you, my dear, I save all my foolishness for you."

Ariana thanked God that she was teaching the next day. For two blessed hours, the lesson got her mind off the principessa.

Vanessa Billings sang Rosina's aria from the *Barber of Seville,* "Una voce poco fa." Ariana sat in her armchair, still, remote, all her faculties focused into a narrow beam of pure attention. Vanessa negotiated the octave-and-more leaps of the cabaletta with no difficulty whatsoever. Yet Ariana sensed something missing. *How am I going to say this?* she thought. *How did DiScelta say it to me?*

"Not bad," she said. "But you're respecting the music too much."

It took nerve to say that in front of Austin Waters, but he kept silently to his role of accompanist, face angled toward the keyboard, allowing her to be the expert.

"I don't mean you should sing it sloppily," Ariana said, "but there has to be a freedom and joy within the exactness. With Rossini—and with Bellini and Donizetti for that matter—everything is in the melody."

Ariana was surprised at the authority in her own voice. *Is this me?* she thought. *Or is it me parroting DiScelta?*

"Granted, this whole school of opera is terribly artificial—verse, refrain, aria, cabaletta—no one makes love or commits suicide in such strict forms. But it doesn't matter. The melodies sweep the listener past any possible reservation, not because they're classics but because they're wonderful *tunes.*"

Vanessa was staring at her. "Of course. I never thought of the aria as a tune." And she sang it again.

She understands, Ariana thought, and her blood exulted.

Three weeks later Nikos took Ariana to a concert at the Grace Rainey Rogers concert hall in the Metropolitan Museum. She was chatting happily when suddenly she realized Nikos's eyes had become distant, sealed. She followed the direction of his gaze.

Seven rows back Principessa Maggie was settling into her seat. She was wearing a huge white mink coat with a collar like a wing chair, and the man helping her out of it was not her husband, but a diamond magnate whose very tanned face had been on page one of the *New York Post* practically all week.

Ariana tried to remember: *When did we decide to come to this concert, who wanted to, Nikos or me, when did we get the tickets, was it before or after we met that girl at Carlotta's?*

The music started. She didn't hear a note of it.

Intermission, at last. They went to the bar.

As the bell began ringing, summoning the audience back to their seats, Nikos turned apologetically to Ariana. "Please go on without me. I'll be right back."

Ariana went back to her seat.

The concert resumed. Nikos didn't return.

She managed to sit still through half of the first movement. When she could bear it no longer, she looked around to where she had seen Maggie sitting. The diamond man was twisting anxiously to look behind him, and there was nothing in the seat beside him but a giant white mink. She excused herself and wedged past her neighbors' knees. Outside the concert hall a bored-looking guard was pacing.

She hurried the length of the corridor and found no one, and then she came to the entrance of an Egyptian tomb. She took another two steps and froze. A woman's voice was speaking. "You'll find a way."

She found the courage to take one step more, and there were Nikos

184

and Maggie, gazing into a child pharaoh's crypt. Their hands were touching on the railing.

Ariana turned and rushed from the museum. It was raining heavily and she stood on the Fifth Avenue steps with drops of rain slapping her in the face.

Nikos appeared with her coat. "You're angry."

She spun. "Yes, I'm angry! You deserted me!"

He wrapped the coat around her. "I have tax shelters in Montenegro. The prince is a copartner in eight of my corporations. I have to be diplomatic to his daughter."

"And tryst with her in the nearest mausoleum?"

The limousine pulled up to the curb and they rode home in silence and took the elevator to the apartment. She sat at her mirror and spread cold cream over her face. Tears welled up in her eyes.

"You're being jealous of a baby," Nikos said.

Fear took her. She could see him receding. The cold cream jar came down onto the table with the weight of a cannon ball and she turned, begging. "I'm so frightened. Of you and her and what might happen."

He was silent. No denial came from him, no assurance.

"Nikos, what's happening to us? We were happy, and now it's all slipping away. Is it my fault?" She reached for his hand. She attempted a smile and felt it deepening the lines of her face.

"I'll let you rest."

"Stay with me, please?"

"Why?" He had someone else's face. A door slammed and she was alone.

When he returned two hours later she had slipped into bed with a novel she wasn't able to concentrate on. He kissed her. "What are you doing for the next two weeks?"

"You know what I'm doing, three *Elisir d'Amore*s and—"

"Cancel everything. We're going to spend two weeks in the Mediterranean. There'll be no operas, no business, no principessas. Just you and me. That is, if you're willing?"

"Oh, Nikos." She fell against him and it was as though she could breathe again. "You know I'm willing."

She went to Richard Schiller's office and tried to explain.

"I'm a professional," he said. "I represent professionals. That means I work. That means they work." Suddenly he was on his feet. "What the hell are you doing, playing?"

She was on her feet shouting right back at him. "Don't you dare preach to me!"

"Telling you to keep your contracts, that's preaching?"

"I'm entitled to sick leave!"

"Then talk to a doctor, not me!"

She talked to a doctor. His smile was wry and helpless in the face of all the cheating in the world and his own part in it. He wrote her an excuse for the insurance company.

DiScelta called her an irresponsible fool.

"It's only three *Elisir d'Amores*," Ariana said.

"It will be more. Much more."

They flew to Paris Thursday and boarded the *Maria-Kristina* Friday morning in Nice. The trip was everything she had dreamed: gentle breezes, the all-enveloping warmth of the sun, translucent blue sea drifting off forever. Gratified desire glowed in every one of her ligaments.

It's going to work out, she told herself. Yet an anxiety was growing in her, and on the fifth day Nikos caught her chin on his fingertip and gazed at her.

"Ariana, what's wrong?"

"Don't you understand? I'm happy. For the first time in my foolish life, I'm truly happy."

"The way you've been acting—is happy?"

She nodded.

"My poor darling. How little you know yourself. And how little you're able to hide. There's a child in you, worrying. I see her face here—and here—" He touched his lips lightly to her forehead and then to her lips. "What can I do to make you smile?"

"You've already done it. You've given me the most beautiful week I've ever known. It makes the rest of my life seem such a waste."

"Don't bother about the rest of your life today."

Far across the blue water, the green palm trees and turrets of Alexandria shimmered like a liquid mirage in the noon sun.

He led her into their stateroom. He slid a tape onto the player and pushed a button.

She recognized the soft strings and clarinets that opened the "Liebestod," the final scene of Wagner's *Tristan and Isolde*. And then, with amazement, she recognized her own voice.

"Nikos," she protested, "I don't want to hear that."

"You won't even notice it," he promised.

He arched her back against the enormous bed, bending over her, trailing kisses across her nipples, her stomach, her navel. Over the stereo speakers her voice sang of the undying love that could find fulfillment only in death.

She felt a curious disorientation, as if she had split in two.

186

Drawing the elastic of her bathing suit away from her thigh, Nikos's fingers entered and stroked. She felt herself yielding to the moist touch of his lips and the moister touch of his tongue and moistest of all, his mouth plunging into her.

She reached for his erection, held it as it swelled, till its wonderful hardness overflowed her hand. He pressed against her, parting her legs. She felt him rigid against her belly. She lifted her knees and opened herself to him.

He rose above her now, his brown-black eyes boring into her, his hair flying like a demonic conductor's. His body was slick with a thin skin of sweat and hers was slippery from him. His hips moved against her, drawing her into motion in time to the music as if he had done it this way with her through all their lovemaking.

The music poured from the speakers, flowing over them like an ocean. As the interwoven melodies climbed higher, the waves of instrumental sound grew in resonance and power. The tempo pushed forward, always forward, her voice cresting above the mass of sonority like a tireless swimmer.

She couldn't tell whether she was surrendering to the music or to Nikos, but she gave herself without inhibition, without shame. It was as though she were erasing all other voices from the "Liebestod," all other women from his memory.

At first gradually and now swiftly, the music rose to climax after climax, first the voice and then all hundred instruments of the Wagnerian orchestra and then, finally together in this most sexual of all musical fulfillments, voice and orchestra soaring to their long-delayed completion.

She came in a single drawn-out explosion, and instants later he followed.

The orchestra subsided. The strings sighed out a high, aching melody. There were two stinging woodwind chords, resolving into a glowing major chord. For a moment a single oboe held a lonely D-sharp. The chord returned and then all was stillness, peace, fulfillment. She closed her eyes.

Later, on the deck, she said, "Can I talk to you honestly, Nikos? Can I let you see what a child I am and will you promise not to change your mind about me?"

"How could I ever change my mind about you?"

"I can't go back to the life I had. And when I look ahead, that's all I see. The same work, the same people, the same lies . . . when all I want is here . . ." She turned and faced him, suddenly paralyzed, unable to say the words *with you* for fear it would be saying too much.

"Don't you love your work?" he asked.

"I love music. I try to pretend it's enough."

He took her hand. "Who are these people, what are these lies?"

"My husband . . . my marriage . . ."

He nodded. "I have a marriage like that too."

"They took our past. Do they have to have our future too? Why can't we be free?"

He gazed toward the shore. The sea stretched around them like a flaming mirror and his arm tightened gently around her. "Maybe we *can* be free. Maybe there is a way."

Though Ariana did not immediately recognize it, freedom arrived by seaplane the following night after dinner, in the form of a tall, white-mustached man whom Nikos introduced as his lawyer.

"Ariana, meet Holly Chambers. Holly, Ariana."

"Delighted, just delighted." The lawyer's shrewd gray eyes peered at Ariana from a deeply crinkled face. "I've been an admirer of yours for a long time." He was dressed for an air-conditioned New York office, not for a warm night on the Mediterranean, and he carried a briefcase.

When they sat down for brandies on the deck, Ariana realized the briefcase was chained to the lawyer's wrist. That interested her. The conversation did not. She couldn't see what was so important about Bolivian manganese that it had to be discussed now, or why this stranger had to sit with them like a member of the family on what was to have been their private, make-believe honeymoon.

"Will you entertain Holly for a moment?" Nikos rose and kissed Ariana behind the ear. She realized she was to be left alone with the lawyer. Grimly, she braced herself for small talk.

What came was something else.

"I gather you want to divorce your husband."

She looked up, lips parted. "Who told you that?"

"Nikos phoned me last night, ship-to-shore."

She breathed in slowly. "Does Nikos—want me to divorce?"

Holly Chambers was gazing at her across the hurricane lamps. "Do you know what the poet Rilke said about marriage?"

She wondered if she ought to trust lawyers who tried to impress her with their knowledge of German poetry. "Unless it was set to music, I'm sure I don't."

"Rilke said in the best marriage each partner stands guard over the solitude of the other. In that sense, I think you and Nikos are already married."

She decided to tell this man the truth. "I want to be married to him."

Holly Chambers leaned back, elbows on the arms of his chair, hands clasped across his stomach. "And he to you."

Her eyes narrowed. "Nikos said that?"

Holly Chambers was playing with a gold pen. "Nikos tells me a great many things."

What was this lawyer saying to her? It sounded like *perhaps* with a *maybe* in it. She gazed out at the rippling black sea, at the whole unchanging universe of stars. "If only I knew what he wanted."

A snapping of silver locks answered her. Holly Chambers's briefcase sprang open. "Nikos asked me to draw up these papers." He handed them to her. "Do you read Spanish?"

She frowned. "No."

"It's a Dominican petition for divorce. All it needs is your signature." He held out his pen and smiled, showing a mouthful of handsome teeth.

Ariana hesitated. "Is Nikos divorcing his wife?"

"Nikos and Maria-Kristina have been up to their necks in divorce for years."

That sounded like a *maybe* with a *yes* in it. "Why won't she let him go?"

"They can't agree on the child. He'd like to share custody; or at least to have visitation rights."

"His wife refuses?"

"So far she hasn't been noticeably cooperative."

"That's unfair." Ariana took the pen. "Renata is his child too." Quickly, before anything could change her mind, Ariana scratched a signature across the page.

Holly Chambers tapped his fingers on the Dominican petition. "Are you sure you want her to divorce?"

"Absolutely," Nikos said. "I don't want her belonging to anyone but me."

They were sitting alone in the ship's library.

"You realize she'll want to marry you," Holly Chambers warned.

"I can handle Ariana and her wants."

That night, in their stateroom, Ariana turned to Nikos. "Tell me about your daughter."

"Why do you want to know about Renata?"

"Because you love her."

Nikos smiled. "She's a wonderful child. She looks like her mother and she thinks like me."

"Is her mother beautiful?"

"Not as beautiful as you."

In the beige-and-mahogany office on the thirty-seventh floor of the Seagram Building, the lanky Texan with the shaggy white mustache extended an ebony box in a suntanned hand. "Cigar?"

They were State Department Havanas, but Boyd Kinsolving shook his head. "A little early for me."

"Something to drink?"

"Maybe a light Scotch."

Holly Chambers ambled to the bar, poured two stiff Chivas Regals, and handed Boyd one of them.

"You know, Boyd, things always connect. I act as minister without portfolio for a great many interests. Please, sit."

They settled into Mies van der Rohe chairs. Holly Chambers gazed a moment at his visitor, taking his measure.

"Your wife asked me to have a word with you. You're surprised?"

Little warnings began piling up in Boyd's mind. "I didn't realize my wife required your services."

"A lot of people require my services." On all the eighteen gleaming square feet of Holly Chambers's Ferrara marble-top desk, there was only a single piece of paper with two lines of type. He moved it two inches to the right. "Was it Santayana who said marriage is like death—nothing prepares you for it?"

"People are always blaming remarks on Santayana."

"Mrs. Kinsolving feels she entered her marriage unprepared. She wants a divorce."

Boyd was quick to mask any facial reaction.

Holly Chambers smiled pleasantly. "Of course, *divorce* is one of those scare words that say a great deal more about our fears than it does about any sort of reality."

"I had no idea my wife was unhappy with her situation."

"Perhaps I should explain the context of all this. Are you aware that Mrs. Kinsolving has been seeing a great deal of Nikos Stratiotis?"

"I do read more in the papers than my own reviews—or Ariana's."

"He's a really delightful guy. His humor is infectious, he's high-spirited and he takes Mrs. Kinsolving's mind off her problems."

"I didn't realize my wife had problems."

"Any artist faces the stress of getting in, getting on, getting ahead, as I'm sure you know." Holly Chambers's glance dug into Boyd. "I gather you've found your own solution."

"If you mean my wife's and my decision to live separately, I can assure you, it's perfectly ami—"

"Yes, that and your present living arrangement with Mr. DiBuono."

At the mention of Egidio, instinct warned Boyd not to panic. He needed every drop of clarity he could muster. The man facing him was not a frightened little oboist he could cow with a shout, but a highly paid, highly successful destroyer of corporations, careers, and reputations. Boyd had no desire to become another of Holly Chambers's triumphs.

"A divorce could be had without your consent. After all, you and your wife have been separately domiciled for almost two years. You're openly residing with a man. There's no shortage of grounds."

"Am I being threatened?" Boyd asked.

"On the contrary, Nikos wants it made clear that—"

"I don't see that Mr. Stratiotis has any say in this."

Holly Chambers's lips shaped a conciliatory smile. "He happens to be a good friend of your wife's and mine, and he asked me to assure you he'll take a friendly, supportive attitude."

Boyd heard the unmistakable jingle of a code word. "How supportive?"

"That would depend whether or not you consented to a Dominican divorce."

"You can't expect me to decide something like this overnight."

"Overnight is just about all the time we've got. Your wife's petition will be presented to the court Thursday. If it has to be presented without your signature, Mr. Stratiotis's offer, naturally, will not hold."

"You haven't told me what his offer is."

"Mr. Stratiotis is prepared to make an immediate cash deposit in your name into any Bahamian or Swiss bank account you care to establish."

"How large a deposit?"

"Three."

"Three?" Egidio repeated.

"Three million," Boyd said.

"*Dollars?*"

Boyd was making real Swedish sandwiches for them—thick slices of pumpernickel topped with fresh sweet butter and pâté and Brie and ripe tomato slices. He nodded, and suddenly he found his lover staring at him, eyes disbelieving.

"You're shitting me."

"No shit. The man said dollars." Boyd arranged two slices of furled cucumber on each plate. "Untaxed."

"*Gran Dio,*" Egidio murmured. "You have deep friend, you have fame, and now with money you have everything."

Boyd had to laugh. Egidio was nothing if not upfront. "Is money all you think about?"

Egidio hung his head like a child. "I think about sex too."

Boyd stepped deftly aside, sensing that Egidio was on the verge of one of his love-in-the-afternoon lunges. He carried the plates to the breakfast alcove.

"*Mangia.*"

"How can I eat? I'm too happy for you." Egidio swung one leg around the bar stool. "You know what this means? You'll never have to conduct in Rochester again!"

Boyd wanted to smile, but he felt his lip trembling.

Amazement crossed Egidio's face. "You're crying about *Rochester?*"

Boyd shook his head. "Ariana and I—we had good times together. And now it's over. I hate it when things end." He couldn't expect Egidio to understand what was being taken from him. He ached. Not so much because he loved his wife, though in his way he did, as because his life was more than half over, and it was the stronger, better half that was gone.

Egidio gazed at him. His expression had turned serious. "One thing must sometimes end to let another begin." He leaned across the table and kissed Boyd lightly on the forehead. The kiss left something behind, something warm and deeper than itself. "If she divorces you, then you belong to me. No more pretending. No more lies."

Boyd went to Holly Chambers's office the next morning and signed his wife's divorce petition.

He returned to the apartment early that afternoon from a photography session with *Vogue.*

"Egidio?" he called.

The apartment was silent except for the peaceful gray buzz of air conditioning. Boyd looked in the bedroom and saw a suitcase lying half packed on the bed. He looked in the kitchen.

Egidio was standing at the counter pouring espresso, the smooth fall of his navy blue blazer ending just where the neatly tailored gray flannel slacks hugged the narrow curve of his hips.

"There's a suitcase on the bed," Boyd said. *An $800 monogrammed pigskin suitcase from Mark Cross that I gave you for your birthday.*

Egidio sipped his espresso. "Yes, I'm packing." He set down his cup. The coffee breathed up a filament of white smoke that floated across the view of Central Park West and then lost itself against the bright steam-colored sky.

"Are you going somewhere?"

"I'm leaving for Italy at five."

It was said calmly, without fanfare. It was hardly even a declaration. But Boyd sensed an evasion buried somewhere.

"For long?"

Egidio nodded.

"Couldn't you have told me a little sooner? The Van Rensselaers are expecting us."

"Please apologize to Dinah. I didn't know till an hour ago."

Boyd followed Egidio and the coffee cup into the bedroom. Egidio leaned over the double canopy bed and lifted down an eight-inch carved ebony Christ.

"Why are you taking your sister's crucifix?"

"Pia is not my sister," Egidio said. "She is my wife."

For an instant Boyd forgot how to breathe.

Egidio smiled guilelessly. "Forgive the lie. But you would not have wanted a man with a real wife."

Boyd fumbled a cigarette to his lips and lit it from a shaking match. He slowly absorbed a new reality. "And might I ask why a man with a real wife wanted *me?* Was it my money?"

Egidio shook his head. "Be realistic. I have three children, a wife, a widowed mother. I want to own a house, start a business, send my sons to school. Your money is not enough for that."

"Whose money, then?"

"Whose do you think?"

"Stratiotis paid you?"

"Not as much as he paid you, but enough."

Egidio went to the bureau and collected the grinning snapshots of three children. He folded them one onto the other like a ladder of credit cards and made a cashmere nest for them in the suitcase.

"Are those nieces and nephews your children then?"

Egidio nodded. "Gian-Carlo, Maria, and Tonio."

A sour taste of losing and hating flooded Boyd's mouth. "You goddamned parasite!"

Egidio's hand paused on the suitcase handle. Steel slid into his eyes. "And you, you're different? Your penthouse, your clothes, your Renoirs—how did you earn those? Waving a stick?"

"Chagalls!" Boyd shouted. "They're Chagalls!"

"My eight-year-old girl paints better. And my seven-year-old boy waves a stick better. Goodbye, Boyd."

"Don't go."

"You'll find others, more sincere than me. You know now what to be on guard against."

"I didn't mean to shout. Please don't go."

A door slammed and Boyd winced and the future was no longer what it used to be.

Shaking, he poured himself a vodka and stumbled out onto the terrace to huddle in a canvas chair beside the marble ledge. There was a breeze coming up. In the street far below he saw the doorman helping Egidio with five suitcases and a trunk into a Checker cab.

He gulped enough vodka to soften the edges of the world. He realized there were decisions to be reached.

But not now.

Just for today, just for tonight, he'd push it all back to the horizon.

In the study, on the shelf behind the Mahler Society editions, was a silver box of cocaine with a tiny jade spoon inside the lid. He pressed a forefinger to his right nostril, lifted a tiny scoop of snow-white powder to the left, inhaled; reversed nostrils, inhaled again.

Gradually the pain in him dulled, as though a gleaming veil had fallen between him and it.

He had never before conducted at Avery Fisher Hall while high. He floated and thrashed through Bruckner's *Seventh Symphony*, lost his place, misturned pages, missed dynamics, stretched the adagio to a crawl and squeezed the finale to a screeching gallop.

Musicians exchanged glances, but three thousand subscribers jumped to their feet screaming approval, and the next day the critics gave Boyd Kinsolving the best reviews he'd had since the early concerts with Ariana.

At 10:45 A.M. the following Thursday, a short man wearing a rumpled black robe strode to the bench in the first district civil court in Ciudad Trujillo, Republica Dominicana. He balanced half-moon spectacles on his nose, squinted at his docket, and asked who was representing Señora Kinsolving.

A lawyer in shirt sleeves rose and identified himself.

The judge asked who was representing Señor Kinsolving.

The lawyer in shirt sleeves rose again.

The judge announced himself ready to hear arguments. He massaged a troublesome nerve at the side of his face. He interrupted the lawyer to ask if Señor Kinsolving opposed his wife's motion.

The lawyer shook his head.

The judge slammed his gavel against the table and pronounced Señora Ariana Kinsolving, under the laws of the Dominican Republic, a divorced woman.

The newspapers and magazines referred to Ariana and Boyd's divorce as amicable. One gossip columnist used the word *loving*.

Professionally, it was no divorce at all. They kept working together, and their agents kept drawing their contracts years in advance. Though they traveled to engagements separately and stayed in different hotels, photographers often caught them sneaking off to share a rehearsal-break espresso or an after-performance supper.

They still took bows together, and audiences gave them greater ovations than ever before.

Time magazine called them a model couple for the '60s. Their earnings doubled.

"Are you happy, sweetums?" Boyd asked Ariana.

They were sitting at a corner table in the Biffi Scala. The first-night audience had just given them twelve curtain calls for their *Puritani*, and diners at other tables were glancing at them with undisguised curiosity.

"I'm happier than I've ever been," she said. "I have my work, I have a wonderful conductor who never hurries me or drowns my voice, and I have Nikos."

"I hope he doesn't hurt you."

"Nikos is the kindest man on earth. And you—are you happy?"

Boyd stared into his glass of Chateau Margaux. "Happy enough. I have a new friend. But sometimes I miss us."

She laid her hand across his. "But we still have each other and we always will. Now tell me about your new friend."

20

"WE'RE MEETING HOLLY CHAMBERS," NIKOS SAID. "I HAVE A SUR-
prise."

Ariana looked at him, his face as composed and blank as the profile
on a Roman coin. A winged telepathy brushed her. *The divorce—he's
gotten it!*

The limousine swung to a smooth stop. The driver held the door.
Ariana stepped out and stared at the spotless façade of a five-story
brownstone. There were thick boxwood hedges and bubble-glass leaded
French windows and balconies of curving wrought iron.

"Has Holly moved his office to an embassy?" she asked.

"It's not an embassy," Nikos said. "And it's not Holly's."

Holly was waiting for them in the entrance hall. He gestured toward
two bronzes set in niches by the front door. "Venus and Adonis, sixteenth century, Renaissance Italy. Attributed by the former owner to
Benvenuto Cellini, but who knows?" He nodded toward two six-foot
china-blue vases flanking the rose marble staircase. "Lowestoft—au-
thenticated by Parke-Bernet. I got the former owner to throw them in.
Why don't we start the tour downstairs?"

Ariana could not believe the thirty-two-room townhouse. There were
two kitchens, ten bedrooms, eight baths. With each room they entered,
she felt a weight of premonition grow heavier.

She turned to Nikos. "Why are you showing me this place?"

"Don't you like it?"

"I've never seen any house so magnificent."

"That had better mean you love it, because it's yours."

Holly handed Ariana a key ring and a heavy envelope. "Your front
door; your deed."

Ariana's hand shook as she opened the envelope. Nikos had put the
house in her name.

She couldn't speak. Her mind was racing back through all the tiny
rooms she had called home. She stared at the deed a long moment and
then she stared at the wall with its carved molding and panels. But she
was gazing past it and seeing the future.

She walked quickly into the next room. It was large enough to be a
ballroom. In the mirrored walls she saw a hundred faintly tarnished re-
flections of herself.

Nikos came after her. "We can change anything you don't like."

"Do we have to move in before we're married?"

"Darling, this is a perfect home for us. You can sing, I can work, we
can entertain, we have ten bedrooms to make love in—"

"Why can't we marry first?"

His eyes glowed darkly. "I can't understand you. You have me already. You think making me a husband will make anything better?"

Her mind curled around a doubt. "Nikos, are you ever going to marry me?"

He sighed. "Maria-Kristina will only consent to a divorce if I give up the right to see my daughter."

"But surely you can persuade her *somehow*."

He cracked his knuckles and in the empty room they sounded like a rifle shot. "I've tried. Believe me. I've tried."

"Then she's holding your daughter hostage."

He nodded. "Unfortunately, that seems to be the case."

"She must love you. She must love you as much as I do."

She told herself she needed his warmth to take the chill out of her life. She moved into the house with him and slipped into the wide spaces of his love. For three months she was happy.

There was a great deal to be done: servants to be interviewed, decorators hired. A wall had to come out of the morning room, and that meant interviewing architects and it meant saying a last-minute no to the Met, who had scheduled her as Donna Anna in a benefit *Don Giovanni* in February.

She had hoped to have Siegliende in *Die Walküre* ready in time for a May opening, but had to wire La Scala her regrets.

She tried to see Austin Waters three times a week for coaching, but for two weeks in March she had a cough and had to cancel everything except a few unavoidable parties, which she went to solely to please Nikos.

One day in April 1970, she thought to check whether the maid had kept the ivories on the Steinway clean. She hit a chord and vocalized on the first phrases of Musetta's waltz. The high B croaked out of her throat like a frog, ugly, grotesque, foreign.

She was swept by a wave of disbelief. *Two weeks have slipped by, and what have I done?* She canceled the decorators and threw herself into work. It took five panicky weeks to get back what she had lost in two.

That was the month of changes. Nikos turned unpredictable. She sensed an impatience budding within him. Deep creases pulled down the corners of his mouth and the wide rooms of the house seemed too narrow to contain whatever it was he was feeling.

"Nikos, how was your day?"

Sullen eyes flicked up at her. "Do we have to talk about it?"

She retreated to her practice studio on the top floor. It was a bright space, private and quiet. In a way it belonged to the girl she had never been allowed to be. There were colorful French lithographs, shelves of exotic plants and hand-painted porcelain dolls, and most important of all, there was a six-and-a-half-octave Boesendorfer spinet with a specially designed rack to hold vocal scores open.

She shut Nikos out of her mind, refused to think about his silence. She inhaled, struck a C-major chord, and vocalized.

The following Thursday, after a long fruitless meeting with the directors of two Manitoba uranium mines, Nikos let himself into the Sutton Place townhouse. A voice floated down from the top story.

"*Pace, pace, mio dio . . .*"

A surge of impatience flashed through him. He slammed the front door. The house was suddenly still. He jabbed the elevator call button twice, hard. A moment later he could hear the elevator sighing softly down the shaft. The door opened. A handsome young woman stepped out. Nikos moved aside, surprised.

She smiled at him. Her pale blond hair was cut short and simply combed.

"I beg your pardon," he said.

"I'm sorry," she said. "I didn't mean to hog the elevator."

He stood staring after her, struck by the gentleness of her voice. A moment later she had vanished through the front door.

Ariana found Nikos standing on the balcony outside the French windows in the living room. A cloud of cigar smoke drifted indoors.

"Who was that young woman?" he asked, not turning. He was scowling down at the dark green of the Sutton Place private park.

"You must mean Vanessa, my pupil. She comes every Thursday."

His lips narrowed into a thin line.

"You slammed a door," she said.

"Haven't I a right to slam doors in my own home?"

She saw in some undefinable way that he was no longer the man she had agreed to live with. "What's annoying you, Nikos?"

He sighed. "Why should I be annoyed? Haven't I got everything? A fine life in a fine house with a fine singer?" He plucked the cigar from his mouth and tossed it angrily to the lawn below.

"Nikos, we share the park with our neighbors."

"We share too much. There's no privacy."

She had an astonished sense that after a mere three months he was turning against the house. "Do you want to sell this place, get another?"

"What good's another house? I'll still hear your voice."

She stepped back from him. "You're angry at—*my voice?*"

He put an arm around her. "I love your voice. I worship your voice. But I can't stand hearing you practice. And in this house, the way we live, there's no way *not* to hear you practice."

"Even when I close the doors?"

He nodded. "It's amazing the neighbors haven't complained."

She felt a sting of embarrassment, as though strangers had been seeing her naked at an unshuttered window. "What should we do, soundproof the room?"

"I don't want workmen here again. We've had too many of them."

"But if you don't want to hear me . . ."

"We'll get you a place of your own to practice. An apartment in a different building."

Through the swell of her own surprise, she could see a sort of justice to the idea. He needed moments to be with himself, just as she needed to be with her music.

"All right," she said. "I'll practice in a studio. But it has to be a beautiful studio—as beautiful as my room here."

He hugged her and she felt he loved her more at that moment than he had in months. "You're an angel," he said. "We'll make it the most beautiful artist's studio in all Manhattan."

Ten days later Nikos excitedly told her that a real estate agent had found the perfect place. It turned out not to be a studio, but a four-room apartment stuffed with carved seventeenth-century French maple furniture. An utterly out of place Steinway concert grand hulked before the north window, practically blotting out the view of Central Park South.

"Nikos," she cried, "who chose these things?"

He looked hurt. "I thought you'd like them."

"They're lovely. But . . ."

When she saw the bedroom, she felt surprise shot through by wariness. The gold silk spread on the four-poster canopy bed matched the draperies and the walls.

"I didn't realize I was expected to spend the night."

"You might want to nap."

In the blue marble bathroom she found a Jacuzzi, a needle-point shower—and a bidet.

"What is it?" Nikos said. "Something you don't like?"

She stared at him and realized he didn't understand, didn't even *see*. "Do you think all you have to do is drown me in mink coats and jewelry and co-op apartments? Is that what you really think?"

"What have I done wrong?"

She kicked the bidet. "Why do I need that thing in a practice studio? Why do I need that bed from a French king's whorehouse? What are you giving me, Nikos—a love nest and carte blanche?"

Understanding seemed finally to come to him. He covered his eyes. "That stupid agent. He misunderstood my directions. I'll have this plumbing torn out. I'll have that bed burned."

"The agent doesn't matter. Don't you see what matters?"

He wore a look of utter pathetic bafflement.

"Won't you ever think of me the way I think of you? Won't you ever understand or care?"

"How can I show you I care?"

"Maybe you can't. Maybe you don't. Oh, Nikos, I didn't mean that. Just hold me."

He held her.

The agent removed the bidet, but Ariana decided, on second thought, the bed was too pretty to let go.

"An Escher retrospective!" Carlotta's cry of disbelief filled the entire front room of "21." "Of all the ways to spend an evening! You might as well wash your hair and watch TV."

Ariana's finger played with the tines of a shrimp fork. "I was between *Toscas*. Nikos was called away on business. I'm always at loose ends when he vanishes like that."

Carlotta's eyes changed. There was a sudden alertness in them. "What night was this opening?"

"The tenth. Last Wednesday."

"Now that's funny. Last Wednesday . . . I'm sure it was last Wednesday . . . Nikos was at Mimsy Maxwell's."

"That couldn't be. Nikos flew to Riyadh Wednesday morning and he wasn't back in New York till Friday."

Carlotta sat straight, distancing herself in her chair. "Darling, I saw him at Mimsy's. I have a feeling I'm putting my foot into something, but three dozen other people saw him too."

It struck Ariana that Carlotta had no reason to make up such a story, let alone to tell an outright lie. She very slowly set down her glass of chilled Chablis. "Did I miss a good party? Tell me who else was there."

Carlotta began running off a list. Ariana cut her short.

"What about that sweet girl from that Italian principality? Was she there?"

It took Carlotta a moment to remember, or to pretend to have to. "You mean Principessa Maggie? Yes, she made quite a sensation. She has lovely taste in colors."

Ariana prodded an olive out of her salade Niçoise. "And Principessa Maggie's husband was there too?"

"The pianist? No, poor thing, he had to play at another party. I have a feeling that marriage is in trouble."

"Then who was Principessa Maggie with?"

"With?"

"Someone must have brought her."

"That handsome, handsome editor who runs four miles every morning around the Central Park reservoir. You've met him—John Thatcher, Thacker, he has adorable brown eyes and a yummy flat tum."

Ariana had a dim memory of an editor with one of the men's magazines who jogged in Central Park and talked about it at dinner parties. "He's gay, isn't he?"

Carlotta adopted a tone of mild reprimand. "Darling, as if it mattered."

It did matter, though not in the way Carlotta meant. "Did Principessa Maggie and Nikos talk?"

Carlotta shrugged. "Now I admit I'm a gossip, but I'm not the CIA—and I didn't have a microphone planted in their corner."

Ariana let two beats go by. "They were in a corner?"

"That little alcove. Mimsy has hung that dreadful Dubuffet in it. What in the world she sees in a hack like Dubuffet—" Carlotta saw Ariana's face and stopped short. "Oh, my dear, I've upset you. Forgive me."

"Just tell me how long," Ariana said softly. "How long were you in the corner with her?"

Nikos moved to the window. "I can't believe I'm hearing this."

She got up from the sofa. Her feet marked out four careful steps on the Aubusson carpet. She whirled. "I can't help what I am, Nikos. I have feelings. Pain is real to me."

Nikos gave a sigh of dwindling patience.

"I bend myself out of shape believing the things you tell me." She heard the thin, berating sound of her own voice and hated it. But it was too late to stem the eruption of words. "You say your flight to Riyadh was delayed eight hours. You didn't want to upset my plans, so you didn't phone. But when you tell me Lucius Griswold happened to be in the VIP lounge, and—"

"And he suggested we go to Mimsy's and kill a couple of hours. What's so incredible about that?" Nikos seized the telephone from the end table and thrust it at her. "Go ahead. Ask Lucius. Let him see how deeply you trust me."

She clung to a narrowing margin of belief. "That's not it, that's not what I mean at all. I trust you, I *do*."

"You certainly have an original way of showing it."

"I'll believe anything you tell me so long as you—"

He was winding his watch, the Patek Philippe she had given him for his birthday. "So long as I what?"

"Can't you—at least respect me?"

"Respect?" He glanced toward her. "You harangue me like this and accuse *me* of disrespect?"

She fought to maintain some sense of direction. It was as though she were onstage, lost and flailing in a welter of screaming brass. *Where am I? What's my next line, my next note?* "Why did you have to go to Mimsy's? Why of all places there?"

"It's my habit to go wherever I'm welcome."

"You arrive without me at a party where we're both known. You spend three hours tucked in a corner with that—that child. Don't you see how it looks?"

"Maggie and I spoke ten minutes. We were not tucked anywhere, we were standing in Mimsy's garden with forty other people. And I very much resent your accusing me of being interested in her, let alone of pursuing her in full view of your friends and mine."

"I didn't mean that, I never said that!"

"Then just what *are* you saying?"

She sank to the sofa. "I'm saying I love you," she whispered. "And I'm so frightened . . . of losing you."

He came and put his arms around her.

She let the silence of the moment fill her. "It feels so good when you hold me like this. When I close my eyes I can't be sure where you end and I begin."

"That's the way it's meant to be. That's the way it could be, if only you'd let it." He took her hands in his. "Why do you hate that little girl? It's unworthy of you."

"I don't hate her." Ariana's eyes lifted uncertainly to meet his. "I don't even know her."

"That's the problem." He didn't speak, and then light flickered in his glance. "I have a solution. Invite her to dinner."

She pulled back. "Nikos, it's not important—truly it's not."

"But it *is* important. When a horse throws you, you have to get right back on. Otherwise the fear stays with you. This little girl has thrown you. We'll have her to dinner next Tuesday."

"I'm in Rio singing next Tuesday."

He squeezed her fingers. "A week from Tuesday then."

Protest lumped in her throat. "But we've invited the Chapins."

"Then we'll make it a party." He placed a quick kiss to the left of her mouth. "I want to show off my brave Ariana."

She made three mistakes. She gave the party. She invited sixty-two guests. And on her right she seated Simmy Simpson, a gossipy, bald, two-time Pulitzer Prize-winning author.

It was during the crayfish bisque that Simmy leaned close and whispered, "I must say, dear heart, you're a sport to have la principessa in your house."

Ariana held her face in a mask. She felt her life about to be wiped out with a single swipe of a gossiping tongue.

"After the way she and Nikos have been flaunting themselves all over town . . . I mean, you *do* know, don't you?"

Simmy sipped at his Perrier, watching her over the rim of the glass, his pink eyes glinting under tweezed eyebrows. Her heart was thumping so hard at the base of her throat that no reply could force itself out.

Simmy read her silence. "Oh, dear," he said, "I do hate to bring bad tidings to a sit-down dinner. I'm always afraid the hostess will signal one of the servants to poison me."

Ariana managed a smile. "I wouldn't poison you tonight, Simmy. We're having white chocolate mousse especially for you. Besides, you're not telling me anything I didn't already know."

"Then you knew they were looking at diamonds at Harry Winston's?"

For one helpless moment, Ariana's eyes scanned the sea of dinner jackets and naked shoulders. She saw Nikos far, far away, smiling and tanned and gracious, deep in conversation with the wife of the Dutch ambassador to the U.N.

Tonight she had wanted to make him proud of her. From head to foot, from silk underwear to Chinese mandarin jacket and embroidered satin pajamas, she had dressed in brand-new clothes. She looked like no one else at the party. She had done it for him, but he hadn't spoken to her all evening, hadn't even noticed.

Somehow she found words. "Of course I knew. I asked Maggie to help Nikos pick out earrings for our anniversary. So he could think he was surprising me."

"Anniversary?" Simmy lifted an eyebrow. He had a connoisseur's ear for falsehood.

"It's twenty-three years since we met."

He smiled. "How romantic. But why ask Maggie to help commemorate the event?"

Ariana glanced across the garden. At the table under the farthest corner of the striped canopy, Principessa Maggie shimmered in black silk, laughing and clinging to the arm of the president of the Chase Bank and waving a champagne glass. Two gold bracelets, broad and bold as leather straps from a Greenwich Village sex shop, flashed on her arm. "Maggie has exquisite taste," Ariana murmured.

Simmy's mouth puckered grimly. "*Entre nous,* dear heart, nail down everything you cherish, and I mean everything. La principessa is going to be needing a husband very soon."

Ariana felt a sudden inward pressure just below the sternum. "What about the one she has?"

"You don't see him here, do you?"

"He couldn't come. He's playing piano at East Hampton."

"Mmm-hmm." A faint smile lopsided Simmy's lips. "My informant tells me Mr. Principessa got home from one of those gigs and did not like what greeted him when he flicked the bedroom light switch. She's a tramp, m'dear, and I can cite chapter and verse." He lowered his voice. "Not a whisper to anyone, but a very au courant friend whose initials are Brewster Cardinal McHenry tells me there's a papal annulment in the works."

Ariana somehow got through dessert and coffee and Simmy's chitchat, and then she slipped upstairs and locked herself in the guest bathroom. A racking cough took her. She bent over the toilet and vomited. When there was nothing left to throw up she washed her hands and face, gargled with cold water, emptied her mouth into the sink.

There was blood running down the drain.

For a moment her fingers wouldn't work. She couldn't turn faucets or wring face cloths dry. She thought, *This is death. I'm dying.* She ran the water loud and sat on the closed toilet and prayed.

Dear God, don't let me die alone.

Finally the burning pressure eased a little in her chest.

The bathroom connected two guest rooms and she opened the door on the river side to let in some air. Music and chatter drifted up from the garden. She straightened the hand towel with its single *A* monogram, not paying attention as the mirrored panel swung outward and reflected the dark bedroom. But then her eye was caught by two figures on the balcony, a man and a woman. They were whispering. The woman stepped into the light.

Ariana recognized Principessa Maggie. She turned quickly, not wanting to recognize the man. But she knew. It was as though she had been stabbed across the face.

She got out of the bathroom and down to the hallway one floor below. She stiffened when she saw Nikos coming down the stairs. He was chatting animatedly with Ron Harkins, the man in charge of raising $20 million for the Metropolitan Museum.

Nikos passed and touched her arm and smiled.

Principessa Maggie strode down the stairs thirty seconds later. She was holding the hand of the editor with the flat tum. Her high-skirted dinner suit showed long flashes of thigh and teasingly narrow peaks of breast. Heads turned up toward her in one continuous ripple. "Can you forgive us, Ariana?" she said. "We've got to run."

Ariana mustered disappointment. "Let me find Nikos—he'll want to say goodnight."

"I honestly haven't time. I'll phone."

Ariana was aware of a valley of silence around them as she saw Principessa Maggie and her escort to the door.

There was a row of limousines double-parked in front of the townhouse. Their taillights glowed. The principessa tossed a Fendi fox skin around her neck. It perfectly matched her hair.

"Nikos said you did this whole party for me."

"Just for you and a few friends."

"You're an angel to go to all that trouble for someone you hardly know." The principessa kissed Ariana on the cheek. "Next time it's my treat, all right?"

Finally they were alone.

"You've been seeing her." The words left an emptiness in Ariana's throat.

Nikos glanced up at her from the sofa. "Who?"

"Your principessa. Everyone knows you've been seeing her."

He smiled tolerantly, almost with amusement. "And when do you think I've had a chance to see her?"

She looked at him, hating his calm. "When you're not home. When you're not at work."

"And when's that?"

"All the time. You've been taking her all over town."

"Where?"

"You were at Harry Winston's looking at diamonds."

"When?"

"Don't lie to me, Nikos. The whole world knows and the whole world's laughing."

Nikos rose and came across the living room to put an arm around her. "Then the whole world's as foolish as you."

She pushed him away angrily. "And just what kind of fool do you take me for?"

His eyes darkened. "A fool who's tossing off accusations a little too easily."

"I've every right to accuse. And I've every right to an answer."

"You're like a phone off the hook. I'm not going to listen until you stop making those terrible noises."

She picked up a crystal cigarette box and swung with it. Nikos caught her arm. They grappled. The box shattered on the floor and cigarettes rolled across the parquetry.

Nikos was shouting now. "I am my own master! Get it through your childish head that I obey no one! If I want to wear a plaid hat, I wear a plaid hat! If I want to drink milk, or go to Tahiti, or buy control of IBM, I ask no one's permission!"

"And if you want to make love to your principessa?"

His gaze passed slowly, silently across her. "I warn you only once more, Ariana, I will not stand for jealousy."

"And I won't stand for humiliation!"

"Then we're in full agreement." He turned his back on her and strode from the room.

"Nikos!" She ran to the empty stairway. She heard the front door slam.

She went to bed. Fears started. At first little fears of not being able to fall asleep, then greater fears of being alone at three o'clock in the morning.

She took a sleeping pill. Two hours later she took another.

He didn't come home all that night.

He didn't come home the next morning.

Panic gnawed at her throughout the day.

She taught Vanessa that afternoon at her studio. All through the lesson she was waiting for the phone, for Nikos.

From the corner of her ear she heard something she didn't like in the coloratura section of "Caro Nome." She cut Vanessa short. "Pay attention to that run in broken sixths. You're cheating on the low notes. A lot of singers think they can get away with that but it doesn't fool anyone who knows how to listen."

Austin Waters struck a chord, and Vanessa began the passage again.

Ariana sat bolt upright in her chair, her eyes narrowed, hearing nothing except the phone not ringing.

She realized Vanessa had finished the aria She rose, turning her head a little away from her pupil, looking at the darkening window.

I can't concentrate, she realized. *I can't concentrate on all this singing. I have a life to worry about.* "We're going to have to change our schedule," she said. "I'll see you every other week from now on."

Her tired, dark eyes tried to meet the girl's brilliant gray-green ones with polite apology. They couldn't, and she looked down at herself in embarrassment.

Her glance fell on the locket. Something drew her finger to the gold and amethysts. They felt cool to her fingertip, almost cold, as though the stones were reproaching her.

Vanessa's deep questioning gaze came up at her anxiously. "Are you unhappy with something I've done?"

"Of course not. I just have some problems that require my attention. We'll get back to our regular schedule in a month or so."

21

THAT EVENING BEFORE THE PERFORMANCE ARIANA FOUND TWO dozen red roses waiting in her dressing room. Relief surged in her like a sudden fever. "How sweet of Nikos!"

The dresser was stitching the frilled blouse that Ariana would be wearing in Act Two of *Adriana Lecouvreur*. Her needle paused. "They're not from Mr. Stratiotis, madame."

Ariana reached between the rose stems, found a note and cut her finger ripping the envelope open.

For an unforgettable evening, untellable thanks—Maggie.

"Madeleine—" She fought to keep her voice from rising. "Take these flowers up to the plaza and burn them."

"But wouldn't you rather send them to the hospital?"

"I want them burnt before I step on that stage." Ariana thrust out the card with its ludicrous royal crest. "And burn this too."

Nikos did not show up in the first intermission. He did not show up in the second. By the final curtain, Ariana had suffered three nervous memory lapses and missed an attack on a high B.

At home she found no note, no apology, no flowers. She questioned the servants. They had had no messages from him.

She went to bed. Sleep did not come. In the morning, when daylight touched the silk brocade of the armchair, the pillow beside her was still empty.

Two nights was all she could take of it. She phoned his office. They claimed not to know where he was. She tried to force herself to think rationally. A lover might vanish, even a husband might vanish, but the ruler of Wall Street could not simply disappear. Someone would know.

The newspapers, she realized.

Not her newspapers, but the servants'. The newspapers servants read always knew things no one else would mention.

She sat down in the chair with the cook's *Post* and the maid's *Daily News*. The print was shaking so hard she could barely read it. She spread the papers on the table. She hated her eyeglasses, but she wore them now. Forefinger guiding her line by line, she bent forward to search the gossip column.

She phoned Austin Waters. "I've got to see you." She could hear a student in the background, vocalizing badly.

"Okay, I can fit you in at four-thirty. And, Ariana, be on time?"

❀ ❀ ❀

When she came in the door, Austin looked at her for one smoky instant, marched to the piano, and clunked a loud A-major chord—her signal to sing the arpeggio.

She closed the keyboard lid over his fingers and slapped the *Daily News* clipping onto the music stand. "Lunch at Delmonico's, tea at the Plaza—dinner at Côte Basque!"

Austin squinted. "The girl must have a tapeworm."

"Look at his arm in that picture—not just touching her—*holding* her!"

"For ten years Mr. Stratiotis has made it a point to be photographed with singers, actresses, models, lady newscasters, and millionairesses. Now will you tell me what is so special about Princess Maggie that she has turned you into a raving bitch?"

"He hasn't been home for two days."

"Who wants to come home to Medusa? He doesn't have to put up with it and he's serving you notice."

"Notice of what? That he's infatuated with that child?"

"Ariana—you're talking about a billionaire. You're talking about one of the biggest *shlongs* outside of porno films. He doesn't have to take crap from anyone, least of all an angry humiliated *pazza* like you. Let's warm up."

Austin hit the A-major chord again. Ariana didn't move or make a sound. He turned around on the bench.

"You have *Faust* in Paris in five days, so will you please *sing?*"

She placed an airline ticket over the open Schirmer score of vocalises. "Come to Paris with me."

"Christ, I have students! Ever hear of students?"

"I need you. I can't face it alone."

"You know, to some people Carnegie Recital and the Ninety-second Street Y can be just as scary as the Paris Opéra."

"Who of your students has a recital next week? Name one, just one, and I'll go to Paris alone."

Austin was silent. He picked up the ticket and flipped it open. "Where am I sleeping?"

"The Ritz—you have the room next to mine."

For four frantic days Ariana and Austin worked on *Faust*. She had mixed feelings about Charles Gounod, the composer. He struck her as a professor who had absorbed the pedantry rather than the inventiveness of Bach. His work was well crafted, noble of its sort, filled with good intentions—and unbelievable dullness. Yet the final trio, where Faust and the Devil fought for Marguerite's soul, was operatic drama of the first order.

Many an opera, Ariana reflected, held the stage simply because it had a knockout finale. *Faust* was one.

The first rehearsal at the Paris Opéra, soloists with piano, went poorly. Ariana could feel it and afterward she could feel Austin not saying it. "Can we walk?" she said.

"You'll be recognized."

An old woman was scrubbing the stairs. Ariana went to her.

"Madame, est-ce que je peux acheter votre fichu?"

The old woman looked up in surprise, saw who wanted to buy her kerchief, and pulled herself awkwardly to her feet. She took the kerchief off and apologized for getting it wet.

"Thank you. It will bring me luck," Ariana explained in her operatic French. She insisted on paying with a hundred-franc note, knotted the kerchief around her hair, and put on her dark glasses.

"Worth every centime," Austin said. "You look dreadful."

The paparazzi at the stage door eyed them and instantly dismissed them. Ariana took Austin's arm. The afternoon sky was cloudless and pale blue. A soft breeze pulsed down the Avenue de l'Opéra, driving the sounds and smells of Paris before it.

"Austin—I'm so goddamned afraid."

"Don't be. You have that role in your voice."

"I'm afraid of losing Nikos. Really losing him. For good."

Austin's look rebuked her. "The only thing that will lose him is that attitude."

"Promise?"

"Promise."

"In that case I want to go to the Tuileries for ice cream."

"Your diet."

"I can't diet before I sing Marguerite."

They strolled along the arcades of the Rue de Rivoli and the sculpted hedges of the Louvre. Screaming youngsters surged around them, and a flying kickball almost hit them. They came to a children's carousel. "Where there are wooden horses," Austin said, "ice cream can't be far."

Ariana went to save a place on one of the benches.

"Vanilla all right?"

She accepted a dripping cone from Austin's hand. "My favorite." She spread a Paris *Herald Tribune* on the bench.

"Where'd you get that paper?"

"Someone left it."

They sat and tasted their cones in silence.

"I wish I could have been a child here," Ariana said. "The ice cream's perfect. Every childhood should have one perfect thing." She licked slowly, making the vanilla last. Her gaze traveled up the sightlines of the garden and out along the distant sidewalks of the Champs Elysées, where cafés and trees and strollers seemed to exist in perfect natural balance.

"They say Paris is the capital of happiness. I can believe it. And I can believe it's the capital of loneliness for people who don't have anyone."

"That's a very Parisian thing to say."

"Thank you for being with me," Ariana said.

"It's my pleasure completely."

As they got up to go, Austin folded up the newspaper they'd been sitting on and placed it in a trash basket.

"You're awfully neat today, Austin."

"We're guests."

His neatness made her suspicious enough to go to the newsstand in the Ritz lobby while he was getting the room keys. She asked for a Paris *Herald* and hid it in her purse.

"I think I'll take a little nap," she said in the elevator.

"See you at six then?"

For all their pastel prettiness and cream trim, the walls of the suite oppressed her. She swung open the windows in the sitting room and pulled a chair into the sun.

She searched the *Herald* page by page, column by column.

In the Social Notes on page seven she read that Princess Maggie of Montenegro was in town, cochairing the International Orphans Ball at the Georges Cinq.

In the Business Notes on page nine she read that Nikos Stratiotis would be flying to Bucharest to discuss a natural gas pipeline with the Rumanians. His plane would be stopping tomorrow morning at Charles de Gaulle airport for refueling.

"Shouldn't have had that ice cream." Austin wagged his finger at her. "Spoiled your appetite."

They were sitting by the open French windows at an early dinner. Day still hovered faintly over the Place Vendôme, and sunset just managed to touch the statue of Napoleon at the top of his column.

"I think I'm coming down with something," Ariana said.

"You don't have a temperature, do you?" Austin's hand was cool and firm on her forehead. "You'd better lie down."

She couldn't even doze.

Nikos is meeting her . . . Nikos is meeting her. . . .

She didn't dare take more than two sleeping pills. Terrors kept tumbling through her.

What if Nikos should leave me?

He won't leave me. Please God. He won't leave me for her.

But what if he should decide to leave me?

He would never leave me for her.

But what if he should decide to leave me for that child? My God, what if he should decide to leave, what if he should decide, what if he should, what if, what then?

In the morning she phoned Austin's room. "My cold is worse. I'm staying in bed."

"What about rehearsal?"

"They'll have to use the girl who's covering for me."

"But the rehearsal is for *you.*"

"I can't do it!" she screamed, and slammed down the phone.

She put on a raincoat and her dark glasses and the cleaning woman's kerchief. She sneaked down the back stairs to the Rue Cambon and slipped into a taxi waiting at the cab rank.

For the next three hours, while seven soloists and the orchestra and chorus of the National Opera rehearsed without her, she raced through Charles de Gaulle airport. She checked arrival gates of flights from New York and departures of flights to Eastern Europe. Once she was certain she saw Nikos and twice she was sure she recognized Princess Maggie's back, but when she caught up with them they turned out to be astonished strangers.

Ariana was in no state of mind or voice to sing *Faust* that night. From the very first act, she knew she was racing toward disaster.

The opera opened as Doctor Faust sat in his study, old and disillusioned after a life spent trying to learn the secrets of the universe. He filled a cup with poison and called on the Devil. In a puff of stage smoke Mephistopheles popped through a trapdoor in the floor and proposed a bargain: youth and the joys Faust had missed in exchange for his soul. As an irresistible temptation, the Devil summoned up a vision of the maiden Marguerite.

At this point Ariana had to stand behind a scrim and be beautiful enough and young enough to induce the greatest intellectual of medieval Germany to give up his soul.

All she could think was, *Nikos doesn't want me . . . he doesn't want me. . . .*

It came almost as a surprise when Faust agreed to the bargain. In a second puff of smoke—long enough to allow Faust's wig and robe to drop through the trapdoor—Mephistopheles transformed him into a handsome young man.

Ariana did not sing until Act Two, the village festival, with citizens, soldiers, and students thronging the market square. Marguerite's brother Valentin, departing to join the army, prayed God to protect his sister. While Mephistopheles baffled the crowd with spectacular feats of magic, Faust offered his arm to Marguerite.

Ariana had to refuse modestly, but her tone came out dark and chesty, like Delilah vamping Samson, and there were titters in the audience.

The third act, the garden scene, went without major mishap. Mephistopheles placed a casket of jewels on Marguerite's doorstep. Musing romantically about Faust, she found the casket, opened it, and was delighted with the sparkling gems. Astonishingly, Ariana negotiated the coloratura of the Jewel Song and thought she even heard some bravas. It seemed to her there would have been more applause if the singer playing Martha, her neighbor, hadn't rushed into the next recitative, telling Marguerite she'd be a fool not to keep the jewels.

Mephistopheles and Faust entered. The Devil lured Martha into a corner of the garden. Faust ardently courted Marguerite, and she promised to meet him the next day. But Mephistopheles urged him not to wait.

Ariana flung open the flimsy stage window and sang of her desire for Faust. He cried, "Marguerite!" and rushed to her. Darkness fell and the Devil laughed.

Something went very wrong in Act Four, when Marguerite, now pregnant and abandoned, entered church and attempted to pray. Mephistopheles interrupted her and warned she would be eternally damned. It was all too close to what Ariana was feeling and fearing: her voice thinned to a hysterical sob.

She could feel waves of bafflement and annoyance sweeping the audience. Fortunately there was a distraction—a rousing soldier's chorus as Valentin returned victorious from war, only to learn of his sister's disgrace. When Mephistopheles sang a mocking serenade outside her house, Valentin rushed into the street, sword drawn, and was mortally wounded dueling with Faust. Marguerite ran to her brother, but with his dying breath he cursed her.

When the applause came at the fall of the curtain, sparse and grudging, Ariana felt the curse had been all too effective.

In the final act, after the witches' Walpurgis Night revel, Mephistopheles took Faust to the prison where Marguerite, now insane, had been sentenced to death for murdering her child. Faust begged her to escape with him, but she drew back in horror from the Devil.

Now came the climactic moment of the opera, the Trio, where Marguerite, repudiating Faust and the Devil, saw a shining angel and called upon him to save her.

Astonishingly, Ariana slipped on the climactic phrase "*Portez mon âme au sein des cieux*"—"Carry my soul to the bosom of heaven"—and sang "*Portez mon homme*," a shift of vowel that laughably changed the line to "Carry my man to heaven."

It didn't matter that her high B rang out secure and pure. There were guffaws and catcalls as Marguerite died. Mephistopheles cried, "Condemned!" and the audience applauded. Offstage angelic voices sang, "Saved!" and the audience hissed.

As the prison walls parted and Marguerite was carried to heaven on a wheezing hydraulic platform the audience was already hurrying in disgust from the house.

The reviews were killers. Reading them over café au lait in her bedroom the next morning, Ariana wished she were lying at the bottom of the Seine.

As she turned a page of *Paris-Matin*, her eye was caught by a photograph of a woman in dark glasses and babushka skulking beside the Bulgarian Airlines gate in Charles de Gaulle airport.

Her heart slammed against her ribs. *Why was the diva playing hooky from rehearsal?* the caption screamed.

Her eyes winced shut and she crumpled the page into the wastebasket. She lifted the phone receiver. "Give me international information, please—Sweden."

Austin answered Ariana's knock in his bathrobe, holding an electric blow-dryer.

"I can't come to dinner," she said.

"You're not going to let those bitchy reviews scare you."

"I still have a fever."

He returned to the mirror and went on drying his hair. "If you don't show up, people are going to think that *was* you in that frumpy photograph."

"I can't be bothered what people think."

Slowly his head turned and he looked toward her. "I think as guest of honor maybe you'd better be bothered."

"Baron Rothschild would be better off serving his guests rotten meat. You'll have to apologize for me."

He cut the dryer. "I'm an ivory-tinkling nobody. They'll murder me if I show up without you."

"Austin, it *was* me in the photograph. I was trying to catch Nikos and Maggie."

Austin stared at her. He sank back onto the bed. "Oh, Jesus."

"I've been crazy these last few days. I'm still crazy. Please phone the baron's house. Tell one of the servants. *Please*, Austin."

Austin glared at her, then crossed the room and phoned. He lowered the receiver slowly and met Ariana's eyes. "I don't think the House of Rothschild will be inviting you to too many more functions."

"It can't be helped." She studied herself in the dresser mirror. "I don't look like that photograph. Tell me I don't."

"You don't."

She kissed him. "Will you take care of Euro-Agency for me?"

He set the dryer down on the bed. "What's to take care of?"

"I can't sing the other *Fausts*. Don't look at me like that. You heard my voice last night."

He came barefoot across the rug to her and placed both hands on her shoulders. He spoke very distinctly, very slowly, like a diction coach. "Your voice is fine. It was a memory lapse."

She slipped free. "I have to get away from here."

"What the hell are you trying to do to your career—hara-kiri?"

"I have to rest!"

"And what do you think that $300 a night bed next door is for?"

"Don't shout at me, Austin!" She turned away from him, dropping her voice. "I thought you were my friend."

"I am your friend—not your manager, not your nursemaid. I'm not changing any more of your diapers. All that shit's between you and your defective superego."

"Why do you always have to get psychoanalytical with me?"

"It's time someone did, you crazy old bat."

She marched quickly to the door and slammed it behind her.

As she came back into her suite the phone was ringing. She didn't answer. A small Vuitton suitcase lay packed on the baggage stand. She opened it, frowned, added a sweater and some overnight items. She looked through her purse and made sure she had her passport and her airline charge card.

The phone rang again. She hesitated, then picked it up.

Austin's voice said, "Love you, honey."

"You called me old."

"All I meant was old enough to know better. You going to leave me some cash to get home on?"

Naturally she was going to leave him cash, but naturally she wasn't going to tell him in the middle of a fight. "No."

"You really have messed up my week, baby."

"And what about my life?"

"You call that madness a life?"

"The only life I have."

"I didn't mess it up, I'm not going to clean it up. That's your job. See you in Nueva York if you decide to honor your contract and sing there next fall."

"I keep my promises," she said quietly. "It's other people who don't keep theirs."

22

FIVE HOURS LATER ARIANA'S SAS JET TOUCHED DOWN UNDER THE mournful, windy sky of Stockholm. She transferred to a two-propeller plane and after an hour's flight she was waiting at a small airport near the Baltic.

She walked out of the shed. Winter lingered in patches of snow alongside the tarmac. A line of telephone poles stretched along the horizon like desolate church steeples.

"*Ti kano edho?*" she asked herself. What am I doing here?

She noticed a figure in the parking lot: a girl was wearing a flannel shirt and a woolen ski hat that made a violent red splash against the bare, white sky.

A wind blew in from the sea, bending the evergreens beside the runway. Ariana raised the collar of her fur.

The girl approached shyly. "Mrs. Kinsolving?"

"Yes?"

"I'm Renata Stratiotis. Mother sent me to meet you." The child had long blond hair and pale, perfect skin and eyes the color of the northern morning sky. "Is that all your luggage?" She couldn't have been more than sixteen years old.

"That's all," Ariana said, thinking *her mother must be beautiful.*

"You take one and I'll take the other. It's only a short walk."

They followed a narrow gravel road to the shore. The girl chatted pleasantly about flying and travel. She spoke English with an extraordinarily cultivated accent. They came to a small dock with a speedboat tied to it. "You first, Mrs. Kinsolving."

"Please, call me Ariana."

The girl placed the bags in the boat, held it steady while Ariana stepped in, and started the motor. She aimed the boat toward the horizon. The rush of ocean air blasted her hair out behind her.

"Care for a smoke?" The girl held out a thin, strangely malformed cigarette. "Panama red."

Ariana quickly shook her head. "No, thanks. I can't. My voice."

The girl opened the throttle full. The boat gouged into the sea with a sudden forward leap, bouncing and slapping and swerving neatly past shoals. By the time they reached the island and nosed to a stop at a stone jetty it was dark. Night had come quickly and early. The girl placed the bags on the dock. She made the boat fast and led the way up a gentle slope to a frame house.

"Mother," she called out.

A woman rose from a chair on the terrace and came forward. "How do you do? I'm Maria-Kristina." She had a friendly voice and pale gray-green eyes that looked closely at Ariana from the bright face of a middle-aged child. Ariana was relieved. Her hostess was beautiful, but not nearly as lovely as her daughter.

Maria-Kristina took Ariana's hand in a warm, firm grip. "What a great honor it is to meet you. It was very kind of you to come."

"I invited myself. You're kind to have me."

"No, no, it's a pleasure. We collect all your records."

A gray-haired woman with a limp appeared, as if by signal, in the doorway of the house.

"Ilse, Mrs. Kinsolving would like some—" Maria-Kristina glanced at Ariana. "Coffee?"

"Thank you. Coffee would be wonderful." Ariana stared up at an astonishingly clear sky. There was something unfamiliar in the way the stars had grouped themselves. They told her she was in a new latitude, a thousand miles from the Paris stage where she was scheduled to perform. She sighed. "I have no business being here."

"This is Nikos's house, and any friend of his is welcome."

"You can't mean that."

"But of course I do."

"Has he spoken about me?"

Maria-Kristina laughed pleasantly. "It's six years since I've heard his voice. But I read the British papers."

The servant appeared with a tray of coffee and vanished again.

Ariana was suddenly aware of the serenity of this moment, this island, this night. "I want to marry Nikos," she blurted.

A speedboat screamed past.

"That's just Renata," Maria-Kristina said. "She loves to drive her speedboat in the dark."

"I want to marry Nikos but he can't divorce you if you won't share custody of Renata. Why are you refusing? She's his daughter too. He loves her as much as you do."

Maria-Kristina leaned forward to set her cup down on the table, and the lamplight suddenly glowed in her red-blond hair. "You've had a long trip. Why don't you rest? Tomorrow we can talk."

"You're not going to give me an answer."

"It's too long an answer for tonight. Come. I'll show you the guest room."

Ariana awoke in the middle of the night. Moonlight was spilling across the goose-down quilt. Her mouth was dry and she felt a need for ice-water. She explored her way through dark rooms and found the kitchen.

Nikos's daughter was sitting at the table, profiled in moonlight. The air had a sweet, herbal smell. An ember winked in an ashtray on the table.

"Am I disturbing you?" Ariana said. "I wanted some ice-water."

The girl's head came around. "I'll get it for you." She went to the cabinet and the refrigerator and the sink, and a moment later she handed Ariana a tall cool glass.

"Do you often sit in the dark?" Ariana said.

"I like the dark. It helps me think."

Ariana sipped, interested in this girl who might one day be her step-daughter. "What do you think about?"

"To tell the truth, I was thinking about you. I envy you. You're doing something with your life."

"I sing. It's not very much."

"It's a gift. People admire that."

"Do you really think it matters what people admire?"

"Father thinks so." The girl sighed. "I wish I had a gift."

"Everyone is gifted in one way or another," Ariana said.

"How am I gifted?"

"I don't know you well enough to say. Do you smoke that marijuana all the time?"

"Not around Mother. She disapproves. Do you disapprove?"

"I don't approve of it for myself. Why do you smoke it?"

"The same reason I sit in the dark. It helps me think. It helps me not think. It helps."

The moonlight caught the girl's eyes, turning them into fragments of shattered glass. For an instant Ariana had a glimpse into a life as troubled as her own.

"You seem lonely," Ariana said.

"Isn't everyone?"

"I'd like to be your friend."

It was a moment before the girl answered. "I think we both need friends. I'd like to be yours." She held out her hand.

Ariana squeezed it.

In the morning a gray fog had settled over the beach, and Ariana could hear gulls chattering on the shale. It was a sunny day, with a touch of Baltic spring. After breakfast Maria-Kristina took her on a tour of the island.

They walked through pastures and pine groves. Maria-Kristina pointed out flowers and plants that grew nowhere else in the world. There was a beautiful outgoing warmth in her eyes. She spoke of herself and how she had come to the island and, gradually, Ariana was able to put together part of the story of Nikos Stratiotis's wife.

The daughter of a well-to-do Stockholm fruit importer, Maria-Kristina had taken her junior college year abroad in America. There she had fallen in love with the dark brown eyes and the big mustache and the six foot one of Nikos Stratiotis. After a long courtship with, on her side, many hesitations, she had married him. Eight months later—she admitted this with a smile—she had given him a daughter. For the next ten years she had been happy with him.

"But as you know, happiness with Nikos is strenuous. He demands perfection. You have to dress right, sound right, not complain when he cancels dinner and vanishes for three weeks."

Their eyes met and Ariana smiled.

"Everything changed when I had to go into the hospital. I thought it was cancer. I didn't tell Nikos."

"Why not?" Ariana asked.

"Because we seemed to have a bargain, and my part was to be perfect. Cancer didn't fit in."

Ariana couldn't help feeling a desire to be close to this woman; and with it the sadness of knowing that it would never happen.

"Luckily it turned out to be a small cystoid fibroid. Coming out of anesthesia I realized that I had faced terror and survived—without any help from my husband. That was as terrifying as the possibility of cancer had been. I realized that not only would I never be able to count on him, I would never need to."

From the woods came the clear, hollow hammering of a woodpecker.

"After that the whole importance of my marriage began to shrink. The day came—I wasn't surprised—when he wanted his freedom. It didn't matter to me. I think maybe that hurt him, that it didn't matter. We separated. He was generous. He's still generous. And for the last six years I've been as happy without him as I ever was with him. I love this little island. For me, it's a little space of order and safety, tucked away from all the noise and heartbreak of the world."

"You didn't fight him on the separation?" Ariana said.

"Why should I have fought him? What did I need?"

"Then why won't you share custody of Renata?"

Maria-Kristina looked carefully at Ariana. "What has Nikos said about Renata?"

"He's said you won't give him visitation rights if there's a divorce."

Long shadows of pines reverberated like echoes in the landscape. Maria-Kristina's eyes, gray-green and speculative, met Ariana's.

"Nikos has never asked me to divorce him. He's never asked to visit Renata. If he wants a divorce, if he wants to share custody, I'll never stand in his way. Renata adores him. I'd be delighted for them to be closer."

It was not surprise that took Ariana's will to speak, but the shock of certainty too long delayed.

"I've made all of that quite clear to Nikos," Maria-Kristina said. "But perhaps he hasn't made it clear to you."

After a moment Ariana felt Maria-Kristina take her hand.

"Tell me the truth, Ariana. You know this man, you know what he is capable of, what he is incapable of. Do you really want Nikos Stratiotis?"

"I want him."

"In that case nothing halfway will work. You must fight for him more than you have ever fought for anything in life."

That evening, heart beating like a drumroll, Ariana placed two long-distance calls from the island. With the first, she instructed her European agent to cancel all appearances for the next two weeks. He howled in three languages, pleaded, cursed her, predicted ruin. With the second, she reserved plane passage home for the following day.

23

ARIANA WAS ABOUT TO FOLLOW THE BUTLER AND HER SUITCASES into the elevator when she heard footsteps. Nikos came down the marble staircase. He was dressed to go out.

She was on the verge of flinging it out in front of him: *I know you've been lying, I know everything!* But she had not realized the power his face had over her. As she met his gaze, every accusation in her melted. "Hello, Nikos. Are you going somewhere?"

"I have a business date."

"Now, in the evening?"

"Yes, now in the evening."

Suddenly she said, "Cancel it. Please."

"Do you cancel your operas for me?"

"Maybe you don't know everything I do for you."

He stared at her, shook his head, and crossed to the front door.

"Are you going to Maggie?" she blurted.

He turned. "Welcome back, Ariana. I'd forgotten what home was like with you."

Each day of that summer Ariana sensed the gap between her and Nikos grow wider. He spent most of his time out of the country. They did not vacation together. When they dined together, which was rare, it was at private dinners for sixty or more.

Her attitudes began changing. They seemed to belong to someone else. She began not caring.

In September she arrived at the Metropolitan for *Pagliacci* with barely time to get into costume, let alone warm up. She was able to vocalize a little during the Prologue, while the tenor singing Tonio stepped before the curtain and reminded the audience that though the drama they were about to see would be played by actors, it concerned human beings with real emotions.

The emotions in *Pagliacci* were jealousy and anger, and for Ariana they were a little too close to home that night. She hurried to her place onstage.

The curtain rose as a troop of actors arrived in a nineteenth-century Calabrian village. Tonio helped Nedda—Ariana's role—down from the wagon. Her husband, Canio, pushed him jealously away. The company went to the inn, and Nedda was left alone, longing to be as free as the birds flying in the sky. Though Ariana's voice pinched on the high note of her "Ballatella," the surging orchestral accompaniment pointed the climax and the audience applauded warmly.

Now Tonio approached and tried to make love to her. She struck him scornfully in the face with a whip.

Ariana was horrified to see blood on the baritone's cheek.

Tonio skulked away far enough to spy on a conversation between Nedda and Silvio, a villager who wanted her to run away with him. Alerted by Tonio, Canio interrupted the lovers, but Silvio managed to escape unrecognized. Canio began shaking his wife violently, but she refused to reveal her lover's name.

The other actors separated the quarreling husband and wife. It was time for the clown show.

Canio, enraged and heartbroken, hiding his feelings behind the clown's face, sang "Vesti la Giubba"—"Put on your costume"—one of the classic tenor showpieces in the repertoire. There were bravos as the curtain fell to mark a brief time lapse. When it rose again the villagers were bustling expectantly to their seats and the clown show began.

Nedda played Columbine, trysting with her lover Harlequin. Her husband Pagliaccio, the clown, played by Canio, burst jealously onto the little traveling stage. Harlequin escaped. Canio, confusing play and real life, cried, "A clown no more—I am a man!"

The audience of villagers stirred in confusion.

Nedda, trying to maintain her character, sang Columbine's teasing song. Canio, dropping all pretense, flung himself at her, demanding her lover's name.

Again, she refused to tell him.

He stabbed her. Silvio leapt onto the stage—too late. Canio killed him too. Then, turning to the horrified spectators, he cried, "*La commedia è finita!*"

Ariana couldn't help wondering, as she took her bows and rode home alone, if the comedy wasn't finishing for her too. There were days when she couldn't practice at all, couldn't move, couldn't even think. She began canceling dates.

At first she canceled unimportant engagements: a *Lakmé* in San Diego; a *Butterfly* in Ghent. But one day the notion of flying seven hours filled her with unbearable queasiness, and she canceled a *Pirata* in Brussels. Two weeks later she found herself at home listening to a broadcast of a *Tannhäuser* at the Met that she should have been singing, and she felt a whisper of panic in her blood.

What am I doing to myself?

Finally Richard Schiller summoned her to his office. "Ariana, what the hell's going on with you? Eight cancellations."

He stared at her and she felt like a little schoolgirl with shame creeping hotly up her face.

"You're burning up a hell of a lot of track record awfully fast. The

Met says if you cancel the *Adriana Lecouvreur* gala, that's it. You'll no longer be *grata*, you'll no longer be hired. And believe me, a thing like that will ripple out. Even Bogotá won't want you. You've got to shape up."

"I know."

"Anything you want to talk to me about?"

She looked at this sweet tough man who knew everything about her career and nothing at all about her. She shook her head. "Thanks, Richard. I'm lucky to have you."

Ariana sang the *Adriana Lecouvreur*. She couldn't find her center, musically or dramatically. The *Times* review was scathing.

DiScelta jabbed her finger at the vocal score. "What in the world do you think you are singing?"

Ariana stopped in midphrase. "Aren't I singing the notes?"

DiScelta gazed a moment at her pupil with disgust, then slammed the score closed on the music stand. The strings of the piano, shocked into sympathetic vibration, sent out a ghostly chord.

"The notes, yes, but Donizetti wrote melody, damn it, melody!" DiScelta shook her head. "I can't make sense of all the senseless things you've been doing. What's wrong with you?"

She made two cups of blackcurrant tea with honey and Ariana tried to tell her.

Finally DiScelta set down her cup. "What are you—an artist or a silly courtesan?"

"I don't know who I am," Ariana whispered.

"Then make up your mind. The reason you are failing now, as a courtesan, as an artist, is that you're not paying attention to details."

Ariana sighed. "How can I bother with details?"

"My child, few things are certain in life except this: if the details are sloppy, the work fails."

"You don't understand—I love him."

"I do understand. You have sunk into love. I cannot help you with love. No one can. Perhaps you cannot even help yourself. But I *can* help you with music. And for you, music is life."

"A nightingale doesn't sing in a storm," Ariana said softly.

DiScelta slammed down her cup. "Nightingales are not professionals. Look at me, Ariana. If you must face life without this—this man—is it so dreadful?"

"For me it's dreadful."

"Then I can only tell you this. Not every problem has a solution, but all have answers."

"And what's the answer?"

"Let him go," DiScelta said, her eyes blazing. "Let him go!"

Ariana tried to keep up her lessons with Vanessa, but she found the endless hours spent rehashing the same old mistakes as difficult and draining as a performance.

"E-flat, Vanessa, it's written in the score, E-flat."

"I'm sorry."

"Let's take it from '*beltà funesta.*'"

Ariana could see Vanessa was scared, desperate to do everything right. And for some reason that made everything worse, and she wouldn't let her pupil do anything right.

"Why do you breathe there?"

Vanessa had no answer. She sank to the piano bench next to Austin. His hand closed gently over hers.

Ariana walked slowly to the window. It was raining. The skyscrapers of New York loomed hard and glistening under a leaden heaven. "Vanessa. We've got to talk about this." She pulled a chair over to the bench and sat down.

Vanessa peeped up at her.

"This isn't working. Our lessons just aren't getting anywhere."

Vanessa gave her a look of sheer terror. "Is it my fault? Am I doing something wrong?"

Ariana noticed a small movement from Austin Waters. His eyes snapped around to narrow on her silently.

She shook her head and realized how much she had dwindled. "No, it's my fault. I'm tired. I need a rest."

After a moment Vanessa rose and began gathering her scores.

Ariana couldn't bear the girl's obvious pain. "Perhaps we can have a lesson next month."

The girl turned quickly, eagerly. "Next month?"

"Or maybe—" Ariana could not meet the hope in her eyes. "Maybe the month after. I'll phone."

And then she was alone with Austin.

"Did you need to do that?" he said.

Ariana stood staring down at the gold chain around her neck, feeling the suddenly insufferable weight of the locket. "Leave me alone," she said. "Please. Just leave me alone."

"You're making a mistake."

"I don't care. Go."

Three rings, and then the principessa's answering machine. "Hi. This is Maggie. Beep."

"Maggie, it's Ariana—"

There was a click and a buzz and Maggie cut in. "Ariana? *Loved* your review this morning."

"Can we meet for a talk?"

The briefest of hesitations; a new wariness in the voice. "How about this morning?"

"Half an hour?"

"Come on over. I'll give you coffee."

The walls of Maggie's penthouse co-op on Beekman Place were light apricot and coffee turned out to be chilled Pouilly Fuissé served by a Norwegian girl. Ariana lifted her wineglass and pretended to smoke a cigarette and made small talk and tried to work up nerve to get to the point.

Maggie said, "Pleasant as this is, Ariana, I do have to think about changing for lunch. Was there something you wanted to talk about?"

Maggie had put on a wrap-around camel's-hair skirt, a beige and white pin-dot blouse with a brown vest flung over it. She wore a single strand of pearls. Ariana sensed it was Maggie's idea of a deliberately dull outfit, that Maggie had dressed down for her. Ariana felt inappropriate in her brand-new Givenchy. She realized that she and Principessa Maggie came from totally different solar systems.

"I came to apologize."

"What in the world for?"

"For resenting you." Ariana couldn't help thinking how good Maggie was at seeming amazed. "You must have known it. I've resented you from the moment we met."

Maggie gave her a hard, questioning look. "Why, because I'm younger?"

"Younger and a lot of other things too. Maybe it's because you've never known a moment's doubt in your life. You've always been attractive, always popular, always done well in private schools and on tennis courts and in ballrooms and rich men's dining rooms." *And bedrooms,* she thought. "I grew up in a slum on East 103rd Street and I never got a thing in life I didn't have to fight for."

Maggie stared at her with uplifted eyebrow. "You had the rough time and I had the easy time, is that it?"

It flashed through Ariana that this mustn't turn into an argument. *Play it like Verdi,* instinct said. *Direct, honest supplication. The waitress entreats the princess.*

"You know what I'm trying to say," Ariana said.

"I'm not sure I do." Maggie pressed her lips together and walked to the mahogany piano and began shuffling sheet music on the rack. It was as though she sensed what was coming and wanted to force Ariana to shout it so that the maid could hear it in the next room.

"Please ..." Ariana said. "Please don't take him from me. Please don't do it just to prove you can."

Maggie turned and gazed at her and the look of astonishment that came into her eyes did not seem forced this time. "You're talking about *Nikos?*"

Ariana nodded.

"I don't have to take things," Maggie said. "I accept them."

There was another silence and then, in a voice that was suddenly, inexplicably faint, Ariana said, "I love him."

"Perhaps you should tell Nikos that, not me."

"I don't see how you could love him the way I do. You don't even know him."

"Did I ever claim to know or love anyone? I'm attracted to a man, he's attracted to me. We flow with it till one of us gets tired of it and then we go our separate ways and it's a nice memory. What's the big fuss?"

"That's all Nikos means to you?"

"Nikos is a friend."

Ariana rose and felt herself swaying on unsteady legs. She took a step and looked out the window as though she had never seen a river before. "Are you going to deny you're sleeping with him?"

"We're friends and we have a marvelous relationship with trust and understanding."

"And you're sleeping with him."

Maggie drew her teeth across her lower lip, then gave her attention to one of her fingernails. "You have got to be one of the most naïve women I've ever met."

"I don't care what you think of me." Ariana knew her eyes must be shining in front of this child like hot spills of candle wax.

Maggie didn't answer. In the next room the pitch of the maid's vacuum cleaner had risen to a loud whine.

"I have a right to know the truth," Ariana said. "*Are you sleeping with him?*"

"Why don't you ask Nikos?"

"Would I be here if I had the courage to ask him?"

Maggie drew her head back to look at Ariana with a cool expression. "Let me give you some advice. You know a great deal about Puccini and Verdi, but you don't know much about men. I've had friendships with some of the outstanding men of our time, and the reason is, I never talk about them to other people."

"Nikos is all I have. You're young, you're beautiful, rich. You can have anyone. Please, let me keep him. Let me marry him."

Maggie shot her a look of almost withering pity. "But my poor little superstar, don't you realize it's not up to me?"

"But don't you realize it *is?*"

In the silence Maggie lifted her cigarette again. "Ariana, I'm going to tell you something about that privileged childhood of mine. A royal palace is as rough as any street in East Manhattan. Every minute you're dealing with people at their phoniest, their most manipulative. I had to be tough and show I wouldn't take bullshit from anyone. And frankly, I won't take it from you."

Suddenly Ariana felt strange and weak. "What do you mean?"

"I mean go to hell."

24

"THE WHOLE THING WAS PURE OPERA," MAGGIE SAID. "TEARS were running down her cheeks, *tears*, as if she were bidding adieu to life itself. I have to give her one thing: she's a real performer."

Nikos dropped into an armchair and closed his eyes. "Yes," he agreed softly, "a real performer."

"She actually has the notion that you're going to marry her."

He could see Maggie expected confirmation or denial.

"If it's none of my business," she said, "just tell me to butt out."

He stared at Maggie. He shook his head. "I never asked her to marry me."

Nikos called to Ariana from the living room when the limousine brought her home that night. She saw that the butler had laid a little table of cheese and fruit and French bread.

"Nikos, what a nice idea." *We're making up*, she thought. She spread some ripe Brie on a thick crust and held it out to him.

He didn't take it. "Are you pleased with your performance?" he asked.

"*Trovatore*'s never been my favorite," she said.

"That's not what I mean. You spoke with Maggie this morning."

The blood thudded so hard in her veins that his image trembled before her eyes. She was swept by a certainty that in two seconds the world was going to end, that her stupidity had caused it to happen.

"Do I have to remind you we're not married? I am free to have whomever I want in my life, and I intend to!"

Ariana felt a scream gathering inside her. She seized the knife from the wheel of Brie and thrust the handle at him. "Then why don't you just kill me and get it over with, for God's sake!"

Nikos looked at her. A strange trembling filled her. She half believed he might actually cry out, *Because I love you.*

"You've always had a flair for the drab," he said.

"You never loved me," she said. "Never. And the worst thing is, you don't love her either. And if you think she loves you . . ." She crossed to the window and stared down at the dark garden, wishing he would come up behind her and put his hand on her, knowing he wouldn't but wishing it anyway.

"I can't go on like this, Ariana—arguing day in, day out."

"You're trying to make it all my fault. But it isn't."

"I frankly don't care whose fault it is. I can't take another minute of this endless battle that you call living together."

She turned to face him. "You've never cared for me, have you? I was just a possession for you to show off."

"I thought I loved you. But maybe you're right. Maybe you're right about everything. Do you want to use my lawyer or do you want to get one of your own?"

At the mention of the word *lawyer* she felt her world racing toward death. "What do I need a lawyer for? We're not married."

"You can have what you want, Ariana. Anything. I don't want to hurt you anymore than I have."

"What makes you think you've hurt me? I'm not a child."

He sighed. "I'm sorry that I'm not made for belonging to someone the way you want me to."

Her eyes drank in the truth in little sips. She finally grasped his utter refusal to compromise. That refusal was his strength. It was him. She had loved a refusal. "You were my life," she said. "I would have done anything for you."

He didn't answer.

"Do you know something? Even now I want to plead. I want to say this is all my fault, I'll do anything to make it right."

"Don't—please."

"Don't worry. You can't humiliate me anymore, Nikos. The most you can do is destroy me."

"I won't sleep here tonight," he said. "I won't sleep here anymore."

She turned and walked to the elevator and pushed the button. She heard his silence behind her, dark like the onset of night. She realized she was alone now. Not just alone waiting for an elevator to take her to her room, but alone for the rest of her life.

She didn't know how long she lay on the bed biting her lip and sobbing. At some point during the night she heard the front door closing, and she knew Nikos had gone.

She pulled herself to her feet and crossed to the oak chest of drawers. With a sidewise swipe of her hand she cleared it of perfume bottles, figurines, dolls, lamps. She smashed her fist into the mirror but she was still there, multiplied into a half-dozen silvered fragments, a Picasso with running mascara and a locket flying like a yo-yo at her bosom.

She felt a surge of hate and rage. She yanked the locket loose and hurled it to the floor. She went into the bathroom, leaned over the sink and let herself collapse like a wave.

The mirrored door of the bathroom cabinet swung open and caught her reflection. She stared at herself. Her eyes were pools of fatigue. She saw there was a bottle of Seconal capsules in her hand.

It was not so much making a decision as carrying out one already made. She shook what seemed two dozen pills into her palm, lifted them quickly to her mouth and took ten long gulps from a glass of water.

She heard a crash.

The woman in the mirror was in violent movement, pummeling the drinking glass against the edge of the sink, stabbing at her wrist with a handful of sawtoothed fragments.

She watched blood whirlpooling down the drain. A sort of peace engulfed her. Nothing hurt. Nothing mattered. *I should have done this long ago,* she thought.

She half closed her eyes. Sounds mingled and faded. And then a figure stepped silently into the bathroom. A man.

For an instant the light enclosed him like the background in a sixteenth-century Flemish painting. He was gazing at her with a kind look, a look she remembered from long ago, a look of caring, of consoling, of being a part of someone.

He was wearing a dark suit, and at his neck was the narrow white strip of an Anglican collar. He took her wrist. "Don't do that."

It was Mark's voice. He looked absurdly young and handsome in his clerical collar and dark jacket.

"Mark?" she said wonderingly.

He pulled in a sigh. "You don't want to die."

"I'm going to die anyway, why not now? I'm alone, there's no one to guide me, no one who even cares, why should I go on?"

"You're not alone. There is someone to guide you. Someone who cares."

She raised her eyes. "You, Mark? Do you care?"

"Someday you'll understand."

Something like a cold steel pin went through her heart. "I'll never understand. You left me and the best part of me died."

"I never left you. I never will."

"Then where have you been? All this time, all these years that I've needed you?"

He kissed her lightly on the cheek. His breath warmed the side of her face. She closed her eyes, remembering. She was a girl again. There was a boy who loved her. The world was full of sun and music and reasons not to die.

He was winding a towel around her wrist. Her blood had made a large rose around the monogram. His hand touching hers felt wonderfully soft, like milk.

Can a touch be imagined, she wondered? *Can a touch be remembered as clearly as this?*

"Hold the towel now," he was saying, "hold it as tight as you can."

"I'm so scared," she whispered.

"Don't be. There's nothing to be afraid of. You're safe."

"Oh, Mark, you left me too soon, years and years too soon."

"I never left you," he said. "Are you strong enough to make it to the other room?"

"I think so."

"Good. I want you to pick up that phone and call the doctor."

She picked up the phone and called the doctor. When she turned Mark was gone. There was only light where his face had been.

An hour later a sleepy butler showed Dr. Worth Kendall, Ariana's latest private physician, into the bedroom. The doctor unwrapped her wrist from the towel and studied it a moment. He opened his bag and began cleaning the cut carefully.

His eyes met hers. "You weren't even trying."

"I feel like an idiot," she said.

"Anything you care to talk about?"

"Nikos has left me."

"Then he's the idiot. Kill him, not yourself." The doctor bandaged her wrist and then prepared a hypodermic.

"Dr. Kendall, I don't need any more sedatives. I swallowed two dozen sleeping pills."

His eyes came up at her. "The Seconals I gave you?"

She nodded.

His only comment was silence. He lifted the sleeve of her dress. She felt the sudden chill of alcohol as though a tiny window had opened on her arm and then the quick sting of the needle.

"Those pills were placebos," he said. "Just in case you ever tried something like this."

She didn't know whether to feel insulted or relieved. "How did you know I'd—?"

A mixture of affection and skepticism played on Dr. Kendall's wrinkled face. "I've been a doctor quite a few years. I know all about human willfullness."

"I am not willful," she said.

"On the contrary." He smoothed a small circular bandage over the puncture. "You performers don't just have feelings, you *insist* on having them—no matter what the cost. But now that you've decided to live after all, I won't have to send you to the hospital, will I?"

As he was snapping his bag shut the empty Seconal cylinder rolled to the floor and he bent down to retrieve it.

"Say, what have we here?" He was holding DiScelta's locket.

Ariana stared. "I must have dropped that."

He handed it to her. As she took it the lid popped open on an unbroken hinge. The face of Alberta Gesualda smiled out from behind an unshattered crystal.

Dr. Kendall watched Ariana's hand shake. "Have you considered getting away for a while?"

"I can't. I have performances till June."

"Perhaps you should cancel a few of those. You can't go forever skipping essentials, you know."

"What sort of essentials am I skipping?"

"Quite a few—air, sun, tranquillity."

She closed the locket and slipped the unbroken chain around her neck. A soothing coolness flowed across her bosom.

"Doctor, is it possible to dream—and be wide awake?"

"For an artistic imagination like yours a great many things are possible. That doesn't mean they're advisable. You'd better lie down, Ariana. That injection's going to hit pretty fast."

25

"HE WON'T MARRY MAGGIE." CARLOTTA BUSCH FOLDED HER Côte Basque menu and flipped it down flat on the table. "Why do you think he pays that wife in Stockholm two million a year? To render him permanently unavailable."

Ariana toyed with the stem of her tulip glass of Perrier. "Marjamaa, not Stockholm. His wife lives on an island in the Baltic. Maybe she's wise. Maybe I should live on an island too."

"Islands are for people who've given up. You're no good at defeat. You're a contender and you were born to win."

"Am I? I'm so tired."

"Stop whining, darling, and listen to me. It's perfectly easy to get Nikos back."

"Don't you dare humor me, Carlotta. There's nowhere on earth I'm going to get blond hair and a body like that *and* a royal pedigree."

"You know perfectly well they can all three be bought—and so, I might add, does Maggie. And anyway that's not what I'm talking about. *You* have something she'll never be able to buy or fake."

"What?"

Carlotta smiled knowingly and let a moment slip by. "You're an achiever. You can eclipse that little bitch with two well-planned galas. Three. Why not arrange a television shot? I doubt Nikos watches the educational stations, so make it one of the networks."

"You really think Nikos is that much of a child?"

"Darling, he's a starstruck peasant from outer Anatolia. He can pyramid companies and corner commercial grade uranium, but beyond that forget it. My take on Nikos is, he has complete contempt for anything he can understand and total awe for anything he can't. Why the hell else do you think he pays three million for a lousy *Mondrian?*" Carlotta gave a contemptuous snap to her breadstick and dolloped butter across the fracture. "And you're the same in reverse. To you, a high D-flat is daily drudgery and a corporate takeover is a work of genius."

It was true. Ariana shook her head. "What an ass I am."

"Welcome to the club. The point is, you and I know we're asses. Most people only think everyone else is."

Ariana made her resolution. "I'm going to fight, Carlotta. I'm going to hold on to that bastard."

"*Ecco un artista!*" Carlotta signaled the waiter and told him they would be having a bottle of Mumm's with the mousse au saumon fumé and then she fixed an approving, measuring gaze on Ariana. "You know, darling, Maggie has the much harder job. She has to make youth last. All you have to do is make press coverage last."

*   *   *

It wasn't so much an unannounced visit to the fifth floor of the Met as it was a surprise invasion.

Ariana stepped out of the elevator armored in a Lope de Trina platinum brocade jacket, a Fidalgo sequin skirt that swirled like an ocean tide at the calves of her Gucci boots, and $40,000 in Cartier baubles that the insurance policy said should never be allowed out of the Chase vault before sundown. With a wave, she ignored the secretary's attempt to stop her and pushed quickly through the mahogany door with its bronze nameplate.

Adolf Erdlich was sitting behind his ebony desk waging war against Milan on one phone and making love to Vienna on another.

"Adolf." She drew in a deep lungful of courage. "I'll do your *Traviata* gala."

In a single continuous movement Adolf hung up Milan and he hung up Vienna and then he crossed the room and hugged her. "If you'd told me two minutes later it would have been too late. Do you know who I had on the phone? Schwarzkopf. She was willing to cancel La Scala and step in."

"You don't need to embroider. I said I'll do it."

He buzzed the intercom and told his secretary to bring in Miss Kavalaris's letter of intent.

"Sign here." Adolf held out a pen.

"Thanks, but I prefer this one." Ariana opened her purse and took out the tooth-marked pen that she'd used, so long ago, to sign her first contract with the Domani Opera.

"Ah, the lucky pen." Adolf smiled.

"It has been so far." Ariana leaned over the desk. She hesitated for an instant, then splashed a signature across the blank line where Adolf's finger was pointing.

"And what is all this?" DiScelta waved a copy of the *Times*.

"They're mounting a new production." Ariana sat huddled in the wing chair. "It has to be publicized with a star."

"That role is no longer yours. It belongs to your pupil."

"I'm not going to sing it. I'm letting them use my name, and then, when Vanessa steps in . . ."

"Vanessa has a contract with the Metropolitan?"

"No, not yet, but I'll see she gets one."

DiScelta lifted her hands slowly and shook her head. It was a stage gesture, and it carried a battery of accusation. "Now I understand. You've lied to the Metropolitan."

"All right, I lied to them." A flash of anger broke through Ariana's control. "It was a small, unimportant lie. Singers do it. Management does it. Do you think when the Met announces Sutherland for six performances she actually sings them all? It's a way of selling subscriptions and everybody understands it."

"You're not doing this for management. And you're not doing it for Vanessa. You're doing it for *him*."

Ariana burst out: "Haven't I a right to *some* happiness?"

"Rights are for children. We're talking about responsibilities."

"Doesn't anyone have any responsibilities toward *me*?"

"How do you dare complain after all life has given you?"

Ariana sprang to her feet. "What has life given me? What kind of friends do I have? Rivals, conductors, flatterers? I'm loved one day, hated the next, rich today, broke tomorrow. I'm overworked without let-up, I can't smoke or take a drink or go dancing or travel just to travel, I have to train like a prizefighter and put my body on the line like a mercenary, and for all I know some malicious critic can shoot me dead tomorrow. Do you call that a life?"

"Yes—I call that the life of a world-class singer."

Ariana turned away from her teacher's shouts.

"Do you know what you have gained with this lie?" DiScelta cried. "Twenty-four hours of fame. And you have mortgaged your career—and hers. I love you, my child. But you must be strong. Weakness becomes a habit. And no lie is ever the last."

Ariana sank back into the chair.

"Retract." DiScelta placed a hand firmly on her shoulder.

"I can't retract. Not yet."

DiScelta sighed deeply. "The only purpose of human acts is to shape a destiny. Be careful, Ariana. You are shaping the wrong destiny."

It might have been the wrong destiny, but it was decidedly the right publicity.

In addition to the *New York Times*, the story of Ariana's gala appeared in the next day's *New York Post* and *News*. Within twenty-four hours it was picked up in Chicago, Washington, Los Angeles, and Houston. The "Today" show asked her to do a live three-minute TV segment.

Eight prominent hostesses invited her to dinners the following week, promising Elizabeth Taylor, Barbara Walters, Happy Rockefeller, and Henry Kissinger. Because live gossip was still the best advertising medium of all, Ariana accepted seven of the dinners and agreed to arrive for dessert at the eighth.

Simmy Simpson looked up at the studio clock. Three seconds to go before air time. He darted a hand toward his hair, fluffing it out across the bald spot. At that instant the commercial came off the monitor and he saw himself. *Not bad, Simmy, not bad, considering we haven't slept for, what is it, two days—no, three.*

"And this morning, ladies and gentlemen," Loretta Jansen, the hostess for the segment, was announcing, "we have a real treat for you—high society's favorite bard and raconteur, Simeon—better known as Simmy—Simpson."

The camera dollied in for a closer look at Simmy, his melon-bald head sprouting like a shaved sunflower from a pleated violet crepe shirt. He waved to the cameraman. "Top of the morning to you, innocent bystanders."

"Simmy," his hostess said, "there's been an awful lot of talk about the role private investment plays in the arts in this country."

Simmy Simpson blew on the Tia Maria in his coffee cup. "You could only mean Nikos Stratiotis," he said.

"And people *like* Nikos Stratiotis."

"*Ma chère amie*, there is no one *like* Nikos Stratiotis."

Simmy Simpson felt himself in form this morning. Riding in from the Hamptons in the studio limousine, he'd had two black beauties, a line of coke, three bloody Marys and two grams of Vitamin C. He was positively bubbling with anecdote.

"Simmy, could you tell us how funding of high culture has changed over the last five years?"

"It hasn't been a change, Loretta, it's been a revolution—and Nikos Stratiotis, if you'll excuse my saying it, has been the Pancho Villa of that revolution."

Loretta Jansen, TV's highest-paid morning talk-show hostess, aimed a flick of her blond hairdo at the control booth, signaling the engineer to roll the archive footage. The film unreeled on the monitor, highlights of Nikos Stratiotis's career with teasing glimpses of Newport balls, Appellate Court hearings, and polo matches.

"Simmy, perhaps you could fill our viewers in on who's who in these pictures?"

"Gladly, Loretta. Gracious *moi*, I see you've uncovered a fascinating link. That tall handsome gent receiving champagne from Nikos's overflowing jeroboam is Desmond FitzGerald, who at the time of this particular celebration was codirector of the CIA and administered millions of dollars in top-secret, unaudited contracts for—"

Suddenly Simmy Simpson drew a blank. Unaudited contracts for *what?*

Hon-eee, he told himself, *think of something fast, the William Morris people did not negotiate us fifteen thousand per appearance for us to draw blanks on live coast-to-coast TV!*

"Certain Latin-American imports of a recreational nature," he heard himself say. *Mother of Dieu, what am I talking about?*

There wasn't time to think. The sluice-gates of free association were open and words were spilling in a flood, fast and startling and very very close to the gutter, the way Simmy Simpson fans expected, and when he

235

stopped to draw breath he hadn't the faintest idea what confidences he had just shattered or invented. He thought he heard Loretta Jansen mention Ariana Kavalaris.

"Ariana's a dear," he said emphatically. "And that *voice!*"

"But are we to understand that Miss Kavalaris told you—?"

"Loretta, dear, everyone tells *moi* everything."

Loretta Jansen stared incredulously at Simmy Simpson. "But Nikos Stratiotis is hardly the sort of man who—"

"Oh, he's big and gallant and I'm sure he believes it's his machismo alone that holds the New York skyscrapers up—but a lover? Forget it. Why do you think no one wants to marry him? Why else do you think he has to chase all those young girls?"

"You say *has to,* Simmy?"

"You think he has a choice?"

"I most certainly do. If I may speak as a female who happens to have sat next to him at dinner, he is a most attractive man and—"

"I am not casting aspersions upon his hormones or yours, Loretta, dear, but I very much doubt that anyone has had to shall we say shoulder his peccadilloes quite so intimately as poor Ariana."

In his penthouse suite in the Hotel Pierre, Nikos Stratiotis whipped his head around. He stared at the gibbering television set. His jaw dropped and he spat out the Greek word for *whore.*

It was as though any rational decision had been taken out of his hands and his instincts had declared war. He strode to the telephone. He snatched up the receiver and punched out a number.

"Hello," he snapped.

"Hello. You sound awful. What's the matter?"

"When shall we marry?"

The air in the conference room had the faint high-priced odor of senior partners' cologne. Nikos glanced for the third time at his watch and then at the other men at the table.

Holly Chambers leaned close to Nikos and whispered, "I hope you realize you took these fellows any from a double cram-down cash election merger. It's costing $15,000 an hour to keep them waiting."

"The money doesn't matter," Nikos said. "She'll be here."

Maggie arrived ten minutes and $2,500 later. She was wearing an old Chanel camel's-hair coat and she was followed by a man whom she introduced as her attorney.

Nikos kissed his bride-to-be.

"Didn't mean to be late," she said breathlessly. "There was a problem with my charge card at Bergdorf's. I wanted to wear something blue. Blue's my lucky color." She opened her collar and showed him the Dior scarf around her neck. "Like it?"

"You don't realize it, Maggie, but that little patch of blue is probably the most expensive square foot of silk in New York City."

"I'm no dummy, dummy. I made them give me a discount."

For an instant Nikos's forehead creased vertically. "I'm afraid these gentlemen are waiting." He held a chair for her.

Maggie smiled at the lawyers and sat, and the work of hammering out a marriage contract began. Negotiations went smoothly for an hour and a half, with lawyers on both sides objecting to one point or another and accepting the necessary compromises, but then Nikos said, "I want Maggie's shares in Syndic Montenegro."

"I'm not allowed to sell those," Maggie said.

Her lawyer spoke. "All of the princess's shares in state corporations are entailed to her descendants."

Nikos stared at Maggie's lawyer. "But there's nothing to prevent Maggie's assigning them to me."

"So long as the marriage lasts," her lawyer said.

"So long as Maggie lives," Nikos answered.

Maggie's lawyer looked at Nikos with cool fatigue. "Time out, please." He beckoned to his client and they went to a corner.

"Don't let him rush you into this," he said.

Maggie was gazing at the lit, glassed-in shelves where one of the partners of the law firm kept his collection of duck decoys. One of the hand-painted wooden birds bore a three-inch gold plaque with a greeting from President John F. Kennedy.

"What do you suggest I do," Maggie said, "call off negotiations and wait for him to come back to me on my terms?"

"That wouldn't be a bad idea."

"I think the biggest mistake I could make would be to give him time to reconsider."

"All negotiation involves risk."

"I'm not going to risk this one," Maggie said.

She turned and walked over to Nikos's chair and began rubbing the back of his neck. His hand closed around hers.

"I have no objection," Maggie said, "provided Nikos is willing to settle irrevocable trusts on my children."

Holly Chambers spoke. "On the children of his marriage to you."

"On them and on any other children I might have."

Nikos rose and went to the window. Across a bright canyon of empty sky the twin façades of the World Trade Center glittered like mile-high transistor radios. "One unreasonable condition deserves another," he said. "I agree. Provided Maggie does not adopt without my consent."

Maggie smiled. "I can live with that provision."

"There's another point," Maggie's lawyer said. "Both parties to this agreement are at the moment married."

"That is in the process of being rectified," Nikos said.

The lawyer's eyes met his. "Mr. Stratiotis is doubtless aware that, traditionally, royalty may not divorce. Will he undertake to pay the costs of obtaining the princess's papal annulment?"

"Don't get into this," Holly whispered.

Nikos shrugged the warning aside. "I'll pay."

"For all I know it might be a damned nice bed to visit—but marry her?" Holly Chambers chalked the tip of the cue and leaned over the billiard table to line up his shot.

"Why don't you just shut up," Nikos said.

"Because I'm your lawyer. Seven ball in the corner pocket." Holly drew the stick back and glanced up at Nikos. "And there's the most god-awful premonition buzzing around inside of me."

"I don't pay you for god-awful premonitions."

"You sure as hell do."

Holly nudged the tip of the stick against the cue ball and sent it spinning into the seven. A crack echoed through the partners' billiard room. The seven ball crawled across the felt and dropped into the pocket.

"It's a question of honor," Nikos said.

Holly looked up. His eyes were deep and sharp beneath their heavy eyebrows. "You mean you argued with Ariana and you want to show her. Nikos, this is a very expensive way of thumbing your nose."

"I am praying for the strength not to bash your face in."

"You really want to go back in there and sign that suicide warrant?"

Nikos raised his cue. "Holly, whatever it costs me, whatever she is, I'm marrying the bitch, all right?"

A crowd of reporters was waiting when Ariana stepped out of the townhouse.

"Miss Kavalaris, any comment on Mr. Stratiotis's engagement?"

She hadn't known. Her heart gave a sickening lurch and she felt herself falling into empty space. "Naturally I wish Nikos good luck in all his undertakings."

"How long have you known he was planning to marry Principessa Maggie?"

Her eyes crinkled but she tried to show not a flicker of surprise. She took her bearings on the limousine parked at the curb and strode forward through the human thicket. "Since they met."

"How in the world did you let a rich hunk like Nikos Stratiotis slip through your fingers?"

Ariana held up her hands and she thanked God for the last-minute insecurity that had made her put on her diamonds.

"I spread my fingers very, very wide."

Someone snapped a picture of the diva with forty-carat, widespread fingers. The chauffeur was holding the door of the limousine for her and she was about to step in.

"Do you have any feelings about Mr. Stratiotis's leaving you for a younger woman?"

She turned and met the eyes of the woman who had asked the question. She knew she was taking the first step beyond a boundary that she would never be able to cross back over. But she had no choice. Nikos had dealt her a public humiliation and she had to reply in kind.

"If you'll allow me to set the record straight, Mr. Stratiotis did not leave me. It was I who left him because of irreconcilable differences. He is understandably lonely and the principessa is understandably eager to console him. Many women are. As to the question of age, the principessa has never struck me as a young person. Younger, yes. But young, no—she is far too wise. And Nikos is not interested in youth. He is attracted only to wisdom. That's why he collects great art and cultured friends."

"Do you predict a happy marriage for them?"

"I foresee no other possibility. The principessa can tell him what life is like in a discothèque. One day she will go to the moon and perhaps she will take him with her. She belongs very much to tomorrow, and now so does Nikos. They both make me very grateful for today."

She got into the limousine and waved to the reporters from the window. As the car pulled into traffic she was overwhelmed by a sense that her sun was setting.

By the time she returned home the reporters had gone. She took the elevator directly up to the music room.

Dear God, please help me.

She sat down at the piano and opened the score of *Traviata* and struck the first chord of Scene One.

DiScelta was seated at the Steinway. "When are they going to announce your cancellation?"

"I'm not canceling," Ariana said quietly.

"But you promised." DiScelta rose, and Ariana instinctively stepped back. "You swore to me you were going to cancel and Vanessa would sing!"

"I'll keep my promise—soon."

"What kind of an artist says *soon?* An artist says *now!*"

"Maybe I'm not an artist. Maybe I'm just a woman."

DiScelta looked at Ariana as though she were some kind of pathetic caged bird. "You're still trying to show him. Hoping he'll read your publicity and come to the stage door and say, 'Oh, Ariana, it was all a mistake, may I have your autograph and your hand in marriage?' And in the meantime, what about the promise you made to *music?*"

"Music isn't enough."

DiScelta wheeled on her. "Not enough? Music is the only thing that lasts! Your loves, your jealousies, your little happinesses and despairs, they come and go—but music is forever!"

Ariana's eyelids dropped. She felt her teacher's hand under her chin, lifting it till their gazes met.

"How can I make you see? A promise is a natural law, like gravity. You cannot tamper with it. If you do this, if you take the role that you swore to give to your pupil, your life as an artist is over—and your life as a woman will not matter."

Ariana did not answer.

"Do you want to spend eternity in hell?" DiScelta screamed.

Ariana broke loose. *"Panagia mou! Voïthia!"*

DiScelta stared at her furiously. "Greek is not one of my languages."

"I'm saying I'm in hell *now*, don't you understand? I'm trying to get *out!*"

"I forbid you to go through with the performance. For your sake—not just hers, not just mine—*I absolutely forbid it!*"

"Forbid all you want," Ariana cried. "I'm singing the role!"

26

AN ICY JANUARY DOWNPOUR RAISED A LATHER IN THE GUTTERS outside the Philadelphia Academy of Music. Inside, the performance of *Traviata* began at 8:07 when the conductor lifted his baton and gave the orchestra the upbeat to the Prelude.

In New York City, the night sky was clear and starry, the air crystal cold. Inside the darkened Metropolitan Opera House Boyd Kinsolving lifted his baton at 8:11, and Verdi's opening measures sighed out from the ethereal, unaccompanied violins.

Vanessa had prepared arduously. She had hoarded her voice, hardly even speaking for the twenty-four hours before the performance.

With her very first phrase, "*Flora, amici, la notte che resta,*" she knew the effort had been well spent. She could sense a warmth flowing from the audience. Her voice felt right, her character felt centered, and she could feel the subscribers settling back securely in their seats.

At 8:13 Ariana stood at the mirror in her dressing room. A clamminess gripped her ribs every time she tried to draw a breath.

The stage manager's assistant had given the warning knocks on her door. There was an instant when she knew she could still send in her understudy. She felt herself suspended between two lives.

Another knock came. "Miss Kavalaris?"

"Coming," she answered.

And she went on. She willed herself into the role of Violetta Valery, one of the most beautiful courtesans of Paris. She was giving a supper party for three dozen nineteenth-century jet-setters and hangers-on.

Her first phrase, welcoming her guests, was a disaster. What came out was barely audible, poorly placed, not projected at all. With her second phrase, "*Lo voglio,*" her voice shook so badly she had to fight an impulse to turn and run from the stage.

All right, she told herself, *so there's no voice.* She would simply have to resort to other tactics.

Alfredo—a handsome newcomer—toasted her and stayed behind as the others went to dance in the adjoining room. A fit of coughing took her. Alfredo declared his love. She pretended to be amused.

All through the scene she forced herself to keep moving, keep gesturing, using her own desperation as the character's. When a B-flat cracked she flung herself onto her tenor as though the cracked note were the point, when she flubbed an entrace she flung herself onto her maid as though the flub were Violetta's, not Kavalaris's, when an A just wasn't there she flung herself onto her couch as though the missed note was an intentional touch.

After the guests had gone she remained by herself, pondering Alfredo and the love he offered. Mustering all her bravado, she decided to forget him and continue her fast, gay life. Missing most of her high notes, not even projecting the low ones, she forced out a hectic "Sempre Libera."

Vanessa took four solo bows after the Act One curtain. The darkness seemed to adore her, like a single worshiping soul. She curtsied deeply, gratefully, confidently.

Ariana took two curtain calls after Act One. She saw the faces in the front rows and tiers, dangling masks of shock against the unforgiving night, and she refused even to attempt a third bow.

A blown fuse delayed the Philadelphia curtain, and the New York curtain rose on Act Two three minutes before Philadelphia's.

The scene was the country villa where Violetta and Alfredo had been living happily together for several months. Alfredo discovered Annina, the maid, sneaking back from Paris. He learned she had been selling Violetta's possessions to pay the cost of running the household. Shamed and shocked, he rushed to Paris to raise money.

His father, Georges Germont, arrived. Accusing Violetta of destroying his son, he beseeched her to break off the affair.

Ariana began the scene poorly. Her pitch was unsteady. She tried to project calm dignity and, when she learned that Alfredo's sister could not marry because of her liaison, pity. For a terrifying instant, on the words "*Ah, morir preferirò*," there was no sound. Her tone simply stopped.

No, she told herself, *I will not die like this.*

Somehow, by sheer dint of refusal to submit, she forced her voice up into life again. It was not so much a sound as a rattle, and she could feel tiny flapping wings against her throat. There was only a pulsation now, but she was able to build the pulsation into a sliding back and forth between two extremely uncertain pitches, neither of them the high B-flat intended by the composer.

Her baritone was staring at her in undisguised horror. Boyd's baton had slowed, and the music hung in suspension. She realized she had reached the turning point, that this note was going to decide not just the rest of her performance, but of her career.

And of her life.

Always, before, she had held something back for later. Now she held nothing back. She needed this note, now. With a last effort she narrowed back the airstream, imagined a steel door in her throat closing down against the stream, tightening it into a single strand of air.

By some miracle, the pitch focused. It was not the pitch she wanted—it was far too low—but at least it was a single, unmistakable note. She was able, by thought, by will, to scoop it up and suddenly, clearly projected like a light through a rift in a storm, was the note Verdi had written: full, warm, unmistakable.

She agreed to Germont's entreaties and wrote a hasty farewell note. Alfredo returned. Declaring her undying love for him, she went. He ripped open the note and read the message: he and Violetta must separate.

His father begged him to return home. Alfredo refused. Seeing an invitation on the table from Violetta's friend Flora, he resolved to go to Flora's and force a confrontation.

Vanessa's first flub came with no warning. Just after the words "*Ah, morir preferirò*," in her duet with Alfredo's father, she felt a pricking, like a needle in her breast. There was an unbelievable instant when no sound came out of her, a split second of absolute silence, as though all the power in her had shut down.

An instant later, the voice came back. In all, the slip and the recovery had taken less than a tenth of a second. The audience out there, most of them, probably had no idea.

But *she* knew.

As Ariana's performance progressed, the notes began coming back, the high B's and C's, the daring attacks, the sustained tones swelling like waves. When she appeared with her former lover, Baron Douphol, in Scene Two of the second act, the party at Flora's, the audience's approval glowed down upon her, giving her an almost unreal sense of confidence.

The baron gambled and lost to Alfredo. Taking Violetta aside, Alfredo demanded to know why she had left him. Lying, she claimed no longer to love him. Announcing to the guests that he was paying Violetta in full, he hurled his winnings at her feet. His father entered and, apologizing to Violetta, rebuked his son for such unworthy behavior.

Vanessa felt it slipping, the mastery that an artist must wield to hold an audience. There was a pressure in her chest. Her voice seemed drawn and shrunken and each note required a throat-filling effort.

Mistakes began piling up: foolish slips of words, notes, phrasing. She listened in horror to herself bungling more and more of the score. She felt hopeless, as though she were waiting for some final, inevitable catastrophe to burst upon her.

And it came.

During the confrontation with Alfredo, two bars before he hurled the money at her feet, she stumbled and fell.

The whole opera house somersaulted around her. Realization came flooding in on her. This was real now: the cast staring numbly, the cue missed, the music flowing on without her, the white-hot blank in her mind where her next note should have been. The dramatic highpoint of the act was aborted, and with it, the opera.

Hands helped her to her feet.

Voices cued her, covered for her. Only the thought that she mustn't disgrace herself totally kept her stumbling on through the last act.

Violetta lay in her bedroom dying of tuberculosis. Though her money was practically gone, she told Annina to give half of what little remained to the poor. She reread a letter from Germont saying that Alfredo had been told the truth and would soon return to beg her forgiveness.

Annina rushed breathlessly in with Alfredo. The lovers embraced and sang of beginning a new life together. The doctor arrived with Germont, who now realized how much and how nobly Violetta had sacrificed. The old man embraced her as a daughter. Violetta felt a last, deceptive flare-up of life and for an ecstatic moment believed she had recovered.

And then, as those around her despaired, she fell dead.

At 11:05, to thundering applause, Ariana took twelve curtain calls with a happy, rather shy smile. Her public had forgiven her Act One and Scene One of Act Two. She had recouped. She was their Ariana again, their darling, their invincible.

There was no way of not taking a curtain call. Vanessa walked toward the gap in the curtain, out into the milky light, and received the monumental contempt pouring from the opera house.

Ariana hurried to her dressing room and closed the door.

"Ariana."

She whipped around. She had not seen the figure in the armchair.

"I didn't think you'd do it." DiScelta's face loomed out of the shadow at her. "That your honor matters nothing to you, I must accept. I misjudged you. You cannot help how you are made. But that you care nothing for anyone else—"

Ariana's hands came up shaped into balled fists. "Do you actually think I did this for myself?"

"No. You broke your word for that man."

"Whatever I do, I do because I love him."

244

"And have you no feeling for your pupil? No responsibility?"

Ariana thought back, but it seemed so far away, so long ago. She could remember teaching a young woman how to sustain the breath column, where to break the phrase in "*Sarò la più bella*," she could remember the voice and the name, but she couldn't call the face up.

"I've done what I could for her."

"You've done what you could to destroy her."

Anger swelled in Ariana, deep and choking. "I sang, that's all I did, I didn't betray anyone, I didn't murder anyone, I opened my mouth and notes came out!"

"And whose notes were they? Who put them there?"

"If I haven't said thank you, I'm saying it now. Thank you."

DiScelta's gaze touched Ariana fiercely. "Saying thanks is not the same as doing thanks. Every act brings its precise equivalent in return. You have been given a gift and you must give a gift back. Otherwise—"

"I don't want to hear this. Not now. Not ever again."

DiScelta took Ariana's hand in an astonishingly tight grip. "If you don't keep your word, we are all lost—not just you, not just her, but all those who came before, who trusted you to keep the promise."

Ariana jerked free. "Will you get it through your head that I am all out of guilt!"

A corpselike stillness fell on the room.

"The world is a clock," DiScelta said. "No wheel moves without moving all the others. When you refuse your destiny, you rob others of theirs. And that is murder."

Ariana brought a fist crashing down on the dresser. A mushroom cloud of face powder exploded up into the mirror fringe of makeup lights. "I'm not going to take any more of your nagging! No one gives a damn about me, and I don't give a damn about anyone—not you, not Vanessa, not your pathetic superstitions! I'm going to sing what I want where I want, when I want; I'm going to show the world I'm not a washed-up old diva like you, you crazy old witch!"

DiScelta's eyes heaped disbelief on her pupil. Her words seemed to fight their way through layers of stone. "You're making the greatest mistake of your life."

Ariana's throat pushed out a harsh, mirthless laugh. "I don't care! I don't care!" She tilted back her head, closing her eyes.

When she opened them again, the old woman was gone, so suddenly and so silently that it seemed she had never been there at all.

Ariana felt a sudden stinging chill on her bosom, as though a blade were pressing into her skin. She lifted the locket and snapped it open. Was it her imagination, or had the face inside changed its expression, was there a hint of contempt in the eyes, in the set of the mouth?

That crazy old witch has me imagining things.

27

IN FEBRUARY ARIANA SANG THREE *MADAMA BUTTERFLYS* IN LIS-
bon. Perhaps superstition had something to do with what happened: Butterfly was one of the roles she had taught Vanessa and
which—in theory at least—she had renounced.

The curtain rose on a set depicting a hill above Nagasaki harbor, a
little house bustling with preparations for a Japanese wedding. The
groom-to-be, U.S. Navy Lieutenant Pinkerton, took the wedding as a
lark, but the American consul warned him that his betrothed, a Japanese geisha, had taken it seriously enough to convert to Christianity.
The bride-to-be, Cio-Cio-San, known as "Madame Butterfly," joyfully
arrived with a crowd of friends and relatives.

There was applause as Ariana, looking surprisingly Oriental and pe-
tite, made her entrance in the title role.

No sooner had the marriage ceremony been performed than Butterfly's uncle, a Buddhist monk, stormed angrily in and cursed his niece for
betraying the religion of her ancestors. Butterfly was reduced to tears.
Pinkerton drove the guests from the house. He comforted his sobbing
bride and led her to the bridal chamber.

As the curtain fell to warm applause Ariana felt a soreness just above
her collarbone. She had a cup of tea in her dressing room.

The Second Act curtain rose on Butterfly's little house. Though Pinkerton had promised to come back "when the robins nest," three
springs had passed, and Butterfly still waited patiently, secure in her
faith that one fine day—"*Un bel di*"—her husband would return to
her.

On the fourth note of the aria, the F-sharp at the top of the staff,
Ariana experienced a sudden choking. It was hardly a difficult note to
sustain, yet for the rest of the act she had a sensation that it simply was
not there.

The consul entered, trying to break the news to Butterfly that Pinkerton had married an American. But Goro, the marriage broker, interrupted, bringing a rich suitor for Butterfly's hand. She angrily left the
stage and returned a moment later, carrying her child by Pinkerton: a
blond, blue-eyed two-year-old. The boy's name, she told the consul, was
Trouble, but when his father returned it would be changed to Joy.

A cannon shot sounded in the harbor, announcing a ship's arrival. Excitedly peering through a telescope, Butterfly recognized Pinkerton's
ship, the *Abraham Lincoln.* In a rapturous duet, Suzuki, her maid,
helped her decorate the house with cherry blossoms.

Ariana's throat felt as though she were shouting through scabs.

By now night was falling. As Butterfly, Suzuki, and little Trouble waited for Pinkerton, their crouching figures were silhouetted against the paper wall and off-stage voices could be heard in the haunting melody of the Humming Chorus.

In the next intermission the house doctor peered down Ariana and said he detected an inflammation. "I wouldn't continue."

"Doctor, I have to complete the performance."

He sighed—"I shouldn't do this"—and gave her cortisone.

The pain in her throat had abated slightly by the time the curtain rose on the final act. It was after dawn, and Pinkerton still had not appeared. Suzuki persuaded Butterfly to rest in the other room. The consul arrived with Pinkerton and his American wife. Realizing Butterfly had remained faithful, Pinkerton fled, unable to face her.

Butterfly entered, saw the American lady in the garden, and asked who she was. Finally grasping the truth, she agreed to give up her child, asking that Pinkerton collect his son in half an hour.

Alone with the infant, Butterfly took her father's hara-kiri dagger and stabbed herself. With her dying breath she crawled to embrace Trouble. Arriving instants too late, Pinkerton found the boy beside his dead mother, playing with a miniature American flag.

Oddly enough, Ariana had five curtain calls, and the reviews were respectful. *Not her best,* said one, *but Kavalaris after all is Kavalaris, a claim that can be made by few others.*

A day later, when she vocalized, the F-sharp was still not there. "How could it be?" she demanded at her next coaching session with Austin Waters. "How can an F-sharp simply vanish?"

"The note is there," he assured her. "You're just nervous."

But it was something more than nerves. She felt like an organism under attack. A month later in Brussels she was singing Desdemona in Verdi's *Otello,* another of the roles she had supposedly abdicated to Vanessa. During Act Three, in her scene with Otello, her A below high C suddenly vanished. Again, she was able to force other tones into the gap, but the sound was strained and ugly.

And again, when she vocalized later, the A was still missing.

"Now I've lost two," she sobbed to Austin. "The F and the A."

"What do you think you just sang?"

"That wasn't an A, that was a B-flat bent down and that was why it sounded horrible."

He gave her a long look. "Sweetheart, you haven't lost anything except your marbles."

But she *was* losing something. She could feel it. So could audiences. Her voice began tearing arias into irregular shapes. She had to break the line more and more frequently to sneak a breath, and soon there was nothing sneaky about the breaths; they were outright gulps slicing into the melody.

Curtain calls became fewer, bravas less spontaneous; and soon critics were commenting that this or that arietta had not been quite up to Kavalaris's usual standard.

One day Richard Schiller asked, "Excuse me for prying, but are you on anything?"

"What do you mean, on anything?" she said.

He shrugged in a way that seemed embarrassed. "Drugola."

"Drugs? Are you crazy?"

"No, but I sometimes get the impression you are."

"I think we'd better continue this discussion another day."

"*After* your vacation. You got three free weeks coming up. Use 'em."

Ariana fled back to her work—what remained of it—not simply for distraction, but for solace and sanity. The Chicago Lyric Opera had mentioned needing a Carmen on short notice, and she began studying the role.

In Carmen Bizet had written the greatest mezzo part ever. The French vowels—usually so hard to project with their closed, nasal quality—were exploited for their sensual effect: an exuberant sexuality sprang from the very sound of the score. Yet there was a classical clarity and perfection that reminded Ariana of Mozart. But how different Bizet was, how modern! *Carmen* held the listener with its story, which Mozart's operas did not, and with its unending stream of irresistible tunes, which unlike Mozart's needed no allowance for style or period.

And yet she was uncertain whether or not to take the role. She was, after all, a soprano—true, a soprano whose high notes were going. But to accept a mezzo role seemed an admission of defeat.

March 3, in the first district court of Ciudad Trujillo, Dominican Republic, Judge G. de Souza y Saavedra granted Señora Maria-Kristina von Heidenstam Stratiotis of Marjamaa, Sweden, an uncontested divorce from Señor Nikos Lykandreou Stratiotis of Ile St-Louis, Paris. Both parties were in absentia at the proceedings.

Twenty-eight days later in Vatican City, the papal curia issued a decree *per extraordinaria* annulling the marriage of Principessa Marghereta di Montenegro and Jean-Baptiste de Grandmont.

On a beautiful Tuesday in early spring with sunlight splintering off the walls of Olympic Tower and flags snapping on the hoods of diplomatic limousines, 1,500 guests gathered at St. Patrick's Cathedral to witness the marriage of Principessa Marghereta di Montenegro and Nikos Stratiotis.

The three television networks stationed cameras on Fifth Avenue, on Forty-ninth Street, and in the nave of the cathedral. Millions of viewers were able to watch as uniformed guards from Cartier's and Harry Winston's brought the bride's jewels to the cathedral in armored trucks; as

beautiful, famous women in bright designer dresses and glistening faceted diamonds stepped out of Continentals and Mercedes-Benzes and
Rolls-Royces on the arms of handsome, suntanned escorts; as Prince Ar-
noldo of Montenegro, dapper and Old World in spats and cutaway,
escorted his daughter Maggie down the aisle. The bride wore a blush
French illusion veil, held in place by a wedding tiara of diamonds, sapphires, and rubies. Television commentators claimed that the matching
lace side panels of her skirt were embroidered in 3,200 seed pearls.

After the ceremony the wedding cortege of limousines and chartered
London buses sped west through Rockefeller Center, where a reception
for eight hundred was held in the world-famous Rainbow Room atop
the RCA building.

By nine o'clock that evening two thousand guests were busily enjoying champagne at the bar, cocaine in the bathrooms, and live disco on
the dance floor. The celebrating showed no signs of slowing down.

In Chicago, one time zone to the west, it was eight o'clock, but in the
opera house the time was noon and the place was Seville. Soldiers and
passers-by thronged the city square as the girls from the nearby cigarette factory returned to work. One of them—Carmen, a hot-blooded,
amoral gypsy—flirted with Don José, commander of the troop, and
teasingly tossed him a red rose. He feigned indifference, but afterward,
unobserved, mused on the flower and hid it in his coat.

Micaela, a simple peasant girl from Don José's village, arrived with a
letter and a kiss from his mother. She gave him the letter; she gave him
the kiss. Alone, he read the letter and discovered, to his pleasure, that
his mother wanted him to marry Micaela.

A commotion broke out in the factory. Girls rushed into the square.
Carmen had stabbed a coworker during an argument. The captain of
the guards arrested her and handed her over to Don José.

Carmen now used all her powers of seduction, all the dark lure of her
insinuating mezzo voice, to win her freedom. In a lilting *seguidilla* she
offered to meet Don José at a tavern on the outskirts of the city if he
would let her go. Fatally snared by her charms, he loosened the rope
around her wrists, allowing her to escape.

Applause was warm. Chicago gave Ariana Kavalaris three bows for
this, the first act of her first stab at Carmen. It had cost her a month's
hesitation to accept Chicago's last-minute offer of the role. She'd had to
persuade herself that it was no surrender to go mezzo, simply a procla-
mation of versatility.

There was also the consideration that the role, lying mostly in the
low range, exposed none of the freak gaps in her high register.

And so she was Carmen the irresistible temptress, singing and dancing with two gypsy friends for the soldiers at Lillas Pastia's tavern on
the outskirts of Seville. When the bullfighter Escamillo entered to the

acclamation of the crowd, she ignored his advances. She was waiting for Don José, due to be released from the jail where he had been imprisoned for letting her escape.

Finally, after the inn had closed, Don José appeared. Carmen urged him to desert the army and join the gypsies. At first he refused; but the captain of the guard arrived to order him back to the regiment. The two men drew swords. Carmen's gypsy cronies overpowered the captain, leaving Don José no choice but to escape with them to the mountains.

Again, three curtain calls.

Ariana was in her dressing room sipping chamomile tea for her nerves when the phone rang. A voice at the switchboard asked if she would talk to Mrs. Busch—urgent from New York.

She took the call.

"Are you near a television set?" Carlotta sounded out of breath.

"Of course not. You know perfectly well I'm performing."

"CBS," Carlotta said. "The wedding's coming up right after the commercial."

"*Panagia mou,*" Ariana whispered. "Did you go?"

"I went to the ceremony and two minutes of the reception. The room was *thick* with cigar smoke and deals. You know the sort of people."

So. It was ended.

Ariana was no longer thinking clearly as she listened to Carlotta's voice spilling from the telephone. All she wanted was for Carlotta to have no notion how deeply she was hurt. She had never for an instant believed that Nikos would go through with it. She had seen everything—the publicity, the gossip, even the engagement—as an elaborate game played solely to test her capacity for being hurt; in an obscure way it confirmed that he loved her after all. But now she saw that the only game had been the one she had played on herself; there was a cold hollow in the pit of her stomach and she realized how completely unprepared she was for this disaster.

"Thank you, Carlotta. Yes, I'll look at it."

A stagehand found a small black-and-white TV. She sat and for the longest three minutes of her life stared at guests streaming into the cathedral. They were the same princes and polo players and playboys who had come to her own wedding; the same women, showing their money, wearing mink coats and diamond bracelets in the daytime.

Could it really be ended? she thought. *Does anything in life end like this, between acts of* Carmen *and commercials on the evening news?*

There was a rap at the door. "Places, Miss Kavalaris."

"Thank you."

Her thoughts moved amazingly quickly in the next thirty seconds: it was as though she were watching a speeded-up film of her entire life with Nikos. Everything stood out sharply, from the evening so long ago when a young man in an absurd fedora had sauntered into a coffee shop on Broadway to the night twenty-three years later when he had slammed the iron grille door of a townhouse on Sutton Place.

What struck her now that the story was finished was a sense that it could have ended no other way.

She hurried onto the stage, into the gypsy smugglers' camp. She was Carmen again, now tiring of Don José, reading and rereading her fortune in the cards and finding only death.

Death, she thought. *Only death.*

Escamillo, Carmen's latest conquest, entered. Don José, wildly jealous, attacked him, but Carmen separated the two.

A frightened Micaela appeared, bringing word that Don José's dying mother was calling for him. The girl had a lovely voice, all purity and innocence.

I used to sing Micaela, Ariana thought, *when I was a student . . . when I was a soprano.*

She realized someone was threatening her. It was Don José, warning that, though he was going home with Micaela, he would never let Carmen leave him.

She sat alone in her dressing room, waiting for the last act.

At 10:40, on the arm of Escamillo, she entered the square where all Seville waited outside the bullring to hail her new lover. Friends warned her that Don José had been seen lurking about. Unafraid, she waited for him.

I want to die, she thought.

Don José appeared, pathetic and beaten, and begged her to return to him. Scornfully she refused, flinging at his feet the ring he had given her. As shouts from the arena acclaimed Escamillo, Don José—blind with jealousy—plunged his dagger into Carmen's heart.

She fell to the hard planking of the stage and lay there, hearing the chorus pour from the bullring, hearing the sobbing Don José give himself up, hearing the curtain whoosh down.

The audience was friendly, polite, only mildly enthusiastic. Ariana took two solo bows. She could tell they were applauding her past, not her Carmen.

28

"REFILL, DARLING?"

Nikos handed Maggie the tulip glass. She sipped and smiled at him and sank deeper into the black marble bathtub.

"Here—lean over," he said, "I'll do your back."

He scrubbed her gently. Gradually the scrubbing turned into an attempted embrace. She slid free, steadied herself with one hand on the gold-plated faucet and climbed out.

He held the towel for her and folded it around her. He drew her to him and kissed her. She pulled away and took a robe from the back of the door. The robe was deep purple lace with frilled cuffs.

"Why are you putting that on?" he asked.

"Because it's pretty."

"You're prettier the way you are."

"You say the nicest things." She kept dressing.

"This is very strange. Do I have to seduce my own bride?"

"What makes you think I want to be seduced?"

"The way you're teasing."

"Is that what I'm doing?"

She looked at herself in the mirror.

"We were married less than seventy-two hours ago. We've spent the last twenty-four hours on trains and planes. Now we're alone. It's a beautiful spring night and here we are in the master stateroom with the windows open to the Adriatic. I should be holding you. Kissing you."

"Then why aren't you?"

"Because you're there and I'm here," he said.

"You can come here."

"I've tried."

"Then you just have to try again."

He went to her and tried to take her in his arms and again she drew back. He gazed at her a long, curious moment. "Don't you love me?" he asked quietly.

"Of course I love you. I'd have to, to marry you, wouldn't I?"

"Then what do you expect of me? Am I supposed to wait and let you come around little by little?"

"If you like waiting, that would be fine. Do you mind if I smoke a joint?"

He stared at her.

"My God, Nikos, don't tell me that shocks you. A lot of people smoke before sex. It makes sex better."

"I've always found sex pretty good by itself."

"Then tonight it's going to be better than pretty good."

He watched her in the mirror. Her negligee had opened. His eye took in the snowy white mound of one breast, the curve of her stomach, the dark glimpse of hair between her legs.

When he turned around, his penis was standing straight out.

She was stretched on the bed now, watching with amused fascination as he crossed the stateroom toward her. "You're not very good at hiding your feelings," she said.

"Why should I have to hide them from my own wife?"

She took another long, relaxed draw on her marijuana. "You've got a good body, Nikos." Her hand reached out and tweaked one of his nipples thoughtfully. She rose up on the bed and pressed her breasts against his chest and made a circular, rubbing motion. The touch of her nipples excited him even further.

She drew back and pushed the joint into his mouth. "Inhale, Nikos."

He inhaled. A lightness gradually filled him. He took her breasts in his hand and began fondling them.

"Kiss them," she said.

He was not used to being told what to do. But she pushed her breasts into his mouth, one after the other, and her smooth firmness filled him, and he liked it.

She gave him three minutes of her breasts, smiling down at him, taking puffs on her joint and knocking the ash off.

"Now—I want *that*."

She laid the joint in an ashtray beside the bed and slid gracefully to a sidesaddle position on the carpet before him, her legs pointing out to one side. She swallowed his whole cock.

When she had made him slick and firm she released him, looking up at him. A tiny smile curved the edge of her lips.

"I want your cock in me. I want your big cock. Now, Nikos. Now."

He hated to hear her talking like that, hated the way it excited him. He pushed her back on the bed and straddled her. She wrapped her legs around him.

As his movements quickened low wordless sounds began to bubble out of her throat. She dug her fingernails into his nakedness. Little welts of blood rose on the brown of his shoulders. His mouth took starved gulps of her. She raked her nails up and down his back. She bit. She scratched. He lunged and thrashed like a goaded beast, till finally he was at the brink.

She began to tremble uncontrollably, screaming, and for him that was the signal. He pumped furiously, sweat blinding him, and then he shot into her and heard her crying, "Yes, yes!"

Afterward she lit another joint. "Wow." She smiled. "You're not so bad."

Morning dawned cloudy and dark, but the weather cleared in the afternoon and Nikos went swimming off the ship. When he pulled himself back on deck, Maggie was sunning herself without a bra. He decided it was too early in their honeymoon to object to things like that.

He settled into the chair next to her. She began to run her hand slowly over his chest and belly.

"You're in damned good shape for a man your age," she said.

In a moment he heard a match strike and smelled the by now very familiar odor of marijuana.

The galley door opened and an immaculate steward stepped on deck. He was carrying a tray of ice tea and sherbet and meringues. It seemed to Nikos that the man sniffed and smiled before setting the tray on the table in front of them.

When the steward had gone, Nikos said, "I wish you wouldn't smoke that stuff in front of the staff."

She laughed like a spoiled child. "But they're only servants. And besides it's my yacht too now, remember?"

He pulled himself up from the chair. He crossed the deck and went into the library. He sat by the window, thinking. Then he reached across the table and lifted the telephone receiver. "Can you connect me with the mainland operator please?"

The *Maria-Kristina* docked at Dubcek, on the Yugoslav coast, at 8:30 that evening. Maggie came on deck in her white chiffon dress and pendant diamond earrings and cast a glance at the tiny harbor. "Nikos, why in the world are we stopping here?"

"Company," he said.

And they poured on board with their luggage and their laughter: Seymour and C. Z. van Slyke, and the Duke and Duchess of Warwickshire, and Stanley Jannings, the playwright, with his wife and his mistress, a pretty Norwegian model, and his wife's lover, who happened to be a member of the British cabinet, and Nikos's old friend Solange, Vicomtesse de Nouilles, who had brought her newest composer, an eighteen-year-old Argentinian.

He introduced Maggie to the people she didn't already know. Her expression suggested she had had plenty of experience smiling in all kinds of situations at all kinds of people but was a little surprised at having to take on guests on her own honeymoon.

The steward showed the new arrivals to their staterooms. Maggie changed into a rainbow-colored Cantonese silk tunic, and just before dinner C. Z. van Slyke came running up to hug her and cried, "You're so lucky—it's the greatest yacht I've ever *seen!*"

"Yes," Maggie said wistfully, "it's great for getting away."

That night in the stateroom Maggie whipped her hair with the silver-and-ruby brush that had been one of Nikos's wedding presents. She glared at his reflection in the mirror. "You pick interesting times to give parties."

He looked up from the company report he was reading in bed. "I thought you needed cheering up."

"Did I say I needed cheering up?"

He turned a page of the report. "I'm sorry, darling, I misunderstood."

Thirty-three hours later, the board of directors of a Sierra Leone zinc mine rebelled against the parent company, a wholly-owned Stratiotis subsidiary. Nikos said goodbye to his guests and to his bride of less than a week and jetted to Geneva.

It took all of nine days to straighten the matter out, too long to be able to resume his honeymoon.

Ariana flubbed again.

"I'm sorry," she said.

It was the twenty-third take on the silly four measures and she was conscious of the musicians' gazes fastened resentfully on her face.

Boyd stood with his head bent. He raised his eyes to look at his former wife and silently lowered his baton.

"Take five," he sighed. He signaled Ariana to come into the engineer's soundproof booth. "What's the problem?"

"My throat . . . won't do it."

"But you've sung Lady Macbeth dozens of times."

"Not in the last two years." Not since she'd coached Vanessa Billings in the role.

"Ariana, what's happening to you?"

"I didn't want to make this recording. It was you who begged me! And now you accuse me of—"

"Sweetums." His arm went around her, but his touch was cool and perfunctory. "No one's accusing. We'd just like to get something on tape we can ship out and market. Now why don't you go home for the day and get a good rest?"

"There was another call from Vanessa Billings," Ariana's secretary told her.

"What's wrong with that girl?"

Roddy hesitated. Ariana smelled embarrassment.

"I said you'd talk to her tomorrow morning at ten."

She had half a mind to fire him on the spot. "I've told you never to make an appointment without consulting me."

"She sounded so desperate. And it's hardly an appointment. Just a simple three-minute phone call."

But it wasn't a simple three-minute phone call. At ten the next day Vanessa appeared at Ariana's door.

"I've got to see you."

"Very well, now that you're here."

Vanessa came into the house. She no longer moved like a young person. "My voice is going," she said.

"Don't be ridiculous. Voices don't go at your age."

"I used to be able to vocalize to high F. Now I can barely reach D. I have trouble sustaining in the upper register."

The bones in Vanessa's face showed bluishly through her skin. Ariana could see that something was very wrong.

"What are you eating?" Ariana asked.

"I haven't any appetite."

"That's your answer. It's a physical problem. Something to do with metabolism. You have to see a doctor, not me."

"But it's more than physical. I have memory slips. Roles I learned by heart aren't in my head anymore. There are gaps."

"What do you expect? A singer's memory is an organ, like a lung. You're not taking care of yourself. All your organs suffer." She took a cigarette from the majolica box on the coffee table.

Vanessa watched her light it. Astonishment crossed her face. "You're smoking?"

"Nerves," Ariana said. "It's a low nicotine brand. I don't inhale." She added, "It's a dreadful habit. Don't you ever start." She followed this with five minutes' practical advice.

Vanessa listened patiently. "But there's something else. Whatever it was I had when I was working with you—whatever it was you gave me—is gone."

Ariana had a fleeting intuition of an existence as painful as her own. She brushed it aside. "You've got to get over this fixation you have on me. Stop making me the center of your problems."

"The center of my problems? Oh, no, you're the center of my hopes. You're the only one who can help me."

"I can't help you. I can't help anyone." Ariana sprang from her chair and went quickly to her desk. She flipped open the album-sized checkbook. Her accountant would kill her for this, but so what. She scribbled her signature across check number 763, left the amount blank, made a note on the stub: *Vanessa B.*

She ripped the check out.

"Here. Get yourself another teacher. Get yourself a fur coat. Get yourself a car, a trip around the world, anything. And, please, forgive me."

When Ariana sang Gilda in Paris that May her voice felt inexplicably slurred and thick. Her tongue had trouble tossing off the articulations in "Caro Nome" and she cracked on her very first E in the coloratura section. She recovered, but on the next E her voice broke entirely and she had to take a very obvious breath in an unaccompanied passage.

It was the same with each E afterward: break after break after break. Her high B and C, even her high C-sharp were perfect, her sixths in the descending passage were easy and crystal clear, but the E kept slipping. Her final trill—E again—refused to materialize: she felt an unbudging gurgle come out of her mouth.

Her ears were filled with roars and hisses and boos.

The next day's reviews were murderous. With uncanny penetration the critic for *Le Figaro* touched her deepest fears.

There is no denying that, at this moment in what was once a spectacular career, Madame Kavalaris is losing her voice. Occasionally the phrasing, the attack, the pitch are the perfection we remember; but in the very next phrase, she is a stumbling amateur. It is perhaps time for this beloved artist to renounce the stage and consider teaching.

The review could not have come at a worse possible time. She was scheduled to sing two performances of the Verdi *Requiem* the following week—one at La Scala, and the other, for a large audience including His Holiness the Pope, at an outdoor concert in the Milan Duomo.

Magazines, television, the international press would be covering the outdoor concert. She was counting on the publicity, for more and more it seemed to her that only publicity could keep her alive.

When the Scala representative phoned to ask if he might call at her suite at the Georges Cinq, Ariana assumed it was to discuss her dress at next Wednesday's performance. Though the Verdi *Requiem* was not liturgical, color would, of course, be inappropriate. She did not need to be told this and as she let Mr. diFilipi into the suite she wondered what sort of an idiot he took her for.

"To get to the point," she said, "I'll be wearing white."

He was a short, stout man of about fifty, with bushy black hair, and he seemed not to understand what she was talking about. She led him into the bedroom and opened the closet. She stripped tissue paper off the dress like bark from a tree.

"As you can see, it's simple, unruffled. There's an extra panel to allow for the diaphragm, but it's hardly decorative."

The Scala representative's face made an effort as if he were not used to smiling at dresses. "The Scala management will let you keep the deposit."

"Of course I'll keep the deposit. Why bring that up now?"

"Because if Madame Kavalaris wishes, she may withdraw from the performances of the *Requiem*."

Ariana carefully put the dress back in the closet. "So, my *Rigoletto* reviews frightened you."

"Scala is willing to pay half your fee, even if you cancel."

"Signore, listen. I signed a contract. I keep my contracts."

"Scala is willing to pay your entire fee even if you cannot perform. We only beg that you let us know now. For your own sake, we suggest that Madama consider taking a short rest."

It took all her self-control to master the anger that flashed through her. "Signore, I must sing the Verdi *Requiem*. I will sing it, I can sing it. For La Scala and for the Pope."

She landed at Milan airport Tuesday night, avoided reporters, had the limousine take her straight to the Principe di Savoy.

She spent the day of the performance in her suite. No interviews, no phone calls. Her head throbbed, her stomach was tight, she was certain she was going to be sick.

She arrived at La Scala two hours before the performance.

The wood-paneled dressing room gave her the comfort of an old friend seen after too long a separation. She prayed, warmed up, got into her white dress, and led the other soloists onto the stage.

As she bowed to the applause, she felt a wave of coldness sweeping from the audience. It was as if they were ready to assess her performance microscopically, like doctors examining body tissue for signs of decay.

Through the opening orchestral and choral measures she tried to ignore the uneasiness in the pit of her stomach. She negotiated her first "Kyrie," with its rapid climb to a fortissimo high B. Her throat was tight and the tone felt strident, but at least she hit the notes.

In the "Salva me" section of the "Rex tremendae" she had her first real trouble: an ominous break in line as she was reaching for a piano A-flat above the staff.

The passage was covered by the other soloists and orchestra, but as the phrases lengthened and the melody climbed to a high C she felt her breath giving out early; she was pulling up strength instead of tone. Before her octave drop she took an extra breath, just a tiny one, and the friendly acoustics of the house lent just enough resonance to cover— though the mezzo soloist shot her a glance.

She had no trouble with her G above the staff, but as the melody dropped back to E—an easy note, well within the range of any singer—the same astonishing thing happened. The breath wasn't there, the note wasn't there. She touched it, and suddenly it was gone.

The acoustics couldn't help this time. Verdi had scored the chord for vocal quartet, and she was the melody note. There were wind and string doublings, but no one was fooled.

The other soloists threw her questioning looks.

A whisper swept the darkened house.

But the real disaster did not come till near the end, in the "Et Lux Perpetua" of the "Libera me."

One of the most affecting moments in the whole requiem, it was scored for soprano solo floating above a cappella chorus. She had loved the passage since childhood; she had sung it at her father's funeral, at her audition for DiScelta, two dozen times since. It summed up for her the meaning of the work, the spirit of mercy and forgiveness overcoming wrath and terror and death.

She tried to project that spirit as she sang the beautiful phrases that Verdi had marked dolcissimo, as gentle as possible. But as she reached the final "requiem" with its astonishing quadruple piano and its upward octave leap to a high B-flat, she lost control of her throat muscles: the sound turned stringy and shot up too quickly, ahead of the chorus, thinning into a batlike squeak.

There was no way to recover, no way to hold the note. The conductor had to cut the chorus short.

Before she could even continue there were cries of *"Vergogna!"*—"Shame!"—and *"Basta!"*—"Enough!"

The choral fugue and her final recitative *senza misura* passed in a nightmare. When her turn came to bow, she was hissed. Somehow, with Roddy's help, she got through the jeering crowds back to her hotel.

The newspapers crucified her the next day, calling her an insult to Verdi, to music, and—not least of all—to God.

The afternoon of the following day the sky was piercingly blue, without a cloud. Ariana told herself that was an omen. But under the arching glass of the Duomo, Milan's great enclosed arcade, the light was a toneless gray.

She told herself that was not an omen.

A platform had been set up for the musicians, bleachers for the reserved seats, a special section for the Pope and his retinue. As she took her place before the orchestra she saw that herds of reporters and paparazzi had swollen the crowd.

In deference to the solemnity of the occasion, there was no applause.

Her eye caught His Holiness smiling and then the gunmetal glint of a camera in the front row. She looked quickly away, down at her hands pressed white in her lap.

The conductor gave the downbeat. Muted cellos sighed out the first descending figure.

As the music spun out in pianissimo, she was aware of the sheer physical bulk of orchestral and choral sound. For the first time in her career she wondered if her voice would be strong enough to cut through.

Blood began pounding through her arteries. She waited through the short choral fugue on *"Te decet hymnus,"* through the modulation back to A-major that was her signal, with the three other soloists, to stand.

She stood. She felt her knees turning liquid.

The tempo quickened slightly and over repeated string chords the solo tenor sang the first "Kyrie." The bass replied with the first "Christe," and then it was Ariana's turn.

She breathed in, organizing strength for her "Kyrie." She had sung the entrance dozens of times, yet today had all the foreboding of a first time. As the sound gathered in her lungs she was aware of an extraordinary time lag between thought and execution.

The notes inched their way up her throat, rising by sheer force of will until they shot out of her, far too loud, almost shrill.

On her fifth note, the G-sharp above the staff of "Eleison," she lost control of her voice and skidded into a scream without finishing the word.

Panic dropped on her like a net.

She stretched out a shaking hand toward the conductor, entreating. He lowered his baton. The music stopped.

She turned toward the Pope. "If His Holiness will forgive me, I cannot continue."

She left the platform. There was something absolutely terrifying about the silence of the crowd. It was as though they were screaming *Burn her! Burn her!*

She pushed her way through them, and a moment later she was running alone up the dazzling avenue with only one thought in her head: to put an ocean between herself and her disgrace.

A figure in white detached itself from the crowd. It came quickly up the center aisle, swerved to kneel an instant before the Pope's chair, and continued directly to the platform where the Scala orchestra, the conductor, and three soloists stood like bewildered refugees in a stranded lifeboat.

A wind of whispers swept alongside her. *"La Rodrigo!"*

"Brava la Rodrigo!"

Clara Rodrigo dropped her white sable coat on the chair that only a moment ago had been Ariana Kavalaris's. She was wearing a simple white gown and a single strand of pearls. She had lost weight. Under her right arm she clutched a score of the *Requiem*.

She embraced the conductor and allowed him to kiss her on both cheeks.

Applause broke out.

La Rodrigo, smiling serenely, sat in her newly claimed chair. The soloists sat. The orchestra sat. The conductor once more raised his baton.

The audience fell silent.

The Pope smiled.

Verdi's *Requiem* began, again, with the pianissimo falling sigh of muted cellos.

They were in line at the boarding gate when Ariana noticed. "You've booked us on Alitalia."

"You said you wanted the first flight to New York."

"I can't fly Alitalia. They'll crash the plane. Book us on another line. I won't fly with a Catholic pilot."

Roddy grimaced. "Your luggage is already on board."

"Splendid—they can take revenge on *it*."

She stepped out of line and planted herself in a chair in the lounge. She sensed whispers around her, heads turning. In less than two hours, the scandal had already reached the Milan airport. She adjusted her kerchief and her dark glasses. She sat quietly, doing nothing but dying.

A half-hour later Roddy returned waving two reticketed folders. "Will El Al do?"

29

THE PLANE REACHED JFK ON SCHEDULE. AT FIRST ARIANA thought she was safe in the sea of travelers embracing their families, but then she saw the reporters waiting, hungry to carve her into a mass of raw skin.

"Nothing to declare," she told the customs inspector.

She strode forward. There was a clicking of shutters, and then a storm of questions and flashbulbs and mikes thrust into her face.

"Miss Kavalaris, why did you walk out on the Pope?"

"I did not walk out on His Holiness."

"What do you think of Clara Rodrigo stepping in for you?"

A voice cut in resonantly: "Miss Kavalaris has no comment and wishes you all a good day."

She spun around. She hadn't seen or even thought of Giorgio Montecavallo for over two years, and here he was with his arm thrown protectively around her in the middle of the El Al terminal.

"Monte, what in the world are you doing here?"

"Meeting you, cara." He was wearing a three-piece suit of tan tropical worsted, a boldly striped shirt and a wide flowered tie. He was gorgeously overweight and she covered him with kisses.

"Is there a new love in your life, Miss Kavalaris?"

Monte raised a hand. "Miss Kavalaris and I are friends." He bullied a way for them through yelling newsmen. They reached the limousine. A chauffeur held the door.

Ariana settled into the back seat. She smiled fondly at Monte as they crawled through expressway traffic. Tears pooled in the corners of her eyes. "Oh, Monte. My oldest, dearest friend. Of all of them, the only one who's lasted."

Two hours later she stood in the living room of the Sutton Place townhouse looking out over the garden and the East River.

"Something to drink?" Monte was at the bar.

"Nothing for me. I'm going to bed."

"Good idea. You're overtired."

She turned. "I know you've a million things to do, Monte. But would you stay with me? Just be in the house till I fall asleep?"

Monte tucked her into bed. Her eyes shut immediately. She was breathing heavily. There seemed to be an enormous weight on her chest.

He unhooked the gold chain and set her locket on the night table.

"Yes," he heard her mumble. "Take it off. Just for a while."

✿　✿　✿

He stayed for the next two days while she tossed in gnarled dreams. He held her hand when she screamed, showed the cook how to make a decent minestrone for a convalescent, personally took charge of everything from doctors to phone calls.

"Carlotta? Yes, cara, she's in a terrible state. The doctor says it's exhaustion."

He appointed himself Ariana's guardian and bulldog. When reporters laid twenty-four-hour siege to her front door, it was he who ushered them five at a time into the private garden, offered drinks, and explained the crisis. "You can't quote me."

"Naturally not," CBS-TV assured him.

"It involves His Holiness the Pope."

Ariana opened her eyes drowsily. Through planes of shifting fog she could make out jungles on fire. A voice spoke of America bombing Vietcong supply routes in Cambodia. She realized she was staring at a TV set.

There was a rich, resonant pop. Monte set a silver ice bucket by the bedside. A fizzing, foil-necked bottle rested on a bed of ice.

"Champagne?" she said. "What's the occasion?"

He handed her a bubbling glass. "Look. Listen."

The image on the TV changed. A woman in black sable with dark glasses was rushing down the corridor of an airline terminal, barely managing to stay ahead of a pack of pursuing reporters.

"It's me!" Ariana reached for her glasses. "I don't look bad, do I?"

"You look *splendida!*"

A microphone shaped like a hornet's nest had bobbed into the picture. The woman in black was swatting it aside. "No comment. Please leave me alone."

"Thursday's evening news," Monte said. "I taped it for you."

"I have a good speaking voice, haven't I?" Her eye flicked back to the screen, where a newscaster with too much makeup was reading from a teleprompter.

". . . because of Vatican objections to Madame Kavalaris's friendship with tenor Giorgio Montecavallo, a man whose civil divorce is considered invalid by the Roman Catholic Church."

She burst out laughing. "They think—oh, good God, they think I stopped singing because I argued with the Pope over *you?*"

He nodded.

She jumped out of bed.

"Ariana, be careful. You're weak."

She flung open the closet doors. Her hand rifled down the row of fifty-seven evening gowns.

"What are you doing?"

"Looking for my reddest, most low-cut, most vulgar gown. Monte, phone La Côte Basque. We're going to make a scandal."

Photographers were waiting outside the townhouse as they stepped into the limousine. Photographers were waiting on Fifty-fifth Street as they stepped onto the sidewalk. They refused to kiss for the cameras but consented to hug. "We're just friends," Ariana said. "Not all the gossip you hear is infallible."

"That was naughty," Monte whispered as they entered La Côte Basque.

The manager shook hands with Monte and embraced Ariana as though they were his long-lost brother and sister. He led them to a table in the best part of the room. The maître d' and headwaiters all came crowding up to say hello. Customers' heads turned, jeweled hands cupped whispers, eyes flashed greetings.

The manager helped Ariana out of her full-length sable. A pail of ice cradling a bottle of Taittinger brut was by their table almost before they had settled into their places.

"Kiss me," Ariana said. "Truman Capote is staring."

When the waiter brought the menus Ariana sighed.

"On the eve of the holocaust," she said, "happiness must be snatched quickly. I'll have a dozen escargots, the crème de carottes, the filet mignon bordelaise à point, pommes croquettes, asparagus hollandaise, the endive salade vinaigrette and perhaps we'd better order the dessert soufflés now."

The rented limo brought them home a little after two in the morning. They were drunk and happy and New York was sparkling in the misty early morning.

Ariana dredged her keys out of her handbag and unlocked the front door. Riding up in the elevator she asked Monte to sleep in her room that night.

"All right, I'll pull the easy chair over to your bed."

When he began moving the chair she caught his hand.

"Sleep in the bed with me. I want to feel you next to me."

He stood there for a second, just looking at her. "You don't want an old wreck like me."

"Old wreck? Monte, you may be a little overweight, but you're a very attractive man. I love your hair and your skin and your sense of humor and I'd love you to make love to me."

He pulled her into a blind, bone-mashing embrace. "I . . . can't."

She saw a crucifixion in his face.

"For some time now I haven't been able to. I thought it might have been because of drink, so I stopped drinking for six months. I went to an analyst, and he couldn't help. I've been to doctors for shots and clinics for rest cures and nothing works. I'm sorry, Ariana. Is that a terrible disappointment?"

She saw the sadness of it, yet she couldn't help smiling at the endlessly repeating pattern of her life: new man, same mess.

"We can still sleep together, can't we?" she said.

"If you don't mind—just sleep."

"Oh, Monte. Just sleep sounds like heaven."

"Monte, move in with me."

"Cara, don't be ridiculous."

"But it makes sense. This house is too big for one person."

"We'd be cutting each other's throat in a week."

"Nonsense. We've been together three weeks without a fight."

"And you've been in Latin America two of those weeks."

"And it made all the difference in the world knowing you'd be here when I opened that front door."

They argued for two days. He explained why it couldn't work: they were both singers, both crazy, there would be no sex. She explained why it couldn't fail: they were both singers, both crazy, there would be no sex.

He finally agreed to a one-month trial and moved in with three laundry bags, a carved lamp, and twelve suit bags bearing the name of a good tailor in Venice.

"Is that all?" she asked.

"The rest has to be shipped."

She understood. He had nothing else in the world.

The next day she took one of his suits to Paul Stuart's. She picked out five pairs of slacks and two lovely Harris tweed sports jackets and asked the fitter to take the size from the suit. While she was in the store she picked out four sweaters and a dozen shirts and three beautifully simple neckties.

There were tears in Monte's eyes when the packages came. He kissed her and rushed up to his room to change.

"You look beautiful," she said.

"I'll take you to lunch," he said. "You can show me off."

They went to La Grenouille; Monte had forgotten his charge card and she paid with hers. He was terribly embarrassed.

"Be quiet, darling," she said. "You're gorgeous and why shouldn't I use my charge card a little."

Over the next weeks, she gave him a nice watch from Tiffany, because all he had was an old one that didn't keep time; and two pairs of decent shoes, because the half-soles were falling off his; and, thinking ahead, an overcoat for autumn.

"You can't keep giving me things. I'm a man and you're a woman and I should be giving you things."

"But, darling, you *are* giving me something. You give me laughter."

And it was perfectly true. He was always saying funny things, pointing out the idiocy of this or that, mimicking people, turning everyday conversations into parodies of operatic scenes.

Ten days later she found him sitting in the living room looking utterly miserable. He wouldn't tell her what the matter was, but finally she wormed it out of him that he owed Internal Revenue $12,000 in back taxes and they were dunning him.

"I'll loan you the $12,000," she said.

"I can't keep draining you."

"It's not as though I were poor yet."

She wrote him a check and he gazed at her.

"Your beautiful eyes," he said.

"What about my beautiful eyes?"

"They're just beautiful, that's all."

He said he wanted to make himself useful to her. He took her checkbook from her and looked after money matters. He wrote the checks for everything: food, insurance, taxes on the house. He did the balancing, went over the statements, deposited the drafts from her agent. She signed and that was all there was to it.

It was a great load off her mind.

"Cara, you pay Roddy $500 a week?"

She looked up. Monte was sitting at the desk. She could see him totaling up figures on a pocket calculator.

"I do half your secretarial work for you," he said. "I could perfectly easily do the rest."

"Monte, I could never ask you to—"

"Cara, I love you, I understand you, I'm quite content to do everything I can for you."

"But Roddy's been with me so long, I couldn't bear to tell him I don't need him anymore."

"Don't worry, cara, I'll tell him myself."

Monte persuaded her to cut back on servants as well: to make do with one maid instead of two; to take a part-time instead of a full-time cook.

"I love to cook," he said. "Tuesday and Thursday can be our cook-in nights."

The Monday after the butler was let go Ariana answered a ringing at the front door. The caller was a big man, smoking a cigar, and his

266

breath smelled of mouthwash. A temple-to-temple eyebrow arched over his eyes. "Monte around?" he asked gruffly.

"Monte's upstairs."

"The name's Degan." The man held out a hand bristling with black hairs. "Mort Degan." He wore a polka-dot bow tie and a dark suit that had a glossy look, as though it had been cleaned too often. He tossed a nod over his shoulder. "They're with me."

An orange Toyota was parked at the curb. A woman in a khaki pants suit and a man in a camouflage jacket were hauling camera equipment from the trunk.

"Monte!" Ariana called.

He appeared at the top of the stairs, knotting the sash of his bathrobe. He slapped a hand to his forehead. "Cara, forgive me—I forgot the photographers were coming today." The explanation came tumbling out. Mort was an old friend; the man and woman carrying lights and tripods into the house were from *Esquire* magazine. "They're here to interview us, cara. Mort arranged it, wasn't that nice of him?"

Ariana sat absolutely still, absolutely smoldering as cameras and lights were set up in the living room.

Monte asked Mort Degan how life had been treating him.

"I sold eight million five in film rights at Cannes."

Monte whistled.

The man in camouflage began darting and crouching about the room, snapping pictures with a little camera that made insectlike buzzes and clicks. The woman in khaki placed a cassette recorder on the coffee table and asked questions about the relationship between opera and fame.

Ariana let Monte do the answering.

He went off at tangents, speaking about the techniques of creating a character, the mystery of personality which is at the core of all art, and of course the God-given thing, the human voice. Ariana became aware of a shadowy space between Monte's words and his actions, of the difference between what he believed himself to be and what she knew he was. She did not like his making a fool of himself. She did not like the look of his friend Mort Degan or of the magazine people. She smiled for Monte's sake, but inside herself she was not smiling at all.

"The key," Monte was saying, "is Ariana's musical integrity. No matter what she is performing—and she has enormous range—she never debases herself or the music."

"Are you really as wonderful as all that, Miss Kavalaris?"

"Monte's being charming. The truth is, I'm dreadful. I'm a gossip, I have terrible moods, and I cheat at pinochle."

The woman smiled tightly. "Any truth to the rumors about the two of you?"

Ariana's glance flicked up at the woman. "Rumors?"

"A joint concert next January?"

"I hadn't heard those rumors," Ariana said icily.

"To tell the truth," Mort Degan said, "I started them."

Ariana took a long drag from a filter-tip cigarette. "Why?"

"Pure self-interest. I want to represent you for the concert."

After dinner they were sitting, just the two of them, in the living room. "He's a peculiar man, your Mr. Degan," Ariana said.

Monte glanced at her. "He's a damned hardworking agent."

"But I already have an agent. Richard and I choose my performing dates—not Mr. Degan, however hardworking he may be, not you, however much I may love you. I very rarely do recitals, and I never do them jointly with anyone."

Monte looked at her a long, sad, silent moment. "In other words you're telling me to go to hell."

"Monte, what's wrong with you? I'm telling you I don't do things Mr. Degan's way and I don't want to get mixed up with him or his schemes."

"You don't trust me."

"Of course I trust you. But my engagement calendar's full for the next year and a half."

"It's not full on January twenty-fourth."

Silence piled upon silence.

"Monte, this is foolish. Please, let's not argue."

"You're a great artist, Ariana, but as a woman . . ." Monte was sitting on the sofa, arms locked around his knees, staring at his Scotch and soda. "You give a man reassurance in one area, you raise doubt in another, you keep his uncertainties alive and stinging. You must be hell to love."

"That's not fair."

"Neither is this hysteria of yours. I was only trying to help."

"What kind of joint recital? I sing 'Sempre Libera' with piano accompaniment and you sing 'Granada' with your guitar? You haven't even vocalized in a year and a half."

Monte drained his Scotch and stood. "Excuse me for trying."

"Oh, Monte, for God's sake—"

But he was gone, and a moment later the elevator was whirring up the shaft.

Not wanting to show his anger just yet, Nikos watched Maggie settle down at the dressing table in her lavender evening gown. It was two in the morning. He had been home four hours, but he was still in his dinner jacket. She was babbling about a birthday party she'd been to at the Carlyle.

"Whose birthday?" he said quietly.

"The party was given by Adela Schatzberg—you know, the painter—she does those large dolls—they were in *New York* magazine—and it was in honor of Putney Wilkes, who does something at the Metropolitan Museum of Art. Runs it, I believe." As her arm lifted to unhook her necklace, two rows of zipper teeth in her gown pulled slightly apart.

"Was it a late birthday party?" Nikos asked.

"No, we left at about seven and went to the costume gala that Pru Delman was giving for her husband—Senator Bruce Delman, you met him at the Vanderbilts'."

"So you went to a birthday party and then to a costume ball."

"I suppose the papers will call it a ball. There was a rock band and a big striped tent. I'd never heard of half the movie stars who were there, they were all children on cocaine. Lady Benson says hello, by the way."

Nikos stood with his eyes half shut. *The rest of my life*, he thought. *I'll have to listen to nonsense like this for the rest of my life.* He wondered for the ten-thousandth time since his wedding night what the hell he had gotten himself into.

"Didn't you forget something?" he said.

"Forget?" She looked at him with a blankness that seemed almost unfeigned.

"We were invited this evening to Buzz Dworkin's reception for his daughter's wedding."

"Buzz Dworkin? I can't stand that man."

"Be that as it may, he's a force in this city and he sent us an invitation over a month ago. The governor and his wife were there. So were the mayor and his wife. So were a good many other men and their wives."

"Poor you. It sounds like cigar smoke and deals and politicians toasting one another."

"And we accepted."

"No, Nikos, you accepted. You never mentioned it to me."

He thrust her Florentine-leather date book under her nose. On that day's page, in looping green felt-tip, she had scrawled *Dworkin recep.* In red ink, running over the green, *Viv/Shatz party.* In pencil, over that, *Delmans.*

Her face tightened like a macadamia in a nutcracker. "How dare you search my desk."

"How dare you embarrass me in that manner."

"How many times have I begged you to come with me to Hobe Sound, or Sag Harbor, or Elaine's? And how many times have you not shown up at parties *we* were giving?"

"Once, only once, and that was because of business."

"And how many times have I had to go to art openings alone or fly to Paris by myself?"

"You're changing the subject."

"Just because you're jealous of Ariana making headlines with that tenor doesn't mean I have to be at your side every time a sleazy tycoon throws a tax-deductible blast. I don't mind your being fixated on her, but I will not have you taking your obsession out on me."

Silence froze the bedroom. Nikos raised his hand and brought the date book swinging against Maggie's face like a fly swatter.

She took a long moment looking at him, and then a sly sort of triumph crept into her narrowed eyes. She turned back to her mirror, finished unhooking her emerald necklace, and laid it neatly to rest in the contoured velvet bed of its enameled box.

"Putney Wilkes heard her Norma. Apparently it was less than excellent." Maggie's gaze attached itself to Nikos and seemed to purr. "Poor Ariana. What's she going to do now that her voice is gone?"

"Sweetums . . ."

Boyd was staring not at Ariana but beyond her, out the window of their first-class compartment in the Flèche d'Or. They—or rather, he—had decided that taking the train ("And such a comfortable train, sweetums, first class only; the Europeans do these things so well") was less trouble than flying from Amsterdam to Paris. ("Who wants to drag all the way out to airports and back, after all we're just going from the Doelen to the Ritz." She had sensed that what he really meant was, *We're just going from bad reviews at the Dutch State Theater to worse reviews at the Paris Opéra, so let's keep a low profile.*

The manicured Belgian countryside was speeding past. Ariana's eye followed three farmhouses and two lonely stands of ancient elms.

"Don't you think Puccini's an awful second-rater?" Boyd's score of *Tosca* was open on his lap and now he shut it with a slam. "I don't care if I ever conduct another *Tosca* again."

Ariana was suddenly alert. For two decades Richard Schiller had arranged her bookings years in advance, and even though her voice was going, she still had future dates to fall back on. Granted, there were fewer and fewer of them, but nonetheless they stretched forward as a dwindling sort of security over the next three years.

Ariana knew her career was over. She had known it since Milan. She knew Boyd was giving her—and himself—an out.

And she hated him for it.

"You mean you don't want to do another *Tosca* with me." Her eyes met his and she watched him muster shock and denial.

"Nothing to do with you, sweetums. I'd just rather dig into something new. Like late Verdi. Like *Falstaff*."

He knew she didn't sing any of the women in *Falstaff*. "You know I won't cancel my contract, so you're going to cancel yours, and that way you won't have to conduct me in *Tosca* . . . or anything else. I'm a sinking ship and you're abandoning me."

"I'm not going to talk to you if you're going to be paranoid."

Twelves days later, when she returned to New York, Ariana found a letter waiting from Richard Schiller. Apparently Boyd's agent had sent word that due to circumstances beyond et cetera et cetera, his client would be forced to cancel next year's *Tosca*s in Covent Garden, Paris, Vienna, Scala, Chicago, and Melbourne.

For three days Ariana's thinking was a fog of self-doubt and terror.

On the fourth day she went to see Richard Schiller. He was pacing behind his desk, trailing the telephone cord back and forth through his fingers. A low indecipherable voice was screaming from the receiver.

"Richard. I need to talk to you." She crossed the room and poised a finger over the cradle, ready to break the connection.

He apologized to the caller, hung up and stood staring at her.

"You're neglecting me," she said. "Admit it. The only dates I have now were booked long before that Duomo fiasco. You're letting my career wind down."

"What do you want, Ariana? Just what is it you expect an agent to do for you?"

"I want to be on television."

"Why? Because your ex-boy friend got married on TV and you have to compete?"

"Leave Nikos out of this."

"I suggest *you* leave Nikos out of this, because in my frank opinion, that is all this *tzimmis* is about."

"That is one hell of way to talk to one of your top clients."

"And *that* is one hell of way to talk to your top agent."

"Then maybe you don't want to represent me anymore."

He waved his hands across his face. "Go home. Just fucking go home."

Without thinking, she was out of her chair, leaning over his desk, pounding her fist on the blotter.

"What is it about you agents? You get a performer helpless and tied up with contracts and completely at your mercy and then you torture them for the sheer fun of it. You've already decided to junk my career but you're taking your own sweet time watching me die, and all the while you could be helping, you're lecturing and ladling advice and sneering. You're a bullying, sadistic psychopath!"

He looked at her a long moment and a genuine sadness seemed to come into his eyes.

"Ariana—honey—it's not me that's killing you, it's this attitude you've gotten into. It's showing in your work and it's showing in the way you're behaving. I'm sorry to be the one to tell you, but it's showing badly. You've got to pull out of this."

"Get me a job and just watch me pull out of it."

"You've got plenty of jobs—San Francisco next month, Hamburg, Milan, Dusseldorf—"

"Those aren't the kind of jobs I want. Richard, I need promotion. What the rock stars get. Ads on busses. Record jackets in windows. Television spots. I could advertise quality products—American Express Cards, Lincoln Continentals . . ."

He sighed heavily. "Hon, you stick to the singing, I'll handle the rest."

"You're not handling it right. People are forgetting my name."

"If you'd show up for a performance once in a while maybe they'd remember it."

"I haven't missed a performance in two months."

"Sutherland hasn't missed one in her whole career."

"I'm not Sutherland."

"Tell me something I don't know." His teeth bit down on his lower lip. He came around the desk to hug her. "Hon, I'm sorry, I didn't mean to bark—only it's a hell of a time to barge in without an appointment. It's the craziest time of the day. You know we do all our calls to the Coast between two and four."

"What's so important about calls to the Coast that you can't take two minutes to talk to an old client and friend?"

"I'll tell you what's so important—I'm trying to save your tush from a couple of goniffs."

She raised her eyebrows and instantly felt him retreating.

"Don't ask for details, please. You don't want to hear, you don't want to know."

"Richard, I want to hear, I want to know."

"Those clowns I was talking to, they want to do a miked concert at the Pyramids, televised, $1,000 a seat, some lousy pop program."

"What does that have to do with me?"

Richard hesitated, his glance darting around the room as though to make sure that all the ashtrays were nailed down. "They want you."

"Will there be publicity?"

"Sure—an abortion like that is nothing *but* publicity."

"Articles in the papers? Interviews? TV guest shots?"

Richard nodded.

Ariana strode to the window. "How many people see an opera? Four thousand in a big house? And how many see a television show? Eighty million, two hundred million? Richard, I'll do it."

His face blanked out. "You don't want to work with these people.

Everything they touch turns to crapola. Believe me, they'll make the Pyramids a garbage dump."

"So, what's ten minutes in a garbage dump?"

For a long moment he didn't answer. "It's scheduled for August. It'll mean canceling Rio del Mar."

"To hell with Rio del Mar."

Still he hesitated.

"Richard, I'm not leaving this office till you call and accept that offer."

30

IT WAS ENOUGH TO RUIN MAGGIE STRATIOTIS'S BREAKFAST. There was a huge article in the *New York Times* on Ariana Kavalaris's favorite way of making fettuccine.

Who chooses these articles? she wondered. *Why doesn't the* Times *ever ask me how I make blender Vichyssoise?*

That same day, at the hairdresser's, she picked up a magazine and saw a photograph of Ariana at a party in the company of "world-renowned tenor Giorgio Montecavallo." At the edge of the picture—it was unclear whether he formed part of the group or not—was "playwright Arthur Miller."

Maggie was suddenly acutely and painfully Ariana-conscious, aware that the woman enjoyed not just fame but a sort of intellectual prestige.

As she sat under the hair dryer she couldn't help reflecting and assessing. New York had unquestionably become the mecca for world celebrity: it was a city bursting with opportunities for fame. But, staring at the photograph, she had to wonder if she had made the most of those opportunities.

"What's that you've got there?" Nikos asked.

Maggie looked up from her Louis Quinze beechwood chair, where she was industriously marking a blue-covered script in red ballpoint. "I've been job hunting. And I've found something just right. Channel Four. Tony McGraw wants me to host some tours of the great Hudson Valley homes." She described the project and the go-aheads that the Rockefeller and Roosevelt estates had given.

"I don't want you getting mixed up with McGraw," Nikos said.

"Why not? You do business with him."

"That's why."

Their eyes locked.

"What do you expect me to do, phone him and say I've decided to drop the whole idea?"

"That's exactly what I expect you to do."

She shook her head. "Sorry, Nikos. I have a life too."

Five thousand miles away, after a night of listening to waves breaking on the rocks, Renata Stratiotis showered and dressed. She tiptoed past her mother's room. The door was open.

In a stream of pale morning sunlight, Maria-Kristina sat by the window brushing her hair. She turned. "Renata? You're up early."

"I've got something to do in town today."

Her mother's eyes narrowed into a quick worried look. "You're not seeing those dope dealers. Please don't get into that again."

"No, Mother, I'm through with them."

Renata walked slowly across the lawn to the little bay. She got into the blue-and-white speedboat tied to the end of the jetty. It rocked a little under her. The Baltic waters shined up at the sky with the even glow of stainless steel.

With a rip of the starting cord she jerked the motor into life.

The poodle jumped barking into the boat. She lifted it gently and set it down on the dock. "Sorry, Cochon, no passengers."

At a café on the mainland she met her dealer, a young man with mirrored glasses. She paid him and crammed 800 kroner worth of pills and marijuana into her traveling satchel.

"You'll like the grass," he said. "It's nerve gas."

She walked in the woods and smoked two joints. From a pay phone by the roadside she placed a call to New York City.

"Collect call for Nikos Stratiotis from Renata Stratiotis," an operator said.

Maggie glanced irritably from the receiver in her hand to the glowing dial of the bedside clock. "I'll accept charges."

"Is my father there?" The voice had that more-than-Oxford accent that Swedish schools teach their nationals.

Oh, God, am I going to have to lie here and listen to a father-daughter reunion? Maggie wondered. *I've got a ten-hour day lined up tomorrow at the Rockefeller estate.* She gloved her voice in kindness. "Renata, this is Maggie. Your father has told me so much about you. Is something the matter?"

"I just need to say hello to him."

Hello hardly sounded like an emergency. Maggie stubbed out her cigarette. "Darling, it's three-fifteen in the morning here. Your father will call you in the morning when he wakes up."

She replaced the receiver. A moment later, when Nikos stepped out of the bathroom, she had rolled onto her side and was pretending to be asleep.

Renata smoked another joint on her way back to the speedboat. She opened the motor full throttle. She stared up at a sky full of mashed-potato clouds. She checked the time by her wristwatch. It was a slender, silver wafer of a watch, sent to her by her father when she'd graduated from grade school university at Göteborg, second highest in her class. He'd been too busy to attend in person.

The island came rushing toward her. The house that Mother and Father had built seemed to be dancing on its foundation. A tall, scholarly woman in a red polka-dot dirndl ran onto the terrace and from her twisted face Renata could see she was screaming.

Mother, I'm sorry, but I didn't sleep all night and Father wouldn't take my call.

For one blinding instant time stopped. With a 60-mile-per-hour splintering of wood and chrome, the speedboat slammed into the stone harbor wall. Renata's skull was split open on impact.

Maria-Kristina's voice nearly broke across the five-thousand-mile satellite connection. It took Nikos a moment to understand, and then the earth fell away beneath him. "But why?" he said.

"Dr. Aakeborg thinks it was depression."

"But she had treatment for the depression."

"We found ninety-two lithium tablets in her medicine cabinet. She'd been lying. She hadn't been taking them."

Memories rushed back to him in a tidal wave, unbidden, eerily vivid: Renata's eighth birthday when he'd given her a white Shetland pony and she'd jumped into his arms and he'd hugged her and said, "Happy birthday, *min lilla flicka.*"

"And were there any other . . . drugs?"

"I don't want to autopsy, Nikos. Unless you insist. I'd like to bury her tomorrow. Here on the island."

"I'll be there." He buzzed his secretary. "Get hold of my wife, please. We have to leave for Sweden in three hours."

Waiting for Maggie in the private plane gave Nikos a strange sort of nausea. Twilight was turning dusty gray. He watched the sun touch the surface of Jamaica Bay.

They were two hours past their scheduled takeoff when a stewardess approached. "Mr. Stratiotis, your wife is with a camera crew in Pocantico Hills. We've been trying since five o'clock, but we can't get through to her."

Nikos let himself sink slowly into acceptance. "All right. We'll leave without Mrs. Stratiotis."

Nikos stood with his ex-wife and her three servants staring down into a grave that seemed a thousand light-years deep. The Lutheran minister read the service in Swedish.

Nikos tried to follow the words, but his thoughts kept going to the little girl. There had never been time to be with her, never time to tell her how very very much he loved her. His only child and he had never said *I love you.*

He found himself praying: *God, please give her back to me so I can tell her I loved her.*

Maria-Kristina threw the first handful of earth, Nikos the second. Afterward they walked along the beach.

"We haven't been together here in a long time," he said.

"Not since we were married."

"It seems a lifetime ago."

"It was."

He looked at the woman who had once been his wife. Her skin had the translucent beauty of middle age but her eyes were the same unfading gray-green he remembered.

"Did you ever think we'd be here again, like this?" he said.

"I try not to think like that. Each day is hard enough without adding others to it."

"I can still remember her as a girl. Little Renata. With golden pigtails. And now she won't even live to be a mother." He suddenly stopped. "How can God let it happen?"

"Maybe someday, with patience, we'll know the reason."

He wondered if she really believed those things. "There's no reason. It's pointless, all the living and dying and suffering and growing old."

The hand that took his was soft and strong. "It's a mystery and we have to endure it. How we endure it makes all the difference."

"I'm not very good at the 'how.'"

"Come up to the house. We'll have coffee. Ilse has baked that raisin cake you love."

Nikos flew back to New York that night. He arrived at the apartment in the morning and found hundreds of letters waiting. One was from Ariana. He was reading it for the third time when Maggie came breezing through the hallway.

She was obviously on her way to an appointment. Already she was beginning to dress like the highest-paid woman in TV history: diamonds, pearls, a pink Mainbocher suit. She saw him and immediately her manner became subdued.

"Nikos, I'm so terribly, terribly sorry. About your daughter and about the mixup. Nobody knew it was *your* secretary phoning." She stopped in front of the mirror. She placed a cartwheel hat on her head and tried it at different angles. It matched her suit and jiggled with dyed egret feathers. "I'd have done anything to be on that plane with you. I could have murdered those fools when I heard they didn't put the call through."

"Read this."

He thrust Ariana's letter at her. Her eyes glanced over it.

"Very sweet." She handed it back. "Very considerate."

"That's all you can say? Sweet, considerate?"

"What do you expect me to say?"

"There is one living person in the world who cares if I or my family live or die—and it isn't you."

"Anyone can write a note."

"Anyone can get to a plane on time."

"Nikos, I didn't know. No one told me."

"You're lying. *You knew.*"

She whirled, eyes mustering denial. "Are you actually accu—"

He seized her head between his hands and bent it back. "*She* is my family. Not you. From now on, Stratiotis watches over Kavalaris. And you—" He flung her away from him.

She stood massaging her neck, crying softly.

"Don't cry, little princess. Maybe someday some TV producer will come along and make you the whore you yearn to be."

That summer—armed with twelve gowns, her *briki*, two pounds of chamomile tea and three of Vassilaros, the only decent Greek coffee available outside of Greece—Ariana gave eighteen sold-out concerts in the Far East. Audiences applauded wildly when she put on a kimono to sing "Un Bel Di." Critics never mentioned that she was transposing everything down.

Five weeks later she sat in a New York screening room. Images of her concert at the Pyramids flooded the screen; the sound came through a small speaker that buzzed on every A-flat.

Her gaze sifted through the darkness, catching the puzzled expressions on the faces around her. One of the junior executives rolled a joint.

The reel finished. The lights came up. The president of Channel 4 stood and shook her hand. "That was a most stimulating experience, Miss Kavalaris."

"When will you air it?"

"It's not quite our sort of material. Well, we knew it was a gamble, didn't we?"

"I want to talk to your friend," Ariana told Monte at dinner that night. "Your friend Mort Degan."

"What happened, hon?" Richard Schiller stood before Ariana and gazed at her with concern. "You used to have savvy. And now you're mixed up with this Degan."

"He's managing a concert for Monte and me, that's all."

"First of all, you shouldn't be singing with that has-been. Second, you don't know Degan. I can understand you're disappointed in last year's bookings. But he's a drunk and a cokehead. You don't need him."

There was an instant's silence in the office and then she drew herself up. "I never thought you'd stoop to that."

"I'm not the one who's stooping, hon. And I'm not letting you do this concert."

"I'm doing it."

"I say no and I'm your agent."

"Were my agent. Goodbye, Richard."

She was moving into new terrain; and if that meant burning a few bridges, so what. She sold three sable coats. She had Sotheby's auction her living room antiques. She took a loss, but since she was backing the concert herself she needed the cash.

Mort Degan handled the production details. Every time she went to his office there was a piece of paper needing her signature.

"Would you just sign this agreement with the stage managers? All three copies. And there's a rider, be sure to initial. And when you're through with that would you sign this?"

"What is it?"

"You're opening a special bank account at Chase."

"What for?"

"Expenses, ever heard of expenses?" Mort smiled. He was a full-time smiler. "Sign where your name's typed. All three. And would you sign this—hate to hit you with so much paper."

"What is it?"

"The bond."

"Bond?"

"In case we burn the house down, they'll want to be reimbursed."

The first ad was a half-page in the *New York Times* the Sunday after Thanksgiving.

MORTON DEGAN ASSOCIATES PRESENT

IN CONCERT

LIVE

THE DREAM DUET

ARIANA KAVALARIS/GIORGIO MONTECAVALLO

FAVORITE ARIAS FROM OPERA, BROADWAY, AND FOLKLORE

MAIL ORDERS NOW. TICKETS AT BOX OFFICE TOMORROW 10 A.M.

The sun was shining the next morning. Ariana and Monte hailed a taxi and asked the driver to go slowly past Carnegie Hall. At 9:00 A.M. the line stretched around two corners and halfway down the block to Sixth Avenue.

Ariana grabbed Monte's arm. "All those people. They remember." Her eyes were beginning to tear.

Monte hugged her to his shoulder. "They never forgot."

❀   ❀   ❀

Mort Degan phoned Ariana at three o'clock that afternoon. "It's a sellout. Scalpers are getting fifty bucks for balcony seats."

There was too much to do: dresses to be chosen and fitted, a white gown for the first half of the concert, a lower-cut black gown for the second; interviews, press agents who had to be lunched with, columnists who had to be cultivated, parties to go to, parties to give, all the day-and-night labor of promoting a concert that was still two months in the future.

It was hard to judge how the concert was shaping up. Ariana was too close to her fears. The numbers she rehearsed with Monte—candy like "La Ci Darem la Mano" and "The Merry Widow Waltz" and "Tonight, Tonight" from *West Side Story*—embarrassed her. With Monte bellowing beside her she felt like the sun setting behind a billboard advertising gelati and tortoni.

It was even worse with her solo numbers.

She attempted "Caro Nome" and her voice felt swollen and damp. Every note above the staff seemed to blister her throat. She closed her eyes and plummeted through the empty space where a high B-natural ought to have been.

I was able to sing it once. What happened?

She listened to her records. They made her thoughtful and sad. As she walked back to her bedroom her back ached. For the first time in her life she felt middle-aged. She lay down and wept silently.

Monte sat on the bed and stroked her forehead.

"Nothing lasts," she said. "Sooner or later everything we have is taken from us."

"Except our appetites," he said. "Let's go out to dinner."

She took to staying up late. She took to getting up late. She took to Monte's set because they didn't know music or, thank God, talk it. Tennessee Williams and Natalie Wood were her friends for an entire week and they didn't raise eyebrows when she lit a cigarette.

She tried to eat well, and Monte arranged that all important discussions took place over meals at Côte Basque, the Russian Tea Room, "21," L'Escargot, or—if they didn't want to be recognized—La Grenouille.

But even nourishing food didn't put energy into her. She was losing weight and turning edgy, overreacting to things: jumping when a teaspoon clattered in a saucer; brooding when the mailman was late. Dreams took her back to her childhood and she kept seeing her father's corpse and waking up in a sweat.

As he stepped into the cubicle Dr. Worth Kendall saw a figure in a green smock perched on the edge of the examining table, her head twisted around to look up at him. Her face might have been drawn with gray chalk and if he hadn't had her chart in his hand he'd never have recognized Ariana Kavalaris.

He was careful to hide his shock. "Hello, Ariana. How are you?"

"I thought I'd come in and find out."

"Good idea." He tapped her, probed her, shone a light in her ears and down her throat. He had a sense that something had broken in her. "Look up. Look down. Look at me."

Dark rings underneath her eyes gave them a ghostly luminosity. "I have pains." She pointed to her chest.

Dr. Kendall probed lightly where the ribs joined the breast bone. "I see a little swelling and some redness. How does it affect your singing?"

"It's hell when I have to take a deep breath."

"Well, relax, it's not a tumor. It's called costochondritis and it's not as bad as the name. It can hurt like hell but it goes away with treatment."

"What's the treatment?"

"Mild pain killers, heat, rest."

"I can't rest. I have a concert next month."

"I don't think you should be giving any concerts."

"You just said that costo-chondro thing isn't serious."

"It's not only the costochondritis. Your weight's down. Your blood pressure's up. Your pulse is irregular, there's a flutter in your heartbeat, I can hear fluid in your lungs. You had TB as a child?"

"I got over it."

He looked at her a moment. "Your reflexes are much too slow. And don't try to blame it on all the coffee you've been drinking or all the cigarettes you've been sneaking."

Her eyes slid away from his. "I haven't been sneaking anything. I make no secret . . . of my morning cigarette."

"A for honesty and E minus for conduct. People shouldn't smoke and singers shouldn't and above all you shouldn't. But we're not here to argue about nicotine. The point is, you're exhausted and you're driving yourself to a collapse. You've got to postpone that concert."

"I can't."

"Then cancel."

"Doctor, if I cancel the concert I might as well cancel my life."

"You have no strength. How the hell do you expect to get up on a stage and sing?"

"You can give me something to get me through the month."

"Nothing can get you through the month except a complete change of lifestyle."

She phoned Mort Degan.

"Glad you called," he said. "I need $850 for lights. Has to be cash. I'd go to the bank myself, but I'm waiting for the features editor from the *Times*."

She sighed. "All right, I'll have a messenger send it over. Mort, I need a doctor. Do you know anyone good?"

"I know someone great."

"What seems to be the problem?" Dr. Ted Gorman had a smile that seemed ready to understand any pain, any confusion in the world. He was a bald, trim man in his late forties, wearing a neatly pressed white linen doctor's jacket.

"I'm having trouble sleeping at night," Ariana said, "and trouble staying awake during the day. I'm very nervous about my concert next month. The tension's affecting my throat muscles."

Dr. Gorman wrote quickly on a prescription pad. "Are you allergic to cortisone?"

"I've never had any reaction to it."

"Planning to do any driving or operate any heavy machinery?"

"I'm a singer, doctor."

He glanced up at her. "Sorry. The heavy machinery was a joke. My wife keeps telling me to leave the comedy to the pros. Will you be driving?"

"No."

"Fine." He began dealing prescriptions at her like playing cards. "You'll take these to sleep. These for energy. These for nervousness. These for your throat and these for general muscle tension. Take off that blouse. I'll give you a shot now and I'd like you to come back twice a week till your concert for more."

31

DR. GORMAN'S SHOTS PROPELLED ARIANA THROUGH THE DAYS. HIS blue pills soothed her through the nights. But tiredness gnawed at her. She had trouble producing an even tone, trouble keeping on pitch in the high register, astonishing trouble with memory.

And then there was trouble with Monte. He was morose, drinking two or three martinis at lunch. When they ran through their duets at Austin's, he did not even know five of the songs. His voice cracked on an A.

Austin was granite-faced. "We can take that down a tone."

In the taxi going home Monte asked her, "Are you still sure you want to do the concert with me?"

She realized how much doubt had seeped into him. She patted his hand. "Of course I'm sure, Monte."

Four days later Monte bustled her to Carnegie Hall. Mort Degan was waiting with a pudgy, balding man with thinning gray curls. His name was Stu Waehner and apparently he was a sound technician. There seemed to be some possibility of putting panels behind the singers, reflecting the sound out into the hall.

"Every house is dead to certain frequencies," Stu Waehner said. "Carnegie happens to be poor from F above middle C up to D."

Which was news to Ariana.

Stu Waehner asked Ariana and Monte to stand on the stage and vocalize. He sat in different seats wearing earphones and holding something in his lap that looked like a tiny recording machine.

"What sort of panels?" Ariana asked afterward.

"Acoustic," Stu Waehner said, too busy jotting equations into a tiny notebook to meet her eyes.

Mort phoned that afternoon. "Good news, Stu can do it. Five panels. It'll cost thirty-two."

"Thirty-two hundred?" Ariana said.

"Thousand. Custom-built. I got him down from thirty-nine. They'll make all the difference. And Monte will feel more secure. Maybe he hasn't told you, but he's pretty nervous."

"Let me call you back, Mort."

She got the *briki* from the kitchen and went into the living room. A small pile of cedar logs was burning in the fireplace. She held the long-handled copper pot over the flames till the water boiled, and then she added Greek coffee and sugar. When the mix foamed up she tipped it into her cup.

She drank the coffee down to the grounds, then clapped a saucer over the cup and inverted it. She stared at the swirls of sediment. They told her that events were in a downward spiral.

We'll need all the help we can get, she realized. *Besides, it's only $32,000.*

She phoned Mort.

"All right, Mort. Have the panels built."

"Come on," Mort Degan said, "I gave you that money." He moved the receiver to his other shoulder and took a bite of his liverwurst.

The voice on the phone disagreed. "According to our records you paid a $1,250 deposit. The $5,000 balance was due last Friday. We need cash today or you're out. Sorry."

Mort hung up the phone and sat stiffly in the swivel chair.

And then it came to him.

He had $3,000 cash in the envelope Ariana had given him for the sound men. He could give Carnegie $2,500, promise to have the rest tomorrow, hold the lighting men with $500 . . .

He opened a desk drawer. No envelope. He foraged through old receipts and contracts and canceled checks. *Mort, you're no good like this. You're not thinking, not functioning. You need something to take the pressure off.*

He locked the office door, opened the bottom desk drawer. He lifted out the petty-cash box, took out the cellophane envelope and the sheet of tinfoil and the one-edged razor blade. He carefully poured the white powder over the tinfoil, then did a series of fast parallel chops with the razor. He rolled an almost-virgin bank note into a cylinder, put one end to his nostril, passed the other over the mound of white powder and inhaled.

Twenty seconds after the first snort he began to feel a lot better about the concert, about himself. He had bent down for a second snort when he noticed what he was holding to his nostril: a rolled $100 bill.

Where the hell did that come from?

And then he saw where it had come from: *From the petty-cash box. Dummy, you stashed Ariana's $3,000 with the coke.*

Suddenly everything was laughter and carnival and can-do. At that moment there was only one thing in Mort Degan's world that mattered, and it was not Ariana Kavalaris's concert or Carnegie Hall's deposit. He lifted the phone and dialed. All the time in the world seemed to pass before the two buzzes and the answering click.

"Lou—hey, Lou—it's Mort. I gotta see you. Like right away."

The phone pushed out a thundering silence. "You're into me for $2,200, Mort," his coke dealer said.

"Look—let me have a gram right away. I can give you $1,200 cash."

* * *

284

The voice on the phone was a woman, full of apology. "I wasn't supposed to, but I like Mort, so I gave him an extension. He never showed. There's no answer at his office."

Ariana turned, holding the phone, and watched Monte in his bathrobe sipping coffee and working out the *Times* crossword puzzle. "But surely, with the house sold out, you can trust us."

Monte looked up at her.

"Miss Kavalaris, we don't have those ticket receipts."

"Who does have them?" Ariana asked, and fear was suddenly running like poison in her veins.

"They went straight into the bank."

"Whose account?"

"You'd have to ask Mr. Degan."

Ariana realized that the one thing that mattered now was to put on a convincing face. "Mr. Degan was called out of town," she said, "and I'm afraid the oversight is mine. The money will be there in an hour." As she hung up the receiver she had a sense of time running out, life running down. "Monte. Phone the bank. Ask for the balance in the concert account."

His tone was instantly defensive. "Cara, why are you so upset?"

"Monte. *Phone.*"

He phoned and asked and then, overweight and shaking, he gazed with numbed eyes at her. "Mort closed the account yesterday."

She drew in a deep breath and let it out in a whisper. "*Panagia mou . . . voïthia.*" This time the words were no unthinking Greek reflex. She needed help and she was calling on the Virgin.

"Everyone's ripping her off. Sound men, lighting men, agents, managers." The informer had stooped shoulders, a tight, damp mouth, a red-veined blob of a nose. "Even the printer's charging her for five thousand flyers that never got printed."

Nikos listened and his soul vomited. It pained him to hear these stories. He had thought her life would be different. He had expected more for her.

"If the rent's not paid by five tonight," the little man said, "they lose the deposit and the hall."

Nikos sat thinking a moment, and then his smile opened up like a little boy's. "That brother of hers—used to strong-arm delicatessens for a bakery—is he still around?"

"Stathis Kavalaris. Changed his name to Stanley Kaye. He owns a liquor store in Brooklyn Heights."

"Have him here in my office in an hour."

"She needs $5,000 to pay for the hall. There could be other expenses too. She's in with sharks."

"Yeah." Stathis Kavalaris, a.k.a. Stanley Kaye, sat uncomfortably erect in the office chair. The Scuff Kote on his shoes didn't quite match the leather. "Well, she never had any business sense."

"I want you to go to her, Stathis. I want you to offer her money. You understand me, Stathis? We've opened an account for you and you sign the checks. Whatever she needs, she gets. But my name is never mentioned."

"Okay. Only . . ." Stathis hesitated. "What do I get?"

"You're my agent, right? Agents get ten percent."

"The big ones are getting fifteen."

"Are you a big agent, Stathis?"

"I think a job like this deserves fifteen."

"I haven't had time to go to the hairdresser." Ariana's eyes met her brother's. "Is that what you're staring at?"

"Hell, no." Stathis shifted nervously. He would never have recognized his little sister in this tired forty-nine-year-old woman with gray carelessly streaking her hair. He laughed uneasily. "Remember that slum we used to live in? And here you are in a house like this. It's funny, isn't it?"

"What are you here for, Stathis?"

"I hear you're having problems. I want to help."

"How do you think you could help?"

"Money."

She looked at him a long moment and then she began to smile.

"I'm not bulling you. How much do you need? Ten thousand? Twenty? I'll write you a check." He snapped a checkbook out of his breast pocket. He leaned over the chest of drawers and mumbled as he wrote. "Twenty . . . five . . . thousand." He handed her the check.

She stared at him and then she began very quietly to cry.

Stathis made his hand soft. Bending toward his little sister, he stroked her to quiet the pain. "Come on, what's a brother for? And don't worry about paying me back. You can have all the time you need—three, six months, no rush."

Ariana arrived with Monte at the artists' entrance two hours before the concert, scheduled for 8:00 P.M. Carnegie Hall was already a mob scene. TV crews had set up minicams on the front steps, in the corridors, waiting to trap the glitterati of two coasts and three continents.

She vocalized in her dressing room. She knelt on the carpet and tried to pray.

"Dear God, I beg you, don't let me disgrace my art. Whether it is Your holy will that I succeed or fail, I only implore You not to leave me on this earth when I am of no further use to music."

She rose and opened her purse. She drew out the locket on its thin gold chain. "Help me," she whispered. "Help me tonight and I swear I'll keep my promise." She kissed the portrait and slipped the chain around her neck.

In the corridor, she embraced Monte. He sang the opening segment of the program. She stood in the wings. She listened with her skin.

He could still stir an audience. They applauded loudly between numbers. They seemed especially to enjoy the "Drink, Drink, Drink" song from *The Student Prince.*

He came bounding off the stage to a sound of rushing applause. "Cara, this will be the greatest moment of our lives. Listen to that audience. They love us."

"It's you they love, Monte. They haven't heard me yet."

The houselights dimmed again. Hovering in the wings, at the outer edge of the dying tumult, she felt her courage falter.

Austin Waters led her out and the entire audience rose on one count.

She stood a moment, harbored in the crook of the piano, then stepped forward and bowed to the applause.

The hall was packed. People had jammed into the seats, onto the railings, onto the steps. She could not see a single empty space—except the center box in the first tier.

She gave Austin the nod to start the introduction. Her voice came out small, but the note held steady. She attacked the next note and swelled it. With gathering confidence she floated a high A-flat. It made a beautiful soaring arc.

I'm singing! she realized. *I'm really singing!*

Suddenly the notes were there: the high B's and B-flats, the F's and A's and E's that she had thought were lost forever; even a high C, secure and radiant and endless (*Where am I getting this breath from?*) and—did she dare? Yes, she dared!—a high D-flat that she held miraculously still and quiet like a firefly barely glowing in the palm of her hand. She tossed in a grace note, the E-flat above, then trilled, and then a high F shot out of her.

A shout broke out from the audience. They were standing, screaming, throwing programs. She glanced again at Austin. He smiled at her. *We did it!*

The next number on the program was "Over the Rainbow."

"Let's take it up a half-tone," Austin whispered.

"Take it up a whole tone," she whispered back, "and up another tone for the second refrain."

Austin rippled her introduction. And then something, someone was chattering. Ariana's eye traced the trickle of sound to the center box of the grand tier. Principessa Maggie, sparkling as though she had walked through a snow of diamonds, stood brandishing a white mink, reaching across three exquisitely golden-haired male companions to hand it to a fourth.

Ariana missed her entrance.

Austin glanced at her. He doubled back through the introduction. Ariana opened her mouth. A note came out, but the chattering from that box filled her head. The melody rose an octave on the second note, and she tried to shape another beautiful arc.

Her voice cracked.

She heard Maggie's stifled laughter.

With Austin's help she faked the song, stumbling dizzily on through humiliation and disintegration to the end.

She stood, waiting for some sort of reaction from the shocked audience. A lonely pair of hands high up in the balcony began clapping. Gradually the rest of the house joined in.

She recognized the sound of mercy applause, and she cut it short by positioning herself for her next number—"Torna a Sorrento." Her voice broke on the very first note.

She heard laughter from the center box.

A blinding mist of anger rushed into Ariana's face. Her composure burst like an aneurysm.

She threw her head back and howled. "Get out!"

For an instant a look of bewilderment swept Principessa Maggie's beautifully young, beautifully made-up face.

"Yes, you! Get out of my concert!"

Bravas, jeers, hurrahs, catcalls broke loose in the audience.

"I will not sing until that woman is thrown out of here!"

The rest was a nightmare that Ariana only dimly remembered. It took four stagehands to subdue her, and she dealt one a savage blow to the shoulder. After the house doctor managed to jab a hypodermic into her arm she quieted and they carried her away, black hair streaming down her white, $4,000 gown.

Twenty minutes before Maggie came home, Nikos had the whole story by phone. He was waiting when she stepped through the front door.

"Why?" Rage came spilling from him. "Why did you have to go to *that* concert?"

She took a step backward. "It was a public event, I had a perfect right to go."

"You didn't have to take those sadistic, idiotic people!"

She opened the closet and hung up her mink. "It's not as though I murdered someone. I went to a concert and one of my guests was a little drunk. What's the crime?"

"You insulted an artist."

"She insulted herself."

Nikos raised a hand and Maggie's eyes flinched. There was a moment when he could have struck her and then the hand fell back.

"Ariana's my friend," he said.

"All right, she's your friend, and yes, I resent her, and I went because I knew it was going to be horrible. Everyone there knew. But I didn't *make* it horrible!"

"You made it worse. You made it much, much worse."

"I'm sorry! What else can I say? It was a mistake and I'm sorry!"

"You always make mistakes and you're always sorry."

"What are we arguing about now? Your daughter again?"

She knew immediately it was a stupid, wrong thing to have said. His face closed down and he hardly seemed to be breathing.

"You'll pay," he said quietly. "And it's going to hurt the one way you can be hurt."

She waited to hear how he thought she could be hurt.

"The hospital bills will come out of your allowance."

Disbelief shot out of her. "What hospital bills? For *her?*"

"For her, Maggie. I've been paying for your friends ever since we were married. This time you'll pay for one of mine."

"She's had enough betrayal for one lifetime. She needs to be some-place safe, where no one can touch her, where she can have peace till she's able to cope again. There's a place in Connecticut like that."

Stathis listened patiently to what he considered sentimentality from the ultrarich. He had $12,000 in debts and with $4,000 he could swing a cocaine deal; he wanted money and he was willing to sit in Nikos Stratiotis's office and flatter him with obedience for as long as it took to get it.

"Sounds good," Stathis said.

"She'd have to be committed by a relative."

Stathis nodded solemnly. "Yeah, well, since Mom died I'm her only relative."

"Are you willing to sign the papers?"

"What does this place cost?"

"Don't worry. That'll be taken care of."

Stathis looked up sharply. "I meant my percentage."

"Of course, your percentage. What was it we agreed on—fifteen?"

Stathis's smile had the shape of a grave. "How about twenty this time?"

"All right. Twenty."

Spring came and summer went and Ariana groped through a Thora-zine fog, barely able to wash or dress or feed herself. The nurses put her in a chair by the window. She stared at trees and lawns and banks of shrub unreal in their tidiness, at nurses and patients strolling along the paths like players on a stage-set.

She understood that something was going on, that in some way she was part of it. But she could not hold on to her impressions long enough to shape them into thoughts. They passed across her mind with no more permanence than clouds.

Dr. Peter Meehan, who directed the clinic, looked in on Ariana every day except Sundays. He was a middle-aged man, broad-shouldered, with a lined face and a sprinkling of gray in his hair and mustache. Their visits were always the same. He moved his chair close to hers, took her hand and raised it three inches from the table. He released it.

The hand stayed in the air, unmoving.

"Ariana, put your hand down."

She didn't seem to hear.

He moved his face very near to hers. "Ariana," he said very distinctly. "Lower your hand."

She drew away, blinking, and the hand dropped back to the table.

"Thank you, Ariana. That was very good."

In the fall Dr. Meehan brought a small portable phonograph.

Ariana glanced up expectantly at him.

He set a record on the turntable. He lowered the tone arm. Her forehead puckered.

From the tiny speaker came the voice of Ariana Kavalaris, singing "Sempre Libera."

Her eyes darkened and something painful came into the curve of her mouth. She suddenly struck the table with a clenched fist.

He lifted the arm from the record and set it back on its rest. "I've always liked that recording. I think it's one of your best. You don't care for it?"

She sank back in her chair. Her eyes closed. "Where did I lose them? Where?"

Finally. He had broken through. "Lose what, Ariana?"

"My F—my A—my E?"

Dr. Meehan sat late at night in his office, puzzling. What did it mean—an F, an A, an E? They were musical notes, of course, but years of delving into twisted souls had taught him there had to be a deeper meaning as well. In the private language of the soul, they spelled something.

He doodled on a scratch pad, trying to arrange the letters into words. AFE. EFA. EAF. All he could come up with was FEA—the Spanish word for "ugly woman." Or possibly an incomplete FEAR?

Doc, he thought, *you're stretching pretty far for that one.* He balled the paper into a wad and lobbed it into the wastebasket.

Four years and six months later, as the nation celebrated its Bicentennial, one of the most respected weekly magazines in the country published the first half of a two-part profile by Alan Cupson, the noted music critic. The article began:

> Ariana Kavalaris is no longer of the slightest importance. It is perhaps in poor taste to scrawl graffiti upon the tomb of an artist while she in a technical sense still lives—but the Kavalaris case so clearly epitomizes the temptations besetting the serious arts in our time, and the disaster of succumbing to them, that it merits detailed autopsy.

The day the article appeared doctors drained more than a half-gallon of fluid from Ariana Kavalaris's right lung and almost a half-pint from a swelling under her umbilicus.

Chest X-rays had revealed lesions in her lungs, the sequelae of a childhood bout with tuberculosis. Now proliferating soft tumors were discovered in her abdomen. Tubercular peritonitis was diagnosed, and—with permission of her brother—appropriate treatment was undertaken.

For ten days, though she was not expected to live, Kavalaris was given transfusions of whole blood. It was not until the week before Christmas that she improved sufficiently to return to the clinic where she had been undergoing treatment for severe depression.

Her doctors did not permit her to see the Cupson article, the second part of which concluded:

> As for Kavalaris the interpreter, her development was the opposite of any genuine artist's: She grew progressively more trivial and shallow, evading not only the operatic repertory, but the very issues which lie at the core of music itself. Long before she drove her voice into ruin—who can remember without a shudder of embarrassment the pathetic high F's, A's, and E's of her last years—she had renounced all claim not only upon her listeners' intelligence, but upon their sympathy as well. As with her art, so with her life. Never has a performer so ferociously squandered unquestionable genius. Of her gifts, of what she might have been, nothing remains. She will be remembered only as a warning.
> It is an immortality of sorts.

32

"PERHAPS YOU'D CARE TO BRING YOUR WIFE?"
"I'm not married, sir."

Ames Rutherford was standing in the office of Justin Crewell, a slender, gray-haired senior partner in the Wall Street law firm of Cudahy Crewell. The older man had just invited him to dinner.

"Perhaps you'd care to bring your fiancée?" Mr. Crewell suggested.

"I doubt I could pass Fran off as my fiancée. We've lived together for seven years and we're both very happy with the arrangement."

Mr. Crewell's face worked like a fist preparing to strike. "I'm a great admirer of your father's."

Ames was used to people admiring his father. "Thank you."

"And I think you might make an admirable junior partner of this firm. Provided you regularize your private life."

"Thank you, sir, but I believe my private life *is* my private life."

When Fran came into the apartment she sensed Ames was furious. "Something the matter?"

"Sorry. Long day. Just a little worn-out."

He went into the bedroom. Fran came to the door and saw him staring out the window. They lived on the fourth floor of a converted landmark townhouse, and for New York in 1977 they had a luxury view: Washington Square, the arch and the fountain, NYU students and joggers and drug people.

Ames's silence was like a cold air mass pressing against her. She knew that silence, and even after all the years they'd lived together, it still had the power to terrify her.

She'd felt it the first time in Cambridge, when he'd been at Harvard Law and she'd taught elementary music at the Longy School. They'd been living in a cheap student sublease and she'd come home and found him gazing at the wall. She'd asked if something was bothering him.

"Professor Hooker," he'd said. "Know how he opened the lecture? 'Everyone look at the person on your right. Then look at the person on your left. Next year, one of you isn't going to be here.'"

She'd sat down on the sofa beside him and one of the springs had twanged. She'd smiled and said, "In two years even if the whole rest of the class drops out, you'll be there."

And she was right. Two years later Ames Rutherford was not only there, but on the *Harvard Law Review*. And in the months before graduation there'd been offers from eighteen firms.

Ames had talked it over with her and they'd decided on New York.

He'd chosen the firm of Cudahy Crewell when they'd topped the next-best offer by $5,000. In the four years he'd been with the firm she'd seen him come home moody now and then, but nothing like this evening.

She watched him go into the living room and pour himself a straight Scotch. He took it in three swallows and poured another. Suddenly she felt she was watching a stranger. "Ames, before you drink yourself speechless would you mind telling me what's gotten you into this mood?"

He dropped onto the sofa. "Crewell invited us to dinner."

"Great," she said. "I'll wear my—"

"Then he disinvited us."

She turned. "Why?"

Ames felt awkward bringing up the marriage question. It hadn't exactly been his idea not to get married and it hadn't exactly been hers. Sometimes he felt guilty about it. Fran was his best friend, he loved making love to her, but marriage . . .

"Because we're not engaged and we're not married and we're not . . . what Mr. Crewell thinks a member of Cudahy Crewell should be."

"A member? You're a member of the firm now?"

"Far from it. He just exiled me to a nice little pro bono job. I'm defending a woman accused of homicide."

All the big firms did a certain amount of unpaid work pro bono—for the public good. Fran couldn't see that it was such a disaster. "Sounds juicier than wills and corporate reorganizations."

"I have no criminal experience, no courtroom experience, and Crewell has put this woman's life in my hands."

"They're damned good hands." Fran sat on the sofa beside him. No springs twanged. "Tell me about her."

"She's an ex-nun, a nurse in a hospice for terminal patients. She's accused of smothering a ninety-two-year-old charity case."

As he spoke, Fran could sense an excitement she hadn't felt in Ames since their first days in Fontainebleau. "Know what I think?" she said. "I think Crewell may be doing you a favor. I have a hunch there's going to be a lot more bono in this than you realize."

The DA's office messengered the evidence against Maria Bartholomew to the Wall Street offices of Cudahy Crewell. Ames studied the documents in the quiet of the firm's air-conditioned library.

The state's case rested on the testimony of a convicted felon and admitted drug user by the unforgettable name of Tex Montana. Mr. Montana claimed that Ms. Bartholomew had sold him drugs stolen from her hospice. Mr. Montana further claimed that Ms. Bartholomew had on three occasions remarked that one of her patients, a ninety-two-year-old with esophageal cancer whose drugs she had been diverting, was "on to her" and would have to be "taken care of."

Ames interviewed Maria Bartholomew in a stifling cinder-block cell in the women's house of detention on Rikers Island. He was impressed by the serenity and acceptance radiating from the gray-haired woman whose seventy-year-old eyes peered at him without shame or apology from behind spotlessly bright spectacles.

After four hours he came out of the cell with a strong impression that she was innocent. The impression was bolstered when he visited St. Anne's Hospice, a brownstone on Horatio Street in Greenwich Village. Maria Bartholomew's coworkers called her a tireless worker, a dedicated comforter of the incurable.

"How do you think the patient died?" Ames asked a cheerful blond-haired girl whose job it was to read to the dying. (Most of them, she said, wanted to hear fairy tales and children's stories.)

"Rolled over in his sleep and asphyxiated in his pillow."

"Does that happen often?"

"We have a lot of close calls."

As Ames turned a corner into the winter sunlight of Hudson Street, he collided with a thin line of picketers. They were carrying signs protesting a proposed change in the neighborhood zoning.

"Hey!" The tip of a flute nudged Ames. He looked up from the papers he had spread across the dining table. Fran was smiling at him. "You're happy, do you know that?"

"I'm working my damned ass off. Don't you sit there twiddling your flute and call me happy!"

"You're happy and you love it." She kissed him on the crown of the head. "And so do I."

"At which point Montana—" Dill Switt broke off his description of a murder trial he'd been covering for a New York publisher and wiped a speck of marinara from his lower lip. "Montana changes his testimony and claims *he* provided Watts with the shotgun."

Ames looked up from his lasagna. "What was that name again?"

They were sitting in Emilio's Italian restaurant on Sixth Avenue. "Montana," Dill said. "Tex Montana."

"Dill," Ames said. "We have to talk. Someplace private."

They talked. They decided something very ugly was going on. And then Dill went digging.

Tex Montana, it appeared, was a professional state's witness. He gave credible testimony and juries had twice convicted on it. But his testimony in the Watts case and his deposition in the Bartholomew case contradicted each other on one essential point.

Mr. Montana would have had to have been in Binghamton dealing shotguns with Mr. Watts at the very hour he was two hundred miles away in New York City dealing drugs with Ms. Bartholomew.

Ames asked Justin Crewell if he could take a week off to attend a trial.

"Anything to do with that pro bono case?"

"I think so, sir."

Ames explained and Mr. Crewell nodded wisely. "I'll see to it."

That afternoon Mr. Crewell's secretary knocked on the door of Ames's windowless office.

"Crewell needs you, Amesie boy." She was a trim woman in her early sixties and she spoke Warner Brothers 1940s dialogue. "He needs you in the Whitney-Strauss cash election merger and that means he needs you off the pro bono. Effective immediately."

Fran could feel it the minute she walked into the apartment: the silence, the anger, the ice-cold machine working in the head of the stranger who stood staring out the window at Washington Square arch.

"Okay," she sighed. "Tell me."

Ames turned. "Point one," he said, "Maria Bartholomew's hospice has a ten-year lease on prime Greenwich Village real estate. Point two, the City Council is ramming through zoning changes in the area. Point three, Fairchild Development, who owns the ground under and around the hospice, has filed plans to rip it down and erect a thirty-story high-rise. It goes without saying they gave heavy financial support to the mayor's last election campaign and the governor's. Point four, Fairchild Development is a client of Cudahy Crewell and point five, as of this afternoon I'm off the Bartholomew case."

Fran sank into a chair. "Those are quite a few points."

"Where did I take a wrong turn, Fran? I set out to work for the good guys and here I am being a gofer for the bad guys."

"And Maria Bartholomew's a good guy?"

"The best. That old man's death was accidental and the DA's under orders to crucify Bartholomew so the city can decertify the hospice and some fat-cat can put up a high-rise."

He was enraged, stirred, alive. She liked him this way.

"Maybe . . ." she said carefully, "maybe you should quit the firm and work for Maria Bartholomew."

"I'm resigning, sir," Ames told Crewell.

Crewell nodded as though nothing in the world had the power to surprise him. "Why don't we view it as a well-earned leave of absence—with pay."

"Frankly, sir, I'd prefer to keep it a simple resignation."

That afternoon Ames went to the women's house of detention on Rikers Island. He asked to see Maria Bartholomew.

"Are you a reporter?" the warden asked. She was a flat-eyed, tough-looking woman with a half-inch scar on her jaw that makeup couldn't quite disguise.

"I'm her attorney."

"Then I'm surprised you don't know. Maria Bartholomew died three days ago."

"Cancer." Ames pounded a fist into the dining table and Fran's pot roast jumped two inches off the platter. "She'd been getting treatment at the hospice for two years."

A line of perplexity ran between Fran's eyebrows. "But why didn't she get treatment in the prison?"

"Because no one in the prison knew. She wanted it that way."

"She wanted to die?"

"She was ready to die."

"But why?"

Ames was silent a moment. "I have my theory."

Fran folded her arms. "I'd like to hear that theory."

For the next two hours Ames told her what he thought had happened and why. She listened. She heard anger and outrage and above all she heard caring. She knew exactly what had to be done. She pushed aside the dinner plates and got her portable Olivetti typewriter and a stack of blank typing paper.

Ames stared. "What's that, dessert?"

"Write down every word you just told me," she said. "It's a hell of a story and what's more it's very probably the truth. Nail those bastards. Fictionalize it, make it a novel, stay just this side of libel. Ames, you *have* to!"

"And in the meantime, how do we live?"

"I have my job at the Manhattan School of Music—and Crewell did say leave of absence with pay, didn't he?"

For seven crazed months Ames banged typewriter keys. He dissected the tangle of social and financial interests in a city like New York, showed how they strangled the sick and the poor and the powerless. His main character was a dying ex-nun fighting for the right to dignity in life and in death, fighting not just for herself but for those around her.

And losing. But in losing, winning.

He called the finished manuscript *The Fortress.* New York was the fortress, unbreachable, unyielding. And so was the ex-nun's faith and her final act, a gift of silence to a cacophonous world.

He stared at the stack of 560 pages and realized that somehow he had gotten the hurt out of himself and onto that paper. It felt good not to hurt.

He smiled at Fran. "All right, doctor, now what?"

"Now we take a two-week break and go to London and Paris and revisit Fontainebleau."

"We can't afford it."

"Our American Express card can afford it."

"Fran, those bills have to be paid."

Fran wouldn't take no for an answer. For the next two days she sent Ames off to museums and movies. She made travel arrangements and took Ames's manuscript to the Madison Avenue office of an agent she had read about in that morning's paper, an old gent (very dapper in his photograph) by the name of Horatio Charles who had just pulled off what the *New York Times* called the most spectacular multibook deal of the decade.

A male secretary accepted the manuscript and assured her it would be quite some time before Mr. Charles could get to it.

"Tell him he has two weeks," she said.

Ames and Fran saw London, which was drizzly. They saw Paris, which was hazy. They saw Fontainebleau, which was hazy-bright and blessedly unchanged from seven years ago, and then they saw the Bordeau country, which was gloriously sunny.

When they returned to New York there was a letter from Horatio Charles in the mailbox: *Please phone me immediately.*

Life rapidly became unreal.

Everything that could happen to a book happened: hardcover, paperback, book clubs, foreign sales, TV miniseries. Which didn't do a hell of a lot for Nurse Maria Bartholomew but which made a lot of things possible for Ames Rutherford: never having to negotiate another corporate merger in his life, a house in the Hamptons, a little co-op in Manhattan, days spent sitting in front of a typewriter wondering what the hell to write about next.

He began drinking more heavily. There was no reason not to—he was free of nine to five forever—and, after a day spent trying to pull prose out of his head he enjoyed the buzz.

From enjoying the buzz he progressed to needing the buzz.

Operationally speaking, there wasn't much difference. Vodka or Scotch, a buzz was a buzz was a buzz.

"Ames, is it me? This thing that's happening between us or not happening or whatever the hell's going on?" She was sitting up now, one foot dangling over the edge of the mattress. "Maybe I don't excite you anymore?"

In answer he took her hand and placed it over his erection.

She pulled back but not quite away. "Ames, this is serious."

He grinned lecherously. "So's this."

"Don't you understand? I want to *help*."

He could feel the moment turning heavy, serious, turning into more than he could cope with.

"Then, my darling"—he smiled—"I suggest this is an excellent opportunity for us both to shut up."

He kissed her—a nice, wet, let's-get-back-to-it kiss. And then he made the best love to her they'd had in a year.

Afterward she was still looking at him that way.

There was nothing he could say, nothing he could do. She was right to look at him, right to wonder. Because he had everything in the world and something was still missing.

There was not a day when Ricarda DiScelta did not dread the idea that her life's work would almost certainly go unfinished. But she resigned herself. The Lord had His reasons. The matter was no longer in her hands.

She spent her mornings with her three remaining pupils—they were good, not gifted, but she needed to feel useful—and afternoons as a volunteer at the Hospital for Special Surgery, pushing a cart of fruit juice through the wards.

There was very little more to her life than that.

But December 19, 1978, was different. On that day Ricarda DiScelta died.

She got up early but felt strangely lethargic. She saw her pupils, saw her patients, and that evening she went to the Metropolitan Opera and watched a new Bulgarian soprano sing Puccini's *Manon Lescaut*.

The performance affected her vision in a peculiar way. She caught herself at one point imagining she was watching Jeritza and, at another, Callas. The illusion was strangely complete, because she seemed to hear their voices as well.

She had to remind herself that Jeritza and Callas were in the other world now, waiting for her and perhaps praying for her.

During Act Three a trembling broke out over her shoulders and down her spine. *I'm coming down with flu,* she thought. Though she had rarely in her life walked out on a performance, she thought it best to leave before Act Four.

She asked her driver if he would mind going out of the way. She wanted to look at the Christmas tree in Rockefeller Center.

She stared at the magnificent Norwegian pine a long while, lost in remembering all the Christmases in her life.

A strange thought came to her. *I wonder if I did the right thing separating Ariana from Mark Rutherford?*

She asked the driver to take her home. She went to bed, and still the thought was there.

Did I do the right thing?

It was her last thought. When the housekeeper found her in the morning, her heart had stopped.

Ariana was with the patients in the television room when the evening news reported Ricarda DiScelta's death. She screamed. Two orderlies had to help her to her room.

Dr. Meehan visited Ariana after his evening rounds. She was sitting huddled and wraithlike in her rocker.

"You look sad, Ariana. Would you like to tell me why?"

He sensed she wasn't seeing him at all. Her gaze was fixed on some horizon far beyond the walls of the room.

"Ricarda DiScelta taught me everything. And I betrayed her."

"How did you betray her?"

"I never believed her. I never believed she would die. I never saw that she had the same hopes and sufferings and fears as the rest of us."

"Tell me about Ricarda's fears."

"She feared what we all fear: life ending too soon, before we've had a chance to do our work."

"And what was her work?"

Ariana buried her face in her hands. *"Ti kano edho? Panagia mou, ti kano edho?"*

"Ariana," the doctor said firmly, not about to let her lapse into a language he did not understand, "what was her work?"

Slowly, Ariana raised her head. "To teach me."

"Then she finished her work, didn't she?"

"She finished. *But I didn't.*" Ariana gazed at the doctor. Sweat beaded her forehead. She was shivering. Her voice came in a whisper, as though she were afraid the walls might overhear. "I don't want to go to hell!"

She bent forward, coughing, and blood exploded in gobbets onto the floor of the room.

In the hospital surgeons slid a tiny balloon into Ariana's throat and blew it up, stanching the flow from the ruptured veins of the esophagus. Nothing could be done about the lungs except to administer clotting agents and give transfusions to replace the blood lost.

It was eight days before she was well enough to return to the clinic. Christmas had come and gone. It was almost the New Year.

She knew she was dying. She shut the door of her room and slid to her knees.

"Dear God, I of all sinners have no right to ask You anything. You showed me the right road and I chose the wrong. I betrayed my teacher. I betrayed my pupil. Only You know what sufferings they are now enduring because of me. But I beg You, hear one last prayer. Add to the few days left me. Give me time to make amends to those I have hurt. Dear God, help me to keep my promise."

Mark let the book drop to the desk. He held his breath, listening, wondering if at age fifty-eight he was developing hearing problems.

The only sounds in the study were a faint hissing from the hearth, the soft recurring ticktock of the grandfather clock, the occasional rattle of wind in the raised blinds.

He glanced toward the window.

He didn't know how long he stared at the torn newspapers swirling in the wind through the courtyard. But he realized it had grown darker. The fire hissed and the clock ticked and the wind rattled and then he heard that other sound again, clearer this time.

Someone was calling his name. The voice reached him in tatters, as if across an ocean of time.

He had trouble pushing himself up. His legs had gone to sleep and he could hardly feel them crossing the carpet. All his efforts had the dreamlike heaviness of pushing himself through water.

The window was an indistinct blur. He leaned out into the night.

"Who's there?"

And suddenly, without her even having to say, he knew.

"Ariana?" Harry Forbes's eyes crinkled in remembered pleasure. "After all these years? You saw her?"

Mark was thoughtful a moment. "No. I only heard her."

For almost thirty-two years Mark and Harry Forbes had been meeting once a month at the Knickerbocker Club, taking their port on the sofa in front of the huge fireplace. It was wintry today, and the steward had lit a fire. Shadows danced across the Christmas tree and bookshelves with their bound sets of Churchill and Galsworthy.

Mark sighted the flames through his port. "I heard her say 'Help me.' "

"Help her? Why? What's the matter?"

"I don't know." Mark sat twisting the stem of his glass. "Harry, this is very hard for me to put into words. I've never discussed it with anyone before, and if you repeat a syllable—"

"You have my word of honor," Harry said.

Mark was silent, gathering his thoughts. "Since we separated thirty years ago, I've been with her two times. Three, counting last night. The first time was in Mexico, twenty-nine years ago. At the opera. She was in some sort of despair and I had to be there. Just to let her see me, to let her know someone cared. We didn't talk. But she saw me, and she got through her performance. Later, when Stratiotis left her, she cut her wrists. I made her phone the doctor. And last night—from wherever she was—she called me for help."

"Just a minute. You said she was at the window of your study."

"No. I heard her, but there was no one there. And I wasn't in Mexico the night of her *Rigoletto,* and I wasn't in her bathroom when she cut her wrists. I haven't been in the same room with her since we separated. Those were dreams, Harry, half-waking dreams so real that reality is dim and dead by comparison. It was only in those dreams that I . . . lived. The rest of my life has been one long sleep."

"Come on, Mark. You're being a tad hyperbolic." Harry unobtrusively signaled the steward for refills.

The two old friends were silent a moment, and then Harry asked, "Did Ariana really sing *Rigoletto* in Mexico City?"

"Yes, she did."

"Did she ever attempt suicide?"

"I have no way of knowing."

"Then maybe the things you call 'half-waking dreams' were her way of contacting you."

"What would you call that, Harry, ESP? Telepathy?"

"Does it matter?"

"Have you ever experienced anything similar?"

"I've had experiences. Like everyone else."

Harry touched his glass to his pale lips and Mark realized how very little, outside of these monthly get-togethers, he really knew about his old classmate. There was a thriving office on Broad Street and an impressive, lonely house on Beekman Place; there'd been a number of affairs down through the years, several with other men's wives, and Mark knew the names of more than a few of the women; but there had never been talk of marriage or even of a real love affair. It was all surface with Harry, all charm and port, and that was the way Harry seemed to want it.

Mark sighed. "Something tells me she needs me and I should go to her. But I'm hoping you'll tell me I'm a fool and should drop it."

Harry shook his head. "Still the same old Mark. I'd be on the next plane to her. Where's she living these days?"

"I hear she's spent the last seven years in a clinic in Connecticut."

"Sometimes the sick enjoy visits, you know."

"She vanished eight days ago." There was a hint of defensiveness in Dr. Meehan's manner. "At night the gates are locked, but during the day our patients are free to come and go. Last Monday Ariana Kavalaris chose to go."

"Do you have any idea where?"

"None. Her brother hasn't heard from her. The police haven't turned up anything. You're a friend, Mr. Rutherford?"

"I knew her thirty years ago."

"Are you aware that she's dying?"

The word had the finality of a slammed door.

"She has advanced tubercular lesions of both lungs. Wherever she's decided to go, I hope to God she's getting treatment."

33

"I'D LIKE YOU TO FIND SOMEONE FOR ME."

"Who'd you have in mind?"

Mark told him.

The detective whistled. A well-made man in his middle forties, he had thinning black hair and the shoulders of a football player. "I still play her album of Puccini heroines. 'O Mio Babbino Caro' always breaks me up."

"Me too," Mark said softly. He looked up hopefully. "Captain Terhune recommended you."

"Al Terhune—New London?"

"He said you had experience tracing runaways from the clinic." Mark had checked the agency's ad in the Yellow Pages. *Joseph Connors. Confidential investigations. Fast, precise, discreet.* He wanted to believe the *fast* and the *discreet.*

The detective prepared to make ballpoint scribbles on a yellow pad. "Okay, I'll need some details."

"Mr. Connors phoned again," Nita said at dinner. "He always seems to phone Friday—four-thirty."

Mark looked at her. Nothing was volunteered.

"Mark, is there anything we ought to talk about?"

He began talking about the vestry committee. In his eyes she saw something unspoken, something echoing the void beneath the heart of her own life.

"The Brussels sprouts are delicious," he said. "Are they fresh?"

Mr. Connors phoned every Friday, and then one Wednesday evening a stranger rang the doorbell and tipped his hat to Nita. The gesture charmed her, as though he had kissed her hand.

"Joseph Connors, to see the bishop?"

"Mr. Connors," she stammered, embarrassed because she had visualized him as fat. "He's in his study. I'll show you the way."

"I'll give you this chronologically," Connors said. There were no niceties, no small talk, just a pause till the door clicked, leaving them alone, and then a dive-bombing into matters at hand. "She came to New York from New London on Monday, January eighth, on a Trailways bus. She registered at the Statler Hotel opposite Penn Station. She used the name Yvonne Clouzot."

Something nudged Mark's memory. "I know the name."

"It was her mother's." Connors flattened his palms against the attaché case that lay nestled on his knees. After a moment he popped the two latches open. Papers came out.

"In twenty-five days in New York, she stayed in eight hotels. Not crème de la crème hotels, but good upper-middling midtown hotels. Those places cost bucks. She paid cash."

"Where'd she get that much?" Mark asked.

"Good question. Her brother controls her checking accounts; she doesn't even sign the checks. Which left only one possibility. She had to have savings accounts, and she had to have the passbooks in her possession. I have a friend at IRS. Everyone should have a friend at IRS. I was able to get last year's interest records on Ariana Kinsolving. She had money squirreled away in seven New York savings banks. She closed out six of those. But the seventh account—Bank for Savings—is the interesting one. She drew a cashier's check on that account for $2,000. Twenty-four days later, the last day we know for sure she was in town, she drew a $3,800 check on the same account. Both checks were made out to the same man. I doubt you would know Barney Medina."

"I don't."

"This morning Medina and I had a talk."

There was a beat of silence, and Mark understood that more than words had been exchanged.

"Does the name Vanessa Billings mean anything to you?"

"Should it?" Mark asked.

"Billings was Kavalaris's pupil. She made a promising start and then she bombed out bad. You might say she retired without a trace. The day after Kavalaris disappeared from New London she hired Barney Medina to locate her ex-pupil. In my opinion, $3,800 is steep for the job he did for Miss Kavalaris. He showed me the records. Looks to me like he did a lot of drinking with hookers in Philly."

"Philadelphia?"

"At present Miss Billings makes her home in the City of Brotherly Love. She works in a piano bar called Danny's."

He told Nita at breakfast that he would be going to Philadelphia that day. She knew instantly it had to do with Mr. Connors and the visit.

"Mark, do you have to? Nancy and Pancho de Grandfont are expecting us and they did invite us three weeks ago."

"I have to go today. Please apologize for me."

He found Danny's bar that night, a run-down dive off Allen Street. A shakily lettered poster in the window announced TONIGHT—AT THE PIANO—AVA.

Beneath the chemical sting of air-freshener his nostrils caught a stale whiff of beer. He saw a bar, some tables, some drunks crammed into a narrow strip of wasteland. Plastic banners and miniature college flags gave the place all the gaiety of a used-car lot.

At the far end, a woman was singing at the piano. He took a table where he could watch.

The spotlight picked out a blond wig, fake black eyelashes, a lot of makeup. She wore a deep-cut pink ruffled blouse. It was a cheap pink but the long lacy sleeves drew attention to her hands floating over the keyboard. She threw back her head and let out the last, long note of "Smoke Gets in Your Eyes."

He was the only one who applauded. She turned from the keyboard and looked at him carefully, and then she riffed a key-change and sang two numbers in perfectly accented French, *"Parlez-moi d'amour"* and *"Je t'attendrai."*

He called, "Brava!" Not an opera house brava, just a polite understated nightclub brava.

She floated him a little smile, and then she reached under the piano stool to pick up a purse that was beginning to lose its sequins. She dug out a filter-tip cigarette and crossed to his table.

"Do you have a light?"

He stood and flicked the lighter his wife had given him. The singer bent into the flame.

They sat and the waitress, unasked, brought another Scotch.

The singer lifted her glass. "Thanks for the brava."

"I meant it. You must have studied classical music."

"I studied a lot of things. What's your name?"

"I'm Mark."

"What brings you to Danny's, Mark—the pretty tunes?"

"I'm looking for someone. Her name's Vanessa Billings."

She finished her Scotch and stood. "So long, Mark."

"That was quick."

"I have to change and catch my bus. Thanks for the drink." She turned and disappeared through the kitchen door.

He paid for the drinks and asked the hatcheck woman when Ava sang her last set.

"You just heard it."

He went outside. It was raining.

Danny's had a front entrance and a back door down an alley by the garbage cans. A little after two the alley door opened. For an instant raindrops flashed like a handful of tossed diamonds. A woman in a slicker and a pulled-down rain hat stepped out.

It was the singer. He followed her.

At the corner she hailed a taxi. It didn't stop.

She turned up a side street and zigzagged through a neighborhood of saloons and boarded-up storefronts and room-to-let signs.

The rain made a sound like buckets of pennies being tossed.

He turned a corner and suddenly she wasn't there. Through the darkness he could make out a dimly lighted archway and a passage beyond. The passageway led to a courtyard. There was a lighted window at the corner of the top story. He counted five flights and knew she couldn't have gotten there that fast.

The light on the top story went out. He blew on his hands and bent to rub his legs. Suddenly there was a reflection on the wet cobblestones. On the third story a light filtered through slatted blinds like an eerie blue flame. He counted windows up and windows across, making sure he had the exact location.

A silhouette moved across the blinds and suddenly there was a distant voice. He listened and his heart tightened.

Through the splattering rain, barely audible above the drumming of water on drainpipes, Ariana Kavalaris was singing "Casta Diva."

"That window there." Mark pointed.

The janitor shielded his face against the morning sun. "Oh, yeah. The nightbird."

Mark gave the janitor ten dollars. "What's her name?"

"Ness." The old man pulled a crumpled pack of Luckies from his workshirt. He offered Mark one and then lit a match on his blackened thumbnail. "Who are you, collection agency?"

"No, I'm just looking for a friend of Miss Ness's."

"You mean the woman that's living with her?"

"Who's that?"

The janitor's bobsled nose crinkled. "Gray-haired. Old. Sick-looking. Don't know her name. She never gets mail. Plays records when the other one's out. Plays the piano too. There's an old spinet up there. They sing. A lot of la-la-la stuff—classical. The neighbors complain. Doesn't bother me, though. Live and let live, I say. Long as they're not burning the place down."

Late that evening Mark returned to Danny's. He knew Ava Ness's escape route and he took the table by the kitchen door. It was Friday, and that meant more of a crowd, more spilled beer, more talk during the numbers.

She sang Irving Berlin: "Always," "Blue Skies," songs of memory and promise that had been over the hill before she was born. After the set she smiled to a spattering of applause. The spotlight clicked off. Her face immediately reverted to a sullen blankness, and she went to sit with a man at a front table.

Something was exchanged. Mark couldn't see whether it was a piece of paper or a matchbook or money—just something small that slid from the man's hand to hers, and then she was coming through the tables toward the kitchen.

Mark rose. "Good evening, Miss Ness. Won't you join me for a minute?"

He signaled for two Scotches. The bartender was watching and that seemed to affect her decision. She sat.

"My janitor says you've been asking about me," she said.

"Your janitor tells me you're living with a sick woman."

"Why don't you leave me alone?"

"How long has she been vomiting, Miss Ness? How much weight does she lose each day? How much strength?"

"There's nothing happening that I can't handle."

"There's nothing happening that you *can* handle. Look at you. You have a God-given voice. You belong in a concert hall or on an opera stage and here you are wandering the belly of the city."

"That's my business," she said in a flat voice that exactly matched her eyes.

"Your friend belongs in a hospital, but you've got her tucked in a slum. Maybe you think that's your business too. I suggest you get it through your head, Miss Billings—"

"You had it right the first time. Ness. The name's Ness."

"Can't you understand I'm trying to help that woman?"

"A lot of people said that. It took a lot of help to get her where she is now."

"And maybe with a different sort of help we can get her *out* of where she is now."

"What's so different about your help?"

"I care about her."

"Oh, Jesus. *Now* you care."

"Now is all she's got left, Miss Ness. And maybe—with the right treatment—a tomorrow or two."

"She's not too interested in those tomorrows."

"You still haven't any right to take them from her."

Miss Ness's mouth narrowed into a grimace of determination. "I'm not taking anything from anyone—least of all crap from you."

"She's dying. And you're as good as killing her, keeping her in that rattrap."

"Screw you, Charley."

"This is my card—don't rip that card, Miss Ness. That's my name, that's my job. My real name, my real job. You can ask your friend about me. Tell her I'm here. Tell her I'm here to help. And then phone me. I'm at the Hilton."

"That figures. In a suite?"

"I have a single bedroom, Miss Ness. The same as you."

He knew from her eyes he'd said just enough.

"Goodnight, Miss Ness." He rose and turned and then he was gone.

✵　✵　✵

At 2:30 in the morning the phone jangled by the bedside and a thin, urgent voice said Miss Billings was in the hotel lobby.

"Send her up." Mark dressed quickly.

There was a knock at the door. Little dark pearls of rain still clung to the raincoat of the woman who had called herself Ava Ness. She gave him a look and he saw terror in it.

"Ariana's vomiting blood," she said. "She's delirious."

A knot formed in his stomach. He went to the phone. "This is Bishop Mark Rutherford. Room 711. I need the hotel doctor right away."

"We'll have to wake him, Bishop."

"Then please do. This is an emergency."

They waited, listening to the rain pulse against the window. It was almost forty minutes before the doctor arrived, a bald man with a dripping umbrella in one hand and a pigskin satchel in the other.

"Okay, which one of you two's dying?"

"The sick woman's across town," Mark said. "We'll take a taxi, unless you have a car."

The doctor's eyes narrowed in disbelief, and Mark noticed a half-inch of pajama top peeking out the back of his shirt collar.

"Now hold it a minute. I only treat hotel guests and my private patients."

Mark had taken the measure of a great many doctors. He knew the profession and he knew its ethic. He pulled a $100 bill from his wallet. He tucked it into the doctor's breast pocket.

The doctor glanced down at his blazer. "The insurance companies give me that much for letting a patient sit in my waiting room."

Mark held out a second hundred. "This is untaxed money, doctor. In your bracket it's worth $400. Four hundred for one house call."

The doctor took the money. "My car's downstairs."

They rushed up the stairs, their shadows rippling beside them over the peeling walls. Vanessa let them into an airless room with a single shuttered window.

To the right was a tiny battered spinet piano, to the left a table with a phonograph. Between these two dark shapes was the dim light of a lowered lamp. On the small bed in the corner a bony figure was stretched, motionless, wrapped in a blanket.

Mark saw with a shock that it was an old woman. She was lying on her back, her head with its gray face, set like stone, flung back on the pillow. Even unconscious, she was making a hacking attempt to breathe.

He stared and took a step forward. "Ariana," he said.

His eyes misted. He remembered a glowing little girl in a frilled white skirt, her black hair hanging to her shoulders.

A spasm racked the body, followed by a convulsive cough. A thin dribble of blood broke at the side of the mouth.

The doctor drew back the sweat-soaked sheet. The abdomen was swollen. He gently tapped the rib cage. There was a sound like a hollow drum being beaten. His lips set in a grim line. He took the wrist between his fingers, delicately, as though it were a brittle stick of candy, and counted the pulse against the second hand of his wristwatch.

"Her heart is giving out. I can't help her here. We have to call an ambulance and get her to a hospital. Is there a phone?"

"There's a pay phone downstairs," Vanessa said. "The dime slot's stuck. It only takes nickels." She went to the table and tipped two nickels from a cracked teacup into her palm. She handed them to the doctor. He made a face, as though walking those two flights again were the grimmest affront yet, and left the room quickly.

Ariana was making a gasping sound. Vanessa leaned over her, took up her limp hand, rubbed it rapidly.

Ariana's eyes opened slowly. She stared at the figure seated on the bed beside her, lit by a thin flow of light from the door.

"Vanessa?" Her voice was a hacking whisper. "I was afraid you'd left me."

"Don't tire yourself trying to talk. We've gotten a doctor. You're going to the hospital."

Ariana shook her head. "It's too late." There was a quick urgency to her movements as she tried to unclasp the locket from her neck. "Help me," she said weakly. "The voice. Quickly. It must not die with me."

Following her teacher's gestured instructions, Vanessa undid the catch and lifted the locket free.

"This locket," Ariana said, "is my voice. I bequeath it to you. Do you accept?"

Vanessa, too startled even to think, nodded.

Her teacher's voice, barely audible now, went on. "You must take a student. Train her in your repertory. Once you have taught her a role you must never perform that role again. Within twenty-five years you must turn your entire repertory over to your pupil."

The locket hung a moment between them, swinging slowly from its golden chain.

"Before you renounce your last role—you may choose the moment—give this locket to your pupil. Make her promise as I now make you promise."

Ariana's fingers dug into Vanessa's arm with such surprising force that the younger woman had to beat back an instinctive impulse to pull free.

"Swear. Keep the promise I left unkept. Finish the life I left unfinished."

Vanessa was certain her teacher had entered the final delirium. She threw a panicked glance behind her, looking for the doctor.

The fingers tugged at her. *"Swear before I die."*

"You're not going to die."

"Swear!"

Vanessa saw unmistakable terror in those failing eyes. What was the harm in swearing, she wondered, if it would bring peace to a suffering woman's last hour?

Her glance met Mark's, and it seemed to her that he nodded.

"I swear," she said.

The locket, its gold and its rubies and amethysts unaged, unflawed, passed from the old woman's hands, wrinkled and spotted with the years, to the graceful smooth hands of the young woman.

"Put it on," Ariana whispered. "Let me see it on you."

Vanessa fastened the locket around her neck.

Ariana smiled. "Yes. That's where it—" She sighed and fell back suddenly against the pillow.

The doctor came hurrying breathlessly through the door. "An ambulance is on its way."

Ariana rolled her head sideways on the pillow, squinting beyond the circle of lamplight. For the first time she seemed to be aware of the man who had been standing there silently watching.

"Who's that?"

The doctor stepped forward. "I'm Dr.—"

Weakly, Ariana waved him aside. "No—there's someone else."

Mark came to her and bent down and put his hand to her hair. She placed her hand on his. Lifting her head with effort, she gazed at him.

His temples had grayed and his skin was lined, but in the dim shadowed light of the sickroom his face for an instant seemed to be that of a young man.

Then in her memory she saw sunlight streaming through a window from a garden, and walking through the gate, back from his studies, a young seminarian with glowing eyes and ruddy cheeks. She heard his steps bounding up the stairs, and the door hinges squeaked the two notes of "Amazing Grace" that meant he was home.

"Mark?" Her voice was strange and wondering. Suddenly her colorless lips parted and a shudder passed through her: her head lifted up from the pillow and a sound almost of pain ripped out of her: "Mark!"

She seized his hand. He bowed his head to her bosom, and he could hear the life racing out of her.

Her voice was scarcely audible now. "Mark. Oh my darling . . ."

Her hand explored him, feeling the thick gray hair at the back of his neck.

As he looked at her time seemed to flow backward, and all anguish seemed to pass out of her face, leaving it smooth as evening sky. He had the impression that she was young again, the same dark-haired girl brimming with hope and fire who had held his hand and walked beside him through springtime streets and told him her dreams and listened to his.

"*Panagia mou*," she whispered. "Now I know. It was your spirit—your unselfishness—that came to me. Thank you, Mark. Thank you for being with me in all my darkest moments. Thank you for being here with me now."

Tears came into his eyes. Feelings poured back, the whole flood of a life unlived. There was a burning just above his heart. He could scarcely speak. "I should never have left you. Never, never."

"You never left me and I never left you. We've never been apart in all our lives since the day we met. And we'll never be apart in death. You do believe that, Mark."

Mark said, "I do."

"Then I am your wife," she whispered. "And you are my husband. And one day we will be married on earth as we are in eternity!"

He lifted her from the pillow—how light she was!—and held her, wishing time would stop then and there. He kissed her and her lips were waiting, soft, soft, soft.

"It's strange," she whispered. "The pain is gone. I feel strength coming back—a new strength." Suddenly she gripped him with surprising force. "I'm going . . . to live!"

He felt a bone-shaking spasm tear her. And then he realized what he was holding in his arms: silence—only silence.

"Sleep well," he whispered.

She had crossed the frontier peacefully, in the safety of his loving face bent over her. It was as though she had done no more than step out of the bright stagelights into the coolness of the wings.

For Ariana Kavalaris it was all over now: all yearning, all striving, all suffering.

He longed to be at rest beside her.

He whispered her name, and his thoughts shaped words that were never uttered. "I've always loved you. Only you. I always will."

Her expression answered him, beautiful and silent and secret.

What had she meant? he wondered, *One day we will be married on earth as we are in eternity.*

And why did he believe her?

Part Four

EXILE: 1979—1981

34

ONE RING.

Ames Rutherford stared at the blank page in his typewriter. Being a writer wasn't working today. He wanted to be a surfer or a tennis bum.

Second ring.

He lunged a hand to snatch up the receiver before the answering machine cut in. He knocked over a stack of research and the research almost knocked over a coffee cup.

"Kavalaris died last night—the singer."

He recognized Greg Hatoff's Class of 1964 Harvard drawl.

"I heard on television." And he remembered feeling just an instant's anger for what the world had done to her.

"The service is day after tomorrow, St. Patrick's Cathedral. Can you cover it for us?"

"That's a crazy idea, Greg."

It was a crazy idea and Ames was thinking. Part of his legend—every writer nowadays had a legend—was that he could stop in the middle of everything and dash off a cover story for *People* or *Atlantic* in an afternoon. Here was a perfect leave of absence from the novel that was about to turn him into a tennis bum.

"Greg, why me? I only met her once, years ago."

There was a hint of apology in Greg's hesitation. "You don't know who's doing the eulogy?"

"Should I?"

"Your father *is* Bishop Mark Rutherford?"

"Dad? But he's Episcopalian. He wasn't even her pastor."

"*Vogue* did call him confessor to the jet set."

"I can't believe Dad would—" Ames realized how very little he actually knew about his father.

"The invitation list is very elegant, kid. Crème de la crème de la crème. She's a very hot ticket. I thought you might like to give us your slant on necro-chic."

Ames arrived at St. Patrick's Cathedral early so that he could observe not just the mourners but the observers too. He spoke his notes softly into a tiny tape recorder that fitted almost invisibly into his fist.

It was strange to see his father stride to the lectern, his plain black suit contrasting almost puritanically with the crimson and white and gold vestments of the cardinal and the archbishop.

It was stranger still to hear him deliver the eulogy, his voice choked with emotion that Ames had never suspected him to be capable of.

"She gave us music. In some ways hers was the sort of music that sounds strongest in memory. We never really hear it till it is gone. Like light that we see only by the shadow it casts, we hear her—know her—mourn her—only by her silence."

A hush fell: the congregation waited.

From somewhere high in the rear of the cathedral, a thread of sound wove itself into the stillness. Softly at first and then with increasing volume, a soprano was singing the "Et Lux Perpetua" of Verdi's *Requiem.*

A wind of unbelieving recognition blew through the crowd. Ames couldn't be sure, but the voice sounded very much like Ariana Kavalaris.

He turned, and suddenly his sight blurred.

It was like a dream seen through shivering layers of memory.

She was standing in the choir loft. The area surrounding her had dimmed out and a white spot seemed to be focused on her. Her face engulfed him. A dazzling light spread from her and she seemed to be alone, silhouetted against a dark sky.

He couldn't tell if he was seeing her or imagining her or, somehow, recalling her. Her blond hair, parted down the center, hung in two long tresses framing the oval of her face. He saw things he knew he couldn't possibly be seeing at that distance: the gray-green of her irises, and a strange, unmistakable plea in her eyes.

He felt something slip inside him, as though a handbrake had been forced loose under violent pressure.

And all at once ideas were racing in him, ideas so foreign to him they might have been someone else's: that there was danger in his remaining seated there; that he must get to his feet, shove his way to the aisle, find the stairway to the choir loft.

One thought above all was so clear in his mind it was a voice commanding him: *I have to reach her this time. This time I have to reach her.*

And suddenly, inexplicably, he was standing at the top of a narrow flight of stairs, and an astonished organist was staring at him, and an old gentleman in morning clothes was pulling at him, saying, "I'm sorry, sir, you're not allowed here."

Fleetingly, through the black-gowned choir, he saw her.

She raised her head and it seemed to him she was about to acknowledge him in some way.

And then the choir shifted, and she vanished from his sight.

A dense, rain-slashed mist cloaked the Long Island shore. As Ames skidded the Mercedes into the driveway he could barely see the house and grounds. He let himself in through the kitchen.

Fran was sitting at the table. She was wearing her bright pink jogging shorts and her dark hair was bound in a towel turban. She set down her cup of tea and looked at him. "Good funeral?"

"Celebrity stuff." As he passed her chair she leaned back and he planted an upside-down-kiss on her forehead. He went into his workroom and closed the door and sat at the typewriter.

For four hours he tried to write a stripped, objective, brief account of the funeral. It missed by thirty miles. He rolled a fresh sheet into the carriage and sat frowning at the blank page.

The thought wouldn't let go of him. *I have to reach her this time. This time I have to reach her.*

The funeral left Nikos Stratiotis in a strange mood. He stayed up late that night, locked in his study, staring at walls, seeing old phantoms. His mind kept replaying the voice from the service.

When he went into the bedroom, Maggie was waiting up for him, reading. She looked at him, closed her book, and crossed to the chest of drawers. His eyes followed her.

At thirty-one, she had the silky body and arrogantly careless grace of a twenty-year-old. She worked for it: exercise classes three hours a day, diets, a bathroom filled with exotically labeled ointments and lotions. Her hair was its natural auburn—had been for the last three years—and it fell in smoothly maintained waves that grazed her shoulders as she took a very slender cigarette from a mother-of-pearl box. She lit it and came back to the edge of the bed and sat beside him.

She inhaled delicately, exhaled. Her dark eyes fixed him questioningly. "Why don't you ease up on yourself, Nikos? Get high."

"Why should I get high?"

"Because you've had a rotten day, and it's made me depressed too, and we should make love and get our minds off . . ."

She didn't say *Ariana*. He'd asked her not to come to the funeral and she'd said she understood. She'd gone shopping instead.

He took the joint and pretended to inhale. In a while he turned down the lights and they began making love.

It was skillful sex, as it always had been, but tonight for the first time in all their troubled marriage it was flavorless. When she gripped him and called his name, a horrible thought occurred to him. *I'll never enjoy making love to her again.*

Afterward, she sat staring at the Matisse still life on the wall.

"Something's bothering you," she said.

"I'm not sure."

"I'm going to smoke another. It helps me sleep."

"Go right ahead."

He fell asleep. In a dream, he heard the voice in the cathedral singing "Et Lux Perpetua." When he awoke shuddering in the dark, Maggie was breathing peacefully beside him.

In the morning he went to Richard Schiller's office at Americana Artists Agency in its glass-faced headquarters on Fifty-fifth Street.

It was hard to believe that they had known each other thirty-two years. Theirs had not been a close friendship, but the sheer accretion of time had become a bond between them. Neither was offended when the other asked a favor. Usually, Nikos wanted theater tickets, and Richard needed backing for a client's show.

But today Nikos asked for something else. "I want you to represent the young woman who sang at Ariana's funeral. Get her dates at the Metropolitan, La Scala, Covent Garden, all the places Ariana sang. I'll pay."

"Nikos, an unknown singer can't just—"

"With the right management this one can. You heard her voice."

"I heard her sing thirty-two bars and beyond that I don't know a damned thing about her. And neither do you."

"I know one thing about her. Ten years ago she was Ariana's pupil."

Richard's eyes narrowed. "You're sure?"

"I'm sure. I came home one day and she was getting out of the elevator." *She smiled.* "I don't forget people. Phone the archdiocese and get her address and go sign her."

"Nikos, it doesn't work like that."

"Make it work like that. I'll pay."

The archdiocese said the singer's name was Vanessa Billings. They had an address for her on Seventeenth Street. Richard Schiller slipped a white carnation into the lapel of his Chesterfield and took a taxi to her apartment. He climbed five dingy flights in a rickety old walkup, knocked on her door, and introduced himself. "I'm an artists' agent. I want to represent you."

Her blond hair was pulled straight back from her forehead and her gray-green eyes looked huge. She backed away from him. "No."

"May we talk about it?" He handed her his card and stepped over the bar of a police lock.

She had one dark room, one window, a view of the factory across the airshaft. "I'm not a singer," she said. "I have no voice."

"If you have no voice, Miss Billings, I have no ears."

"You haven't heard me."

"I heard you at St. Pat's."

"But that wasn't . . . the real me."

"Okay—whoever it was, I want to represent her."

"Why?"

"Because the voice that I heard at Ariana's funeral is going to have a career."

"How can you be so sure?"

"Thirty years in the business."

Something flickered in her eyes. "Would you like some coffee?"

"Sure. Milk, no sugar."

There was a two-burner gas range in what looked like a closet. She fixed coffee in a Chemex. He was surprised how rich and good it tasted.

"There's something you should know about me." She looked at him. "I'm no good onstage. I mean that. No good. I've tried."

"You need a little coaching, a little confidence, a little experience in front of audiences. It'll all come together."

"I've had some experiences in front of audiences that were pretty . . . dreadful."

"But you're a real singer. We both know that."

"Do we?"

"Sure. You studied with Ariana."

"Long ago. Only for a little while."

"And she believed in you."

"Maybe."

"Maybe, hell. That's her locket around your neck. Her teacher gave it to her, and now you're wearing it. That tells me she wanted you to go on from where she left off."

Miss Billings's finger went to the locket and touched it nervously.

"I represented Ariana," he said. "I represented her for twenty-four years. And what's more I was her friend for twenty-four years. And I want to represent you for twenty-*five* years. And I have a hunch I'll want to be your friend too."

He set his coffee cup down. She sat motionless there at the table but he could feel something inside her beginning to sway.

"Here's my card." He placed it in front of her. "Call me."

She appeared at Richard Schiller's office one week later.

"I'll sign." Her voice was calm. It didn't match her eyes, which were drops of seawater spinning with life.

Richard managed to keep from shaking. He had his secretary bring in the contract. "Do you want a lawyer to read it?"

"No."

"Want my pen?"

"Thanks."

She signed and he pointed out the riders, and she initialed those, and when she handed the contract back to him he felt he was picking up a thread from the tapestry of the past.

He opened his desk drawer and handed her an envelope. "This is yours. You'll be getting one the first of every month."

She opened it and stared at the cashier's check. "I don't understand. I haven't earned this."

"There's a certain someone who doesn't want you having to sell perfumes at B. Altman's when you should be home practicing."

"Who is this someone?"

"They prefer to be anonymous."

"I don't see how I can accept."

"How much money do you have now? Be honest."

"Ninety-seven dollars."

"Then take it as a loan."

For the rest of the afternoon Richard Schiller purred, shouted, told some lies and a few truths, answered phones, slammed down phones, shot off a two-word note to the manager of a regional opera house who had balked at his demands, informed La Scala they would have to bid against Hamburg if they wanted their favorite *Sonnambula* for the next season's opening.

And all the while, in his memory, he kept seeing Ariana Kavalaris running across a stage, Isolde's sun-streaked hair flying out behind her. He buzzed his secretary. "Find me Kavalaris's 'Leibestod,' will you?"

She found the tape. He sat and listened.

God made that voice, he thought. *He never gave that power to any other voice again. And yet, this Billings . . .* He phoned Boyd Kinsolving, music director of the Metropolitan Opera. "Meet me at the Russian Tea Room at six-thirty. I've got something you want."

"All right, what's this mysterious something that I want?"

"This." Richard slipped the earphones over Boyd's head and pressed the *start* button. He'd put nearly dead batteries in the cassette player, so Kavalaris's "Liebestod" sounded only intermittently like Kavalaris. The rest sounded like shortwave during a nuclear blitz.

Boyd monkeyed with volume controls and listened. His eyes searched Richard's. "Lousy sound. Who is it? Ariana?"

"Are you kidding? Ariana never sang with a pit band like that. It's Billings. Her pupil. The girl who sang at the funeral."

Boyd's face went white. "You've signed her?"

"Of course. Think I'd let you get to her first?"

Over two more rounds of drinks, Richard coaxed the deal to ripeness. "Three Santuzzas," he insisted.

"But she'll understudy six Neddas."

"Provided she covers two Marschallins in Washington."

Boyd grimaced. "One. I promised Columbia Artists—"

"Do you want her or don't you want her?"

Boyd drained his Scotch. "I want her. Two Marschallins."

"You're looking well, Boyd."

"You're looking well too, Clara."

Boyd removed his bifocals. He didn't like to be seen in them, and while Clara Rodrigo was in his office he was obviously not going to be able to continue working on Shostakovich's orchestration of Moussorgsky's *Boris Godunov.*

"Thank you for your nice tempo change in *Turandot* last night."

She'd run out of breath on the climactic phrase, cutting short the high C in the Riddle Duet. He'd rushed the accompaniment to make the gaffe less obvious. There had been knowing boos.

He smiled graciously. "My pleasure, sweetums."

"I understand you've found me a new cover for Nedda?"

He'd made the deal barely forty-eight hours ago and already she knew. There had to be a leak in the contract department.

"Tell me about her." Clara sat massaging her diamond rings.

"She's . . . promising."

"Have I heard her?"

"Possibly."

Clara seemed to have stored up only a limited number of smiles and she had obviously now exhausted her supply. She rose to her full five foot three, four inches of which were heels. "I am a reasonable woman, yes? I do not expect to live forever. *Nor do I expect to fade so soon as you would like!*"

"What in the world are you talking about, sweetums?"

"Three Santuzzas and six Neddas. Opening and closing night on the Washington tour—as the Marschallin!"

"She's only understudying the Marschallin," Boyd said.

"That makes no difference." Clara's head snapped back into a stare that bored into his skull. "Maybe her future is great. But she cannot leap into it. She must crawl like anyone else!"

"Now, Clara, you hardly had to crawl into the Metropolitan."

She was jabbing diamond-crusted fingers dangerously near his eyes. "Three years in Palermo, four years with the Barcelona Lyric, never a Marschallin in New York—and this Billings, with one arioso at a funeral—you give her everything!"

"Why does she frighten you?"

"I am not frightened," she screamed, "I am disgusted!"

A strange excitement exploded in Boyd Kinsolving's chest. It began to dawn on him just how good the Billings girl really was.

"I will not sing at this house if she does. You hear me, Boyd?"

"Yes, sweetums. You've made everything quite plain."

It took Boyd Kinsolving till three that afternoon to break through Richard Schiller's phone defenses. "I can't hire the Billings girl. If she sets foot on this stage, Clara walks."

Richard muttered, "That piggy little bitch."

"But there's another possibility. Can you bring Billings to Côte Basque for lunch tomorrow?"

*　　*　　*

Richard asked Vanessa to meet him in the restaurant at one. His heart broke when he saw her sitting there in a pretty white dress, bursting with anticipation.

He talked slowly, explaining. He reached across the table and took her hand. She sat silent, motionless.

Boyd Kinsolving sauntered in twenty minutes late, wearing a red ski jacket. "Miss Billings?" He took her hand. "You've got a terrific agent and I love your work and I'm sick about the mixup." He sat and opened the menu. "Excuse me if I seem a little high, but I've just been rehearsing Strauss with the Philharmonic. God, that man is the *sun*."

"The sun?" Vanessa said pleasantly. "I've always thought he was a satellite of Wagner."

"*Satellite?*" Boyd Kinsolving laid down his half-moon glasses and peered at this young lady who not only sang but talked back.

She said that Wagner captured the psychology of the human race, but Strauss never got further than the individual. "Take the 'Ride of the Valkyries'—it's a universal cataclysm. Compared to those pages, Elektra's dance of triumph and Salomé's 'Dance of the Seven Veils' are strictly local events."

Boyd Kinsolving placed his glasses back onto his nose. "I'm scheduled to record in London next month. But my soprano has decided to have a baby. Can you sing *Manon* for me?"

"Puccini's or Massenet's?" she asked.

Both composers had written operas—*Manon Lescaut* and *Manon*, respectively—based on Abbé Prevost's novel. It wasn't unusual for two composers to take the same subject. What *was* unusual was for both operas to achieve lasting popularity. Usually one ousted the other: Verdi's *Otello* had wiped out Rossini's; Puccini's *Bohème* had kept Leoncavallo's in permanent shade. But the two *Manons*—one raw Italian passion, the other pure French elegance—had thrived.

"Massenet's," Boyd said.

"I don't know the role," she said quietly.

"Of course, you won't have to memorize," Boyd said, "and it's all going to be short takes anyway. You'll be singing with the London Philharmonic. To my mind, they're the most sensitive opera orchestra in the world bar none. Your tenor will be Lucco Patemio. He's still good in the recording studio. Richard, tell her to do it."

Richard nodded. "Do it."

"May I think about it? Overnight at least?"

Boyd Kinsolving smiled a charming smile that said *no*. "Don't worry about learning anything. We'll get Austin Waters to coach you. He taught that role to Callas in—was it three weeks, Richard?"

"Two."

"Then it's settled? Good. Let's celebrate. Champagne with our oysters?"

For the first time in his career as a working writer, Ames Rutherford dead-ended.

He sat at his desk and nothing came. He walked two thousand miles around his desk and nothing came.

Something was gone: the will, the trick, the ability. He couldn't call it back. When he shut his eyes and tried to summon up words, all that came was the image of that face in the choir loft.

After twelve days dribbled away like cat piss in a litterbox, he knew he would never write this article, and after thirteen he began to wonder if he would ever write anything again. He went to the man at *Knickerbocker* magazine who thought he had the makings of a features writer. "Greg, I just can't lick this one."

Rising from his desk, Greg Hatoff pulled the after-lunch cigar out of his mouth. He was a large man, his face tanned even in winter, his brown eyes nested in a web of smile lines. "Maybe you don't want to dish the dirt on your dad. I can understand that. Hell, I can even admire it."

Ames had come prepared for an argument and instead the manipulative bastard gave him understanding.

"I'll have my agent return the advance."

Greg threw an arm around Ames's shoulder. "Hey, keep the money. It'll be a retainer for your next."

For ten days Vanessa Billings studied Jules Massenet's *Manon*, and Boyd Kinsolving assumed the score was causing his new star no insurmountable difficulties. A week before the recording date he invited Vanessa's coach to dinner just to make sure.

Austin Waters sat at the long dining table and seemed to be trying to bring himself to say something very difficult. "How well do you know this Billings?"

"Oh, Christ." Boyd set down his fork and reached for his wineglass. "She can't read music. She has no memory. She has no top. No bottom. Will you please get that spooked look off your face and tell me the bad news?"

"Why'd you hire her?"

"Instinct. Plus she sounded good at the funeral. Plus—I don't know. There's something about her . . ."

Austin Waters was silent in the flickering candlelight. He had gray hair and penetrating eyes and something was definitely troubling him. "I worked with her when she was Ariana's pupil. She's changed. There's no way I can coach her in this role."

Boyd stared in shocked silence and felt the earth give way beneath him. Austin was one of the best coaches in opera. He'd taught beginners, he'd restored old-timers, he was known to work magic. And here he was admitting defeat. "Oh, Jesus."

"Did she tell you she'd sung *Manon* before?"

"No. She was honest. She admitted she'd never sung it."

"Then she's lying." Austin leaned forward. He spoke almost in a whisper. "Boyd, she's not learning the score. She *knows* it. Every note, every intonation—from day one, she had it down pat. Not to mention that her French is beautiful. But this is the bizarre part. It's Ariana's performance."

Boyd stared at him, not understanding. "But Ariana never sang Massenet's *Manon*."

"Believe me, if she had, it would have sounded like this."

Boyd sank back into his chair. A tightness lifted from his chest. "Then you're telling me she's good."

"She's not just good. She's the best."

Boyd Kinsolving flew to London eight days later.

Vanessa Billings astonished him.

She wore a light dress to the recording studio and her blond hair was pulled back with a blue ribbon like a little girl's. She was completely at ease in front of one hundred of the most experienced, critical musicians in the world.

She didn't strive, she glided into the role. She had scrupulous phrasing, clean attack; she refused to swoop into notes; she projected not just the melodic quality, but the drama of each tone. Everything—timbre, shading, phrasing—was there.

Her work was perfect on the first take. In three eight-hour work days they taped the major arias of Acts One and Two.

On the fourth day Boyd took Vanessa to a light lunch at Claridge's. They chatted about opera, or, rather, she chatted and he tried to listen without showing amazement.

She told him that she didn't think of opera as music. "Its roots are musical, but it's really theater and emotion and sensation. Don't you think that's why so many musicians mistrust it?"

Boyd asked what she thought melody was if not music.

"Operatic melody *began* as music," she said. "But compare a melody of Strauss and a melody of Mozart, or of Puccini and Donizetti. Look how the later composers have broken free of musical logic and substituted emotional impact. Look how they rely on harmony and orchestration to buttress their melodic line. You can transcribe the arias of early opera or even sing them without accompaniment. Melodies of later opera exist only in the environment their composers have set them in."

Boyd tried to look wise and suitably unimpressed. "You have a point," he conceded, and he caught the waiter's eye to signal for more wine.

By 3:00 P.M. on the fifth day of recording they had reached Manon's gavotte, "Profitons de la jeunesse"—"Let's enjoy youth while we have it." Vanessa took all the optional high runs, including a spectacular rippling scale from low E to D above high C. At another point she attacked a climactic note mezzo forte, then without warning she made a diminuendo, bringing the sound down almost to a whisper. The effect was hypnotic, like a bright blaze of light suddenly narrowing to a burning infinitesimal pinpoint.

And then she brought the tone up and out, steady and strong and absolutely even, building it to a mass of sound that pulsed through the entire space of the studio, a physical presence so huge, so solid, so tangible that every musician in the room could feel its shimmering weight pressing down on him.

And then—where any other soprano would be stretching the effect, slugging it home—silence. No sound.

Boyd wondered why she had cut the note short, but so far the take was perfect, and he was willing to go with her. He gave the downbeat for the next measure. On the second beat Vanessa glanced at him and he knew immediately that something was wrong.

He signaled the orchestra to cut.

"Vanessa, that was beautiful, just ravishing. What went wrong? You can hold that note as long as you like—I'll follow you."

She shook her head. "It can't be held. The oboe enters there and the voice will drown it."

He looked down at his score. She was right. The oboe entered on the fourth beat, a three-note phrase that the composer had marked *avec douleur*—"with sadness." He had never noticed the entrance before, and he was certain he had never heard it in any performance or recording. "Oboe, three bars after H, fourth beat, what do you have?"

The player bent toward his music stand and squinted. "A rest."

Boyd frowned. Apparently there was a mistake in the publisher's orchestral parts. "There should be an E-flat tied across the bar line."

The oboist bent forward again and jotted the note on his part.

"Can we take that again, just the orchestra?" Boyd raised his baton and gave the downbeat.

The music surged, and at the climactic dissonance, the oboe added a sting of regret. Suddenly, a musical passage that had been simple melodrama was pure emotion.

"Perfect." Boyd lowered his baton. "Absolutely perfect."

He wondered how Billings could have known. She couldn't have memorized the orchestral score. It was enough work just learning her own part. He had never in all his years of conducting opera known a singer who bothered to learn the orchestral part.

Except Ariana.

Afterward he asked Vanessa, "How did you know about that oboe?"

"It's my business to know. The orchestra is one of the most important characters in opera—don't you agree?"

He mused a moment. "I'd never thought of it that way."

"The orchestra is like the narrator in a novel. It knows the past, the present, the future—the causes, the outcomes, the reasons. And it always tells the truth, the whole truth, and nothing but the truth."

He stared at her and had the impression he was seeing someone else.

"You amaze me," he said.

35

IN HER CENTRAL PARK WEST CO-OP, CLARA RODRIGO WAS RUN-
ning out of breath. Her voice clawed its way up toward the A-
flat, got as far as G, and—with a grotesque squawk—cracked.

Her accompanist, who made house calls twice weekly, looked at her
with an odd arch to his eyebrow. "Excuse me, madame, it's difficult to
sustain the line unless you breathe *before* the E-flat. In fact, Bellini in-
serts the rest for that reason."

Clara squinted at the score and wondered why she had never noticed
that rest before. "Kavalaris never breathed before the E-flat and my
breath control is far better than hers."

The accompanist drew himself absolutely straight on the piano
bench and was silent.

"You're useless," Clara said. "You're all useless. None of you understands what I'm trying to achieve. Well, there's always Austin Waters. I
don't like him, but *he* at least understands the voice."

She phoned Austin Waters. She got his answering service, who said
he was in London and would not be back for ten days. She slammed
down the phone. How dare he go off without telling her? Didn't he
know she might need him?

She made another phone call, this time to one of Austin's students.
She chatted. She offered passes for her performance of *Cavalleria*
Thursday. Finally, "And what do you hear of dear Austin?"

She listened, and her mind became like a magnifying glass. She began
to perceive the tiny links in the plot against her. "Thank you, my dear.
Do enjoy the tickets."

She hung up. A scream ripped out of her.

Clara hired a limousine and got to JFK airport barely in time for the
8:30 evening flight to London. She stopped at Claridge's and freshened
up, and at 10:00 A.M. she strode into the HMV Kingsway studio as
though she owned controlling interest in the company. She waved a
jeweled hand at the guard. He let her pass. She went directly to the
control room and stood listening.

The Billings girl was floating a long arc of sound over a murmuring
string accompaniment. The ache that went through Clara was part admiration, part envy, but mostly despair. She knew she would never
again sing those notes as this girl did, in one unbroken breath.

She touched the engineer's shoulder. "Stop the recording."

A goateed face lifted two eyes of shock at her.

"She should have sung A-flat on *douce*," Clara said.

The engineer hesitated, then leaned toward the mike and raised his voice over the torrent of sound. "Mr. Kinsolving, sorry to interrupt. We seem to have a problem."

Clara refused the chair to which Boyd gestured her. "Boyd, you're a rascal. Didn't we agree she wouldn't sing with you?"

"We agreed she wouldn't sing at the Met."

Steel edged into her voice. "But, dear Boyd, you *are* the Met."

He looked into her eyes and saw the madness of Lady Macbeth, of Medea and Lucia. "Now Clara, we're in London. Our orchestra is British."

"You gave me your word. Either you keep your word, or I break my contract." She opened her purse, took out a document, and began ripping.

Boyd went through a rapid calculation. For six years now Clara had been abusing her voice, jetting across continents and oceans to five engagements a week, taking on roles she couldn't handle. Her pitch was insecure on the top notes and she had the beginnings of a wobble. On the other hand, she still had a following, and she could still count on reviews. Vanessa Billings had as yet no following, no friends among the critics.

For the moment, Boyd needed Clara more than he needed Vanessa.

He reached out and stayed her hand. "Clara, you've made your point. Stop ripping."

They were sitting at a table in the Waldorf bar. Boyd was drinking his gin tonic, Vanessa was stirring hers.

"I believed in this project," she said. "I believed in you and for the first time in ten years I believed in myself. I learned the role and I really thought we were going to do something wonderful."

"And we did do something wonderful." He put his hand over hers. He could feel her pulling her strength back into herself.

"Have you had dinner?" he offered.

"No, thanks. I'll eat on the plane tonight."

Richard Schiller listened and nodded with carefully measured sympathy. He didn't need her feeling sorry for herself. "Boyd Kinsolving made a mistake," he said. "That's his problem."

Vanessa huddled in the chair. "Sometimes I feel so powerless."

"Then sometimes you're an idiot. You're going to give a recital. We'll book Alice Tully Hall. We'll buy ads on the classical stations—and we'll use your Manon tapes. You'll sing some lieder, some folksongs, and since you went to all the trouble of learning them, you'll sing Manon's three big arias."

For a moment she didn't react. "I'm not sure I can face . . ."

"To hell with you. You're going to do this for Ariana."

"Hey, honey," Ames called.

Fran raised a questioning smile. "Mmm-hmm?"

He was stretched in his bathrobe, leafing through the entertainment section of the Sunday *Times*. They were on the glassed-in sun terrace, and a pot of coffee was steaming on the table.

"How'd you like to go to a concert on the twenty-third?"

"We can't. Cathy and Sid Guberman invited us for dinner."

He groaned. "Dinner and slides of their trip to Egypt? Say your mother's in town. Say mine just died. Say anything."

"What's so great about this concert?"

"It's that woman I heard at Kavalaris's funeral."

"Since when are you such an enthusiast for song recitals?"

"I'm not going to miss this one, Fran. If you want to watch slides at Cathy's, watch slides. But I'm going."

Alice Tully Hall was sold out the evening of the concert, and Fran and Ames squeezed into their seats just as a rising wave of applause welcomed the singer on stage.

Vanessa Billings stood erect and slender in a pool of light, graceful and smiling in a plain white gown that showed strong shoulders and a good throat. She bowed twice and then turned and nodded to her accompanist.

The concert opened with three Schubert lieder.

Fran knew nothing about voice, but she had spent eight years studying the flute, and halfway through the first song, "An die Musik," she knew that this voice had all the qualities of a fine instrument: security and timbre and the indefinable something that separated the great from the good.

At the end of the set, applause ripped through the hall. Fran was surprised at its intensity, but she joined in and clapped.

Ames didn't clap.

She looked at him. Suddenly there was nothing connecting her to him. Something was happening in the air. She felt a presence, like a shadow. A prickling current ran along her skin.

She realized that he was staring at the singer.

And the singer was staring straight back at him.

At that moment Vanessa Billings's voice rose like a fountain of sound in the opening measures of Schumann's "Frauenliebe und Leben."

The last applause was slowly dying when Vanessa hurried into the green room. She dumped herself into a chair and mouthed a silent groan. Richard Schiller embraced her and was surprised how limp she felt in his arms.

"Hey, pull yourself together. You're going to have visitors."

"Do I have to meet them? Now?"

"Glory has its tiring side."

She sighed and pulled herself into the bathroom. He heard a long, drumming splash of water in the sink. She looked a little better when she came back.

He gave her a hug. "And remember—be nice to the critics."

"How do I know who's a critic?"

"I'm going to have to teach you everything, aren't I."

"You're going to have to hold me up."

He opened the doors. People were lined up into the hallway and down the stairs. He let them in ten at a time.

He could see it was difficult for her to meet strangers. At least thirty people asked her to autograph their programs, and six or seven even gave her little gifts: flowers, candy, sheet music. When she made a nervous and mildly humorous remark they all laughed. That seemed to confuse her. He had a sense this was her first taste of being a big deal.

Alan Cupson of the *Times* made an elaborate show of kissing her hand. He had grown a gray goatee since Richard had last seen him. "I'm not reviewing you, Miss Billings. Just here for pleasure. And what a pleasure it was. What about that high F in 'Der Gärtner'? I never heard anyone but Kavalaris interpolate it. Were you by any chance imitating her?"

"High F?" She seemed confused.

"Don't misunderstand me. I'm not criticizing. Certain liberties are entirely appropriate. Particularly with a middling composer like Wolf. He often needs a little—enhancement." The critic caught her hand and his eyes held hers a moment. "I thank you for a lovely evening."

Richard was about to open the door to another ten visitors when Vanessa stopped him. "I feel doped with all these people around me. I really have to lie down. Richard—*please?*"

She looked much too pale and he could believe she was about to faint. "Okay. Take five."

In thirty-five years he had never waited more than two minutes for anyone. But Nikos Stratiotis stood almost a half-hour in the corridor. It was a little past eleven. He was the last admirer still waiting when the door of the green room finally opened.

"Sorry to keep you," Richard said.

A small light was burning on a table. Vanessa Billings was sitting up on a chaise longue. Richard made the introductions.

Nikos bent to kiss her hand. "Thank you for the concert. I admire your music very much."

She raised her eyes to him and there was an instant of contact. "Thank you."

"Are you hungry? Could I offer you dinner?"

"That's very kind of you, but . . ."

"Or, if you're tired, I could drive you home."

She hesitated, and Richard quickly cleared his throat.

"That's all right, Nikos. I was planning to take Vanessa home myself."

"Of course." Nikos took her hand once again and kissed it. "In that case, goodnight."

He was at the door when her voice stopped him.

"Mr. Stratiotis—I'd like to drive with you. But could we walk just a little first?"

They walked south along Broadway, and the limousine crawled alongside them. It was a warm night, and the streetlights glowed like peacock's spots in the hovering mist. For three blocks they were silent.

She looked at him, and he saw the eyes of someone else questioning him. "It's you, isn't it?" she said. "You paid for the hall and the ads. It was your money that got the critics there and filled the house and bought the applause."

"You're wrong. No one bought that applause. I've been giving you $800 a month. I rented the hall and paid $5,000 for publicity. Your agent says that's standard."

She stopped. "Why are you helping me?"

"It's a debt."

"You don't owe me anything."

"I owe it to someone else."

They reached Fifty-ninth Street. A horse-drawn carriage was waiting at the curb, the driver and animal both dozing. "Would you like to ride in that?" he said.

She smiled, and Nikos woke the driver.

The clipclopping horse took them on a leisurely tour of the park and the avenues around it. Sometimes they spoke, sometimes they lapsed into long silences. There was a strange lack of tension between them. It was as though they were old friends reunited after a long separation, sifting through separate memories of the same events.

They rode for well over an hour. It was close to one in the morning when Nikos pointed and said, "Look, there's a newsstand. Let's see if your reviews are out."

He stepped down from the cab and bought the papers. He read her reviews to her. They were good. The *Times* predicted that Vanessa Billings would be moving to the front ranks of America's young vocalists. The *News* said she was Kavalaris without the flaws.

"You're going to be very busy now," he said. "But some evening— when you have time—may I see you again, Miss Billings?"

＊　　＊　　＊

331

Richard Schiller's desk was an island of inefficiency. He had to dig through notes on five contracts to find the letter that had come for Vanessa that morning.

She stood at the window. She read it and then she reread it. The words had a counterfeit ring. Like the sender.

"I'm gratified," she said. "I'm very flattered Boyd Kinsolving liked my reviews. But . . . when I think of that man and what he's put me through . . ."

She tore the letter up. She came around the desk and opened her fist and let the confetti rain down into the wastebasket.

Richard watched her. "There isn't room in your career right now for a grudge. You're going to sit right down and write him a sweet little thank-you note."

"I'm not going to write him a sweet little anything."

"Then I'll forge it myself, because he's the best game in town and I want you working for him."

"I'll never work for that man again."

"Hey, I make the deals, you stick to making the music, okay? I don't care who you hate or who hates you, you'll be singing for him on the Metropolitan stage in three months."

Fran walked in from the kitchen carrying a tray of yogurt and fresh strawberries. She saw Ames ripping something out of the *Times*.

"What's that you're tearing out?" she said.

He threw her an almost startled glance. "Nothing," he said, folding the piece of paper. "Just an ad for Dill's book."

"Didn't know he'd published it yet."

"Sure. Last week."

Ames took the article into his study and reread it for the twelfth time. Vanessa Billings had sung a recital at a veterans' hospital. There was a photograph of her and he spent a long time looking at it.

He closed the study door and then he opened the metal cabinet. From behind the IRS forms he withdrew a folder that was beginning to bulge with clippings on Vanessa Billings.

He added the article to the file.

36

THE FIRST TUESDAY OF EVERY MONTH RICHARD SCHILLER AND
Meyer Colby, a fellow agent, met for lunch in the grill room at
the Four Seasons. They always sat at the same little round table just behind the boxwood screen, always drank one martini each, and always
ate whatever Julian, the maître d', recommended.

This Tuesday Julian recommended the gravlax. Meyer looked unhappy and Richard had a hunch it was not just because he hated fish.

"That bitch is driving me crazy."

"Come on, Meyer, no one drives you crazy."

"You don't know Clara Rodrigo. Why the hell did I ever want to represent her? She canceled a recital at Bloomington, Indiana, last week.
In fact she's canceling all her Great Artists dates."

The Great Artists University series was one of Meyer Colby's biggest
moneymakers. College kids bought series tickets to umpteen flutists, recorder consorts, fledgling pianists and lutenists, and as a reward they
got one or two artists they really wanted to hear, or thought they did:
like Clara Rodrigo belting "Vissi d'arte." Meyer Colby had sold a lot of
zitherists that way.

"Is she allowed to do that?"

"If it's medical she's allowed."

"Is it medical?"

Colby's lips were narrow and taut below the small brown mustache.
"You tell me. Thursday she's due to sing in Peoria and she comes down
with strep throat and a roaring fever. Saturday she's due to sing at the
Chicago Lyric and she's fine."

"Who's her doctor?" Richard asked.

On rare occasions, it pays to have a sister-in-law. Richard phoned his
brother's wife Frieda. "Aren't you a friend of that Abscheid woman, the
doctor's wife?"

"Henrietta? I took care of her cat when they went to Nice."

"I need to meet her husband."

"I'll expect two grand tier passes at the Met opening this fall."

"How do you know it's worth two grand tier passes?"

"If you're asking, I know."

Three evenings later, on his agency charge card, Richard took his sister-in-law and Dr. and Mrs. Gunter Abscheid to dinner at Le Lavan-
dou. For three courses the women gossiped about old friends and cats,
and Richard watched Dr. Abscheid stare somberly at his filet of flounder. Promptly after dessert (they all ordered raspberry mousse) Frieda

333

had a dizzy attack and asked Henrietta to walk her around the block.

Richard emptied two envelopes of Sweet 'n Low into his café exprès. "Why's Clara Rodrigo canceling so many dates?"

The doctor looked at the ceiling. "The question is, why's she singing so many?" He shook his head. "It's a crime."

"Is that a musical opinion?"

"God, no, it's a medical opinion pure and simple."

Richard leaned across the table. "What's wrong with her?"

Dr. Abscheid scratched nervously under his chin. And then it came spilling out. "Her throat is a mess. It's a miracle she can swallow, let alone get a note out of it." He described the condition. Richard listened and understood and not for a moment was he tempted to feel pity for Clara Rodrigo. She had hurt far too many people with far too little thought.

"What's keeping her going?"

"Cortisone. I shouldn't be giving it to her, but she's such a . . ." The doctor's fingers were tapping on his pony of Armagnac. "I've never been so manipulated by a patient ever in my career."

Richard made a sympathetic face. "She's good at that."

"I give her shots before the big dates. She doesn't bother with the little dates anymore. The shots mask the symptoms for a few hours. She's wrecking her throat. Already I've seen irreversible damage. But she won't give up the big dates."

"How long can she last?"

"She can't last. Listen to her. Call that singing?"

Richard sensed that Dr. Abscheid had had it with Madame Rodrigo, which meant he was ready to deal. "She's singing a *Hoffmann* next week. The role's a killer, even for a healthy voice. Don't give her the shot. Make her cancel."

"She'll never accept that. She's terrified of letting her understudy go on. The girl's twenty-one and sings like a pro."

"Who's the understudy?"

"Camilla someone—Seaton. Great voice. She'll go places."

"I can help," Richard said. "Give Clara a placebo shot. I'll arrange it so Seaton doesn't go on. I'll get a newcomer into the role, someone who's never sung at the Met before."

"A newcomer who happens to be a client of yours?"

"As it happens, yes."

"And we'd be even?"

"Almost. Could you arrange two grand tier passes for my sister-in-law to the Met opening next fall?"

Dr. Abscheid phoned Wednesday. "I gave her a placebo shot this morning. She won't be able to sing tomorrow night."

"I'll take care of the rest. And remember, two passes?"

They met at Adolf Erdlich's favorite wheeling and dealing spot, a sidewalk café on West Sixty-seventh Street that served what Erdlich said was the only truly Viennese coffee in New York.

The deal: "How are you, Adolf?"

"What do you want, Richard?"

"And your wife?"

"Please get to the point."

A chubby-cheeked waitress set two cups of steaming Wiener schlag before them. The director of the Metropolitan Opera smiled at her. Quite possibly his only smile that week. He measured exactly one level teaspoon of sugar and let it rain down onto the whipped cream.

"Off the record, Adolf, Clara will be canceling tomorrow."

Adolf Erdlich stared at pedestrians. With a lifting of his chin he managed to give the impression that in the old Viennese days Sigmund Freud and Gustav Mahler had strolled past his sidewalk table. Now it was punks on skate boards and flashy black hookers. "In the first place, Clara never cancels at the Met. In the second place, we have a standby."

"And in the third place I have someone better. Vanessa Billings. You heard her at Ariana's funeral. You read her Tully Hall reviews."

Erdlich's cup touched his lips and left a tiny bloom of whipped cream on his neat white pencil-line mustache.

"We're talking a handshake deal. No contract, no guarantees. You're not obligated in any way. Vanessa will be at the house tomorrow night at six-thirty, ready to go on. Don't tell anyone. Just make an announcement three minutes before the curtain goes up."

Erdlich sat stiffly, his head erect in its starched collar, his gray hair slicked to his skull as though it had been laid there with a paintbrush. When he finally spoke, it was with elegant world-weariness. "In the first place, we can't throw neophytes onto the stage of the Metropolitan Opera. In the second place, she hasn't rehearsed our production."

Richard commenced to embroider. "She's seen it three times."

"She doesn't know the blocking."

"She'll go through it tomorrow afternoon."

"One walk-through? You're joking."

Richard decided to lie outright. "It's the Spoleto blocking. She covered it last summer. She can get through it in her sleep."

Erdlich's dark eyes narrowed and there was a quivering at the edges of his well-veined nostrils. "Bring her to rehearsal room three tomorrow afternoon at two."

It took Richard two hours to track Vanessa down to a Greek laundromat on the corner of Twenty-second Street. "How'd you like to sing *Tales of Hoffmann*? All three heroines?"

She was sitting with a vocal score of "Amore dei tre re," waiting for a dryer, and she almost dropped the score. "All three?"

It was a killer assignment: a singing doll; a Venetian courtesan; a doomed, tubercular beauty. They were all sopranos, but each so different vocally and psychologically from the others that very few singers ever attempted all three.

"At the Met," Richard said. "Tomorrow night."

Something wilder than panic was written into her white face. Disbelief. "You know I can't."

"I know you can. You're blocking at two, you're reporting for makeup at six-thirty, you go on at eight."

"Richard, I don't—know the roles."

He touched a finger to her neck chain and drew it out. Ariana's locket swung free from the collar of her blouse.

"The hell you don't know the roles."

At three the next afternoon Boyd took Clara's call on the terrace of his penthouse. "Boyd darling, I have a bit of a cold. I could sing Olympia tonight, but I think it would be wiser to save my strength for Giulietta and Antonia. After all, they're the audience's favorite roles."

And the easiest of the three, Boyd thought. "Of course. We'll alert your understudy."

She phoned again two hours later. Boyd took the call in the sauna.

"Boyd darling." Every syllable seemed to be hacking its way through layers of stratified phlegm. "You couldn't by any chance take Giulietta's aria down a tone? I really think I should save my high C-sharp for Antonia."

"We'd have to copy the parts, and there isn't time. We'd better let your understudy handle it."

"Poor girl, she has *no* experience. I hope the audience won't be too disappointed."

"Not when they have your Antonia to look forward to."

An hour later, in a voice that seemed to be croaking its way from inside a coffin, Clara phoned to cancel her Antonia.

By five after eight the crowds had swarmed down the aisles to their seats. At seven after, the chandeliers of the Metropolitan Opera House dimmed and slowly rose to the ceiling. A tall man in evening clothes stepped onto the stage and announced a cast change.

Thirty seconds later Adolf Erdlich knocked at dressing room nine. Camilla Seaton, about to make her debut in the triple role of Olympia, Giulietta, and Antonia, answered the door in a costume of rustling mauve taffeta. Her face glowed.

Adolf Erdlich told Miss Seaton she would not be going on. His words fell like stones into the sudden silence. He laid his hand on Miss Seaton's trembling shoulder. In his Viennese version of Oxbridge English, he dredged up his usual speech for these not very unusual occasions.

"Come, my dear. It's not the end. You'll have other chances."

The members of the orchestra had finished tuning their instruments and were fidgeting silently when at the back of the pit a door flew open. In strode Boyd Kinsolving. As he passed the violas the follow spot picked him out and escorted him up to the stand. He faced the audience, bowed his head with enough of a snap to send a floating wave through his handsomely graying hair.

He turned to the music stand, raised his baton, held an audience of four thousand and an orchestra of seventy-two captive in an instant of absolute soundlessness. His wrist flicked out the downbeat.

He conducted the Prologue almost absentmindedly, beating time with his left hand, turning pages with his right.

The brief opening scene took place in a beer cellar in Nuremberg. Lindorf, sung by the same baritone who would play the hero's nemesis in each of the following acts, intercepted a note from the opera singer Stella to the poet Hoffmann, inviting him to meet her after her performance and enclosing a key to her dressing room.

Lindorf resolved to make use of both the key and the invitation.

Hoffmann entered with his friend Nicklausse. A group of students asked Hoffmann to regale them with his amorous adventures. Though at first reluctant, he began to drink and finally agreed to tell the stories of his three great, tragic loves.

The first act, which followed immediately, was Hoffmann's first tale. The curtain rose on the fantastic candlelit laboratory of opera's one and only mad scientist, the doll-maker Spalanzani. It was one of the Met's most spectacular sets, and the audience applauded enthusiastically.

Though he had seen her only once through a window, Hoffmann was entranced with Spalanzani's daughter, Olympia. Spalanzani promised that, thanks to science, Hoffmann would meet the girl. As guests began arriving for Olympia's coming-out party, Nicklausse warned Hoffmann not to fall in love too fast.

The understudy playing Olympia entered. Boyd threw a glance toward her. At least wardrobe had made the costume fit.

For the next half-scene Olympia had to cling to her father's arm amid approving whispers.

She clung to his arm. So far, so good. Hoffmann declared his love for her. She had to sing two words: *Oui* and *Oui*.

She sang "*Oui*" and "*Oui*."

To Boyd's surprise, the audience laughed both times. He glanced again toward the stage, a little baffled by the quality of attention that the audience seemed to be focusing on her.

Not hostility, not boredom, but expectancy.

Spalanzani lumbered offstage and returned carrying a magnificently improbable harp. Silence rushed into the house like a tide. Spalanzani sat at the harp and mimed arpeggios.

In the pit the flute and the harp began the introduction of the Doll Song, one of the most demanding arias in the coloratura repertory. Boyd braced himself for a train of tiny mishaps. God only knew, the aria was mined with vocal traps.

The understudy didn't fall into one of them.

There was a comic moment when her voice faltered and a servant touched her. A whirring spring was heard and she began singing again.

With no sign of effort whatsoever, she executed the leaps and trills and runs, employed every form of vocal attack from sustained legato to fleet pinprick staccato, dipped to low E-flat at the bottom of the staff, rose to an unbelievably brilliant high E-flat.

Boyd realized she could not possibly be the girl he had auditioned two weeks ago. The musical discrepancies were too great. This was no nervous understudy's first run-through before a paying audience. This was a seasoned performance, every breath, every note, every attack calculated and sure.

She finished the first refrain on a glittering high A-flat. He could feel the audience wanting to break into the music, to applaud right then. He sensed something passing from her to them, some signal of the eyes, of the posture, of the voice itself. It was as though she had stepped to the footlights and said, *Not yet. You'll have your chance in a moment. For now, let me have mine.*

But she hadn't moved.

She had simply stood there, faced her audience, attacked her note clean and cut it clean. And now, in the eight measures of harp and flute, she moved. She took two sideways steps, swung out a hand and, turning as though to pirouette, collided with the harp.

The harp did not go over, she did not go over, but for one breath-stopping instant it seemed as though everything might go over.

Boyd Kinsolving had seen that bit of business only once before in his life, when Ariana Kavalaris had last sung the role, in this very house. The baton fell from his hand. It clacked against the edge of the music stand and clattered to the floor of the pit.

She saw. She slid him a glance. Her eyes gleamed. Not with malice, not with triumph. With humor.

Vanessa Billings, he realized, and his heart skipped a beat. *But how?*

Offenbach's delicate waltz continued with no help from Boyd. The first cellist handed him back his baton. He rejoined the music.

It was traditional for singers to interpolate high notes on the second refrain, but she was singing higher than any interpolations he had ever heard. Higher than Ponselle. Higher than Lily Pons, who had been perhaps the greatest coloratura of the mid-twentieth century. E-flats, E-naturals, F's. Higher than anyone . . . except Kavalaris.

A stunning high E-flat brought the audience shrieking to its feet.

Olympia completed her song, danced exquisitely, and withdrew.

A violent argument now broke out between Spalanzani and his co-worker, Coppelius. A moment later there was a noise of shattering machinery. Coppelius entered carrying Olympia—a broken doll. As the curtain fell, Hoffmann realized he had been deceived by an automaton.

The next act took place in the courtesan Giulietta's palazzo on the Grand Canal in Venice. This time Billings played Giulietta, the beautiful pawn of the evil Dappertutto, who used her to capture men's souls. She had already stolen the shadow of her lover Schlemil and was now setting a trap for Hoffmann.

Again, Nicklausse warned his friend, and again Hoffmann was too blindly in love to listen. Giulietta urged him to come to her room: Schlemil had the key and Hoffmann had only to duel him for it. Hoffmann challenged Schlemil, killed him, and took the key. He ran to Giulietta's balcony just in time to see her floating away in her gondola, laughingly embracing another man.

This time when Boyd's eyes met Vanessa Billings's, he smiled back at her like an old friend.

Camilla Seaton, the understudy for the understudy, stayed in her dressing room, changing her costume for each act. There was always the chance they might need her.

As the last act began she moved through the long silent stretches of the backstage corridors, feeling hollow and alone. Among all the singers and stagehands bustling through the wings, she was the one person with nothing to do. She stood by the electrician's booth. She listened to her rival.

The scene on stage was the home of Crespel the lute-maker, in Munich. This time Hoffmann was smitten with Crespel's lovely but fragile daughter, Antonia. She was sitting at the harpsichord singing a plaintive song about a turtledove. Camilla had expected the voice to go through her like a knife. Instead, it was as though the sun had peeped over a dark horizon.

Crespel reminded Antonia that the exertion of singing had killed her famous mother and could spell her doom as well. She promised not to sing.

Hoffmann entered. Antonia embraced him passionately. They joined voices in their favorite love song, but—suddenly weak—she clasped her hand to her heart.

She's better than I am. Inwardly, Camilla Seaton sighed. *She's much, much better. And she couldn't be that much older. Maybe ten years. I wonder if I'll ever be that good?*

Hearing her father returning, Antonia fled to her room. Hoffmann hid and eavesdropped on a conversation between Crespel and Dr. Miracle, the mysterious quack whose treatment had resulted in the death of Antonia's mother. Cynically, Miracle inquired after the girl's health. Crespel drove him from the house.

But when Antonia was alone, Miracle suddenly appeared and urged her to sing. She appealed to her dead mother for help. Miracle brought to life the portrait of Antonia's mother on the wall: the portrait encouraged her to sing. Miracle seized a violin and accompanied. The portrait, the diabolical doctor, and the doomed Antonia now joined in a heartrending trio.

Camilla tried to analyze Vanessa Billings's voice.

It was lofty enough and vast enough to fill a cathedral. There was flow, there was clarity, there was rhythmic exactness and absolute precision of detail.

But there was something else, something disturbing and beautiful. The voice seemed to articulate an unheard melody—the true melody— that lay behind the sounding notes.

Exhausted, Antonia fell to the floor. Hoffmann rushed to take her into his arms. He called for a doctor. Miracle appeared once more and triumphantly pronounced the girl dead.

The brief epilogue took place in the tavern. Hoffmann's tales were ended. His friends had gone, leaving him in an alcoholic stupor. The Muse of Poetry appeared and urged him to belong to her alone, for she alone loved him. The door opened and Stella, Hoffmann's last love, entered with Lindorf. Lindorf pointed sardonically to the poet—passed out drunk—and led Stella away.

The curtain dropped like swift nightfall. Boyd laid down his baton.

The audience, like a single being, held its breath. There was a moment of absolute silence, when the music seemed to hang in the air, and then a great steady roar of applause and bravos and stamping.

The curtains parted.

The soloists stepped single-file through the gap to take their bows. There was applause for the supporting singers—the mezzo, the baritones, the second tenor.

Vanessa took her bow.

Bravas ripped loose. Programs were flung to the stage. Torn paper fluttered down from the front balconies spinning like butterflies in the air currents.

She faced the house, curtsied deeply and perfectly. Her face glowed with an incredible serenity, like a figure in a Renaissance painting.

Boyd mopped his face with an already soaked handkerchief. He had expected disaster, and instead . . . this. *Home free*, he thought.

They called Vanessa Billings back eight times. The tenor, Lucco Patemio, tagged along for eight bows too.

Boyd caught his breath, allowed himself a moment to believe that this was real, this screaming stamping hysteria of approval was actually happening. He loved the sound. He loved the moment. He wanted his share.

He strode from the podium, past the string players politely tapping their bows against their instruments. As he hurried through the doorway and up the steps to the stage he could hear the ongoing screams, the bravos, the change in resonance as the audience moved down to the front orchestra and stood shouting.

Billings and Patemio were waiting for him. He gave them each one of his hands, and they marched forward through the gap in the curtain that took all of a stagehand's weight to hold open.

"Brava, my darling, absolute brava." Boyd kissed his new star on the cheek. He remembered to give Patemio's hand a quick squeeze. "You too, Lucco."

Patemio, now well over sixty years old, had had an astonishingly long career for an opera singer—some four decades. His voice had lost its beauty but little of its power. He wore an obvious toupee, but it was no worse than the wigs he wore onstage. He was a jealous beast, worse than a household pet, and he had to be coddled; but he knew the repertory, and to the tone-deaf among the public he had become an institution—Mr. Opera.

"You were absolutely brilliant," Boyd assured him.

They moved smiling into the pool of spotlight. Boyd could feel the damp skin of Vanessa's palm, her pulse hammering against his hand. "You're a miracle!" he shouted in her ear.

For one moment her eyes met his and it seemed to him something like recognition flashed between them: *We have been here before, you and I. We have shared this moment, this applause . . .*

And then she fell against him.

"Vanessa, are you all right? Lucco, help me. She's fainted."

But she hadn't fainted; she had just lost her balance. They got her offstage. She was able to stand, her bosom rising and falling like the wing of a fluttering bird.

The house was still applauding, still screaming.

"Both of you, take another bow." Boyd gave his tenor and soprano a push. "Lucco, hold her up. Just a short bow now. It's almost midnight and we don't want to go into overtime."

A Niagara of thumping and screaming tore loose. The sound was almost terrifying, as though Bolsheviks were ripping a palace apart.

It was almost two minutes of bravos and shrieks before Lucco helped Vanessa back behind the curtain.

A figure stood beside Boyd. He recognized the little understudy, as tiny and lost and trembling as a snowflake in an avalanche.

"She's magnificent," the girl said quietly.

Boyd put a fatherly arm around the girl's shoulder. He felt a twinge of sympathy. Tonight might have been *her* night. "You're right, sweetums," he agreed. "Magnificent and then some."

The girl looked at Vanessa shyly and Boyd caught the glance.

"Vanessa, this is Camilla Seaton, Clara's understudy."

"How do you do." Vanessa smiled weakly. "You would have sung if it hadn't been for me."

"I wouldn't have sung nearly as well as you."

"You're very kind."

"I'm not kind, Miss Billings, just telling the truth. I've studied *Hoffmann* for two years, but I've never really heard it till tonight. Could I ask you something?"

"Of course."

"Would you coach me?"

Silence pooled, thick and sudden.

"I know you're very busy, but I could be available whenever you have a moment. I'm a hard worker and a fast learner."

Boyd had seen manipulation before, but this child brimming with hope and gall took his breath away. He stepped between the two women. "Perhaps this could be discussed another time. Vanessa has had an exhausting two days."

Vanessa pulled free of his arm. "I'm all right now." She took the girl's hand. "That's the kindest compliment you could give me."

She was staring into the girl's eyes. There was a silence, but it was a silence between the two women, no one else. Boyd sensed something pass through the air.

"May I phone you?" Vanessa said. "We'll talk about it."

"You didn't have to do that," Boyd said afterward, walking Vanessa to her dressing room. "You don't owe her a thing."

She looked at him strangely. "How do you know what I owe?"

Boyd shook his head. "A word of advice from a seasoned opera survivor. Sentiment belongs on the stage. Not off."

37

FOR THREE MONTHS CLARA RODRIGO WATCHED THE BILLINGS girl mount the climbing wave of fame. *Vanessa Billings possesses an unearthly versatility,* the *New York Times* cooed. *Her voice can as effortlessly encompass the dark tones of a Tosca as it can the silvery filigree of a Norma. Not since Kavalaris has this listener heard such an astonishing instrument, and Kavalaris, we would do well to remember, excelled in this regard even the magnificent Maria Callas.* The magazines, always more sensational, openly predicted a golden future: *the next Kavalaris.*

As chance would have it, the evening came when Clara and the Billings girl appeared in the same opera at different houses: Clara at the Met in a new gala production, Billings at the City Opera just across Lincoln Plaza in a scaled-down revival. The opera was *Turandot,* and as Clara was hurrying across the plaza two hours before curtain, a small, dark, bearded man approached her. His jacket was rumpled and stained and he had the aura of a ratty sorcerer.

"Hey, lady." The voice was secretive. "Got a ticket for Billings? I'll give you four Rodrigos for a Billings."

Fury took her breath. She gave him a look of pure hatred, yanked her mink tight around her, strode past him.

"Five Rodrigos! Hey lady! Five Rodrigos and cash!"

Billings's reviews the next day were better than hers. She was troubled and she decided to go to a fortune teller who had been recommended to her, a woman said to have occult powers who worked near B. Altman's department store on Thirty-fourth Street.

The sun was going down as Clara climbed the stairs over the Chinese restaurant. She moved aside a beaded curtain and groped her way into the dimness. A transistor radio was blaring salsa and it was very hot inside the room.

At first she could barely make out the huge dark woman wrapped in lace. A surprisingly deep voice commanded, *"Siéntese."* Sit.

The woman turned down the radio. Clara could begin to see her: the eyes were milky, practically without irises, and half the teeth were missing from the upper jaw. Behind her was a shelf of carnival dolls: bears and rabbits and babies with blond hair.

The two women spoke in Spanish: not the Castilian of Clara's conservatory days, but the harsh Santurce dialect of her childhood.

"Who sent you?"

Clara named the Haitian woman who cleaned her apartment.

There was a moment's silence. *"¿Por qué has venido, hijita?"*—"Why have you come, little daughter?"

Clara talked for twenty minutes, telling everything.

The old woman instructed her what to do.

Two days later Clara climbed the stairs again. She gave the woman a live chicken tied in a ribbon that she had worn in *La Fille du Régiment*.

"Come back in one week at the same hour," the woman said.

"Next week I have to be in Chicago."

"Come back in one week."

The next evening at City Opera Vanessa Billings sang another role that Clara regarded as rightfully her own, Magda in *La Rondine*. To believe the critics, the performance was faultless. After studying the reviews, Clara canceled Chicago.

On the day commanded she again climbed the stairs. The fortune teller held Clara's hands in a tight grip and passed them over a pot of sickening dark goo.

"There are forces behind her," the woman said. "They are powerful. More powerful than you can imagine."

"Do these forces have a name?"

"They have the name of the unnamable."

Clara had expected the name of an agency or manager, but she saw she was not going to get it. "How can these forces be defeated?"

"Only love can defeat these forces."

Clara sprang up from her chair. "Love thine enemy, is that what you're telling me? I could have gone to a priest for that!" She yanked back her hand and realized the woman had somehow worked the ring off her finger. "Give me back my ring."

"I have told you the truth," the woman warned. "If you do not pay me now, you will have to pay much more later."

"I'll pay you $25, not a ten-carat diamond ring."

The woman handed back the ring. "In one year," she warned, "Billings will be a star and you will have lost your voice."

That winter Ames Rutherford finally published his second novel. Critics said it more than fulfilled the promise of his first. They called his prose muscular, strong, free-wheeling. *People* ran a two-page spread. He made TV appearances. He worried about being inadequate on the little screen, having nothing to say, but talk-show hosts liked him and on the TV screen he looked even handsomer than the photo on his book jacket. His eyes televised dark and alert, his mouth full-lipped, his nose narrow and Anglo-Saxon, and his light brown hair darkened to chestnut. His movements, like his answers to interviewers, were minimal and confident, and at six foot one he appeared to be in perfect physical shape.

The book went into a fifth printing.

Now I have everything I ever wanted, he thought.

Yet he felt an unanswerable dissatisfaction, a restlessness that went to the bone. Something was eluding him.

One Friday when the rain was a smear of winter gray over Long Island he lay on the living room rug, his eye absently running down the columns of the *New York Times* Weekend section. Fran had put a steaming mug of coffee and amaretto by his side and he was turning pages without seeing words.

A photograph of a strangely familiar dark-haired woman suddenly caught his eye. *Tuesday night,* the caption stated, *Vanessa Billings will don a black wig to sing the role of Santuzza, the excommunicated Sicilian beauty, in Pietro Mascagni's* Cavalleria Rusticana.

Tuesday Ames lied to Fran and made an excuse to be out. He wanted to go to the City Opera and he wanted to go alone.

An usher pointed Ames to his seat. Light shone in soft patches across the rows of red velvet seats.

There was an overture and a serenade by the tenor, Turiddu, to his love Lola, before the curtain rose on a Sicilian town square: upstage, the church; stage right, the tavern; stage left, Mama Lucia's house. Time: an Easter morning in the late nineteenth century.

As the chorus of celebrating peasants cleared the stage, Santuzza crept on. The audience broke into applause. She knocked hesitantly at Mama Lucia's door and asked for news of Lucia's son, Turiddu.

Lola's husband, the cheerful cart-driver Alfio, entered, singing of the joys of work and a faithful wife. He mentioned having seen Turiddu that morning near his home. Santuzza quickly silenced Mama Lucia. It was not until Alfio and the other villagers had gone into the truth that she revealed her shame: Turiddu, returning from the army after his sweetheart Lola had married Alfio, had become Santuzza's lover. But Lola had succeeded in winning him back.

Disgraced, heartbroken, abandoned, Santuzza now begged Mama Lucia to pray for her in church.

Alone, Santuzza waited in the deserted square till Turiddu arrived. She accused and pleaded with him. Lola appeared, mocking and flirting. Throwing Santuzza aside, Turiddu followed Lola into the church. Prostrate on the steps, Santuzza screamed a curse after him.

Alfio entered. Santuzza revealed his wife's infidelity. Alfio swore vengeance, *fortissimo.*

The stage was empty as the Intermezzo—probably the best-loved melody in the score—came soaring out of the orchestra. The villagers spilled onstage from church. Turiddu invited his friends to drink with him. Refusing, Alfio challenged him to a duel. Turiddu gave the Sicilian sign of acceptance—he bit Alfio's ear.

Turiddu begged his mother to look after Santuzza, kissed the old woman farewell, and left for the dueling ground.

Santuzza entered. As mother and betrayed sweetheart waited in trembling premonition, there was a cry from the wings: "They have murdered Turiddu!" Swooning, Santuzza fell to the stage. The curtain dropped.

Ames was on his feet, applauding and shouting. *"Brava!"*

"Jean Stern wants us to come to a housewarming." Fran handed him a square of Tiffany vellum, engraved, with blanks inked in in Jean Stern's best Farmington penmanship. *You are invited to* and then, in red with exclamation points, A BASH!!

"Let's go," he said.

Fran was watching him with amazement. "You said you couldn't stand her or her jet-setting friends."

"So? Let's go anyway."

Years later, he would still be wondering why he made that decision.

Jean Stern greeted them at the door of her new apartment in the Dakota. "Angels, you actually made it!" Her hair was in pigtails and she was wearing a jade-green gown with black peacocks. She sounded happy and high and she looked very happy and very, very high. "Loved your reviews, Ames. Did you write them yourself?"

"Bitch," he said sweetly, kissing her on the cheek.

She took Ames and Fran in hand and made introductions. Most of the guests were rich or extraordinarily famous—or *New Yorker* Profile writers who had helped them get that way. The heiress of a perfume fortune, dripping pearls and cigarette ashes, told Ames, "You know, I've always wanted to write. I have a wonderful story, but I need a collaborator."

What the hell am I doing here? he wondered.

"You wanted to come," Fran said. "Don't blame me."

"I'm not complaining, am I?"

"But you're not mixing either. You're a celebrity this month. Jean expects her celebrities to mingle. And that way I get to talk to all those old classmates of mine who bore you silly."

"Okay, I can take a hint. Go talk."

He explored. Joints were being passed in the library. Cocaine was being snorted in the bath of the master bedroom. From the sound of it, three or more people were having sex in the guest-room john. He didn't see a thing or person at the party that wouldn't be improved by being dropped out of a speeding fire truck.

By nine o'clock he was sitting morosely on a sofa, busily not listening to the perfume heiress and her idea for a novel, staring across the flowered Oriental carpet into the far corner of the living room. Through a shifting sea of tailored jackets and shoulders with off-season tans, he saw a small pillared archway.

Suddenly he sat forward. Standing in the archway was a little girl with long black hair and huge dark eyes.

He could see her with almost hallucinatory clarity, as though he were looking through the wrong end of a pair of binoculars. She was as familiar to him as if he had dreamt of her every night of his life. She couldn't have been more than six. She wore long white socks and a frilled white skirt that spoke of another time. Her smile reached to him like an outstretched hand.

He had the feeling he had had at Kavalaris's funeral, the sensation of a handbrake coming loose, something inside him racing beyond his control. He heard himself say, "Excuse me." And then he was rising quickly from the sofa and pushing through the crowd.

"*There* you are." Jean Stern took his hand. "Come meet someone."

"Jean, who's that little girl?"

"Sorry, darling, no little girls at *this* party. Vanessa, this is my dear friend Ames Rutherford. Ames, Vanessa Billings."

"Hello," he said. "You make quite a Santuzza."

"In that awful black wig?" she smiled.

At the mention of the wig a jolt went through him. Vanessa Billings was a grown woman, her hair blond and her eyes gray-green, but *she was the dark-haired little girl he had just seen.*

"Moving right along, Ames," Jean was saying, "this is Nikos Stratiotis."

Stratiotis was a solidly built middle-aged man with dark waving hair just beginning to gray. He looked handsomer than his photographs, and healthier, and there was unmistakable murder in his eyes.

"You two were in the *New York Times* together," Jean chirped. "Face to face in the Weekend section." She realized she'd lost two members of her audience. "Hey, Vanessa. Hey, Ames." She waved a hand. "I'm talking to you both?"

Nikos realized almost immediately that Ames Rutherford was no stranger. An image came back to his mind: a brilliantly blue June day eleven years ago. A crowd milling after commencement in Harvard Yard. Ariana rising on tiptoe to kiss a young man and explaining later that he was no one, "Just the son of an old friend."

Now that he knew the name, a piece of an old puzzle fell into place. This was the son of the man she had loved. A Greek sense of fatality whispered in Nikos's blood. He and Ames Rutherford were bound by too much history, too much pain. This crossing of paths was no meaningless coincidence. *This curly-headed young man in the Brooks Brothers shirt and old blue jeans and new jogging shoes is my nemesis.*

He moved closer to Vanessa. "Let's go," he whispered.

She looked at him, startled. "But, Nikos, we just got here."

"Say goodbye. I'll get your coat."

She frowned at him in the elevator. "Don't you think we were a little bit rude?"

"Do you know that young man from somewhere?"

"No."

In the limousine he raised the glass partition. "You're sure you haven't met him before?"

She stared out the window at the awnings on Seventy-second Street. A secret smile hovered around her lips. "He's seen me onstage. Some people have, you know."

"He was looking at you as though you two shared some kind of . . . I don't know. Some kind of history."

She laughed. "You're very attractive when you're jealous."

"I'm not jealous." His tan darkened. "It's just that I have little enough time with you and I don't intend to share you with every ambitious little writer who pops up at a party."

She took his hand and leaned across the seat to rest her head on his shoulder. "Stay jealous. It makes me feel safe. I'm going to hire that ambitious little writer to pop up everywhere we go."

The study on the top floor of the Fifth Avenue triplex was half-firelight, half-dark. Nikos went to the desk and took a long, lined yellow legal pad. He turned on a lamp. In a tight neat hand that he had been taught by Armenian nuns he made notes, listing everything he would need to know about Ames Rutherford and a few things he was simply curious about.

Twenty minutes later Maggie appeared in the open door, peeling diamonds off her neck. "Still working?"

"Mmm-hmm." He didn't glance up. "How was the show?"

"You didn't miss a thing. Are you going to come in tonight?"

"I don't want you to catch my bug."

"Okay. Get a good night's sleep."

The next morning, in the back seat of a limousine speeding to JFK airport, Nikos handed an assistant three long sheets of lined yellow legal paper that had been covered with meticulous handwriting.

"Get me this information as quietly and as quickly as you can."

The report was waiting on his desk when he returned from Brussels. He read it slowly.

Ames Rutherford had gotten top grades at the Buckley School in Manhattan; top grades at Phillips Exeter Academy in New Hampshire; top grades at Harvard University; top grades at Harvard Law; had served in the army reserve; worked four years with a top New York law firm; published two best-selling novels; lived with the same woman eleven years; never married her (*Why not?* Nikos wondered); never cheated on her (*Why not?*); drank heavily but not, for this day and age, abnormally; had friends who took drugs but was not reputed to be a drug user himself.

Nikos stared at the neatly word-processed pages. They filled him with uneasiness. He went to the window and for a long while stood gazing forty stories down at the East River.

The following evening Nikos sat in his study listening to music. The sounds washed like soothing water into the caverns of his mind.

He heard his wife's voice and opened his eyes.

"We haven't been spending much time together." Maggie was dressed in a red Oscar de la Renta as if she were going out.

"Does that bother you?"

"It bothers me when people notice. Are you having an affair?"

"Please, Maggie. I'm trying to listen to music."

"Will you at least pay attention to me tonight?"

"Why tonight?"

"Because as you perfectly well know we're having company."

"I forgot." He sighed. "I'm sorry. And disappointed. I'd hoped to listen to *Bohème.*"

"Hans has laid your clothes out on your bed. The guests will be arriving in forty minutes."

Nikos couldn't bear the party. Maggie's guests made noises about real estate and art as though they were deciding the fate of Western civilization. Fingerbowls were passed after the Scotch salmon and the women clunked their rings down by their place settings and it was like being in a washroom.

"I had my sapphires redone," the woman on Nikos's left said. She was said to be an up-and-coming anchorperson on NBC news, and she had lectured him for twenty minutes about the situation in Salvador. "I kept the setting but changed the stones. What do you think?"

He excused himself before the dessert soufflés were served. Maggie intercepted him in the hallway. "Where are you going?" she said.

"To the opera. I can still make the last act of *Adriana Lecouvreur.*"

She stared at him for one instant of hooded fury. "I suppose Vanessa Billings is singing."

"Yes. And after three hours of your friends I very much need to hear a human voice."

"Nikos, if you walk out of this party, I warn you—"

He didn't wait for the warning. He walked out of the party.

The next morning Maggie Stratiotis stopped in at Cartier's. Her eye fell on a Venetian cross of diamonds and rubies set in gold. "What's that delicious-looking thing?"

The salesman unlocked the glass display case. "Benvenuto Cellini designed this. It belonged to the Medicis." He slipped the chain around her neck. "We've restored three of the stones."

She stared at her reflection. "Would you charge it, please, and wrap it?"

The salesman telephoned the Stratiotis office.

"What was that figure again?" Nikos said.

"One million, two hundred fifty thousand dollars, sir."

"Couldn't you ship it to New Jersey and save me the sales tax?"

"She took it from the store, sir."

Nikos sighed. "I see." He broke the connection, sat a moment, then asked his secretary to phone Richard Schiller's office. "Richard, what kind of opera could the Metropolitan put on for $1,250,000, plus eight percent?"

"One hell of an opera."

"Starring Vanessa?"

Adolf Erdlich outlined the proposal. Instead of its scheduled fall production of *Manon Lescaut,* the Metropolitan would borrow the San Francisco production, with sets by Chagall; there would be seven stage rehearsals with augmented orchestra; and all costs would be underwritten by Mr. Stratiotis's foundation.

"For which generosity we are, needless to say, deeply indebted."

Adolf Erdlich crossed to his desk and took four fine cigars from the humidor. He handed one to Meyer Colby and one to Richard Schiller; one to Boyd Kinsolving and one to Nikos Stratiotis. "Clara, do I dare offer you one?"

Not bothering to smile, Clara Rodrigo shook her head sharply. Adolf Erdlich lit his own cigar, sat down again, and continued. Clara Rodrigo listened, a tiny mountain of diamonds and silence, and when Adolf Erdlich had finished she drew herself up.

"My answer, as you knew it would be, is no. And, Boyd, I am shocked you are a party to this."

Adolf Erdlich placed an arm around Clara. "Why must we argue? Can't we be a family, just this once? Don't we all want what's best for the Metropolitan?"

"It is my impression that Mr. Stratiotis wants what's best for his friend."

"Which in this case is what's best for all of us."

Clara turned slowly to look at each of the five men who had betrayed her. "I have a contract to sing that production. Whether the sets come from San Francisco or the moon, whether they are paid for by Mr. Stratiotis or the Abominable Snowman, that production is *mine.*"

"Clara," Meyer Colby said, "cooperate just this once. Please."

Adolf Erdlich spoke softly, with concern. "Clara, we all pray God it's only a temporary condition, but you do not at the moment have a voice. You've had to cancel your last three performances."

"Is a sore throat such a crime? Anyone can get a sore throat!"

"And anyone who expects to be paid $70,000 a performance can get *over* a sore throat."

"By the time the production's ready, I'll be well."

"No, Clara. You've canceled three times."

La Rodrigo rose to her feet, trembling. "Meyer, are you my agent or are you working for these men?"

"There's nothing I can do, Clara."

"Then I'll sue all of you."

Adolf Erdlich shrugged and turned his dark weary gaze on the woman who had once been his *prima donna assoluta*. "Sue all you want, Clara. But Vanessa Billings sings this production."

The *Manon Lescaut* dress rehearsal that fall went perfectly until the fourth act, when Manon lay dying on what Puccini called "the plains of Louisiana." Boyd rapped his baton on the music stand, silencing the orchestra. "Vanessa, the tempo changes at '*sei tu*'—the value of the quarter note is 72, not 69. Otherwise you're dragging."

She moved toward the apron of the stage. "It feels wrong to speed up there."

"Sorry, sweetums. If you want to see my score—"

Boyd looked down at his conductor's score, the score from which he had conducted all of Ariana's *Manon Lescaut*s. In a red marker, in Ariana's handwriting, overriding Puccini's tempo indication, he saw an X slashed through the 72 and the emphatically gashed command: *Quarter equals 69 sempre!! Boyd, this is my moment and don't you dare screw me up!*

Vanessa's eyes met Boyd's across the footlights and for one heart-stopping instant, seeing her in the powdered wig and torn gray deportee's uniform, he thought she was his dead wife.

He cleared his throat. "Well, sweetums, we could try 69. Orchestra, make a note." He raised his baton again. "All set, harp? Take it from where the meter changes to 2/4. Give it guts, gentlemen."

At 8:26 P.M. on the evening of October 23 on the stage of the New York Metropolitan Opera, Vanessa Billings, glittering in the traveling clothes of an eighteenth-century schoolgirl, stepped from the carriage that was to carry her to the convent.

The audience stirred like a wind-brushed forest.

From the moment she opened her mouth, they were hers. She knit the arias and recitatives of her role into a character, a fierce amalgam of innocence and willfulness that came hurtling across the footlights like a demonic angel. Her slightest movement, her softest utterance was

351

charged with seduction, as though all the world's sexual longing had, for that evening, incarnated in her flesh and voice.

Like the four thousand other men and women in the house, Ames Rutherford in his third row seat in the grand tier sat spellbound, fascinated, amazed at how fresh and new the performance made Puccini seem. Each note Billings sang was like a faceted jewel sending out brilliant shafts of melody.

Fran rested against him, her hand touching his for most of the first act. But as Des Grieux proposed to Manon, *"Fuggiamo, fuggiamo"*— "Let's flee, let's flee"—Ames drew away.

Something is about to happen. Watch out.

The feeling of foreboding came out of nowhere. There was no reason for it. He didn't know the opera, didn't know the performers, he certainly didn't know the future; yet he was suddenly certain that everything happening now had happened before—the music, the movement, the bustle and the light on the stage, the rapt silence and the soft floating perfumes in the audience.

An almost claustrophobic panic rose in him and he had no walls to contain it. It was as though he were on the very edge of knowing something he couldn't bear to know.

He rose, pushed his way past knees and purses, felt Fran reaching out after him, found the aisle and the steps leading up through the darkness to the light-etched outline of the exit door.

He went to the grand tier bar, the only customer. His heart was pounding in his throat. The stillness was dense with muffled Puccini. He took a hard swallow of Stolichnaya on the rocks. Instead of calming him, it hit him like a triphammer, ramming his pulse up through his skull.

The bartender was making a wise face. "They say Billings is going to be the next Kavalaris. Do you agree, sir?"

"Highly probable. Could you pour me another of these, please?"

Fran came hurrying across the red carpeting. "Ames, what happened to you? Are you all right?" She stood looking at him. Something had changed in his eyes. They were like the hollows in Greek statues, with no one behind them.

"Just a moment of claustrophobia," he said. "It's pretty stuffy in there."

At that moment applause broke out in the house. Jeweled dowagers and tuxedoed escorts began streaming toward the bar.

"Would you like to go home?" Fran asked.

Ames downed his second vodka. "Hell no. I'm fine now."

He had another vodka in the next intermission, another in the third. Fran, watching him with anxious eyes, drank soda with lime.

At 11:20, as the curtain fell on the final act, Ames and Fran hurried out to Broadway to beat the crowd to a taxi, and Billings was called back for twelve curtain calls.

The frantic dresser hurried Dr. Abscheid into the dressing room.

Vanessa was lying full-length on the settee, her face buried in the pillow. The doctor rolled her over. Her skin was deathly white. He loosened the bodice of her costume, felt for the pulse in her neck.

At first he thought she had lapsed into coma but then as her breathing deepened he realized she had simply fallen asleep after an exhausting performance.

She stretched and turned over onto her side. Her eyes opened. There was an instant of dazzling gray-green incomprehension.

"Was I dreaming?" She sat up.

Dr. Abscheid coiled the tube of his stethoscope. "I don't know. Were you?"

"That was no dream." Richard Schiller handed her a bouquet of three dozen white roses. "You brought down the house."

"I was really all right?"

Richard smiled at the others. "You hear the little girl?"

Nikos took her home in his limousine.

"Thank you for the roses," she said. "They were beautiful. And thank you for this evening."

"Thank *you* for this evening. It gave me such joy." He settled his arm across the top of the seat, spanning the space between them but not touching her. "You know, it's strange. I used to hate opera. And now I never seem to think of anything else."

A faint breath of rose scent came up from the air-conditioning duct. She could feel him wanting to draw her closer. After a moment she rested her head against his shoulder.

"Nikos," she said quietly, "what was Ariana like?"

He sighed. "I'm sure you knew her better than I ever managed to."

"No. To me she was a teacher—always distant, always unreal. To you she was flesh and blood."

His gaze came around gravely to her face. "Why do you ask?"

"Isn't it natural for a woman to be curious about her predecessor?"

He was silent, looking out the limousine window through glass so polished it seemed not to be there at all. The glistening high-rises of Central Park West sparkled in the night.

"I was twenty-five." His voice was soft with remembering. "I walked into a coffee shop on Broadway. There she was. Dark hair, dark eyes that looked at me like a wounded little girl's. She wasn't a star then. But she had spirit . . . intelligence . . . independence . . . ."

"And beauty?"

He nodded. "Beauty. Oh, yes, she had beauty. And twenty-one years later, when we finally made love . . . she was more beautiful still."

He spoke about their meetings, their courtship, their living together. He spoke of the happiness that had turned to unhappiness and of the gradual coming-apart.

"Why did it go sour?" Vanessa asked. "Because of Maggie?"

"No." He shook his head. "Because of me. I was never able to . . ." He fell silent.

"Able to what, Nikos?"

He was staring at his hands, squeezed together in his lap. His voice was tight. "To admit how much I loved her. I've never been able to admit how much I loved anyone . . . until it was too late. I'm good at everything else but that."

She raised her head and touched her lips to the side of his neck. "There are other ways of saying it than words."

He turned and held her in his gaze. "I wish tonight could last. The performance. The applause. The way you sounded. The way you look. Riding home, like this, with you. If only it could last."

"It will last, Nikos. We can make it last."

38

"YOU'RE MAKING TOO MUCH SCANDAL," HOLLY CHAMBERS SAID IN April. He was sitting with Nikos in the New York office, drinking espresso and reviewing strategy on next week's stock offering.

"I can afford scandal," Nikos said quietly.

"We've persuaded a very conservative brokerage house to underwrite us. They don't appreciate their client showing up in tabloids between the disco gossip and the cocaine busts."

"It's a changed world, Holly. Fame is an asset nowadays. Any kind of fame. A mass murderer could franchise hamburgers. A dictator's mistress could put her name on a line of blue jeans. And a hundred banks would be waiting in line to back them."

Holly shook his head dubiously. "I still wish you'd slow down a little with the singer."

Nikos paced to the window and turned. "She's an oasis for me. She gets my mind off work. She gets my mind off all the nonsense, all the parties and cruises and people I can't stand. Most of all she gets my mind off my ridiculous marriage. I'm crazy without her and with her I'm sane. I don't understand it and I don't want to understand it. All I know is, I need her."

The phone rang. Nikos snatched up the receiver, listened an instant, shot off commands. "She'll be singing at the Paris Opéra Wednesday. It's a late curtain. Have the limousine waiting at the stage door. And make sure the plane's waiting at the airport."

Nikos hung up and his counsel's blue eyes pierced him. "And you'll be waiting on your yacht in Cannes, I suppose?"

Nikos didn't deny it.

Holly smiled a cynical, accepting smile. "Face it. You've never had sense where women are concerned, you never will."

"What's the point to women if I have to have sense? I have sense in business. I've earned a little madness."

"And if the principessa's on that yacht, a little madness is exactly what you're going to get."

Nikos had done all the inviting himself. He had persuaded the Marquis and Marchioness of Ava to come on board for three days. Sir Herbert Parry, who painted the royal family and did society portraits, was staying at the Angleterre in Nice and Nikos had gotten him to join the party for Thursday and Friday and bring Lady Parry, Britain's first woman Chancellor of the Exchequer. He felt reasonably sure that with a British cabinet minister on board Maggie would behave herself and not slip into one of her famous public pouts.

Vanessa arrived by seaplane from the airport Thursday night. She seemed to shine in her plain white dress, and even at night her wide-brimmed red straw hat threw a warm glow on her face.

Nikos made introductions.

Maggie hid her shock well. "You could have warned me," she hissed later, as they were going to their stateroom.

"And spoil the surprise?"

"Don't you dare humiliate me, Nikos. Not in front of these people."

He made no attempt to seek Vanessa out. But the next day he saw her on the deck just after sunset. She was standing at the railing some distance from the others, staring out at the sea, her face sweet and serious. He joined her.

The sky was hushed and the lights and sounds of Nice seemed to come across an enormous gulf of space and time.

"I'd like to stand here beside you forever," he said.

She smiled. "You'd get bored with that."

"I'd never be bored with you."

He ached to press her close to him and cover her face and throat with kisses. But he sensed that was not the way.

"Oh, Nikos, I'm so insignificant compared to your friends. They run empires and I . . . warble."

"You're more significant than any of them, and you know it."

She squeezed his hand for just a moment, gratefully. "Why are you so good for my ego?"

"Why are you so good for mine?"

After dinner Maggie rose and clapped her hands for silence. "Vanessa, could I possibly persuade you to sing a few songs in the ship's lounge? I'm sure our guests would love it as much as I would."

The guests applauded, and Vanessa felt a burn of anger creeping up her neck and face. She was tempted to say she never sang except on-stage; but she realized that this was exactly the reply her hostess hoped to force out of her.

Vanessa gathered all her graciousness into a smile. "I'd be delighted to sing."

Instinct told Nikos not to applaud too loudly, not to court Vanessa Billings too openly. He excused himself and went to his stateroom after her third selection.

Through the open porthole he heard a soprano voice floating effortlessly through "Regnava nel Silenzio," from Donizetti's *Lucia di Lammermoor.* The sound came to him above the waves, like a memory. His book fell to his lap and he dozed off smiling.

Maggie came into the stateroom a little after two in the morning. She was stripping off jewels, talking irritably as Nikos woke up. "I don't care for the way your Miss Billings carries on. She treated our guests as if they were a backers' audition."

"How so?"

"Monopolizing things, singing all those dull songs."

"Be fair, Maggie. It was you who asked her to sing."

"But not all those *arias*."

"What did you expect? 'Melancholy Baby'?"

"At least that would have been *short*. I thought she'd never shut up. Did you invite her to annoy me? Are you having an affair with her?"

"Do you see me in her bed?"

"Not yet."

Nikos opened a book. "Then why don't you just relax about Vanessa and enjoy her?"

"Why on earth should I enjoy that woman?"

"A lot of hostesses would kill to have her for five days."

"You invited her for *five days*?"

Nikos nodded and turned a page of his book.

Maggie thumped a gold bracelet down onto the bureau. "Then I'm getting off this ship and you can entertain La Billings and all your old bores yourself."

The *Maria-Kristina* docked at Corfu three days later. Principessa Maggie disembarked, carrying her overnight case, and dropped into the back seat of the only taxi at the dock.

Rage beat in her heart. "Take me into town."

The taxi honked its way through twisting cobbled streets. Maggie gazed at perfume shops, liquor shops, souvenir shops. She gazed at an art shop with a window full of local-looking paintings and sculptures and handicrafts.

She realized she was staring at the solution.

"Driver—stop here, please."

The air over New York City's Jamaica Bay had turned misty and smoggy as Air France Flight 546 from Paris touched safely down. The terminal swarmed with travelers. Press and TV reporters added to the congestion, clustering like bees in the exit corridor.

A figure in black mink raised a hand to her face as she passed through customs, placing dark glasses over her eyes. Too late. A woman from *Newsweek* recognized her, and then CBS and the *Washington Post* took up the shout: "Miss Billings!"

They rushed with her in a wave, leaving no lane of clearance.

"Are you having an affair with Nikos Stratiotis?"

She removed the glasses and faced them. "I'll tell you if you tell me who wrote *La Traviata*."

"Richard Wagner."

"There will be no June wedding."

Ames had been sitting at his typewriter for three hours and nothing had flowed but crumpled sheets into the wastebasket. He snapped the power switch off and went to get a beer.

Fran was in bed with a book and she called out as he passed the open door. "Coming to bed soon?"

"Depends if I get lucky at the typewriter."

He pulled a beer from the fridge and went to the study and dropped down in front of the TV. He played with the remote control, channel-hopping to see what they had on this late at night.

He was slumped in the Barcalounger, peering at commercials and late movies, when a woman's mocking voice drew him up with a start. "There will be no June wedding."

As he stared at Vanessa Billings's face her lips parted in a luminous smile. He realized he had been daydreaming about that smile, following it in his half-conscious thoughts for days now. He leapt up from the chair, pressed the "record" button on the VCR, was able to get just a snippet of her before a commercial cut her short.

He ran the tape back, stopped the frame on her, stared. He sat half an hour gazing at her face.

"This is crazy."

He gulped the last of the now-warm beer and went and took a long hot stinging shower. When he came into the bedroom the light was out and he could hear Fran's breathing, regular and untroubled in sleep.

He got another beer, dropped down again in front of the TV, lit a cigarette and began staring again at the face.

"I'm sorry to trouble you, Mr. Stratiotis, but the shipping agent won't release the statues unless he's paid cash."

Nikos glanced up from his desk. "What statues?"

"The Cupids Mrs. Stratiotis ordered in Corfu." His secretary handed him the duplicate invoice.

His eyes quickly scanned the column of figures—$132,000 to ship stones first-class letter rate. He felt the unreality of it and a dull fatigue cut into him. "From now on, Mrs. Stratiotis's expenses are her own affair—not mine, not this company's. And Miss Owens—I mean *all* her expenses. Please see to it."

In absolute rigidity Principessa Maggie listened as the shipping agent explained why the Cupids could not be sent by limousine to the apartment. She pressed another button on the phone.

"Tell the chauffeur I need him to take me shopping."

✿ ✿ ✿

Maggie was looking at rings when a cabochon sapphire engraved with a tiny figure caught her eye.

The salesman showed it to her under a magnifying glass. "Diana, goddess of the hunt."

Maggie pulled off two rings, making room, and slipped Diana onto her finger. "It's loose."

"We can tighten the band."

She sighed. "How long will that take?"

"Would tomorrow noon be convenient?"

"No, I need it for a party tonight." She handed back the ring and stalked around the display counters like a starved lioness. And then she saw a display case full of necklaces. "How very pretty," she said. "How very, very pretty."

"If Madame is considering sapphires, we have a lovely—"

She cut the salesman short, pointing to a gold necklace of eight emerald-cut solitaire diamonds. She tried it on. "How much?"

The salesman coughed softly into his fist. "One million, one hundred twenty-five thousand."

She walked to a mirror by the window and studied herself. No doubt about it, her chinline was getting a little soft. Damn, that meant another trip to Brazil.

"I'll take it. Can you put it in a box for me?"

"Certainly. And how does Madame prefer to pay?"

"Charge, as usual."

The salesman's teeth came down against his lower lip for one instant of hesitation. "Just one moment, please."

She pretended to be studying brooches but in the mirror she was watching the salesman confer with the manager. She sensed a hush come over the two men. Finally the manager approached.

"Madame wishes to charge the necklace?"

"As I charge all my purchases."

The manager's face took on a grave expression. "Then Madame is unaware that Mr. Stratiotis has issued instructions?"

"What sort of instructions?"

"His office has ordered Madame's charge account closed. Of course, if Madame would care to pay by check—"

A wave of rage and incredulity swept her. She felt the catch pop as she ripped the necklace off and flung it onto the display case.

"Thank you very kindly, but Madame does *not* care to."

The party that night was one of Carlotta Busch's typical mixes of old guard America and new New York. Saltonstalls and Randolfs and Pinkneys rubbed shoulders with the new TV anchorwoman from CBS, fashion designers, Broadway composers. Maggie sensed sudden silences when she joined groups, eyes following her that averted themselves when she returned a glance. She suspected that word had already gotten around, but she didn't know for sure until after dinner.

She was in one of the bathrooms on the second story. Through double doors, in the neighboring bathroom, she heard laughter.

And then a woman's voice. "Mimsy Hoyt and Happy Blumenthal were there when the manager told her. She made a disgusting scene."

And another woman. "Couldn't happen to a sweeter princess."

Maggie returned quickly to the party, wanting to burst into tears and commit murder at the same time. She felt she had been walked over with cleats and after three minutes chatting with the man who Rolfed all the stars in Hollywood she had to excuse herself and go outdoors. She walked with conscious, straightbacked grace, wondering how early she dared go home.

The lights of Queens were not commanding, but the view of them from Carlotta's terrace was. A puff of wind blew the light material of Maggie's dress against her, outlining for an instant firm breasts and a waist not quite as small as she would have wished. A tugboat hooted on the river.

A voice behind her said, "Do you mind, ma'am?"

She turned and found herself facing a tall man, six foot two or so, with a long face and close-set penetrating green eyes. She'd seen him somewhere, couldn't remember where.

He took a cigar from his inner breast pocket, extracted it from its cylindrical case, waited for her permission.

"Go right ahead," she said. "Smoke never bothers me."

"The name's Johnny Day Hill."

Now Maggie remembered. The trial lawyer. He'd just gotten an heiress acquitted of a murder charge in Baton Rouge. Typical of Carlotta to have snagged him for dinner the day of the verdict.

"I'm Maggie Stratiotis."

"Heard lots about you." He placed the cigar in the corner of his mouth, took a moment coaxing it to light. "You've got a case. Closing your charge accounts. That's nonsupport."

She stiffened. It was too much. Even perfect strangers knew.

"Refusing to pay shipping on your purchases and then letting the press know. That's defamation." He spoke with a husky voice and an easy smile. "I advise you to bring suit, young lady."

She let the mask of noncomprehension fall. "How much could I get?"

"A sizable allowance based on reasonable expenses."

"What's reasonable?"

"How much has he ever let you spend in a month? Double it."

"That might be $150,000."

"We'll try for a quarter-million. I get a third."

At 2:30 P.M. on May 3, in judge's chambers in fourth district civil court in Manhattan, attorney Johnny Day Hill asked the court to grant his client Maggie Stratiotis $250,000 a month in temporary living expenses.

Attorney Holly Chambers, representing Nikos Stratiotis, asked his honor if the court might have a breakdown of those expenses.

Johnny Day Hill crossed his Texas boots and consulted the jottings in his memorandum pad. "Mrs. Stratiotis requires $27,000 a month to maintain her Manhattan co-op; $1,400 a month for club memberships; $1,200 for American Express; $1,200 for Diners Club. And $3,600 for travel and lodging; $12,000 for entertaining; $8,000 for staff; $5,000 for contributions to charity; $25,000 for clothing."

"A month?" his honor asked, eyebrows flexing.

"A month, Your Honor. And $37,000 for jewelry and furs."

Holly Chambers punched buttons on a pocket calculator. "That leaves $128,600 a month unaccounted for."

Johnny Day Hill smiled. "My client has a great many incidentals."

Holly Chambers returned the smile. "*My* client would like to have those incidentals spelled out."

Johnny Day Hill tucked his thumbs into his pearl-studded belt. "Your Honor, Mrs. Stratiotis is a public figure. Incidentals for public figures are astronomic. If the court wishes, my client can provide an audited accounting—"

The judge waved Mr. Hill silent. "This matter is not in court. We're conducting an informal hearing."

"Give her twice what she's asking," Nikos Stratiotis said.

Both attorneys' heads shot around. Even Maggie Stratiotis, glowing in her blue picture hat, glanced across the room at her husband, a wrinkle of perplexity marring her flawlessly smooth brow.

"Your Honor," Holly Chambers said, "may I confer with my client?" Holly took Nikos to the window with its seventeenth-story view of rain sluicing down on the traffic-jammed Brooklyn Bridge. "What the hell are you doing? I can get her down to $50,000."

"I don't want to haggle, Holly. I've got to be free of her. I don't care what it costs."

"I do care what it costs and that's why you pay me."

"You're not hearing me, Holly."

Nikos explained exactly what he had in mind and, shaking his head, Holly Chambers returned to the bench.

"Your Honor, my client attaches one condition to his offer. Mrs. Stratiotis must agree to an immediate, uncontested, no-fault divorce. She must agree here and now, in these chambers. Otherwise tomorrow morning my client will sue for divorce on grounds of adultery. He is prepared to introduce into open court evidence collected by the investigative firm of Meyers and O'Reilly."

Maggie's picture hat lifted itself a degree. She asked his honor if she might confer with her attorney.

A moment later Johnny Day Hill cleared his throat. "Your Honor, my client is willing to accept divorce plus $750,000 a month."

"Your Honor!" Holly Chambers cried.

"Holly," Nikos said, "shut up. Tell Mr. Hill his client has a deal."

The refrigerator was jammed with Fran's neatness: Tupperware containers of leftovers, bottles of whole milk and all-natural no-additive juice, wheels and wedges and rectangles of cheeses, Baggies of fruit and bowls of Cuisine-Arted veg.

Ames decided on a trapezoid of chèvre and a bowl of julienned carrots, and, why not, a beer; and took the armload back to his workroom.

He sat a long while, the curtains open to the darkening May afternoon, not eating, not writing, not really thinking, just sipping beer and massaging his knuckles and wondering how the hell he'd gotten a callus on his right palm.

A car honked in the drive. There were voices at the front door, and then Greg Hatoff was striding past Fran into the workroom, hand out, a big grin on his face.

"Hiya, Amesie. I just happened to be in the neighborhood, and . . ."

A lie. No New York magazine editor just happened to be in the Hamptons on a drizzly May weekday.

Greg glanced toward the sheet of paper in the typewriter carriage. "*Scarlet Letter* or *Gone With the Wind?*"

Ames forced a smile. "A little too early to say."

Greg settled himself into the armchair. "How'd you like to slay a few giants for the magazine?"

"I'd love to. But I'm on a book."

Undaunted, Greg tapped his fingers together. "Here's the situation. Nikos Stratiotis, your favorite capitalist and mine, is ditching his wife, Maggie. Rumor hath it it's the highest out-of-court settlement since Napoleon sacked Josephine. The selling point of this story is that anything this cheap could happen to such expensive people. And you're the man to put it in words. Twenty-five thousand."

"Words?"

"Dollars, dummy."

"Talk to my agent."

"You're not hearing me out. There's a quality edge. The same rumor hath it that Nikos is going to marry your favorite coloratura and mine, Vanessa affectionately known as *La* Billings."

At that instant everything in the room, in the world, changed. It was as though Ames were suddenly alive, a warm body pressing against him, connections coming through his skin.

"All you have to do," Greg said, "is interview her. We'll set it up."

It amazed Ames how many rationalizations were already there, waiting. The assignment would be a release from the commonplaces of his existence. It would help him through his block. It would be a glimpse of a world he'd never otherwise know.

But there was a deeper reason, a shape in his mind so dim and inexplicable he could barely articulate it even to himself. *Stratiotis isn't going to marry her. I'm going to.*

He heard himself answer, in a voice not quite his own, "I'll do it."

39

WEDNESDAY EVENING AMES RUTHERFORD WATCHED TWO ACTS of Puccini's *Manon Lescaut* from a seat in the Metropolitan grand tier. This time he suffered no premonitions, no claustrophobia. In a simpleminded way he even enjoyed the opera—more for its sumptuously spun-out melody than for its moral, which seemed to be that passion never pays.

At 9:55 he threaded his way backstage through a mob of cheering Manhattan nabobs, gave his name to a guard, and was ushered into Vanessa Billings's dressing room to wait for his quarry.

After three minutes the most famous American soprano in the world walked in and glanced at him. "Hello," she said. "Haven't we met?"

The earth didn't shake, there was no bolt of lightning. Yet that one glance told him his whole life had just changed direction.

"We met at Jean Stern's," he said.

She was wearing a powdered wig and a hooped, low-bosomed dress of satin the color of sun on snow. She had a beauty mark on her cheek.

Why do I feel like an eight-year-old with a crush? he wondered.

She lifted her wig. With a smile and a thank-you she handed it to a young man who went to work combing it and readjusting curls. "We can take our time," she told Ames. "I wear the same costume to jail in Act Three. Would you like something to drink?"

He felt excited and anxious out of all proportion to anything that was happening. He didn't need to pour fuel on top of that. "Thanks, I'm not drinking."

"I didn't mean a drink drink. But I've got some apple juice."

"Apple juice sounds great."

She poured two glasses from a pitcher on the dresser top and handed him one. "It's room temperature. Pretty icky, but singers have to be careful what they drink between acts. A burp onstage could be disastrous."

"May I quote you?"

She laughed, and instantly there was warmth in the room. Stranger still, there was warmth in a space inside him where he had never felt warmth before, where he had never even known there was a space.

"What sort of people do you usually interview?" she asked brightly. "Do they walk right up to the guillotine and lie down?"

"Some do. It's up to them."

Her wide mouth curved wryly. "Thanks for the warning. You're not going to ask embarrassing questions, are you?"

"That depends what sort of things embarrass you."

"That depends what sort of things you want to know."

"What do you want to tell me?"

"There's not much to tell. I'm just an amateur from Hempstead, Long Island, who turned pro." The remark sounded like outrageously phony modesty until she burst out laughing. "I'm sorry, that was too dumb, wasn't it? I'm trying to be interview material and I haven't the faintest idea what that is."

He tried to analyze the attraction he felt for her. It wasn't just the beauty, the suggestion of intelligence, the slightly aloof informality. It was something far less tangible. He wasn't looking at a simple middle-class girl from Hempstead or a French coquette or one of the world's greatest artists. He was seeing someone else, someone she was creating especially for this moment. For him.

"May I ask a corny question?" he said.

"Why not? After all, we're in an opera house."

"Are you one of the greats?"

"Ask them, not me." She pointed to the walls, where she had hung up pictures of divas of the past and present. "As far as I'm concerned, all I am is one tiny link in a long, long chain."

"But you broke into the chain. A lot of people don't. What made the difference? Or was it a who that made it happen?"

"You mean, was it my mother, or my teacher, or some secret backer . . . ?"

Their eyes met.

"Please," she said, "let's not discuss *those* rumors."

"Was it Kavalaris?" he asked.

"Ariana played a very great role in my life. She taught me."

"Some people say she formed you in her image."

"Some people are fools. I don't even come within envying distance of her. But I'm trying my damnedest."

From then on it went smoothly. He sat there trying not to gaze too openly at her, asking questions, pulling answers out of her. In a quarter-hour he had enough for a decent five-page article: the hopes, the breaks, the disappointments, all the colorful superficial stuff. And then there was a knock on the door and a voice called, "Ten minutes, Miss Billings."

She rose from her chair and went to the wig stand. "Funny. I was dreading this, but you turned out to be nothing like what I expected. In fact I had a good time."

"Thanks . . . I enjoyed it too."

He was at the door, one hand reaching for the knob, when she said, "I'm on TV a week from Friday—Channel Thirteen. Doesn't that impress the hell out of you?"

He smiled. "I'll watch."

"Look, I didn't give you much. I'm not very good at talking. But if you'd like to—I don't know—follow me around one day and see how a prima donna buys chuck in the supermarket . . ."

"I'd like to," he said. He knew he'd like to very much.

"I don't know my schedule right now. I'll phone you as soon as I have a day free."

He gave her his number.

The night Vanessa Billings was on television, it turned out, Fran had invited Ellen Stern and friend for dinner. Ames pushed lobster around his plate and tried to be fascinated by Ellen and her blond beau, a drawling stockbroker by the name of Chasen Montgrade.

"Art is the creation of its outlaws," Chasen said.

Ames bit back a reply, excused himself and went into the library. Five minutes later Fran came after him and found him in front of the television set.

"Ames Rutherford, what's the matter with you? We've got guests. If you're watching something important, tape it and look at it later."

The rest of the evening felt like a slow trudge through snow. Ellen and Chasen didn't leave till 1:30. Fran followed Ames into the library, talking about Ellen and the old days at Vassar.

He rewound the Betamax tape and pushed the play button. The black-and-white image of a woman's face composed itself on the screen. It wasn't Vanessa's face. He realized they were filling in background on her teacher. He pushed the fast-forward button.

Fran yawned. "I'm going to bed."

"I'll come in a little while," he said.

But it wasn't a little while. He sat playing and replaying Vanessa's interview till four in the morning.

He spent Saturday waiting for Vanessa's call. She didn't phone. He tried to work. The pieces of the article wouldn't come together and he couldn't concentrate for more than a half-hour at a time.

She didn't phone Sunday.

He played and replayed her tape. He watched her tell the interviewer why she had chosen opera. "I believed in the feeling of wonder and the sense of romance I'd known as a kid. I wanted the world to be that way. And in opera, it is."

She didn't phone Monday, and he began to be frightened at the importance she had in his life.

"Is something wrong?" Fran had a mystified, concerned look.

His mind came back from the other end of the solar system. "I can't seem to get a handle on that damned article."

"Don't think too hard."

He kissed her guiltily and hoped the guilt didn't show. Then he shut himself in his workroom with the phone and a notepad. He got nothing written, and there was no call.

That night he drank.

The next morning Fran brought him a cup of coffee in bed. She was silent, watching him with the patient eyes of a woman waiting for someone who was never going to be there.

"There's a message on the phone for you," she said.

He tried to show no excitement, tried to take a very long time getting to the answering machine and pressing the playback button.

"I'm calling for Vanessa Billings. Could Ames Rutherford meet her at noon today at 89 Perry Street, apartment 2A?"

It was a woman's voice, but it wasn't Vanessa's. It was dark and urgent, unfamiliar in an oddly familiar way. He played the message again and wrote down the address.

Fran was standing there in her pink jogging shorts, watching him. "You have a lunch date with your agent," she reminded him.

"Damn it. Forgot about that." He phoned Horatio Charles and asked if they could move lunch back an hour.

He shaved and showered and threw appropriate notebooks and his cassette player into his briefcase. Fran bade him an oddly subdued goodbye.

The house at 89 Perry Street was a four-story stucco walkup, painted pink and covered in ancient wisteria vines. There was no answer when Ames buzzed apartment 2A, so he buzzed the super.

The slight humpbacked woman who unlatched the wrought-iron gate must have been in her eighties, but she had thick white hair and lively eyes that observed him closely.

"Miss Billings asked me to meet her in apartment 2A."

Limping slowly, the old woman led him through a narrow passageway. They crossed a noon-bright courtyard. Birds were chirping with energy that was almost crazy. There were trees of paradise and beds of blue and pink petunias and a splashing marble fountain with an ivy-covered Pan tilting nonchalantly far from the vertical.

She took him up a flight of stairs and stopped at a wooden door with the Gothic brass A.

He experienced a dreamlike certainty that he had walked through this courtyard, up these stairs, to this very door before.

The old woman gave the door a push, and as it swung inward the un-oiled hinges sang two notes. He could have sworn he remembered those notes from a long time ago: the first two notes of "Amazing Grace."

The apartment was dusty and dim and furnished like a motel room. Bafflement swept him. "She's not here?"

"You're the first," the old woman said. "Take your time. I'll be downstairs if you want the place."

With a shuffling step she was gone, and it came to Ames that he was standing in a furnished apartment for rent.

Why did Vanessa ask me to meet her here?

He walked to the next room. There was a wooden-frame bed with a cotton spread printed in imitation of a quilt. The closet door was open. He had a surprisingly definite feeling there should have been a piano, a carved upright, against the wall by the window.

He sat on the bed. The quarter-hour chimed from a nearby church, and in a while another quarter-hour chimed. He heard the gate in the courtyard swing open and a dog barked and he thought, *It's her.* But he ran to the window and it was a fat woman in pink curlers.

The church chimes rang again, and he knew she wasn't going to come. He went down the staircase and gave the old woman his best smile. "If my friend comes, will you tell her she can catch me at Gino's restaurant down on Bleecker?"

The meal was very quiet except for the sound of knives and forks scraping plates. Horatio Charles had on a perfectly tailored, very light gray suit, and he talked in his very soft Princeton voice about a French deal on the novel.

Ames kept looking at the door, but Vanessa Billings didn't walk in, breathless with apology and explanation. His heart felt like a burning stone in his chest.

He drank deeply from his glass of beer. Talk drifted along, but in his mind he kept seeing the apartment on Perry Street, and the wall where a piano should have been, and the gate that she should have walked through at noon.

Horatio Charles paid for the meal. "Shall I send the papers out to East Hampton or do you want to stop by and sign?"

"Send them out," Ames said, and he hadn't the slightest idea what he'd agreed to.

He tried calling Vanessa from a phone booth. He reached her answering machine, and he was too hurt to speak to it and admit he was hurt. He drove home much too fast and replayed the day's messages. There were the usual hangups and wrong numbers, one partial erasure that made him wonder if something was wrong with the machine, and a man saying, "Please call Timothy."

That was it. One Timothy, whoever *he* was, and no Vanessa.

When Fran got home from tennis Ames asked if she'd erased any of his messages. She looked at him and in that one moment of explosive silence he realized, *She knows. She knows the thing that never happened between us has happened between me and someone else.*

"I don't erase other people's messages," she said.

That was all there was to it: a question, an answer, and they both knew they had crossed to the downhill side.

Just before noon, he heard the front door slam as Fran went out. He phoned Vanessa again and again her machine answered. This time he left a message. "It's Ames Rutherford. Please phone me."

From that moment on his office was no longer the room where he worked: it was the room where she didn't phone.

After two hours he called her agent. Richard Schiller said it was a very difficult period for Miss Billings. She had commitments in Europe and South America as well as a Kundry this June in Bayreuth, and quite frankly interviews were not a first priority; in fact, she didn't give them.

"She gave me one last week," Ames said.

"In that case, could I ask why you need to see her again?"

"I need some personal background."

"Miss Billings is a very private person."

"She promised."

There was a pause, and Ames waited for a *drop dead* or a disconnect. What came instead was almost ingratiating.

"Well, if it's background you want, her parents are real characters. They live out on Long Island. Hold on, I'll get you the phone number."

The little white frame house stood on a corner lot. There were trellised morning glories and a flagstone path leading to an immaculate birdbath, and a gray-haired man in a Hawaiian shirt stopped pushing his lawnmower and jogged over to the curb.

"Hi, I'm Stan Billings." A red, friendly hand came through the open Mercedes window and Ames shook it. "Put your car in the drive and come on in and meet Ella-Viola."

Ella-Viola had pink hair and glitter-framed bifocals and a chubby face that seemed made for smiling. She offered iced tea. "Unless you'd like something stronger?"

Ames noticed a Bless-This-House sampler above the stairway. "Iced tea will be fine, thanks."

Ella-Viola sat in a rocker and plunked a half-finished needlepoint rose onto her lap. "It wasn't overnight success for Vanessa, the way the magazines tell it. She's been working since she was a child, and it was always two steps forward and three backward, and after she sang that horrible *Traviata* in Philly, she was ready to give up."

"Now, Ella," Stan said, "let Mr. Rutherford ask questions."

Ella-Viola took the advice with admirable serenity. "What would you like to know, Mr. Rutherford?"

Ames looked around the living room full of stuffed dolls and bowling trophies and shelves of Tony Bennett records, and he couldn't help wondering, *A world-class operatic soprano came out of this?* It seemed as likely as an orchid growing in a clover patch.

"Please, call me Ames." He knew from interviewing dozens of parents that childhood was the can opener. "Tell me about Vanessa as a little girl."

And for the next two hours Stan and Ella-Viola were talking about a living person and not a national shrine.

One point more than any other caught his interest, because it was a mystery that the parents made no attempt to explain away. Vanessa had failed in *Traviata*, failed in the role that was ten years later to become her greatest triumph, failed so completely that she had disappeared, severing all contact with opera, with friends, with family, until her astonishing comeback at her teacher's funeral.

"What was she doing during those years?" Ames asked.

"She never talks about it," Ella-Viola said. "We thought she was dead."

The sun's last rays were pouring across the wall-to-wall carpet when Ames finally said thank you to Stan and Ella-Viola, packed up his notebooks and cassette recorder, and got back into the Mercedes.

He drove three blocks. At the intersection of Albemarle and Kingston a black stretch limousine cut him off. A tall man in chauffeur's livery stepped out and motioned Ames to pull over to the curb.

"Mr. Rutherford?" His voice was low and without expression. He opened Ames's door. "Mr. Stratiotis would appreciate your company for a moment."

Ames saw no way of refusing. He didn't want a fistfight, and the reporter in him said, *go ahead*. The chauffeur escorted him to the limousine and he stepped from the sweltering afternoon into the creamy air conditioning of the black Lincoln Continental.

Ames and Nikos Stratiotis stared at each other from opposite ends of the back seat. An antique tabletop hinged to the partition held a silver tray of bottles and glasses and ice. Stratiotis leaned forward and poured a Chivas on the rocks.

"This is what you drink, right?"

Ames accepted the glass. "Thanks. Why not."

Stratiotis lifted his own glass in an unspoken toast. Ames suspected from the look of the bubbles that it held Perrier and lime.

"You've been phoning Vanessa Billings," Stratiotis said.

"I've been phoning her answering machine."

"Why?"

"I'm writing an article on her."

"I'd appreciate it if you didn't."

"It's my job."

"Who's paying you?"

"Sorry."

"I can find out."

"But not through me."

"Mr. Rutherford, you seem to have enough to keep you busy already." Stratiotis's black-with-iron-gray hair lay in a beautifully cut wave across his forehead. "You have a woman you're busy breaking up with, you have dope-smoking literary friends, and people say you have an impressive drinking problem. You don't need to add Vanessa Billings to all that."

Ames glanced toward the chauffeur on the other side of the raised glass panel. "I don't know who gives you your information, but they're full of crap."

"My sources are reliable. Please drop the article."

The *please* did not impress Ames. Stratiotis was ordering, not requesting. In a way it was touching. The man was obviously in love and was simply trying to protect his property; only he made the mistake of doing it, as he did everything in his life, with a bulldozer.

Ames had to wonder: *What is it about Vanessa that makes this man love her; is it the same thing that fascinates me? Why does she have me swimming against the stream like a salmon?*

There was no question of dropping the article, but he knew better than to give a man of Stratiotis's power an outright no.

"I'll drop it when my employer asks for his advance back." Which, if he knew Greg Hatoff, would be never.

"In that case," Stratiotis said, "your employer will be in touch with you."

But Greg Hatoff did not get in touch, and the Stratiotis encounter turned out to be the prod Ames needed.

He burrowed into the local library for all the pop journalism he could find on Vanessa from the last eleven months. He spent three days in New York Xeroxing articles from the *Times* and the *Post* morgues. He had four boozy lunches with an opera maven and took down all the Billings scuttlebutt on his cassette recorder.

Then he hung the GENIUS AT WORK sign on his office and began putting it all together.

All the while, he was aware of Fran watching silently, uneasily.

He was into his second week of binge-writing when the phone, with exquisitely wrong timing, rang and derailed a very intricate train of thought. He was sick of his own voice on the answering tape and snatched up the receiver before the machine could cut in.

"Ames?"

It was Vanessa. He knew her voice right away. He could feel the room brighten as though the sun had flown in through the window.

"How have you been?" she asked.

How've I been? I've been going crazy waiting for you to phone and now that you're on the line I feel eight times crazier. Not the time to go into all that. Don't want you to see what an idiot I am. Time to be strong, attractive, successful. "Oh, I've been fine. And you?"

"I've been away—Chicago needed me for three *Trovatores*; it's *not* my favorite role. The part lies just wrong for my voice, but don't tell anyone."

"I guess that's why you forgot our date?"

"Date? We had a date? Ames, I'm sorry. My secretary must have forgotten to tell me. We've all been going crazy around here, my coach has had the flu and I'm working with a real madman, and I'm looking for a new apartment, and nothing's been sane. Do you still want to meet or am I on your enemies list now?"

"I don't keep an enemies list and if I did you'd never be on it."

"I wish critics were as nice as you. Would you like to meet tomorrow? Noonish?"

"Sure."

"Where?"

"Well, why not 89 Perry Street?"

"I'll be there."

Vanessa hung up and then remembered something astonishing: she had a rehearsal of *Salomé* tomorrow at the Met at 10:00 A.M. *How in the world could I have forgotten that?*

A strange weight fell on her at the thought of calling Ames Rutherford back and canceling.

She asked herself why she felt so attracted to him. It had something to do with his easy, relaxed laugh; and with his eyes. She remembered intelligence in his gaze, and mystery. She remembered feeling that this stranger saw deeper into her than she saw into herself, that he knew everything about her past, her thoughts, her hopes.

She went to the window and opened it wide enough to lean out. It was a dazzlingly clear afternoon. From the street came a confused but unchanging noise, like a soft chord held on an organ.

She phoned her agent.

"Richard, I can't rehearse tomorrow. I have some kind of intestinal bug." It was an outright lie, yet she felt wistful and happy and truthful. Tomorrow Ames Rutherford, not Salomé, would be her reality. "Can you cancel for me?"

A very practiced sigh of a very practiced agent came across the line. "You know they're going to have to pay the chorus."

"There's no chorus in Salomé, and it's only a piano rehearsal. Please, Richard? Just this once?"

"One thing I've learned in my long tragic career is that in opera there's no such thing as just this once. But just this once, okay."

40

AMES AND HIS NOTEBOOKS AND HIS CASSETTE RECORDER AR-
rived at the pink house on Perry Street at quarter of twelve.
By five of twelve she still hadn't shown up.

She's not going to come.

At noon a Checker cab pulled up and she stepped out. She was
dressed completely in pale raspberry and she glowed and he felt his
eyes sticking to her.

"Hi," she said.

"Hi."

They approached each other a little too rapidly for a simple, friendly
glad-to-see-you. He realized they were about to hug, and he felt her realize it too. Then each pulled back a half-step and she held out her
hand.

"What a great day not to be singing Salomé," she said.

"And a great day not to be sitting at a typewriter."

Ames buzzed the super and the old woman appeared and opened the
gate. "We'd like to see that apartment again," he said.

The old woman led them into the little garden. She stared at Vanessa,
her eyes squinting against the sun. "You know where it is," she
said.

Ames took Vanessa up the stairs. He sensed her hanging back. He
pushed the door with the Gothic brass A. It swung in, and the hinges
sang two notes of "Amazing Grace."

She walked into the room slowly. As her eyes scanned the walls,
Ames noticed things about her: the smoothness of her slightly suntanned skin, the deep gray-green of her eyes, the way she carried her
head high, as though four thousand people were watching. She seemed
to shine against the walls.

"What's the verdict?" Ames said. "Will the apartment do?"

She looked at him, confused. "Do for what?"

"You're looking for a new place, aren't you?"

"Yes, I am, but . . . not a furnished walkup in the Village."

He frowned. Something wasn't making sense. "Then why did you ask
me to meet you here?"

She stared at him. "But you asked me to meet *you.*"

"Last time your secretary told me to come at noon. I came and you
never showed."

"But my secretary said she never phoned you."

"Come on, someone phoned."

"Ames, it wasn't Cynthia. Besides, if I were meeting someone, why in
the world would it be here?"

"Hey, don't look at me. I'm innocent."

But she kept staring at him, and it occurred to him she had the same odd sensation he'd had the first time he walked into the place.

"Without all the tacky furniture it could be a homy old apartment, couldn't it," he said.

"I don't know. A place never feels like home to me without a piano."

He had no idea why he said what he did next. In some unfathomable way he wanted to test her. "There's a piano."

She threw him a look, then went to the closed door and opened it. She turned toward the empty wall. "Where?"

"Why did you go straight to that corner?"

"Because it seemed a logical place for a little . . ."

Say it, he thought: a *carved little upright.*

But she drew herself together and stood absolutely motionless and stared at him. "Are you playing games?"

"Of course. Don't all interviewers?"

"You're interviewing me here?"

"Why not? It's more private than any restaurant."

She smiled, and it was as though a storm cloud had passed. They sat and he put his cassette recorder on the glass-top table.

"You're probably more interested in Billings than in me."

"Is there a difference?" he said.

"Billings sings. I eat fudge and watch soap operas."

"Let's start with Billings."

It was as if she were making affectionate fun of a person who wasn't there. She told him of the years of unrelenting discipline, of the obsessive will that enabled Billings to condition the muscles of the body and voice. "Billings never finishes learning anything—not technique, not a role. And when she's in shape she can never hold it long: maybe four hours; for Götterdämmerung, six. Then she has to start from the beginning with the same dumb do-re-mi's. Behind every hour when she's in form on that stage are thirty when she's killing herself."

She refused to discuss her own period of eclipse after the disastrous *Traviata* in Philadelphia. On the other hand, she told him stories that no journalist had ever written about her.

"Billings is a real bitch about her hot milk and blackstrap molasses after every performance. It does absolutely no good, of course; in fact milk causes mucus. But her granny gave it to her as a child and no diva likes to give up her bad habits."

She told him of songs that had stayed in her memory since childhood, the popular songs, the folksongs, the easy classics everyone starts with, music that even today could pull her up from depression and restore her faith in life.

"I can't believe you've ever been depressed or lost your faith in anything," Ames said.

She gave him a long look. For a moment they held each other in the cool trembling of their gazes.

And suddenly he wasn't thinking of any interview. He felt all the emptiness in himself, all the space, all the hungering past, waiting to be filled.

And now, suddenly, he was very sexually aware of her. *Not yet. I could kiss her now, but I'm not going to.*

But that wasn't what happened. To his surprise he found himself getting up from his chair. The act involved no will, no choosing. It was as though someone else were walking over to her.

She reached out a hand. As it grazed his cheek, he felt a pinpricking of excitement run along his skin. Neither of them moved, and he knew with absolute sureness that she felt the same desire as he did.

He put his hands on her shoulders and studied her troubled face for a long moment, then bent forward and lightly touched her lips with his. For a moment she did not respond, then with a tiny moan she locked her arms around him, pressing their bodies together as her lips parted hungrily.

He tasted the cool tip of her tongue. The kiss did not stop. It was a kiss with no turning back after it. He went and locked the door.

"In here," he said, leading her into the bedroom.

Again, it was not he whose heart was pounding, he who lifted her blouse and kissed her breasts. It was not he who unhooked her skirt and gave her his hand as she stepped out of it.

And yet, a moment later, it was he who became her lover.

Vanessa rushed into her apartment, confused, worn out, and exhilarated all at the same time. Her eye fell on a bowl of roses like none she had ever seen before. They were shell pink, with a birthmark of fiery red at the base of each petal. As she bent down to smell them she saw a note. The handwriting was Nikos's. *Sorry you aren't feeling well. N.*

A phone was ringing in the other room. Cynthia, her secretary, came into the hallway, her bun of gray hair trembling. "He's been calling every hour since eleven this morning."

Vanessa took the call.

"You're not feeling well?" Nikos said.

"I'm all right. Just a little exhausted."

"It's not like you to cancel a rehearsal."

She felt a great sadness. He had moved from the center of her life to the margin. "Nikos, I'm dead tired. Can we talk tomorrow?"

"Of course. I love you."

She was silent just a moment too long. Then, "I love you too."

The next day Ames shut himself in his study. He knew what he wanted: not the usual celebrity guff about mansion and jewels and limousines but Vanessa herself, an image caught in the blink of a camera's lens.

He reviewed his notes. Whole stretches came back to him with astonishing clarity.

Not just the conversation. How she'd smiled. The moment they had touched. The way her eyes had met his. But he couldn't get anything down. It was like trying to nail clouds to a board.

Fran took to appearing at the door. Sometimes she brought coffee or a sandwich and sometimes she was just there, and he had a disturbing sense that she was checking up on him.

"It's a beautiful day," she said. "Want to walk?"

"Sorry."

"Come on. It feels like you've been away a month. I miss you."

"Why do you have to start missing me just when I'm trying to write?"

She stared at him and her voice took on the tautness of a stretched cord. "I've lived with you twelve years and do you know something ridiculous? Sometimes I still haven't the foggiest idea who you are or what you want me to be."

He sighed, gathering his patience. "I'm Ames Rutherford, I'm trying to be a writer, and you can be anything you want so long as you let me get this article done."

Silence dropped, and he realized he'd raised his voice at her.

Her color deepened and suddenly she was out the door and a slam followed her, and then she was back looking at Ames with a prayer in her eyes. "Oh, Jesus. Hold me. Please."

He got up and held her.

"I'm so scared," she said. "I never see you and we haven't made love in eighteen days. I hate this article and I hate the way it involves you and I'm scared I'm going to lose you."

"Lose me to an article?"

"To her."

"Who the hell are you talking about?"

He knew who the hell and he could see she knew he knew but her eyes thanked him for the lie.

He atoned the only way he knew how: he made dinner. Lobster tails with thick daubs of mustard and Parmesan broiled under a high flame. They ate on the terrace with cool breezes fanning them.

"Do I dare ask how the article's coming?" she said.

"Better," he lied. "Much better."

After dinner he went back to work. He said it would only be for an hour or so, but it was 4:00 A.M. before he came to the bedroom.

There was a crack of light underneath the bathroom door. He could see Fran's face against the pillow. She was on her side, breathing deeply.

"Fran?"

No answer.

He undressed and showered, then switched off the light and groped his way carefully through the dark. He got into bed very quietly so as not to disturb her. But she moved and he felt her breasts pressing against his back, and he realized she had been waiting for him.

He turned and shut his eyes, praying to be able to love her.

His arms went around her. His lips passed over her mouth, touching, not kissing. He could feel her beginning to respond and he could feel himself withdrawing, his thoughts fleeing to Vanessa.

He passed his lips over Fran's cheeks, then very slowly in a circling movement down to her breasts. Usually it worked for him, but it didn't work tonight.

His fingertips moved up to her face. Her eyes were closed and he could feel dampness. She had begun to cry.

"I'm sorry," he whispered.

She rolled away, pushing out silence like a wall. He felt an ocean of misunderstanding wash between them.

"Go to sleep," she said. "Please go to sleep. I love you and it doesn't matter."

But it did matter. It mattered very much.

She had seen too many changes in him happening too quickly, and they had begun with his work on the opera article.

She waited till he drove into town for his monthly haircut, then—swallowing her self-reproach—threw herself headlong into a search of his study. She played a quick sampling of his tape cassettes. They appeared to be four stultifyingly ordinary hours of *where-did-you-study* and *what-do-you-eat*.

She leafed rapidly through his notebooks, the "in" and "out" mail trays on his desk where he kept manuscripts in progress. She combed the desk drawers, the closets, the shelves. She searched the wastebasket. She even looked under cushions and behind pictures.

In an hour and a half she turned up nothing.

Nothing typed, nothing handwritten, nothing jotted or scrawled or even doodled. He had been locked in the room, shutting her out for three days, and there was nothing on paper.

Just as she heard his car coming back, the wheels crunching on the gravel drive, her eye went one last time to his desk. She noticed his address book. A sudden instinct told her to open it.

A piece of typing paper, neatly folded, fell out.

She bent and picked it up.

She had expected an explosion, and instead there was only a whisper. On the paper, in printing that was not Ames's, was a New York City telephone number. Below that, in loops that danced and leapt across the page, the name Vanessa was written, how many times? She counted.

Twenty-seven times.

The handwriting was Ames's.

41

DINNER WAS FRESH SHAD ROE WITH BACON AND PERFECTLY steamed string beans and silence. Ames answered Fran's attempts at conversation in civilized monosyllables. She knew it was the wrong moment to talk and she knew when she was angry she was not her own pilot. But she couldn't hold it in any longer.

"Don't you have any stake at all in *us*? Am I the only one who's trying to save this love affair or whatever it is we have?"

"Fran, please, I know I've been lousy company, but as soon as I've finished my article—"

She knew she had to fight and she had no weapons: no guile, no celebrity, no mystery. She had nothing but the truth. "Come *off* it, Ames. You've been working in there three days and nights and your pages are blank."

He stared at her as though she had kicked the breath out of him.

"Except for this one." She held out the page.

"Where did you get that?"

"I searched your room."

He didn't answer.

"Are you having an affair with her?" she asked.

He rose. "I don't think this is the time to—"

"Because if you are, I want to know. I'm not going to take another twelve years of feeling guilty and responsible every time you pull away from me when you're the one who should be guilty and responsible!"

"You're accusing me? You with your Timothy?"

Her jaw dropped. "Timothy?"

"He phones and you erase his messages so I won't suspect."

"Oh, my God, you think Timothy—is an *affair*?"

" 'Call me back when you can talk. . . . When can we meet. . . .' What the hell am I supposed to think?"

"Timothy is a sweet, white-haired seventy-year-old married man and he's my Al-Anon sponsor."

"Run that past me again? Your Al-what?"

"I've been going to Al-Anon meetings. It's a self-help group for families and friends of alcoholics."

For an instant Ames had the eyes of a trapped animal. "You're telling people *I'm* an alcoholic?"

"You drink, Ames. Look at yourself now. You can't even get up from the table without a glass in your hand."

He looked at the glass. "That doesn't make me an alcoholic."

"You drink and you're killing yourself and I'm not going to let you kill me too. Yes, I go to meetings. Twice a week. And yes I tell Timothy everything—and he helps me get through this mess of a life we're living."

Rage blinded him. The last thing he remembered about that night was barricading himself in his study with a bottle of vodka.

In the morning when he staggered into the kitchen for coffee, his head felt like a drum and Fran's silence beat a funeral march on it. "I think I owe someone an apology," he said.

"You don't remember the things you said, do you." From the way she was looking at him he knew whatever he wasn't remembering must have been pretty dreadful.

The phone rang. "Ames, it's Vanessa. Is our interview still on?"

Fran was pouring herself another cup of coffee, carefully measuring a teaspoon of organic honey into it and stirring.

"Sure," he said.

"Same place?" the voice asked.

"Sure."

"Twelve-thirty?"

"Sure."

Fran turned her head and watched him. For an instant there was remarkable beauty in her pain and suddenly he was torn.

He hung up the phone and began moving with energy and speed. He put on a clean Brooks Brothers shirt and clean jeans. He put the right papers into his briefcase. He went for the car keys.

Fran was looking at her coffee with a sad sort of acceptance. "Remember we're having dinner with the Currys tonight. Six-thirty. We were two hours late last time. They won't be giving us another chance."

It took him a moment to get back into the world of dinner and tonight. "I'll be on time."

Vanessa was in the Perry Street apartment before him, standing by the window looking down at the garden. She turned when he came in. "I was beginning to think you weren't coming."

"The traffic held me up."

"I missed you."

"I missed you too."

It was a strange moment, awkward and beautiful.

He started his cassette recorder, fingers fumbling, and asked some dumb question or other about critics.

"Ames, would you turn that machine off?"

He turned the machine off.

"I wish you'd come over here next to me."

He closed his notebook and crossed the room. "A minute ago I was sitting over there thinking I'd sell my soul just to hold your hand again, and now I'm holding your hand."

"Stand close to me," she said. "Hold all of me."

He stood close to her, held her. "Do you know I haven't thought about anything but you for the last week?"

"I don't know. Tell me."

"When I close my eyes I see you, when there's no sound in the middle of the night I hear you. Oh God, if you knew how much I want to make love to you . . ."

"Ames—that's what I want too."

He kissed her. First on the forehead, lightly, and over the eyes, gently, one at a time, and then on her cheeks, less gently, and finally on the mouth, full and deep and not gently at all.

She pulled back and led him through the doorway to the bedroom.

He was hard before they even reached the bed. They undressed quickly, and then she opened her embrace to him.

"Oh, yes, Ames, oh, yes."

Without pulling away from each other they made love three times, each act flowing without boundary into the next.

Afterward, they lay on the bed. "I guess it's happened," he said. "We're having an affair. Meeting secretly, making love. Isn't that what an affair's supposed to be?"

"I wanted it to happen," she said.

"So did I."

Her arm tightened around him. "When did you first want it?"

"When I first saw you."

"Me too." And then she was silent. "But you have a friend."

"You do too."

"Do you love her?"

"Not anymore. Not for a long time. Do you love him?"

She didn't answer.

"It would kill me if I thought you loved him."

"Why?"

"Because I've fallen in love with you." He knew what he wanted to hear from her, and he didn't hear it. "What about you?"

"All I know, Ames, is that I want to spend the rest of my life with you, and if I don't . . . I'll die."

He was still lying beside her on the bed when he saw that the light in the courtyard had darkened to evening.

"Oh, God." He reached to the pile of clothes on the floor where he had laid his watch. "I'm in trouble. Where's a phone?"

"Call me later this week?"

"Tomorrow, okay?" He kissed her and she held out his cassette recorder. He looked at her and his heart missed a beat. "You're goddamned wonderful, you know that?"

"What are you, some kind of critic?"

"Just someone who's been waiting a long, long time for someone exactly like you." He made a move to kiss her again but she held him away with surprising firmness.

"Corner of Bleecker. Phone booth." She pushed him out the door.

The booth was right where she said it would be. He dropped the coins in, dialed. After a moment the line buzzed.

"Hello?"

"Fran, I'm sorry, I got held—"

She cut him short. "I was raised with the old-fashioned notion that when we promise something it matters."

"I'm on my way now. You go to the party. I'll meet you there."

"Take your time. I told them we wouldn't be coming. I'm going to my Al-Anon meeting instead."

"Come on, Fran, it was an accident, you don't need to punish me."

"I love you, Ames. And you don't love me. You don't love anyone. I shouldn't say that. Maybe you love your opera singer. But you've never loved me. No one's to blame and the punishment's over."

"What are you talking about?"

"I'm talking about us. We're through, Ames. I'm moving out."

"Because I was late for a dinner date?"

"Because you were late for a dinner date. And ten million other reasons."

The line went dead. He dialed information. "Operator, is there a listing for Al-Anon in East Hampton?"

He found Fran's Al-Anon meeting just as it was breaking up. A dozen or so people, mostly women, were hanging around chatting on the lawn in front of a Methodist Church.

Fran was wearing dinner clothes and her favorite little Tiffany starburst and he felt a pang of guilt.

"Ames, this is Timothy. I've told you about him."

A short and solid white-haired man with rimless glasses was holding out his hand. "Hi," he said in a friendly voice.

"Hi," Ames said. He didn't trust Timothy. He sensed masks beneath masks.

"Timothy is coming home with me," Fran said. "He's going to help me pack a few things."

Ames nailed a smile to his face. "Can't we talk?" he said.

She hesitated. "Timothy, I'll meet you at the house." She got into Ames's car.

They drove in silence. It was not that large a front seat, and yet there was a great deal of space between them. He took the curves carefully. "I'm sorry," he said.

"I'm tired of your being sorry and my being sorry. I've sunk twelve years into you and me, and what do I have—a dumb degree in music, no kids, no husband, a couple of months in Al-Anon—it's not enough!"

"I guess the world's tough for all of us."

"The world's tough, but it doesn't have to be absurd. I can't live in Kafka-land anymore, wondering if you'll be cold or if you'll be warm, wondering if you've stopped off in a bar and forgotten we had a dinner, praying you're alive and wishing you were dead."

"I never knew you wished I was dead."

"I don't wish anything. I don't even care if you touch me or give me the silent treatment or fall in love with someone else. You can keep tearing little shreds off yourself and throwing them away and it will never hurt me again. I prayed to be able to detach from you and now thank God I can."

"Have I been that awful?"

"You've gotten pretty awful over the years."

"Then why did you want me?"

"Because you make love beautifully. Or used to. And for some reason you seemed to need me." She sighed. "Why did you need me, Ames? Why did you hold on to me for twelve years?"

"I loved you."

"No, you didn't."

"All right—I didn't."

"Do you know what I think, Ames? You're afraid of love. It's something you picked up from your father. Love is dangerous, don't do it. I was your defense against falling in love. Well, the defense has failed. You've met your opera singer."

When they got back to the house, night was closing in. He made himself a drink and watched as she piled the last clothes into the last bags and made everything fit. Finally a few toiletries went into the little overnight Gucci he had given her for the second anniversary of the night they'd decided to live together. It was battered and a little ragged now, but she'd kept it.

He followed her to the front door.

"Goodbye, Ames." She went up on tiptoe and kissed him. "I'll send my address when I have one."

"Fran, I'm sorry."

"Don't be. It's not your fault, it's not mine. We tried to prove we could have a life; we can't."

She turned and ran quickly outside to the station wagon where Timothy was warming the motor. Ames stood motionless in the hallway, waiting, and then he heard the car door slam on twelve years that were suddenly no longer there.

With the help of a quart of vodka Ames fell into a restless sleep. No one said "Good morning" when he awoke and rolled over in bed. There was no coffee on the bedside table, sending up its friendly cloud of steam.

He staggered into the kitchen. The day was already a bright square of light on the counter. The wall seemed naked in new places.

He squinted at the crumbs from last night, the half-eaten peanut butter sandwich that he didn't remember slapping together, the beer cans and the crazily stacked dishes in the sink.

He'd left tens of thousands of dirty plates in that sink, and they'd always wound up magically in the dishwasher or back on the shelves. These plates hadn't budged all night. They were serving him notice: *the universe has changed.*

He made himself a cup of instant coffee with hot water from the tap. He picked up the telephone and dialed the New York City area code and the seven digits of Vanessa's number.

For a moment there was no ring.

It's too early. I'll wake her.

He hung up and made an agreement with himself not to phone her before ten.

But what if she's out by ten?

Okay, nine-thirty. But not a minute earlier.

At 9:29 he dialed Vanessa's number again.

It makes no sense for me to love her. Every sign is against it. I should at least wait a decent interval after Fran.

He hung up and then he thought, *What kind of bullshit am I giving myself? Fran is over. I don't need to wait for anyone or anything.*

He dialed a third time. There was an instant of absolute stillness. His stomach had the sensation of free fall. On the fifth ring a voice answered. "May I help you?"

Not Vanessa; a man.

"Miss Billings, please."

"Miss Billings is away, may I take a message?"

Away—where's away? "Could you tell me where I can reach her?"

"Who's calling, please?"

"This is Ames Rutherford. I'm interviewing her."

"Yes, Mr. Rutherford. Miss Billings is very sorry. She won't be giving interviews this summer. She's with friends in Monte Carlo and will be touring till September."

What's happened? She never said anything about Monte Carlo.

"She's written you a note. I mailed it this morning. You should have it tomorrow."

But the note didn't come the next day or the day after or even the day after that. Four days went by, days of listening to waves and going crazy and running out to the mailbox in sun and downpour every time a passing car slowed down. There were fliers and bills and ads for Fran, but for four days there was nothing from Vanessa Billings.

On the fifth day he found a letter lying alone in the mailbox. The paper was thick and soft with the comfortable skinlike feel of vellum. It was Vanessa's handwriting on the envelope, a rectangle of soft gray that reminded him of dawn. He brought the letter up to his face and inhaled and smelled her perfume.

Suddenly he was as weak as a dog panting beside a stream. He felt he'd run four hundred miles for that letter. He took it and collapsed in the easy chair by the fireplace. His hand was shaking. His insides were shaking. He opened the envelope neatly along the flap.

My dearest Ames,

These are the hardest words I think I've ever had to write in my life. I feel more strongly for you than I've ever felt for anyone or anything, including music. And that is the problem.

Music is not just my career—music is my life, the best part of me. It is everything that is good and strong and honest in me.

The rest is fear and dishonesty and shame, things I cannot bear even to look at.

Music brought me back from the dead to the living. I owe music my life and soul. I made a promise, Ames, a promise that leaves no room in my life for more than a halfway love.

Till I met you I was never tempted to betray that promise. And since meeting you I've wanted to betray it a thousand times over. But betrayal would be the death of all that I have become, of everything that you love in me.

I cannot love you halfway. Any other man I could, but not you.

And so there is no choice. I can never see you again.

I shall never forget you. You have made me happier than I ever deserved. Please forgive me, Ames. I will always love you.

Vanessa

Part Five

RETURN: 1981–1985

42

AMES READ THE LETTER A HUNDRED TIMES THAT DAY, BUT EACH time it said the same unbelievable thing.

Why? *Why?*

He put Vanessa's tape on the Betamax and sat staring at her, hearing her, looking for an answer in that image.

Suddenly a strange voice filled the living room. "Of course I shall sing again. I must—I will—I can."

There was something arresting in the face that stared out of the screen at him. It was part of the black-and-white introductory segment on Vanessa's tape that he had always skipped. Someone was asking Vanessa's teacher about her proposed comeback.

His heart thumped in his chest and his breath caught. He knew that voice.

He jabbed the stop button and ran the film back to replay her. The face hung motionless on the screen. There was an instant of explosive silence and then, again, the voice that he somehow knew.

"I must—I will—I can."

Dill Switt got Ames Rutherford's phone call at four in the afternoon and, breaking his ass, he was able to make the five o'clock train.

Potbellied, unshaved, squint-eyed, nursing a three-day hangover, Dill knew that his grooming and dress were pretty casual, but he was nonetheless shocked by what greeted him when his oldest and best drinking buddy opened the front door.

Ames Rutherford had shed ten pounds and the lines in his face had gained at least as many years. Beard stubble flecked his chin and the hand he clapped on Dill's shoulder trembled badly. "Dill, babe."

"Ames, babe."

The two Harvard men fell into each other's arms.

"Hungry after that lousy train ride?" Ames slurred.

The kitchen looked like the site of a terrorist bombing. The sink was piled with unwashed dishes and punctured beer cans.

"I've missed you, old pal." With a sweep of the arm Ames cleared a space on the counter. He wrenched a couple of two-inch steaks from the freezer and slapped them unthawed into a skillet.

"Get yourself a drink. Glasses in the cupboard."

Dill drank and watched. For twelve minutes Ames lurched around the kitchen, slopping a coffee cup of vodka down his front and, now and then, down his throat. He adjusted flames and threw ingredients into a blender and never measured or timed a thing.

Drink was funny, Dill reflected. It hurt a lot of men's writing, but rarely a man's cooking.

They ate their salad and steaks on the terrace under the stars, passing the wine and the coarse black pepper back and forth. Dill brought Ames up-to-date on all the gossip, who had sold a new book, who hadn't, who was breaking up and who was making out.

He sensed he was boring his host.

"You said you wanted to talk about something, Ames?"

Ames brought a six-pack of Bud from the kitchen and snapped the tops off two of the cans. He angled two deck chairs toward the Atlantic and gestured Dill to one of them. Feet propped on the little stone wall, Ames began quietly speaking about Vanessa.

A six-pack and a half later, Dill wiped his mouth on the back of his hand. "You're not the first man who's been in love."

Ames's gaze nailed him. "It's not the first time I've been in love with Vanessa Billings."

The moon was reflecting off the high tide. The waves were breaking close to shore with long spaces between the splashes.

"When was the first time?"

"Dill, I've never *not* been in love with this woman. The minute I saw her, I knew this was the one."

Dill thumped his feet on the flagstone. "Sweetheart, I know the tune. You're not the first who's sung it."

"I don't mean like that. I mean I *knew* this woman. Knew what made her laugh, made her cry, what her favorite flower was, what it would be like to make love to her."

"Okay, this Vanessa gives you a strong case of déjà vu."

"I'm not buying that reductionist shit, Dill."

"You're in love with someone you don't know. You're filling in the blanks. Ames, *I* could fill in the blanks. This woman has been on eight magazine covers in the last year and the *Times* has run umpteen profiles on her, and you've been saving her clippings. No wonder you know her favorite flower—you know her favorite *recipe*, for God's sake."

"How did I know about making love to her?"

"There are two kinds of sex. Good sex, bad sex. Good sex is always the same. Déjà screw. Don't you see, you're making her up. The word for it is *projection*. Ask Freud. Ask Jung. Ask anyone."

"You think I'm crazy."

"We're all crazy. We're writers, we have to be. What we *don't* have to be is dumb. You threw away a woman you'd lived with for twelve years, for fantasy; and you lost the fantasy to boot. Now that's dumb, and if you want my opinion, that's what's hurting. Pick up the phone and get Fran back."

"Fran and I have been over for years."

"Which you didn't know until Vanessa made it all very clear."

"It would have happened with or without Vanessa."

"Sure—you would have met someone else—and you would have known all about her, what perfume, what flower, what the hell. Ames, you were *ready*. You made it happen. You can make it un-happen, and if you want my advice, that's exactly what you'll do."

"It's too late. I love Vanessa. I always have, I always will. And she loves me. Her letter says she loves me."

"Sure she loves you. That's why dishes are piling up in your sink and she's off with her billionaire on the French Riviera."

"She wants me. That letter is a cry for help."

"That letter is a cry to leave her the hell alone."

Ames sighed. Far away two waves broke in quick succession, like a gunshot and its echo. "Come inside."

He led the way into the house, past the living room liquor cabinet where he picked up a bottle of Stolichnaya, into a room that reeked of sweat and pot and spilled beer.

"Take a seat," Ames said. "I want you to see something."

The something was a grainy black-and-white tape of Ariana Kavalaris's last, pathetic TV interview, the famous one where she'd said, *I'll sing again. I must—I will—I can.*

Ames was pushing the buttons on a phone-answering machine. "Now listen to this."

Dill listened to a man selling magazine subscriptions for the Police Athletic League.

"Crap, not that one." Ames jabbed another button. Up came a wrong number in Spanish. Then Fran said she'd be home at 6:30. And then a woman's voice.

"I'm calling for Vanessa Billings. Could Ames Rutherford meet her at noon today at 89 Perry Street?"

That was all.

"So?" Dill said.

"You don't hear it?" Ames reran the television tape and then the woman on the answering machine.

Dill didn't react. He wasn't exactly refusing comment, but he wasn't rushing in with a verdict either.

"They're the same voice," Ames said.

"Wait a minute. Ariana Kavalaris is not phoning people to make appointments for Miss Billings. That is not her line of work. For another thing, she had to be dead when you got that message."

"That's Ariana Kavalaris on my answering machine."

"How the hell can it be her?"

"How the hell can it *not* be her?" Ames shouted. Now he was pushing buttons crazily, running the tapes simultaneously.

Dill raised his hands in surrender. "All right—all right. There's a resemblance. Maybe Billings hired this secretary because the voice reminded her of Kavalaris."

"Vanessa's secretary never phoned me. We checked."

"You're telling me Ariana Kavalaris phoned you all the way from the grave with that dinky message?"

"Not Ariana Kavalaris. Her *voice*."

"Listen to me, Ames. They've tested astrology. They've tested Tarot and I Ching."

"I'm not talking about extrasensory crap. I'm talking about ..." Ames fell into a chair. "Hell, I don't know what I'm talking about." He began crying softly.

Dill's heart went out to his old, suffering friend. The guy's life was a mess. It seemed a very good moment to switch to a less painful subject. "So tell me, old buddy, how's your writing?"

Ames shrugged.

"Maybe you should get back to that article. All the stewing you've been doing about Vanessa Billings, it'd be a shame to waste it. Put it down on paper."

Ames drained his glass and then his eyes came up at Dill with sudden hopefulness. "If I write this article, she'll see it, won't she."

In the morning Ames drove Dill to the 10:30 train, waved goodbye, and came home and placed his hands on the typewriter. He felt its gunmetal stillness creep up into him. He took a drink—just one—for luck, for lubricant, for the road.

He could feel his brain loosen up, words ready to trickle.

He lifted his hands over the keyboard—and dove.

He knew what he wanted the article to say. He wanted to underscore the parallels between Ariana Kavalaris and her pupil, to make them if anything eerier and more uncanny than in life. He wanted to present Vanessa as the supreme artist, caught in the clutches of commercial mediocrities, repeating all her teacher's mistakes. He didn't fool himself about his own role. He was a self-appointed Galahad, rescuing the fair damsel by publishing the piece.

For the next three days he slept four hours a night, downed twenty cups of coffee and a fifth of vodka a day, and ignored the phone. He lived on canned tuna and hard-boiled eggs.

On the morning of the fourth day he carried 143 pages out into the sunshine and sat under a great burst of summer leaves and tried to focus his eyes on what he had somehow done. That afternoon he drove into East Hampton and mailed the article overnight express.

Seventy-two hours later the phone pulled Ames out of a three-day sleep. Greg Hatoff was screaming. "I love it! I love you! You even made me love that screwed-up little diva!"

Painfully, Ames opened the other eye. "Hope all that loving means you like it."

"Wise-ass. We're having the lawyers check it for libel, and if all's well we'll run it in the July Fourth issue."

Ames dug into isolation and waited. His proofs came June 21, and the July Fourth issue of *Knickerbocker* hit the stands June 28.

On June 29 Greg phoned. "The newsstands sold out in twenty-four hours. We had to run off another hundred thousand."

Tear sheets from clipping services started showing up in the mailbox: a columnist in Chicago said Ames knew all about ambition and the heartbreak behind it. The *Washington Post* said no one had raunchier wit than Ames Rutherford or a keener feel for the extravagant vulgarities of our time.

Ames filed the clippings, but only one thing interested him: Vanessa Billings's reaction. It didn't come. He wondered how long it took *Knickerbocker* to reach Monaco.

He spent the Fourth of July alone, waiting by the phone. He actually hoped she'd phone to say *Happy Fourth—oh, and I saw our article.*

She didn't phone. By 10:00 P.M. that night he figured everyone was asleep in Monaco anyway, and he went down the beach to George Plimpton's fireworks party to see if there was any gossip about her.

He heard she was preparing *Turandot* for La Scala.

He heard she was in Australia shooting a movie for British TV.

He drank too much and came home with an heiress from Barbados and a very bad headache. There was a message on the answering machine.

"Hello, Ames. This is your father. Can you give me a ring?"

"I read your article," Bishop Rutherford said the next day. "It touched me."

Ames stood with the phone, staring out the open window at the Atlantic. His head throbbed with hangover. He managed to say, "Thanks."

"I'd like to talk to you about it. Could you have dinner with me tonight?"

Ames hesitated. "Look, I haven't got my calendar here, but—"

"*Please.*" The voice was tight with urgency.

It was the first time in his life Ames could remember his father's ever begging. "Okay, but I can't stay long."

They finished their dinner and went to the study. The bishop crossed slowly to the sideboard. He fumbled with a latch, produced a bottle and two handsome snifters. As he poured, his movements seemed tired and a little sad.

It occurred to Ames with pained surprise that his father was becoming old. *I wonder how long I have before I'm old too?*

The bishop handed him a snifter. "To your very good health."

"And yours."

A conversation waited to be started. Ames tipped his head back and took half the brandy in a gulp.

His father stood looking at him in the half-darkness, and Ames sensed in him a solitude that was strong and resigned and impenetrably patrician.

"How are you getting along with Fran?"

"You don't have to pretend, Dad. I know you don't like her."

"I don't dislike Fran."

"She's left me," Ames said.

Concern flickered in the bishop's eyes. "I'm sorry."

"We've been breaking up a long time. Ever since we met, I guess."

"Do you love her?"

"No."

"I hope—I hope you'll love someone, someday."

"I do love someone."

The bishop looked at his son a moment, then walked to the window and stood gazing down through the graceful wrought-iron bars at evening strollers in the street below. They were mostly blacks and Spanish, peaceful tonight. It was a changed neighborhood. Once it had been a white, Protestant, patrician suburb of a white, Protestant, patrician New York. Only the cathedral remained from those days, and the blacks and Spanish rarely came to worship in it.

The bishop sighed. "That was a fine article, Ames. Oh, I know you were poking fun a little, but that's your right." He came back to his leather armchair. "You were wrong about one thing, though—the reason I did the eulogy. It wasn't that I'm father-confessor to some jet set. She was a friend—and I felt I owed her *something*."

Suddenly, Ames was interested. For years he'd thought of his father as a completed puzzle, no pieces missing, and without warning here was a brand-new piece.

"It must seem strange to you," the bishop said, "your father and . . . an opera singer. Sometimes it seems strange to me. As though it all happened to someone else."

But somehow it didn't seem strange to Ames; not strange at all. In fact it seemed like something that a part of him had known all his life. "Dad, how well did you know Kavalaris?"

"How well?" The bishop was silent a moment, his eyes lost in memory. "Long ago—when we were very young, and very full of hope, Ariana and I—were in love."

In a soft voice that only occasionally trembled, Bishop Mark Rutherford told his son the story.

43

BY THE TIME THE BISHOP FINISHED, THE ROOM WAS DARK. HE walked slowly to the desk and turned the lamp on.

Ames honored the moment by keeping silent.

The bishop picked up a pipe. "I sometimes wonder if the road I've traveled all my life has been a detour, not the main road."

Ames recognized that it was a question, and that more than anything else his father needed the answer. He began to understand the sense he had always had of Mark Rutherford as a man waiting by the wayside of life, huddled, shutting things out. He began to understand things about his own life too, and about the part of himself that had always seemed to be missing.

"Dad, the apartment that you shared with her—was it at 89 Perry Street?"

The bishop looked surprised. "Yes—it was."

Ames rose and came across the room and embraced his father.

"Thank you," the bishop whispered. "Thank you for letting me say everything." He began crying.

His son didn't speak, just held him close.

"Silence is death. I've lived so much of my life in silence. No one's to blame for it but me. It was my choice." The bishop dried his eyes. "Excuse me for breaking down like this."

"Thank you, Dad." Ames had a sense that those tears and those four hours of truth were the first real thing his father had ever given him. "From the bottom of my heart, thank you."

The next day Ames went to his father's old seminary. His eye swept iron fences, trees that had grown undisturbed for a hundred years, buildings of ancient brick. A sudden conviction froze him.

I've been here before.

He knew what he would see if he followed the path around the turning. *A boxwood hedge. Beyond it, a tennis court. A tall oak tree, as tall as these buildings. Beyond that, a jungle gym.*

He turned the corner.

Three little children were scrambling on a jungle gym, too busy to glance at him. Two seminarians in swimsuits and T-shirts were batting a tennis ball across a net in the fading evening light.

He sat musing on a bench under the oak.

How could I have dreamed this? Why would I have dreamed it? Aren't dreams fulfillments of wishes? What wish of mine is this place?

Thoughts came to him that were not his own. A sadness filled him.

He seemed still to be listening to his father. A weight pulled in his chest.

He didn't know how long he sat there. He sensed a shadow beside him on the bench, and then realized the sky was darkening. Drizzle was clicking against the leaves. He bolted for cover to the nearest doorway. Rain began slapping down. He pushed through the door.

As his eyes adjusted to the blackness he could make out two candles shedding a pale light on a distant altar. Above it, chunks of the past peered out of a half-restored stained-glass window. He stood hunched and frowning. *What the hell am I doing in a church?*

He slid down into a pew and emptied his lungs in a sigh.

"Whoever You are, whatever You are," he whispered, "help my father." He hadn't intended to ask anything more. He was surprised to hear the same voice whisper, "And help me."

The very first thing Vanessa saw when she opened the door that fall was a rumpled magazine on the music stand of the piano.

"What kind of friends does my agent rent my apartment to?" She frowned. "Isn't *Knickerbocker* a drug magazine?"

Cynthia looked at her sharply—too sharply. "It prints a lot of gossipy trash about a lot of gossipy trashy people."

Vanessa held up the cover with her name on it. "You mean gossipy trash about me."

"Don't bother reading it," Cynthia said.

"Honestly, it's not going to break my bones." Vanessa plunked herself down in the comfortable chair and turned on the reading light. She came to the byline. *Ames Rutherford.*

His image floated before her mind. He seemed to have happened decades and not just a summer ago.

It's over, she thought. *I chose for it to be over. I've always stuck by my choices.*

She began reading.

The article glowed with affection and bristled with an accuracy that astonished her. There were details she was certain she'd never discussed with anyone. Time and time again she stopped and wondered how he could have known so much about voice, about the people around her, and strangest of all, about her own feelings.

I could phone him, she thought. *There's no harm in that. Just a phone call to say I liked it.*

Ames stared at the page where he had typed eight fumbling attempts at the same sentence. The room suddenly seemed warm. He threw open the window. Gulls were swooping over the Atlantic. He thrummed his fingers on the sill.

The second hand of the electric wall clock glided evenly past Roman numerals. As it touched the *V* the sound of a bell crashed in on him like waves.

For an instant there was nothing in the universe but one jangling phone. He saw a shadow in the air, a ripple of blond hair, the turning of a head. He lunged a hand for the receiver, but the answering machine had already cut in. *Hello, you have reached . . .*

No, Vanessa thought; *I don't want to speak to his machine.*

Ames snatched up the receiver.
There was only a droning dial tone.

During the year till Nikos's Dominican divorce became final under the laws of New York State, Vanessa buried herself in song and success. She spent the winter season fulfilling engagements in New York, Paris, Milan, and Munich. There were slack and empty weeks in May and her thoughts drifted back to the young reporter who had interviewed her so many months ago and to the turning her life had almost taken.

She caught herself gazing out windows and one Wednesday afternoon she found herself, for no reason at all, standing on Perry Street in front of the door of 89.

A jolt went through her. She marched to the nearest pay phone. "Austin, it's time for me to learn *Lulu.*"

"You're kidding."

"When can you run through the score with me?"

"Baby, no one runs through *that* score, but come over at two-thirty this afternoon and we can try limping."

Vanessa allowed herself only one week's vacation that year, seven serene September days with Nikos under the cloudless blue skies of Bad Luzern. And then she plunged into an October of *Aïdas* and *Turandots* in Australia and South America.

"It's no use, Austin. I can't pull it together." It was spring again, and the change in weather had made her edgy.

"Come on, now. Take it from '*al fin son tua.*' "

"I've been taking it from '*al fin son tua*' for three weeks!"

"And one of these weeks you're going to get it right."

Vanessa's voice broke on the first note. She sat down on the bench beside her coach and began crying. "Why can't I breathe before the B-flat?"

"Only fakes do that."

"No one does it in one breath."

"Kavalaris did."

"I'm not Ariana!"

He was staring at her. "There's nothing she did that you can't do. I taught her to sing this passage the way Donizetti wrote it, and I'm going to teach you." He nodded another upbeat and his fingers rippled into the accompaniment again.

Vanessa slammed her fist into the keys.

Austin closed the piano lid. "Five-minute break. Spill."

She sat trembling, wanting to let tears come. "I'm sorry. The whole winter's been off. No, that's a lie. The whole year's been off. Sometimes I think my whole life's been off."

"You're tense." His hand was on her shoulder, massaging. "You've got a big debut coming up. There's not an artist in the world who doesn't have moments of self-doubt."

"It's worse than doubt. It's fear."

"Fear of what?"

She had to tell someone. It might as well be her coach. He knew everything else about her.

"When I go onstage, I never know what's going to come out of my mouth."

"The score's going to come out of your mouth."

"But sometimes . . ." What was the use trying to explain something she could barely put into words? It was like trying to describe a shadow that hovered just beyond the periphery of vision. "In La Scala last May, in *I Puritani*, the end of the mad scene, I sang an E-flat—"

"That Bellini indicated in the score."

"He didn't indicate it in *my* score."

"Go to the library of the Accademia di Santa Cecilia and look up the manuscript."

"To hell with the manuscript! I held that note nine measures over an orchestral and choral tutti."

"So? You brought the house down."

"I don't have that kind of lungs!"

"You do now, sweetheart."

"Austin, I never prepared it, no one taught me, I don't read composers' manuscripts, there's no *basis*. And it's not just notes. There are bits of stage business I find myself doing and I don't know where they come from."

"Such as?"

She shut her eyes. "Lisbon. *Traviata.* Who ever sang 'Addio del Passato' from the floor?"

"Are you trying to make a mystery out of it?"

"I'm trying to make sense out of it."

"Okay. Sit. Let's make sense." Austin got up and poured two cups of coffee. "In Athens Kavalaris sang 'Addio del Passato' from the floor—trying to pull herself to the bed, like a broken doll—clinging to the spot where she and Alfredo first made love. She did it in Amsterdam too.

398

And Rio. And it was damned effective. What's the problem? There's a lot of Kavalaris in you. Consider yourself lucky. She was the best, and she knew you were going to be the best. That's why she taught you."

"Austin—*she didn't teach me those things.*"

"She didn't need to. You saw her performances, you read about them, you have the same instincts she did."

"You're not understanding me, Austin. I'm not trying to imitate Kavalaris. I'm not performing when those things happen. They just happen—" She dropped her saucer to the rug. "Like that."

"Sorry, honey, that was phony. They happen—" Austin slapped her across the face and she dropped the coffee cup. "Like *that.*"

She stared at the stain on the rug and then at him and then she buried her face in her hands and began crying.

"It's okay. It's okay." He hugged her to him. "It's called losing yourself in the role. It's called going to the heart of the music. It's called genius. You've got it. Keep it."

She pulled away. "But the person singing *isn't me*. What comes out of my throat is someone else's voice—singing *through* me."

He sucked at his unlit pipe. "It's not that rare. DiScelta used to say that two or three times in every career—when conditions are perfect—the singer has that sensation of another voice singing through him or her. Usually it turns out to be his or her top performance. All that's happening is, you're giving a lot of top performances."

She sighed, shaking her head. "Austin, the voice isn't *me*. And it's not just the voice that feels wrong. The performances aren't me. What's more, half the time my goddamned *life* isn't me."

Austin looked thoughtfully at her. "Tell me about your goddamned life."

"Have you ever had experiences you knew by heart before they even happened?"

"Give me an example."

"I recognized Ames Rutherford the minute he came into my dressing room. I felt I'd loved him longer than I've loved anyone in the world."

Austin shrugged. "He wrote a great article. He called you great names. I'd love him too."

"Austin, I saw him three times in my life. No, four times. Once was at a party. How could I have loved a stranger?"

"There must be something damned attractive about him."

"His eyes . . . seemed to know everything about me: my past, my secrets, my hopes . . . my dreads. As though I'd been confiding in him since we were six years old. And when he made fun of opera—it made me laugh. Laughter feels so good in this profession."

"I'll say amen to that."

"And when he made love to me . . . Am I awful to tell you all this? He was so damned confident of himself. As though he knew every pore of my body. It . . . excited me. Why do I hate to admit that?"

Austin shrugged. "And Nikos? Does he excite you?"

"Yes, but . . . Austin, I feel like some kind of tramp saying this. With Ames I was outside of myself, I was someone else. With Nikos . . . it's wonderful, but I'm still plain old me."

Austin took a long reflective drag from his unlit pipe. "You're an intelligent woman. You're facing a painful dilemma. Maybe Ames Rutherford is your diplomatic way out."

"Out of what?"

"Nikos has been generous to you. He's a charming man, a lonely man. You're grateful to him. You don't want to hurt him."

"I don't and I won't."

"But you're not going to marry him either."

She looked at her coach wonderingly. "Of course I'm going to marry him."

"That's not what you just got through telling me."

She blinked as though he'd slapped her again and then she rose quickly to her feet. "Then I'm telling you now. I'm going to marry Nikos."

"Nikos—marry me today."

He smiled. "I have to be in Zurich today."

"I'll come with you."

"And who'll sing *Tosca* tonight? They're not paying to hear your understudy." He put his arm around her shoulder and drew her against him.

Nuzzled against his cheek, she felt a fleeting sense of safety. "Will you marry me when you get back?"

"Of course. Why do you think I'd change our plans?"

"I mean the minute you get back. *Please*, Nikos."

He took off his glasses. His eyes met hers carefully. "Darling. Sometimes we have to wait for the things we really want."

You don't understand, she thought. *You don't realize. How can I make you see things I can't even believe myself?*

"It's only a week," he soothed.

"But what if something changes?"

"Are you afraid the world will blow up? North America will sink beneath the ocean? I promise you, nothing will change."

The world did not blow up. North America did not sink under the ocean. Nikos returned a week later, exactly on schedule. The following afternoon Vanessa went with him to the Greek Orthodox Church on Fifth Avenue and Ninety-second Street. There, in front of a very bearded patriarch by the name of Father Gregorios Lampodoupolos, they rehearsed their wedding.

It went without a hitch.

The hitch came three minutes later, on a Manhattan street with the sun pouring down.

Nikos helped Vanessa into the limousine and the chauffeur pushed the door shut after them. Vanessa felt the car close in on her: her adopted world.

The bar was open, the table down. A champagne bottle lay on a bed of shaved ice in a silver bucket. Beside it waited two beautiful pale-green goblets, slender and long-stemmed like roses.

Nikos lifted the bottle, peeled aside the foil and mesh, and began gently working the cork loose. The pop came, and champagne was foaming down the side of the bottle. He poured quickly, wasting not a drop, and handed Vanessa her glass.

"To happiness," he said quietly.

She felt the thin tap of one crystal membrane against another. Her lips curved to the rim of the goblet. A thousand unbelievably fine bubbles exploded against her tongue. It was like tasting chilled sparks.

Nikos took a small, flat object from his breast pocket and held it out to her.

A tiny wave of hesitation pulsed through her. She opened the black velvet jeweler's box. Light flashed across her hand. She lifted up a necklace of diamonds in three braided strands. It swayed like a pendulum marking the earth's rotation.

"It's lovely," she whispered.

"Here. Let me."

Nikos fastened the diamonds around her neck. They touched her skin like fingers coolly pressing her throat.

"I've only one thing to ask," Nikos said. "After we're married you must never see Ames Rutherford again."

She stared at Nikos, her adoring aging Greek god in his beautiful dark business suit, his black curls singed in gray. Then she laid her head against him, very still.

"Ames Rutherford must never try to see you again, never try to communicate with you in any way, never write anything about you."

Never again, she thought dully. "I can't control another person."

"He's reckless, but he's still a man of honor. You can get his promise."

She dialed the East Hampton area code and the number. The ten digits seemed to have been lying in her memory waiting for this moment.

There were four rings, and then the answering machine came on.

Remembrance stirred in her, aching. The beep came and she realized she hadn't planned what to say.

"Ames . . . this is Vanessa . . . Vanessa Billings . . . I'm calling to . . . I'd like to . . ."

There was a click, and the rattle of a phone snatched up, and then, "Hello? Hello?" He didn't sound angry, as she'd thought he might: just shocked—very, very shocked. "Vanessa?"

She'd never expected to hear his voice saying her name again. Something in her twisted. "I want to see you."

Silence slammed down.

"Do you want to come out here?" he said.

She wanted to, she realized. She wanted to very much. And that scared her. "No," she said quickly. "Someplace nearer. Someplace quiet . . . but public."

There was an instant's hesitation. "Do you know the seminary on Ninth Avenue and Twenty-first Street?"

She wondered why on earth he'd expect her to know a seminary in Chelsea. She wondered why on earth she had a feeling she had heard of one, or glimpsed one. . . .

"I'll find it," she said.

"I'll meet you there tomorrow morning at ten, okay?"

The limousine came to a smooth halt before the wrought-iron gates. The chauffeur hopped out and came around to hold the door. A cool draft swept along Vanessa's legs. She drew her fur around her.

Nikos remained mountainous, staring, a mask. "I'm not going in."

"Nikos—*please!*"

He made his hand soft and cupped it to her face. "You're not a child anymore. Papa can't do this for you."

Vanessa saw finality in Nikos's eyes and pain for them both. An overwhelming aloneness filled her. She stepped obediently from the car and went slowly to the gates.

She walked quickly inside.

44

A BAFFLING FEELING OF FAMILIARITY STAINED EVERYTHING: THE buildings, the paths, the elms and oaks making their strange sighing sounds in the breeze. And then Vanessa saw Ames.

He was pacing under a tree. She watched him light one cigarette from another, then flip the first one away.

He turned, saw her. He came quickly toward her. "You sounded awful on the phone. What's the matter?"

Suddenly everything was impossible—movement, speech, even breathing. They faced each other, frozen in silence.

"Vanessa." He was shaking her and then, without warning, they were pressed together, kissing, whimpering.

"Don't ever let me slip away again." Her hands were pulling at him, holding to him as though if she let go for even an instant he would vanish.

"My car's outside," he said.

"Not that gate. Is there another?"

"In back. Behind the chapel."

Rain clouds were moving rapidly across the sky and there was a dull rumble of thunder as Ames's Mercedes shot across the state line into Maryland. They found a jewelry store in a shopping mall and bought a $30 gold ring.

"I'll get you a real one later," Ames said.

Vanessa kissed him. "This one's real enough."

Ames asked the salesman where you went to get a marriage license in this town. The salesman smiled and drew them a map on the back of the receipt.

The wood-frame house stood on the corner of High Street and River. An old man dressed in a pair of blue jeans and a workshirt answered the doorbell. He had tiny angel's wings of white hair at the sides of his head and he walked with a stoop. "Help you?"

"Marry us," Ames said, handing him the license.

The old man put on his spectacles. "Can do. Come on in."

The house was tidy, with a faint smell of cat. The justice called his wife in from the kitchen. "Mildred, we need a witness."

Mildred nodded hello. She had a thin, masklike face, with large, luminous eyes. As she listened to the ceremony, she dried her hands absentmindedly on her dough-stained apron.

The justice read from a tattered-looking pamphlet. Every time a car passed the house Vanessa's eyes crept to the window and she held her breath, listening to hear if it was slowing down.

"Do you, Ames, take this woman to be your lawfully wedded wife?"

"I do."

"Do you, Vanessa Billings, take this man to be your lawfully wedded husband?"

There was no voice in her. She could only nod her head.

"Was that a yes, Vanessa?"

"Yes," she whispered.

"Ames, you may place the ring on Vanessa's finger."

She felt the warmth of his hand and then a band of coolness sliding onto her finger.

At last, something in her sighed; *at long, long last*.

The justice's voice seemed to come from a great, echoing distance. "By the powers vested in me by the state of Maryland and Cecil County I pronounce you man and wife."

Ames kissed her, and Vanessa saw the reflection of her own eyes shining in his. She had an overpowering, uncanny sense that something had been restored.

When Vanessa and Ames got back to New York, bullets of rain were spattering the sidewalk. They ran into the building.

She'd left a standing lamp on, and a comfortable twilight glow filled the apartment. He peeled her out of her coat.

"There's just one thing I have to do," she said.

"Mmmm, there's just one thing *I* have to do."

"I mean before that. It'll only take a second."

She went to the phone and dialed her answering service. "Molly, it's Vanessa—any messages?"

When she finally replaced the receiver, Ames was smoking a cigarette, watching her.

"Eighteen calls." She sighed. "All from Nikos."

Silence filled the space between them. Ames blew a smoke ring.

"I have to go to him."

Ames didn't answer.

"I have to tell him. I owe him at least that much."

The maid led Vanessa to the library. Nikos greeted her with fond, mournful eyes. "I was worried," he said.

"I'm sorry, Nikos, I—" She realized she was going to hurt him and there was no way of softening the pain. "I've married Ames."

He gazed at her. His chest swelled and a sigh came out of him. "I wanted you free, or not at all. I took a risk and I knew it was a risk. I have no right to complain."

"We didn't plan it. We didn't intend it." She tried to explain, but each word seemed to be a stone piled on him.

"I wish you every happiness," he said.

"Are you going to hate me?"

"I'm not sure. I'm entitled to hate you a little." He kissed her forehead and turned her face so that the lamplight shone in her eyes. "I want to be part of your life, Vanessa."

"You are," she said softly. "You are."

"Will you let me keep helping you? No one need ever know." He touched a finger to her chin and lifted her face up. "It would help me atone for what I never gave *her*."

A whisper came out of her. It came without her will. It came because she had hurt him and at that moment would have done anything never to hurt him again. "Please never stop helping me, Nikos."

Vanessa told her first married lie that night.

Ames had insisted on taking her to Côte Basque for dinner. They were talking animatedly by the time the waiter brought the bottle of Mumm's, and they laughed when spray from the popped cork caught Ames in the face.

"To us," Ames said. "To Mr. and Mrs. Mark Ames Rutherford the Third."

They clinked glasses.

Ames was watching her. "What did Nikos say when you told him?"

The smile froze on her face. She could have said, *He wants to set up a foundation to fund my performances.*

Instead she said, "He wished us every happiness."

"He said that? Every happiness?" Ames smiled. "Here's to Nikos— for losing like a gentleman. God bless him."

That summer, in the Hamptons, they were happy.

Ames actually got to work on the research for his new novel. Vanessa prepared her fall roles: Lucia for Covent Garden; Marguerite for Brussels; Donna Anna for New York. For three sunny months the house rang with clattering typewriter keys and high C's.

"You're singing a helluva lot of crazy ladies this year," Ames joked, and she slapped him on the butt with a score of *Jenufa*. "Another crazy," he said, then added, "Let's make love."

"Later. I'm working and so should you be."

"It's one-thirty on a sunny afternoon and we'll never be this young again. Come on. Please? I'll cook dinner."

She hesitated. "Broiled lobster?"

She awoke in the middle of night. He was not beside her. She got out of bed, curious, and padded barefoot into the corridor.

The door of his workroom was open. He was bent over the typewriter, gazing at a page curling out of the carriage.

She could sense he was stuck. She went quietly and sat down on the floor by his chair.

She'd read his books. They articulated human hope in the face of suffering and she had been moved by them. To her he had the same power as the composers whose melodies she sang. They and Ames brought something beautiful into the world that had never been there before.

She embraced his leg and laid her head on his thigh.

After a moment his hand came down and touched the back of her neck. And then his touch vanished, and the typewriter sprang to life, spitting out a furious rhythm of clicks and bells and slamming carriage returns.

She couldn't help thinking: *I did that for him.*

The next day Ames brought her a tiny bouquet of wild flowers.

"You're my center," he said. "Never leave me."

She couldn't say exactly when she was first aware of changes in her singing, but they began within six months of her marriage.

Occasionally it was just a note placed carelessly—an uncontrolled high B-natural in her Marguerite that broke into a hard cracking sound when she released it. Occasionally it was an entire aria—a "Mi chiamano Mimi" in Brussels that she sang cheaply, not knowing why, doing it anyway, bringing down the house.

She mentioned it to Austin Waters the next time she went to his studio.

He looked over at her and spoke gently. "Audiences like you. And the public is never entirely wrong."

"Austin, stop being tolerant. My performances have been getting cheap. I hear myself doing things . . ."

Ever the diviner of her unspecified demons, he understood the uncompleted thought and laid a paternal hand on her shoulder. "All you can do is prepare, be ready, go on. A performance isn't a master class. You can't be on top of yourself every minute. At some point the performance shapes *you*, not vice versa."

"My performances have been shaping me very strangely lately."

"You've been through a lot of stress. Your life is changing. You're developing."

She sighed. "I'm so damned tired of *developing.*"

"Know what I think you should do?"

She waited to hear the secret of his centeredness, half expecting the name of a guru or a masseur or miracle herb.

"You should take a pupil. Believe me, there's nothing like it for getting your mind off yourself. And you'd be surprised what it can do for your own singing."

* * *

Vanessa found the phone number of the understudy who'd asked to study with her. "Camilla, would you still like me to coach you?"

The presence on the other end of the line seemed to die, then revive. "I sure as hell would—I mean, yes—I mean, when?"

"We'll have to fit it into my schedule, but for a start, how about tomorrow?"

Camilla was willing to take the Long Island Railroad out to the house; no small degree of willingness, considering that it was the slowest and filthiest railroad in the East. There were evenings when she missed her early train back and stayed on for dinner (prepared, deliciously and with good grace, by Ames).

Vanessa loved the lessons, looked forward to them. As a teacher, she was like an accountant with an eye for small change, using a microscope on every detail of the score, seeing things for the first time in the very act of making Camilla see them.

Nothing got past her. Was it correctly phrased? Was the rhythm exact? Was the length of the rest right? Was the *T* articulated? A tone poorly placed, an A-flat just a little too flat, a dotted eighth note not dotted quite long enough—all were enough to cause her to wave Camilla silent and face her, hands on hips.

"Might I ask, Miss Seaton, what the hell was *that*?"

As Camilla trained, she began to be able to do a hundred things that had been too hard for her at first. And little by little the uneasiness rolled off Vanessa and she was at ease again in her own performances.

"Hey, tell me something." Ames turned to her in the car one Thursday in March after they'd delivered Camilla to the last train. "Did I marry a world-famous star or a teacher?"

"You married a world-famous star who's learning to be a terrific teacher."

"Sure you're not spreading yourself a little thin?"

"If it helps my performing, why not?"

"But *does* it help your performing?"

"Come see my *Tosca* run-through and judge for yourself."

As Ames took his seat in the grand tier of the New York Metropolitan, he was full of expectancy and curiosity. Three sinister chords crashed from the orchestra and the curtain rose swiftly. He sat forward, fixing his attention on the action.

Angelotti, a political escapee, rushed into the Church of Sant' Andrea, Rome, where the artist Cavaradossi was painting a portrait of the Madonna. Cavaradossi promised to help Angelotti and hid him in the crypt.

Vanessa entered as Tosca, a celebrated opera singer and Cavaradossi's mistress. She had heard whispering and suspected her lover of deceiving her. When she recognized the model in the portrait as the beautiful Marchesa Attavani, Angelotti's sister, she was convinced of her lover's infidelity. In a soaring duet he managed to appease her jealousy, saying he loved only her, and promised to meet her that night at his villa.

Ames found something inexplicable happening to him. He loved Puccini, he loved *Tosca*, he loved his wife. Yet he couldn't believe Vanessa's character for an instant, couldn't believe she saw value in this—the posturing, the screaming, the exaggeration of emotions that were never credible in the first place. He felt a sort of embarrassment for her.

The elaborate sets struck him as ridiculous, the expensive costumes as foolish and vulgar. *People are starving in the world*, he thought, *and foundations are spending money on this.*

When Tosca made her exit, he didn't applaud.

What the hell's happening to me? he wondered. *Am I turning into an opera-hating curmudgeon?*

Uneasiness whispered through him, and it wasn't just because a cannon boomed offstage, signaling that Angelotti's escape had been discovered. It was because he could feel himself turning into someone else, someone he didn't know.

Cavaradossi exited, spiriting Angelotti with him to the safety of his villa outside Rome.

Scarpia, the chief of police, entered in a black cloak. He found the Marchesa Attavani's fan, bearing the family's coat of arms. Recognizing her as the model in the portrait and knowing that Cavaradossi was sympathetic to the revolutionary cause, he suspected that the painter might be involved in Angelotti's escape.

As Act One wore on Ames broke into a cold sweat. His heart began thudding like an eight-foot bass drum. The music which had once seemed so melodious and sweeping and passionate suddenly sounded thin, with no point except the resounding high notes. Though as operas went the story was not nearly so fraught and phony as most of the standard repertoire, today it struck him as the worst sort of melodrama, with coincidences scattered like raindrops in a storm.

Tosca returned. Scarpia showed her the fan as proof that her lover was deceiving her. Convinced, she set off in a rage to find Cavaradossi. Scarpia dispatched an agent to follow her. To the counterpoint of a church choir, Scarpia blasphemously plotted with a crony to execute Cavaradossi and make Tosca his own mistress. "Tosca, you make me forget my God!" Then, in an access of sexual fervor, he joined in the *Te Deum.*

The curtain fell.

Ames stayed in his seat through the first intermission. A hatred filled him stronger than any he had ever known in his life. It was a slashing, annihilating hatred that wanted to rip apart curtains, knock over sets, tear pages from scores, burn down opera houses.

After a stomach-churning eternity the houselights dimmed to the halfway mark, warning the audience back to their seats. The theater went dark and the curtain rose on Scarpia's office in the Farnese Palace.

As Scarpia dined, his agents dragged in Cavaradossi. Scarpia interrogated him, but the painter refused to reveal Angelotti's whereabouts.

Tosca entered, and Scarpia ordered Cavaradossi into the next room to be tortured. Unable to bear the sounds of her lover's screams, Tosca revealed that Angelotti was hiding in the well at her lover's villa. As the guard led him through the room, Cavaradossi turned on her furiously, accusing her of betrayal.

Alone with Tosca now, Scarpia stated his bargain: her lover would be executed unless she consented to become his mistress.

Like a trapped animal, Tosca fled to the window that only moments before she had threatened to throw herself from. Across the room, the gloating Scarpia reminded her that her lover had only one hour to live.

In the distance a military drum rapped out the cadence of a death march. Tosca raised her head and listened.

There is a silent beat to music that underlies the heard beat. It is not the inanimate ticktock of a metronome or the movement of a conductor's baton marking off measures, but the pumping of a living heart. All musicians hear it and follow it. Thanks to this silent beat an entire orchestra can rise out of dead silence and attack a note together, slow down or hasten a phrase together, or meet the soprano just as she brings her trill to a safe finish. Thanks to this beat vocalists can hold together during the wildest stretches of the wildest duets.

Vanessa listened now for this beat.

The near-emptiness of the house answered her.

For an instant she saw the dim glitter of the tiered balconies, and perhaps it was only her imagination, but she had a flash of Ames with his elbows propped on one of the railings. It seemed to her he had a disgusted look on his face.

What must he think of all this hollering? she wondered.

Her lungs expanded, drawing in air, but for a moment only. She felt a ripple of disorientation. In one glance she saw the baritone, oozing operatic menace in his eighteenth-century costume, and just beyond him in the wings, scratching his ear and radiating boredom, a stagehand in overalls.

What nonsense this is. What am I standing here for?

She was ludicrously aware that she was moving across a false set in the false glow of electric lights surrounded by false shadows.

She missed her entrance.

Boyd Kinsolving rapped his baton on the music stand, silencing the orchestra. "Can we take it again from number 34?" He gazed questioningly at Vanessa. "Sweetums, are you all right?"

Even with the house dark and still, Ames could feel her not sleeping, could feel the racing of her thoughts on the pillow beside him. Finally he flicked the light on.

"Okay," he said, "let's both stop pretending. I know you're not asleep, you know I'm not asleep. We'd better talk about it."

She sat up, stared at him. "I felt something happen in the opera house today. Just before I missed my cue."

He nodded. "I felt it too."

"What was it, Ames?"

He shook his head helplessly. "I don't know."

"It was as though something were pouring out of you—something terrible and almost . . . *hating*."

He sighed. "Sometimes I wish you weren't so damned intuitive."

"What were you hating, Ames?"

"It just came over me that I was going to lose you."

She stared in drop-jawed amazement. "Lose me how?"

"I don't know. But I could feel the music taking you from me, swallowing you up like quicksand."

"Come on, I know Puccini can be soupy, but *quicksand* . . ." She was silent a moment. "Ames, how many of my performances have you been to?"

"I don't know. Dozens, I suppose."

"Have you ever felt this hatred before?"

"Never."

She gazed at him a long, searching moment. "Today was the first time you've heard me perform since we were married."

"How could that have anything to do with—"

"I'm not certain, but when we married, something changed in my voice. I know it sounds superstitious, but damn it, Ames, singers *are* superstitious. At least *this* singer is."

He was silent.

"I love you, Ames. I've loved you from the very first moment we met. Sometimes I feel I've loved from long before that first moment. I'd do anything in the world for you."

He caught something held back in her. "But?" he said.

"But today I was terrified."

"And?"

"And I don't want you to come to any of my performances ever again."

The surprising thing to Ames was that he *wasn't* surprised.

He felt darkness encroaching, he felt Vanessa drifting away from him, but he felt no surprise at all.

He reached to the bedside table, lit a cigarette, blew out smoke. "So it would appear I'm a big bad magician and I put curses on pretty little singers."

"Do you think I'm just being neurotic?"

He shook his head. "If anyone should be seeing a shrink it's me. Something crazy came over me today and you felt it."

"And everything in me stopped and the sound wouldn't come. Ames, I've failed so often, I can't afford another failure."

He kissed her as though it were all very understandable. "Look, you're not going to fail. And I won't come to any more of your performances, okay?"

"Are you angry?"

"I love you."

"But are you angry?"

"Not angry—a little mystified, that's all."

The baritone reminded her, chillingly, that her lover had only an hour to live.

Vanessa stood at the window staring out for three bars.

When she turned back toward the audience she was different. Everything about her had somehow altered during those few seconds.

It was difficult to describe what the difference was, but going to the window she had been Vanessa Billings playing a better-than-decent Tosca, and when she turned around again a totally changed person presented herself to the audience.

She crossed to the sofa, sank slowly down onto it.

Scarpia, cold and cynical, poured his coffee and sipped.

The orchestra subsided.

The audience sat forward in their seats, hushed.

There was an instant's total silence.

She raised her head. A sound came out of her, startling in its purity.

"*Vissi d'arte, vissi d'amore* . . ."—"I have lived for art, I have lived for love . . ."

What happened in the opera house was something beyond the words, beyond the musical notes. The aria seemed to lose its identity feature by feature, to dissolve into a sort of limitless music that in turn dissolved into pure supplication.

Listening, the audience changed. It was as though every man and woman in that dark house were recalling the time when as children they had begged most hopelessly for the life of a pet or for a wish, or as adults for the life of another person, or for a dream, or perhaps for love itself.

And when God had, inexplicably, refused.

"Perchè, Signor, ah perchè me ne rimuneri cosi?"—"Why, ah why, Lord, do you repay me thus?"

The question hung in the air, unanswered.

Applause did not come immediately. Too many of the audience were holding back sniffles. There was a moment of handkerchiefs slipping back into pockets and purses before the bravas and screams ripped through the dark.

And then a police agent entered with word that Angelotti had committed suicide. Scarpia asked Tosca her decision: Would she become his mistress or would she let her lover die?

Grimly, she nodded. She would become his mistress.

Scarpia instructed the agent to arrange a mock execution, with blanks instead of bullets. The agent went, and Tosca demanded a safe-conduct for herself and Cavaradossi. Scarpia quickly wrote it out. Tosca took a knife from the dining table and hid it behind her. As Scarpia came to embrace her, she plunged the blade into his stomach. He crumpled. She searched frantically for the safe-conduct, found it. Suddenly she thought to set two candles beside the dead body and a crucifix on the breast.

And then she fled.

In her dressing room Vanessa settled down uneasily into a chair and looked across at her understudy. "How am I doing?"

Camilla stared at her unbelievingly. "You have to ask?"

"It's such a can't-miss act they applaud even when I'm lousy."

"You're never lousy."

"My rehearsal was lousy and I feel I'm lousy tonight."

"You're terrific tonight."

"Am I? I don't seem to be there for the big moments. I remember going to the window. I remember stabbing Scarpia—but in between's a blank. I don't remember singing 'Vissi d'arte.'"

Camilla looked at her teacher in amazement. "You're kidding. That was the best 'Vissi d'arte' I've ever heard."

Vanessa felt herself floating through the last act.

The curtain rose on the battlements of Castle Sant' Angelo, where the guards were preparing Cavaradossi for execution. Tosca entered with her safe-conduct and told him the execution would be a hoax. The lovers sang rapturously of their future happiness.

The firing squad arrived. Tosca instructed Cavaradossi how to die realistically. The soldiers fired. Cavaradossi fell to the ground.

"Ecco un artista!"—"That is an artist!" Tosca exclaimed.

But when she rushed to Cavaradossi's side he didn't move. She realized Scarpia had tricked her: the bullets had been real. Her lover was dead.

Guards rushed in to arrest her. She ran to the parapet, pausing only to cry: *"Scarpia, avanti a Dio!"*—"Scarpia, we will meet before God!" And then she jumped to her death.

The audience called her back for eight solo bows. The next day the *Times* called Vanessa's the *most sensational Tosca since Callas. This was opera at its most unabashedly grand. Brava, Billings!*

45

WHEN VANESSA SANG IN NEW YORK AMES COULD SURVIVE THE seven-hour stretches without her. But when she sang in Europe there were twelve-day stretches without her, chunks of blank time when he wandered the house listening to waves, trying to write, not writing, trying to eat and not eating, looking at the level in the vodka bottle going down and not knowing how it was going down so fast.

And then one morning he lifted his head from the typewriter and found her bending over him.

"Please be happy, Ames. You've got the best of me. What's onstage isn't me. It's just something I have to do. Come to bed."

"I'm sorry," he slurred, thinking, *What in God's name am I turning into?*

When he woke up, hangover and guilt pressed on him like a metal sky. She had errands that kept her out of the house, and he was glad of it. He prepared dinner: rolled veal stuffed with sage and sausage and grated lemon peel, zucchini with lemon butter, potato croquettes handmade from first peel to final sizzle; hot sourdough rolls; a nice chilled jug of German Riesling.

He set sandalwood-scented candles on the table and lit them and had just one glass of wine and waited and wondered what was keeping her.

What was keeping her was her seventeen-year-old lover.

One hundred and eighty miles away, at the Metropolitan Opera House, Vanessa was singing the Marschallin in Act One of *Der Rosenkavalier*—the Knight of the Rose—a bitter-sweet comedy set in eighteenth-century Vienna.

The curtain had risen on a sumptuous bedroom. Just as the Marschallin and her cousin Octavian were awakening from a night of rapturous lovemaking, a man could be heard pushing his way past the servants into her chamber. Octavian slipped into one of the Marschallin's dresses, disguising himself as a chambermaid, "Mariandel."

The intruder turned out to be another cousin of the Marschallin, the pompous and oafish Baron Ochs, requesting a favor. Always short of cash, he had become engaged to the daughter of a newly ennobled merchant. He needed a young nobleman to present the traditional silver rose to his fiancée. The Marschallin suggested he use Octavian.

Throughout the discussion Ochs flirted outrageously with "Mariandel." Since the role of Octavian was sung by a mezzo, the baritone playing Ochs was in fact ogling a woman playing a man pretending to be a woman.

The Marschallin's morning reception began. A horde of petitioners and shopkeepers surged in. Among them were Valzacchi and Annina, two professional intriguers offering to sell the Marschallin a scandal sheet. Ochs hired them to investigate his bride-to-be.

The crowd finally departed, leaving the Marschallin in a sad mood. She reflected that Octavian would soon tire of her and fall in love with a younger woman. Octavian tried to reassure her, but after he left she realized they had forgotten to kiss goodbye. She sent her page after him with the box containing Ochs's silver rose.

Ames went into the kitchen and checked the calendar on the side of the refrigerator where Vanessa wrote her engagements. He wondered how he could have missed it. The date was clearly marked. She was singing that night at the Metropolitan.

He went to the garage and got into the car and backed into the driveway and drove. Just drove.

Vanessa, like most sopranos able to sing her, loved the Marschallin. The character had beauty, intelligence, humor, and generosity—not to mention some of the loveliest pages Richard Strauss had ever composed and—a big plus—though she opened and closed the opera, she didn't appear in the middle act.

Which gave Vanessa time to rest, time to sip fruit juice, time to write letters.

Two stories above her the opera continued. In her father's palace, young Sophie van Faninal eagerly awaited her first meeting with her fiancé. Octavian entered and ceremoniously presented her with the silver rose. The two instantly fell in love.

Ochs arrived, oozing crudeness and shocking his fiancée. While he discussed the terms of the marriage contract with Faninal, Sophie—repelled—begged Octavian to save her from the baron. The young nobleman swore to stand by her.

Valzacchi and Annina alerted Ochs. The baron tried to pull Sophie from the room, but Octavian drew his sword, challenged the old lecher, and nicked him in the arm. Crying "Murder!" the baron called for a doctor.

Defying her father, Sophie flatly refused to marry Ochs. Faninal threatened to send her to a convent.

Octavian hit upon a plan.

Annina entered and handed the baron a note from "Mariandel," the Marschallin's supposed chambermaid, requesting a tryst. The baron, delighted, promised to reply.

* * *

Ames checked his Mercedes into the parking lot under Lincoln Center. Up on the plaza, an old woman with a mink as frizzy as her hair was hawking a balcony seat for the last act of *Der Rosenkavalier.*

The seat was practically at the top of the house. Ames sat tapping his fingers together, staring at the stage.

Why am I doing this? he suddenly thought. *Why am I here?*

The curtain rose on a private room in a rather shady tavern where Valzacchi and Annina were arranging the final details of Ochs's rendezvous. Octavian, dressed as "Mariandel," tossed them a purse. He returned on the arm of Baron Ochs, who—to save money—dismissed the waiters.

"Mariandel" and Ochs settled down to dinner and seduction, but "she" refused to drink and resisted Ochs's advances, pointing out that he was, after all, engaged.

On prearranged signals, Octavian's accomplices popped out of chests and openings in walls. The baron was convinced he was hallucinating. Annina burst in, insisting that Ochs was her husband and had abandoned her. Four children rushed in, loudly claiming Ochs as their father.

Outraged, the baron called for the police.

The knock came on the door and the call, "Three minutes, Miss Billings."

Vanessa moved toward the mirror, glancing one last time at her costume. A sudden nausea gripped her. She began to sway. Her dresser caught her and helped her back into the chair.

She knew what the matter was. *Ames is here—in the house.* She could barely force sound out of her throat. "Call my understudy," she told the dresser. "I can't go on."

It was like coming out of a blackout.

"Excuse me." Ames rose and, ignoring his neighbors' annoyance, squeezed his way into the aisle. It was a long dark walk down to the exit.

As abruptly as the spell had come, it passed. Vanessa drew in a breath, drinking up air. *He's gone.*

Another knock at the door. "Places."

She was able to rise, to walk, to cross to the door and turn the handle. She saw relief on her dresser's face.

"Tell Camilla it was a false alarm. I'm going on."

Faninal and Sophie, summoned by Valzacchi, arrived at the tavern, followed by the Marschallin. Immediately grasping the situation, the

Marschallin assured the police commissar that the whole affair was only a farce. Then, with kind firmness, she advised Ochs that he had lost Sophie and had better accept the fact.

Ames walked through traffic and fumes, passed signs and shops that were strange to him. He came to a stone wall between two ivied brick buildings. There was an iron gate and it seemed to him this was his destination. He opened the gate and went through.

The young lovers and the Marschallin were now alone on the stage. Their voices rose in a sublime trio, Octavian and Sophie lost in their love for one another, the Marschallin gracefully accepting the inevitable.

The Marschallin departed with Faninal. A moment later Sophie and Octavian followed. The Marschallin's page returned to retrieve a handkerchief Sophie had dropped. The curtain fell to a final sparkle of melody.

Ames wasn't home when the limousine brought Vanessa back to the house in East Hampton. She found the table set for dinner, candles long gutted onto the mahogany, food ice-cold. She put the veal and vegetables away and made herself some Sanka.

Ames came through the door at 2:30.

"Pull up a cup," she said.

They sat sipping and chewing and finally she mentioned the obvious. "That was quite some feast somebody made and didn't eat."

"Would've been."

"You're home late."

"Sorry about that. How was the performance?"

"So-so." After a silence, "You took the car?"

"I went into New York."

He was in the opera house tonight, she thought. And then, *No, he promised . . . he wouldn't have . . .*

"I went to that old seminary," he said. "Remember, where we met the day we got married?"

"Why in the world did you want to go there?"

"It's a beautiful old place. It doesn't seem to be part of New York at all. I just sat there and watched the night get darker."

He broke off and she had a sense that he was only halfway to the center of his thought.

"I don't care for that seminary," she said. "It reminds me of a graveyard." She wanted to say something stupid. She wanted to say that the dead cast longer shadows than the living. She wanted to say, *I wish you wouldn't go there ever again.*

She said it in her own roundabout way. "Next week's our anniversary—April ninth. If I canceled some performances, we could have the whole week to ourselves."

"Come on, you can't cancel."

"Sure I can." *No I can't, no, I shouldn't, no, I mustn't, but I'm going to.* "It's only two *Toscas*. Camilla can go on for me."

"Why, you irresponsible little superstar. Honey, I love you." He leaned across the table and kissed her and then he grabbed her. "You know why I've been acting so rotten lately? I was thinking you'd . . . I don't know, forgotten me."

"Ames, you beautiful fool."

"I don't know about beautiful, but sometimes I am undeniably a fool."

The next morning Vanessa phoned Richard Schiller and told him she was going to be sick for the week of the ninth.

He was icily silent.

"Richard, at this point my marriage needs me more than those *Toscas* do."

"Let's pack a picnic and take a hike," Ames said. The sky was blue and the weather was freakishly warm for the season—almost summery. It was the first day of their vacation, their hooky, and he felt a crazy, schoolboyish excitement.

"You're on," she said.

They went barefoot on the shore. The air had the clean salt smell of ocean. They followed the dark line of the outgoing tide, past the beach houses, and then they turned and went up into the dunes and spread their checkered tablecloth on the grass.

They shared a loaf of French bread and a sixth of a wheel of runny Brie. The weather was warm, the air mild, the wind seemed to have a shine on it. They passed a bottle of *vino rosso da tavola* back and forth.

The sound of waves was heavy and muffled. He followed the direction of her eyes. "What are you seeing?"

"Over the horizon," she said. "London and Paris and Frankfurt."

"Don't. Pretend the horizon isn't there."

"It came back just then, that feeling. Being penned in. November. Three *Lulus* and seven *Esclarmondes*."

"A bitch and a witch do not a death sentence make."

"Hamburg one day, Milan the next, San Francisco the day after and never a stop. Sometimes it seems like forever."

"Forever can be a lot of things. Forever is the next six days, too."

He pulled her down beside him and they lay side by side, the sun warm on their backs, the windborne seaspray a faint mist on their skins. They made lingering lazy love in the open air. There were tears in her eyes and he looked down at her and saw a little girl, astonishment floating on her face like a moon in the sky.

"You know what we're having?" she said. "Our second affair."

"I can't think of any better way of picking up a marriage, can you?"

It was perfect till seven o'clock on the fourth day.

Afternoon had become an evening light saturated with purple. Vanessa and Ames were together on the terrace. In the distance a car hummed past and then stopped and made a backing-up sound. There was a crunch of wheels on gravel.

"Visitor," Ames groaned.

A figure was coming across the lawn. It was Camilla Seaton. "I'm sorry," she said. "I should have phoned, but . . ."

"This one's for you," Ames whispered. He excused himself, saying he had a date with a flounder in the kitchen.

Camilla sat. There was emptiness in her eyes.

"What's the matter?" Vanessa said.

It took Camilla a long moment to begin speaking. She said her *Tosca* had bombed. There'd been dead silence after her "Vissi d'arte." She hadn't been able to find the knife to stab Scarpia and, startled by the snaredrum roll, she had dropped the crucifix instead of placing it on his chest.

"That's all?" Vanessa said, though it was plenty.

"Will you go over the role with me? Tonight?" Suddenly Camilla was sitting forward in her chair. "I brought my score, I have a tape, and if you could just show me where I'm going wrong . . ."

Vanessa's eye went to the kitchen window, to Ames's shadow cutting back and forth through the light. "Not tonight." She couldn't bear to look at the girl. Couldn't bear to say that for the first time in her life she was happy. "I'm having difficulties of my own."

Camilla sat absolutely still, enclosed in a pocket of silence.

"We'll work on it later," Vanessa said. "Next month."

"Not till next *month?*"

"We'll go over the score note by note," Vanessa said, hating herself, hating this life that always demanded you hurt yourself or hurt someone else, and then thinking, *No, the whole point is I love my life.*

"What was that all about?" Ames asked over a candlelit dinner of filet of flounder stuffed with crab.

"Nothing. She was just a little nervous."

It was cool and fresh and sunny the next morning, their anniversary. A golden omen. Ames fried eggs for breakfast and managed to break only one of the yolks. They walked barefoot along the shore, saw dew glittering on the beach grass and felt lucky.

"Hey, honey," he said, "I have an idea for tonight. Let's stay home and stuff ourselves silly on all sorts of great food no one in their right minds would eat . . ."

"Like lobster thermidor?"

"And wine and pastry, a lot of pastry. That should keep us busy till eleven or so, and then we can forget about the dishes and sit out on the terrace and look at the moon and . . ."

He kissed her, a long teasing kiss.

"I like that *and*," she said.

"I have to go into town and pick up a few things. You stay right here, okay?"

"I haven't got anything else planned."

"Promise?"

She laughed and closed her eyes. "Promise."

He drove into East Hampton. As he walked along the main street happiness enveloped him like an invisible coat.

He had to wait in the fish store for the lobster and in the pastry shop for hazelnut tortes. He thought of a dozen other little surprises like the set of Pierre Deux napkins he knew she wanted and he had to wait in a dozen other shops. He didn't mind the waiting one bit. He kept seeing her laughing with her eyes shut in the sun.

Adolf Erdlich phoned. "Vanessa, you've got to sing tonight."

"No way, Adolf. I'm sick. Officially."

"And your understudy is sick, genuinely. Camilla spent the night in emergency at Lenox Hill. Apparently she mistook sleeping pills for vitamin pills."

"Oh, my God—no. Will she be all right?"

"She'll be all right. Her *Tosca* is another matter. Over a third of our subscribers have phoned in donating their seats to the musicians' fund."

Light fell through the window lattice of wood and putty. Vanessa's eye followed the slope of the lawn down to the shore. The sun was at noon in the sky, flinging a brilliant path in the Atlantic between East Hampton and all the opera houses of Europe.

"There's no one else who can sing tonight?"

"You contracted to perform two *Tosca*s this week," the voice on the phone said. "We've let you out of one of them. We need you very, very badly tonight. A car will be at your house to pick you up at three o'clock."

Vanessa heard herself say, "I'll be ready."

She wanted to explain. She *had* to explain.

But Ames wasn't there and Adolf Erdlich's onyx-black limousine was. She made the driver wait fifteen minutes and then another fifteen minutes and Ames's car still hadn't turned into the drive.

At 3:30 she scrawled a note and taped it to the Chemex in the kitchen.

Ames returned a little after four.

"Vanessa?"

His glance moved from room to room, scanning.

"Honey?"

His insides went from hope to uncertainty to foreboding. He had an unlit cigarette in his mouth when he found the piece of paper taped to the Chemex.

Darling—I waited till three-thirty. Camilla is badly hurt and can't go on. They need me. Please forgive. I love you, I'll make it up to you. Promise. XXXXX OOOOO Vanessa

In the ten seconds it took him to read the looping scrawl he aged from a little boy filled with love to an old man with nothing but hate in his heart. He smashed the Chemex against the wall, then stared in disbelief at his bleeding hand.

What the hell is happening to me?

An inkling came to him, a tiny last pin-speck of hope. He picked up the phone in his workroom and dialed.

"Dad, it's Ames. I've got to talk to you. Can you see me right away?"

46

"DAD, WHAT I HAVE TO ASK YOU MAY SOUND STRANGE."

"Ask it."

"After you left Ariana, what were your feelings toward music?"

"Music?" The bishop inhaled deeply. "I felt music had taken her from me. For ten horrible years I hated it. Vocal music enraged me. Opera . . . destroyed me. I wanted to kick down the sets and throttle the singers."

For an instant there was not a breath of air in the study, and then a soft wind sighed through the curtains.

"And now?"

"Now?" The bishop smiled a smile touched with pain long dead. "Now I'm as musical as the next prelate."

"You can go to concerts?"

"Certainly."

"Opera?"

"I go now and then if I'm invited."

"And you've stopped hating?"

"I had no choice. There's an awful lot of Bach in my business."

"How did you manage to change?"

"I prayed for the strength. I built up a tolerance, listened to records, made myself go to symphonies. One day I went to a vocal recital. It wasn't easy, but it didn't kill me. And then I took a real plunge and went to the opera. It hurt, but I survived."

Ames couldn't help but feel admiration for his father, this man who might have been a stockbroker but who had kicked over the traces and put on a clerical collar and cantered so far from Wall Street, who had faced disappointment and broken himself of it as one would a bad habit. "Did you ever go to any of her performances again?"

The bishop exhaled. "Only . . . in my mind. But I bought all her recordings. Sometimes . . . I play them."

Late that night, Ames walked around the edge of the woods and down to the water. Cool foam lapped at his bare feet.

A car engine growled. A moment later, up where the beach threaded into the dunes, Vanessa's shape was moving toward him. They kissed. He asked about her performance.

"Ames, I'm sorry—"

"Hey, don't be sorry. Work's work. Did you knock 'em dead?"

She smiled. "I knocked 'em dead."

They strolled a moment. She asked about his day.

"Know something funny? My day was goddamned wonderful."

For three days longer they were happy.

And then Camilla phoned Vanessa in tears over pans she'd gotten from the critics for a *Pagliacci* in Philadelphia.

Vanessa made reassuring sounds ("No one can sing that role two days out of the hospital"), but the conversation left her feeling it was her fault, that if she would only lead Camilla through the score point by point all would be well.

For two days guilt obsessed her. Finally she phoned Richard Schiller. "I've got to take next week off."

"You can't. You're singing in San Francisco."

"You have to get me out of it."

"Why?"

What could she tell him? That she felt a compulsion to give lessons to her pupil? "I feel queasy. Jinxed."

"Let's have lunch. You can tell me about it."

They had lunch at a quiet corner table in the little French place down Fifty-fifth Street from the agency. Richard listened to her.

"You're not Camilla's mother. Her performances are her responsibility, not yours."

"She's my pupil. She helped me."

"*She* helped *you?* This I'd like to hear."

"She let me teach her."

Richard's eyebrows arched. "She *let* you teach her?"

"Yes, let me. And then I dropped her."

He shook his head. "So? If it's that important you'll teach her after San Francisco." He reached across the tablecloth to squeeze her hand. "Relax, will you? You're happily married, you're in perfect health, you're in the best voice you've ever been, you'll be carried by satellite and two hundred million people will be watching and do you know what that will do to your record sales?"

"Then why do I feel so rotten?"

"Artists are supposed to feel rotten. Now eat your vichyssoise. It's getting warm."

Four days later, despite misgivings, Vanessa yielded to her agent's advice and boarded Eastern Airlines Flight 309 from New York to San Francisco.

A ghostly voice was talking in the empty office. "Mark Ames Rutherford the Third, trailblazing author of *The Fortress*, is the first writer to explore the hidden and insidious links behind the vaults of Chase Manhattan and the Trevantine marble walls at Lincoln Center."

The sound was coming from the phone-answering machine and it very much resembled Dill Switt in one of his antic moods.

Ames couldn't resist lifting the receiver. "*Hidden, insidious?* I do believe you're a little bit high, Dill."

"*Looped* is the polite word. I've been sitting in the Lion's Head drinking chilled Beaujolais with a young lady who happens to be an ace reporter for the *Wall Street Journal* and, here's the interesting part, an opera buff. Now pay close heed. The price of a glass of chilled Beaujolais just dropped thirty percent. And why did the price just drop? Because the French devalued the franc ten days ago. And why did they do that? Because of the collaboration, witting or un-, of well-intentioned solid citizens like your lovely wife the songbird with international sleaze like Niko the Greeko."

"Dill, I'd rather you didn't make jokes like that."

"Who's joking? You gotta know that Nikos Stratiotis uses his dollar holdings as margin to speculate against European currencies."

"So does every bank in New York City and Zurich."

"But Stratiotis hasn't paid a cent in American corporate taxes in twenty years. He has charitable foundations to offset income."

"That happens to be how the big boys do it."

"The other big boys don't do it with Stratiotis's flair. To quote from a program of the Chicago Opera: 'This production of *Il Trovatore* was made possible by the deeply appreciated generosity of the Stratiotis Foundation for the Fine Arts.' I translate freely from a recent program of the Paris Opéra: 'The management wishes to acknowledge the extraordinary generosity of the Foundation Stratiotis in the preparation of this production of *Romeo et Juliette*.' "

"Okay," Ames conceded. "Some men back horses. Stratiotis backs opera. What's your point?"

"Stratiotis backs your wife's productions, dumbo. Hers and hers alone."

Ames fought to muster disbelief. *I'm not hearing this. Dill's lying. No, not lying. Mistaken. An honest mistake.*

"That's not true," he heard himself saying. "Vanessa hasn't had anything to do with Stratiotis for over a year."

"Oh, no? Look at the programs of the Barcelona Lyric, Teatro Colón, La Scala. Look at last week's program at the New York Metropolitan, for God's sake. 'The Metropolitan Opera wishes to acknowledge—' "

Ames tried to blot out the words, tried to concentrate on the waves breaking softly forty feet from the house. But something twisted in him and then collapsed. "I want to meet your friend from the *Wall Street Journal*. I want to see these programs."

"Lisa and I are having dinner at Carnaby's at eight-thirty. The table can seat three."

❁   ❁   ❁

Ames met them at the restaurant, the newest, innest dining spot in SoHo. He studied five opera programs while Dill and his date shared a rack of lamb. The programs were all recent, in different languages but with two things in common: Billings singing, Stratiotis funding.

"I have others at home," the girl said. "Cartons full. He's been backing her for years."

Ames decided to speak to Stratiotis directly. He phoned the Wall Street office and, using a forgivable bit of subterfuge, identified himself as Stan Billings, Vanessa's father.

The secretary's voice suddenly glowed with pleasantness. "You can reach Mr. Stratiotis in San Francisco, sir. I'll give you his number."

The flight across the continent was a dark, dreamlike glide of six hours, and then the buildings and streets of San Francisco were moving past the taxi window like unreal shadows on glass.

A spring rain was slanting down and it was 7:55 when Ames arrived at the opera house, a small jewel of a building on Van Ness. He threaded his way through streams of opera patrons. An usher handed him his program and showed him his seat. He sat and opened the program. *Please, God, let me be wrong. Let it all be my paranoid imagination.*

His eye skimmed quickly down the names of the performers.

And there it was, the small italicized mention at the bottom of the page. *This performance of* La Traviata *is made possible by a deeply appreciated grant from the Stratiotis Foundation for the Fine Arts.*

In her dressing room, Vanessa felt uneasy, curiously remote, her eyelids shut down over a foreboding she couldn't quite articulate.

The makeup woman daubed with a powder puff at her forehead.

And suddenly Vanessa knew. "He's here. He's in the house . . ."

The dresser threw her a startled glance before tilting her chin up and correcting the shading of her brow. "Yes indeed, ma'am, Callas used to feel just like that before she sang Violetta."

Ames shifted in his seat, glanced at his watch. The second hand seemed to crawl. *All right, so Stratiotis happens to be in the same city where she's singing a performance. What does that prove?*

Finally the houselights dimmed. From the orchestra pit came soft rustlings. An oboe chirped. There was applause as the conductor entered the pit.

Ames made a deeply concentrated effort to listen.

So he happens to be in the same city where she's singing a performance he happened to finance. So maybe he's been in a few cities where

425

she's been singing performances he happened to finance. Maybe quite a few cities. What does that prove?

He was suffocating. He couldn't endure not moving.

I don't want to see this.

Vanessa's hands made a protective circle around the locket, drawing strength from it. The premonition lifted, leaving a merciful blank. She couldn't even remember what had been bothering her—something frightening and fantastic and foolish.

A knock came at the door and the cry, "Places, Miss Billings!"

Vanessa rose. With a smile, the dresser pulled the door open.

Impulsively, Vanessa kissed her.

Ames drank three double martinis. The bartender had a bushy mustache and the bar had a rich mahogany glow.

Every now and then a door opened and her voice rocketed through the silence, soaring so lightly, so swiftly that Ames's ear could hardly follow its flight.

The performance ended. Applause broke like a storm. Vanessa's tenor took her hand and led her through the curtain.

For a moment the whole world blazed up into glory. She stood in the spotlight with the applause and torn programs and tossed flowers raining down. With a smile she acknowledged the deafening acclamation and made a deep curtsy.

Ames could hear the crowd calling her name like wind in a forest. He stretched a twenty-dollar bill out flat on the bar and snapped a finger to catch the bartender's attention.

"How do I get backstage?"

The air in the corridor pressed down heavy and stagnant. Ames found the door. He raised his hand and gave two knocks, and it was opened by a little gray-haired woman.

"Yes, sir?"

Behind her he could see Vanessa relaxing in an armchair, still in costume. And then she saw him.

For a split second she stared in open horror and then she stretched out a hand and attempted a smile. "Ames."

In the instant that she moved toward him he was aware of the other presence in the room, the tall figure in a dark suit waiting near the dimly lit window.

Nikos Stratiotis turned to face him. Their eyes locked.

"I understand," Ames said quietly. "I finally understand."

"Ames," Vanessa whispered, "no!"

Nikos moved a three-legged stool toward him. "You don't understand anything. Sit down."

Ames swiped the stool aside. It fell with a sideways crash to the floor. "Do you know how lonely and empty I felt when you were with him? I knew there had to be a reason you didn't want me at your performances, but I never dreamed it was Stratiotis!"

Terror splashed Vanessa's face. "Ames, you're wrong."

"And drunk," Nikos said. "A pity you can't keep your mouth as closed as your mind for ten seconds and let us explain—"

Ames whirled on him. "I wanted this woman, I loved her, and unlike you I married her!"

Vanessa reached out. "Ames, I swear!"

"You swore to love, honor, and cherish me—me, not him! What the hell did you want me for, a false front?"

"Ames, you have it all wrong!"

She tried to explain, but he strode from the dressing room and didn't even bother slamming the door behind him.

It seemed an eternity later that the knocking came.

"Miss Billings." The assistant stage manager had an apologetic expression. "We've raised the houselights, but they're still applauding. Would you mind one more curtain call?"

Nikos interposed himself. "Miss Billings is exhausted."

"It's all right, Nikos." She moved past him. "They're my friends. I owe them this."

He couldn't read her intention, but he felt something in her, firm and formed and secret.

"You go on to the party," she said. "Sally will help me change."

The dresser smiled, liking to be needed. "Yes, ma'am."

Vanessa kissed Nikos lightly. "I'll meet you there in half an hour."

The opera house roared. Rising to their feet, the cheering, glittering crowd gave her three more curtain calls.

It had been the most brilliant performance of a brilliant career: a faultless *Traviata*. They knew it; she knew it.

At that instant she was, arguably, what half the critics in the world called her: the greatest soprano of the day.

Vanessa hurried back to her dressing room. She leaned a moment against the shut door and closed her eyes. Her knees began to buckle. She held the back of a chair an instant before sitting.

Sally brought a glass of warm milk flavored with molasses. Vanessa sipped. Sally watched with a satisfied look and took the glass.

"Shall I draw your bath?" Sally offered.

"No, thanks, I'll do it. I'd like to be by myself for a while."

Alone, Vanessa began undressing. Her movements were automatic, the unthinking reflex of a singer protecting her costume and at the same time divesting herself of what she had been onstage.

She unhooked the thin gold chain from around her neck and let it slide through her fingers. The locket slipped down onto the dressing table. She lost her eyes a moment in it. The tiny gems gleamed back at her, hard and unyielding as justice without mercy.

A last sickening conviction settled itself onto her mind. *I can never have both. It will always be music or life. Never both.*

She knew what had to be done. There was nothing to be gained by delay.

With a quick swipe of her arm she swept the locket aside. It thudded lightly against the carpet.

She ripped a piece of paper from the notepad on the dresser.

She scrawled three words.

Forgive me, Ariana.

She drew a hot bath and sprinkled the tub with a handful of verbena salts. It was like a scene in an opera in which she was performer and audience at the same time. She observed her actions with detachment and a strange sense of completion.

She took a tape cassette from the dressing table. She did not look at herself in the mirror. She slid the cassette into the player and pressed a button.

A moment later a pure soprano voice filled the room like a soft fountain of prayer.

The bathroom was misty, like early morning. A silver haze shimmered and trembled over the tub. The air was laden with the fragrance of verbena. The temperature was like a caress.

She took a razor blade from the cabinet.

Hesitation suddenly gripped her. She caught the edge of the commode. The smell of bath salts tightened sharp around her, like arms strengthening her.

She stepped into the tub and lay back. She shut her eyes and pressed close to Verdi's music.

Requiem aeternam dona eis, Domine, et lux perpetua luceat eis. . . . Give them eternal rest, Lord, and may perpetual light shine upon them.

She lifted the razor blade.

It wasn't hard to do. It was as though life were a fabric and she were slipping through a secret opening in it. She had done the same thing a thousand times when she stepped out onto the stage. This time it was a different stage, that was all.

A half-hour later, Sally knocked. There was no answer.

She tried the door. It was locked. The wood felt hot to her touch. She called for the security guard to bring a passkey.

The room was filled with steam.

Vanessa lay in the tub, surrounded by pink foam. She looked waxen, lifeless. Her eyes were closed.

Sally screamed.

It was Charley Zymanowski, the security guard, who phoned for the ambulance. He had been with the San Francisco Opera for over twenty years and he had never seen anything like this.

A team of emergency medics from San Francisco General rushed Vanessa Billings out on a stretcher. Charley stayed behind. He told Sally he'd clean up.

Ten minutes later he found a scrawled note on the dressing table and a locket on the floor.

Nikos did not bother to use the house phone. He paid the night manager of the St. Francis $100 to let him into Ames's room.

Ames was sitting in his shirt sleeves by the window, staring down at the park.

"I have one question to ask you," Nikos said. "Do you want her?"

Ames turned slowly. "Butt out, Croesus."

Nikos felt a hot flash down his back, the same flash he got when it was deciding point in a squash match or when he was closing a long and arduous deal. "You'll be proud to know she attempted suicide after your little discussion."

Ames rose unsteadily from his chair.

"She'll recover," Nikos said. "But she's going to need care. I've made arrangements for her to go to a clinic in New Jersey."

"Decent of you."

"She flies east tomorrow. One of us is going to be on that plane with her. And that's the last choice in her life I'll ever give you."

Ames was on the plane with her. He was hungover and shaky and filled with a million stinging repentances, but he was with her, holding her hand for six hours and three thousand miles.

429

47

AMES FOLLOWED DOWN THE LONG CORRIDOR OF WHITEWASHED concrete. The orderly knocked on a door and stood aside. Ames went in.

The room was low-ceilinged. An orange rug and framed watercolors tried to fight the flat white of the walls. Sunlight shone through the open barred window. The air smelled of formaldehyde.

Vanessa sat stiffly on the quilted bed, holding herself back from the light. Ames approached. She didn't move.

He prepared a smile and then he put his arms around her. She turned her head and let him kiss her.

He sat in the chair facing the bed and held her hand. "Sunny today. Did you go walking this morning?"

He had never seen such eyes as hers had become. They had the emptiness of wells reflecting the starless night sky. He stared into them and felt the utter absence of her.

"Everyone asks how you are. Everyone misses you. Especially me. You don't know how much I miss you." He squeezed her hand. "Come back to me, Vanessa. Come back soon."

She seemed to be looking beyond him, watching the sunlight as it fell slanting on the linoleum tiles. There was only silence. After a long moment he rose and walked to the door.

"She's an extraordinary woman and right now she's in extraordinary pain."

Dr. Carl Sandersen's voice possessed the quiet resonance of power. So did his office, a chilly room of gray carpet and chrome and leather. Ames noticed only one area that had warmth, the bookshelves where several volumes had been put back on their sides.

"I wish you'd tell me about the pain," Ames said.

"Two forces are battling for her spirit: the normal human will to survive, and a devastating fear that there's no longer any reason whatsoever to go on living."

"Has she said she's afraid? Has she actually told you that?"

The doctor's brow wrinkled. He was a well-built man, his jet-black hair crew-cut like a soldier on active duty. "Indirectly."

"Has she spoken to you? If she has, quite honestly I'm jealous."

"There's no need to be jealous. She doesn't talk to anyone."

"This is all my fault. If I hadn't been so damned self-centered . . ."

Dr. Sandersen's voice became kinder. "Guilt is just a way of pretending we're in control. It hurts to admit we're powerless."

"But it was because of me that she tried to . . ."

"The predisposition was already there. It could have been anything that sent her over. Look, what she's suffering from is awful, but it's not rare and it's no mystery. It's an epidemic in this country. There are more depressives in hospitals than schizophrenics."

"Has she gotten any better in the year she's been here?"

Dr. Sandersen wished he could say something encouraging. "All recoveries hit plateaus. It may not look as though she's moving ahead right now, but she is. And believe me, it's damned hard work—so give her the benefit of your doubts. She needs them."

Dr. Sandersen touched Vanessa's arm. "I had a chat with your husband yesterday."

Her gaze did not move from his face. He went on just as though she had answered.

"He's a likable man."

She did not agree, did not deny. The sun made dusty yellow patterns on the wall behind her, like thrown pollen.

"Would you like to tell me about your husband?" He wondered why he could never sustain a doctorly tone with her, never muster the false caring or the cool curiosity he could with the others. With her the caring and curiosity were real.

She seemed to be staring at the space cutting him off from her.

Dr. Sandersen had to remind himself that silence is simply a message in a language we do not recognize.

He thought of what she must have been in the full fury of performance, igniting the hush of the opera house with the flame of her voice. He'd had a glimmer of it. He owned her recordings. He'd seen her on television three times. She had acted out passions that most human beings only dreamt in the secrecy of their hearts. She had loved, sacrificed, betrayed, and murdered. She had done it fortissimo and in front of a million witnesses.

He couldn't stand the thought of letting all that wither into silence.

"I have a confession to make," he said.

He had been saving this. He sensed a flicker of interest in his direction. A shyness came into him that was almost like awe.

"I collect autographs. Perhaps, when you're better . . ."

He'd been hoping the word *autograph* would summon up some reflex, some neural imprint that bypassed thought. But she sat catatonic and mute like a strip of movie film trapped in a broken projector.

He had seen it in patients before, the willed renunciation of consciousness, the flight from life into the seamless finality of psychosis.

Tonight, he thought, *I pray for a miracle.*

Sunday the third of August was Wanda Zymanowski's fifty-sixth birthday, and she and Charley celebrated the event with a little barbe-

431

cue in the backyard. It was not a large backyard, but this time of year it caught the late afternoon Bay Area sun perfectly.

"You take it easy, sweetie," Charley called. "I'll do the work."

Wanda settled into a deck chair and Charley brought out steaks and salt and coarse pepper. He set the sack of charcoal and can of lighter fluid down beside the grill. He made sure the charcoal was perfectly placed and the fluid perfectly squirted. Then he struck a match, and soon the fire was going.

He came up to Wanda's chair, smiling. "Happy birthday, sweetie."

He handed her a package. It was a small pyramid of red-and-green striped paper, tied with a blue ribbon. The pyramid turned out to be two smaller packages, a little jeweler's box on top of a larger wallet-sized box.

She opened the jeweler's box first.

He had given her a locket on a gold chain. She wondered why the dickens he'd thought she'd like it. It was flea market stuff. The amethysts were probably genuine, but she wondered about all the little rubies set in something that was probably meant to look like gold.

She forced out a gasp of delight. "Oh, Charley, I love it!" She jumped up from the chair to kiss him. "It'll go so well with—" She had to think. "It'll be perfect with my red dress."

"Open the other box," Charley said.

This time Charley's thinking had her totally buffaloed. He had given her a piece of scratch paper, ripped jagged from a lined notepad. He had had it mounted on velvet and framed under glass in beautiful gold-leafed maplewood.

There was handwriting on the paper. She had to angle the glass away from the afternoon sun to read the words.

Forgive me, Ariana.

"Charley, I don't get it."

Eagerness pulsed from him. "The note's what they call an autograph letter. Vanessa Billings wrote it herself. They auction stuff like that for hundreds of dollars."

Wanda's heart was pushing uncomfortably at her ribs. "Charley, where did you get these?"

Charley's glance wavered. "She left them in the dressing room the night she—you know."

"You took these from Vanessa Billings's dressing room?"

"You collect opera stuff. Look at that Melba postcard you have framed in the living room."

Wanda stared at her husband. "But, Charley, they're hers."

"Come on, she left them behind. No one ever asked for them."

"It's not right, Charley."

He was wounded now. "You don't like them."

"Oh, Charley, they're the nicest presents anyone has ever given me. But we have to give them back."

Something honked.

Ames had been staring at his typewriter for three hours. He swung around in his chair and looked out the window. Through the pines he could see the tiny red flat standing up on the mailbox. The mailman's station wagon made a faint grunting down the road. He put on his shorts and sprinted, avoiding the puddles from yesterday's rain. A lumpy, buff-colored envelope was lying in the mailbox on top of the *New York Review of Books.* Through the heavy paper he could feel ridges.

It was from the San Francisco Opera, which gave him a jolt, and it was addressed to him, not to her.

He returned to the house. He found the letter opener and poked the flap loose.

Inside was a second envelope addressed to Vanessa Billings, care of the San Francisco Opera. The return address indicated it was from a Mrs. Charles Zymanowski on Pine Street, S.F.

It was too bulky to be a fan letter.

Ames hesitated. *Hell, I have her power of attorney.*

He ripped Mrs. Zymanowski's letter open.

Dr. Sandersen stared down at the note. His eyebrows knitted. " 'Forgive me, Ariana.' Why would she have written that?"

"I don't know."

"Who's Ariana?"

"Vanessa studied with Ariana Kavalaris. Long ago."

"But Kavalaris has been dead for years now. Are you telling me your wife wrote this note to a dead woman?"

"If she wrote it that night . . . yes, she wrote it to a dead woman."

A pair of horn-rimmed spectacles began swaying from the doctor's fingers.

"There was something else in the package." Ames reached a hand into his pocket.

Dr. Sandersen stared at the ruby and amethyst locket. It was a striking little piece of jewelry.

"It belonged to Kavalaris," Ames explained. "Vanessa used to wear it all the time. It was like a good luck charm to her. That night, for some reason, she took it off."

The doctor was silent a moment.

"Doctor, the cassette she was playing in her dressing room—it was Kavalaris's recording of the Verdi *Requiem.*"

Dr. Sandersen's swinging spectacles came to a dead stop. "May I borrow the note and the locket?"

Dr. Sandersen stood a moment in the hallway, listening. There was no sound. He pushed the door inward and stepped into the room.

Vanessa was sitting on the bed.

"Good evening, Vanessa," he said pleasantly.

Her gaze floated toward him.

He put the cassette player on the table, and then he placed the tape cassette beside it. Taking all the time in the world, letting her see every move and the purpose of it, he loaded the tape into the player. He pushed the start button.

The machine made a whirring sound. Then the music started.

She held her face in a calm rigidity. There was no indication of anything living or aware behind it.

Now came the entry of the first human voices, the chorus.

Something changed in her. Her gaze seemed suddenly grayer, softer, and then she blinked and he saw it was because her eyes had moistened.

The voice of Ariana Kavalaris detached itself from the chorus, like a single spark flying upward from a flame.

For six minutes Vanessa was silent, her face angled downward like a nun's at prayer. Dr. Sandersen was reminded that hearing is any living animal's first link with the outer world.

The music finished. Silence fell. Dr. Sandersen took the locket from his jacket and placed it on the table in front of her.

Her jaw tightened. Her knuckles were white knots. He could sense some power gathering in her, coming out against him, at long last forcing a crack in that wall of concealment she had faced toward the world.

"Vanessa." He whipped her around to face him. "Why did you write 'Forgive me, Ariana'?"

Her mouth hid behind pinching fingers. He yanked her hand aside, shook her with all his strength, determined to shatter the answer loose.

"Why were you wearing her locket? Why did you take it off that night? *Why did you need her forgiveness?*"

She looked at him and it was as though her eyes were screaming.

He heard the shriek, but for an instant he was so surprised he couldn't tell where it had come from.

"Because I broke my promise!"

His heart was thudding, practically breaking through his ribs. "What promise, Vanessa?" Neither his eyes nor his hands nor his will let go of her. "What promise did you break? *What promise?*"

48

"SUBCONSCIOUSLY SHE BELIEVES HERSELF BOUND BY THIS PROM- ise; and because her pupil failed, she believes she broke the promise. It amounts to a delusion that her teacher's spirit is in control of her."

Ames Rutherford was silent. "Doctor, is she insane?"

"Insane is not a medical term."

"But is she?"

"She's severely depressed."

"How's that different from insane?"

"It's a defense *against* insanity. The ego can overreact."

"To what?"

"In this case, feelings."

"And where do these feelings come from?"

"From . . ." Dr. Sandersen hesitated, wondering how best to put it in layman's terms. "From within."

Ames Rutherford shook his head. "Psychiatry giveth, psychiatry taketh away. Every time it answers one question another pops up. Tell me, doctor, will she ever get out of here?"

Dr. Sandersen steepled his fingers together. "Once she recognizes that her ideas are delusions, that she projects them onto the world around her, we might consider a sort of provisional release. With one major caveat. Contact with music is forbidden."

"But there's music everywhere. In elevators, in the supermarket, in the street. She can't be shielded from all that."

"Obviously, casual exposure to music is inevitable. It's the structured musical situations that concern me: opera houses, concert halls. We have to rule them out."

"For how long?"

"Till we're sure the projected material has been dealt with."

"How can we be sure of that?"

"If she can get through a year without relapse or depression, that would be a pretty good indication."

"Will she be able to perform again after the year?"

Dr. Sandersen studied Ames Rutherford. "Do you want her to perform again?"

"Yes. I want that more than anything else in the world."

"Then in time—with your help and understanding—she may be able to."

Dr. Sandersen's office was quiet and peaceful. It always seemed peaceful to him when Vanessa was there. The reddish light from the setting sun bathed the bookcases. Her hands rested in her lap among the dark folds of her skirt. The light caught the gold of the wedding ring on her finger.

"Anything you'd care to talk about?" he asked.

"My dreams have been pretty dull lately. Let's see. There's a little cat wandering the grounds; I think it's been abandoned."

"What about that?"

"What about what?"

"Being abandoned."

"Oh, doctor, come off it." She was smiling at him.

"Why did you mention the cat?"

"Because I saw it. It was real, doctor, not a fevered projection of my anxious imagination."

"Why do you say anxious? Do you think I think you're anxious?"

"It's your business to find anxieties in your patients."

He smiled. "Well, have you got any good ones?"

"What's there for me to be anxious about? I've got no roles to learn. No blocking to unlearn. No tenors to argue with, no conductors to mess up my tempi. No agents, no contracts, no autograph hunters. Just blessed rest. It's a singer's dream."

"I should think most singers would get a little anxious if too much time went by between performances."

"You're trying to get me to say something, aren't you?"

"What am I trying to get you to say?"

"Oh, that I'm scared of sleeping, scared of being awake, scared of swallowing, scared of seeing my husband."

"And scared of never performing again?"

Vanessa gave a tiny shrug. Dr. Sandersen understood the gesture. It signaled capitulation.

"That most of all," she sighed.

"Vanessa, you will perform again. And I hope it will be soon." Dr. Sandersen clasped his hands behind his neck and explained. What it boiled down to was one year of no music.

She listened in silence. "And if I agree to all this—what can I expect?"

"To use the layman's term—recovery."

"What's recovery? Not being mad?"

"That's a fairly good definition."

She sat with her hands in her lap and looked at him. "I can bear madness. According to you, I've borne it for over a year now. I can live possessed: thousands stronger than me have done it. But I can't live separated from music. You might as well amputate my hearing, toss away a fifth of my life."

"Only for a year."

"Don't you mean *maybe* another year, doctor? Maybe longer? Maybe for as long as I live?"

"There's always a maybe."

"And if the sanity you offer me turns out to be—a premature burial?"

"It's possible. Not at all probable."

"Yet I could bear even that if only I could teach."

"Why is teaching so important to you, Vanessa?"

"I was given gifts. They have to be passed on."

"You believe that?"

"I believe I swore to do it."

"And if I told you that you swore nothing of the sort?"

"Why should I believe anything you tell me? Why should I trust you? You forbid me to perform, you forbid me to teach. You want to kill the only part of me that matters."

"No one says you can't teach. You can teach very soon."

"How soon?"

"As soon as you're able to recognize the delusory nature of your beliefs. And with rest, and care, and willingness, you'll learn to. It's like reeducating the eye after an implant. Vision returns. You begin to see the difference between light and dark."

"How will you know that I recognize my delusions as delusions?"

"Because you'll say so."

She was silent a moment. "You'll believe me?"

"We have to trust each other, Vanessa."

Three days later Vanessa seemed preoccupied, cautiously distant sitting in the chair. "I've been crazy, haven't I?"

"Crazy's a strong‑word, Vanessa." Dr. Sandersen crumpled the wrapper of a candy bar into his ashtray and smiled at her pleasantly.

"But believing those things—" Her shoulders were tensed together and her hands had wrestled one another to a standstill in her lap. "There's no other word. It's crazy."

He didn't answer. She was lying, of course. Her body screamed it. Still, the very fact of lying, of telling *this* lie, showed a willingness to compromise with reality, to meet it halfway.

It was a start.

"What do you want to do, Vanessa?"

"I want to go home."

It was a cold day in September, pure and brilliant, when Ames took her back to the house in East Hampton. They put her bags in the front hall and she stood and looked around at the familiar but somehow strange walls and then she crossed the living room and looked out the window at the ocean.

"Same old Atlantic," Ames said.

She turned. "Aren't you even going to get angry at me?"

"Why should I get angry at you?"

"For going crazy."

"I've been angry enough for a lifetime."

She looked at him. Her eyes were soft and tentative. "What if I'm not me anymore? What if I'm not the person you married?"

"But you are."

"Ames, they did everything but drill holes in my head. Sometimes I feel so different I wonder if they put someone else inside me."

He took her jaw in his hand and stared into her eyes. "Hey. Honey. There's no one in there but you."

"Are you sure you want me here?"

"I'm very, very sure."

That night, he guided her gently through lovemaking that was careful and fragile and their first in over a year and a half.

Afterward, she swore to him that the affair with Nikos had ended with her marriage.

"I know," he said, ashamed he had ever been jealous. He smiled to reassure her, to show her he had recovered just as she had. He kissed her. "Do you know how much I love you?" he said.

"Do you?" she whispered. She blinked as her eyes teared over.

He nodded and then very slowly he took her in his arms again.

"Beautiful," Ames said.

And she *did* look beautiful. In the six weeks that she'd been home she'd shed her hospital pallor and put on just enough weight to lose the haggardness around her eyes and cheekbones. But she kept frowning at her reflection in the hall mirror. "I wonder if they all know. I suppose they do."

"Honey, what if they do? It's no disgrace."

"I wish this wasn't the first party. I wish it was the third or the fourth and I didn't have to care so much."

"Well, we'll just have to give more parties."

"Hold my hand."

Three o'clock came, zero hour, and then there was a heart-crunching quarter-hour when nobody showed up and Ames kept resetting his watch by the grandfather clock and resetting the grandfather clock by his watch. Vanessa stood by the pantry window and counted hors d'oeuvres and trays and watched the driveway; and the man they had hired to tend bar, a lean and hungry-looking German named Hansl, arranged olives and ice cubes and polished glasses that didn't need polishing.

At twenty after the first car crunched down the drive—a blue Mercedes—and out stepped the Cavanaughs: Morgan and his wife Morgan—they both really had the same name—and then tumbling out of a red Audi were Pia Schrameck and her husband Wystan, who stuttered when he got really excited. And then Frank Bauer, Ames's real estate broker, who had walked from his house down the road and had brought a striking Eurasian palm reader named Harmony Ching, and then Pablo and Leo—one of them painted and the other . . . Vanessa forgot.

"You look wonderful, Vanessa, just wonderful."

As though they were all very carefully telling her something. And then Burt and Julia O'Connor and Julia's cousin Erin, who must have come from another party because they were already a little giddy, and Vanessa found herself thinking that the house was filling up with artists and brokers and writers and lawyers, and not one musician, not so much as a cocktail pianist or a strolling accordionist.

She made introductions and astonished herself by actually remembering names: "Pablo, Leo, Harmony, Allan, Eleanor, Wystan, Morgan, Morgan—Julia and Burt and Erin."

And no musicians.

And then Mandy van Slyke arrived in a chauffeured Rolls, apologizing for being late and hoping Vanessa wouldn't mind, but she'd brought an old friend—"Of *yours*, dear."

Vanessa turned. Her heart stopped. "Boyd."

"How are you, sweetums."

He looked thinner and grayer than she remembered and his face was beginning to show a few too many years' polite dissipation. But she couldn't believe the relief she felt at seeing him.

"We've got to talk," she said.

It was a half-hour before they could get away and walk along the beach. She asked what was happening at the Met.

"Strikes," he said. "Clara Rodrigo. A lot of *Bohème.* The usual. When are you going to come back and sing for us?"

"Who knows."

"Have you seen our new *Don Carlos?*"

"I don't get out much."

He looked at her, surprised. "Sweetums, what the hell's wrong with you?"

"You really don't know? I went crazy for over a year."

"Are you still crazy, sweetums?"

"We don't know. We're waiting to find out."

"I don't see why crazy people can't go to the opera. They sure as hell sing in it."

She laughed and kissed him. "Thank you, Boyd—for being you."

He took her hand and they strolled along the shore. He could sense there was something she was trying very hard to say.

Gradually, it came out.

"Boyd, during the years you were married to Ariana, did you ever know her to be—a mystic?"

"A mystic?" He drew his collar up against a gust of ocean wind. "If you mean did she walk on nails and chant—"

"I mean what sort of things did she believe in?"

"She believed in giving a good performance, keeping a good tempo, getting good pay."

"Those aren't the sort of things I mean." Vanessa's finger went to the gold thread around her neck. "On her deathbed she gave me this locket. She said it was her voice."

Boyd shrugged. "Ariana was always an original."

"She made me swear to keep the promise she'd left unkept and complete the life she'd left unlived. I gave my word. She seemed delirious. I thought I was humoring her. But now I'm not sure."

They walked on.

"Boyd, do you know about the promise Ariana made her teacher?"

Boyd stopped a moment. "Ariana mentioned something once about taking a pupil."

"She promised DiScelta to take a pupil, teach her, and launch her. What do you know about the life she left unlived?"

"I have no idea."

The sun glinted off the Atlantic like sparks.

"Could I tell you something spooky?" Vanessa said. "Time and again, ever since I met Ames Rutherford, I've felt I've been living someone else's life, not my own." She turned to face Boyd. "Does that sound as though I should be back in the nuthouse?"

"Not at all. We've all had feelings like that now and then."

They stood listening to the waves, and she asked, "Boyd, how much do you know about Mark Rutherford?"

"Mark Rutherford was Ariana's lover. He abandoned her after her Mexico City *Aïda*."

"Why?"

"I always suspected Ricarda DiScelta was mixed up in it. She couldn't stop meddling in Ariana's life. It wouldn't have been beyond her to play on Mark's sense of honor and persuade him to give up Ariana for the sake of her music."

Gulls swooped, calling mournfully.

"Till the moment she died," Vanessa said, "Ariana never stopped being in love with Mark Rutherford. I was there. I saw it."

Boyd's eyes seemed to change depth of focus. He didn't speak.

"Boyd, what if Mark was the same? What if he stayed in love with Ariana all his life, even when he was married to another woman? Don't you think his son would have picked up on it?"

"Picked up on it how?"

"Wouldn't Ames have sensed something unspoken, something unre-

440

solved in his father? What if he sensed it so early in life that it formed his own reactions to love and sex and women?"

"And to you?"

Vanessa nodded.

"It cuts both ways, sweetums. Ames is Mark Rutherford's son, but—in an artistic sense—you're Ariana's daughter. The son falls in love with the daughter of his father's lost love. And the daughter falls in love with the son of the mother's lost love. Wouldn't a psychiatrist call that oedipal rivalry? Succeeding where the parents failed? Well, who knows about you or Ames or psychiatrists? I certainly don't."

"Boyd, be honest with me. What do you make of my husband?"

"He's handsome. Nice sense of humor. He obviously adores you."

"Thank you. What do you really think of him?"

"The truth?"

"The truth."

"I see him as a figure in a pattern. On the one hand there are Ariana and Mark, on the other you and Ames. It's almost as though the children were playing out their parents' story, picking it up at the point where it broke off thirty-four years earlier. As for Ames personally, I doubt he much cares for me."

"It's because you're a musician. Ames dislikes anything to do with music at all. Once when I was rehearsing *Tosca* at the Met, he was watching from the balcony. There was a malevolence streaming from him that stopped me cold and wrecked the whole run-through. I had to ask him never to come to a performance of mine again."

"Curious," Boyd said. "It's like a seesaw balancing itself. Mark gave Ariana to music: Ames is trying to take you back from it."

"Sometimes I feel Ames hates music as though it were a rival."

"But, sweetums, don't you see? That's exactly what it *is*."

It was 6:30 when Ames realized Vanessa was missing, and almost seven when he saw her coming in from the beach on Boyd Kinsolving's arm. She looked happier than he had seen her in a year and a half, and he didn't have the heart to take that away from her.

He waited till the guests had gone home. "Who invited Boyd Kinsolving?"

"No one. Mandy brought him."

"What were you two talking about?"

"Music."

He was silent.

"Ames, I wasn't singing. Scout's honor."

It surprised him how hard it was to smile back at her.

In the weeks after the party Vanessa took down old curtains, put up new curtains, went to a garage sale and found a Mission rocking chair for the living room. She spent three days covering the shelves in the pantry with new Contact paper and putting the glasses where the plates had been and the plates where the glasses had been.

She didn't complain, didn't talk much, just smiled when Ames happened to come into a room where she was pottering around.

He phoned Dr. Sandersen, who said, "Maybe it's time to let a little more life trickle in from the outside."

A phone call came two days later. A man by the name of James Draper said he'd been Ricarda DiScelta's assistant for over fifty years; he apologized for calling; Boyd Kinsolving had given him the number, he hoped he wasn't intruding.

"I hope you aren't either," Ames said coolly.

There was an instant's fluttery embarrassment, and then Draper explained that he had a project that might interest Vanessa.

"My wife isn't working at present."

"I didn't mean *work* work. Look, could we meet?"

"I'll be in town seeing my agent day after tomorrow."

"I'm in Carnegie Hall Studios. Why don't you stop by for tea?"

James Draper turned out to be a small elderly man, ruddy and still robust, bald and with a gray mustache. He sat on the sofa in a kind of boyish squat, hugging his knees, petting his Abyssinian cat, his feet tucked under him.

He explained what he had in mind: a scholarly work, to be printed by the Oxford University Press, setting forth in meticulous detail the interpretation of twelve different roles by twenty divas of the past and present. "I could speculate and theorize all I want, but when you get right down to it, no one but a performer who's been there can give you the inside view of how it's done."

"What would you expect Vanessa to do?"

"Listen to tapes. Comment."

"No singing?"

The old man was indignant at the idea. "Naturally not."

Ames realized he had been praying for weeks for some little sign from somewhere, from someone. And here it was. This funny little man was offering him salvation.

"I'll ask her," Ames said.

49

VANESSA CAME INTO THE ROOM IN A BILLOWING SKIRT OF BLUE brocade.

A short, bald man with glasses and a polka-dot bow tie rose to take her hand. "I'm so grateful you were able to see me. For many years I was Ricarda DiScelta's assistant, and of course she taught your teacher. So this is auld lang syne for me."

"Yes," Vanessa said, "Ariana often spoke of DiScelta. She admired her enormously."

The cleaning woman had set out tea and two cups. Vanessa served. "Milk or lemon?"

"Lemon, please. I've brought tapes. I thought we could play them, and you could comment, and if you don't mind, I'll record what you say. I've got the most god-awful memory and we don't want lawsuits if I misquote you!"

James Draper had a traveling case on the sofa beside him with a great many wires and microphones spilling out of it.

"Why don't we start with a little *Turandot?* I've got some really splendid cuts here."

He began with tapes of "In questa reggia": Tebaldi; then Callas; then Sutherland. "Do you think Sutherland gets to the innerness of the role?" he asked.

Vanessa thought herself into the role of expert. "It's a curious role. There's less innerness there than in Puccini's other heroines. It would be a mistake to sing it like Tosca. Remember Liù, the rival soprano, calls her '*tu che di gel sei cinta*'—'you who are girdled in ice.' Personally, I find Callas's recording too warm, too emotional. But that's a subjective opinion. What the role really takes is power—not much else."

"Power." James Draper's glasses were glinting at her.

"For example, Nilsson sings it very coldly, but my God how effectively."

He nodded and in a moment he was playing more tapes. She commented when he asked for comments. Time floated by. And then a pure soprano voice arched up into the silence.

She lifted her head, listening. She recognized the music, of course: Violetta's solo scene from Act One of *Traviata*.

"Who's that?" she asked.

"You."

"Me? My God. I was good."

"Oh, you're excellent. Truly excellent."

I'll get it back, she thought. *I'm scarred, but I'll mend.*

443

James Draper changed cassettes. And then she was hearing Violetta's farewell to Alfredo.

She felt more than a little uncomfortable at recognizing herself in this singing puppet. The vocal inflections were banal, without any sense of the aching might-have-been. There was no passion in the phrasing, no memory of the long, sweet tenderness the lovers had shared. She felt even more uncomfortable when she heard Ariana singing the same passage. It was almost too much, a fiery outpouring of nightmare and dread and the terror of abandonment.

James Draper stopped the tape. "This is one of the clearest examples I've been able to find of diametrically opposed interpretations—yours and hers."

"Yes . . . they are different."

"And the difference is all the more curious in view of the fact that she coached you in that role."

At that moment Vanessa felt a whispering trickle of certainty. There was something on those two tapes . . . something she had to understand.

"Why did you choose to do such a pastel shading of that scene?" James Draper asked.

"I didn't choose anything. It's just not a very good performance." She fixed her gaze upon the cassette player. "Could I borrow those tapes? Just the *Traviata*s. Ariana's and mine."

She awoke in the middle of the night. Ames stirred in his sleep. She crept downstairs. She got James Draper's tapes out of the piano bench and looked at the neatly lettered labels.

The date was the same on both: *January 12, 1971*. The night she'd spent thirteen years trying to forget.

She got the cassette player from the study. She slid one of the Kavalaris cassettes into the machine. There was a hypnotic moment of dead sound. Strange, she thought, how every opera house had its own special silence: the silence of the Met was huge, cavernous, cool, broken after a moment by applause for the conductor. An instant's stillness, and then the familiar descending string chords of the Prelude.

She closed her eyes. She was there, in the Met.

The cellos sobbed out the haunting, big tune of the Prelude. The violins added their skittering, nervous countermelody. And then the curtain rose on the party at Violetta's Paris townhouse.

Ariana Kavalaris was in terrible voice, muffing entrances, dodging high notes, missing lows, swooping into phrases, garbling text. Vanessa slipped her own tape into the machine. The orchestra wasn't quite as polished as the Met's, but she was in far better voice than her teacher. Initially. And then came that awful moment in *"Ah! fors'è lui,"* the B-flat that wasn't there.

She forced herself to listen to the whole act; and then Ariana's second act; and then her own. And then Act Three. An intuition kept teasing her: there was a connection between the two performances, a link so strong it was almost cause and effect.

But what?

She spent the morning listening to the tapes and still not knowing what it was she was listening for. After lunch she got paper and pencil, taking careful notes.

After four hours she looked over her scribblings: *Act One: Libiamo. Ariana, lousy. Me: terrific. Sempre Libera. Ariana—lousy lead-in, good cabaletta. Me: good lead-in, good cabaletta. Ah! fors'è lui: Ariana— lousy; me—sensational.* And so it went throughout the opera: both sopranos sang erratically; but Ariana improved phenomenally, going from a terrible Act One to a superb Act Three, and Vanessa slid from a sparkling Act One to a dismal last act.

But she was certain there was something else. She needed to *see* the music.

She got the score from the library.

She replayed the "Libiamo," marking Ariana's mistakes on the score in green, her own one slip, a B-flat cut short, in red.

No pattern there.

She went through the act, marking. A lot of green, not too much red. A premonition began stirring inside her.

Act Two: by midpoint the green and red were running equal.

Act Three: not much green, a sea of red.

She stared at the two colors. She had the impression a pattern was there, staring right back at her. But she couldn't see it.

She looked out the window. The sun was down. How many hours had she spent on this madness?

She glanced toward the grandfather clock. *My God, nine hours.*

She spun the tape backward.

Where had Ariana's B-flat been so weak? "*Gioir.*" Act One. And where had it come out ringingly strong? She changed cassettes. Act Three. That crucial B-flat at the end of the final quintet.

Now she replayed her own tapes. "*Gioir*" again. B-flat was damned good. Now the quintet. She winced. The B-flat was like an old lady in a church choir.

She made notations on her paper: the good B-flats, the bad B-flats, whose was which and where.

All right, let's go for the high C's.

Two hours later she had an approximate run-down on her and Ariana's notes from the top of the staff up, F's through high C's. There was the glimmering of a sort of pattern: When Ariana finally got her A-flat, Vanessa lost hers; when Ariana finally managed a high C, Vanessa's cracked.

But the pattern didn't quite hold. Ariana managed a decent B-flat in "*E Dio cancello*," and ninety-seven bars later Vanessa was still singing good B-flats in "*Ah, morir preferirò.*"

Unless . . .

She telephoned Boyd Kinsolving, talked her way past a very possessive-sounding male secretary, and finally got the Great Man on the line. "Is there some way I can find out the starting and finishing times of the acts of a performance at the Met and the Philadelphia Opera?"

"What date?" he said.

Boyd phoned back the next day. "You sly little devil, you. I conducted that performance at the Met. Ariana was singing. And you were singing in Philly."

"Believe me, I know. Do you have those times?"

He read her the curtain up and curtain down times for each act. "This is all very mysterious, Vanessa. Are you going to let me in on what's up?"

"You'll be the first to know when I know."

"Can't wait."

The next step was to make two Xerox copies of the score. That entailed a trip to the public library. She scissored out the vocal lines. She marked one *Ariana* and the other *Me*, and using a stopwatch and Boyd's curtain-up and curtain-down times, marked the minute-by-minute timing of each measure. The results were approximate, but a comparison of the two vocal lines was enough to show the connection.

Her hands were shaking as she phoned, but she managed to keep her voice steady. "Boyd, can you come down to the house for lunch tomorrow? I need to talk to you."

Ariana's voice came in great waves of sound, traveling out from the stage across the darkness, across the years . . .

"*Ah! io ritorno a vivere—oh gioia!*"—"I live again—oh joy!"

Verdi's final, tragic chords thundered out of the tiny speaker. The cassette player snapped off, and Ariana was gone.

Boyd sat feeling the poignancy of live performance, the loss of the woman who had been his wife. For a long, aching moment his thoughts were in the past.

"Of course," he said, "both performances have their rough spots. Yet there are moments on those tapes when I couldn't say for sure who I was hearing—you or her."

Vanessa sat watching him.

"In some flukey way you caught not just her style but something else too—her timbre, her intonation. Of course, you went on to develop and you became original and marvelous too."

"You don't need to be polite, Boyd."

"She *was* your teacher, and it's perfectly natural to be influenced. She herself had a great many of DiScelta's mannerisms." He was thoughtful a moment. "As do you."

"Boyd, there's one voice on both those tapes."

He had to remind himself she was only recently out of her nerve clinic. "That's an interesting notion, sweetums. You're saying you and Ariana shared the same tradition?"

"We shared the same voice, Boyd. It's not her, it's not me. But whenever we're good—and I mean really good—it's that voice. At moments she has it, at other moments I have it. *And we never both have it at the same time.*"

"Run that past me again, sweetums?"

"At first I have the voice and she's got nothing but that squawk, and then bit by bit she gets the voice and I—well, you heard what happened to me."

"Anyone can have an off night. You don't need to get metaphysical to explain it."

"It's not metaphysical. It's note for note and I've documented it." She opened a notebook and read: "New York, 8:47: Ariana hits her first successful B-flat. Philly, 8:47: Vanessa loses her first B-flat." She looked at him. "I never have a decent B-flat after that, and hers are all fantastic."

"It's an awfully baroque theory to erect on a B-flat."

"It's not just B-flat. It's every note above the staff." She tossed him the notebook.

He glanced at the neatly penned pages. What they added up to, he couldn't be quite sure.

"When James Draper played me those tapes all I heard was me going from wonderful to horrible and Ariana going from horrible to sublime. Then I noticed the dates. They were both the same night. Then I began listening with the score. Ariana started out with no notes. I started out with all the notes. As the evening went on, I lost my B-flat, she got her B-flat. I lost my A, she got her A. It went beyond coincidence. It checked out for every note in the score. And the times checked out too. She got the notes as I lost them. *She was taking them from me.*"

Boyd tried to put things together in his mind. The voices on the tape were real. All the notes, right and wrong, beautiful and ugly, were really there. Vanessa wasn't imagining them. She heard what she said she heard, and what she heard disturbed her—as well it might. It disturbed him as well.

"You've made a brilliant case," he said. "But it's impossible. Not to be tactless, sweetums, but you were . . . *recovering* when these ideas came to you."

"Boyd, did you know that common law says *the dying don't lie?* Ariana told me about that promise on her deathbed. And she told me

447

the conditions. Once her pupil sang a role onstage, Ariana could never sing that role again. She broke that part of the promise the night we sang those *Traviatas*."

A silence fell on the living room. Boyd lit a cigarette.

Vanessa paced to the window, turned, faced him. "In the months before she died, Ariana finished teaching me her roles. Boyd, this may sound insane; but at the end she was trying to keep faith with Di-Scelta—and I intend to keep faith with Ariana. But I can't do it without your help. Will you find Camilla Seaton for me?"

"Why?"

"Because I've already taught her and we can pick up where we left off. Because teaching her will be the surest way of paying my debt to Ariana and freeing myself."

"Freeing yourself from what?"

"From . . . what I'm caught in."

"Camilla Seaton is not worth your while. She's a has-been."

"She failed because I failed her—just as I failed when Ariana failed me."

"I can't believe you take that hocus-pocus seriously."

Vanessa's voice was very even, very soft. "Boyd, I have a last chance to keep my promise. If I don't, I'll wind up in that madhouse again, and this time I *won't* get out. Besides—I gave my word."

"To a madwoman. Ariana was on the knife-edge all her life."

"Mad people can know the truth! Sometimes that's what makes them mad! My God, what do you call those tapes, if not evidence?"

He paused. "Well, there's undeniably something there—something extraordinary. But it's hardly evidence."

"Omigod." Vanessa was standing with her fist pressed against her mouth. "It just came to me." She sat down next to him. "After that *Traviata*, Ariana lost her F, then her A, then E. Don't you see?"

He stared at her blankly. "See what?"

"Solfège, Boyd."

Solfège, he thought, remembering the long-ago days when he had had to study that grabbag of musical fundamentals—rhythm tapping and sight-singing and calling the notes *do-re-mi* instead of C, D, E.

"The solfège syllables for F, A, E are *fa-la-mi*," she said. "*Follow me*. The voice was *calling* her."

Boyd drew in a long, slow breath. "Let's just keep that little theory a secret between thee and me, okay?"

"All right, Boyd, you don't have to believe me. But if you'll help me find Camilla, I'll come back to the Met."

His gaze came around and took hold of her. "What role?"

"What do you want?"

"Isolde."

I can find Camilla, he thought. *Someone will know where she is.*

448

"All right," he said. "I'll do my best, sweetums."

He hurried out of the house and across the lawn to his car.

He drove west, straight into the blinding November sunset. Hamlets and townships and potato fields and produce stands raced past.

She's crazy. All singers are crazy.

But one thought kept coming back to him.

Isolde. Billings.

Boyd phoned Vanessa five days later. "Camilla Seaton is teaching autistic children at a special school in Bronxville."

"Have you spoken with her?"

"Yesterday. She looks well—maybe a tad chubby, but it's becoming—and she's willing to meet with you. To tell the truth, I think she feels sorry for you."

"Good, I can use some sympathy. Can you bring her here next Tuesday? Ames will be in town and we'll have the house to ourselves."

There was an instant when former pupil and former teacher might have kissed but the hesitation stretched a fraction of a second too long. "You look wonderful," Vanessa said.

"You too." Camilla came into the hallway. "I haven't been here in—what is it, two years? You've redecorated."

"Just a lot of new knickknacks from barn sales."

"It looks cozy. So—country and comfortable."

They went into the living room. Vanessa offered drinks. Boyd asked for a highball, Camilla asked if tea would be too much trouble. For a while they chitchatted, saying the unimportant, polite little things: Where have you been, what have you been doing with yourself?

Vanessa sensed she would have to attack head-on. Nothing would be accomplished by evasion. "I want to teach you again."

Camilla put her teaspoon back into the saucer and set the cup back on the table. "I haven't time for music. I work with brain-damaged children. I'm on call twenty-four hours a day. I don't sing anymore. I don't go to operas. The closest I get to the Met is the Saturday afternoon broadcasts when I have a weekend free."

Vanessa stared at the young woman. "Then why did you come here today?"

"Because Boyd was on my back. Eighteen phone calls in three days. We've got to clear up a misunderstanding for once and all. You two think I'm still a singer. I'm not."

"I don't believe a person with your gifts, with your promise, can just stop," Vanessa said.

"Opera doesn't need me. The children do."

"I disagree." Boyd sprawled back comfortably on the sofa with his legs loosely crossed. "Camilla, you're here because music is still a part of you. You want to sing. You want to perform. You want to put your gifts to use. There's a need in you and you can't satisfy it by service to brain-damaged children."

Camilla's eyes slitted. "Music is a luxury. I haven't time."

Vanessa lowered her voice, made it conciliatory. "You're angry at me. And with every right. I let you down. And now I'm asking you for forgiveness. I'm asking to make amends."

"There's nothing to forgive. I thought I could accomplish something in opera, I couldn't. So I've turned to something that I *can* do."

Vanessa and Boyd exchanged glances.

"I never was a singer," Camilla said. "All I was was promising. Hundreds of people are promising. Little girls singing at birthday parties are promising. I had my chance. I didn't have the stuff. It took me two years to accept that fact. Two years when I hated music, when I couldn't stand records or radio or anything that reminded me of opera. And then, somehow, acceptance came. I admitted what I'm not. I found out what I can be. I've built a new life, I'm happy."

"You're not happy," Vanessa said.

The green eyes bored into Vanessa. "Camilla Seaton opera star is dead. She was a bright flash of promise. Leave her in her grave. And leave me . . . in Bronxville."

"You belong on the stage," Boyd said. "I knew it the minute I heard you phrase that '*Mio superbo guerrier*' section two years ago."

"I phrased it the way Verdi marked it."

"No," Boyd said, "you gave a wonderful lift on the A-flat. The tone floated. The whole phrase floated. In fact the whole duet floated, just because of that note. You took that scene from Otello and he knew it."

"No Desdemona takes a performance from Otello."

"You did. I wonder what the critics would have said if you'd been singing it at the Met."

"Well, I wasn't singing it at the Met. And in time the critics said plenty. Besides which, not only haven't I vocalized in over a year, I've lost any sense of pitch I ever had."

"I doubt that," Boyd said. "What's your bottom note, G below the staff, isn't it?"

"I used to be able to manage it."

"Your ear may forget, but the throat muscles never do." Boyd rose and went to the piano, blocking her view with his back. He struck a note.

"That's not G," Camilla said, "it's A-flat."

Suddenly she was silent.

"So much for no ear." Boyd struck another note.

"E above the staff," Camilla said.

He struck a chord.

"B dominant seventh. All right, I still have an ear. But the voice is gone."

"I'm going to coach you," Vanessa said. "The voice will return."

"I live in Bronxville. I can't commute here, it's three hours each way."

"I'm sure Austin Waters would let us use his studio," Vanessa said. "And Manhattan's one twenty-five minutes from Bronxville."

"I couldn't bear—" Camilla stared down into her teacup. "I couldn't bear to go through it all again, all the working and hoping and learning—and fail again."

"You won't fail," Vanessa said. "You never did fail. It was I who failed you."

"Adolf? It's Boyd."

"Yes, Boyd. What can I do for you?"

"No, sweetums. It's what can I do for you. Closing night, Vanessa Billings singing Isolde."

"My dear Boyd, I've lived through too much in this job to go on believing in miracles."

"I have her letter of intent. And, Adolf, she's in *great* voice. It's going to be the high-voltage Isolde of the *decade*."

A thoughtful, hungry pause. "Of course Clara is already scheduled for closing night," Adolf Erdlich said.

"Clara can't sing anymore."

"We know that, audiences are beginning to know it, but Clara has a great desire to be remembered as Isolde. On the other hand, she's feuding with us over air conditioning and still hasn't signed the contract."

"Ah! *Vanitas vanitatum!* Which of us has his desire in this world, or, having it, is satisfied? I say better four thousand happy subscribers than one deluded Clara."

"I agree."

"One stipulation, Adolf. It has to be kept hush-hush till the last possible moment."

Vanessa phoned the day after the contract was signed. "Boyd, I want Camilla to understudy me."

"I knew it, I knew there'd be a catch."

"Fix it with Adolf."

"After that abortion of a *Tosca* two seasons ago you think he'd let her near the Met?"

"Boyd—arrange it."

50

TWO WEEKS BEFORE THANKSGIVING AMES AND VANESSA WERE having breakfast in the kitchen when she suddenly said, "I want to join Women for Recovery. It's a self-help group of ex-mental patients. Mandy van Slyke told me about it."

"Do you think you need it?"

"Can't hurt, can it?"

"Why don't you phone and check with Dr. Sandersen?"

The next day she said Dr. Sandersen had assured her it was all right to go to the group. "We meet in New York. Twice a week."

He gave her a look.

"Don't worry," she said, "I can survive the Long Island Railroad."

On March 5 Clara Rodrigo returned to New York from a series of European performances. She found the Metropolitan Opera revised rehearsal schedule in her mail, forwarded by her accompanist.

"*Puta!*" she screamed. "*Coño!*"

The next morning she entered Adolf Erdlich's office with the brisk air of a ruling queen. "Adolf, we agreed last May. The closing performance of the season is mine."

He stared at her. "Our contract hasn't been signed."

"Because you haven't fixed the air conditioning in my dressing room."

"Nevertheless, it hasn't been signed."

"I have told managers I am singing that Isolde. I have told magazines. I have told friends. I must sing it. I will sing it!"

Adolf Erdlich gave her a motionless look that held the shadow of a pitying smile. "There is no contract."

Clara's black leather telephone book had three numbers listed for Billings: the first two were crossed out and the third appeared to be Long Island, with a 516 area code.

A machine answered. She waited for the beep. "I'm going to fight you, Vanessa. You will not sing my Isolde."

Ames played the message.

You will not sing my Isolde.

He erased it before Vanessa could hear it.

Once again, Clara made her way up the dimly lit stairs over the Chinese restaurant near B. Altman's department store. She pushed through the beaded curtain into the hot, suffocating space.

The huge dark woman reached to turn down the radio. Her milky eyes fixed unseeingly on her visitor. *"Siéntese,"* she commanded.

Clara sat. *"Soy yo—Clara,"*—"It's me—Clara."

"Te recuerdo."—"I remember you."

Clara slipped the diamond ring off her finger and pressed it into the woman's hand. "Now Billings wants to sing my Isolde."

"I warned you. It is too late. No power on earth can help you now."

"What shall I do? At least tell me that!"

The old woman sighed and pocketed the ring. "All you can do is to accept what must be." And, in terrifying detail, she went on to describe what resistance to the inevitable would entail.

"Clara—cara!"

She had summoned Giorgio Montecavallo to a 10:00 A.M. conference on her terrace. As he bent to kiss her, sunlight struck the tiny hairline scars of his recent face lift.

"Two hundred thousand dollars, Monte?" She held the letter that had arrived three months ago outlining the request.

"An investment, cara—not a loan."

"Tell me about this restaurant you want to open."

Monte described it. He had an option on a prime lot in Bergen County. The restaurant would serve the best fettuccine and saltimbocca in all New Jersey. And twice nightly Giorgio Montecavallo would sing favorite arias from grand opera.

Clara was thoughtful. "This comes at a good moment. I'm thinking of semiretirement."

Monte's face was very good at showing shock. "You, cara?"

"It's best to leave the stage while one is still at the height of one's fame and power." She poured coffee, thick rich-smelling espresso with three spoons of sugar in each cup. "The restaurant will be called Clara and Monte's. We will sing arias and duets."

He nodded. "Yes, duets are popular."

"And I think—for publicity purposes—we should be married."

Ames could not get the phone message out of his mind.

That Thursday, while Vanessa was with her group, he phoned the subscription department of the Metropolitan and asked if there had been any cast changes in upcoming productions of *Tristan and Isolde*. He was told Rodrigo would not be singing, but that a replacement had not yet been announced.

Tuesday he followed Vanessa into New York.

She went to an old Victorian apartment building on West Fifty-fifth Street. A younger woman was waiting for her. Ames recognized Camilla Seaton. The doorman let them go up.

Ames went into the building and asked for Dr. Harry Woolrich.

"No Dr. Harry Woolrich here, sir."

"Are you sure? This was the address my dentist gave me."

The doorman stepped aside to let him look down the row of buzzers. Ames caught the name that resonated: A. Waters. Vanessa's old voice coach.

He went to a pay phone and rang Austin Waters on Fifty-fifth Street. A man answered. In the background Ames heard Vanessa, unmistakably Vanessa with her high vocal filigree.

He apologized. "I must have the wrong number."

He saw the women come out of the building together, talking with the animation of old friends catching up on years' absence. They said goodbye on the sidewalk and Vanessa went to a garage on Fifty-eighth Street. A small chauffeured sedan was waiting for her.

The sedan dropped her at the train station at East Hampton, and from there she drove back to the house.

When Ames came through the door and Vanessa gave him a warm kiss and asked how his day had been, he said, "So-so. And yours?"

She began describing how tiresome it was rapping for three hours with a bunch of crazy ladies.

He cut her short. "I followed you."

Vanessa met his gaze. "Then you know Austin's coaching me."

"I figured that out."

"You know I'm singing Isolde?"

At that moment he felt the ground giving way beneath him, he felt her slipping back into that world of high C's and mad Lucias. "I think you ought to talk to Dr. Sandersen about that."

"Ames, I'm through being a patient."

He could hear tidal waves roaring out of the orchestra pit and the whole *Social Register* in gowns and cutaways springing to their feet screaming bravas. He could feel her wanting that world more than she wanted recovery, more than she wanted Ames Rutherford, more than she wanted anything else on this earth.

"Doesn't it mean anything to you what we have," he said, "what we've built in these last six months?"

"What have we built?"

He couldn't believe she'd said it like that, so calmly and matter-of-factly. "We've built a recovery," he said.

"Ames, I'm not what you think. Maybe I'm not even the woman you married. I know I'm not the case of delusional psychosis Dr. Sandersen's got you believing I am."

"Dr. Sandersen never said that about you."

"Of course not. He didn't need to. It's self-evident that I'm a poor overworked madwoman with some crazy idea that she made a deathbed promise to her teacher. Well, let me ask you one thing. If I'm deluded, what was that phone call on your machine?"

"Hey, will you calm down?"

"No, I will *not* calm down. You played me the tape the week we moved out here. That voice on the phone telling you to meet me at Perry Street—it was *her*, Ames. It was Ariana using me just the way she used me onstage. Don't you see? I wasn't imagining!"

His mind was spinning wheels. He remembered the phone message, remembered matching the voice to Ariana Kavalaris's. But he'd been on a bender when he did that, he'd been drunk, crazy.

Dear God, he prayed, *don't let Vanessa be mad, don't let Vanessa be mad.*

"I only want you to be well," he said.

She looked at his entreating eyes, his sun-streaked hair, his trembling mouth, and something in her cried out to bridge the emptiness between them. She felt his aching fear.

Yet she knew she had to stand her ground. If she yielded now she would be yielding forever.

She went into the bedroom and began packing.

Ames stood watching her from the doorway. "I'm not threatening, but you'd better face realities. You have no money, no property. Everything's in my name."

She closed the one suitcase.

"Where are you going?"

"Ames, I made a promise. I have to keep it. Under the circumstances that obviously means I can't stay with you. I'm sorry. I love you, but as you just got through saying, I have to face reality—only I'm facing *my* reality, not yours."

He marshaled a thousand arguments against her going. She granted that they were all wise, all just, all in her best interest.

Ames watched disbelievingly as she walked out of the house, got into the car, and drove away.

Nikos came to the door in his dinner jacket. She could hear by the sounds pouring from the apartment that he was giving a party.

"Vanessa." It was a soft, pained cry. "What's the matter?"

He had aged. His face was longer, the eyes and mouth more lined. His hair was paler; in two years it had shaded to white.

A word she had never heard before, never spoken before, ripped itself from her throat. *"Voïthia!"*

He recoiled from her. "Ariana?"

"Not Ariana. Vanessa."

"But what did you just say? That was . . . her voice."

She felt sudden strength. It was as if Ariana were crying out through her, commanding him to help her. *"Voïthia!"*

His face went white. *"Pos?"*

She knew he had agreed: he was asking how he could help.

"Afise mou na kathiso sto spithi sou," she said, not understanding what she was saying or how she was able to say it, knowing only that he had to take her into his home.

He stood aside. *"Ela,"* he said. *"Ela."*

For an instant she didn't move.

And then he said it in English. "Come in. Please. Come in."

She walked into his apartment with one suitcase. He gave her the guest room.

He provided everything: the piano, the accompanists, the listening, the advice, the encouragement.

And he was glad.

Dr. Sandersen learned at his breakfast table, pouring himself a second cup of coffee. The headlines in the *New York Times* proclaimed another day of last straws: crime was up, taxes were up, unemployment and prices were up. Everyone was broke and hurting and no one cleaned the streets or cared about the government's billion-dollar wars.

He turned for relief to the entertainment page.

Vanessa Billings's photograph smiled at him from the third column. He was on the phone thirty seconds later. "You're playing games with her sanity."

"I had no say in it," Ames Rutherford answered. "She's left me."

"You're still her husband, aren't you?"

"Technically I am."

"Then you have the power to stop her. I'll execute any affidavits you need."

"Your husband phoned me," Nikos told Vanessa. "He says Dr. Sandersen doesn't want you to sing."

"Dr. Sandersen hasn't seen me in over a year."

"All the same, just to be on the safe side, I think we should talk with Holly Chambers."

"The fact that we can blow Ames Rutherford off the map doesn't mean he can't still make trouble."

"What sort of trouble, Holly?" Nikos said.

"The worst sort. And I doubt Vanessa wants to spend these next weeks agonizing over whether or not she can legally sing Isolde."

They were sitting in Chez Claudine, a new little French restaurant on Second Avenue. They'd all ordered the day's specialty, ragout, and the chilled young Beaujolais. Their corner table was bright with flowers and checkered cloth; the terrine maison and the main course had proved peasant-hearty; and the conversation, for the last five minutes, painful.

Vanessa raised a gently protesting palm. "Holly, the one thing I'm not agonizing over is whether or not I can sing that role. So long as my lungs don't desert me, I'll be on that stage."

"Don't be so sure of it."

"I have a contract with the Met."

"And you also have a contract with Ames Rutherford that legally takes precedence."

She set down her fork firmly against her plate. "I never signed a contract with Ames."

"You married him. In court, that's a contract."

"But we're separated."

"Legally?"

"If you mean have we brought lawyers into it, no."

"Then under certain circumstances Ames Rutherford has the right to exercise custody of Vanessa Rutherford."

"That's ridiculous. I'm not a child."

"Age isn't the criterion. If a court judges you mentally incompetent, your husband becomes your custodian."

"But why would a court—"

"You were hospitalized."

"That was over a year ago."

"Doesn't matter. If your husband can find a doctor willing to swear that you're still mentally incompetent, the court will grant him custody. He'll have power of attorney; power to revoke contracts you entered into; power to recommit you to the hospital."

Vanessa fought off images of white cells and barred windows. "But Ames wouldn't—" Her eyes went to Nikos.

"Holly, show her," Nikos said.

Holly moved butter dishes and wineglasses and set the document on the table.

It was only a Xeroxed copy. Vanessa reached a hand and picked it up by the corner. She read it slowly, incredulity building in her. "They could stop me with this?"

Holly nodded. "It's a sad and unjust thing. But that's the law. He may be a bastard but you're his spouse and in that situation the bastard has the power."

"I never called him a bastard," Vanessa said softly. "He just doesn't understand."

Holly shrugged.

"There must be *something* I can do," she said.

"Sure. Shoot him."

Nikos spoke. "Not funny, Holly."

"Sorry." Holly sighed. "I've given this a lot of thought, and I can only see one sure way Vanessa can go onstage. Ask the court for a separation. Do it immediately. Once you're legally separated, Ames Rutherford and all the doctors in the world can't keep you from singing Isolde."

Vanessa glanced up at Nikos. He was faceless against the glare of sunlight in the restaurant window. "Nikos?" she said.

He shook his head. "It's up to you. You have my full support whatever you decide."

"All I want to do is to sing."

Vanessa saw Ames the day before her performance.

He was sitting across the courtroom in a rumpled raincoat and it wasn't even raining. He was wearing the South American sweater she had given him for his birthday and a necktie that didn't go with it and she had a feeling he was wearing sneakers too.

She felt sad. *Poor Ames—he'll always need someone to dress him.*

Holly Chambers was sonorously outlining his client's petition.

Vanessa stared at the man she was asking to be separated from.

It all seemed hopelessly unreal to her, meeting him, loving him so much that the thought of him had obliterated every other thought, living with him, feeling the love change in a way she couldn't begin to understand or control, and now seeing him across a courtroom while her attorney explained she wasn't asking for his money or his car or his house, wasn't asking for anything except never to be approached by him again.

She had said to Holly, "I only need till after the performance," and he had said, "But legally you have to ask for never again."

Ames sat listening, alone and still in a spill of sunlight from the window. He looked across at Vanessa and she looked across at him.

She felt they had known each other for centuries, and still she could remember the first time, the little boy in his navy blue private school blazer that she had glimpsed through the crowd at a matinee in the old Metropolitan Opera House, and suddenly she thought, *I was never in that old house,* and surprise jerked her back to the present.

"Is Mr. Rutherford's counsel in the courtroom?" the judge asked.

Ames rose. His voice was so soft it could hardly be heard. "I have no counsel, Your Honor."

"Speak up, please?"

"I have no counsel, Your Honor."

"Are you representing yourself?"

"I suppose so, Your Honor."

"Do you oppose Vanessa Rutherford's motion?"

"No, Your Honor."

"Motion granted."

❀   ❀   ❀

After the hearing Ames went to the twenty-ninth floor of the World Trade Center. It was 1:15, lunchtime, and several men and women were sitting in a small conference room with a view of the Hudson River.

The speaker today was an elderly woman, a clerical worker with an architectural firm. Ames slipped into a chair and listened to her gentle voice telling the old familiar story of loss and loneliness and booze . . . and recovery.

There were smiles and applause when she finished, and then anyone who had anything to say put his or her hand up in the air.

She called on Ames.

"Hi. My name is Ames. I'm an alcoholic."

He had been coming to this room, and to rooms like it, for the seven weeks since Vanessa had left him and he had woken up in a wrecked Mercedes with an empty vodka bottle beside him and no memory of how he'd wound up in that potato field.

"Just an hour ago the court granted my wife a legal separation. I don't feel like drinking over it, but I feel angry and scared and very much alone. I've been holding onto the hope that somehow I'd get her back, but now the prospects don't look too bright. I don't know what I'll do if I lose her."

The woman nodded. "It's okay to be angry. It's okay to be scared. You'll do the right thing whatever happens. You're not alone, you're here. And the court's not God. You may not lose her."

"They changed the New York divorce law. The only grounds used to be adultery. You had to have a guilty party and an innocent party."

She wondered why Nikos was mentioning it. "That doesn't affect me, Nikos. I'm not divorced. I'm only separated."

"Once the court grants a separation, if the parties don't live together or change their minds, they're automatically divorced in a year."

Her mind played with the idea as though it were a strange object, like a chunk of meteor that had landed at her feet. "Holly didn't mention that." She walked out of the study onto the terrace and stared down forty stories at Central Park. At first she could only see darkness and then she saw lights lacing the trees beside the paths.

Footsteps came close and slowed. Nikos's voice was beside her. "I've loved having you here."

"Thank you for letting me stay. I don't know what I would have done without you."

"After you married I was dragging myself around like an emotional paraplegic."

"I'm sorry."

"It wasn't your fault. Maybe after all the years I've ridden roughshod through other people's lives I needed to learn what it was to need someone else."

"You've been good to me. I had no right to ask for anything and you've been wonderful."

"You and Ames are virtually divorced now. Do you understand that?"

"I can't think about it now."

She said it gently. She was grateful to Nikos. There was caring in him and warmth. She took his hand. His fingers curled around hers.

"Have you ever been to Georgetown?" he said. "In the Bahamas?"

"I've never been to the Caribbean."

"It's beautiful down there. I have a plane waiting for us at JFK."

Sometimes he struck her as a child. He would never understand that people had lives and responsibilities of their own, that they couldn't just drop everything because he had an impulse to play.

"It sounds wonderful, but I'm singing tomorrow."

"Just for tonight. We can fly back right away."

"Why go all that way for a night?"

"The law's different down there. We could marry in Georgetown. It wouldn't carry legal weight in New York, but in a year we could marry here too and then we'd be man and wife in all fifty states."

She thought how defenseless he had made himself to her. "That's the most beautiful thing you could offer me. Thank you, Nikos."

"That's it? Thank you?"

"Thank you and I love you. You've been very good to me."

"Will you marry me? At long, long last?"

She looked at him, his eyes soft and dark and hopeful, his hair curling and thick and white. She thought how easy he would be to wound at this moment and how she must never hurt him again.

"I can't decide anything, Nikos. Not till I get through what I have to get through."

51

THEY WERE IN HER DRESSING ROOM, WITH BARELY THREE MIN-
utes before the Prelude. There was a light knock at the door.

Vanessa frowned into the mirror, trying to adjust her headband.
"Would you see who that is?"

An usher handed Camilla a small gift-wrapped package.

Vanessa glanced over her shoulder. "Open it, would you?"

A necklace of cabochon diamonds sparkled in a bed of contoured
purple velvet. Vanessa stared. The jewels seemed to have been thrust
by accident into the wrong universe. She looked at the card.

"Nikos."

"Don't you want to try it on—for luck?" Camilla said.

"No, this is my good luck jewel." Vanessa lifted the locket from the
dressing table. She clicked it open. Her eyes met those of the woman in
the portrait. As she put on the locket an easy temporary immortality
flowed into her. She smiled at Camilla's perplexed look.

"Is my toothbrush around somewhere? I don't like to pray with dirty
teeth."

The chandeliers dimmed, rising to the ceiling. Latecomers hurried to
their seats. There was applause for Boyd Kinsolving as he entered the
pit. He raised his baton.

The Prelude surged out, faded to two plucked notes of the cellos and
basses. The huge golden curtain rose on a ship becalmed on the Irish
Sea.

The knight Tristan was taking Isolde, daughter of the Irish king, to be
married to King Mark of Cornwall. She had remained strangely silent
and refused food throughout the voyage. Finally—tall, head up, her
cape streaming out behind her—she explained her behavior to her
bewildered servant, Brangaene.

Isolde told how her fiancé, Morold, had gone to Cornwall to exact
tribute. Tristan had scornfully slain him and sent his head as payment
to Ireland. Later a wounded man calling himself Tantris had landed on
the Irish coast and sought Isolde's help, since she was famed for her
knowledge of potions and healing. She had noticed a nick in his sword. It
matched a piece of steel taken from Morold's head. She knew he was Tristan. She raised the sword to kill him. His eyes met hers. She could not
strike the death blow. Instead she healed him. He promised eternal gratitude. But his uncle, King Mark, impressed by his description of Isolde,
decided to marry her and sent Tristan back to Ireland to fetch her.

Now, her voice cutting through the dense orchestral sound as though
there were a light within it, Isolde revealed that she was still in love

with Tristan and felt he had betrayed her. Resolving to kill herself and him, she commanded Brangaene to brew a deadly poison. She summoned Tristan and, deceptively, proposed they drink a toast of reconciliation.

But Brangaene had substituted a love potion for the poison. As Tristan and Isolde drained their cups and looked into each other's eyes, they fell helplessly in love.

The audience had listened hushed, unmoving, and at the end of one hour and ten minutes their applause broke like a wave hurling itself against the land.

"Flowers for Miss Billings."

The guard at the artists' entrance glanced at the man in the raincoat whose eyes seemed so strangely patient and lonely. "Leave them here."

"The instructions are to deliver personally."

"Sorry, we can't—"

The man thrust out the yellow duplicate of the florist's invoice. The guard's eyes took in the boldly hand-printed DELIVER IN PERSON FIRST INTERMISSION and the name of the sender—Nikos Stratiotis.

"Okay. Take a right, another right, and it's the third dressing room on the left."

He knocked. It was the dresser who opened the door. Vanessa turned, saw the florist's package, saw who was carrying it.

"Ames." Her hands tightened.

He tried to tell her with his eyes all that she would never believe from his lips: that he loved her, had never meant to harm her.

Nikos burst into the room. "How the hell did you get in here?"

The two men began shouting. Vanessa screamed.

A guard knocked at the door. "Miss Billings?"

"It's all right," she called. "I was just—practicing."

Nikos dropped shamefaced into a chair, and Ames took up position by the doorway.

"I'm in the middle of a performance," she said. "Neither of you is helping."

They both looked embarrassed and hurt. It was Nikos who finally spoke. "You've got to choose, Vanessa. Take one of us or the other."

"No, Nikos. It's the two of you who have to choose—between me and the woman you really love." She looked from Nikos to Ames. She could see that neither of them understood. "Leave me alone till midnight. Let me finish my performance, and I'll belong to whichever one of you chooses me over Ariana Kavalaris."

Nikos and Ames watched Act Two from opposite wings of the stage.

Isolde, married to King Mark, had arranged to meet Tristan while the king was away hunting. Together they prayed to the night to guard their love. Brangaene, keeping watch from the castle turret, warned that day was near. They ignored her. As their song rose ecstatically, Brangaene screamed and Tristan's groom Kurwenal rushed in to warn that the king's hunting party was returning.

With heartbroken dignity, King Mark confronted the lovers. Tristan asked if Isolde was willing to follow him to the land of oblivion. She replied she would happily follow wherever he led. As they kissed, one of King Mark's knights drew his sword. The guilt-ridden Tristan allowed himself to be mortally wounded.

Stepping back from her curtain call, Vanessa saw him in the wings, his eyes fixed on her.

The realization jolted her that she had sung an entire act with Ames Rutherford standing no more than thirty feet away.

Something has changed, she realized. *He didn't make me freeze up.*

Without a word, she hurried past him, past props and flats of a dozen other operas.

"So you see," Vanessa said, "the story of this locket is quite special. It's the story of a life that never reached its goal and had to be lived again." The dressing room had the silence of a vacuum pressing in. "Are you frightened?"

"No," Camilla answered. "Just scared to death."

From far away came the lonely, unsupported notes of the violins, ascending as though into endless space. Act Three was beginning.

"Do you accept?" Vanessa asked.

She could feel the smallest seed of hesitation drop before Camilla silently bowed her head in acquiescence.

Vanessa handed the locket over, ensuring that there would be no turning back for her as there had been for Ariana. She fastened the thin gold chain around her pupil's neck. "Now it's yours, Camilla—the gift, the promise—and the duty."

Vanessa turned now to Richard Schiller.

"Did you bring the contracts?"

He nodded and placed them on the dressing table.

Vanessa's eyes skimmed, running down the list of roles and operas. Isolde came first. Then came the heroines in *Tales of Hoffmann;* then Nedda in *Pagliacci* and Marguerite in *Faust;* and on and on, four pages listing every role she had ever learned.

After each came a date and the identical stipulation: from the day specified onward, Vanessa Billings would never again sing the role; thenceforth Americana Artists Agency would use its best efforts to promote Camilla Seaton in said role.

Vanessa signed, then handed the pen to Camilla.

Camilla signed quickly and handed the pen to Richard.

He shook his head. "Twenty years. No one ever signs a twenty-year contract."

But he signed.

At a desolate castle on the rock-strewn Brittany coast, Kurwenal kept watch over the dying Tristan while the two waited for Isolde's ship. She had promised to come heal her lover. Tristan was on the verge of despair when a shepherd's pipe signaled that a ship had finally been sighted.

Delirious, Tristan ripped off his bandages. With his last strength he staggered to his feet to meet Isolde. They embraced. He died in her arms.

King Mark arrived. He had learned of Brangaene's potion and had come to forgive the lovers. But it was too late.

Across the stage, in the opposite wing, Nikos could see Ames Rutherford pacing.

In the distance, from the direction of the dressing rooms, a solitary woman approached. She walked along slowly, very small in a hooded black woolen cloak. She passed within a foot of Nikos.

He hardly glanced at her.

The grief-stricken white-garbed Isolde bent over the body of her dead knight. Her eyes closed. She began the "Liebestod"—the "Love-death."

The shining line of her voice detached itself from the waves of orchestral sound and arched in a forever of longing. Note by note, then in a steady stream, the music entered the senses and nerves of the audience. It was as if they could hear time itself welling up. For a soaring quarter-hour, eternity was a place—that stage.

Wombed in mystery, rising into the sun's glory, the voice threw itself outward toward the universe.

There was a war of climaxes, music and voice rising to separate peaks, finally peaking together, then falling back.

The voice faded and was still. Isolde sank to the floor and—following Tristan to the land of oblivion—fell across her lover's body, dead.

The orchestra subsided. The strings sighed out a high, aching melody. There were two stinging woodwind chords, the longing motif, resolving into the final transcendant B-major chord. For a moment a single oboe held a lonely D-sharp. The chord returned and then all was stillness, peace, fulfillment.

The curtain fell in silence. Applause ripped loose.

❖　❖　❖

464

The musicians filed out of the pit, the houselights were raised, it was five after midnight, then ten after, and still the curtain calls went on and torn programs and flowers rained down on the stage.

In the wings, Nikos and Ames waited to see which way she would turn. The curtain fell back for the last time. The applause died. She hesitated, then came quickly toward Ames.

He rushed forward, arms open. Then stopped. The woman in Isolde's costume, the woman beneath Isolde's makeup, was not Vanessa.

Camilla Seaton looked at Ames Rutherford curiously, then smiled. "Excuse me." And stepped around him.

From deep in the shadow of the wings, the figure in the cloak watched the well-wishers flocking to Camilla Seaton. She couldn't help feeling a surge of pride.

I taught her. I passed that on to her.

Then her eyes went to Nikos and Ames, still disbelieving, still lost on the outskirts of the confusion. Though she openly met both their gazes, neither seemed to recognize her. It was as though they were looking too far beyond her to see her.

And no wonder. Now she was only Vanessa Billings, the girl from a little town called Hempstead; she was Ariana no longer.

Ariana was there in the wings where she belonged, glowing from the face of Camilla Seaton.

Vanessa's eyes misted. *Goodbye, Nikos and Ames, you who thought you loved me; it was Ariana you really loved.*

And she wondered, *What about me? Did I ever love them? Or was that Ariana too?*

Vanessa adjusted her hood and passed quietly through the stage door, raising scarcely a nod from the guard on duty.

She turned for one moment and whispered her goodbye.

On the underground sidewalk a mob of newsmen had collected. A man with a minicam shoved her aside in his rush to line up a better shot of the artists' entrance.

She went slowly out to the street.

It was a clear early spring night. She raised her arm and hailed a taxi. She got in.

As the cab pulled into the Broadway traffic she turned to stare back at the opera house, at the arched glass façade with the bright red and yellow splashes of the Chagall murals on the grand tier.

I'm free now.

An emptiness ached in her.

Twenty feet down Broadway, a figure darted crazily into the traffic. The driver slammed on his brakes. Car horns blared angrily behind them.

A man was rapping at the passenger window, pulling at the door handle. Through the shield of glass, Vanessa's eyes met Ames Rutherford's.

In her memory a young man, flushed and eager, bolted up the steps of a choir loft; a little boy in a school blazer stared at her across the crowded promenade of an old opera house.

She unlocked the door.

Ames slid into the back seat beside her, out of breath. "Why did you run off like that? I panicked when I realized Camilla wasn't you."

"When did you realize?"

"During the curtain calls. You were standing by the artists' entrance. You stopped and said goodbye."

"You heard me?"

"I felt it. Don't say goodbye, Vanessa. Please don't ever say goodbye again."

For a moment nothing moved in her face. Then she smiled and it was as though a rose were slowly opening its petals. There was memory and sadness in that smile but there was hope too.

"I was only saying goodbye to Isolde. She's been good to me; and I'll never sing her again." Sadness brushed her. "One by one, I'll have to say goodbye to all my roles. In twenty years . . . they'll be gone."

She was silent. He took her hand.

"Twenty years can be a lifetime," he said.

She stared at him, sensing he was beginning to understand as she understood; to believe as she believed.

"Where are you going now?" he asked.

"I'm not sure."

"We can catch the last train to the Hamptons."

She hesitated.

"Vanessa, I'm not the person I was."

It was as though for the first time she was hearing the voice that was truly his. And then there came a sound almost as surprising, the voice that was truly hers. "I'm not the person I was either."

Her fingers closed tight around his. A strange wondering peace began slowly to fill them both—a peace of reconciliation that had been over a half-century in coming.

Somewhere far away a little boy in a school blazer kissed a little girl in a white skirt. A young seminarian held a dark-eyed voice student in his arms, at last, forever.

Ames leaned forward to the partition. "Driver, we've changed our minds. Take us to Penn Station, please."

Edward Stewart is the author of nine novels, including *They've Shot the President's Daughter!*, *Launch!*, and *Ballerina.* His novels have been published throughout the British Commonwealth and have been translated into twelve different languages; his articles and fiction have appeared in *Esquire, Saturday Review,* and *Ladies' Home Journal.* An opera and dance aficionado, Mr. Stewart is a graduate of Harvard and a lifelong resident of New York City.